Marcius Willson

Outlines of History

Marcius Willson

Outlines of History

Reprint of the original, first published in 1874.

1st Edition 2024 | ISBN: 978-3-36884-975-7

Verlag (Publisher): Outlook Verlag GmbH, Zeilweg 44, 60439 Frankfurt, Deutschland
Vertretungsberechtigt (Authorized to represent): E. Roepke, Zeilweg 44, 60439 Frankfurt, Deutschland
Druck (Print): Books on Demand GmbH, In de Tarpen 42, 22848 Norderstedt, Deutschland

OUTLINES OF HISTORY;

ILLUSTRATED BY NUMEROUS

GEOGRAPHICAL AND HISTORICAL NOTES AND MAPS

EMBRACING

PART I. ANCIENT HISTORY.
PART II. MODERN HISTORY.

BY MARCIUS WILLSON,

AUTHOR OF "AMERICAN HISTORY," "HISTORY OF THE UNITED STATES," ETC.

SCHOOL EDITION.

IVISON, BLAKEMAN, TAYLOR & CO.,
NEW YORK AND CHICAGO.
1874.

NOTE TO THE REVISED UNIVERSITY EDITION OF 1872.

IN the revision to which the present work has been subjected, those points in the history of the Reformation, and in the philosophy of its causes and effects, to which our Roman Catholic friends have taken exception, have been carefully re-examined and re-written, with the most earnest desire to do the strictest justice to all of them, and, if possible within the limits of fidelity to historic truth, to give offense to none. Some omissions of statements believed now to be wrong, or doubtful, have been made ; all undue harshness of expression has been avoided ; and we hope the spirit of Christian charity has been thrown over all. To Prof. Fisher, of Yale College, who kindly consented to revise my revision, I am under great obligations for the happy manner in which his amendments have contributed to the carrying out of my wishes, which are also those of my Publishers.

With these explanations, the work is again submitted to the judgment of a discriminating public.

M. WILLSON.

Stereotyped by SMITH & McDOUGAL, 82 Beekman Street, N. Y.

PREFACE TO THE UNIVERSITY EDITION.

The author of the following work submits it to the Public with a few remarks explanatory of its Plan, and of the endeavors of the writer to prepare a useful and interesting text-book on the subject of General History.

In the important departments of Grecian and Roman History he has aimed to embody the results of the investigations of the best modern writers, especially Thirlwall and Grote in Grecian, and Niebuhr and Arnold in Roman History; and in both Ancient and Modern History he has carefully examined disputed points of interest, with the hope of avoiding all important antiquated errors.

By endeavoring to keep the attention of the student fixed on the history of the most important nations—grouping around them, and treating as of secondary importance, the history of others,—and by bringing out in bold relief the main subjects of history, to the exclusion of comparatively unimportant collateral details, he has given greater fulness than would otherwise be possible to Grecian, Roman, German, French, and English history, and preserved a considerable degree of unity in the narrative; while the importance of rendering the whole as interesting to the student as possible, has been kept constantly in view.

The numerous Notes throughout the work were not only thought necessary to the geographical elucidation of the narrative, by giving to vents a distinct "local habitation," but they also supply much useful explanatory historical information, not easily attainable by the student, and which could not be introduced into the text without frequent digressions that would impair the unity of the subject.

In addition to the Table of Contents, which contains a general analysis of the whole work, a somewhat minute analysis of each Chapter or Section, given at the beginning of each, is designed for the use of teachers and pupils, in place of questions.

* In the "School Edition," Part III., containing "Outlines of the Philosophy of History" is omitted.

The author has devoted less space to the History of the United States of America than is found in most similar works, for the reason that he has already published for the use of schools, a " History of the United States," and also a larger " American History ;" and, furthermore, tha. as the present work is designed as a text-book for American students, who have, or who should have previously studied the separate history of their own country, it is unnecessary, and, indeed, impossible, to repeat the same matter here in detail; and something more than so meagre an abridgment of our country's annals as a *General* History must necessarily be confined to, is universally demanded.

The author is not ignorant that he will very probably be charged with presumption in heading Part III. of the present work with the ambitious title of " Philosophy of History," although he professes to give only its " Outlines ;" nor is he ignorant that a great critic has expressed the sentiment, that as the vast Chaos of Being is unfathomable by Human Experience, so the Philosophy of all History, could it be written, would require Infinite wisdom to understand it. But although the whole meaning of what has been recorded lies far beyond us, the fact should not deter us from a plausible explanation of what *is* known, if, haply, we may thereby lead others to a more just appreciation of the true spirit—the *Genius* of History—and the great lessons, social, moral, and political, which it teaches. With the explanatory remark that our brief and very imperfect sketches of the Philosophy of History were not designed to enlighten the advanced historical scholar, but to lead the *student* beyond the narrow circle of facts, back to their causes, and onward to some of the important deductions which the greatest historians have drawn from them, we present these closing chapters as a brief compend of the history of Civilization, in which we have aimed to do justice to the cause of Religion, Intelligence, and Virtue, and the cause of Democracy,—the great agents of regeneration and Human Progress ;—and we commend this portion of our work to the candor of those who have the charity to appreciate our object, and the liberality to connect with it our disclaimer of any other merit than that of having laboriously gathered and analyzed the results of the researches of others, and reconstructed them with some degree of unity of plan, and for a good purpose, into these forms of our own.

TABLE OF CONTENTS.

PART I.

ANCIENT HISTORY.

CHAPTER I.

CHAPTER II.

CHAPTER III.

CHAPTER IV.

CHAPTER V.

CONTENTS.

CONTENTS.

CHAPTER III.

GENERAL HISTORY DURING THE SIXTEENTH CENTURY.

CHAPTER IV.

THE SEVENTEENTH CENTURY.

CHAPTER V.

THE EIGHTEENTH CENTURY.

CONTENTS.

CHAPTER VI.

THE NINETEENTH CENTURY.

SECTION I.—THE WARS OF NAPOLEON : 1800—1815.

GENERAL GEOGRAPHICAL AND HISTORICAL VIEWS, ILLUSTRATED
BY THE FOLLOWING MAPS.

NOTE. For the "Index to the Geographical and Historical Notes" see end of the volume.

PART III.

OUTLINES OF THE PHILOSOPHY OF HISTORY

[OMITTED IN THE SCHOOL EDITION.]

CHAPTER I.

THE ANTEDILUVIAN WORLD.

CHAPTER II.

EARLY EGYPTIAN, ASSYRIAN, AND BABYLONIAN CIVILIZATION.

CHAPTER III.

CHARACTER AND EXTENT OF CIVILIZATION DURING THE FABULOUS
PERIOD OF GRECIAN HISTORY,

CHAPTER IV.

CHARACTER AND EXTENT OF CIVILIZATION DURING THE UNCERTAIN
PERIOD OF GRECIAN HISTORY.

CHAPTER V.

THE GLORY AND THE FALL OF GREECE.

CHAPTER VI.

THE FIRST PERIOD OF ROMAN HISTORY: FROM THE FOUNDING OF ROME
TO THE CONQUESTS OF GREECE AND CARTHAGE.

PART I.

ANCIENT HISTORY.

CHAPTER I.

THE EARLY AGES OF THE WORLD, PRIOR TO THE COMMENCE MENT OF GRECIAN HISTORY.

ANALYSIS. 1. THE CREATION. The earth a chaotic mass. Creation of light. Separation of land and water.—2. Vegetable life. The heavenly bodies. Animal life. —3. God's blessing on his works. Creation of man. Dominion given to him. Institution of the sabbath.—4. ANTEDILUVIAN HISTORY. The subjects treated of.—5. The earth immediately after the deluge. The inheritance given to Noah and his children.—6. The building of Babel. [Euphrates. Geographical and historical account of the surrounding country.] Confusion of tongues, and dispersion of the human family.—7. Supposed directions taken by Noah and his sons.—8. EGYPTIAN HISTORY. Mis'raim, the founder of the Egyptian nation. [Egypt.] The government established by him Subverted by Ménes, 2400 B. C.—9. Accounts given by Herod' otus, Joséphus, and others [Memphis and Thebes. Description of.] Traditions relating to Ménes. His great celebrity. [The Nile.]—10. Egyptian history from Ménes to Abraham. The erection of the Egyptian pyramids. [Description of them.] Evidences of Egyptian civilization during the time of Abraham.—11. The Shepherd Kings in Lower Egypt. Their final expulsion, 1900 B. C. Joseph, governor of Egypt. [Goshen.] Commencement of Grecian history.—12. ASIATIC HISTORY. [Assyria. Nineveh.] Ashur and Nimrod. [Babylon.] The worship of Nimrod.—13. Conflicting accounts of Ninus. Assyria and Babylon during his reign, and that of his successor.—14. Account of Semir'amis. Her conquests, &c. [Indus R.] The history of Assyria subsequent to the reign of Semir'amis.

1. THE history of the world which we inhabit commences with the first act of creation, when, in the language of Moses, the earliest sacred historian, "God created the heavens and the earth." We are told that the earth was "without form, and void"—a shapeless, chaotic mass, shrouded in a mantle of darkness. But "God said, let there be light; and there was light." At the command of the same infinite power the waters rolled together into their appointed places, forming seas and oceans; and the dry land appeared.

I. THE CREATION.

2. Then the mysteries of vegetable life began to start into being; beautiful shrubs and flowers adorned the fields, lofty trees waved in the forests, and herbs and grasses covered the ground with verdure

The stars, those gems of evening, shone forth in the sky; and two greater lights were set in the firmament, to divide the day from the night, and to be "for signs, and for seasons, and for days and for years." Then the finny-tribes sported in "the waters of the seas,' the birds of heaven filled the air with their melody, and the earth brought forth abundantly "cattle and creeping things," and "every living creature after its kind."

3. And when the Almighty architect looked upon the objects of creation, he saw that "all were good," and he blessed the works of his hands. Then he "created man* in his own image;" in the likeness of God, "male and female created he them;" and he gave them "dominion over the fish of the sea, and over the fowl of the air, and over every living thing that moveth upon the earth." This was the last great act of creation, and thus God ended the work which he had made; and having rested from his labors, he sanctified a sabbath or day of rest, ever to be kept holy, in grateful remembrance of Him who made all things, and who bestows upon man all the blessings which he enjoys.

4. The only history of the human family from the creation of
II. ANTEDI-
LUVIAN HIS-
TORY.
Adam to the time of the deluge,[b] a period of more than two thousand years, is contained in the first six chapters of the book of Genesis, supposed to have been written by Moses more than fourteen hundred years after the flood. The fall of our first parents from a state of innocence and purity, the transgression of Cain and the death of Abel, together with a genealogy of the patriarchs, and an account of the exceeding wickedness of mankind, are the principal subjects treated of in the brief history of the antediluvian world.

5. When Noah and his family came forth from the ark, after the deluge had subsided, the earth was again a barren waste; for the waters had prevailed exceedingly, so that the hill-tops and the mountains were covered; and every fowl, and beast, and creeping thing, and every man that had been left exposed to the raging flood, had been destroyed from the earth. Noah only remained alive, and they that had been saved with him in the ark; and to him, and his three sons, whose names were Shem, Ham, and Japheth, the whole earth was now given for an inheritance.

6. About two hundred years after the flood, we find the sons of Noah and their descendants, or many of them, assembled on the

a. 5411 B. C.   b 3155 B. C.

banks of the Euphrates,[1] in a region called the " Land of Shinar,"
and there beginning to build a city,—together with a tower, whose
top, they boasted, should reach unto heaven. But the Lord came
down to see the city and the tower which the children of men in
their pride and impiety were building; and he there confounded the
language of the workmen, that they might not understand one another; and thus the building of the tower, which was called Babel,
was abandoned, and the people were scattered abroad over the whole
earth.

7. It is generally supposed that Noah himself, after this event,
journeyed eastward, and founded the empire of China; that Shem
was the father of the nations of Southern Asia; that Ham peopled
Egypt; and that the descendants of Japheth migrated westward
and settled in the countries of Europe, or, as they are called in
Scripture, the " Isles of the Gentiles."

8. Soon after the dispersion of mankind from Babel, it is supposed
that Mis'raim, one of the sons of Ham, journeyed into
Egypt,[2] where he became the founder of the most ancient
and renowned nation of antiquity. The government established by him is believed to have been that of an aristocratic

III. EGYPTIAN HISTORY.

---

1. The *Euphrates*, the most considerable river of Western Asia, has its sources in the table
lands of Armenia, about ninety miles from the south-eastern borders of the Black Sea. The
sources of the *Tigris* are in the same region, but farther south. The general direction of both
rivers is south-east, to their entrance into the head of the Persian Gulf. (*See Map, p.* 15.) So
late as the age of Alexander the Great, each of these rivers preserved a separate course to the
sea, but not long after they became united about eighty miles from their mouth, from which
point they have ever since continued to flow in a single stream. Both rivers are navigable a
considerable distance,—both have their regular inundations; rising twice a year—first in December, in consequence of the autumnal rains; and next from March till June, owing to the
melting of the mountain snows. The Scriptures place the Garden of Eden on the banks of the
Euphrates, but the exact site is unknown.

We learn that soon after the deluge, the country in the vicinity of the two rivers Tigris and
Euphrates, where stood the tower of Babel, was known as the *Land of Shinar* : afterwards the
empire of Assyria or Babylon flourished here; and still later, the country between the two
rivers was called by the ancient Greeks, *Mesopotamia*,—a compound of two Greek words,
(*mesos* and *potamos*,) signifying "between the rivers." In ancient times the banks of both
rivers were studded with cities of the first rank. On the eastern bank of the Tigris stood
Nineveh; and on both sides of the Euphrates stood the mighty Babylon, "the glory of kingdoms," and "the beauty of the Chaldee's excellency." Lower Mesopotamia, both above and
below Babylon, was anciently intersected by canals in every direction, many of which can still
be traced; and some of them could easily be restored to their original condition. (*See
Map, p.* 15.)

2. Ancient EGYPT, called by the Hebrews *Mis'raim*, may be divided into two principal portions; Upper or Southern Egypt, of which Thebes was the capital, and Lower Egypt, whose
capital was Memphis. That portion of Lower Egypt embraced within the mouths or outlets of
the Nile, the Greeks afterwards called the *Delta*, from its resemblance to the form of the
Greek letter of that name. (Δ) Ancient Egypt probably embraced all of the present Nubia,
and perhaps a part of Abyssinia. Modern Egypt is bounded on the North by the Mediterra-

priesthood, whose members were the patrons of the arts and sciences and it is supposed that the nation was divided into three distinct classes,—the priests, the military, and the people ;—the two former holding the latter and most numerous body in subjection. After this government had existed nearly two centuries, under rulers whose names have perished, Ménes, a military chieftain, is supposed to have subverted the ancient sacerdotal despotism, and to have established the first civil monarchy, about 2400 years before the Christian era. Ménes was the first *Pharaoh*, a name common to all the kings of Egypt.

9. Upon the authority of Herod' otus[1] and Joséphus,[2] to the first king, Ménes, is attributed the founding of Memphis,[3] probably the most ancient city in Egypt. Other writers ascribe to him the building of Thebes[4] also ; but some suppose that Thebes was built many

___

nean, on the east by the Isthmus of Suez and the Red Sea, on the south by Nubia, and on the west by the Great Desert and the province of Barca.

The cultivated portion of Egypt, embraced mostly within a narrow valley of from five to twenty miles in width, is indebted wholly to the annual inundations of the Nile for its fertility and without them, would soon become a barren waste. The river begins to swell, in its higher parts, in April ; but at the Delta no increase occurs until the beginning of June. Its greatest height there is in September, when the Delta is almost entirely under water. By the end of November the waters leave the land altogether, having deposited a rich alluvium. Then the Egyptian spring commences, at a season corresponding to our winter, when the whole country, covered with a vivid green, bears the aspect of a fruitful garden. (*Map, p. 15.*)

1. *Herod' otus*—the earliest of the Greek historians: born 484 B. C.

2. *Joséphus*—a celebrated Jewish historian: born at Jerusalem, A. D. 37.

3. *Memphis*, a famous city of Egypt, whose origin dates beyond the period of authentic history, is supposed to have stood on the western bank of the Nile, about fifteen miles south from the apex of the Delta—the point whence the waters of the river diverge to enter the sea by different channels. But few relics of its magnificence now occupy the ground where the city once stood, the materials having been mostly removed for the building of modern edifices. At the time of our Saviour, Memphis was the second city in Egypt, and next in importance to Alexandria, the capital ; but its decay had already begun. Even in the twelfth century of the Christian era, after the lapse of four thousand years from its origin, it is described by an Oriental writer as containing "works so wonderful that they confound even a reflecting mind, and such as the most eloquent would not be able to describe." (*Map, p. 15.*)

4. The ruins of *Thebes*, "the capital of a by-gone world," are situated in the narrow valley of the Nile, in Upper Egypt, extending about seven miles along both banks of the river. Here are still to be seen magnificent ruins of temples, palaces, colossal statues, obelisks, and tombs, which attest the exceeding wealth and power of the early Egyptians. The city is supposed to have attained its greatest splendor about fifteen hundred years before the Christian era. On the east side of the river the principal ruins are those of Carnac and Luxor, about a mile and a half apart. Among the former are the remains of a temple dedicated to Ammon, the Jupiter of the Egyptians, covering more than nine acres of ground. A large portion of this stupendous structure is still standing. The principal front to this building is 368 feet in length, and 148 feet in height, with a door-way in the middle 64 feet high. One of the halls in this vast building covers an area of more than an acre and a quarter ; and its roof, consisting of enormous slabs of stone, has been supported by 134 huge columns. The roof of what is supposed to have been the sanctuary, or place from which the oracles were delivered, is composed of three blocks of granite, painted with clusters of gilt stars on a blue ground. The entrance to this room was marked by four noble obelisks, each 70 feet high, three of which are now standing. At Luxor

centuries later. Ménes appears to have been occupied, during most of his reign, in wars with foreign nations to us unknown. According to numerous traditions, recorded in later ages, he also cultivated the arts of peace; he protected religion and the priesthood, and erected temples; he built walls of defence on the frontier of his kingdom— and he dug numerous canals, and constructed dikes, both to draw off

MAP ILLUSTRATIVE OF EARLY HISTORY.

are to be seen the remains of a magnificent palace, about 800 feet in length by 200 in width. On each side of the doorway is a colossal statue, measuring 44 feet from the ground. Fronting these statues were two obelisks, each formed of a single block of red granite, 80 feet in height, and beautifully sculptured. A few years ago one of these obelisks was taken down, and conveyed, at great expense, to the city of Paris, where it has been erected in the Place de la Concorde. Among the ruins on the west side of the river, at Medinet Abou, are two sitting colossal figures, each about 50 feet in height, supported by pedestals of corresponding dimensions. On the same side of the river, in the mountain-range that skirts the valley, and westward of the ruins, are the famous catacombs, or burial-places of the ancient inhabitants, excavated in the solid rock. (*Map, p. 15.*)

the waters of the Nile[1] for enriching the cultivated lands, and to prevent inundations. His name is common in ancient records, while many subsequent monarchs of Egypt have been forgotten. Monuments still exist which attest the veneration in which he was held by his posterity.

10. From the time of Ménes until about the 21st century before Christ, the period when Abraham is supposed to have visited Egypt,[1] little is known of Egyptian history. It appears, however, from hieroglyphic inscriptions, first interpreted in the present century, and corroborated by traditions and some vague historic records, that the greatest Egyptian pyramids[2] were erected three or four hundred years before the time of Abraham, and eight or nine hundred years before the era of Moses,—showing a truly astonishing degree of power and grandeur attained by the Egyptian monarchy more than four thousand years ago. When Abraham visited Egypt he was re-

1. The *Nile*, a large river of eastern Africa, is formed by the junction of the White River and the Blue River in the country of Sennaar, whence the united stream flows northward, in a very winding course, through Nubia and Egypt, and enters the Mediterranean through two mouths, those of Rosetta and Damietta, the former or most westerly of which has a width of about 1800 feet; and the latter of about 900. The Rosetta channel has a depth of about five feet in the dry season, and the Damietta channel of seven or eight feet when the river is lowest. Formerly the Nile entered the sea by seven different channels, several of which still occasionally serve for canals, and purposes of irrigation. During the last thirteen hundred miles of its course, the Nile receives no tributary on either side. The *White* river, generally regarded as the true Nile, about whose source no satisfactory knowledge has yet been obtained, is supposed to have its rise in the highlands of Central Africa, north of the Equator. (*Map, p.* 15.)

2. The *pyramids* of Egypt are vast artificial structures, most of them of stone, scattered a' irregular intervals along the western valley of the Nile from Meroe, (Mer-o-we) in modern Nubia, to the site of ancient Memphis near Cairo. (Ki-ro.) The largest, best known, and most celebrated, are the three pyramids of Ghizeh, situated on a platform of rock about 150 feet above the level of the surrounding desert, near the ruins of Memphis, seven or eight miles south-west from Cairo. The largest of these, the famous pyramid of Cheops, is a gigantic structure, the base of which covers a surface of about eleven acres. The sides of the base correspond in direction with the four cardinal points, and each measures, at the foundation, 746 feet. The perpendicular height is about 480 feet, which is 43 feet 9 inches higher than St. Peters at Rome, the loftiest edifice of modern times. This huge fabric consists of two hundred and six layers of vast blocks of stone, rising above each other in the form of steps, the thickness of which diminishes as the height of the pyramid increases, the lower layers being nearly five feet in thickness, and th upper ones about eighteen inches. The summit of the pyramid appears to have been, originally, a level platform, sixteen or eighteen feet square. Within this pyramid several chambers have been discovered, lined with immense slabs of granite, which must have been conveyed thither from a great distance up the Nile. The second pyramid at Ghizeh is coated over with polished stone 140 feet downwards from the summit, thereby removing the inequalities occasioned by the steps, and rendering the surface smooth and uniform. Herodotus states, from information derived from the Egyptian priests, that one hundred thousand men were employed twenty years in constructing the great pyramid of Ghizeh, and that ten years had been spent, previously, in quarrying the stones and conveying them to the place. The remaining pyramids of Egypt correspond, in their general character, with the one described, with the exception that several of them are constructed of sun-burnt brick. No reasonable doubt now exists that the pyramids were designed as the burial places of kings.

a. 2077 b. C.

ceived with the hospitality and kindness becoming a civilized nation; and when he left Egypt, to return to his own country, the ruling monarch dismissed him and all his people, "rich in cattle, in silver, and in gold."

11. Nearly a hundred years before the time of Abraham's visit to Egypt, Lower Egypt had been invaded and subdued[a] by the Hyc'sos, or Shepherd Kings, a roving people from the eastern shores of the Mediterranean, —probably the same that were known, at a later period, in sacred history, as the Philistines, and still later as the Phœnicians　Kings of this race continued to rule over Lower Egypt during a period of 260 years, but they were finally expelled,[b] and driven back to their original seats in Asia.　During their dominion, Upper Egypt, with Thebes its capital, appears to have remained under the government of the native Egyptians.　A few years after the expulsion of the Shepherd Kings, *Joseph* was appointed[c] governor or regent of Egypt under one of the Pharaohs; and the family of Jacob was settled[d] in the land of Goshen.[1]　It was during the residence of the Israelites in Egypt that we date the commencement of Grecian history, with the supposed founding of Argos by In'achus, 1856 years before the Christian era.

12. During the early period of Egyptian history which we have described, kingdoms arose and mighty cities were founded in those regions of Asia first peopled by the imme- IV. ASIATIC diate descendants of Noah.　After the dispersion of HISTORY. mankind from Babel, Ashur, one of the sons of Shem, remained in the vicinity of that place; and by many he is regarded as the founder of the Assyrian empire,[2] and the builder of Nineveh.[3]　But

1. "The land of *Goshen* lay along the most easterly branch of the Nile, and on the east side of it; for it is evident that at the time of the Exode the Israelites did not cross the Nile.　(Hale's Analysis of Chronology, i. 374.)　"The 'land of Goshen' was between Egypt and Canaan, not far from the Isthmus of Suez, on the eastern side of the Nile."　(*See Map, p. 15.*)　(*Cockayne's Hist. of the Jews, p. 7.*)

2. The early province or kingdom of ASSYRIA is usually considered as having been on the eastern bank of the river Tigris, having Nineveh for its capital.　But it is probable that both Nineveh and Babylon belonged to the early Assyrian empire, and that these two cities were at times the capitals of separate monarchies, and at times united under one government, whose territories were ever changing by conquest, and by alliances with surrounding tribes or nations.

3. The city of *Nineveh* is supposed to have stood on the east bank of the Tigris, opposite the modern city of Mosul.　(*See Map, p. 15.*)　Its site was probably identical with that of the present small village of Nunia, and what is called the "tomb of Jonah;" which are surrounded by vast heaps of ruins, and vestiges of mounds, from which bricks and pieces of gypsum are dug out, with inscriptions closely resembling those found among the ruins of Babylon.

Of the early history of Nineveh little is known.　Some early writers describe it as larger than Babylon; but little dependence can be placed on their statements.　It is believed, however,

a. 2159 B. C.　　　b. 1900 B C.　　　c. 1872 B. C.　　　d. 1863 B. C.

others[1] ascribe this honor to Nimrod, a grandson of Ham, who, as they suppose, having obtained possession of the provinces of Ashur, built Nineveh, and encompassing Babel with walls, and rebuilding the deserted city, made it the capital of his empire, under the name of Babylon,

that the walls included, besides the buildings of the city, a large extent of well-cultivated gardens and pasture grounds. In the ninth century before Christ, it was described by the prophet Jonah, as "an exceeding great city of three days' journey," and as containing "more than six score thousand persons that could not distinguish between their right hand and their left." It is generally believed that the expression here used denoted *children*, and that the entire population of the city numbered seven or eight hundred thousand souls.

Nineveh was a city of great commercial importance. The prophet Nahum thus addressed her: "Thou hast multiplied thy merchants above the stars of heaven." (iii. 16.) Nineveh was besieged and taken by Arbaces the Mede, in the eighth century before Christ; and in the year 612 it fell into the hands of Ahasuerus, or Cyaxares, king of Media, who took great "spoil of silver and gold, and none end of the store and glory, out of all her pleasant furniture," making her "empty, and void, and waste." (*Map, p.* 15.)

1. According to our English Bible (Genesis, x. 11), "*Ashur* went forth out of the land of Shinar (Babylon) and builded Nineveh." But by many this reading is supposed to be a wrong translation, and that the passage should read, "From that land he (Nimrod) went forth into Ashur, (the name of a province,) and built Nineveh." ("De terra illa egressus est Assur et ædificavit Nineveh." (See Anthon's Classical Dictionary, article Assyria. See, also, the subject examined in Hale's Analysis of Chronology, i. 450-1.)

2. Ancient *Babylon*, once the greatest, most magnificent, and most powerful city of the world, stood on both sides of the river Euphrates, about 350 miles from the entrance of that stream into the Persian Gulf. The building of Babel was probably the commencement of the city, but it is supposed to have attained its greatest glory during the reign of the Assyrian queen, Semiramis. Different writers give different accounts of the extent of this city. The Greek historian Herod' otus, who visited it in the fourth century before Christ, while its walls were still standing and much of its early magnificence remaining, described it as a perfect square, the walls of each side being 120 furlongs, or fifteen miles in length. According to this computation the city embraced an area of 225 square miles. But Diodórus reduces the supposed area to 72 square miles;—equal, however, to three and a half times the area of London, with all its suburbs. Some writers have supposed that the city contained a population of at least five millions of people. Others have reduced this estimate to one million. It is highly improbable that the whole of the immense area inclosed by the walls was filled with the buildings of a compact city.

The walls of Babylon, which were built of large bricks cemented with bitumen, are said to have been 350 feet high, and 87 feet in thickness, flanked with lofty towers, and pierced by 100 gates of brass. The two portions of the city, on each side of the Euphrates, were connected by a bridge of stone, which rested on arches of the same material. The temple of Júpiter Belus, supposed to have been the tower of Babel, is described by Herod' otus as an immense structure, square at the base, and rising, in eight distinct stories, to the height of nearly 600 feet. Herod' otus says that when he visited Babylon the brazen gates of this temple were still to be seen, and that in the upper story there was a couch magnificently adorned, and near it a table of solid gold. Herod' otus also mentions a statue of gold twelve cubits high,—supposed to have been the "golden image" set up by Nebuchadnezzar. The site of this temple has been identified as that of the ruins now called by the Arabs the "Birs Nimroud," or *Tower of Nimrod.*

Later writers than Herod' otus speak of a tunnel under the Euphrates—subterranean banqueting rooms of brass—and hanging gardens elevated three hundred feet above the city; but as Herod' otus is silent on these points, serious doubts have been entertained of the existence of these structures.

Nothing now remains of the buildings of ancient Babylon but immense and shapeless masses of ruins; their sites being partly occupied by the modern and meanly built town of Hillah, on the western bank of the Euphrates. This town, surrounded by mud walls, contains a mixed Arabian and Jewish population of six or seven thousand souls. (*Map, p.* 15.)

about 600 years after the deluge, and 2555 years before the Chris
tian era. After his death, Nimrod was deified for his great actions,
and called Belus : and it is supposed that the tower of Babel, rising
high above the walls of Babylon, but still in an unfinished state, was
consecrated to his worship.

13. While some believe that the monarch Ninus was the son of
Nimrod, and that Assyria and Babylon formed one united empire
under the immediate successors of the first founder; others regard
Ninus as an Assyrian prince, who, by conquering Babylon, united
the hitherto separate empires, more than four hundred years after
the reign of Nimrod; while others still regard Ninus as only a personification of Nineveh.[a] During the reign of Ninus, and also
during that of his supposed queen and successor, Semir' amis, the
boundaries of the united Assyrian and Babylonian empires are said
to have been greatly enlarged by conquest; but the accounts that
are given of these events are evidently so exaggerated, that little reliance can be placed upon them.

14. Semir' amis, who was raised from an humble station to become the queen of Ninus, is described as a woman of uncommon
courage and masculine character, the main object of whose ambition
was to immortalize her name by the greatness of her exploits. Her
conquests are said to have embraced nearly all the then known world,
extending as far as Central Africa on the one hand, and as far as
the Indus,[1] in Asia, on the other. She is said to have raised, at one
time, an army of more than three millions of men, and to have employed two millions of workmen in adorning Babylon—statements
wholly inconsistent with the current opinion of the sparse population
of the world at this early period. After the reign of Semir' amis,
which is supposed to have been during the time of the sojourn of
the Israelites in Egypt, little is known of the history of Assyria for
more than thirty generations.

1. The river *Indus*, or Sinde, rises in the Himmaleh mountains, and running in a south west
erly direction enters the Arabian Sea near the western extremity of Hindostan.

a. Niebuhr's Ancient Hist. I. 55.

CHAPTER II.

THE FABULOUS AND LEGENDARY PERIOD OF GRECIAN HISTORY:

ENDING WITH THE CLOSE OF THE TROJAN WAR, 1183 B C.

ANALYSIS. 1. Extent of Ancient Greece. Of Modern Greece. The most ancient names of the country.—2. The two general divisions of Modern Greece. Extent of Northern Greece Of the Morea. Whole area of the country so renowned in history.—3. The general surface of the country. Its fertility.—4. Mountains of Greece. Rivers. Climate. The seasons. Scenery Classical associations.

5. GRECIAN MYTHOLOGY, the proper introduction to Grecian history.—6. Chaos. Earth, and Heaven. The offspring of Earth and U'ranus. [U'ranus; the Titans: the Cyclopes.]—7. U'ranus is dethroned, and is succeeded by Sat'urn. [The Furies: the Giants: and the Melian Nymphs. Venus. Sat'urn. Jupiter. Nep'tune. Pluto.]—8. War of the Titans against Sat'urn. War of the Giants with Jupiter. The result. New dynasty of the gods.—9. The wives of Jupiter. [Juno.] His offspring. [Mer'cury. Mars. Apol'lo. Vul'can. Diana. Miner'va.] Other celestial divinities. [Ceres. Ves'ta.]—10. Other deities not included among the celestials. [Bac'chus. Iris. Hebe. The Muses. The Fates. The Graces.] Monsters. [Harpies. Gor'-gons.] Rebellions against Jupiter. [Olym'pus.]—11. Numbers, and character, of the legends of the gods. Vulgar belief, and philosophical explanations of them.

12. EARLIEST INHABITANTS OF GREECE. The Pelas'gians. Tribes included under this name.—13. Character and civilization of the Pelas'gians. [Cyclopean structures. Asia Minor.]—14. FOREIGN SETTLERS IN GREECE. Reputed founding of Ar'gos. [Ar'gos. Ar'-golis. Oceanus. In'achus.] The accounts of the early Grecian settlements not reliable.—15. The founding of Athens. [At'tica. Ogy'ges.] The elements of Grecian civilization attributed to Cecrops. The story of Cecrops doubtless fabulous.—16. Legend of the contest between Min-er'va and Nep'tune.—17. Cran'aus and Amphic'tyon. Dan'aus and Cad'mus. [Bœotia. Thebes.]—18. General character of the accounts of foreign settlers in Greece. Value of these tra-ditions. The probable truth in relation to them, which accounts for the intermixture of foreign with Grecian mythology. [Ægean Sea.]

19. The HELLENES appear in Thessaly, about 1384 B. C., and become the ruling class among the Grecians.—20. Hellen the son of Deucalion. The several Grecian tribes. The Æolian tribe. —21. The HEROIC AGE. Our knowledge of Grecian history during this period. Character and value of the Heroic legends. The most important of them. [1st. Hercules. 2d. Theseus. 3d. Argonautic expedition. 4th. Theban and Ar'golic war.]—22. The Argonautic expedition thought the most important. Probably a poetic fiction. [Samothrace. Euxine Sea.] Proba-bility of naval expeditions at this early period, and their results. [Minos. Crete.]—23. Open ing of the Trojan war. Its alleged causes. [Troy. Lacedæ'mon.]—24. Paris,—the flight o Helen,—the war which followed.—25. Remarks on the supposed reality of the war. [The fable of Helen.]—26. What kind of truth is to be extracted from Homer's account.

COTEMPORARY HISTORY.—1. Our limited knowledge of cotemporary history during this period. Rome. Europe. Central Western Asia. Egyptian History.—2. The conquests of Sesos'tris. [Libya. Ethiopia. The Ganges. Thracians and Scythians.] The columns erect-ed by Sesos'tris.—3. Statues of Sesostris at Ipsam'boul. Historical sculptures.—4. Remarks on the evidences of the existence of this conqueror. The close of his reign. Subsequent Egyptian history.—5. The Israelites at the period of the commencement of Grecian history. Their situation after the death of Joseph. Their exodus from Egypt, 1648 B.'C.—6. Wander ngs in the wilderness Passage of the Jordan. [Arabia. Jordan. Palestine.] Death of

1. GREECE, which is the Roman name of the country whose history we next proceed to narrate, but which was called by the natives *Hel'las*, denoting the country of the *Hellénés*, comprised, in its most flourishing period, nearly the whole of the great eastern peninsula of southern Europe —extending north to the northern extremity of the waters of the Grecian Archipelago. Modern Greece, however, has a less extent on the north, as Thes'saly, Epírus, and Macedónia have been taken from it, and annexed to the Turkish empire. The area of Modern Greece is less than that of Portugal; but owing to the irregularities of its shores, its range of seacoast is greater than that of the whole of Spain. The most ancient name by which Greece was known to other nations was *Iónia*,—a term which Josephus derives from Javan, the son of Japhet, and grandson of Noah: although the Greeks themselves applied the term *Iónes* only to the descendants of the fabulous *I'on*, son of Xúthus.

I. GEOGRAPHI-CAL DESCRIP-TION.

2. Modern Greece is divided into two principal portions :—Northern Greece or Hel'las, and Southern Greece, or Moréa—anciently called Peloponnésus. The former includes the country of the ancient Grecian States, Acarnánia, Ætólia, Lócris, Phócis, Dóris, Bœótia, Eubœ'a, and At'tica; and the latter, the Peloponnesian States of E'lis, Acháia, Cor'inth, Ar'golis, Lacónia, and Messénia; whose localities may be learned from the accompanying map. The greatest length of the northern portion, which is from north-west to south east, is about two hundred miles, with an average width of fifty miles. The greatest length of the Moréa, which is from north to south, is about one hundred and forty miles. The whole area of the country so renowned in history under the name of Greece or Hel'las, is only about twenty thousand square miles, which is less than half the area of the State of Pennsylvania.

3. The general surface of Greece is mountainous; and almost the only fertile spots are the numerous and usually narrow plains along the sea-shore and the banks of rivers, or, as in several places, large basins, which apparently once formed the beds of mountain lakes. The largest tracts of level country are in western Hel'las, and along the northern and north-western shores of the Moréa.

4. The mountains of Greece are of the Alpine character, and are remarkable for their numerous grottos and caverns. Their abrupt summits never rise to the regions of perpetual snow. There are no navigable rivers in Greece, but this want is obviated by the numerous gulfs and inlets of the sea, which indent the coast on every side, and thus furnish unusual facilities to commerce, while they add to the variety and beauty of the scenery. The climate of Greece is for the most part healthy, except in the low and marshy tracts around the shores and lakes. The winters are short. Spring and autumn are rainy seasons, when many parts of the country are inundated; but during the whole summer, which comprises half the year, a cloud in the sky is rare in several parts of the country. Grecian scenery is unsurpassed in romantic wildness and beauty; but our deepest interest in the country arises from its classical associations, and the ruins of ancient art and splendor scattered over it.

5. As the Greeks, in common with the Egyptians and other Eastern nations, placed the reign of the gods anterior to the race of mortals, therefore Grecian mythology[1] forms the most appropriate introduction to Grecian history.   II. GRECIAN MYTHOLOGY.

6. According to Grecian philosophy, first in the order of time came Cháos, a heterogeneous mass containing all the seeds of nature; then "broad-breasted Earth," the mother of the gods, who produced U'ranus, or Heaven, the mountains, and the barren and billowy sea. Then Earth married U'ranus[2] or Heaven, and from this union came a numerous and powerful brood, the Títans[3] and the Cyclópes,[4] and the gods of the wintry season,—Kot'tos, Briáreus, and Gy'ges, who had each a hundred hands,—supposed to be personifications of the hail, the rain, and the snow.

1. MYTHOLOGY, from two Greek words signifying a "*fable*" and a "*discourse*," is a system of myths, or fabulous opinions and doctrines respecting the deities which heathen nations are supposed to preside over the world, or to influence its affairs.

2. U'ranus, from a Greek word signifying "heaven," or "sky," was the most ancient of all the gods.

3. The Titans were six males—Oceanus, Coios, Crios, Hyperion, Japetus, and Kronos, or Sat'urn, and six females,—Théia, Rhéa, Thémis, Mnemos'yne, Phœ'be, and Téthys. Océanus or the Ocean, espoused his sister Téthys, and their children were the rivers of the earth, and the three thousand Oceanides or Ocean-nymphs. Hypérion married his sister Théia, by whom he had Auróra, or the morning, and also the sun and moon.

4. The Cyclópes were a race of gigantic size, having but one eye, and that placed in the centre of the forehead. According to some accounts there were many of this race, but according to the poet Hesiod, the principal authority in Grecian mythology, they were only three in number, Bron'tes, Ster'opes, and Ar'ges, words which signify in the Greek, Thunder, Lightning, and the rapid Flame. The poets converted them into smiths—the assistants of the fire-god Vulcan. The Cyclópes were probably personifications of the energies of the "powers of the air."

HEATHEN DEITIES.

JUPITER.   NEPTUNE.   PLUTO.

MERCURY.   MARS.   VULCAN.

APOLLO.   DIANA.   MINERVA.

JUNO.   CERES.   VESTA.

ANDERSON SC.

7. The Titans made war upon their father, who was wounded by Sat' urn,[1] the youngest and bravest of his sons. From the drops of blood which flowed from the wound and fell upon the earth, sprung the Furies,[2] the Giants,[3] and the Melian nymphs;[4] and from those which fell into the sea, sprung Venus,[5] the goddess of love and beauty U' ranus or Heaven being dethroned, Sat' urn, by the consent of his brethren, was permitted to reign in his stead, on condition that he would destroy all his male children: but Rhéa his wife concealed from him the birth of Júpiter,[6] Nep' tune,[7] and Plúto.[8]

1. *Sat' urn*, the youngest but most powerful of the Titans, called by the Greeks, Krónos, word signifying "Time," is generally represented as an old man, bent by age and infirmity, holding a scythe in his right hand, together with a serpent that bites its own tail, which is an emblem of time, and of the revolution of the year. In his left hand he has a child which he raises up as if to devour it—as time devours all things.

When Sat' urn was banished by his son Júpiter, he is said to have fled to Italy, where he employed himself in civilizing the barbarous manners of the people. His reign there was so beneficent and virtuous that mankind have called it the *golden age*. According to Hesiod, Sat' urn ruled over the Isles of the Blessed, at the end of the earth, by the "deep eddying ocean."

2. The *Furies* were three goddesses, whose names signified the "Unceasing," the "Envier," and the "Blood-avenger." They are usualy represented with looks full of terror, each brand ishing a torch in one hand and a scourge of snakes in the other. They torment guilty consciences, and punish the crimes of bad men.

3. The *Giants* are represented as of uncommon stature, with strength proportioned to their gigantic size. The war of the Titans against Sat' urn, and that of the Giants against Júpiter, are very celebrated in mythology. It is believed that the Giants were nothing more than the energies of nature personified, and that the war with Júpiter is an allegorical representation of some tremendous convulsion of nature in early times.

4. In Grecian mythology, all the regions of earth and water were peopled with beautiful female forms called nymphs, divided into various orders according to the place of their abode. The *Melian* nymphs were those which watched over gardens and flocks.

5. *Vénus*, the most beautiful of all the goddesses, is sometimes represented as rising out of the sea, and wringing her locks,—sometimes drawn in a sea-shell by Tritons—sea-deities that were half fish and half human—and sometimes in a chariot drawn by swans. Swans, doves, and sparrows, were sacred to her. Her favorite plants were the rose and the myrtle.

6. *Júpiter*, called the "father of men and gods," is placed at the head of the entire system of the universe. He is supreme over all: earthly monarchs derive their authority from him, and his will is fate. He is generally represented as majestic in appearance, seated on a throne, with a sceptre in one hand, and thunderbolts in the other. The eagle, which is sacred to him, is standing by his side. Regarding Júpiter as the surrounding ether, or atmosphere, the numer ous fables of this monarch of the gods may be considered allegories which typify the great gen erative power of the universe, displaying itself in a variety of ways, and under the greatest diversity of forms.

7. *Nep' tune*, the "Earth-shaker," and ruler of the sea, is second only to Júpiter in powe. He is represented, like Júpiter, of a serene and majestic aspect, seated in a chariot made of a shell, bearing a trident in his right hand, and drawn by dolphins and sea-horses; while the tritons, nymphs, and other sea-monsters, gambol around him.

8. *Pluto*, called also Hades and Or' cus, the god of the lower world, is represented as a man of a stern aspect, seated on a throne of sulphur, from beneath which flow the rivers Letho or Oblivion, Phleg' ethon, Cocy' tus, and Ach' eron. In one hand he holds a bident, or sceptre with two forks, and in the other the keys of hell. His queen, Pros' erpine, is sometimes seated by him. He is described by the poets as a being inexorable and deaf to supplication, and as

8. Th? Titans, informed that Sat'urn had saved his children, made war upon him and dethroned him; but he was restored by his son Jupiter. Yet the latter afterwards conspired against his father, and after a long war with him and his giant progeny, which lasted ten full years, and in which all the gods took part, he drove Sat'urn from the kingdom, and then divided, between himself and his brothers Nep'tune and Plúto, the dominion of the universe, taking heaven as his own portion, and assigning the sea to Nep'tune, and to Plúto the lower regions, the abodes of the dead. With Júpiter and his brethren begins a new dynasty of the gods, being those, for the most part, whom the Greeks recognised and worshipped.

9. Júpiter had several wives, both goddesses and mortals, but last of all he married his sister Júno,[1] who maintained, permanently, the dignity of queen of the gods. The offspring of Jupiter were numerous, comprising both celestial and terrestrial divinities. The most noted of the former were Mer'cury,[2] Mars,[3] Apol'lo,[4] Vul'can,[5]

object of aversion and hatred to both gods and men. From his realms there is no return, and all mankind, sooner or later, are sure to be gathered into his kingdom.

As none of the goddesses would marry the stern and gloomy god, he seized Pros'erpine, the daughter of Céres, while she was gathering flowers, and opening a passage through the earth tarried her to his abode, and made her queen of his dominions.

1. *Juno*, a goddess of a dignified and matronly air, but haughty, jealous, and inexorable, is represented sometimes as seated on a throne, holding in one hand a pomegranate, and in the other a golden sceptre, with a cuckoo on its top; and at others, as drawn in a chariot by peacocks, and attended by I'ris, the goddess of the rainbow.

The many quarrels attributed to Júpiter and Júno, are supposed to be physical allegories— Júpiter representing the ether, or upper regions of the air, and Júno the lower strata—hence their quarrels are the storms that pass over the earth: and the capricious and quick-changing temper of the spouse of Jove, is typical of the ever-varying changes that disturb our atmosphere.

2. *Mer'cury*, the confident, messenger, interpreter, and ambassador of the gods, was himself the god of eloquence, and the patron of orators, merchants, thieves and robbers, travellers and shepherds. He is said to have invented the lyre, letters, commerce, and gymnastic exercises. His thieving exploits are celebrated. He is usually represented with a cloak neatly arranged on his person, having a winged cap on his head, and winged sandals on his feet. In his hand he bears his wand or staff, with wings at its extremity, and two serpents twined about it.

3. *Mars*, the god of war, was of huge size and prodigious strength, and his voice was louder than that of ten thousand mortals. He is represented as a warrior of a severe and menacing air, dressed in the style of the Heroic Age, with a cuirass on, and a round Grecian shield on his arm. He is sometimes seen standing in a chariot, with Bellona his sister for a charioteer. Terror and Fear accompany him; Discord, in tattered garments, goes before him, and Anger and Clamor follow.

4. *Apol'lo*, the god of archery, prophecy, and music, is represented in the perfection of manly strength and beauty, with hair long and curling, and bound behind his head; his brows are wreathed with bay: sometimes he bears a lyre in his hand, and sometimes a bow, with a golden qu'ver of arrows at his back.

5. *Vul'can* was the fire-god of the Greeks, and the artificer of heaven. He was born lame, and his mother Júno was so shocked at the sight that she flung him from Olym'pus. He forged the thunderbolts of Júpiter, also the arms of gods and demi-gods. He is usually represented as of ripe age, with a serious countenance and muscular form. His hair hangs in curls

Diána,[1] and Miner'va.[2]　There were two other celestial divinities,
Céres[3] and Ves'ta,[4] making, with Júno, Nep'tune, and Plato, twelve
in all.

10. The number of other deities, not included among the celestials,
was indefinite, the most noted of whom were Bac'chus,[5] I'ris,[6] Hebe,[7]
the Muses,[8] the Fates,[9] and the Graces;[10] also Sleep, Dreams. and
Death.　There were also monsters, the offspring of the gods, pos
essed of free will and intelligence, and having the mixed forms of

to his shoulders. He generally appears at his anvil, in a short tunic, with his right arm bare
and sometimes with a pointed cap on his head.

1. *Diána*, the exact counterpart of her brother Apol'lo, was queen of the woods, and the
goddess of hunting. She devoted herself to perpetual celibacy, and her chief joy was to speed
like a Dórian maid over the hills, followed by a train of nymphs, in pursuit of the flying game
She is represented as a strong, active maiden, lightly clad, with a bow or hunting spear in her
hand, a quiver of arrows on her shoulders, wearing the Crétan hunting-shoes, and attended by
a hound.

2. *Miner'va*, the goddess of wisdom and skill, and, as opposed to Mars, the patroness and
teacher of just and scientific warfare, is said to have sprung, full armed, from the brain of Jú
piter. She is represented with a serious and thoughtful countenance; her hair hangs in ring
lets over her shoulders, and a helmet covers her head: she wears a long tunic or tunicle, and
bears a spear in one hand, and an ægis or shield, on which is a figure of the Gorgon's head, in
the other.

3. *Céres* was the goddess of grain and harvests. The most celebrated event in her history is
the carrying off of her daughter Pros'erpine by Pluto, and the search of the goddess after her
throughout the whole world. The form of Ceres is like that of Juno. She is represented bear
ing poppies and ears of corn in one hand, a lighted torch in the other, and a crown on her head
a garland of poppies. She is also represented riding in a chariot drawn by dragons, and dis
tributing corn to the different regions of the earth.

4. *Ves'ta*, the virgin goddess who presided over the domestic hearth, is represented in a long
flowing robe, with a veil on her head, a lamp in one hand, and a spear or javelin in the other.
In every Grecian city an altar was dedicated to her, on which a sacred fire was kept constantly
burning. In her temple at Rome the sacred fire was guarded by six priestesses, called the
Vestal Virgins.

5. *Bac'chus*, the god of wine, and the patron of drunkenness and debauchery, is represented
as an effeminate young man, with long flowing hair, crowned with a garland of vine leaves,
and generally covered with a cloak thrown loosely over his shoulders. In one hand he holds a
goblet, and in the other clusters of grapes and a short dagger.

6. *Iris*, the "golden winged," was the goddess of the rainbow, and special messenger of the
king and queen of Olympus.

7. The blooming *Hebe*, the goddess of Youth, was a kind of maid-servant who handed around
the nectar at the banquets of the gods.

8. The *Muses*, nine in number, were goddesses who presided over poetry, music, and all the
liberal arts and sciences. They are thought to be personifications of the inventive powers of
the mind, as displayed in the several arts.

9. The *Fates* were three goddesses who presided over the destinies of mortals:— 1st. Cló'tho
who held the distaff; 2d, Lach'esis, who spun each one's portion of the thread of life; and 3d,
At'ropos, who cut off the thread with her scissors.

> "Clótho and Lach'esis, whose boundless sway,
> With At'ropos, both men and gods obey!"—Hesiod.

10. The *Graces* were three young and beautiful sisters, whose names signified, respectively,
Splendor, Joy, and Pleasure. They are supposed to have been a symbolical representation of
all that is beautiful and attractive. They are represented as dancing together, or standing with
their arms entwined.

animals and men. Such were the Har'pies;[1] the Gorgons;[2] the winged horse Peg'asus; the fifty, or, as some say, the hundred head ed dog Cer'berus; the Cen'taurs, half men and half horses; the Ler'nean Hy'dra, a famous water serpent; and Scyl'la and Charyb' dis, fearful sea monsters, the one changed into a rock, and the other into a whirlpool on the coast of Sicily,—the dread of mariners. Many rebellious attempts were made by the gods and demi-gods to dethrone Júpiter; but by his unparalleled strength he overcame all his enemies, and holding his court on mount Olym'pus,[3] reigned su preme god over heaven and earth.

11. Such is the brief outline of Grecian mythology. The legends of the gods and goddesses are numerous, and some of them are of exceeding interest and beauty, while others shock and disgust us by the gross impossibilities and hideous deformities which they reveal. The great mass of the Grecian people appear to have believed that their divinities were real persons; but their philosophers explained the legends concerning them as allegorical representations of general physical and moral truths. The Greek, therefore, instead of wor shipping nature, worshipped the powers of nature personified.

12. The earliest reliable information that we possess of the country denominated Greece, represents it in the possession of III. EARLIEST a number of rude tribes, of which the Pelas'gians were INHABITANTS the most numerous and powerful, and probably the most OF GREECE. ancient. The name Pelas'gians was also a general one, under which were included many kindred tribes, such as the Dol'opes, Chá ones, and Græ'ci; but still the origin and extent of the race are in volved in much obscurity.

13. Of the early character of the Pelas'gians, and of the degree of civilization to which they had attained before the reputed found ing of Ar'gos, we have unsatisfactory and conflicting accounts. On the one hand they are represented as no better than the rudest bar barians, dwelling in caves, subsisting on reptiles, herbs, and wild fruits, and strangers to the simplest arts of civilized life. Other and more reliable traditions, however, attribute to them a knowledge of

1. The *Har'pies* were three-winged monsters who had female faces, and the bodies, wings and claws of birds. They are supposed to be personifications of the terrors of the storm—de mons riding upon the wind, and directing its blasts.

2. The *Gor'gons* were three hideous female forms, who turned to stone all whom they fixed their eyes upon. They are supposed to be personifications of the terrors of the sea.

3. *Olympus* is a celebrated mountain of Greece, near the north-eastern coast of Thessaly. To the highest summit in the range the name Olympus was specially applied by the poets. It was the fabled residence of the gods; and hence the name "Olym'pus" was frequently used for "Heaven."

agriculture, and some little acquaintance with navigation; while there is a strong probability that they were the authors* of those huge structures commonly called Cyclopean,[1] remains of which are still visible in many parts of Greece and Italy, and on the western coast of Asia Minor.[2]

14. Ar' gos,[3] the capital of Ar' golis,[4] is generally considered the most ancient city of Greece; and its reputed founding by In' achus, a son of the god Océanus,[5] 1856 years before the Christian era, is usually assigned as the period of the commencement of Grecian history. But the massive Cyclópean walls of Ar' gos evidently show the Pelas' gic origin of the place, in opposition to the traditional Phœnician origin of In' achus, whose very existence is quite problematical. And indeed the accounts usually given of early foreign settlers in Greece, who planted colonies there, founded dynasties, built cities, and introduced a

IV. FOREIGN SETTLERS IN GREECE.

1. The Cyclópean structures were works of extraordinary magnitude, consisting of walls an 1 circular buildings, constructed of immense blocks of stone placed upon each other without cement, but so nicely fitted as to form the most solid masonry. The most remarkable are certain walls at Tir' yns, or Tiryn' thus, and the circular tower of At' reus at Mycéna, both cities of Ar' golis in Greece. The structure at Mycéna is a hollow cone fifty feet in diameter, and as many in height, formerly terminating in a point; but the central stone and a few others have been removed. The Greek poets ascribed these structures to the three Cyclópes *Bróntes*, *Ster'-opes*, and *Ar' ges*, fabulous one-eyed giants, whose employment was to fabricate the thunderbolts of Jupiter. (*See Cyclópes*, p. 22.)

2. *Asia Minor*, (or Lesser Asia,) now embraced mostly in the Asiatic portion of Turkey comprised that western peninsula of Asia which lies between the waters of the Mediterranean and the Black Sea. (*See Map*, No. IV.)

3. *Ar' gos*, a city of southern Greece, and anciently the capital of the kingdom of Ar' golis, is situated on the western bank of the river In' achus, two miles from the bottom of the Gulf of Ar' gos, and on the western side of a plain ten or twelve miles in length, and four or five in width. The eastern side of the plain is dry and barren, and here were situated Tir' yns, from which Her' cules departed at the commencement of his "labors," and Mycéna, the royal city of Agamem' non. The immediate vicinity of Ar' gos was injured by excess of moisture. Here, near the Gulf, was the marsh of *Ler' na*, celebrated for the Ler' nean Hy' dra, which Her' cules slew.

But few vestiges of the ancient city of Ar' gos are now to be seen. The elevated rock on which stood the ancient citadel, is now surmounted by a modern castle. The town suffered much during the revolutionary struggle between the Greeks and Turks. The present population is about 3,000. (*See Map*, No. I.)

4. *Ar' golis*, a country of Southern Greece, is properly a neck of land, deriving its name from its capital city, Ar' gos, and extending in a south-easterly direction from Arcádia fifty-four miles into the sea, where it terminates in the promontory of Scil' læum. Among the noted places in Ar' golis have been mentioned Ar gos, Mycénæ, Tir' yns, and the Ler' nean marsh. *Némea*, in the north of Ar' golis, was celebrated for the *Némean lion*, and for the games instituted there in honor of Nep' tune. *Naúplia*, or Napoli di Romani, which was the post and arsenal of ancient Ar' gos during the best period of Grecian history, is now a flourishing, enterprising, and beautiful town of about 16,000 inhabitants. (*See Map*, No. I.)

5 *Océanus*. (See "The *Titans*," p. 22) *In' achus* was probably only a river, personified into the founder of a Grecia i state.

a. Thirwall's Greece I. p. 52; Anthon's Classical Dict. articles *Pelasgi* and *Ar' gos*; also Heeren's Manual of Ancient History, p. 119.

knowledge of the arts unknown to the ruder natives, must be taken with a great degree of abatement.

15. Cécrops, an Egyptian, is said to have led a colony from the Delta to Greece about the year 1556 B. C. Two years later proceeding to At'tica,[1] which had been desolated by a deluge a century before, during the reign of Og'yges,[2] he is said to have founded on the Cecrópian rock, a new city, which he called Athens,[3] in honor of the Grecian goddess Athe'na, whom the Romans called Miner'va. To Cecrops has been ascribed the institution of marriage, and the introduction of the first elements of Grecian civilization; yet, not only has the Egyptian origin of Cécrops been doubted, but his very existence has been denied,[a] and the whole story of his Egyptian colony, and of the arts which he is said to have established, has been attributed, with much show of reason, to a homesprung Attic fable.

16. As a part of the history of Cécrops, it is represented that in his days the gods began to choose favorite spots among the dwellings of men for their residences; or, in other words, that particular deities began to be worshipped with especial homage in particular cities; and that when Miner'va and Nep'tune claimed the homage of At'tica, Cécrops was chosen umpire of the dispute. Nep'tune asserted that he had appropriated the country to himself before it had been claimed by Miner'va, by planting his trident on the rock of the Acrop'olis of Athens; and, as proof of his claim, he pointed

1. *At'tica*, the most celebrated of the Grecian States, and the least proportioned, in extent of any on the face of the earth, to its fame and importance in the history of mankind, is situated at the south-eastern extremity of Northern Greece, having an extent of about forty-five miles from east to west, and an average breadth of about thirty-five. As the soil of At'tica was mostly rugged, and the surface consisted of barren hills, or plains of little extent, its produce was never sufficient to supply the wants of its inhabitants, who were therefore compelled to look abroad for subsistence. Thus the barrenness of the Attic soil rendered the people industrious, and filled them with that spirit of enterprise and activity for which they were so distinguished. Secure in her sterility, the soil of At'tica never tempted the cupidity of her neighbors, and she boasted that the race of her inhabitants had ever been the same. Among the advantages of At'tica may be reckoned the purity of its air, the fragrance of its shrubs, and the excellence of its fruits, together with its form and position, which marked it out, in an eminent degree, for commercial pursuits. Its most remarkable plains are those of Athens and Mar'athon, and its principal rivers the Cephis'sus and Ilys'sus. (*See Map*, No. 1.)

2. *Og'yges* is fabled to have been the first king of Athens and of Thebes also. It is also said that in the time of Og'yges happened a deluge, which preceded that of Deucálion; and Og'yges is said to have been the only person saved when Greece was covered with water.

3. *Athens.* (*See Map* No. 11. *and description.*)

a. "Notwithstanding the confidence with which this story (that of Cécrops) has been repeated in modern times, the Egyptian origin of Cécrops is extremely doubtful."—*Thirwall i. p. 53* "The story of his leading a colony from Egypt to Athens is entitled to no credit."—"The whole series of Attic kings who are said to have preceded Théseus, including perhaps Théseus himself, are probably mere fictions."—*Anthon's Clas. Dict., article* "*Cécrops.*"

to the trident standing there erect, and to the salt spring which had issued from the fissure in the cliff, and which still continued to flow. On the other hand, Miner' va pointed to the olive which she had planted long ago, and which still grew in native luxuriance by the side of the fountain which, she asserted, had been produced at a later period by the hand of Nep' tune. Cécrops himself attested the truth of her assertion, when the gods, according to one account, but according to another, Cécrops himself, decided in favor of Miner' va who then became the tutelary deity of Athens.

17. Cran' aus, the successor of Cécrops on the list of Attic kings, was probably a no less fabulous personage than his predecessor; and of Amphic' tyon, the third on the list, who is said to have been the founder of the celebrated Amphictyonic council, our knowledge is as limited and as doubtful as of the former two.[a] About half a century after the time of Cécrops, another Egyptian, by name Dan' aus, is said to have fled to Greece with a family of fifty daughters, and to have established a second Egyptian colony in the vicinity of Ar' gos; and about the same time, Cad' mus,[1] a Phœnician, is reported to have led a colony into Bœótia,[2] bringing with him the Phœnician alphabet, the basis of the Grecian, and to have founded Cad' mea, which afterwards became the citadel of Thebes.[3]

1. There is no good reason for believing that *Cad' mus* was the founder of Thebes, as his history is evidently fabulous, although there can be little doubt that the alphabet attributed to him was originally brought from Phœnicia. (See Thirwall, i. p. 107.) We may therefore venture to dismiss the early theory of Cad' mus, and seek a Grecian origin for the name of the supposed founder of Thebes.

2. *Bœótia*, lying north-west of At' tica, is a high and well-watered region, mostly surrounded by mountain ranges, of which the most noted summits are those of Hel' icon and Cithæ' ron in the south-west. Bœótia is divided into two principal basins or plains, that of Cephis' sus in the north-west, watered by the river of the same name, and containing the lake of Copais; and that of Thebes in the south-east, watered by the river Asópus. As many of the streams and lakes of Bœótia find their outlet to the sea by subterranean channels, marshes abound, and the atmosphere is damp, foggy, oppressive, and in many places unhealthy. The fertility of Bœótia, however, is such, that it has always an abundant crop, though elsewhere famine should prevail. Bœótia was the most populous of all the Grecian states; but the very productiveness of the country seems to have depressed the intellectual and moral character of the Bœótians, and to have justified the ridicule which their more enterprising neighbors of barren At' tica heaped upon them. (*See Map*, No. I.)

3. *Thebes*, the ancient capital of Bœótia, was situated near the small river (or brook) Ismenus, about five miles south of the lake Hyl' ica. The city was surrounded by high walls, which had seven gates, and it contained many magnificent temples, theatres, gymnasiums, and other public edifices, adorned with statues, paintings, and other works of art. In the most flourishing period of its history, the population of the city amounted to perhaps 50,000. The modern town of Thebes, (called Thiva,) contains a population of about 5,000 souls, and is confined mostly to the eminence occupied by the Acropolis, or citadel, of the ancient city. Prodigious ramparts and artificial mounds appear outside of the town: it is surrounded by a deep fosse

a. "There can be scarcely any reasonable doubt that this Amphic' tyon is a merely fictitious person." — *Thirwall*, i. p. 149

18. These and many other accounts of foreign settlers in Greece during this early period of Grecian history, are so interwoven with the absurdest fables, or, rather, deduced from them, that no reliance can be placed upon their authenticity. Still, these traditions are not without their value, for although the particular persons mentioned may have had no existence, yet the events related can hardly have been without some historical foundation. It is probable tha after the general diffusion of the Pelas'gic tribes over Greece, an while the western regions of Asia and northern Africa were in an unsettled state, various bands of flying or conquering tribes foun their way to the more peaceful shores of Greece through the islands of the Æ'gean,[1] bringing with them the arts and knowledge of the countries which they had abandoned. It is thus that we can satisfactorily account for that portion of Grecian mythology which bears evident marks of Phœnician origin, and for that still greater portion of the religious notions and practices, objects and forms of Grecian worship, which, according to Herod'otus, were derived from the Egyptians.

19. At the time that colonies from the East are supposed to have been settling in Greece, a people called the *Hel-*　v. THE *lénes*, but whether a Pelas'gic tribe or otherwise is un-　HELLÉNES. certain, first appeared in the south of Thes'saly,[2] about 1384 years before the Christian era, according to the received chronology, and

and remains of the old walls are still to be seen; but the sacred and public edifices of the ancient city have wholly disappeared. Previous to the late Greek Revolution the city had some handsome mosques, a bazaar shaded by gigantic palm-trees, and extensive gardens, but these were almost wholly destroyed by the casualties of war. (*See Map,* No. I.)

1. The *Æ'gean Sea* is that part of the Mediterranean lying between Greece and Asia Minor now called the Grecian Archipelago. (*See Map,* No. III.)

2. *Thes'saly,* now included in Turkey in Europe, was bounded on the north by the Cambunian mountains, terminating, on the east, in the loftier heights of Olympus, and separating Thes'saly from Macedonia; on the east by the Æ'gean Sea, which is skirted by ranges of Ossa and Pelion; on the south by the Malian gulf and the mountain chain of Œta; and on the west by the chain of Pindus, which separated it from Epirus. In the southern part of this territory between the mountain chains of Œta and Othrys, is the long and narrow valley of the river Sperchius, which, though considered as a part of Thes'saly, forms a separate region, widely distinguished from the rest by its physical features. Between the Othrys and the Cambunian mountains lies the great basin of Thes'saly, the largest and richest plain in Greece, encompassed on all sides by a mountain barrier, broken only at the north-east corner by a deep and narrow cleft, which parts Ossa from Olympus—the defile so renowned in history as the pass, and in poetry as the *Vale of Tem'pe.* Through this narrow glen, of about five miles in length, the Peneus, the principal river of Thes'saly, finds its way to the sea; and an ancient legend asserts that the waters of the Peneus and its tributaries covered the whole basin of Thes'saly, until the arm of Her'cules, or, as some assert, the trident of Nep'tune, rent asunder the gorge of Tem'pe, and thus afforded a passage to the pent-up streams. Herod'otus says. "To me the separation of these mountains appears to have been the effect of an earthquake." See *Map,* No. I.)

gradually diffusing themselves over the whole country, became, by their martial spirit, and active, enterprising genius, the ruling class, and impressed new features upon the Grecian character. The Hel lénes gave their name to the population of the whole peninsula, al though the term *Grecians* was the name applied to them by the Romans.

20. In accordance with the Greek custom of attributing the origin of their tribes or nations to some remote mythical ancestor, Hel'len, a son of the fabulous Deucálion, is represented as the father of the Hel'lenic nation. His three sons were Æ' olus, Dórus, and Xúthus, from the two former of whom are represented to have descended the *Æólians* and *Dórians*; and from Achæ' us and I' on, sons of Xúthus, the *Achæ'ans* and *Iónians*,—the four tribes into which the Hel'lenic or Grecian nation was for many centuries divided, and which were distinguished from each other by many peculiarities of language and institutions.[a] Hel'len is said to have left his kingdom to Æ' olus, his eldest son; and the Æólian tribe was the one that spread the most widely, and that long exerted the greatest influence in the affairs of the nation, although at a later period it was surpassed by the fame and power of the Dórians and Iónians.

21. The period from the time of the first appearance of the Hel·lénes in Thes'saly, to the return of the Greeks from the expedition against Troy, is usually called the Heroic Age. Our only knowledge of Grecian history during this period is derived from numerous marvellous legends of wars, expeditions, and heroic achievements, which possess scarcely the slightest evidence of historical authenticity; and which, even if they can be supposed to rest on a basis of fact, would be scarcely deserving of notice, as being unattended with any important or lasting consequences, were it not for the light which they throw upon the subject of Grecian mythology, and the gradual fading away, which they exhibit, of fiction, in the dawn of historic truth. The most important of these legends are hose which recount the Labors of Her'cules[1] and the exploits of the

VI. THE
HEROIC AGE.

---

1. *Her' cules,* a celebrated hero, is reported to have been a son of the god Júpiter and Alcmena. While yet an infant, Júno, moved by jealousy, sent two serpents to devour him; but the child boldly seized them in both his hands, and squeezed them to death. By an oath of Júpiter, imposed upon him by the artifice of Júno, Her' cules was made subservient, for twelve years, to the will of Eurys'theus, his enemy, and bound to obey all his commands. Eurys' theus commanded him to achieve a number of enterprises, the most difficult and arduous ever known, generally called the "twelve labors of Her'cules." But the favor of the gods had com

a. "We believe Hel'len, Æ' olus, Dórus, Achæ' us, and I' on, to be merely fictitious persons, representatives of the races which bore their names."—*Thir wall,* l. 1. 66.

Athenian Théseus;[1] the events of the Argonautic expedition;[2] of the Théban and Ar'golic war of the Seven Captains;[3] and of the succeeding war of the Epig'onoi, or descendants of the survivors, is

pletely armed him for the undertaking. He had received a sword from Mer'cury, a bow from Apol'lo, a golden breastplate from Vul'can, horses from Nep'tune, a robe from Miner'va and he himself cut his club from the Némean wood. We have merely room to enumerate his twelve labors, without describing them.

1st. He strangled the Némean lion, which ravaged the country near Mycénæ, and ever after clothed himself with its skin. 2d. He destroyed the Lernean hydra, a water-serpent, which had nine heads, eight of them mortal, and one immortal. 3d. He brought into the presence of Eurys'theus a stag, famous for its incredible swiftness and golden horns. 4th. He brought to Mycénæ the wild boar of Eryman'thus, and during this expedition slew two of the Centaurs, monsters who were half men and half horses. 5th. He cleansed the Augean stables in one day, by changing the courses of the rivers Al'pheus and Péneus. ("To cleanse the Augean stables" has become a common proverb, and is applied to any undertaking where the object is to remove a mass of moral corruption, the accumulation of which renders the task almost impossible.") 6th. He destroyed the carnivorous birds which ravaged the country near the Lake Stymphálus in Arcádia. 7. He brought alive into Peloponnésus a prodigious wild bull which ravaged the island of Crete. 8th. He brought from Thrace the mares of Dioméde, which fed on human flesh. 9th. He obtained the famous girdle of Hippol'yta, queen of the Amazons. 10th. He killed, in an island of the Atlantic, the monster Géryon, who had the bodies of three men united, and brought away his purple oxen. 11th. He obtained from the garden of the Hesper'ides the golden apples, and slew the dragon which guarded them. 12th. He went down to the lower regions, and brought upon earth the three-headed dog Cer'berus.

1. To *Théseus*, who is stated to have become king of Athens, are attributed many exploits similar to those performed by Her'cules, and he even shared in some of the enterprises of the latter. By his wise laws Théseus is said to have laid the principal foundation of Athenian greatness; but his name, which signifies the *Orderer*, or *Regulator*, seems to indicate a *period* in Grecian history, rather than an individual.

2. The *Argonautic Expedition* is said, in the popular legend, to have been undertaken by Jason and fifty-four of the most renowned heroes of Greece, among whom were Théseus and Her'cules, for the recovery of a *golden fleece* which had been deposited in the capital of Col'chis, a province of Asia Minor, bordering on the eastern extremity of the Euxine. The adventurers sailed from Iol'cos in the ship Ar'go, and during the voyage met with many adventures. Having arrived at Col'chis, they would have been unsuccessful in the object of their expedition had not the king's daughter, Medea, who was an enchantress, fallen in love with Jason, and defeated the plans of her father for his destruction. After a long return voyage, filled with marvellous adventures, most of the Argonauts reached Greece in safety, where Her'cules, in honor of the expedition, instituted the Olym'pic games.

Some have supposed this to have been a piratical expedition; others, that it was undertaken for the purpose of discovery, or to secure some commercial establishment on the shores of the Euxine, while others have regarded the legend as wholly fabulous. Says Grote, " I repeat the opinion long ago expressed, that the process of dissecting the story, in search of a basis of fact, is one altogether fruitless."—*Grote's Hist. of Greece*, i. 243.

3. The following are said to have been the circumstances of the *Théban and Ar'golic war*. After the death of Œ'dipus, king of Thebes, it was agreed between his two sons, Etéocles and Polynices, that they should reign alternately, each a year. Etéocles, however, the elder, after his first year had expired, refused to give up the crown to his brother, when the latter, fleeing to Ar'gos, induced Adras'tus, king of that place, to espouse his cause. Adras'tus marched an army against Thebes, led by himself and seven captains; but all the leaders were slain before the city, and the war ended by a single combat between Etéocles and Polynices, in which both brothers fell. This is said to have happened twenty-seven years before the Trojan war. Ten ears later the war was renewed by the *Epig'onoi*, descendants of those who were killed in the first Théban war. Some of the Grecian states espoused the cause of the Ar'gives, and others aided the Thébans; but in the end Thebes was abandoned by its inhabitants, and plundered by the Ar'gives.

which Thebes is said to have been plundered by the confederate Greeks.

22. Of these events, the Argonautic expedition has usually been thought of more importance than the rest, as having been conducted against a distant country, and as presenting some valid claims to our belief in its historical reality. But we incline to the opinion, that both the hero and the heroine of the legend are purely ideal personages connected with Grecian mythology,—that Jason was perhaps no other than the Samothrácian[1] god or hero Jásion,[a] the protector of mariners, and that the fable of the expedition itself is a poetic fiction which represented the commercial and piratical voyages that began to be made, about this period, to the eastern shores of the Euxine.[2] It is not improbable that voyages similar to that represented to have been made by the Argonauts, or, perhaps, naval expeditions like those attributed to Mínos,[3] the Crétan[4] prince and lawgiver, may first have led to hostile rivalries between the inhabitants of the Asiatic and Grecian coasts, and thus have been the occasion of the first conflict between the Greeks and the Trojans.[b]

23. The Trojan war, rendered so celebrated in early Grecian his-

1. *Samothráce* (the Thracian Sámos, now Samothraki,) is an island in the northern part of the Æ'gean Sea, about thirty miles south of the Thracian coast. It was celebrated for the mysteries of the goddess Cyb'ele, whose priests ran about with dreadful cries and howlings, beating on timbrels, clashing cymbals, and cutting their flesh with knives. (*See Map* No. III.)

2. The *Euxine* (Pon'tus Euxinus) is now called the *Black Sea*. It lies between the southwestern provinces of Russia in Europe, and Asia Minor. Its greatest length, from east to west, is upwards of 700 miles, and its greatest breadth about 400 miles. Its waters are only about one-seventh part less salt than the Atlantic—a fact attributable to the saline nature of the bottom, and of the northern coast. The Euxine is deep, and singularly free from rocks and shoals. (*See Map* No. V.)

3. *Minos* is said, in the Grecian legends, to have been a son of Júpiter, from whom he learned those laws which he delivered unto men. It is said that he was the first among the Greeks who possessed a navy, and that he conquered and colonized several islands, and finally perished in an expedition against Sicily. Some regard Minos simply as the concentration of that spirit of order, which, about his time, began to exhibit, in the island of Créte, a regular system of laws and government. He seems to be intermediate between the periods of mythology and history, combining, in his person, the characteristics of both.

4. *Créte* (now called Candia) is a large mountainous island in the Mediterranean Sea, 90 miles south-east from Cape Matapan in Greece—160 miles in length from east to west, with a breadth averaging about 20 miles. Créte was the reputed birth-place of Júpiter, "king of gods and men." The laws of Minos are said to have served as a model for those of Lycur'gus; and the wealth, number, and flourishing condition of the Crétan cities, are repeatedly referred to by Homer. (*See Map* No. III.)

a. Thirlwall's Greece, i. 77-79.

b. According to *Herod'otus*, i. 2, 3, the abduction of Hel'en, the cause of the Trojan war, was in retaliation of the abduction of Medea by Jason in the Argonautic expedition. But Herod'otus goes farther back, and attributes to the Phœnicians the first cause of contention between the Asiatic and the Grecians, in carrying away from Ar'gos, Io, a priestess of Júno.

tory by the poems of Homer,[1] is represented to have been undertaken about the year 1173 before the Christian era, by the confed
erate princes of Greece, against the city and kingdom of Troy,[2]
situated on the western coast of Asia Minor. The alleged causes
of this war, according to the Grecian legend, were the following:
Hel'en, the most beautiful woman of her age, and daughter of Tyn'-
darus, king of Lacedæ'mon, was sought in marriage by all the
princes of Greece; when Tyn'darus, perplexed with the difficulty of
choosing one without displeasing all the rest, being advised by the
sage Ulys'ses, bound the suitors by an oath that they would approve
of the uninfluenced choice of Hel'en, and would unite together to
defend her person and character, if ever any attempts were made to
carry her off from her husband. Menelaus became the choice of
Hel'en, and soon after, on the death of Tyn'darus, succeeded to the
vacant throne of Lacedæ'mon.[3]

24. After three years, Paris, son of Priam king of Troy, visited
the court of Menelaus, and taking advantage of the temporary absence of the latter, he corrupted the fidelity of Hel'en, whom he
induced to flee with him to Troy. Menelaus, returning, prepared to
avenge the outrage. He assembled the princes of Greece, who,
combining their forces under the command of Agamem'non, brother
of Menelaus, sailed with a great armament to Troy, and after a siege
of ten years finally took the city by stratagem, and razed it to the
ground. (1183 B. C.) Most of the inhabitants were slain or taken
prisoners, and the rest were forced to become exiles in distant
lands.

1. *Homer*, the greatest and earliest of the poets, often styled the *father* of poetry was prob
ably an Asiatic Greek, although seven Grecian cities contended for the honor of his birth. No
circumstances of his life are known with any certainty, except that he was a *wandering* poet,
and *blind*. The principal works of Homer are the *Iliad* and the *Od'yssey*,—the former of
which relates the circumstances of the Trojan war; and the latter, the history and wanderings
of Ulys'ses after the fall of Troy.

2. *Troy*, the scene of the battles described in the Iliad, stood on a rising ground between the
small river Simois (now the Dumbrek) and the Scaman'der, (now the Mendere,) on the coast
of Asia Minor, near the entrance to the Hel'lespont. New Ilium was afterwards built on the
spot now believed to be the site of the ancient city, about three miles from the sea. (*See Map
No. III. and No. IV.*)

3. *Lacedæ'mon*, or *Spar'ta*, the ancient capital of Laconia, was situated in a plain of con
siderable extent, embracing the greater part of Laconia, bounded on the west by the mountain
chain of Taygetus, and on the east by the less elevated ridge of mount Thornax, between which
flows the Eurotas, on the east side of the town. In early times Spar'ta was without walls, Lycur'gus having inspired his countrymen with the idea, that the real defence of a town consisted
solely in the valor of its citizens; but fortifications were erected after Sparta became subject
to despotic rulers. The remains of Spar'ta are about two miles north-east of the modern town
of Mistro. (*See Map No. I.*)

25. Such is, in brief, the commonly-received account of the Trojan war, stripped of the incredible but glowing fictions with which
the poetic genius of Homer has adorned it.   But although the
reality of some such war as this can hardly be questioned, yet the
causes which led to it, the manner in which it was conducted, and its
issue, being gathered, even by Homer himself, only from traditional
legends, which served as the basis of other compositions besides
the Iliad, are involved in an obscurity which we cannot hope to
penetrate.   The accounts of Hel'en are various and contradictory
and so connected with fabulous beings—with gods and goddesses—as
clearly to assign her to the department of mythology; while the
real events of the war, if such ever occurred, can hardly be separated
from the fictions with which they are interwoven.[1]

26. But although little confidence can be placed in the reality of
the persons and events mentioned in Homer's poetic account of the
siege of Troy, yet there is one kind of truth from which the poet
can hardly have deviated, or his writings would not have been so acceptable as they appear to have been to his cotemporaries;—and
that is, a faithful portraiture of the government, usages, religious notions, institutions, manners, and general condition of Grecian society,
during the heroic age.[a]

1. Thus the most ancient account of Hel'en is, that she was a daughter of the god Jupiter, hatched from the egg of a swan; and Homer speaks of her in the Iliad as "begotten
of Jupiter."   When only seven years of age, such were her personal attractions, that Theseus,
king of Athens, having become enamored of her, carried her off from a festival at which he
saw her dancing; but her brothers recovered her by force of arms, and restored her to her
family. After her marriage with Menelaus, it is said that Jupiter, plotting a war for the purpose of ridding the earth of a portion of its overstocked inhabitants, contrived that the beauty
of Hel'en should involve the Greeks and Trojans in hostilities.   At a banquet of the gods, Discord, by the direction of Jupiter, threw into the assembly a golden apple, on which was inscribed, "The apple for the Fair one," (Τῇ καλῇ τὸ μῆλον,) or, as in Virgil, *Pulcherrima me
habeto,* "Let the most beautiful have me."   The goddesses Juno, Miner'va, and Venus, claiming it, Paris, the son of Priam, king of Troy, was made the arbiter. He awarded the prize to
Venus, who had promised him the beautiful Hel'en in marriage, if he would decide in her
favor. Venus (the goddess of love and beauty) caused Paris and Hel'en to become mutually
enamored, and afterwards aided the Trojans in the war that followed. Homer represents the
heroes as performing prodigies of valor, shielded and aided by the gods; and the gods themselves as mingling in the strife, and taking part with the combatants. The goddess Miner'va,
an unsuccessful competitor for the prize which Paris awarded to her rival Venus, planned the
stratagem of the wooden horse, which concealed within its side a band of Greeks, who, borne
with it into the city, were thus enabled to open the gates to their confederates without.

a. "Homer was regarded even by the ancients as of historical authority."—"Truth was his
object in his accounts and descriptions, as far as it can be the object of a poet, and even in a
greater degree than was necessary, when he distinguishes the earlier and later times or ages. He
is the best source of information respecting the heroic age."—*Heeren's Politics of Greece,* p. 88

COTEMPORARY HISTORY

1. During the period of early Grecian history which we have passed over in the present chapter, our knowledge of the cotemporary history of other nations is exceedingly limited. Rome had not yet a beginning:—all Europe, except the little Grecian peninsula, was in the darkness of barbarism: in Central Western Asia we in deed suppose there existed, at this time, large cities, and the flourishing empires of Assyria and Babylon; but from them we can gather no reliable historic annals. In north-eastern Africa, indeed, the Egyptian empire had already attained the meridian of its glory; but of the chronological detail of Egyptian history during this period we know comparatively nothing. What is known relates principally to the conquests of the renowned Sesos''tris, an Egyptian monarch, who, as nearly as can be ascertained, was cotemporary with Oth'niel, the first judge of Israel, and with Cécrops, the supposed founder of Athens, although some modern authors place his reign a hundred years later.[a] This monarch is said to have achieved many brilliant conquests as the lieutenant of his father. After he came to the throne he made vast preparations for the conquest of the world, and raised an army which is said to have numbered six hundred thousand foot and twenty-four thousand horse, besides twenty-seven thousand armed chariots. He conquered Lib'ya[1] and Ethiópia,[2] after which, entering Asia, he overran Arabia, subdued the Assyrians and Medes, and even led his victorious hosts beyond the Ganges:[3]

1. Lib'ya is the name which the Greek and Roman poets gave to Africa. In a more restricted sense, however, the name was applied to that part of Africa, bordering on the Mediterranean, which lies between Egypt on the east and Tripoli on the west,—the most important part of which territory is embraced in the present Barca.

2. Ancient Ethiópia comprised, principally, the present countries of Nubia and Abyssinia, south of Egypt.

3. The Ganges, the sacred river of the Hindoos, flowing south-east through the north-

a. The era of the accession of Sesos'tris, may be placed at 1565 B. C.; that of Oth'niel at 1564; and the supposed founding of Athens at 1556,—the latter two in accordance with Dr. Hales. In Rollin the date for Sesos'tris is 1491; Hereen "about 1500"; Russell's Egypt, 1306 Mure, "between 1400 and 1410"; Gliddon's Egypt, 1565; and Champollion Figeac (making Sesos'tris the same as Ramses IV., at the head of the 19th dynasty), 1473. Eusebius, followed by Usher and Playfair, supposes that Sesos'tris was the immediate successor of the Pharaoh who was drowned in the Red Sea; while Marsham, followed by Newton, attempts to identify him with the Shishak of Scripture who invaded Judea—a difference, according to various systems of chronology, of from 500 to 800 years. Mr. Bryant endeavors to prove that no such person ever existed.

Since the interpretation of the hieroglyphics, however, the principal ground of dispute on this subject among the learned, appears to be, whether the Sesos'tris so renowned in history was the same as Ramses III., the fourteenth king of the 18th dynasty, or the same as Ramses IV., the first king of the 19th dynasty there being a difference between the two of about a hundred years.

he is also said to have passed over into Europe, and to have ravaged the territories of the Thracians and the Scythians,[1] when scarcity of provisions stopped the progress of his conquests. That the fame of his deeds might long survive him, he erected columns in the countries through which he passed, on which was inscribed, "Sesos' tris, king of kings, and lord of lords, subdued this country by the power of his arms." Some of these columns were still to be seen in Asia Minor in the days of Herod' otus.

3. The deeds and triumphs of Sesos' tris are also wrought, in sculpture and in painting, in numerous temples, and on the most celebrated obelisks, from Ethiopia to Lower Egypt. At Ipsamboul,[2] in Nubia, is a temple cut out of the solid rock, whose front or façade is supported by four colossal figures of exquisite workmanship each sixty feet high, all statues of Sesos' tris, the faces of which bear a perfect resemblance to the figures of the same king at Mem' phis. The walls of the temple are covered with numerous sculptures on historical subjects, representing the conquests of this prince in Africa. Among them are processions of the conquered nations, carrying the riches of their country and laying them at the feet of the conqueror; and even the wild animals of the desert—antelopes, apes, giraffes, and ostriches—are led in the triumphs of the Egyptians.

4. Were it not for the many similar monumental evidences of the reign of this monarch, which have been recently discovered, corroborative of the deeds which profane authors attribute to him, we might be disposed to regard Sesos' tris as others have done, as no more than a mythological personification of the Sun, the god of day, "the giant that rejoiceth to run his course from one end of heaven to the other." But with such an amount of testimony bearing on the subject, we cannot doubt the existence of this mighty conqueror, although probably his exploits have been greatly exaggerated by the vanity of his chroniclers; and it is not improbable that the deeds of several monarchs have been attributed to one. After the return of Sesos' tris from his conquests, he is said to have employed his time to the close of his reign, in encouraging the arts, erecting tem-

eastern part of Hindostan, enters the Bay of Bengal, through a great number of mouths, near Calcutta.

1. *Thrace,* a large tract of country now embraced in Turkey in Europe, and bordering on the Propontis, or sea of Marmora, extended from Macedonia and the Æ' gean Sea on the south-west, to the Euxine on the north-east. North of the Thracians, extending along the Euxine to the river Danube, was the country of the *Scythians.*

2. *Ipsamboul,* so celebrated for its well-known excavated temples, is in the northern part of Nubia, on the western bank of the Nile. ·

ples to the gods, and improving the revenues of his kingdom. After his time we know little of the history of Egypt until the reign of Pharaoh-Necho, in the beginning of the seventh century, who is re markable for his successes against Jerusalem.

5. At the period which we have assigned, somewhat arbitrarily, for the commencement of Grecian history, 1856 years before the Christian era, Joseph, the son of the patriarch Jacob, was governor over Egypt; and his father's family, by invitation of Pharaoh, had settled in Goshen, on the eastern borders of the valley of the Nile. This is supposed to have been about three centuries before the time of Sesos' tris. On the death of Joseph, the circumstances of the descendants of Jacob, who were now called Israelites, were greatly changed. "A king arose who knew not Joseph;"[a] and the children of Israel became servants and bondsmen in the land of Egypt. Two hundred years they were held in bondage, when the Lord, by his servant Moses, brought[b] them forth out of Egypt with a mighty hand and an outstretched arm, after inflicting the most grievous plagues upon their oppressors, and destroying the pursuing hosts of Pharaoh in the Red Sea. (1648 B. C.)

6. Forty years the Israelites, numbering probably two millions of souls,[c] wandered in the wilderness on the north-western confines of Arabia,[1] supported by miraculous interposition; for the country was then, as now, "a land of deserts and of pits, a land of drouth and of the shadow of death, a land that no man passed through, and where no man dwelt;"[d] and after they had completed their wanderings, and another generation had grown up since they had left Egypt, they came to the river Jordan,[2] and passing through the bed of the

1. *Arabia* is an extensive peninsula at the south-western extremity of Asia, lying immediately east of the Red Sea. It is mostly a rocky and desert country, inhabited by wandering tribes of Arabs, the descendants of Ishmael. They still retain the character given to their ancestor. The desert has continued to be the home of the Arab; he has been a man of war from his youth; "his hand against every man, and every man's hand against him." (Gen. xvi. 12.)

2. The river *Jordan* (See Map, No. VI.) rises towards the northern part of Palestine, or the western slope of Mount Hermon, and after a south course of about forty miles, opens into the sea of Galilee near the ancient town of Bethsaida. After passing through this lake or sea, which is about fifteen miles long and seven broad, and on and near which occurred so many striking scenes in the history of Christ, it pursues a winding southerly course of about ninety miles through a narrow valley, and then empties its waters into the Dead Sea. In this river valley was the dwelling of Lot, "who pitched his tents toward Sodom" (Gen. xiii. 11, 12; and "in the vale of Siddim, which is the salt sea," occurred the battle of the "four kings with five." (Gen. xv.) The Israelites passed the Jordan near Jericho (Josh. iii. 14–17); the prophets Elijah

a. Paraphrased by Josephus as meaning that the kingdom had passed to another dynasty.
b. 1648, B.C.
c. They had 603,550 men, above 20 years of age, not reckoning Levites. Ex. xii, xxviii. 9.
d. Jeremiah, ii. 6

stream, which rolled back its waters on their approach, entered the promised land of Palestine.¹ The death of Moses had left the government in the hands of Joshua. And "Israel served the Lord all the days of Joshua, and all the days of the elders that outlived Joshua, and which had known all the works of the Lord that he had done for his chosen people."ᵃ

7. From the time of the death of Joshua to the election of Saul as first king of Israel, which latter event occurred about seventy years after the supposed siege of Troy, Israel was ruled by judges, who were appointed through the agency of the priests and of the divine oracle in accordance with the theocratic form of government established by Moses. After the death of Joshua, however, the Israelites often apostatized to idolatry, for which they were punished by being successively delivered into the hands of the surrounding nations. First they were subdued by the king of Mesopotámia,ᵇ after which the Lord raised up Oth'niel to be their deliverer (1564 B. C.). a second defection was punished by eighteen years of servitude to the king of the Móabites,² from whom they were delivered by the enter-

and Elisha afterwards divided the waters to prove their divine mission (2 Kings, xi. 8) ; the leper Naaman was commanded to wash in Jordan and be clean (2 Kings, iv. 10) ; and it is this stream in which Jesus was baptized before he entered on his divine mission. (Matt. iii. 16, &c.) The Dead Sea, into which the Jordan empties, is so called from the heaviness and consequent stillness of its waters, which contain one-fourth part of their weight of salts. The country around this lake is exceedingly dreary, and the soil is destitute of vegetation. Sodom and Gomorrah are supposed to have stood in the plain now occupied by the lake, and ruins of the overthrown cities are said to have been seen on its western borders. (*Map* No. VI.)

1. *Palestine,* a part of modern Syria, now embraced in Turkey in Asia, lies at the eastern extremity of the Mediterranean Sea ; extending north and south along the coast about 200 miles, and having an extreme breadth of about 80 miles. Though in antiquity the northern part of Palestine was the seat of the Phœnicians, a great commercial people, yet there are now few good harbors on the coast, those of Tyre and Sidon, once so famous, being now for the most part blocked up with sand. The country of Palestine consists principally of rugged hills and narrow valleys, although it has a few plains of considerable extent. There are many streams falling into the Mediterranean, the largest of which is the Orontes, at the north, but none of them are navigable. The river Jordan, on the east, empties its waters into the Asphaltic Lake, or Dead Sea, which latter, about 55 miles in length, and 20 in extreme width now fills the plain where once stood the cities of Sodom and Gomorrah. North of the Dead Sea is the Lake of Gennesareth, or Sea of Galilee, the theatre of some most remarkable miracles. (Matthew viii.; Luke viii.; and Matthew xix. 25.) The principal mountains of Palestine are those of Lebanon, running in ranges nearly parallel to the Mediterranean, and finally connecting with mounts Horeb and Sinai, near the Gulf of Suez. Jerusalem, the capital city of Palestine or the Holy Land, will be described in a subsequent article. (*See p.* 164, *McCulloch ;* articles Syria, Said, or Sidon, Dead Sea, Lebanon, &c.) (*Map* No. VI.)

2. The *Moabites,* so called from Moab the son of Lot (Gen. xix. 37), dwelt in the country on the east of the Dead Sea. (*Map* No. VI.)

a. Joshua, xxiv. 31.

b. Numbers, iii. 8. Some think that the country here referred to was in the vicinity of Damascus, and not "beyond the Euphrates," as Mesopotámia would imply. *See Cockayne' Civil Hist. of the Jews* 29–33.)

prising valor of Ehud.[a]   After his death the Israelites again did evil
in the sight of the Lord, and " the Lord sold them into the hand of
Jabin king of Canaan,"[1] under whose cruel yoke they groaned twenty
years, when the prophetess Deborah, and Barak her general, were
made the instruments of their liberation.   The Canaanites were
routed with great slaughter, and their leader Sisera slain by Jael, in
whose tent he had sought refuge.[b]

8. Afterwards, the children of Israel were delivered over a prey
o the Midianites and Amalekites,[2] wild tribes of the desert, who
" came up with their cattle and their tents, as grasshoppers for multitude."   But the prophet Gideon, chosen by the Lord to be the
liberator of his people, taking with him only three hundred men,
made a night attack on the camp of the enemy, upon whom such fear
fell that they slew each other ; so that a hundred and twenty thousand men were left dead on the field, and only fifteen thousand escaped by flight.   In the height of their joy and gratitude, the people would have made Gideon king, but he said to them, " Not I, nor
my son, but JEHOVAH shall reign over you."[c]

9. Again the idolatry of the Israelites became so gross, that the Lord
delivered them into the hands of the Philistines[3] and the Ammonites,[4]
from whom they were finally delivered by the valor of Jephthah.[d]
At a later period the Philistines oppressed Israel forty years, but the
people found an avenger in the prowess of Samson.[e]   After the
death of Samson the aged Eli judged Israel, but the crimes of his
sons, Hophni and Phinehas, whom he had chosen to aid him in the
government, brought down the vengeance of the Lord, and thirty
thousand of the warriors of Israel were slain in battle by the Philis-

1. The *Canaanites*, so called from Canaan, one of the sons of Ham (Gen. x. 6-19), then dwelt
in the lowlands of the Galilee of the Gentiles, between the sea of Galilee and the Mediterranean.
Barak, descending from Mount Tabor (see Map), attacked Sisera on the banks of the river
Kishon. (*Map* No. VI.)

2. The *Midianites*, so called from one of the sons of Abraham by Keturah, dwelt in western
Arabia, near the head of the Red Sea. The *Amalekites* dwelt in the wilderness between the
Dead Sea and the Red Sea. (*Map* No. VI.)

3. The *Philistines* (see Map) dwelt on the south-western borders of Palestine, along the coast
of the Mediterranean, as far north as Mount Carmel, the commencement of the Phœnician
territories. Their principal towns were Gaza, Gath, Ascalon, and Megiddo, for which see Map.
The Israelite tribes of Simeon, Dan, Ephraim, and Manasseh, bordered on their territories.
"The whole of the towns of the coast continued in the hands of the Philistines and Phœnicians,
and never permanently fell under the dominion of Israel."—*Cockayne's Hist. of the Jews*, p. 44.

4. The *Ammonites* (see Map) dwelt on the borders of the desert eastward of the Israelite
tribes that settled east of the Jordan.

a. Judges, iii. 15-30.   b. Judges, iv.   c. Judges, vi. ; vii.; viii.
d. Judges, x. 7; xi. 33.   e. Judges, xiii. 1 ; xiv.; xv.; xvi.

tines.[a]   The prophet Samuel was divinely chosen as the successor of
Eli. (1152 B. C.)   His administration was wise and prudent, but
in his old age the tyranny of his sons, whom he was obliged to employ as his deputies, induced the people to demand a king who
should rule over them like the kings of other nations.   With reluctance Samuel yielded to the popular request, and by divine guidance,
anointed Saul, of the tribe of Benjamin, king over Israel[b] (1110
B. C.)

10. We have thus briefly traced the civil history of the Israelites
down to the period of the establishment of a monarchy over them,
in the person of Saul, at a date, according to the chronology which
we have adopted, seventy-three years later than the supposed destruction of Troy.   It is, however, the religious history, rather than the
civil annals, of the children of Abraham, that possesses the greatest
value and the deepest interest; but as our limits forbid our entering upon a subject so comprehensive as the former, and the one cannot be wholly separated from the other without the greatest violence,
we refer the reader to the Bible for full and satisfactory details of
the civil and religious polity of the Jews, contenting ourselves with
having given merely such a skeleton of Jewish annals, in connection
with profane history, as may serve to render the comparative chronology of the whole easy of comprehension.

a. 1 Sam. iv. 18.   b. x. 1.

CHAPTER III.

THE UNCERTAIN PERIOD OF GRECIAN HISTORY:

EXTENDING FROM THE CLOSE OF THE TROJAN WAR TO THE FIRST WAR WITH PERSIA
1183 TO 490 B. C. = 693 YEARS.

ANALYSIS. 1. Introductory.—2. Consequences of the Trojan war.—3. THESSA' LIAN CON QUEST.—[Epirus. Pin' dus. Penéus.]—4. BŒO' TIAN CONQUEST.—Æo' LIAN MIGRATION. [Les' bos. 5 Dóris.] RETURN OF THE HERACLI' DÆ.—6. Numbers and military character of the Dórians.—Passage of the Corinthian Gulf.—[Corinthian Isthmus.—Corinthian Gulf.—Naupac' tus.]—7. Dórian conquest of the Peloponnésus. [Arcádia. Achâia.] Iónian and Dórian mi grations.—8. Dórian invasion of At' tica.—[Athens. Delphos.] Self-sacrifice of Códrua. Government of At' tica.—9. [Lacónia.] Its government. Lycur' gus.—10. Travels of Lycur' gus. [The Brahmins.] INSTITUTIONS OF LYCUR' GUS.—11. Plutarch's account—senate assemblies—division of lands.—12. Movable property. The currency.—13. Public tables. Object of Spartan education, and aim of Lycur' gus.—14. Disputes about Lycur' gus. His supposed fate, [Delphos, Créte, and E' lis.]—15. The three classes of the Lacónian population Treatment of the Hélots.—16. The provincials. Their condition.—17. [Messénia. Ithóme FIRST MESSE' NIAN WAR. Results of the war to the Messenians.—18. Its influence on the Spartans. SECOND MESSE' NIAN WAR. Aristom' enes.—19. The Poet Tyrtæ' us. [Corinth. Sic' yon.] Battle of the Pamisus. The Arcádians. 20. Results of the war.—21. Government of Athens. DRA' CO.—22. Severity of his laws.—23. Anarchy. LEGISLATION OF SOLON. Solon's integrity.—24. Distresses of the people. The needy and the rich—25. The policy of Solon. Debtors—lands of the poor—imprisonment. Classification of the citizens.—26. Disabilities and privileges of the fourth class. General policy of Solon's system.—27. The nine archons. The Senate of Four Hundred.—28. Court of the Areop' agus. Its powers. Institutions of Solon compared with the Spartan code.—29. Party feuds. Pisis' tratus.—30. His usurpation of power. Opposition to, and character of, his government.—31. The sons of Pisis' tratus Conspiracy of Harmódius and Aristogeiton.—32. EXPULSION OF THE PISISTRATIDS. Intrigue of Hip' pias. [Lyd' ia. Per' sia.]—33. The Grecian colonies conquered by Crœ' sus—by the Persians. Application for aid.—34. ION' IC REVOLT. Athens and Eubœ' a aid the Iónians. [Eubœ' a. Sar' dis. Eph' esus.] Results of the Iónian war. [Milétus.] Designs of Darius.

COTEMPORARY HISTORY.—I. PHŒNI CIAN HISTORY. 1. Geography of Phœnicia.—2. Early his tory of Phœnicia. Political condition. Colonies.—3. Supposed circumnavigation of Africa.— 4. Commercial relations. II. JEWISH HISTORY—continuation of.—6. Accession of Saul to the throne. Slaughter of the Am' monites. [Jábesh Gil' ead. Gil' gal.] War with the Philistines.—7. Wars with the surrounding nations. Saul's disobedience.—8. David—his prowess. [Gath.] Saul's jealousy of David. David's integrity.—9. Death of Saul. [Mount Gil' boa.] Division of the kingdom between David and Ish' bosheth. [Hébron.] Union of the tribes.—10. Limited posses sions of the Israelites. [Tyre. Sidon. Joppa. Jerusalem.] David takes Jerusalem.—11. His other conquests. [Syria. Damascus. Rabbah.] Siege of Rabbah. Close of David's reign.—12. Solomon. His wisdom—fame—commercial relations.—13. His impiety. Close of his reign.— 14. Revolt of the ten tribes. Their subsequent history.—15. Rehoboam's reign over Judah. Reign of Ahaz. Hezekiah. Signal overthrow of the Assyrians.—17. Corroborated by pro fane history.—18. Account given by Herod' otus.—19. Reigns of Manas' seh, A' mon, Josiah, and Jehóahaz.—20. Reign of Jehoiakim—of Jechoniah.—21. Reign of Zedekiah. Destruc tion of Jerusalem.—22. Captivity of the Jews.—23 Rebuilding of Jerusalem. III. RO MAN HISTORY.—24. Founding of Rome.—IV. PERSIAN HISTORY.—25. Dissolution of the As syrian empire.—26 Establishment of the empire of the Medes and Babylonians. First and

1. Passing from the fabulous era of Grecian history, we enter upon a period when the crude fictions of more than mortal heroes, and demi-gods, begin to give place to the realities of human exist-ence; but still the vague, disputed, and often contradictory annals on which we are obliged to rely, shed only an uncertain light around us; and even what we have gathered as the most reliable, in the present chapter, perhaps cannot wholly be taken as undoubted his-toric truth, especially in chronological details.

2. The immediate consequences of the Trojan war, as represented by Greek historians, were scarcely less disastrous to the victors than to the vanquished. The return of the Grecian heroes to their coun-try is represented by Homer and other early writers to have been full of tragical adventures, while their long absence had encouraged usurpers to seize many of their thrones; and hence arose fierce wars and intestine commotions, which greatly retarded the progress of Grecian civilization.

3. Among these petty revolutions, however, no events of general
ı. THESSA'LIAN interest occurred until about sixty years after the fall of
CONQUEST. Troy, when a people from Epirus,[1] passing over the mountain chain of Pin'dus,[2] descended into the rich plains which lie along the banks of the Penéus,[3] and finally conquered[a] the country, to

---

1. The country of *Epirus*, comprised in the present Turkish province of Albánia, was at the north-western extremity of Greece, lying along the coast of the Adriatic Sea, or Gulf of Venice, and bounded on the north by Macedónia, and on the east by Macedónia and Thes'saly. The inhabitants in early times were probably Pelas'gic, but they can hardly be consid-ered ever to have belonged to the Hellénic race, or Grecians proper. Epirus is principally distinguished in Roman history as the country of the celebrated Pyr'rhus (see p. 149.) The earliest oracle of Greece was that of Dodóna in Epirus, but its exact locality is unknown There was another oracle of the same name in Thes'saly. (*Map* No. I.)

2. *Pin'dus* is the name of the mountain chain which separated Thes'saly from Epirus. (*Map* No. I.)

3. *Penéus*, the principal river of Thes'saly, rises in the Pin'dus mountains, and flowing in a course generally east, passes through the vale of Tem'pe, and empties its waters into the Ther maic Gulf, now the gulf of Salonica, a branch of the Æ'gean Sea, or Archipelago. (*Map* No. I.)

a. About 1124 B. C.

which they gave the name of Thes saly; driving away most of the inhabitants, and reducing those who remained to the condition of serfs, or agricultural slaves.

-*. The fugitives from Thes'saly, driven from their own country passed over into Bœótia, which they subdued after a long II. BŒO'TIAN struggle, imitating their own conquerors in the disposal CONQUEST. of the inhabitants. The unsettled state of society occasioned by the Thessálian and Bœótian conquests was the cause of collecting to gether various bands of fugitives, who, being joined by adventurers from Peloponnésus, passed over into Asia,[a] constituting the *Æólian migration*, so called from the race which took the prin- III. ÆO'LIAN cipal share in it. They established their settlements in MIGRATION. the vicinity of the ruins of Troy, and on the opposite island of Les'bos,[1] while on the main land they built many cities, which were com prised in twelve States, the whole of which formed the Æólian Con federacy.

5. About twenty years after the Thessálian conquest, the Dórians, a Hellénic tribe, whose country, Dóris,[2] a mountainous region, was on the south of Thes'saly, being probably harassed by their northern neighbors, and desirous of a settlement in a more fertile territory, commenced a migration to the Peloponnésus, accompanied by portions of other tribes, and led, as was asserted, by descendants of Her'cules, who had formerly been driven into exile from the latter country. This important event in Grecian history is IV. RETURN called the *Return of the Heraclídœ.* The migration of the OF THE Dórians was similar in its character to the return of the HERACLI'DÆ. Israelites to Palestine, as they took with them their wives and children, prepared for whatever fortune should award them.

6. The Dórians could muster about twenty thousand fighting men, and although they were greatly inferior in numbers to the inhabitants of the countries which they conquered, their superior military tactics appear generally to have insured them an easy victory in the

1 *Les'bos*, one of the most celebrated of the Grecian islands, now called Mytiléne, from its principal city, lies on the coast of Asia Minor, north of the entrance to the Gulf of Smyrna. Anc'*. v, Les'bos contained nine flourishing cities, founded mostly by the Æólians. The Les'b as were notorious for their dissolute manners, while at the same time they were distinguished for intellectual cultivation, and especially for poetry and music. (*Map No. III.*)

2. *Dóris*, a small mountainous country, extending only about forty miles in length, was situated on the south of Thes saly, from which it was separated by the range of mount Œ' ta. The Dórians were the most powerful of the Hellénic tribes. (*Map No. I.*)

a. About 1040 B. C.

open field. Twice, however, they were repelled in their attempts to break through the Corinthian isthmus,[1] the key to Southern Greece, when, warned by these misfortunes, they abandoned the guarded isthmus, and crossing the Corinthian Gulf[2] from Naupac' tus,[3] landed safely on the north-western coast of the peninsula. (B. C. 1104).

7. The whole of Peloponnésus, except the central and mountainous district of Arcádia[4] and the coast province of Acháia,[5] was eventually subdued, and apportioned among the conquerors,—all the old inhabitants who remained in the country being reduced to an inferior condition like that of the Saxon serfs of England at the time of the Norman conquest. Some of the inhabitants of the southern part of the peninsula, however, uniting under valiant leaders, conquered the province of Acháia, and expelled its Iónian inhabitants, many of whom, joined by various bands of fugitives, sought a retreat on the western coast of Asia Minor, south of the Æólian cities, where, in

1. The *Corinthian Isthmus*, between the Corinthian Gulf (now Gulf of Lepan' to) on the north-west, and the Saron' ic Gulf (now Gulf of Athens, or Ægina) on the south-east, unites the Peloponnésus to the northern parts of Greece, or Greece Proper. The narrowest part of this celebrated Isthmus is about six miles east from Corinth, where the distance across is about five miles. The Isthmus is high and rocky, and many unsuccessful attempts have been made to unite the waters on each side by a canal. The Isthmus derived much of its early celebrity from the *Isthmian games* celebrated there in honor of Palæ' mon and Nep' tune. Ruins of the temple of Nep' tune have been discovered at the port of Schæ' nus, on the east side of the Isthmus. (*Map* No. I.)

2. The *Corinthian Gulf* (now called the Gulf of Lepan' to) is an eastern arm of the Adriatic, or Gulf of Venice, and lies principally between the coast of ancient Phócis on the north, and of Acháia on the south. The entrance to the gulf, between two ruined castles, the Roumé la on the north, and the Moréa on the south, is only about one mile across. Within, the waters expand into a deep magnificent basin, stretching about seventy-eight miles to the south-east, and being, where widest, about twenty miles across. Near the mouth of this gulf was fought, in the year 1570, one of the greatest naval battles of modern times. (*Map* No. I.)

3. *Naupac' tus* (now called Lepan' to) stands on a hill on the coast of Lócris, about three and a half miles from the ruined castle of Roumélia. It is said to have derived its name from the circumstance of the Heraclidæ having there constructed the fleet in which they crossed over to the Peloponnésus. (*Naus*, a ship, and *Pégo*, or *Pégnumi*, to construct.) It was once a place of considerable importance, but is now a ruinous town. (*Map* No. I.)

4. *Arcádia*, the central country of the Peloponnésus, and, next to Lacónia, the largest of its six provinces, is a mountainous region, somewhat similar to Switzerland, having a length and breadth of about forty miles each. The most fertile part of the country was towards the south, where were several delightful plains, and numerous vineyards. The Alphéus is the principal river of Arcádia. Tégea and Mantinéa were its principal cities. Its lakes are small, but among them is the Stymphálus, of classic fame. The Arcádians, scarcely a genuine Greek race, were a rude and pastoral people, deeply attached to music, and possessing a strong love of freedom. (*Map* No. I.)

5. *Acháia*, the most northern country of the Peloponnésus, extended along the Corinthian Gulf, north of E lis and Arcádia. It was a country of moderate fertility; its coast was for the most part level, containing no good harbors, and exposed to inundations; and ts streams were of small size, many of them mere winter torrents, descending from the ridges of Arcádia. Originally Acháia embraced the territory of Sic' yon, on the east, but the latter was finally wrested from it by the Dórians. The Achæ' ans are principally celebrated for being the originators of the celebrated Achæan league. (*See* p.107.) (*Map* No. I.)

process of time, twelve Iónian cities were built, the whole of which were united in the Iónian Confederacy, while their new country received the name of Iónia. At a later period, bands of the Dórians themselves, not content with their conquest of the Pelopcnnésus, thronged to Asia Minor, where they peopled several cities on the coast of Cária, south of Iónia; so that the Æ'gean Sea was finally circled by Grecian settlements, and its islands covered by them.

8. About the year 1068, the Dórians, impelled, as some assert, by a general scarcity, the natural effect of long-protracted wars, invaded At'tica, and encamped before the walls of Athens.[1] The chief of the Dórian expedition, having consulted the oracle of Del'phos,[2] was told that the Dórians would be successful so long as Códrus, the Athenian king, was uninjured. The latter, being informed of the answer of the oracle, resolved to sacrifice himself for the good of his country; and going out of the gate, disguised in the garb of a peasant, he provoked a quarrel with a Dórian soldier, and suffered himself to be slain. On recognizing the body, the superstitious Dórians, deeming the war hopeless, withdrew from At'tica; and the Athenians, out of respect for the memory of Códrus, declared that no one was worthy to succeed him, and abolished the form of royalty altogether.[a] Magistrates called archons, however, differing little from kings, were now appointed from the family of Códrus for life; after a long period these were exchanged[b] for archons appointed for ten years, until, lastly,[c] the yearly election of a senate of Archons gave the final blow to royalty in Athens, and established an aristocratical government of the nobility. These successive encroachments

---

1. *Athens*, one of the most famous cities of antiquity, is situated on the western side of the At'tic peninsula, about five miles from the Saron'ic Gulf, now the Gulf of Ægina. Most of the ancient city stood on the west side of a rocky eminence called the Acrop'olis, surrounded by an extensive plain, and, at the time when i. had attained its greatest magnitude, was twenty miles in circumference, and encompassed by a wall surmounted, at intervals, by strongly-fortified towers. The small river Cephis'sus, flowing south, on the west side of the city, and the river Ilis'sus, on the east, flowing south-west, inclosed it in a sort of peninsula; but both streams lost themselves in the marshes south-west of the city. The waters of the Ilis'sus were mostly drawn off to irrigate the neighboring gardens, or to supply the artificial fountains of Athens. (*Map* No. I. See farther description, p. 564.)

2. *Del'phos*, or *Del'phi*, a small city of Phócis, situated on the southern declivity of Mount Parnas'sus, forty-five miles north-west from Cor'inth, and eight and a half miles from the nearest point of the Corinthian Gulf, was the seat of the most remarkable oracle of the ancient world. Above Del'phi arose the two towering cliffs of Parnas'sus, while from the chasm between them flowed the waters of the *Castalian* spring, the source of poetical inspiration. Below lay a rugged mountain, past which flowed the rapid stream Plis'tus; while on both sides of the plain, where stood the little city, arose steep and almost inaccessible precipices. (*Map* No. I.)

a. 1068 B. C.   b. 752 B. C.   c. 682 B. C.

on the royal prerogatives are almost the only events that fill the meagre annals of Athens for several centuries.[a]

9. While these changes were occurring at Athens, Lacónia,[1] whose capital was Sparta, although often engaged in tedious wars with the Ar'gives,[2] was gradually acquiring an ascendancy over the Dórian states of the Peloponnésus. After the Heraclídæ had obtained possession of the sovereignty, two descendants of that family reigned jointly at Lacedæ'mon, but this divided rule served only to increase the public confusion. Things remained, however, in this situation until some time in the ninth century B. C., when Polydec'tes, one of the kings, died without children. The reins of government then fell into the hands of his brother Lycur'gus, but the latter soon resigned the crown to the posthumous son of Polydec'tes, and, to avoid the imputation of ambitious designs, went into voluntary exile, although against the wishes of the best of his countrymen.

10. He is said to have visited many foreign lands, observing their institutions and manners, and conversing with their sages—to have studied the Cretan laws of Mínos—to have been a disciple of the Egyptian priests—and even to have gathered wisdom from the Brahmins[3] of India, employing his time in maturing a plan for remedying the evils which afflicted his native country. On his return he applied himself to the business of framing a new constitution for Sparta, after consulting the Delphic oracle, which assured him that " the constitution he should establish would be the most excellent in the world." Having enlisted the aid of the most illustrious citizens,

V. INSTITU-TIONS OF LYCUR'GUS. who took up arms to support him, he procured the enactment of a code of laws, by which the form of government, the military discipline of the people, the distribution of property, the education of the citizens, and the rules

1. *Lacónia*, situated at the southern extremity of Greece, had Ar'golis and Arcádia on the north, Messénia on the west, and the sea on the south and east. Its extent was about fifty miles from north to south, and from twenty to thirty from east to west. Its principal river was the Eurótas, on the western bank of which was Sparta, the capital; and its mountains were the ranges of Par'non on the north and east, and of Tayg'etus on the west, which rendered the fertile valley of the Eurótas, comprising the principal part of Lacónia, exceedingly difficult of access. The two southern promontories of Lacónia were Maléa and Tænárium, now called St. Angelo and Matapan. (*Map* No. I.)

2. The Ar'gives proper were inhabitants of the state and city of Ar'gos; but the word is often applied by the poets to all the inhabitants of Greece. (*Map* No. I.)

3. The *Brahmins* were a class of Hindoo priests and philosophers, worshippers of the Indian god Brama, the supposed creator of the world. They were the only persons who understood the Sanscrit, the ancient language of Hindoostan, in which the sacred books of the Hindoos were written.

a. Thirwall, i. p. 175.

of domestic life, were to be established on a new and immutable basis.

11. The account which Plutarch gives of these regulations asserts that Lycur'gus first established a senate of thirty members, chosen for life, the two kings being of the number, and that the former shared the power of the latter. There were also to be assemblies of the people, who were to have no right to propose any subject of debate, but were only authorized to ratify or reject what might be proposed to them by the senate and the kings. Lycur'gus next made a new division of the lands, for here he found great inequality existing, as there were many indigent persons who had no lands, and the wealth was centred in the hands of a few.

12. In order farther to remove inequalities among the citizens, and, as far as possible, to place all on the same level, he next attempted to divide the movable property, but as this measure met with great opposition, he had recourse to another method for accomplishing the same object. He stopped the currency of gold and silver coin, and permitted iron money only to be used ; and, to a great quantity and weight of this he assigned but a small value, so that, to remove one or two hundred dollars of this money would require a yoke of oxen. This regulation put an end to many kinds of injustice, for " Who," says Plutarch, " would steal or take a bribe; who would defraud or rob, when he could not conceal the booty,— when he could neither be dignified by the possession of it, nor be served by its use ?" Unprofitable and superfluous arts were excluded, trade with foreign States was abandoned; and luxury, losing its sources of support, died away of itself.

13. To promote sobriety, all the citizens, and even the kings, ate at public tables, and of the plainest fare ; each individual being obliged to bring in, monthly, certain provisions for the common use. This regulation was designed, moreover, to furnish a kind of school, where the young might be instructed by the conversation of their elders. From his birth, every Spartan belonged to the State sickly and deformed infants were destroyed, those only being thought worthy to live who promised to become useful members of the community. The object of Spartan education was to render children expert in manly exercises, hardy, and courageous ; and the principal aim of Lycur'gus appears to have been to render the Spartans a nation of warriors, although not of conquerors, for he dreaded the effects of an extension of territory beyond the boundaries of Laconia

C

14. Lycur' gus left none of his laws in writing; and some of the regulations attributed to him were probably the results of subsequent legislation. It is even a disputed point in what age Lycur' gus lived, some making him cotemporary with the Heraclídæ, and others dating his era four hundred years later, after the close of the Messénian wars; but the great mass of evidence fixes his legislation in he ninth century before the Christian era. It is said that after he ad completed his work, he set out on a journey, having previously bound the Spartans by an oath to make no change in his laws until his return, and, that they might never be released from the obligation, he voluntarily banished himself forever from his country, and died in a foreign land. The place and manner of his death are unknown, but Del' phos, Créte, and E' lis,[1] all claimed his tomb.

15. There were three classes among the pópulation of Laconia :— the Dórians of Sparta; their serfs, the Hélots; and the people of the provincial districts.[a] The former, properly called Spartans, were the ruling caste, who neither employed themselves in agriculture nor commerce, nor practiced any mechanical art.[b] The Hélots were slaves, who, as is generally believed, on account of their obstinate resistance in some early wars, and subsequent conquest, had been reduced to the most degrading servitude. They were always viewed with suspicion by their masters, and although some were occasionally emancipated, yet measures of the most atrocious violence were often adopted to reduce the strength and break the spirits of the bravest and most aspiring, who might threaten an insurrection.

16. The people of the provincial districts were a mixed race, composed partly of strangers who had accompanied the Dórians, and aided them in their conquest, and partly of the old inhabitants of the country who had submitted to the conquerors. The provincials were under the control of the Spartan government, in the administration of which they had no share, and the lands which they held were tributary to the State; they formed an important part of the

1. Del' phos and Créte have been described. The summit of Mount I'da, in Créte, was sacred to Jupiter. Here also Cyb' ele, the "mother of the gods," was worshipped. (The Mount I' da mentioned by the poets was in the vicinity of ancient Troy.) E' lis was a district of the Peloponnésus, lying west of Arcádia. At Olym' pia, situated on the river Alphéus, in this district, the celebrated Olympic games were celebrated in honor of Jupiter. E' lis, the capital of the district, was situated on the river Penéus, thirty miles north-west from Olym' pia. Map No. I.)

a. Thirwall, i. 129.   b. Hill's Institutions f Ancient Greece, p. 158.

military force of the country, and, on the whole, had little to complain of but the want of political independence.

17. During a century or more after the time of Lycur'gus, the Spartans remained at peace with their neighbors, except a few petty contests on the side of Arcádia and Ar'gos. Jealousies, however, arose between the Spartans and their brethren of Messénia,[1] which, stimulated by insults and injuries on both sides, gave rise to the first Messénian war, 743 years before the Christian era. VI. FIRST MESSÉNIAN WAR. After a conflict of twenty years, the Messénians were obliged to abandon their principal fortress of Ithóme,[2] and to leave their rich fields in the possession of the conquerors. A few of the inhabitants withdrew into foreign lands, but the principal citizens took refuge in Ar'gos and Arcádia; while those who remained were reduced to a condition little better than that of the Lacónian Hélots, being obliged to pay to their masters one-half of the fruits of the land which they were allowed to till.

18. The Messénian war exerted a great influence on the character and subsequent history of the Spartans, as it gave a full development to the warlike spirit which the institutions of Lycur'gus were so well calculated to encourage. The Spartans, stern and unyielding in their exactions from the conquered, again drove the Messénians to revolt (685 B. C.), thirty-nine years after the termination of the former war. The latter found a worthy VII. SECOND MESSÉNIAN WAR. leader in Aristom'enes, whose valor in the first battle struck fear into his enemies, and inspired his countrymen with confidence. The Spartans, sending to the Delphic oracle for advice, received the mortifying response, that they must seek a leader from the Athenians, between whose country and Lacónia there had been no intercourse for several centuries.

19. The Athenians, fearing to disobey the oracle, and reluctant to further the cause of the Spartans, sent to the latter the poet Tyrtæ'us, who had never been distinguished as a warrior. His patriotic odes, however, roused the spirit of the Spartans, who, obtaining Dórian auxiliaries from Corinth,[3] commenced the war anew. The

---

1. *Messénia* was a country west of Lacónia, and at the south-western extremity of the Peloponnésus. It was separated from E'lis on the north by the river Néda, and from Arcádia and Lacónia by mountain ranges. The Pamisus was its principal river. On the western coast was the deep bay of Py'lus, which has become celebrated in modern history under the name of *Navarino* (see p.517)—the only perfect harbor of Southern Greece. (*Map* No. 1.)

2. *Ithóme* was in Central Messénia, on a high hill on the western side of the vale of the Pamisus. (*Map* No. 1.)

3. *Cor'inth* was situated near the isthmus of the same name, between the Gulf of Lepan'to

Messénians, on the other hand, were aided by forces from Sic'ycn[1] and Ar'gos, Arcádia and E'lis, and, in a great battle near the mouth of the Pamísus,[2] in Messénia, they completely routed their enemies. In the third year of the war the Arcádian auxiliaries of the Messénians, seduced by bribes, deserted them in the heat of battle, and gave the victory to the Spartans.

20. The war continued, with various success, seventeen years, throughout the whole of which period Aristom'enes distinguished himself by many noble exploits; but all his efforts to save his country were ineffectual. A second time Sparta conquered (668), and the yoke appeared to be fixed on Messénia forever. Thenceforward the growing power and reputation of Sparta seemed destined to undisputed preëminence, not only in the Peloponnésus, but throughout all Greece.

21. At the period of the close of the second Messénian war, Athens, as previously stated, was under the aristocratical government of a senate of archons-magistrates chosen by the nobility from their own order, who possessed all authority, religious, civil, and military. The Athenian populace not only enjoyed no political rights, but was reduced to a condition but little above servitude, and it appears to have been owing to the anarchy that arose from ruinous extortions of the nobles on the one hand, and the resistance of the people on the other, that Dráco, the most eminent VIII. DRA'CO. of the nobility, was chosen to prepare the first written code of laws for the government of the State. (622 B. C.)

on the north-west, and of Ægina on the south-east, two miles from the nearest point of the former, and seven from the latter. The site of the town was at the north foot of a steep rock called the Acrop'olis of Cor'inth, 1,336 feet in height, the summit of which is now, as in antiquity, occupied as a fortress. This eminence may be distinctly seen from Athens, from which it is distant no less than forty-four miles in a direct line. Cor'inth was a large and populous city when St. Paul preached the Gospel there for a year and six months. (Acts, xviii. 11.) The present town, though of considerable extent, is thinly peopled. The only Grecian ruin now to be seen there is a dilapidated Doric temple. (Map No. 1.)

> "Where is thy grandeur Corinth? Shrunk from sight,
> Thy ancient treasures, and thy rampart's height,
> Thy god-like fanes and palaces! Oh, where
> Thy mighty myriads and majestic fair!
> Relentless war has poured around thy wall,
> And hardly spared the traces of thy fall!"

1. Sic'yon, once a great and flourishing city, was situated near the Gulf of Lepan'to, about ten miles north-west from Cor'inth. It boasted a high antiquity, and by some was considered older than Ar'gos. The ruins of the ancient town are still to be seen near the small modern village of Basilico. (Map No. I.)

9 The Pamisus (now called the Pimatza) was the principal river of Messénia. (Map No. I.)

22 The severity of his laws has made his name proverbial. Their character was thought to be happily expressed, when one said of them that they were written, not in ink, but in blood. He attached the same penalty to petty thefts as to sacrilege and murder, saying that the former offences deserved death, and he had no greater punishment for the latter. It is thought that the nobles suggested the severity of the laws of Dráco, thinking they would be a convenient instrument of oppression in their hands ; but human nature revolted against such legalized butchery, and the system of Dráco soon fell into disuse.

23. The commonwealth was finally reduced to complete anarchy, without law, or order, or system in the administration of justice, when Solon, who was descended from the line of Códrus, was raised to the office of first magistrate (594 B. C.), and, by the consent of all parties, was chosen as a general arbiter of their differ- IX. LEGISLA-
ences, and invested with full authority to frame a new TION OF
constitution and a new code of laws. The almost unlim- SOLON.
ited power conferred upon Solon might easily have been perverted to dangerous purposes, and many advised him to make himself absolute master of the State, and at once quell the numerous factions by the exercise of royal authority. And, indeed, such a usurpation would probably have been acquiesced in with but little opposition, as offering, for a time at least, a refuge from evils that had already become too intolerable to be borne. But the stern integrity of Solon was proof against all temptations to swerve from the path of honor, and betray the sacred trust reposed in him.

24. The grievous exactions of the ruling orders had already re duced the laboring classes, generally, to poverty and abject depend- ence : all whom bad times or casual disasters had compelled to bor- row, had been impoverished by the high rates of interest ; and thousands of insolvent debtors had been sold into slavery, to satisfy the demands of relentless creditors. In this situation of affairs the most violent or needy demanded a new distribution of property, as had been done in Sparta ; while the rich would have held on to all the fruits of their extortion and tyranny.

25. But Solon, pursuing a middle course between these extremes, relieved the debtor by reducing the rate of interest, and enhancing the value of the currency, so that three silver minæ paid an indebt- edness of four : he also relieved the lands of the poor from all in- cumbrances · he abolished imprisonment for debt ; he restored to

liberty those whom poverty had placed in bondage; and he repealed all the laws of Dráco, except those against murder. He next ar ranged all the citizens in four classes, according to their landed property; the first class alone being eligible to the highest civil offices and the highest commands in the army, while only a few of the lower offices were open to the second and third classes. The latter classes, however, were partially relieved from taxation; but in war they were required to equip themselves for military service, the one as cavalry, and the other as heavy armed infantry.

26. Individuals of the fourth class were excluded from all offices but in return they were wholly exempt from taxation; and yet they had a share in the government, for they were permitted to take part in the popular assemblies, which had the right of confirming or reject- ing new laws, and of electing the magistrates; and here their votes counted the same as those of the wealthiest of the nobles. In war they served only as light troops, or manned the fleets. Thus the system of Solon, being based primarily on property qualifications, provided for all the freemen; and its aim was to bestow upon the commonalty such a share in the government as would enable it to protect itself, and to give to the wealthy what was necessary for re- taining their dignity;—throwing the burdens of government on the latter, and not excluding the former from its benefits.

27. Solon retained the magistracy of the nine archons, but with abridged powers; and, as a guard against democratical extravagance on the one hand, and a check to undue assumptions of power on the other, he instituted a Senate of Four Hundred, and founded or remodelled the court of the Areop′agus. The Senate consisted of members selected by lot from the first three classes; but none could be appointed to this honor until they had undergone a strict ex- amination into their past lives, characters, and qualifications. The Senate was to be consulted by the archons in all important mat- ters, and was to prepare all new laws and regulations, which were to be submitted to the votes of the assembly of the people.

28. The court of the Areop′agus, which held its sittings on an eminence on the western side of the Athenian Acrop′olis, was com- posed of persons who had held the office of archon, and was the supreme tribunal in all capital cases. It exercised, also, a general superintendence over education, morals, and religion; and it could suspend a resolution of the public assembly which it deemed fraught with folly or injustice, until it had undergone a reconsideration

Such is a brief outline of the institutions of Solon, which exhibit a mingling of aristocracy and democracy, well adapted to the character of the age, and the circumstances of the people. They exhibit less control over the pursuits and domestic habits of individuals than the Spartan code, but at the same time they show a far greater regard for the public morals.

29. The legislation of Solon was not followed by the total extinction of party spirit, and ere long the three prominent factions in the State renewed their ancient feuds. Pisis' tratus, a wealthy kinsman of Solon, who had supported the measures of the latter by his eloquence and military talents, had the art to gain the favor of the populace, and constitute himself their leader. When his schemes were ripe for execution, he one day drove into the public square, his mules and himself disfigured with recent wounds inflicted by his own hands, but which he induced the multitude to believe had been received from a band of assassins, whom his enemies, the nobility, had hired to murder the friend of the people. An assembly was immediately convoked by his partizans, and the indignant crowd voted him a guard of fifty citizens to protect his person, although warned by Solon of the pernicious consequences of such a measure.

30. Pisis' tratus took advantage of the popular favor which he had gained, and, arming a larger body, seized the Aerop' olis, and made himself master of Athens. But the usurper, satisfied with the power of quietly directing the administration of government, made no changes in the constitution, and suffered the laws to take their ordinary course. The government of Pisis' tratus was probably a less evil than would have resulted from the success of either of the other factions; and in this light Solon appears to have viewed it, although he did not hesitate to denounce the usurpation; and, rejecting the usurper's offers of favor, it is said that he went into voluntary exile, and died at Sal' amis.[1] (559 B. C.) Twice was Pisis' tratus driven from Athens by a coalition of the opposing factions; but as the latter were almost constantly at variance with each other, he finally returned at the head of an army, and regained the sovereignty, which he held until his death. Although he tightened the reins of government, yet he ruled with equity and mildness, courting popularity by a generous treatment of the poorer citizens, and gratifying the national pride by adorning Athens with many useful and magnificent works.

. *Sal' amis* is an island in the Gulf of Ægina, near the coast of At' tica, and twelve or fifteen r m south-west from Athens. (*See Map* No. I.)

31. On the death of Pisis tratus (528 B. C.), his sons Hip' pias, Hippar' chus, and Thes' salus succeeded to his power, and for some years trod in his steps and prosecuted his plans, only taking care to fill the most important offices with their friends, and keeping a standing force of foreign mercenaries to secure themselves from hostile factions and popular outbreaks. After a joint re'gn of fourteen years a conspiracy was planned to free At' tica from their rule, at the head of which were two young Athenians, Harmódius and Aristogeíton, whose personal resentment had been provoked by an atrocious insult to the family of the former. Hippar' chus was killed but the two young Athenians also lost their lives in the struggle.

32. Hip' pias, the elder of the ruling brothers, now that he had injuries to avenge, became a cruel tyrant, and thus alienated the affections of the people. The latter finally obtained aid from the

X. EXPULSION OF THE PISISTRATIDS. Spartans, and the family of the Pisistratids was driven from Athens, never to regain its former ascendency; although but a few years after its expulsion, Sparta, repenting the course she had taken, made an ineffectual effort to restore Hip' pias to the throne of which she had aided in depriving him. Hip' pias then fled to the court of Artapánes, governor of Lyd' ia,¹ then a part of the Persian dominions of Daríus, where his intrigues greatly contributed to the opening of a war between Greece and Persia.²

33. Nearly half a century before this time, Crœ' sus,³ king of Lyd' ia, had conquered the Grecian colonies on the coast of Asia Minor; but he ruled them with great mildness, leaving them their political institutions undisturbed, and requiring of them little more than the payment of a moderate tribute. A few years later they experienced a change of masters, and, together with Lyd' ia, fell, by conquest, under the dominion of the Persians. But they were still allowed to retain their own form of government by paying tribute to their conquerors; yet they seized every opportunity to deliver them-

1. *Lyd' ia* was a country on the coast of Asia Minor, having Mys' ia on the north, Phryg' ia r the east, and Cária on the south. The Grecian colony of Iónia was embraced within Lyd' ia and the northern part of Cária, extending along the coast. (*Map* No. IV.)

2. Modern *Persia*, a large country of Central Asia, extends from the Caspian Sea on the north, to the Persian Gulf on the south, having Asiatic Turkey on the west, and the provinces of Affghanistan and Beloochistan on the east. For the greatest extent of the Persian empire, which was during the reign of Darius Hystas' pes, see the *Map* No. V.

3. *Crœ' sus*, the last king of Lyd' ia, was famed for his riches and munificence. Herod' otus (I. 30-33, and 36, &c.) and Plutarch (life of Solon) give a very interesting account of the visit of the Athenian Solon to the court of that prince, who greatly prided himself on his riches and vainly thought himself the happiest of mankind.

?elves from this species of thraldom, and finally the Iónians sought the aid of their Grecian countrymen, making application, first to Sparta, but in vain, and next (B. C. 500) to Athens, and the Grecian islands of the Æ'gean Sea.

34. The Athenians, irritated at this time by a haughty demand of the Persian monarch, that they should restore Hip'pias to the throne, and regarding Daríus as an avowed enemy, gladly took part with the Iónians, and, in connection with Eubœ'a,[1] fur- XI. IONIC
nished their Asiatic countrymen with a fleet of twenty- REVOLT.
five sail. The allied Grecians were at first successful, ravaging Lyd'ia, and burning Sar'dis,[2] its capital; but in the end they were defeated near Eph'esus;[3] the commanders quarrelled with each other; and the Athenians sailed home, leaving the Asiatic Greeks divided among themselves, to contend alone against the whole power of Persia. Still the Iónian war was protracted six years, when it was terminated by the storming of Milétus,[4] (B. C. 494,) the capital of the Iónian confederacy. The surviving inhabitants of this beautiful

1. *Eubœ'a*, (now called Neg'ropont',) a long, narrow, and irregular island of the Æ'gean Sea, (now Grecian Archipel'ago,) extended one hundred and ten miles along the eastern coast of Bœótia and At'tica, from which it was separated by the channel of Euripus, which, at one place, was only forty yards across. The chief town of the island was Chal'cis, (now Neg'ropont',) on the western coast. (*Map* No. I.)

2. *Sar'dis*, the ancient capital of Lyd'ia, was situated on both sides of the river Pactólus, a southern branch of the Her'mus, seventy miles east from Smyr'na. In the annals of Chris-'ianity, Sar'dis is distinguished as having been one of the seven churches of Asia. A miserable village, called *Sart*, is now found on the site of this ancient city. (*Mcp* No. IV.)

3. *Eph'esus*, one of the Iónian cities, was situated on the south side, and near the mouth of the small river Cays'ter, on the coast of Lyd'ia, thirty-eight miles south from Smyr'na. Here stood a noble temple, erected in honor of the goddess Diana; but an obscure individual, of the name of Heros'tratus, burned it, in order to perpetuate his memory by the infamous notoriety which such an act would give him? The grand council of Iónia endeavored to disappoint the incendiary by passing a decree that his name should not be mentioned, but it was divulged by the historian Theopom'pus. A new temple was subsequently built, far surpassing the first, and ranked among the seven wonders of the world. When St. Paul visited Eph'esus, still the cry was, "Great is Diana of the Ephésians" (Acts, xix. 28, 34); but the worship of the goddess was doomed speedily to decline, and here St. Paul founded the principal of the Asiatic churches. But war, the ravages of earthquakes, and the desolating hand of time, have completed the ruin of this once famous city. "The glorious pomp of its heathen worship is no longer remembered; and Christianity, which was there nursed by apostles, and fostered by general councils, until it increased to fulness of stature, barely lingers on in an existence hardly visible." (*Map* No. IV.)

4. *Milétus*, the most distinguished of the Iónian cities of Asia Minor, and once greatly celebrated for its population, wealth, commerce, and civilization, was situated in the province of Cária, on the southern shore of the bay into which the small river Lat'mus emptied, and about thirty-five miles south from Eph'esus. St. Paul appears to have sojourned here a few days; and here he assembled the elders of the Ephésian church, and delivered unto them an affectionate farewell address. (Acts, xx. 15, 38.) Milétus is now a deserted place, but contains the ruins of a few once magnificent structures, and still bears the name of *Palat*, or the *Palace*. (*Map* No. IV.)

and opulent city were carried away by order of Darius, and settled near the mouth of the Tigris.   Darius next turned his resentment against the Athenians and Eubœ' ans, who had aided the Ionian revolt,—meditating, however, nothing less than the conquest of all Greece (B. C. 490).   The events of the " Persian War" which followed, will next be narrated, after we shall have given some general views of cotemporary history, during the period which we have passed over in the preceding part of the present chapter.

COTEMPORARY HISTORY : 1184 to 490 B. C.

[I. Phœnician History.]—1. The name Phœnicia was applied to the north-western part of Palestine and part of the coast of Syria, embracing the country from Mount Carmel, north, along the coast, to the city and island Arádus,—an extent of about a hundred and fifty miles.   The mountain ranges of Lib' anus and Anti-Lib' anus formed the utmost extent of the Phœnician territory on the east. The surface of the country was in general sandy and hilly, and poorly adapted to agriculture ; but the coast abounded in good harbors, and the fisheries were excellent, while the mountain ranges in the interior afforded, in their cedar forests, a rich supply of timber for naval and other purposes.

2. At a remote period the Phœnicians, who are supposed to have been of the race of the Canaanites,[a] were a commercial people, but the loss of the Phœnician annals renders it difficult to investigate their early history.   Their principal towns were probably independent States, with small adjacent territories, like the little Grecian republics ; and no political union appears to have existed among them, except that arising from a common religious worship, until the time of the Persians.   The Phœnicians occupied Sicily before the Greeks ; they made themselves masters of Cy' prus, and they formed settlements on the northern coast of Africa ; but the chief seat of their early colonial establishments was the southern part of Spain, whence they are said to have extended their voyages to Britain, and even to the coasts of the Baltic.

3 It is also related by Herod' otus, (B. IV. 42,) that at an epoch which is believed to correspond to the year 604 before the Christian era, a fleet fitted out by Pharaoh Necho, king of Egypt, but manned and commanded by Phœnicians, departed from a port on

a. Niebuhr's Lect. on Ancient Hist. i. 113.

the Red Sea, and sailing south, and keeping always to the right, doubled the southern promontory of Africa, and, after a voyage of three years returned to Egypt by the way of the straits of Gibral·tar and the Mediterranean.   Herod'otus farther mentions that the navigators asserted that, in sailing round Africa, they had the sun on their right hand, or to the north, a circumstance which, Herod' otus says, to him seemed incredible, but which we know must hav been the case if the voyage was actually performed, because southern Africa lies south of the equatorial region.   Thus was Africa prob·ably circumnavigated by the Phœnicians, more than two thousand years before the Portuguese voyage of De Gama.

4. The Phœnicians of Tyre and Sidon had friendly connections with the Hebrews; and through the Red Sea, and by the way of the Arabian desert, and across the wilderness of Syria, they for a long time carried on the commercial exchanges between Europe and Asia.   From the time of the great commotions in Western Asia, which caused the downfall of so many independent States, and their subjection to the monarchs of Babylon and Persia, the com·mercial prosperity of the Phœnicians began to decline; but it was the founding of Alexandria by the Macedonian conqueror, which proved the final ruin of the Phœnician cities.

[II. JEWISH HISTORY.]—5. The history of the Jews, which has been brought down to the accession of Saul as king of Israel, pre·sents to the historian a fairer field than that of the Phœnicians, and is now to be continued down to the return of the Jews from their Babylonian captivity, and the completion of the rebuilding of the second temple of Jerusalem.

6. Saul, soon after his accession to the throne, (B. C. 1110,) which was about the time of the Dórian emigration, or the " Return of the Heraclídæ" to the Peloponnésus, gave proof of his military qualifications by a signal slaughter of the Ammonites, who had laid siege to Jábesh-Gil'ead.[1]   In a solemn assembly of the tribes at Gil'gal,[2] the people renewed their allegiance to their new sovereign, and there Samuel resigned his office.   During a war with the Phil·istines soon after, Saul ventured to ask counsel of the Lord; and assuming the sacerdotal functions, he offered the solemn sacrifice,

---

. 1. *Jábesh-Gil'ead* was a town on the east side of the Jordan, in Gil'ead. (*Map* No. VI.)

2. The *Gil'gal* here mentioned appears to have been a short distance west or north-west of Shechem, near the country of the Philistines. (*Map* No. VI.)

a duty which the sacred law assigned to the high-priest alone For this violation of the law the divine displeasure was denounced against him by the prophet Samuel, who declared to him that his kingdom should not continue ; and so disheartened were the people, that the army of Saul soon dwindled away to six hundred men ; but by the daring valor of Jonathan, his son, a panic was spread among the Philistines, and their whole army was easily overthrown.

7. During several years after this victory, Saul carried on a suc cessful warfare against the different nations that harassed the fron· tiers of his kingdom ; but when Agag, the king of the Amalekites, had fallen into his hands, in violation of the divine command he spared his life, and brought away from the vanquished enemy a vast booty of cattle. For not fulfilling his commission from the Lord, he was declared unfit to be the founder of a race of kings, and was told that the sovereign power should be transferred to another family.

8. David, of the tribe of Benjamin, then a mere youth, was di- vinely chosen for the succession, being secretly anointed for that purpose by Samuel. In the next war with the Philistines he dis- tinguished himself by slaying their champion, the gigantic Goliath of Gath.[1] Saul, however, looked upon David with a jealousy bor- dering on madness, and made frequent attempts to take his life ; but the latter sought safety in exile, and for a while took up his residence in a Philistine city. Returning to Palestine, he sought refuge from the anger of Saul in the dens and caves of the moun- tains ; and twice, while Saul was pursuing him, had it in his power to destroy his persecutor, but he would not " lift his hand against the Lord's anointed."

9. After the death of Samuel, the favor of the Lord was wholly withdrawn from Saul ; and when the Philistines invaded the country with a numerous army, several of the sons of Saul were slain in battle on Mount Gil′boa,[2] and Saul himself, to avoid falling alive into the hands of his enemies, fell upon his own sword. On the death of Saul, David repaired to Hébron,[3] and, with the support of the tribe of Judah, asserted his title to the throne ; but the north· ern tribes attached themselves to Ishbosheth, a son of Saul ;—" and

---

1. *Gath*, a town of the Philistines, was about twenty-five miles west from Jerusalem. (*May No. VI.)

2. *Mount Gil′ boa* is in the southern part of Galilee, a short distance west of the Jordan (*Map No. VI.)

3. *Hébron*, a town of Judah, was about twenty miles south of Jerusalem. (*Map N. VI.*)

there was long war' between the house of Saul and the house of David; but David waxed stronger. and stronger, and the house of. Saul waxed weaker and weaker." The death of Ishbosheth, who fell by the hands of two of his own guards, removed the obstacles in the way of a union of the tribes, and at Hebron David was publicly recognized king of all Israel.

10 After all the conquests which the Israelites had made in the land of promise, there still remained large portions of Palestine of which they had not yet gained possession. On the south-west were the strongholds and cities of the Philistines; and bordering on the north-western coast was the country of the Phœnicians, whose two chief cities were Tyre[1] and Sidon.[2] Joppa[3] was the only Mediterranean port open to the Israelites. Even in the very heart of Palestine, the Jeb'usites, supposed to have been a tribe of the wandering Hyk'sos, possessed the stronghold of Jébus, or Jerusalem, on Mount Zion, after David had become king of "all Israel," But

1. *Tyre*, long the principal city of Phœnicia, and the commercial emporium of the ancient world, stood on a small island on the south-eastern or Palestine coast of the Mediterranean, about forty miles north-east from Mount Carmel. The modern town of Sûr, (Soor,) with fifteen hundred inhabitants, occupies a site opposite the ancient city. The prophets Isaiah, Jeremiah, and Ezekiel, represent Tyre as a city of unrivalled wealth, "a mart of nations," whose "merchants were princes, and her traffickers the honorable of the earth." (Isaiah, xxiii. 3, 8.) After the destruction of the old city by Nebuchadnezzar, New Tyre enjoyed a considerable degree of celebrity and commercial prosperity; but the founding of Alexandria, by diverting the commerce that had formerly centred at Tyre into a new channel, gave her an irreparable blow, and she gradually declined, till, in the language of prophecy, her palaces have been levelled with the dust, and she has become "a place for the spreading of nets in the midst of the sea." (Ezek. xxvi. 5.) The prophet Ezekiel has described, in magnificent terms, the glory and the riches of Tyre. (See Ezek. xxvii.) (*Map* No. VI.)

2. *Sidon*, (now called *Said*,) was situated near the sea, twenty-two miles north of Tyre, of which it was the parent city, and by which it was early eclipsed in commercial importance. The modern town contains four or five thousand inhabitants. The site of the ancient city is supposed to have been about two miles farther inland. Sidon is twice spoken of in Joshua as the "great Sidon" (Josh. xi. 8, and xix. 28); and in the time of Homer there were "skillful Sidonian artists" (Cowper's Il. xxiii. 891). In the division of Palestine, Sidon fell to the lot of Asher; but we learn from Judges, (i. 31,) corroborated also by profane history, that it never came into the actual possession of that tribe. In the time of Solomon there were none among the Jews who had "skill to hew timber like unto the Sidonians." (1 Kings, v. 6.) The modern town of *Said*, the representative of the ancient city, is on the north side of a cape extending into the Mediterranean. (*Map* No. VI.)

3. *Jop' pa*, (now called Jaffa, a town of about four thousand inhabitants,) stands on a tongue of land projecting into the Mediterranean, and rising from the shore in the form of an amphitheatre, thirty-two miles north-west from Jerusalem. The "border before Joppa" was included in the possessions of the tribe of Dan (Josh. xix. 46). In the time of Solomon it appears to have been a port of some consequence. Hiram, king of Tyre, writing to Solomon, says, "We will cut wood out of Lebanon as much as thou shalt need; and we will bring it thee in floats by sea to Jop' pa, and thou shalt carry it up to Jerusalem." (*Map* No. VI.)

4. *Jerusalem*, first known as the city of the Jeb'usites, is in the southern part of Palestine, nearly intermediate between the northern extremity of the Dead Sea and the Mediterranean, and thirty-two miles east from Jaffa. (See farther description p. 164.)

David, having resolved upon the conquest of this important city, which its inhabitants deemed impregnable, sent Joab, his general, against it, with a mighty army; " and David took the stronghold of Zion ;" and so pleased was he with its situation, that he made it the capital of his dominions.

11. After the defeat of the Jeb' usites, David was involved in war with many of the surrounding nations, whom he compelled to be some tributary to him, as far as the banks of the Euphrátes Among these were most of the States of Syr' ia,[1] on the north-east, with Damas' cus,[2] their capital, and also the E' domites, on the south eastern borders of Palestine. It was in the last of these wars, dur ing the siege of Rab' bah,[3] the Ammonite capital, that David pro-voked the anger of the Lord by taking Bath' sheba, the wife of Uriah, to himself, and exposing her husband to death. The re-mainder of David's life was full of trouble from his children, three of whom, Amnon, Absalom, and Adoníjah, died violent deaths—the latter two after they had successively rebelled against their father David died after a troubled but glorious reign of forty years, after having given orders that his son Solomon should succeed him.

12. By the conquests of David the fame of the Israelites had spread into distant lands, and Solomon obtained in marriage the daughter of the king of Egypt. So celebrated was the wisdom of Solomon, that the queen of Sheba[a] came to visit him from a dis

1. Ancient *Syr' ia* embraced the whole of Palestine and Phœnicia, and was bounded on the east by the Euphrátes and the Arabian desert. Syr' ia is called in Scripture *Aram*, and the inhabitants Aramæans. The term Syr' ia is a corruption or abridgment of Assyria. (*Map No. V.*)

2. *Damas' cus*, one of the most ancient cities of Syr' ia, existed in the time of Abraham, two thousand years before the Christian era. (See Gen. xiv. 15.) It was conquered by David, but freed itself from the Jewish yoke in the time of Solomon, when, becoming the seat of a new principality, it often harassed the kingdoms both of Judah and Israel. At later periods it fell successively under the power of the Persians, Greeks, and Romans. As a Roman city it attained great eminence, and it appears conspicuously in the history of the Apostle Paul. (Acts, ix.) It is now a large and important commercial Mohammedan city, containing a population of more than a hundred thousand inhabitants. The city is situated in a pleasant plain, watered by a river, the Syriac name of which was *Pharphar*, on the eastern side of the Anti-Lib' anus mountains, a hundred and fifty miles north-east from Jerusalem. (*Map No. VI.*)

3. *Rabbah*, (afterwards called Philadelphia by the Greeks, when it was rebuilt by Ptolemy Philadelphus,) was about thirty miles north-east from the northern extremity of the Dead Sea, at the source of the brook Jabbok. Extensive ruins, at a place now called *Ammon*, consisting of the remains of theatres, temples, and colonnades of Grecian construction, mark the site of the Ammonite capital. The ancient city is now without an inhabitant, but the excellent water found there renders the spot a desirable halting-place for caravans, the drivers of which use the ancient temples and buildings as shelter for their beasts, literally fulfilling the denunciation

a. The queen of Sheba is supposed by some to have come from Southern Arabia, but is more generally thought to have been the queen of Abyssinia, which is the firm belief of the Abys-sinians to this day.— *Kitto's Palestine*

tant country, and the most powerful princes of the surrounding nations courted his alliance.   With Hiram, king of Tyre, the chief
city of the Phœnicians, and the emporium of the commerce of the
Eastern world, he was united by the strictest bonds of friendship.
Seven years and a half was he occupied in building, at Jerusalem, a
magnificent temple to the Lord.   He also erected for himself a palace of unrivalled splendor.   A great portion of his immense wealth
was derived from commerce, of which he was a distinguished patron
From ports on the Red Sea, in his possession, his vessels sailed to
Ophir, some rich country on the shores of the Indian Ocean.   By
the aid of Phœnician navigators he also opened a communication
with Tar'shish, in western Europe, while the commerce between
Central Asia and Palestine was carried on by caravans across the
desert.

13. But even Solomon, notwithstanding all his learning and wisdom, was corrupted by prosperity, and in his old age was seduced
by his numerous " strange wives" to forsake the God of his fathers.
He became an idolater : and then enemies began to arise up against
him on every side.   A revolt was organized in E'dom :' an independent adventurer seized Damascus, and formed a new Syrian kingdom there ; and the prophet Ahijah foretold to Solomon that the
kingdom of Israel should be rent, and that the dominion of ten of
the twelve tribes should be given to Jeroboam, of the tribe of Ephraim, although not till after the death of Solomon.

14. Accordingly, on the death of Solomon, when Rehoboam his
son came to the throne, the ten northern tribes chose Jeroboam for
their king ; and Israel and Judah, with which latter was united the
tribe of Benjamin, became separate kingdoms.   The separation thus
effected is called " The Revolt of the Ten Tribes." (990 B. C.)
The subsequent princes of the kingdom of Israel, as the Ten Tribes
were called, were all idolaters in the sight of the Lord, although
from time to time they were warned of the consequences of their
idolatry by the prophets Elijah, Elisha, Hosea, Amos, Jonah, and
others.   The history of these ten tribes is but a repetition of
calamities and revolutions.   Their seventeen kings, excluding two

of Ezekiel : " I will make Rabbah of the Ammonites a stable for camels, and a couching place
for flocks." (Ezekiel, xxv. 5.) (*Map* No. VI.)

1. The E' domites, inhabitants of Idumea, or *E' dom*, dwelt, at this time, in the country south
and south-east of the Dead Sea.   During the Babylonian captivity the E' domites took possession of the southern portion of Judea, and made Hebron their capital.   They afterwards embraced Judaism, and their territory became incorporated with Judea although in the time of
our Saviour it still retained the name of Idumea. (*Map* No. VI.)

pretenders, belonged to seven different families, and were placed on the throne by seven sanguinary conspiracies. At length Shalmanézer, king of Assyria, invaded the country; and Samária,[1] its capital, after a brave resistance of three years, was taken by storm. The ten tribes were then driven out of Palestine, and carried away captive into a distant region beyond the Euphrátes, 719 years before the Christian era. With their captivity the history of the ten tribes ends. Their fate is still unknown to this day, and their history remains un written.

15. After the revolt of the ten tribes, Rehobóam reigned seven teen years at Jerusalem, over Judah and Benjamin, comprising what was called the kingdom of Judah. During his reign he and his subjects fell into idolatry, for which they were punished by an invasion by Shíshak, king of Egypt, who entered Jerusalem and carried off the treasures of the temple and the palace. We find some of the subsequent kings of Judah practising idolatry, and suffering the severest punishments for their sins: others restored the worship of the true God; and of them it is recorded that " God prospered their undertakings."

16. At the time when Shalmanézer, the Assyrian, carried Israel away captive, the wicked Ahaz was king over Judah. He brought the country to the brink of ruin, but its fall was arrested by the death of the impious monarch. The good Hezekiah succeeded him, and, aided by the advice of the prophet Isaiah, commenced his reign with a thorough reformation of abuses. He shook off the Assyrian yoke, to which his father Ahaz had submitted by paying tribute. Sennachérib, the son and successor of Shalmanézer, determining to be revenged upon Judah, sent a large army against Jerusalem (711 B. C.); but " the angel of the Lord went forth, and smote, in the camp of the Assyrians, a hundred and fourscore and five thousand men." The instrument by which the Lord executed vengeance upon the Assyrians, is supposed by some to have been the pestilential samoom of the desert; for Isaiah had prophesied of the king of Assyria: " Thus saith the Lord; behold, I will send a blast upon him."[a]

17. It is interesting to find an account of the miraculous destruction of the Assyrian army in the pages of profane history. Senna

1. Samária, (now called Sebustieh,) the capital of the kingdom of Israel, stood on Mount Sameron, about forty miles north from Jerusalem. (Map No. VI.)

a. Isaiah, xxxvii. 6, 7

chérib was at this time marching against Egypt, whose alliance had been sought by Hezekiah, when, unwilling to leave the hostile power of Judah in his rear, he turned against Jerusalem. It was natural therefore, that the discomfiture which removed the fears of the Egyptians, should have a place in their annals. Accordingly, Herod' otus gives an account of it, which he had learned from the Egyptians themselves; but in the place of the prophet Isaiah, it is an Egyptian priest who invokes the aid of his god against the enemy, and predicts the destruction of the Assyrian host.

18. Herod' otus relates that the Egyptian king, directed by the priest, marched against Sennachérib with a company composed only of tradesmen and artizans, and that "so immense a number of mice infested by night the enemy's camp, that their quivers and bows, together with what secured their shields to their arms, were gnawed in pieces;" and that, "in the morning the enemy, finding themselves without arms, fled in confusion, and lost great numbers of their men." Herod' otus also relates that, in his time, there was still standing in the Egyptian temple of Vulcan a marble statue of this Egyptian king, having a mouse in his hand, and with the inscription : "Learn from my fortune to reverence the gods."[a]

19. Hezekiah was succeeded on the throne of Judah by his son Manas' seh, who, in the early part of his reign, revelled in the grossest abominations of Eastern idolatry. Being carried away captive to Babylon by Sardanapálus, the Assyrian king, he repented of his sins, and was restored to his kingdom. The brief reign of his son A' mon was corrupt and idolatrous. The good Josíah then succeeded to the throne. His reign was an era in the religious government of the nation; but during an invasion of the country by Pharaoh Necho, king of Egypt, he was mortally wounded in battle. Jerusalem was soon after taken, and Jehóahaz, who had been elected to the throne by the people, was deposed, and carried captive to Egypt, where he died.

20. Not long after this, during the reign of Jehoíakim, the Egyptian monarch, pursuing his conquests eastward against the Babylonians, was utterly defeated by Nebuchadnez' zar near the Euphrátes, —an event which prepared the way for the Babylonian dominion over Judea and the west of Asia. Pursuing his success westward, Nebuchadnez' zar came to Jerusalem, when the king, Jehoíakim, submitted, and agreed to pay tribute for Judah ; but as he rebelled

---

a. Herod' otus, Book II. p. 141.

after three years, Nebuchadnez'zar returned, pillaged Jerusalem and carried away certain of the royal family and of the nobles as hostages for the fidelity of the king and people. (B. C. 605.) Among these were the prophet Daniel and his companions. Jehoniah, the next king of Judah, was carried away to Babylon, with a multitude of other captives, so that "none remained save the poorest people of the land."

21. The throne in Jerusalem was next filled by Zedekiah, who joined some of the surrounding nations in a rebellion against Nebuchadnez'zar; but Jerusalem, after an eighteen months' siege, whose miseries were heightened by the horrors of famine, was taken by storm at midnight. Dreadful was the carnage which ensued. Zedekiah, attempting to escape, was made prisoner; and the king of Babylon slew the sons of Zedekiah before his eyes, and put out the eyes of Zedekiah, and bound him with fetters of brass, and carried him to Babylon. Nearly all the wretched inhabitants were made companions of his exile. Jerusalem was burned, the temple levelled with the ground, and the very walls destroyed. (586 B. C.)

22. Thus ended the kingdom of Judah, and the reign of the house of David. Seventy years were the children of Israel detained in captivity in Babylon, reckoning from the time of the first pillaging of Jerusalem by Nebuchadnez'zar, a period that had been declared in prophecy by Jeremiah, and which was distinguished by the visions of Nebuchadnez'zar, the prophetic declarations of Daniel, Belshazzar's feast, and the overthrow of the kingdom of Babylon by the Medes and Persians. The termination of the Captivity, as had been foretold by the prophets, was the act of Cyrus, the Persian, immediately after the conquest of Babylon. (536 B. C.)

23. The edict of Cyrus permitted all Jews in his dominions to return to Palestine, and to rebuild the city and temple of Jerusalem. Only a zealous minority, however, returned, and but little progress had been made in the rebuilding of the temple, when the work was altogether stopped by an order of the next sovereign; but during the reign of Darius Hystas'pes, Zerub'babel, urged by the prophets Hag'gai and Zechariah, obtained a new edict for the restoration of the temple, and after four years the work was completed, 516 years before the Christian era. The temple was now dedicated to the worship of Jehovah, the ceremonies of the Jewish law were restored, and never again did the Jews, as a people, relapse into idolatry.

[III. Roman History.]—24. Having thus brought the events of Jewish history down to the time of the commencement of the wars between Greece and Persia, we again turn back to take a view of the cotemporary history of such other nations as had begun to acquire historical importance during the same period. Our attention is first directed to Rome—to the rise of that power which was destined eventually to overshadow the world. Rome is supposed to have been founded 753 years before the Christian era, about the time of the abolition of the hereditary archonship in Athens—twenty years before the commencement of the first war between Sparta and Messénia, and about thirty years before the reign of Hezekiah, king of Judah. But the importance of Roman history demands a connected account, which can better be given after Rome has broken in upon the line of history we are pursuing, by the reduction of Greece to a Roman province; and as we have already arrived at a period of corresponding importance in Persian affairs, we shall next briefly trace the events of Persian history down to the time when they became mingled with the history of the Grecians.

[IV. Persian History.]—25. In the course of the preceding history of the Jews we have had occasion to mention the names of Shalmenésar, Sennachérib, and Sardanapálus, who were the last three kings of the united empire of Assyria, whose capital was Nineveh. Not long after Sardanapálus had attacked Judah, and carried away its king Manas'seh into captivity, the governors of several of the Assyrian provinces revolted against him, and besieged him in his capital, when, finding himself deserted by his subjects, he destroyed his own life. (671 B. C.) The empire, which, during the latter part of the reign of Sardanapálus, had embraced Média, Persia, Babylónia, and Assyria, was then divided among the conspirators.

26. Sixty-five years later, the Medes and Babylonians, with joint forces, destroyed Nineveh (B. C. 606),[a] and Babylon became the capital of the reunited empire. The year after the destruction of Nineveh, Nebuchadnez'zar, a name common to the kings of Babylon, as was Pharaoh to those of Egypt, made his first attack upon Jerusalem (B. C. 605), rendering the Jews tributary to him, and carrying away numbers of them into captivity, and among them the prophet Daniel and his companions. Nineteen years later (B. C. 586), he

<hr />

a. Clinton, i. 269. Grote, iii. 255, Note, says, " During the last ten years of the reign of Cyaxares":—and Cyaxares, the Mede reigned from 636 to 595.

destroyed the very walls of Jerusalem and the temple itself, and carried away the remnant of the Jews captive tc Babylon.

27. Soon after the conquest of Judea, Nebuchadnez'zar resolved to take vengeance on the surrounding nations, some of whom had solicited the Jews to unite in a confederacy against him, but had afterwards rejoiced at their destruction. These were the Am'monites, Moabites, E'domites, Arábians, Sidónians, Tyr'ians, Philistines, Egyptians, and Abyssin'ians. The subjugation of each was particularly foretold by the prophets, and has been related both by sacred and profane writers. In the war against the Phœnicians,·after a long siege of thirteen years he made himself master of insular Tyre, the Phœnician capital (B. C. 571), and the Tyr'ians became subject to him and his successors until the destruction of the Chaldean monarchy by Cyrus.[a]

28. In the war against Egypt (B. C. 570), Nebuchadnez'zar laid the whole country waste, in accordance with previous predictions of the prophets Ezekiel and Jeremiah. The prophecy of Ezekiel, that, after the desolations foretold, " there shall no more be a prince of the land of Egypt," has been verified in a remarkable manner; for the kings of Egypt were made tributary, and grievously oppressed, first by the Babylonians, and next by the Persians; and since the rule of the latter, Egypt has successively been governed by foreigners —by the Macedonians, the Romans, the Mamelukes, and lastly, by the Turks, who possess the land of the Pharaohs to this day.

29. It was immediately after his return from Egypt that Nebuchadnez'zar, flushed with the brilliancy of his conquests, set up a golden image, and commanded all the people to fall down and worship it. (B. C. 569.) Notwithstanding the rebuke which his impiety received on this occasion, after he had adorned Babylon with magnificent works, again the pride of his heart was exhibited; for as he walked in his palace he said, in exultation, " Is not this great Babylon that I have built for the head of the kingdom, by the might of my power, and for the honor of my majesty ?" But in the same hour that he had spoken he was struck with lunacy, and all his glory departed from him. Of his dreams, and their prophetic interpretation by Daniel, we shall have occasion to speak, as the predictions are successively verified in the progress of history.

a. The common statement that it was the inland town that was reduced by Nebuchadnezzar, and that most of the inhabitants had previously withdrawn to an island where they built "New Tyre," seems to be erroneous. See Grote's Greece, iii. 366-7.

30. Not long after the reign of Nebuchadnez'zar, we find Bel shaz'zar, probably a grandson of the former, on the throne of Baby lon.   Nothing is recorded of him but the circumstances of his death, which are related in the fifth chapter of Daniel.   He was probably slain in a conspiracy of his nobles. (B. C. 553.)   In the meantime, the kingdom of Media[1] had risen to eminence under the successive reigns of Phraor'tes, Cyax'ares, and Asty'ages,[2] the former of whom is supposed to be the Ahasuérus mentioned in the book of Daniel.[a]   While some writers mention a successor of Asty'ages, Cyax'ares II., who has been thought to be the same as the Darius of Scripture, others assert that Asty'ages was the last of the Median kings.   In accordance with the latter and now generally-received account, Cyrus, a grandson of Asty'ages, but whose father was a Persian, roused the Persian tribes against the ruling Medes, defeated Asty'ages, and transferred the supreme power to the Persians. (558 B. C.)[b]

31. Cyrus the Great,[c] as he is often called, is generally considered the founder of the Persian empire.   Soon after his accession to the throne his dominions were invaded by Crœ'sus, king of Lydia but Cyrus defeated him in the great battle of Thymbria, and after wards, besieging him in his own capital of Sardis, took him prisoner, and obtained possession of all his treasures. (B. C. 546.)   The sub jugation of the Grecian cities of Asia Minor by the Persians soon followed.   Cyrus next laid siege to Babylon, which still remained an independent city in the heart of his empire.   Babylon soon fell be neath his power, and it has been generally asserted that he effected the conquest by turning the waters of the Euphrátes from their chan nel, and marching his troops into the city through the dry bed of the stream; but this account has been doubted, while it has been thought quite as probable that he owed his success to some internal revolu tion, which put an end to the dynasty of the Babylonian kings (B C. 536.)   The prophetic declarations of the final and utter de

1. *Media*, the boundaries of which varied greatly at different times, embraced the country immediately south and south-west of the Caspian Sea, and north of the early Persia. (*Map No. V.*)

2. These kings were probably in a measure subordinate to the ruling king at Babylon.

a. Daniel, ix. 1.   Hale's Analysis, iv. 81.

b. Niebuhr's Lect. on Ancient Hist. i. 135.   Grote's Greece, iv. 183.

c. The accounts of the early history of Cyrus, as derived from Xen'ophon, Herod'otus, Ctésias, &c., are very contradictory   The account of Herod'otus is now generally preferred, as containing a *greater proportion* of historical truth than the others.   Grote calls the Cyropæ'dia of Xen'ophon a "philosophical novel."   Niebuhr says, "No rational man, in our days, can look upon Xen'ophon's history of Cyrus in any other light than that of a romance."

struction of Babylon, which was eventually to be made a desolate waste—a possession for the bittern—a retreat for the wild beasts of the desert and of the islands—to be filled with pools of water—and to be inhabited no more from generation to generation, have been fully verified.

32. In the year that Babylon was taken, Cyrus issued the famous decree which permitted the Jews to return to their own land, and to rebuild the city and temple of Jerusalem—events which had been foretold by the prophet Isaiah more than a century before Cyrus was born. Cyrus is supposed to have lived about seven years after the taking of Babylon—directing his chief attention to the means of increasing the prosperity of his kingdom. The manner of his death is a disputed point in history, but in the age of Strabo his tomb bore the inscription: " O man, I am Cyrus, who founded the Persian empire : envy me not then the little earth which covers my remains."

33. Camby'ses succeeded his father on the throne of Persia (530 B. C.) Intent on carrying out the ambitious designs of Cyrus, he invaded and conquered Egypt, although the Egyptian king was aided by a force of Grecian auxiliaries. The power of the Persians was also extended over several African tribes : even the Greek col ony of Cyrenáica[1] was forced to pay tribute to Camby'ses, and the Greek cities of Asia Minor remained quiet under Persian governors ; but an army which Camby'ses sent over the Libyan desert to subdue the little oasis where the temple of Júpiter Am'mon[2] was the centre of an independent community, was buried in the sands ; and another army which the king himself led up the Nile against Ethiopia, came near perishing from hunger. The Persian king would have attempted the conquest of the rising kingdom of Carthage, but his Phœnician allies or subjects, who constituted his naval power, were unwilling to lend their aid in destroying the indepen- dence of their own colony, and Camby'ses was forced to abandon the roject.

34. On the death of Camby'ses (B. C. 521), one Smer'dis an

i. *Cyrenáica,* a country on the African coast of the Mediterranean, corresponded with the western portion of the modern Barca. It was sometimes called *Pentap'olis,* from its he i ng five Grecian cities of note in it, of which Cyréne was the capital. (See p. 95, also *Map* No. V.)

2. The *Temple of Júpiter Am'mon* was situated in what is now called the Oasis of Siwah, a fertile spot in the desert, three hundred miles south-west from Cairo. The time and the cir- cumstances of the existence of this temple are unknown, but, like that of Delphi, it was fr ned for its treasures. A well sixty feet deep, which has been discovered in the oasis, is supposed to mark the site of the temple.

impostor, a pretended son of Cyrus, seized the throne; but the Persian nobles soon formed a conspiracy against him, killed him in his
palace, and chose one of their own number to reign in his stead.
The new monarch assumed the old Median title of royalty, and is
known in history as Daríus, or Daríus Hystas' pes.   Babylon having
revolted, he was engaged twenty months in the siege of the city
which was finally taken by the artifice of a Persian nobleman, who
pretending to desert to the enemy, gained their confidence, and
having obtained the command of an important post in the city,
opened the gates to the Persians : Daríus put to death three thousand of the citizens, and ordered the one hundred gates to be pulled
down, and the walls of the proud city to be demolished, that it might
never after be in a condition to rebel against him.   The favor which
this monarch showed the Jews, in permitting them to rebuild the
walls of Jerusalem, has already been mentioned.

35. The attention of Daríus was next turned towards the Scythians,[1] then a European nation, who inhabited the country along the
western borders of the Euxine, from the Tan'ais or Don[2] to the northern boundaries of Thrace.[3]   Daríus indeed overran their country,
but without finding an enemy who would meet him in battle ; for the
Scythians were wise enough to retreat before the invader, and desolate the country through which he directed his course.   When the
supplies of the Persians had been cut off on every side, and their
strength wasted in useless pursuit, they were glad to seek safety by
a hasty retreat.

36. The next important events in the history of Daríus we find
connected with the revolt, and final subjugation, of the Greek colonies
of Asia Minor, an account of which has already been given.   Still
Daríus was not a conqueror like Cyrus or Camby'ses, but seems
to have aimed rather at consolidating and securing his empire, than

1. *Scythia* is a name given by the early Greeks to the country on the northern and western
orders of the Euxine. In the time of the first Ptolemy, however, the early Scythia, together
with the whole region from the Baltic Sea to the Caspian, had changed its name to *Sarmatia*,
while the entire north of Asia beyond the Himalaya mountains was denominated Scythia
(*Map* Nos. V. and IX.)

2. The *Don* (anciently Tan'ais), rising in Central Russia, flows south-east until it approach es
within about thirty-six miles of the Volga, when it turns to the south-west, and enters the
north-eastern extremity of the Sea of Azof (anciently Palus Mœotis). (*Map* No. IX.)

3. *Thrace*, embracing nearly the same as the modern Turkish province of Rumilia, was
bounded on the north by the Hæmus mountains, on the east by the Euxine, on the south by
the Propon'tis and the Æ'gean Sea, and on the west by Macedónia. Its principal river was
the Hèbrus (now Maritza), and its largest towns, excepting those in the Thracian Chersom ese
(see p. 96.) were Hadrianopolis and Byzantium. (*Map* No. III. and IX.)

at enlarging it. The dominions bequeathed him by his predecessors comprised many countries, united under one government only by their subjection to the will and the arbitrary exactions of a common ruler; but Darius first organized them into one empire, by dividing the whole into twenty satrapies or provinces, and assigning to each its proper share in the burdens of government.

37. Under Darius the Persian empire had now attained its greatest extent, embracing, in Asia, all that, at a later period, was contained in Persia proper and Turkey; in Africa, taking in Egypt as far as Nubia, and the coast of the Mediterranean as far as Barca; and in Europe, part of Thrace and Macedonia—thus stretching from the Æ'gean Sea to the Indus, and from the plains of Tartary[1] to the cataracts of the Nile. Such was the empire against whose united power a few Grecian communities were to contend for the preservation of their very name and existence. The results of the contest may be learned from the following chapter. (See *Map* No. VII.)

1. Tartary is a name of modern origin, applied to that extensive portion of Central Asia which extends eastward from the Caspian Sea to the Pacific Ocean.

CHAPTER IV.

THE AUTHENTIC PERIOD OF GRECIAN HISTORY.

SECTION I.

GRECIAN HISTORY FROM THE BEGINNING OF THE FIRST WAR WITH PERSIA TO THE ES-
TABLISHMENT OF PHILIP ON THE THRONE OF MACEDON:
490 TO 360 B. C. = 130 YEARS.

ANALYSIS. FIRST PERSIAN WAR. 1. Preparations of Darius for the conquest of Greece.
Mardonius. Destruction of the Persian fleet. [Mount A' thos.] Return of Mardonius.—2. Re-
newed preparations of Darius. Heralds sent to Greece. Their treatment by the Athenians and
Spartans. The Æginétans. [Ægina.]—3. Persian fleet sails for Greece. Islands submit.
Eubœ' a. Persians at Mar' athon. The Plata' ans aid the Athenians. Spartans absent.
[Mar' athon. Plata' a.]—4. The Athenian army. How commanded.—5. Battle of Mar' athon.
—6. Remarks on the battle. Legends of the battle.—7. The war terminated. Subsequent
history of Miltiades. [Paros.] Themis' tocles and Aristides. Their characters. Banishment of the latter. [Ostracism.]—9. Death of Darius. SECOND PERSIAN WAR. Xerxes invades Greece. Opposed by Leon' idas. [Thermop' ylæ.] Anecdote of Dien' eces.—10. Treachery.
Leon' idas dismisses his allies. Self-devotion of the Greeks.—11. Eurytus and Aristodémus.
—12. The Athenians desert Athens, which is burned by the enemy. [Trezéne.] The Greeks
fortify the Corinthian isthmus.—13. The Persian fleet at Sal' amis. Eurybiades, Themis' tocles,
and Aristides.—14. Battle of Sal' amis. Flight of Xerxes. [Hel' lespont.] Battle of Plata' a
—of Myc' ale. [Myc' ale.] Death of Xerxes.—15. Athens rebuilt. Banishment of Themis'-
tocles. Cimon and Pausánias. The Persian dependencies. Ionian revolt. [Cy' prus. Byzan' tium.]—16. Final peace with Persia.—17. Dissensions among the Grecian States. Per'
icles. Jealousy of Sparta, and growing power of Athens.—18. Power and character of Sparta.
Earthquake at Sparta. Revolt of the Hélots. THIRD MESSE' NIAN WAR. Migration of the
Messénians.—19. Athenians defeated at Tan' agra. [Tan' agra.] Subsequent victory gained by
the Athenians.

20. Causes which opened the FIRST PELOPONNE' SIAN WAR. [Corcy' ra. Potidæ' a.]—21.
The Spartan army ravages At' tica. The Athenian navy desolates the coast of the Peloponné-
rus. [Meg' ara.]—22. Second invasion of At' tica. The plague at Athens, and death of Per'-
icles. Potidæ' a surrenders to Athens, and Plata' a to Sparta.—23. The peace of Nicias. Pretexts for renewing the struggle.—24. Character of Alcibiades. His artifices. Reduction of
Mélos. [Mélos.]—25. THE SICILIAN EXPEDITION. Its object. [Sicily. Syracuse.] Revolt
and flight of Alcibiades.—26. Operations of Nicias, and disastrous result of the expedition.

27. SECOND PELOPONNE' SIAN WAR. Revolt of the Athenian allies. Intrigues of Alcibiades.
Revolution at Athens. [Erétria Cys' icus.] Return of Alcibiades.—28. He is again banished.
The affairs of Sparta are retrieved by Lysan' der. Cyrus the Persian.—29. The Athenians are
defeated at Æ' gos-Pot' amos. Treatment of the prisoners.—30. Disastrous state of Athenian
affairs. Submission of Athens, and close of the war.—31. Change of government at Athens.
The Thirty Tyrants overthrown. The rule of the democracy restored.—32. Character, accusation, and death of Soc' rates.—33. The designs of Cyrus the Persian. He is aided by the Greeks
—34. Result of his expedition.—35. Famous retreat of the Ten Thousand.—36. The Greek cities
of Asia are involved in a war with Persia. The THIRD PELOPONNE' SIAN WAR. [Coronéa.]
The peace of Antal' cidas. [Im' brus, Lem' nos, and Scy' rus.]—37. The designs of the Persian
king promoted by the jealousy of the Greeks. Athens and Sparta—how affected by the peace
—38. Sparta is involved in new wars. War with Mantinéa. With Olyn' thus. [Mantinéa

D

1. After the subjugation of the Ionian cities of Asia Minor, Daríus
made active preparations for the conquest of all Greece. A mighty
armament was fitted out and intrusted to the command
of his son-in-law Mardónius, who, leading the land force in
person through Thrace and Macedonia, succeeded, after being once routed
by a night attack,[a] in subduing those countries; but the Persian fleet,
which was designed to sweep the islands of the Æ'gean, was checked
in its progress by a violent storm which it encountered off Mount
A'thos[1], and which was thought to have destroyed three hundred vessels and twenty thousand lives. Weakened by these disasters, Mardónius abruptly terminated the campaign and returned to Asia.

2. Daríus soon renewed his preparations for the invasion of Greece,
and, while his forces were assembling, sent heralds through the
Grecian cities, demanding earth and water, as tokens of submission.
The smaller States, intimidated by his power, submitted;[b] but Athens
and Sparta haughtily rejected the demands of the eastern monarch,
and put his heralds to death with cruel mockery, throwing one into a
pit and another into a well, and bidding them take thence their earth
and water. The Spartans threatened to make war upon the Æginétans[2] for having basely submitted to the power of Persia, and compelled them to send hostages to Athens.[c]

1. *Mount A'thos* is a lofty summit, more than six thousand feet high, on the most eastern of
three narrow peninsulas which extend from Macedonia into the Æ'gean sea. The peninsula
which is about twenty-five miles in length by about four in breadth, has long been occupied
in modern times by a number of monks of the Greek Church, who live in a kind of fortified
monasteries, about twenty in number. No females are admitted within this peninsula, whose
modern name, derived from its supposed sanctity, is *Monte Santo,* "sacred mountain."
(*Map* No. I.)

2. *Ægina,* (now *Egina* or *Engia,*) was an island containing about fifty square miles, in the
centre of the Saron'ic Gulf, (now Gulf of Athens,) between Attica and Ar'golis, and sixteen
miles south-west from Athens. The remains of a temple of Jupiter in the northern part of
the island are among the most interesting of the Grecian ruins. Of its thirty-six columns,
twenty-five were recently standing. (*Map* No. I.)

a. By the Brygi, a Thracian tribe. Mardónius wounded
b. Among them, probably, the Thebans and Thessalians; also most of the islands, but not
Eubœ'a and Nax'os. The Persians desolated Nax'os on their way across the Æ'gean.
c. At this time Thebes and Ægina had been at war with Athens fourteen years. Ar'gos,
which had contested with Sparta the supremacy of Greece, had recently been subdued; and
Sparta was acknowledged to be the head of the political union of Greece against the Persians. Grote's Greece, iv. 311-328.

3. In the third year after the first disastrous campaign, a Persian fleet of six hundred ships, conveying an army of a hundred and twenty thousand men, commanded by the generals Dátis and Artapher'nes, and guided by the exiled tyrant and traitor Hip'pias, directed its course towards the Grecian shores. (B. C. 490.) Several islands of the Æ'gean submitted without a struggle; Eubœ'a was punished for the aid it had given the Iónians in their rebellion; and without farther opposition the Persian host advanced to the plains of Mar'athon, within twenty miles of Athens. The Athenians probably called on the Platæ'ans' as well as the Spartans for aid :ᵃ—the former sent their entire force of a thousand men; but the latter, influenced by jealousy or superstition, refused to send their proffered aid before the full of the moon.

4. In this extremity the Athenian army, numbering only ten thousand men, and commanded by ten generals, marched against the enemy. Five of the ten generals had been afraid to hazard a battle, but the argumentsᵇ of Miltíades, one of their number, finally prevailed upon the polemarch Callim'achus to give his casting vote in favor of fighting. The ten generals were to command the whole army successively, each for a day. Those who had seconded the advice of Miltíades were willing to resign their turns to him, but he waited till his own day arrived, when he drew up the little army in order of battle.

1. *Mar' athon,* which still retains its ancient name, is a small town of Attica, twenty miles not heast from Athens, and about three miles from the sea-coast, or Bay of Mar'athon. The plain in which the battle was fought is about five miles in length and two in breadth, inclosed on the land side by steep slopes descending from the higher ridges of Pentel'icus and Párua, and divided into two unequal parts by a small stream which falls into the Bay. Towards the middle of the plain may still be seen a mound of earth, twenty-five feet in height, which was raised over the bodies of the Athenians who fell in the battle. In the marsh near the sea-coast, also, the remains of trophies and marble monuments are still visible. The names of the one hundred and ninety-two Athenians who were slain were inscribed on ten pillars erected on the battle-field. (*Map* No. I.)

2. *Platæ' a,* a city of Bœótia, now wholly in ruins, was situated on the northern side of the Cithæ'ron mountains, seven miles south from Thebes. This city has acquired an immortality of renown from its having given its name to the great battle fought in its vicinity in the year 79 B. C. between the Persians under Mardónius, and the Greeks under Pausánias the Spartan. (See p. 80.) From the tenth of the spoils taken from the Persians on that occasion, and presented to the shrine of Delphi, a golden tripod was made, supported by a brazen pillar resembling three serpents twined together. This identical brazen pillar may still be seen in the Hippodrome of Constantinople. (*Map* No. I.)

a. Thirwall says: " It is probable that they summoned the Platæ'ans." Grote says: " We are not told that they had been invited."

b. Herod'otus describes this debate as having occurred at Mar'athon, after the Greeks had taken post in sight of the Persians; while Cornelius Nepos says it occurred before the army left Athens. Thirwall appears to follow the former: Grote declares his preference for the latter, as the most reasonable.

5. The Persians were extended in a line across the middle of the plain, having their best troops in the centre. The Athenians were drawn up in a line opposite, but having their main strength in the extreme wings of their army. The Greeks made the attack, and, as had been foreseen by Miltíades, their centre was soon broken, while the extremities of the enemy's line, made up of motley and undisci. plined bands of all nations, were routed, and driven towards the shore, and into the adjoining morasses. Hastily concentrating his two wings, Miltíades next directed their united force against the flanks of the Persian centre, which, deeming itself victorious, was taken com. pletely by surprise. In a few minutes victory decided in favor of the Greeks. The Persians fled in disorder to their ships; but many perished in the marshes; the shore was strewn with their dead,—and seven of their ships were destroyed. The loss of the Persians was 6,400: that of the Athenians, not including the Platæ'ans, only 192.

6. Such was the famous battle of Mar'athon; but the glory of the victory is not to be measured wholly by the disparity of the numbers engaged, when compared with the result. The Persians were strong in the terror of their name, and in the renown of their conquests; and it required a most heroic resolution in the Athenians to face a danger which they had not yet learned to despise. The victory was viewed by the people as a deliverance vouchsafed to the Grecians by the gods themselves: the marvellous legends of the battle attributed to the heroes prodigies of valor; and represented Théseus and Her'cules as sharing in the fight, and dealing death to the flying barbarians; while to this day the peasant believes the field of Mar'a- thon to be haunted with spectral warriors, whose shouts are heard at midnight, borne on the wind, and rising above the din of battle.

7. The victory obtained by the Greeks at Mar'athon terminated the first war with Persia. Soon after the Persian defeat, Miltíades, who at first received all the honors which a grateful people could be- stow, experienced a fate which casts a melancholy gloom over his history. Being unfortunate in an expedition which he led against Pá- ros,[1] and which he induced the Athenians to intrust to him, without informing them of its destination, he was accused of having deceived

---

1. *Páros* is an island of the Æ'gean sea, of the group of the Cyc'lades, about seventy-five miles south east from Attica. It is about twelve miles in length by eight in breadth, rugged and uneven but generally very fertile. Páros was famous in antiquity for its marble, although that obtained from Mount Pentel'icus in Attica was of the purest white. In modern times Páros has become distinguished for the discovery there of the celebrated "Parian or Arunde- lian Chronicle," cut in a marble slab, and purporting to be a chronological account of Grecian

the peop.e, or, as some say, of having received a bribe. Unable to defend his cause before the people on account of an injury which he had received at Páros, he was impeached before the popular judicature as worthy of death; and although the proposition of his accusers was rejected, he was condemned to pay a fine of fifty talents. A few days later Miltíades died of his wound, and the fine was paid by his son Címon.

8. After the death of Miltíades, Themis' tocles and Aristídes become, for a time, the most prominent men among the Athenians. The former, a most able statesman, being influenced by ambitious motives, aimed to make Athens great and powerful, that he himself might rise to greater eminence with the growing fortunes of the state ;—the latter, a pure patriot, had, like Themis' tocles, the good of Athens at heart, but, unlike his rival, he was wholly destitute of selfish ambition, and knew no cause but that of justice and the public welfare. His known probity acquired for him the appellation of The Just; but his very integrity made for him secret enemies, who, although they charged him with no crimes, were yet able to procure from the people the penalty of banishment against him by ostracism.[1] His removal left Themis' tocles in possession of almost undivided power at Athens, and threw upon him chiefly the responsibility of the measure for resisting another Persian invasion, with which the Greeks were now threatened.

9. Daríus made great preparations for invading Greece in person, when death put an end to his ambitious projects. Ten years after the battle of Mar' athon, Xerxes, the son and successor II. SECOND of Daríus, being determined to execute the plans of his PERSIAN WAR. father, entered Greece at the head of an army the greatest the world has ever seen, and whose numbers have been estimated at more than two millions of fighting men. This immense force, passing through Thes' saly, had arrived, without opposition, at the strait of Thermop'ylæ,[2] where Xerxes found a body of eight thousand men, command

history from the time of Cécrops to the year 264 B. C. The pretence of Miltíades in attacking l'áros was that the inhabitants had aided the Persians; but Herod' otus assures us that his real motive was a private grudge against a Párian citizen. The injury of which he died was caused by a fall that he received while attempting to visit by night, a Párian priestess of Ceres, who had promised to r:veal to him a secret that would place Páros in his power. (Map No. III.

1. The mode of *Ostracism* was as follows: The people having assembled, each man took a shell (*ostrakon*) and wrote on it the name of the person whom he wished to have banished. If the number of votes thus given was less than six thousand, the ostracism was void; but if more, then the person whose name was on the greatest number of shells was sent into banishment for ten years.

2. *Thermop' ylæ* is a narrow defile on the western shore of the Gulf which lies between Eubœa and Thessaly, and s almost the only road by which Greece can be entered on the

ed by the Spartan king Leon' idas, prepared to dispute the passage Xerxes sent a herald to the Greeks, commanding them to lay down their arms; but Leon' idas replied with true Spartan brevity, "come and take them." When one said that the Persians were so numerous that their very darts would darken the sun, " Then," replied Dienéces, a Spartan, " we shall fight in the shade."

10. After repeated and unavailing efforts, during two days, to break the Grecian lines, the confidence of Xerxes had changed into despondence and perplexity, when a deserter revealed to him, for a large reward, a secret path over the mountains, by which he was enabled to throw a force of twenty thousand men into the rear of the Grecians. Leon' idas, seeing that his post was no longer tenable, dismissed all his allies who were willing to retire, retaining with him only three hundred fellow Spartans, with some Thes' pians and Thebans, in all about a thousand men. The Spartans were forbidden by their laws ever to flee from an enemy ; and Leon' idas and his countrymen, and their Thes' pian allies,[a] prepared to sell their lives as dearly as possible. Falling suddenly upon the enemy, they penetrated to the very centre of the Persian host, slaying two brothers of Xerxes, and fighting with the valor of desperation, until every one of their number had fallen. A monument was afterwards erected on the spot, bearing the following inscription : " Go stranger, and tell at Lacedæmon that we died here in obedience to her laws "

11. Previous to the last attack of the Spartans, two of their number, Eúrytus and Aristodémus, were absent on leave, suffering from a severe complaint of the eyes. Eúrytus, being informed that the hour for the detachment was come, called for his armor, and directing his servant to lead him to his place in the ranks, fell foremost in the fight. Aristodémus, overpowered with physical suffering, was carried to Sparta ; but he was denounced as a coward for not imi-

---

north east, by way of Thessaly. This famous pass, which is shut in between steep precipices and the sea, at the eastern extremity of Mount Œ' ta, is about five miles in length, and, where narrowest, was not anciently, according to Herodotus, more than half a plethron, or fifty feet across, although Livy says sixty paces. The pass has long been gradually widening, however, by the deposits of soil brought down by the mountain streams. In the narrowest part of the pass were hot springs, from which the defile derives its name. (*Thermos*, " hot," and *pulè*, a " gate" or " pass.") (*Map* No. L.)

a. The Thebans took part in the beginning of the fight, to save appearances, but finally surrendered to the Persians, loudly proclaiming that they had come to Thermop' ylæ against their consent. The story that Leon' idas made a night attack, and penetrated nearly to the royal tent, is a mere fiction. (See *Grote*, v 92. Note.)

tating his comrade—no one would speak or con.municate with him, or even grant him a light for his fire. After a year of bitter dis grace, he was at length enabled to retrieve his honor at the battle of Platæ' a, where he was slain, after surpassing all his comrades in heroic and even reckless valor.[a]

12. After the fall of Leon' idas, the Persians ravaged At' tica, and soon appeared before Athens, which they burned to the ground, but which had previously been deserted of its inhabitants,—those able to bear arms having retired to the island of Sal' amis, while the old and infirm, the women and children, had found shelter in Trezéne,[1] a city of Ar' golis. The allied Grecians took possession of the Corin- thian Isthmus, which they fortified by a wall, and committed to the defence of Cleom' brotus, a brother of Leon' idas.

13. Xerxes next made preparations to annihilate the power of the Grecians in a naval engagement, and sent his whole fleet to block up that of the Greeks in the narrow strait of Sal' amis. Eurybiades, the Spartan, who commanded the Grecian fleet, was in favor of sail- ing to the isthmus, that the naval and land forces might act in con- junction, but Themis' tocles finally prevailed upon him to hazard an engagement, and his counsels were enforced by Aristides, now in the third year of his exile, who crossed over in a small boat from Ægina with intelligence of the exact position of the Persian fleet ;—a cir- cumstance that at once put an end to the rivalry between the two Athenians, and led to the restoration of Aristides.

14. Xerxes had caused a royal throne to be erected on one of the neighboring heights, where, surrounded by his army, he might wit- ness the battle of Sal' amis, in which he was confident of victory ; but he had the misfortune to see his magnificent navy almost utterly an- nihilated. Terrified at the result, he hastily fled across the Hel' les- pont,[2] and retired into his own dominions, leaving Mardónius, at the head of three hundred thousand men, to complete, if possible, the conquest of Greece. Mardónius passed the winter in Thes' saly, but in the following summer his army was totally defeated and him-

---

1. *Trezéne* was near the south-eastern extremity of Ar' golis. Its ruins may be seen near the small modern village of *Damala*.

2. The *Hel' lespont* (now called *Dardanelles*), is the narrow strait which connects the sea of Marmora with the Æ' gean. It is about forty miles in length, and varies in breadth from three quarters of a mile to ten miles. The *Dardanelles*, from which the modern name of the strait is derived, are *castles*, or forts, built on its banks. The strait, being the key to Constantinople and the Black Sea, has been very strongly fortified on both sides by the Turks. (*Map* No IV.

self slain in the battle of Platæ' a. (B. C. 479.) Two hundred thousand Persians fell in battle, and only a small remnant escaped across the Hel' lespont—the last Persian army that gained a footing on the Grecian territory. On the very day of the battle of Platæ' a, the remains of the Persian fleet which had escaped at Sal' amis, and which had been drawn up on shore at Myc' ale,[1] on the coast of Iónia, were burned by the Grecians, and Tigránes, the Persian commander, and forty thousand of his men, slain. Six years later the career of Xerxes was terminated by assassination, when he was succeeded on the throne by his son, Artaxerx' es Longim' anus.

15. In the meantime, Athens had been rebuilt by the vigor and energy of Themis' tocles, and the Piræ' us fortified, and connected, by long walls, with the town, while Sparta looked with ill-disguised jealousy upon the growing power of a rival city. But the eminence which Themis' tocles had attained provoked the envy of some of his countrymen, and he was condemned to exile by the same process of ostracism which he himself had before directed against Aristídes Being afterwards charged with conspiring against the liberties of Greece, he sought refuge in Persia, where he is said to have ended his life by poison. Címon, the son of Miltíades, succeeded Themis'. tocles in the chief direction of Athenian affairs, while Pausánias, the hero of Platæ' a, was at the head of the Spartans. Under these leaders the confederate Greeks waged successful war upon the dependencies of Persia in the islands of the Æ' gean, and on the coasts of Thrace and Asia Minor. The Iónian cities were aided in a successful revolt; Cy' prus[2] was wrested from the power of the Persians; and Byzan' tium,[3] already a flourishing city, fell, with all its wealth, into the hands of the Grecians. (B. C. 476.)

16. Címon carried on a successful war against Persia many years later, during which the commercial power and wealth of the Athenians were continually increasing; but both parties finally becoming tired of the contest, after the death of Címon a treaty of peace was concluded with the Persian monarch, which stipulated that the Iv

1. *Myc' ale* was a promontory of Iónia in Asia Minor, opposite the southern extremity of the Island of Sámos. (*Map* No. IV.)

2. *Cy' prus* is a large and fertile Island near the north-eastern angle of the Mediterranean between Asia Minor and Syria :—greatest length, one hundred and thirty-two miles: average breadth, from thirty to thirty-five miles. Under the oppressive rule of the Turks, who conquered the island from the Venetians in 1571, agriculture was greatly neglected, and the population reduced to one-seventh of its former number. (*Maps* Nos. IV. and V.)

3. *Byzan' tium*, now *Constantinople*. See description, p. 218.

nian cities in Asia should be left in the free enjoyment of their inde
pendence, and that no Persian army should come within three days'
march of the sea-coast.[a]

17. While the war with Persia continued, a sense of common dan
gers had united the Grecks in a powerful and prosperous confederacy,
but now jealousies broke out between several of the rival cities,
particularly Athens and Sparta, which led to political dissensions
and civil wars, the cause of the final ruin of the Grecian republics.
The authority of Címon among the Athenians had gradually yielded
to the growing influence of his rival Per'icles, who, bold, artful, and
eloquent,—a general, philosopher, and statesman,—managed the
multitude at his will, and by his patronage of literature and the arts,
and the extension of the Athenian power, raised Athens to the summit of her renown. Sparta looked on with ill-disguised jealousy as
island after island in the Æ'gean yielded to the sway of Athens, and
saw not with unconcern the colonies of her rival peopling the winding shores of Thrace and Macedon. Athens had become the mistress of the seas, while her commerce engrossed nearly the whole
trade of the Mediterranean.

18. But Sparta was also powerful in her resources, and in the
military renown and warlike character of her people, and she disdained the luxuries that were enervating the Athenians. Complaints
and reclamations were frequent on both sides; and occasions for
war, when sought by both parties, are not long delayed. But while
the Spartans were secretly favoring the enemies of Athens, although
still in avowed allegiance with her, Lacónia was laid waste by an
earthquake (464 B. C.), and Sparta became a heap of ruins. A re
volt of the Hélots followed; Sparta itself was endan- III. THIRD
gered; and the remnant of the Messénians, making a MESSÉNIAN
vigorous effort to recover their freedom, fortified the WAR.
memorable hill of Ithóme, the ancient citadel of their fathers.
Here, for a long time, they valiantly defended themselves; and the
Spartans were compelled to invoke the Athenians and others to their
assistance. (461 B. C.) After several years' duration, the third and
last Messénian war was terminated by an honorable capitulation of
the Messénians, who were allowed to retire from the Peloponnésus

a. The story of this famous treaty, however, generally called the Cimonian treaty, and attributed to Cimon himself, has been regarded by some writers as a fiction, which, originating in
the schools of Greek rhetoricians, was transmitted thence through the orators to the historians
(See *Thirwall*, i. p. 305, and note.) Grote, however, v. 336-43, admits the reality of the treaty
but places it after the death of Cimon.

with their property and their families, and to join the Athenian colony of Naupac'tus.

19. While the Athenians were engaged in hostilities with several
of their northern neighbors, Sparta sent her forces into the Bœótian territory, to counteract the growing influence of Athens in
that quarter. The indignant Athenians marched out to meet them,
but were worsted in the battle of Tan'agra.[1] In the following year
however, they were enabled to wipe off the stain of their defeat by
victory over the aggregate Theban and Bœótian forces then in alliance with Sparta; whereby the authority and influence of Sparta
were again confined to the Peloponnésus.

20. Other events soon occurred to embitter the animosities of the
rival States, and prepare the way for a general war. Corinth, a
Dórian city favorable to Sparta, having become involved in a war
with Corcy'ra,[2] one of her colonies, the latter applied for and obtained assistance from Athens. Potidæ'a,[3] a Corinthian colony tributary to Athens, soon after revolted, at the same time claiming and
obtaining the assistance of the Corinthians; and thus in two instances were Athens and Corinth, though nominally at peace, brought
into conflict with each other as open enemies. The Corinthians, now
accusing Athens of interfering between them and their colonies,
charged her with violating a treaty of the confederated
States of the Peloponnésus, and easily engaged the Lacedæmónians in their quarrel. Such were the immediate
causes which opened the *First Peloponnésian War.*

IV. FIRST
PELOPONNÉ-
SIAN WAR.

21. The minor States of Greece took sides as inclination or interest prompted, and nearly all were involved in the contest. The
Spartans and their confederates were the most powerful by land
the Athenians by sea; and each began the war by displaying its
strength on its peculiar element. While a Spartan army of sixty
thousand, led by their king, Archidámus, ravaged At'tica, and sat
down before the very gates of Athens, the naval force of the Athen

---

1. *Tan'agra*, a city near the south-eastern extremity of Bœótia, was situated on an emi
nence on the northern bank of the river Asópus, and near its mouth. (*Map* No. 1.)

2. *Corcy'ra*, now *Corfu*, the most important, although not the largest, of the Iónian Islands
is situated near the coast of Epirus, in the Iónian Sea. At its northern extremity it is separated
from the coast by a channel only three-fifths of a mile wide. The strongly-fortified *city* of Corfu,
the capital of the Iónian Republic, stands on the site of the ancient city of Corcy'ra, on the
eastern side of the island.

3. *Potidæ'a* was situated on the isthmus that connects the most western of the three Macedonian peninsulas in the Æ'gean with the main land. There are no remains of the city existing. (*Map* No. I.)

ians, consisting of nearly two hundred galleys, desolated the coasts of the Peloponnésus. (B. C. 431.) The Spartans being recalled to protect their own homes, Per' icles himself, at the head of the largest force mustered by the Athenians during the war, spread desolation over the little territory of Meg' ara,[1] then in alliance with Sparta.

22. In the following year (B. C. 430) the Spartan force a second time invaded At' tica, when the Athenians again took refuge within their walls; but here the plague, a calamity more dreadful than war, attacked them, and swept away multitudes of the citizens, and many of the principal men. In the third year of the war, Per' icles himself fell a victim to its ravages. Before this, Potidæ' a had surrendered to the Athenians (B. C. 430), who banished the inhabitants, and gave their vacant lands and houses to new colonists; and when Platæ' a, after a siege of three years, was compelled to surrender to the Spartans, the latter cruelly put the little remnant of the garrison to death, while the women and children were made slaves (B. C. 427.)

23. After the struggle had continued with various success ten years, both parties became anxious for peace, and a treaty, for a term of fifty years, called the peace of Nic' ias, was concluded, on the basis of a mutual restitution of all conquests made during the war. (421 B. C.) Yet interest and inclination, and the ambitious views of party leaders among the Athenians, were not long in finding plausible pretexts for renewing the struggle. The Bœótian, Megárian, and Corinthian allies of Sparta, refused to accede to the terms of the treaty by making the required surrenders, and Sparta had no power to compel them, while Athens would accept no less than she had bargained for.

24. At the head of the party which aimed at severing the ties that bound Athens and Sparta together, was Alcibíades, a wealthy Athenian, and nephew of Per' icles,—a man ambitious, bold, and eloquent,—an artful demagogue, but corrupt and unprincipled, and reckless of the means he used to accomplish his purposes. By his artifices he involved the Spartans in a war with their recent allies the Ar' gives, and induced the Athenians to send an armament against the Dórian island of Mélos,[2] which had provoked the enmity

1. Meg' ara, a city of At' tica, and capital of a district of the same name was about twenty-five miles west, or north-west, of Athens, and was connected with the port of Nis' æa on the Saron' ic Gulf by two walls similar to those which connected Athens and the Piræ' us. The miserable village of Meg' ara occupies a part of the site of the ancient city. (Map No. I.)

2. Mélos now called Milo, is an island belonging to the group of the Cyc' lades, about seventy

of Athens by its attachment to Sparta, and which was compelled, after a vigorous siege, to surrender at discretion. With deliberate cruelty the conquerors, imitating the Spartans at the reduction of Platæ'a, put to death all the adult citizens, and enslaved the women and children—an act which provoked universal indignation throughout Greece. (B. C. 416.)

25. Soon after the surrender of Mélos, the Athenians, at the instigation of Alcibíades, fitted out an expedition against Sicily,[1] under the plea of delivering a people in the western part of the island from the tyranny of the Syracúsans,[2] a Dórian colony; but, in reality, to establish the Athenian supremacy in the island. (415 B. C.)

v. SICILIAN EXPEDITION. The armament fitted out on this occasion, the most powerful that had ever left a Grecian port, was intrusted to the joint command of Alcibíades, Nic'ias, and Lam'achus; but ere the fleet had reached its destination, Alcibíades was summoned home on the absurd charge of impiety and sacrilege, connected with designs against the State itself. Fearing to trust himself to the giddy multitude in a trial for life, he at once threw himself upon the generosity of his open enemies, and sought refuge

miles east from the southern part of Laconia. It has one of the best harbors in the Grecian Archipelago. Near the town of Castro have been discovered the remains of a theatre built of the finest marble, and also numerous catacombs cut in the solid rock. (*Map* No. III.)

1. *Sicily*, the largest, most important, most fruitful, and most celebrated island of the Mediterranean, is separated from the southern extremity of Italy by the strait of Messina, only two miles across, and is eighty-five miles distant from Cape Bon in Africa. It is of a triangular shape, and was anciently called *Trinacria*, from its terminating in three promontories. Sicily, the name by which it is usually known, seems to have been derived from the *Siculi*, its earliest known inhabitants. Its length east and west is about two hundred and fifteen miles;—greatest breadth, one hundred and fifty miles. The volcano Ætna, the most celebrated of European mountains, near the eastern coast of the island, rises to the height of nearly eleven thousand feet above the level of the sea. (*Map* No. VIII. For history of Sicily, see p. 115.)

2. *Syracuse*, the most famous of the cities of Sicily, was situated on the south-eastern coast, partly on a small island, and partly on the main land. Among the existing remains of the ancient city are the prisons, cut in the solid rock, which have been admirably described by Cicero in his oration against Verres. The catacombs, also excavated in the solid rock, and consisting of one principal street and several smaller ones, are of vast extent, and may be truly called a city of the dead. The modern city, however, containing a population of twelve or fifteen thousand inhabitants, has little except its ancient renown, its noble harbor, and the extreme beauty of its situation, to recommend it. (*Map* No. VIII.) "Its streets are narrow and dirty; its nobles poor; its lower orders ignorant, superstitious, idle, and addicted to festivals. Much of its fertile land is become a pestilential marsh; and that commerce which once filled the finest port in Europe with the vessels of Italy, Rhodes, Alexandria, Carthage, and every other maritime power, is now confined to a petty coasting trade. Such is modern Syracuse. Yet the sky which canopies it is still brilliant and serene; the golden grain is still ready to spring almost spontaneously from its fields; the azure waves still beat against its walls to send its navies over the main; nature is still prompt to pour forth her bounties with a liberal hand; but man, alas! is changed; his liberty is lost; and with that, the genius of a nation fades, sinks, and is extinguished."—*Hughes' Greece.*

at Sparta. When, soon after, he heard that the Athenians had condemned him to death, " I hope," said he, " to show them that I am still alive."

26. By the death of Lam' achus, Nic' ias was soon after left in sole command of the Athenian forces before Syracuse, but he wasted his time in fortifying his camp, and in useless negotiations, until the Syracusans, having received succor from Corinth and Sparta under the famous Spartan general Gylip' pus, were able to bid him defiance. Although new forces were sent out from Athens, yet the Athenians were defeated in several engagements, when, still lingering in the island, their entire fleet was eventually destroyed by the Syracusans, who thus became masters of the sea. The Athenian forces then attempted to retreat, but were overtaken and compelled to surrender. (B. C. 413.) The generals destroyed themselves, on learning that their death had been decreed by the Syracusan assembly. The common soldiers, to the number of seven thousand, were crowded together during seventy days in the gloomy prisons of Syracuse, when most of the survivors were taken out and sold as slaves.

27. The aid which Gylip' pus had rendered the Syracusans again brought Sparta and Athens in direct conflict, and opened the second Peloponnesian war. The result of the Athenian expedition was the greatest calamity that had fallen upon Athens. Several of her allies, instigated by Alcibíades, who was now active in the Spartan councils, revolted; and the power of Tisapher' nes, the most powerful satrap of the king of Persia in Asia Minor, was on the point of being thrown into the scale against the Athenians, when a rupture between the Spartans and Alcibíades changed the aspect of affairs, and for awhile revived the waning glory of Athens. By his intrigues, Alcibíades, who now sought a reconciliation with his countrymen, detached Tisapher' nes from the interests of Sparta, and effected a change of government at Athens from a democracy to an aristocracy of four hundred of the nobility; but the new government, dreading the ambition of Alcibíades refused to recall him. Another change soon followed. The defeat of the Athenian navy at Erétria,[1] and the revolt of Euboe' a, produced a new revolution at Athens, by which the government of the four hundred was overthrown, and democracy restored. Alcibíades was immediately recalled; but before his return he aided in destroying

VI. SECOND PELOPONNESIAN WAR.

_____

1. _Erétria_ was a town on the western coast of the island of Euboe' a. Its ruins are still to be seen ten or twelve miles south-east from the present Neg' ropont. (_Map No. I._).

the Peloponnésian fleet in the battle of Cys'icus.[1] (B. C. 411.)
Soon after, Alcibíades was welcomed at Athens with great enthusiasm, a golden crown was decreed him, and he was appointed com·
mander-in-chief of all the forces of the commonwealth both by land
and by sea.

28. Alcibíades was still destined to experience the instability of
fortune, for when one of his generals, contrary to instructions, attacked
the Spartan fleet and was defeated, an unjust suspicion of treachery
fell upon Alcibíades ; the former charges against him were revived,
and he was deprived of his command and again banished. The
affairs of Sparta were retrieved by the crafty Lysan'der, a general
whose abilities the Athenians could not match since they had deprived themselves of the services of Alcibíades. The Spartan
general had the art to gain the confidence and coöperation of Cyrus,
a younger son of Daríus No'thus, the Persian king, whom the latter
had invested with supreme authority over the whole maritime region of Asia Minor.

29. Aided by Persian gold, Lysan'der found no difficulty in man
ning a numerous fleet, with which he met the Athenians at Æ'gos-
Pot'amos.[2] Here, during several days, he declined a battle, but
seizing the opportunity when nearly all the Athenians were dispersed
on shore in quest of supplies, he attacked and destroyed all their
ships, with the exception of eight galleys, and took three thousand
prisoners. The fate of the prisoners is a shocking proof of the barbarous feelings and manners of the age, for all of them were remorselessly put to death, in revenge for some recent cruelties of the
Athenians, who had thrown down a precipice the crews of two captured
vessels, and had passed a decree for cutting off the right thumb of
the prisoners whose capture they anticipated in the coming battle.

30. Thus, in one short hour, by the culpable negligence of their
generals, were the affairs of the Athenians changed from an equality
of resources with their enemy, to hopeless, irretrievable ruin. The
maritime allies of Athens immediately submitted to Lysander, who
directed the Athenians throughout Greece to repair at once to
Athens, with threats of death to all whom he found elsewhere, and

1. *Cys'icus* was an island of the Propon'tis, (now sea of Marmora,) on the northern coast
of Mys'ia. It was separated from the main land by a very narrow channel, which has since
been filled up and it is now a peninsula. (*Map* No. IV.)

2. *Æ'gos-Pot'amos*, ("goat's river") was a small stream of the Thracian Chersonésus, which
flows into the Hellespont from the west. The place where the Athenians landed, appears to
have been "a mere open beach, without any habitations." (Thirwall, i. 485.) (*Map* No. IV)

when famine began to prey upon the collected multitude in the city, he appeared before the Piræ'us with his fleet, while a large force from Sparta blockaded Athens by land. The Athenians had no hopes of effectual resistance, and only delayed the surrender to plead for the best terms that could be obtained from the conquerors. Compelled at last to submit to whatever terms were dictated to them, they agreed to destroy the long walls, and the fortifications of the Piræ'us; to surrender all their ships but twelve; to restore their exiles; to relinquish their conquests; to become a member of the Peloponnésian confederacy; and to serve Sparta in all her expeditions, whether by sea or by land. (B. C. 404.) Thus closed the second Peloponnésian war, in the profound humiliation of Athens.

31. A change of government followed, as directed by Lysander and conformable to the aristocratic character of the Spartan institutions. All authority was placed in the hands of thirty archons, known as the Thirty Tyrants, whose power was supported by a Spartan garrison. Their cruelty and rapacity knew no bounds, and filled Athens with universal dismay. A large band of exiles soon accumulated in the friendly Theban territories, and choosing Thrasybulus for their leader, they resolved to strike a blow for the deliverance of their country. They first seized a small fortress on the frontiers of Attica, when, their numbers rapidly increasing, they were enabled to seize the Piræ'us, where they defeated the force which was brought against them. The rule of the tyrants was overthrown, and a council of ten was elected to fill their places; but the latter emulated the wickedness of their predecessors, and, when the populace turned against them, applied to Sparta for assistance. But the Spartan councils were divided, and eventually, by the aid of Sparta herself, the ten were deposed, when, the Spartan garrison being withdrawn, Athens again became a democracy, with the power in the hands of the people. (B. C. 403.)

32. It was during the rule of democracy in Athens that the wise and virtuous Socrates, the best and greatest of Grecian philosophers, was condemned to death on the absurd charge of impiety, and of corrupting the morals of the young. His accusers appear to have been instigated by personal resentment, which he had innocently provoked, and by envy of his many virtues; and the result shows not only the instability, but the moral obliquity also, of the Athenian character. The defence which Socrates made before his judges is in the tone of a man who demands rewards and honors, instead of

the punishment of a malefactor ; and when the sentence of death had been pronounced against him, he spent the remaining days which the laws allowed him in impressing on the minds of his friends the most sublime lessons in philosophy and virtue ; and when the fatal hour arrived, drank the poison with as much composure as if it had been the last draught of a cheerful banquet.

33. Cyrus has been mentioned as one of the sons of Darius No'thus and governor of the maritime region of Asia Minor. As his ambi tion led him to aspire to the throne of Persia, to the exclusion of his older brother, Artaxerxes Mnémon, he had aided Sparta in the Peloponnésian war, with the view of claiming, in return, her assistance against his brother, should he ever have occasion for it. When, therefore, the latter was promoted to the throne in accordance with the dying· bequest of his father, Cyrus prepared for the execution of his design by raising an army of a hundred thousand Persian and barbarian troops, which he strengthened by an auxiliary force of thirteen thousand Grecians, drawn principally from the Greek cities of Asia. On the Grecian force, commanded by the Spartan Clear'chus, Cyrus placed his main reliance for success.

34. With these forces he marched from Sardis in the Spring of the year 401, and with little difficulty penetrated into the heart of the Persian empire, when he was met by Artaxerx'es, seventy miles from Babylon, at the head of nine hundred thousand men. In the battle which followed, this immense force was at first routed ; but Cyrus, rashly charging the centre of the guards who surrounded his brother, was slain on the field, when the whole of his barbarian troops took to flight, leaving the Greeks almost alone in the midst of a hostile country, more than a thousand miles from any friendly territory.

35. The Persians proposed to the Grecians terms of accommodation, but having invited their leaders to a conference they mercilessly put them to death. No alternative now remained to the Greeks but to submit to the enemy, or fight their way back to their native country. Where submission was death or slavery they could not hesitate which course to pursue. They chose Xen'ophon, a young Athenian, for their leader, and under his conduct ten thou· sand of their number, after a march of four months, succeeded in reaching Grecian settlements on the banks of the Eux'ine. Xen'ophon himself, who afterwards became the historian of his country, has left an admirable narrative of the " Retreat of the Ten Thou

sand," written with great clearness and singular modesty. It is one of the most interesting works bequeathed us by antiquity, as the Retreat itself is the most famous military expedition on record.

36. The part which the Greek cities of Asia took in the expedition of Cyrus involved them in a war with Persia, in which they were aided by the Spartans, who, under their king Agesiláus, defeated Tisapher'nes in a great battle in the plains of Sárdis (B. C. 395); but Agesiláus was soon after recalled to aid his countrymen at home in another Peloponnésian war, which had been fomented chiefly by the Persian king himself, VII. THIRD PELOPONNÉSIAN WAR. in order to save his own dominions from the ravages of the Spartans Artaxerx'es supplied Conon, an Athenian, with a fleet which defeated the Spartan navy; and Persian gold rebuilt the walls of Athens On the other hand, Athens and her · allies were defeated in the vicinity of Corinth, and on the plains of Coronéa.¹ (B. C. 394). Finally, after the war had continued eight years, articles of peace were arranged between Artaxerx'es and the Spartan Antal'cidas, hence called the peace of Antal'cidas, and ratified by all the parties engaged in the war, almost without opposition. (387 B. C.) The Greek cities in Asia, together with the islands Clazom'enæ² and Cy'prus, were given up to Persia, and the separate independence of all the other Greek cities was guaranteed, with the exception of the islands Im'brus, Lem'nos, and Scy'rus,³ which, as of old, were to belong to Athens.

37. The terms of the peace of Antal'cidas, directed by the king of Persia, were artfully contrived by him to dissolve the power of Greece into nearly its original elements, that Persia might thereafter have less to fear from a united Greek confederacy, or the preponderating influence of any one Grecian State. It was the unworthy jealousy of the Grecians, which the Persian knew how to stimulate, that prompted them to give up to a barbarian the free cities of Asia; and this is the darkest shade in the picture. Both Athens and Sparta lost their former allies; and though Sparta was

---

1. *Coronéa* was a city of Bœótia, to the south-east of *Chæronea*, and two or three miles south-west from the Copaic Lake. South of Coronéa was Mount Helicon. (*Map* No. I.)

2. The *Clazom'enæ* here mentioned was a small island near the Lydian coast, west of Smyrna, and in what is now called the Gulf of Smyrna. (*Map* No. IV.)

3. *Im'brus, Lem'nos,* and *Scy'rus,* (now Imbro, Statimene, and Scyro,) are islands of the Æ'gean. The first is about ten miles west from the entrance to the Hel'lespont, and the second about forty miles south-west. Scy'rus is about twenty-five miles north-east from Eubœ'a. (*Map* No. III.)

the most strongly in favor of the terms of the treaty, yet Athens was the greatest gainer, for she once more became. although a small, yet an independent and powerful State.

38. It was not long before ambition, and the resentment of past injuries, involved Sparta in new wars. She compelled Mantinéa,[1] which had formerly been her unwilling ally, to throw down her walls, and dismember the city into its original divisions, under the pretext that the Mantinéans had supplied one of the enemies of Sparta with corn during the preceding war, and had evaded their share of service in the Spartan army. The jealousy of Sparta was next aroused against the rising power of Olyn'thus,[2] which had become engaged in hostilities with some rival cities; and the Spartans readily accepted an invitation of the latter to send an army to their aid. As one of the Spartan forces was marching through the Theban territories on this errand, the Spartan general fraudulently seized upon the Cadméia, or Theban citadel, although a state of peace existed between Thebes and Sparta. (B. C. 382.)

39. The political morality of the Spartans is clearly exhibited in the arguments by which Agesiláus justified this palpable breach of the treaty of Antal'cidas. He declared that the only question for the Spartan people to consider, was, whether they were gainers or losers by the transaction. The assertion made by the Athenians on a former occasion was confirmed, that, "of all States, Sparta had most glaringly shown by her conduct that in her political transactions she measured honor by inclination, and justice by expediency."

40. On the seizure of the Theban citadel the most patriotic of the citizens fled to Athens, while a faction, upheld by the Spartan garrison, ruled the city. After the Thebans had submitted to this yoke four years they rose against their tyrants and put them to death, and being re-enforced by the exiles, and an Athenian army, soon forced the Spartan garrison to capitulate. (B. C. 379.) Pelop'-idas and Epaminon'das now appeared on the field of action, and by their abilities raised Thebes, hitherto of but little political impor ·

---

1. *Mantinéa* was in the eastern part of Arcádia, seventeen miles west from Ar'gos. It was situated in a marshy plain through which flowed the small river A'phis, whose waters found a subterranean passage to the sea. Mantinéa is wholly indebted for its celebrity to the great battle fought in its vicinity in the year 362 between the Spartans and Thebans. (See p. 91.) The locality of the battle was about three miles southwest from the city. The ruins of the ancient town may be seen near the wretched modern hamlet of *Palaiopoli*. (*Map* No. I.)

2. *Olyn'thus* was in the south eastern part of Macedónia, six or seven miles north-east from Potidæ'a. (*Map* No 1)

ance, to the first rank in power among the Grecian States. Al
though Athens joined Thebes in the beginning of the contest, yet
she afterwards took the side of the Spartans. At Teg' yra,[1] Pelop' idas defeated a greatly superior force, and killed the two Spartan
generals, at Leuc' tra,[2] Epaminon' das, with a force of six thousand
Thebans, defeated the Lacedæmo' nian army of more than double
that number. (B. C. July 8, 371.)   Epaminon' das afterwards invaded Laconia, and appeared before the very gates of Sparta, where
a hostile force had not been seen during five hundred years; and at
Mantinéa he defeated the enemy in the most sanguinary contest ever
fought between Grecians.   (B. C. 362.)   But Epaminon' das fell in
the moment of victory, and the glory of Thebes perished with him.
A general peace was soon after established, on the single condition
that each State should retain its respective possessions.

41. Four years after the battle of Mantinéa the Grecian States
again became involved in domestic hostilities, known as the Sacred
War, the second in Grecian history to which that epi- VIII. SECOND
thet was applied.[a]   During the preceding war, the Phó- SACRED WAR.
cians,[3] although in alliance with Thebes by treaty, had shown such a
predilection in favor of Sparta, that the animosity of the Thebans
was roused against their reluctant ally, and they availed themselves
of the first opportunity to show their resentment.   The Phócians
having taken into cultivation a portion of the plain of Del' phos,
which was deemed sacred to Apóllo, the Thebans caused them to
be accused of sacrilege before the Amphictyon' ic council, which con
demned them to pay a heavy fine.   The Phócians refused obedience,
and, encouraged by the Spartans, on whom a similar penalty had
been imposed for their treacherous occupation of the Theban citadel,
took up arms to resist the decree, and, under their leader, Philomélus, plundered the sacred treasures of Del' phos to obtain the means
for carrying on the war.

1. *Teg' yra* was a small village of Bœótia, near the northern shore of the Copaic Lake
(*Map* No. I.)

2. *Leuc' t~a* (now *Lefka*) was a small town of Bœótia, about ten miles south-west frcm
Thebes, and four or five miles from the Corinthian Gulf.   It is now only a heap of ru,ns,
(*Map* No. I.)

3. *Phócis* was a small tract of country, bounded on the north by Thes' saly, east by Bœótia,
south by the Corinthian Gulf, and west by Lócris, Ætólia, and Dóris.   (*Map* No. I.)

a. The first sacred war was carried on against the inhabitants of the town of Cris' sa, on the
northern shore of the Corinthian Gulf, in the time of Solon.   The Crisscans were charged with
extortion and violence towards the strangers who passed through their territory cn their way
to the Delphic sanctuary.   "Cris' sa was razed to the ground, its harbor choked up, and its
fruitful plain turned into a wilderness."—*Thirwall*, i. 152

42. The Thebans, Lócrians,[1] Thessálians, and nearly all the States of Northern Greece, leagued against the Phócians, while Athens and Sparta declared in their favor, but gave them little active assistance. At first the Thebans, confident in their strength, put their prisoners to death, as abettors of sacrilege; but Philomélus retaliated so severely upon some Thebans who had fallen into his power, as to prevent a repetition of the crime. After the war had continued five years, a new power was brought forward on the heatre of Grecian history, in the person of Philip, who had recently established himself on the throne of Mac'edon, and whom some of the Thessálian allies of Thebes applied to for aid against the Phócians. The interference of Philip forms an important epoch in Grecian affairs, at which we interrupt our narrative to trace the growth of the Macedónian monarchy down to the time when its history became united with that of its southern neighbors.

* * *

SECTION II.

GRECIAN HISTORY FROM THE ESTABLISHMENT OF PHILIP ON THE THRONE OF MAC'EDON TO THE REDUCTION OF GREECE TO A ROMAN PROVINCE: 360 TO 146 B. C. = 214 YEARS.

ANALYSIS. 1. Geographical account of Macedónia.—2. Early history of Macedónia. Grecian rulers. PHILIP OF MAC'EDON.—3. Philip's residence at Thebes.—4. His usurpation of the kingdom of Mac'edon. His wars with the Illyr'ians and other tribes. His first efforts against the Phócians.—5. Philip reduces Phócis. Decree of the Amphictyon'ic council against Phócis. Growing influence of Philip.—6. The ambitious projects of Philip. [Illyr'ia. Epirus. Acarnánia.]—7. Rupture between Philip and the Athenians. [Chersonésus.] Devotion of the orator Æs'chines to Philip. [Amphis'sa.] Philip throws off the mask. [Elatéia.]—8. Thebes and Athens prepare to oppose him. Dissensions.—9. The masterly policy of Philip. The confederacy against him dissolved by the battle of Chæronéa. [Chæronéa.]—10. Philip's treatment of the Thebans and the Athenians. General congress of the Grecian States, and death of Philip.

11. ALEXANDER succeeds Philip. He quells the revolt against him. His cruel treatment of the Thebans.—12. Servility of Athens. Preparations of Alexander for his career of Eastern conquest.—13. Results of his first campaign. [Gran'icus. Halicarnas'sus.]—14. He resumes his march in the spring of 333. Defeats Darius at Is'sus. [Cappadócia. Cilic'ia. Is'sus.] Results of the battle. Effect of Alexander's kindness.—15. Reduction of Palestine. [Gaza.] Expedition into Egypt. [Alexandria.] Alexander returns and crosses the Euphrátes in search of Darius.—16. The opposing forces at the battle of Arbéla. [Arbéla. India.]—17. Results of the battle, and death of Darius.—18. Alexander's residence at Babylon. His march beyond

1. The *Lócrians* proper inhabited a small territory on the northern shore of the Corinthian Gulf, west of Phócis. There were other Lócrian tribes north-east of Phócis, whose territory bordered on the Euboe'an Gulf. (*Map* No. I.)

the Indus. [Hyphāsis R.]—19. His return to Persia. [Persian Gulf. Gedrosia.] His measures for consolidating his empire.—20. His sickness and death.—21. His character.—22. As judged of by his actions. The results of his conquests. [Seleucia.]—23. Contentions that followed his death.—24. Grecian confederacy against Macedonian supremacy. Sparta and Thebes. Athens is finally compelled to yield to Antip'ater.—25. Cassan'der's usurpation. Views and conquests of Antig'onus. Final dissolution of the Macedonian empire. [Ip'sus. Phryg'ia.]

26. The four kingdoms that arose on the ruins of the empire. Those of Egypt and Syria the most powerful.—27. The empire of Cassan'der. Usurpation of Demétrius. Character of his government. The war carried on against him.—28. Unsettled state of Mac'edon, Greece, and Western Asia.—29. Celtic invasion of Mac'edon. [Adriat'ic. Pannónia.]—30. Second Celtic invasion. The Celts are repelled by the Phócians. Death of Brennus, their chief.—31. Antig'onus, son of Demétrius, recovers the throne of his father. Is invaded by Pyr'rhus, king of Epirus.—32. Pyr'rhus marches into Southern Greece. Is repulsed by the Spartans. He enter Ar'gos. His death.—33. Remarks on the death of Pyr'rhus. Ambitious views of Antig'onus

34. THE ACHÆ'AN LEAGUE. Arátus seizes Sicyon, which joins the league.—35. Arátus rescues Corinth, which at first joins the league. Conduct of Athens and Sparta.—36. Antig'onus II.—37. League of the Ætólians, who invade the Messénians. [Ætólia.] Defeat of Arátus. General war between the respective members of the two leagues.—38. Results of this war. The war between the Romans and Carthaginians. Policy of Philip II. of Mac'edon.—39. He enters into an alliance with the Carthaginians. His defeat at Apollónia. [Apollónia.]—40. He causes the death of Arátus. Roman intrigues in Greece.—41. Overthrow of Philip's power. The Romans promise independence to Greece.—42. Remarks on the sincerity of the promise. Treatment of the Ætólians. Extinction of the Macedonian monarchy. [Pyd'na.]—43. Unjust treatment of the Achæ'ans. Roman ambassadors insulted.—44. The Achæ'an war, and reduction of Greece to a Roman province. Remarks of Thirwall.—45. Henceforward Grecian history is absorbed in that of Rome. Condition of Greece since the Persian wars. In the days of Strabo.

COTEMPORARY HISTORY.—1. Cotemporary annals of other nations:—Persians—Egyptians.—HISTORY OF THE JEWS.—2. Rebuilding of the second temple of Jerusalem. The Jews during the reigns of Xerxes and Artaxerxes. Nehemiah's administration.—3. Judea a part of the sat'rapy of Syria. Judea after the division of Alexander's empire. Judea invaded by Ptolemy Soter.—4. Judea subject to Egypt. Ptolemy-Philadelphus. The Jews place themselves under the rule of Syria.—5. Civil war among the Jews. Antiochus plunders Jerusalem. Attempts to establish the Grecian polytheism.—6. Revolt of the Mac'cabees.—7. Continuation of the war with Syria. [Bethóron.] Death of Judas Maccabéus.—8. The Syrians become masters of the country. Prosperity of the Jews under Simon Maccabéus.—9. The remaining history of the Jews.

10. GRECIAN COLONIES. Those of Thrace, Mac'edon, and Asia Minor. Of Italy, Sicily, and Cyrenáica. 11. MAGNA GRÆCIA. Early settlements in western Italy and in Sicily. [Cumæ. Neap'olis. Nax'os. Géla. Messána. Agrigen'tum.]—12. On the south-eastern coast of Italy. History of Syb'aris, Crotóna, and Taren'tum. [Description of the same.]—13. First two centuries of Sicilian history. [Him'era.] Géla and Agrigen'tum. The despot Gélo.—14. Growing power of Syracuse under his authority.—15. The Carthaginians in Sicily—defeated by Gélo. [Panor'mus.]—16. Hiero and Thrasybūlus. [Ætna.] Revolution and change of government.—17. Civil commotions and renewed prosperity. [Kamarina.]—18. Syracuse and Agrigen'tum at the time of the breaking out of the Peloponnésian war. The Ion'ic and Dórian cities of Sicily during the struggle. Sicilian congress.—19. Quarrel between the cities of Selinus and Eges'ta. [Description of the same.] The Athenian expedition to Sicily. [Cat'ana.]—20. Events up to the beginning of the siege of Syracuse.—21. Death of Lam'achus, and arrival of Gylip'pus, the Spartan.—22. Both parties reinforced—various battles—total defeat of the Athenians.—23. Carthaginian encroachments in Sicily—resisted by Dionys'ius the Elder. Division between the Greek and Carthaginian territories. [Him'era.]—24. The administration of Timóleon. Of Agath'ocles. The Romans become masters of Sicily.

25. CYRENA'ICA.—Colonized by Lacedæmónians. Cyréne its chief city. Its ascendancy over the Libyan tribes. War with the Egyptians.—26. Tyranny of Agesiláus—founding of Bar'ca—the war which followed. Agesiláus. Civil dissensions. Camby'ses.—27. Subsequent history of Cyréne and Bar'ca. Distinguished Cyréneans. Cyréneans mentioned in Bible history

1. Mac' edon, or Macedónia, whose boundaries varied greatly at different times, had its south-eastern borders on the Æ' gean Sea, while farther north it was bounded by the river Stry' mon, which separated it from Thrace, and on the south by Thes' saly and Epí-rus. On the west Macedónia embraced, at times, many of the Il-lyrian tribes which bordered on the Adriatic. On the north the natural boundary was the mountain chain of Hæ' mus. The prin-cipal river of Macedónia was the Axius (now the Vardar), which fell 'nto the Thermáic Gulf, now called the Gulf of Salon' iki.

2. The history of Macedónia down to the time of Philip, the father ot Alexander the Great, is involved in great obscurity. The early Macedónians appear to have been an Illyr' ian tribe, differ-ent in race and language from the Hellénes or Greeks : but Herod'. otus states that the Macedónian monarchy was founded by Greeks from Ar' gos; and according to Greek writers, twelve or fifteen

ι. PHILIP OF Grecian princes reigned there before the accession of
MAC' EDON. Philip, who took charge of the government about the year 360 B. C., not as monarch, but as guardian of the infant son of his elder brother.

3. Philip had previously passed several years at Thebes, as a hostage, where he eagerly availed himself of the excellent oppor-tunities which that city afforded for the acquisition of various kinds of knowledge. He successfully cultivated the study of the Greek language ; and in the conversation of such generals and statesmen as Epaminon' das, Pelop' idas, and their friends, became acquainted with the details of the military tactics of the Greeks, and learned the nature and working of their democratical institutions. Thus with the superior mental and physical endowments which nature had given him, he became eminently fitted for the part which he after-wards bore in the intricate game of Grecian politics.

4. After Philip had successfully defended the throne of Mac' edon during several years, in behalf of his nephew, his military successes nabled him to take upon himself the kingly title, probably with the unanimous consent of both the army and the nation. He annexed several Thracian towns to his dominions, reduced the Illyr' ians and other nations on his northern and western borders, and was at times an ally, and at others an enemy, of Athens. At length, during the sacred war against the Phócians, the invitation which he received from the Thessálian allies of Thebes, as already noticed afforded him a pretence, which he had long coveted, for a more active inter

ference in the affairs of his southern neighbors. On entering Thes'-saly, however, on his southern march, he was at first repulsed by the Phócians and their allies, and obliged to retire into Macedónia, but, soon returning at the head of a more numerous army, he defeated the enemy in a decisive battle, and would have marched upon Phócis at once to terminate the war, but he found the pass of Thermop'ylæ strongly guarded by the Athenians, and thought it prudent to withdraw his forces.

5. Still the sacred war lingered, although the Phócians desired peace; but the revengeful spirit of the Thebans was not allayed; Philip was again urged to crush the profaners of the national religion, and having succeeded, in spite of the warnings of the patriotic Demosthenes, in lulling the suspicions of the Athenians with proposals of an advantageous peace, he marched into Phócis, and compelled the enemy to surrender at discretion. The Amphictyon'ic council, being now reinstated in its ancient authority, with the power of Philip to enforce its decrees, doomed Phócis to lose her independence forever, to have her cities levelled with the ground, and her population, after being distributed in villages of not more than fifty dwellings, to pay a yearly tribute of sixty talents to the temple, until the whole amount of the plundered treasure should be restored. Finally, the two votes which the Phócians had possessed in the Amphictyon'ic council were transferred to the king of Mac'edon and his successors. The influence which Philip thus obtained in the councils of the Grecians paved the way for the overthrow of their liberties.

6. From an early period of his career Philip had aspired to the sovereignty of all Greece, as a secondary object that should prepare the way for the conquest of Persia, the great aim and end of all his ambitious projects; and after the close of the sacred war he accordingly exerted himself to extend his power and influence, either by arms or negotiation, on every side of his dominions; but his intrigues in At'tica, and among the Peloponnésian States, were for a time counteracted by the glowing and patriotic eloquence of the Athenian Demosthenes, the greatest of Grecian orators. In his military operations Philip ravaged Illyr'ia[1]—reduced Thes'saly more nearly to a Macedónian province—conquered a part of the

---

1. The term *Illyr'ia*, or Illyr'icum was applied to the country bordering on the eastern shore of the Adriatic, and extending from the northern extremity of the Gulf south to the borders of Epirus. (*Map* No. VIII.)

Thracian territory—extended his power into Epírus and Acarnánia —and would have gained a footing in E'lis and Acháia, on the western coast of the Peloponnésus, had it not been for the watchful jealousy of Athens, which concerted a league among several of the States to repel his encroachments.

7. The first open rupture with the Athenians occurred while Philip was engaged in subduing the Grecian cities on the Thracian coast of the Hel'lespont, in what was called the Thracian Chersoné- sus.[2] A little later, the Amphictyon'ic council, through the influ- ence of Æs'chines, an orator second only to Demosthenes, but secretly devoted to the interests of the king of Mac'edon, appointed Philip to conduct a war against Amphis'sa,[3] a Lócrian town, which had been convicted of a sacrilege similar to that of the Phócians It was now that Philip, hastily passing through Thrace at the head of a powerful army, first threw off the mask, and revealed his de- signs against the liberties of Greece by seizing and fortifying Elatéia[4] the capital of Phócis which was conveniently situated for commanding the entrance into Bœótia.

8 The Thebans and the Athenians, suddenly awaking from their dream of security, from which all the eloquent appeal of Demosthe- nes had not hitherto been able to arouse them, prepared to defend their territories from invasion; but most of the Peloponnésian States kept aloof through indifference, rather than through fear. Even in Thebes and Athens there were parties whom the gold and persua- sions of Philip had converted into allies; and when the armies marched forth to battle, dissensions pervaded their ranks. The spirit of Grecian liberty had already been extinguished

9. The masterly policy of Philip still led him to declare that the sacred war against Amphis'sa, with the conduct of which he had

---

1. *Acarnánia*, lying south of Epirus, also bordered on the Adriatic, or Iónian sea. From Ætólia on the east it was separated by the Achelóüs, probably the largest river in Greece. The Acarnánians were almost constantly at war with the Ætólians, and were far behind the rest of the Greeks in mental culture. (*Map* No. I.)

2. The *Thracian Chersonésus* ("Thracian peninsula") was a peninsula of Thrace, between the Melian Gulf (now Gulf of Sáros) and the Hel'lespont. The fertility of its soil early attracted the Grecians to its shores, which soon became crowded with flourishing and popular cities. (*Map* No. III.)

3. *Amphis'sa*, the chief town of Lócris, was about seven miles west from Delphi, near the head of the Crissean Gulf, now Gulf of Salóna, a branch of the Corinthian Gulf. The modern town of Salóna represents the ancient Amphis'sa. (*Map* No. I.)

4. *Elatéia*, a city in the north-east of Phócis, on the left bank of the Cephis'sus, was about twenty-five miles north-east from Delphi. Its ruins are to be seen on a site called Elephta. (*Map* No. I.)

been intrusted by the Amphictyon'ic council, was his only object, and he had a plausible excuse for entering Bœótia when the Thebans and Athenians appeared as the allies of a city devoted by the gods to destruction.   At Chæronéa[1] the hostile armies met, nearly equal in number; but there was no Per'icles, nor Epaminon'das, to match the warlike abilities of Philip and the young prince Alexander, the latter of whom commanded a wing of the Macedónian army.   The day was decided against the Grecians, although their loss in battle was not large; but the event broke up the feeble confederacy against Philip, and left each of the allied States at his mercy.

10. While Philip treated the Thebans with some severity, and obliged them to ransom their prisoners, and resign a portion of their territory, he exercised a degree of lenity towards the Athenians which excited general surprise—offering them terms of peace which they themselves would scarcely have ventured to propose to him.   He next assembled a congress of all the Grecian States, at Corinth, for the purpose of settling the affairs of Greece.   Here all his proposals were adopted, war was declared against Persia, and Philip was appointed commander-in-chief of the Grecian forces; but while he was making preparations for his great enterprise he was assassinated on a public occasion by a Macedónian nobleman, in revenge for some private wrong.

11. Alexander, the son of Philip, then at the age of twenty years, succeeded his father on the throne of Mac'edon.   At once the Illyr'ians, Thracians, and other northern tribes that had been made tributary by Philip, took up arms to recover their independence; but Alexander quelled the spirit of revolt in a single campaign.   During his absence on this expedition, the Grecian States, headed by the Thebans and Athenians, made preparations to shake off the yoke of Mac'edon; but Alexander, whose marches were unparalleled for their rapidity, suddenly appeared in their midst. Thebes, the first object of his vengeance, was taken by assault, in which six thousand of her warriors were slain.   Ever distinguished by her merciless treatment of her conquered enemies, she was now

II. ALEXANDER THE GREAT.

---

1. The plain of *Chæronéa*, on which the battle was fought, is on the southern bank of the Cephis'sus river, in Bœótia, a few miles from its entrance into the Copáic lake.   In the year 447 B. C. the Athenians had been defeated on the same spot by the Bœótians; and in the year 86 B. C. the same place witnessed a bloody engagement between the Romans under Sylla, and the troops of Mithridátes.   (*Map* No. I.)

doomed to suffer the extreme penalties of war which she had often inflicted on others. Most of the city was levelled with the ground and thirty thousand prisoners, besides women and children, were condemned to slavery.

12. The other Grecian States which had provoked the resentment of Alexander, hastily renewed their submission; and Athens, with servile homage, sent an embassy to congratulate the youthful hero on his recent successes. Alexander accepted the excuses of all, renewed the confederacy which his father had formed, and having intrusted the government of Greece and Mac'edon to Antip'ater, one of his generals, set out on his career of eastern conquest, at the head of an army of only thirty-five thousand men, and taking with him a treasury of only seventy talents of silver. He had even distributed nearly all the remaining property of his crown among his friends; and when he was asked by Perdic'cas what he had reserved for himself, he answered, " My hopes."

13. Early in the spring of the year 334, Alexander crossed the Hel'lespont, and a few days later defeated an immense Persian army on the eastern bank of the Gran'icus,[1] with the loss on his part of only eighty-five horsemen and thirty light infantry. Proceeding thence south towards the coast, the gates of Sardis and Eph'esus were thrown open to him; and although at Milétus and Halicarnas'sus[2] he met with some resistance, yet before the close of the first campaign he was undisputed master of all Asia Minor.

14. Early in the following spring (B. C. 333), he directed his march farther eastward, through Cappadócia[3] and Cilic'ia,[4] and on the coast of the latter, near the small town of Is'sus,[5] again met

1. The *Gran'icus*, the same as the Turkish *Demotiko*, is a a small stream of Mys'ia, in Asia Minor, which flows from Mount I'da, east of Troy, northward into the Propon tis, or Sea of Marmóra. (*Map* No. IV.)

2. *Halicarnas'sus*, the principal city of Cária, was situated on the northern shore of the Cer'amic Gulf, now Gulf of Kos, one hundred miles south from Smyrna. Halicarnas'sus was the birth-place of Herod'otus the historian, of Dionys'ius the historian and critic, and of Heraclitus the poet. It was Artemis'ia, queen of Cária, who erected the splendid mausoleum, or tomb, to her husband, Mausólus. The Turkish town of *Boodroom* is on the site of the ancient Halicarnas'sus. Near the modern town are to be seen old walls, exquisite sculptures, fragments of columns, and the remains of a theatre two hundred and eighty feet in d'ameter, which seems to have had thirty-six rows of marble seats. (*Map* No. IV.)

3. *Cappadócia* was an interior province of Asia Minor, south-east of Galátia. (*Map* No. IV.)

4. *Cilic'ia* was south of Cappadócia, on the coast of the Mediterranean. (*Map* No. IV.)

5. *Is'sus* (now Aiasse, or Urzin) was a sea-port town of Cilic'ia, at the north-eastern extremity of the Mediterranean, and at the head of the Gulf of Is'sus. The plain between the sea and the mountains, where the battle was fought, was less than two miles in width,—a sufficient space for the evolutions of the Mac'edonian phalanx, but not large enough for the manœuvres of so great an army as that of Darius. (*Map* No. IV.)

the Persian army, numbering seven hundred thousand men, and commanded by Daríus himself, king of Persia. In the battle which followed, Alexander, as usual, led on his army in person, and fought in the thickest of the fight. The result was a total rout of the Persians, with a loss of more than a hundred thousand men, while that of the Greeks and Macedónians was less than five hundred. The Persian monarch fled in the beginning of the engagement, leaving his mother, wife, daughters, and an infant son, to the mercy of the victor, who treated them with the greatest kindness and respect. When, afterwards, Daríus heard, at the same time, of the generous treatment of his wife, who was accounted the most beautiful woman in Asia,—of her death from sudden illness, and of the magnificent burial which she had received from the conqueror,—he lifted up his hands to heaven and prayed, that if his kingdom were to pass from himself, it might be transferred to Alexander.

15. The conqueror next directed his march southward through northern Syria and Palestine. At Damascus a vast amount of treasure belonging to the king of Persia fell into his hands: the city of Tyre, after a vigorous siege of seven months, and a desperate resistance, was taken by storm, and thirty thousand of the Tyrians sold as slaves. (B. C. 332.) After the fall of Tyre, all the cities of Palestine submitted, except Gaza,[1] which made as obstinate a defence as Tyre, and was as severely punished. From Palestine Alexander proceeded into Egypt, which was eager to throw off the Persian tyranny, and he took especial care to conciliate the priests by the honors which he paid to the Egyptian gods. After having founded a new city, which he named Alexandria,[2] and crossed the

---

1. *Gaza,* an early Philistine city of great natural strength in the south-western part of Palestine was sixteen miles south of Ascalon, and but a short distance from the Mediterranean. The place was called Constantia by the Romans, and is now called *Rassa* by the Arabs. (*Map* No. VI.)

2. *Alexandria* is about fourteen miles south-west from the Canopic, or most western branch of the Nile, and is built partly on the ridge of land between the sea and the bed of the old Lake Mareotis, and partly on the peninsula (formerly island) of Pháros, which projects into the Mediterranean. Alexandria, the site of which was most admirably chosen by its founder, the only port on the Egyptian coast that has deep water, and that is accessible at all seasons. Lake Mareotis, which for many ages after the Greek and Roman dominion in Egypt was mostly dried up, and whose bed was lower than the surface of the Mediterranean, had no outlet to the sea until the English, in the year 1801, opened a passage into it from the Bay of Aboukir, when it soon resumed its ancient extent. The ancient canal from Alexandria to the Nile, a distance of forty-eight miles, was reopened in 1819. While the commerce of the Indies was carried on by way of the Red Sea and the Isthmus of Suez, Alexandria was a great commercial emporium, but it rapidly declined after the discovery of the passage to India by way of the Cape of Good Hope. It is probable that the commerce of the east, through the agency of steam, will again flow, to a great extent, in the ancient channel, and that Alexandria will again become a great commercial emporium. (*Map* No. V.)

Libyan desert to consult the oracle of Júpiter Am' món, he returned to Palestine, when, learning that Darius was making vast preparations to oppose him, he crossed the Euphrátes, and directed his march into the very heart of the Persian empire, declaring that " the world could no more admit two masters than two suns."

16. On a beautiful plain twenty miles distant from the town of Arbéla,[1] whence the battle derives its name, thé Persian monarch, surrounded by all the pomp and luxury of Eastern magnificence, had collected the remaining strength of his empire, consisting of an army, as stated by some authors, of more than a million of foot soldiers, and forty thousand cavalry, besides two hundred scythed chariots, and fifteen elephants brought from the west of India.[2] To oppose this force Alexander had only forty thousand foot soldiers, and seven thousand cavalry, but they were well armed and disciplined, confident of victory, and led by an able general who had never experienced a defeat, and who directed the operations of the battle in person. (B. C. 331.)

17. Darius sustained the conflict with better judgment and more courage than at Is' sus, but the cool intrepidity of the Macedónian phalanx was irresistible, and the field of battle soon became a scene of slaughter, in which, some say, forty thousand, and others, three hundred thousand of the barbarians were slain, while the loss of Alexander did not exceed five hundred men. Although Darius escaped with a portion of his body-guard, yet the result of the battle decided the contest, and gave to Alexander the dominion of the Persian empire. Not long after, Darius himself was slain by one of his own officers.

18. Soon after the battle of Arbéla, Alexander proceeded to Babylon, and during four years remained in the heart of Persia, reducing to subjection the chiefs who still struggled for independence and regulating the government of the conquered provinces. Ambitious of farther conquests, he passed the Indus, and invaded the country of the Indian king Pórus, whom he defeated in a sanguinary engagement, and took prisoner. When brought into the presence of Alexander, and asked how he would be treated, he replied, " Like a king ;" and so pleased was the conqueror with the lofty demeanor

1. *Arbéla* was about forty miles east of the Tigris, and twenty miles south-east from the plain of Gaugaméla, where the battle was fought. Gaugaméla, a small hamlet, was a short distance south-east from the site of Nineveh.

2. The term *India* was applied by the ancient geographers to all the part of Asia which is east of the river Indus. (*Map* No. V.)

of the captive, and with the valor which he had shown in battle, that he not only re-instated him in his royal dignity, but conferred upon him a large addition of territory. Alexander continued his march eastward until he reached the Hyphásis,[1] the most eastern tributary of the Indus, when his troops, seeing no end of their toils, refused to follow him farther, and he was reluctantly forced to abandon the career of conquest which he had marked out for himself to the eastern ocean.

19. Resolving to return into Central Asia by a new route, he descended the Indus to the sea, whence, after sending a fleet with a portion of his forces around through the Persian Gulf[2] to the Euphrátes, he marched with the rest of his army through the barren wastes of Gedrósia,[3] and after much suffering and considerable loss, arrived once more in the fertile provinces of Persia. For some time after his return his attention was engrossed with plans for organizing, on a permanent basis, the government of the mighty empire which he had won. Aiming to unite the conquerors and the conquered, so as to form out of both a nation independent alike of Macedónian and of Persian prejudices, he married Statira, the oldest daughter of Daríus, and united his principal officers with Persian and Median women of the noblest families, while ten thousand of his soldiers were induced to follow the example of their superiors.

20. But while he was occupied with these cares, and with dreams of future conquests, his career was suddenly terminated by death. On setting out to visit Babylon, soon after the decease of an intimate friend, which had caused a great depression of his spirits, he was warned by the magicians that Babylon would be fatal to him; but he proceeded to the city, where, haunted by gloomy forebodings and superstitious fancies, he endeavored to dispel his melancholy by indulging more freely in the pleasures of the table. Excessive drinking at length brought to a crisis a fever, which he had probably con

---

1. The *Hyphásis*, now called *Beyah*, or *Beas*, is the most eastern tributary of the Indus, The *Sutledge*, which enters the Beyah from the east, has been mistaken by some writers for the ancient Hyphásis. (*Map* No. V.)

2. The *Persian Gulf* is an extensive arm of the Indian ocean, separating Southern Persia from Arabia. During a long period it was the thoroughfare for the commerce between the western world and India. The navigation of the Gulf, especially along the Arabian coast, is tedious and difficult, owing to its numerous islands and reefs. The *Bahrein* islands, near the Arabian shore, are celebrated for their pearl fisheries, which yield pearls of the value of more than a million dollars annually. (*Map* No. V.)

3. *Gedrósia*, corresponding to the modern Persian province of *Mekran*, is a sandy or barren region, extending along the shore of the Indian Ocean from the river Indus to the mouth of the Persian Gulf. (*Map* No. V.)

tracted in the marshes of Assyria, and which suddenly terminated his life in the thirty-third year of his age, and the thirteenth of his reign. (B. C. May, 324.)

21. The character of Alexander has afforded matter for much discussion, and is, to this day, a subject of dispute. At times he was guilty of remorseless and unnecessary cruelty to the vanquished, and in a fit of passion he slew the friend who had saved his life; but on other occasions he was distinguished by an excess of lenity, and by the most noble generosity and benevolence. His actions and character were indeed of a mixed nature, which is the reason that some have regarded him as little more than a heroic madman, while others give him the honor of vast and enlightened views of policy, which aimed at founding, among nations hitherto barbarous, a solid and flourishing empire.

22. If we are to judge by his actions, however, rather than by his supposed moral motives, he was, in reality, one of the greatest of men; great, not only in the vast compass and persevering ardor of his ambition, which " wept for more worlds to conquer,"-but great in the objects and aims which ennobled it, and great because his adventurous spirit and personal daring never led him into deeds of rashness; for his boldest military undertakings were ever guided by sagacity and prudence. The conquests of Alexander were highly beneficial in their results to the conquered people; for his was the first of the great monarchies founded in Asia that contained any element of moral and intellectual progress—that opened a prospect of advancing improvement, and not of continual degradation, to its subjects. To the commercial world it opened new countries, and new channels of trade, and gave a salutary stimulus to industry and mercantile activity: nor were these benefits lost when the empire founded by Alexander broke in pieces in the hands of his successors; for the passages which he opened, by sea and by land, between the Euphrátes and the Indus, had become the highways of the commerce of the Indies; Babylon remained a famous port until its rival, Seleu'cia,[1] arose into eminence; and Alexandria long continued to receive and pour out an inexhaustible tide of wealth.

---

1. *Seleu' cia*, built by Seleu' cus, one of Alexander's generals, was situated on the western bank of the Tigris, about forty-five miles north of Babylon. Seleu' cus designed it as a free Grecian city; and many ages after the fall of the Macedonian empire, it retained the characteristics of a Grecian colony,—arts, military virtue, and the love of freedom. When at the height of its prosperity it contained a population of six hundred thousand citizens, governed by a senate of three hundred nobles.

23. The sudden death of Alexander left the government in a very unsettled condition. As he had appointed no successor, several of his generals contended for the throne, or for the regency during the minority of his sons; and hence arose a series of intrigues, and bloody wars, which, in the course of twenty-three years, caused the destruction of the entire family of Alexander, and ended in the dissolution of the Macedónian empire.

24. When intelligence of the death of Alexander reached Greece, the country was already on the eve of a revolution against Antip'-ater; and Demosthenes, still the foremost advocate of liberty, now found little difficulty in uniting several of the States with Athens in a confederacy against Macedónian supremacy. Sparta, however, was too proud to act under her ancient rival, and Thebes no longer existed. Antip'ater attempted to secure the straits of Thermop'ylæ against the confederates, but he was met by Leos'thenes, the Athenian general, and defeated. Eventually, however, Antip'ater, having received strong reinforcements from Mac'edon, attacked the confederates, and completely annihilated their army. Athens was compelled to abolish her democratic form of government, to receive Macedónian garrisons in her fortresses, and to surrender a number of her most famous orators, including Demosthenes. The latter, to avoid falling into the hands of Antip'ater, terminated his life by poison.

25. Antip'ater, at his death, left the government in the hands of Polysper'chon, as regent during the minority of a son of Alexander; but Cassan'der, the son of Antip'ater, soon after usurped the sovereignty of Greece and Mac'edon, and, for the greater security of his power, caused all the surviving members of the family of Alexander to be put to death. Antig'onus, another of Alexander's generals, had before this time overrun Syria and Asia Minor, and his ambitious views extended to the undivided sovereignty of all the countries which had been ruled by Alexander. Four of the most powerful of the other generals, Ptol'emy, Seleu'cus, Lysim'achus, and Cassan'der, formed a league against him, and fought with him the famous battle of Ip'sus,[1] in Phryg'ia,[2] which ended in the defeat and death of Antig'onus, the destruction of the power which he had raised, and the final dissolution of the Macedónian empire, three hundred and one years before the Christian era.

[1] Ip'sus was a city of Phryg'ia, near the southern boundary of Galatia, but its exact locality is unknown. (Map No. IV.)

[2] Phryg'ia was the central province of western Asia Minor. (Maps Nos. IV. and V.)

26. A new partition of the provinces was now made into four in dependent kingdoms. Ptol'emy was confirmed in the possession of Egypt, together with Lib'ya, and part of the neighboring territories of Arabia; Seleu'cus received the countries embraced in the eastern conquests of Alexander, and the whole region between the coast of Syria and the Euphrátes; but the whole of this vast empire soon dwindled into the Syrian monarchy: Lysim'achus received the northern and western portions of Asia Minor, as an appendage to his kingdom of Thrace; while Cassan'der received the sovereignty of Greece and Mac'edon. Of these kingdoms, the most powerful were Syria and Egypt; the former of which continued under the dynasty of the Seleu'cidæ, and the latter under that of the Ptol'emies, until both were absorbed in the growing dominion of the Roman empire Of the kingdom of Thrace under Lysim'achus, we shall have occasion to speak in its farther connection with Grecian history.

27. Cassan'der survived the establishment of his power only four years. After his death his two sons quarrelled for the succession, and called in the aid of foreigners to enforce their claims. Demétrius, son of Antig'onus, having seized the opportunity of interference in their disputes, cut off the brother who had invited his aid, and made himself master of the throne of Mac'edon, which was enjoyed by his posterity, except during a brief interruption after his death, down to the time of the Roman conquest. Demétrius possessed in addition to Mac'edon, Thes'saly, At'tica, and Bœótia, together with a great portion of the Peloponnésus; but his government was that of a pure military despotism, which depended on the army for support, wholly independent of the good will of the people. Aiming to recover his father's power in Asia, he excited the jealousy of Seleu'cus, king of Syria, who was able to induce Lysim'achus, of Thrace, and Pyr'rhus, king of Epírus, to commence a war against him. The latter twice overran Macedónia, and even seized the throne, which he held during a few months, while Demétrius was driven from the kingdom by his own rebellious subjects; but his son Antig'onus maintained himself in Peloponnésus, waiting a favorable opportunity of placing himself on the throne of his father.

28 During a number of years Mac'edon, Greece, and Western Asia, were harassed with the wars excited by the various aspirants to power. Lysim'achus was defeated and slain in a war with Seleu'cus; and the latter, invading Thrace, was assassinated by Ptol'emy Cerau'nus, who then usurped the government of Thra

and Mac'edon. In this situation of affairs, a storm, unseen in the distance, but which had long been gathering, suddenly burst upon Mac'edon, threatening to convert, by its ravages, the whole Grecian peninsula into a scene of desolation.

29. A vast horde of barbarians of the Celtic race had for some time been accumulating around the head waters of the Adriat'ic,¹ making Pannónia² the chief seat of their power. Influenced by hopes of plunder, rather than of conquest, they suddenly appeared on the frontiers of Mac'edon, and sent an embassy to Cerau'nus, offering peace if he were willing to purchase it by tribute. A haughty defiance from the Macedónian served only to quicken the march of the invaders, who defeated and killed Cerau'nus in a great battle, and so completely routed his army that almost all were slain or taken. (B. C. 280.) The conquerors then overran all Mac'edon to the borders of Thes'saly, and a detachment made a devastating inroad into the rich vale of the Penéus. The walled towns alone, which the barbarians had neither the skill nor the patience to reduce by siege, held out until the storm had spent its fury, when the Celts, scattered over the country in plundering parties, having met with some reverses, gradually withdrew from a country where there was little left to tempt their cupidity.

30. In the following year (279 B. C.) another band of Celts, estimated at two hundred thousand men, under the guidance of their principal *Brenn* or chief, called Bren'nus, overran Macedónia with little resistance, and passing through Thessaly, threatened to extend their ravages over southern Greece; but the allied Grecians, under the Athenian general, Cal'lipus, met them at Thermop'ylæ, and at first repulsed them with considerable loss. Eventually, however the secret path over the mountains was betrayed to the Celts as it had been to the Persian army of Xerxes, and the Grecians were forced to retreat. A part of the barbarian army, under Bren'nus, then marched into Phócis, for the purpose of plundering Delphi, but their atrocities roused against them the whole population, and they found their entire march, over roads mountainous and difficult,

---

1. The *Adriat'ic* or *Hadriatic* (now most generally called the *Gulf of Venice*) is that large arm of the Mediterranean sea which lies between Italy and the opposite shores of 'Illyr'ia, Epirus, and Greece. The southern portion of the gulf is now, as anciently, called the *Iónian sea*. The Adriat'ic derived its name from the once flourishing sea-port town of A'dria north of the river Po. The harbor of A'dria has long been filled up by the mud and other deposits brought down by the rivers, and the town is now nineteen miles inland. (*Map* No. VIII.)

2. *Pannónia,* afterwards a Roman province, was north of Illyr'ia, having the Danube for its northern and eastern boundary (*Map* No. VIII & IX.)

B*

beset with enemies burning for revenge. The invaders also suffered greatly from the cold and storms in the defiles of the mountains. It was said that the gods fought for the sacred temple, and that an earthquake rent the rocks, and brought down huge masses on the heads of the assailants. Certain it is that the invaders, probably acted upon by superstitious terror, were repulsed and disheartened. Bren'nus, who had been wounded before Delphi, is said to have killed himself in despair; and only a remnant of the barbarians regained their original seats on the Adriat'ic.

31. After the repulse of the Celts, Antig'onus, the son of Demé-trius, was able to gain possession of the throne of Mac'edon, but he found a formidable competitor in Pyr'rhus, king of Epírus, who resolved to add Mac'edon, and, if possible, the whole of Greece to his own dominion. · Pyr'rhus had no sooner returned from his famous expedition into Italy, of which we shall have occasion to speak in Roman history,[a] than he seized a pretext for declaring war against Antig'onus, and invaded Macedónia with his small army, (274 B. C.) the remnant of the forces which he had led against Rome, but which he now strengthened with a body of Celtic mercenaries. When Antig'onus marched against him, many of his troops, who had little affection or respect for their king, went over to Pyr'rhus, whose celebrated military prowess had won their admiration.

32. Antig'onus then retired into Southern Greece, whither he was followed by Pyr'rhus, who professed that the object of his expe dition was merely to restore the freedom of the cities which were held in subjection by his rival; but when he reached the borders of Lacónia he laid aside the mask, and began to ravage the country, and made an unsuccessful attempt to surprise Sparta, which was lit-tle prepared for defence. He then marched to Ar'gos, whither he had been invited by one of the rival leaders of the people, but he found Antig'onus, at the head of a strong force, encamped on one of the neighboring heights. Pyr'rhus gained entrance into the city by night, through treachery, but at the same time the troops of Antig'-onus were admitted from an opposite quarter—the citizens arose in arms, and a fierce struggle was carried on in the streets until day-light, when Pyr'rhus himself was slain (272 B. C.) by the hand of an Ar'give woman, who, exasperated at seeing him about to kill her son, hurled upon him a ponderous tile from the house-top The greater part of the army of Pyr'rhus, chiefly composed of Macedónians,

a See age 149.

then went over to their former sovereign, who soon after gained the throne of Mac' edon, which he held until his death.

33. The death of Pyr' rhus forms an important epoch in Grecian history, as it put an end to the struggle for power among Alexander's successors in the West, and left the field clear for the final contest between the liberty of Greece and the power of Mac' edon, which was only terminated by the ruin of both. When Antig' onus returned to Mac' edon, its acknowledged sovereign, he cherished the hope of ultimately reducing all Greece to his sway, little dreaming that the power centered in a recent league of a few Achæ' an cities was destined to become a formidable adversary to his house.

34. The *Achæ' an League* comprised at first twelve towns of Achàia, which were associated together for mutual safety, forming a little federal republic—all the towns having an equality **III. ACHÆ' AN** of representation in the general government, to which **LEAGUE.** all matters affecting the common welfare were intrusted, each town at the same time retaining the regulation of its own domestic policy. The Achæ' an league did not become of sufficient political importance to attract the attention of Antig' onus until about twenty years after the death of Pyr' rhus, when Arátus, an exile from Sic' yon, at the head of a small band of followers, surprised the city by night, and without any bloodshed delivered it from the dominion of the tyrants who, under Macedónian protection, had long oppressed it with despotic sway. (251 B. C.) Fearful of the hostility of Antig' onus, Arátus induced Sic' yon to join the Achæ' an league, and although its power greatly exceeded that of any Achæ' an town, it claimed no superiority of privilege over the other members of the confederacy, but obtained only one vote in the general council of the league, a precedent which was afterwards strictly adhered to in the admission of other cities. Arátus received the most distinguished honors from the Achæ' ans, and, a few years after the accession of Sic' yon, was placed at the head of the armies of the confederacy. (B. C. 246.)

35. Corinth, the key to Greece, having been seized by a stratagem of Antig' onus, and its citadel occupied by a Macedónian garrison, was rescued by a bold enterprise of Arátus, and induced to join the league. (243 B. C.) Other cities successively gave in their adherence, until the confederacy embraced nearly the whole of Peloponnésus. Although Athens did not unite with it, yet Arátus obtained the withdrawal of its Macedónian garrison. Sparta opposed the league—induced Ar' gos and Corinth to withdraw from it—and by

her successes over the Achæ' ans, eventually induced them to call in the aid of the Macedónians, their former enemies.

36. Antig' onus II., readily embracing the opportunity of restoring the influence of his family in Southern Greece, marched against the Lacedæmónians, over whom he obtained a decisive victory, which placed Sparta at his mercy. But he used his victory moderately, and granted the Spartans peace on liberal terms. On his death, which occurred soon after, he was succeeded on the throne of Mac' edon by his nephew and adopted son, Philip III. a youth of only seventeen.

37. The Ætólians,[1] the rudest of the Grecian tribes, who had acquired the character of a nation of freebooters and pirates, had. at this time formed a league similar to the Achæ' an, and counting on the inexperience of the youthful Philip, and the weakness of the Achæ' ans, began a series of unprovoked aggressions on the surrounding States. The Messénians, whose territory they had invaded by way of the western coast of the Peloponnésus, called upon the Achæ' ans for assistance, but Arátas, going to their relief, was attacked unexpectedly, and defeated. Soon after, the youthful Philip was placed at the head of the Achæ' an League, when a general war began between the Macedónians, Achæ' ans, and their confederates, on the one side, and the Ætólians, who were aided by the Spartans and E' leans, on the other.

38. The war continued four years, and was conducted with great cruelty and obstinacy on both sides; but Philip and the Achæ' ans were on the whole successful, and the Ætólians and their allies became desirous of peace, while new and ambitious views more eagerly inclined Philip to put an end to the unprofitable contest. At this time the Carthaginians and Romans were contending for mastery in the second Punic war, and Philip began to view the struggle as one in which an alliance with one of the parties would be desirable, by opening to himself prospects of future conquest and glory. By siding with the Carthaginians who were the most distant party, and from whom he would have less to fear than from the Romans, he hoped to be able eventually to insure to himself the sovereignty of all Greece, and to make additions to Macedónia on the side of Italy. He therefore proposed terms of peace to the Ætólians; and a treaty

---

1. *Ætólia* was a country of Northern Greece, bounded on the north by Thes' sa'y, on the east by Dória, Phócis, and Lócris, on the south by the Corinthian Gulf, and on the west by Acarnánia. It was in general a rough and mountainous country, although some of the valleys were remarkable for their fertility. (*Map* No. I.)

was concluded at Naupac'tus, which left all the parties in the war in the enjoyment of their respective possessions. (217 B C.)

39. After the great battle of Can'næ,[a] which seemed to have extinguished the last hopes of Rome, Philip sent envoys to Hannibal, the Carthaginian general, and concluded with him a treaty of strict alliance. He next sailed with a small fleet up the Adriat'ic, and while besieging Appollónia,[1] a town in Illyr'ia, was met and defeated by the Roman prætor, M. Valérius, who had been sent to succor the Illyr'ians. (215 B. C.) Philip was forced to burn his ships, and retreat over land to Macedónia, leaving his baggage, and the arms of many of his troops, in the enemy's hands. Such was the unfortunate issue of his first encounter with the Roman soldiery.

40. Soon after his return to Macedónia, finding Arátus in the way of his projects against the liberties of Southern Greece, he contrived to have the old general removed by slow poison ;—a crime which filled all Greece with horror and indignation. In the meantime, the Romans, while recovering ground in Italy, contrived to keep Philip busy at home, by inciting the Ætólians to violate the recent treaty, and inducing Sparta and E'lis to join in a war against Mac'edon. Still Philip, supported for awhile by the Achæ'ans, under their renowned leader, Philopœ'men, maintained his ground, until, first, the Athenians, no longer able to protect their fallen fortunes, solicited aid from the Romans; and finally, the Achæ'ans themselves, being divided into factions, accepted terms of peace.

41. Philip continued to struggle against his increasing enemies, until, being defeated in a great battle with the Romans,[b] he purchased peace by the sacrifice of the greater part of his navy, the payment of a tribute, and the resignation of his supremacy over the Grecian States. At the celebration of the Isth'mian games at Corinth the terms of the Roman senate were made known to the Grecians, who received, with the height of exultation, the proclamation that the independence of Greece was restored, under the auspices of the Roman arms. (196 B. C.)

42. Probably nothing was farther from the intention of the Roman senate than to allow the Grecian States to regain their ancient power and sovereignty, and it was sufficient to damp the joy of the more

1. *Apollónia* was situated on the northern side of the river Aóus (now Vojutza, near the mouth. Its ruins still retain the name of *Pollini.* Apollónia was founded by a colony from Corinth and Corcyra, and, according to Strabo, was renowned for the wisdom of its laws.

a. See p. 158.   b. Battle of Cynocephalæ, 197 B. C. See p 161

considerate that the boon of freedom which Rome affected to bestow was tendered by a master who could resume it at his pleasure. At the first opportunity of interference, therefore, which opened to the Romans, the Ætólians, who had espoused the cause of . Antíochus, king of Syria, the enemy of Rome, were reduced to poverty and deprived of their independence. At a later period Per' seus, the successor of Philip on the throne of Mac' edon, being driven into a war by Roman ambition, finally lost his kingdom in the battle of Pyd' na,‘ in which twenty thousand Macedónians were slain. and ten thousand taken prisoners, while the Roman army, commanded by Lúcius Æmil' ius Paúlus, lost scarcely a hundred men. (168 B. C.) The Macedónian monarchy was extinguished, and Per' seus himself, a wanderer from his country, was taken prisoner in an island of the Æ' gean, and conveyed to Rome to grace the triumph of the conqueror.

43. Soon after the fall of Per' seus, the Achæ' ans were charged with having aided him in the war against Rome, and, without a shadow of proof, one thousand of their worthiest citizens, among whom was the historian Polyb' ius, were sent to Rome to prove their innocence of this charge before a Roman tribunal. (167 B. C.) Here they were detained seventeen years without being able to obtain a hearing, when three hundred of the number, the only surviving remnant of the thousand, were finally restored to their country. The exiles returned, burning with vengeance against the Romans ; other causes of animosity arose ; and when a Roman embassy, sent to Corinth, declared the will of the Roman senate that the Achæ' an League should be reduced to its original limits, a popular tumult arose, and the Roman ambassadors were publicly insulted.

44. War soon followed. The Achæ' ans and their allies were defeated by the consul Mum' mius near Corinth, and that city, then the richest in Greece, after being plundered of its treasures, was consigned to the flames. The last blow to the liberties of the Hellénic race had been struck, and all Greece, as far as Epírus and Macedónia, now become a Roman province, under the name of Acháia. (146 B. C.) "The end of the Achæ' an war," says Thirwall, "was the last stage of the lingering process by which Rome enclosed her victim in the coils of her insidious diplomacy, covered it with the

1. *Pyd' na* was a city near the south-eastern extremity of Macedónia, on the western shore of the Thermaic Gulf, (ne v Gulf of Saloniki.) The ancient Pydna is now called *Kidros.* Dr Clarke observed here a vast mound of earth, which he considered, with much probability, as marking the site of the great battle fought there by the Romans and Macedónians. (*Map No. L.*

slime of her sycophants and hirelings, crushed it when it began to struggle, and then calmly preyed upon its vitals."

45. W) have now arrived at the proper termination of Grecian history. Niebuhr has remarked, that, "as rivers flow into the sea, so does the history of all the nations, known to have existed previously in the regions around the Mediterranean, terminate in that of Rome." Henceforward, then, the history of Greece becomes involved in the changing fortunes of the Roman empire, to whose early annals we shall now return, after a brief notice of the cotemporary history of surrounding nations. With the loss of her liberties the glory of Greece had passed away. Her population had been gradually diminishing since the period of the Persian wars; and from the epoch of the Roman conquest the spirit of the nation sunk into despondency, and the energies of the people gradually wasted, until, no later than the days of Strabo,[1] Greece existed only in the remembrance of the past. Then, many of her cities were desolate, or had sunk to insignificant villages, while Athens alone maintained her renown for philosophy and the arts, and became the instructor of her conquerors;—large tracts of land, once devoted to tillage, were either barren or had been converted into pastures for sheep, and vast herds of cattle; while the rapacity of Roman governors had inflicted upon the sparse population impoverishment and ruin.

COTEMPORARY HISTORY: 490 TO 146 B. C.

1. Of the cotemporary annals of other nations during the authentic period of Grecian history, there is little of importance to be narrated beyond what will be found connected with Roman affairs in a subsequent chapter; although the Grecian cities of Italy, Sicily, and Cyrenaica, considered not as dependent colonies of the parent State, but as separate powers, will require some further notice. Of the history of the Medes and Persians we have already given the most interesting portion. Of Egyptian history little is known, beyond what has been narrated, until the beginning of the dynasty of the Ptol'emies (301 B. C.,) and of the events from that period down to the time of Roman interference in the affairs of Egypt, we have room for only occasional notices, as connected with the more important ₁ HISTORY histories of other nations. Of the civil annals of the OF THE JEWS. Jews we shall give a brief sketch, so as to continue, from a preced

<hr />

1. Strabo was a celebrated geographer, born at Amasia in Pontus, about the year 54 B. C.

ing chapter. the history of Judea down to the time when that country
became a province of the Roman empire.

2 It has been stated that the rebuilding of the second temple of
Jerusalem was completed during the reign of Darius Hystas' pes,
about twenty-five years before the commencement of the war between
the Greeks and Persians.   During the following reign of Xerxes, the
Jews appear to have been treated by their masters with respect, and
also during the early part of the reign of Artaxerx' es Longimánus
who had taken for his second wife a Jewish damsel named Esther
the niece of the Jew Mor' decai, one of the officers of the palace.
The story of Háman, the wicked minister of the king, is doubtless
familiar to all our readers.   After the Jews had been delivered from
the wanton malice of Háman, Nehemíah, also an officer in the king's
palace, obtained for them permission to rebuild the walls of the holy
city, and was appointed governor over Judea.   With the close of
the administration of Nehemíah the annals embraced in the Old
Testament end, and what farther reliable information we possess of
the history of the Jews down to the time of the Roman conquest is
mostly derived from Josephus.

3. After Nehemíah, Judea was joined to the satrapy of Syria, although the internal government was still administered by the high
priests, under the general superintendence of Persian officers—the
people remaining quiet under the Persian government.   After the
division of the vast empire of Alexander among his generals, Judea,
lying between Syria and Egypt, and being coveted by the monarchs
of both, suffered greatly from the wars which they carried on against
each other.   At one time the Egyptian monarch, Ptol' emy Sóter,
having invaded the country, stormed Jerusalem on the Sabbath day,
when the Jews, from superstitious motives, would not defend their
city, and transported a hundred thousand of the population to
Egypt,—apparently, however, as colonists, rather than as prisoners.

4. During the reigns of Ptol' emy Sóter, Ptol' emy Philadel' phus.
Ptol' emy Euer' getes, and Ptol' emy Philop' ater, Judea remained
subject to Egypt, but was lost by Ptol' emy Epiph' anes.   Ptol' emy
Philadel' phus, by his generous treatment of the Jews, induced large
numbers of them to settle in Egypt.   He was an eminent patron of
learning, and caused the septuagint translation of the scriptures to be
made, and a copy to be deposited in the famous library which he established at Alexandria.   On the accession of Ptol' emy Epiph' anes
to the throne, (204 B. C.) at the age of only five years, Antíochus

the Great, king of Syria, easily persuaded the Jews to place themselves under his rule, and in return for their confidence in him he conferred such favors upon Jerusalem as he knew were best calculated to win the hearts of the people.

5. Antíochus Épiph' anes, the successor of Antíochus the Great, having invaded Egypt, a false rumor of his death was brought to Jerusalem, whereupon a civil war broke out between two factions of the Jews who had long been quarrelling about the office of the high priesthood. The tumult was quelled by the return of Antíochus, who, exasperated on learning that the Jews had made public rejoicings at his supposed death, marched against Jerusalem, which he plundered, as if he had taken it by storm from an enemy. (169 B. C.) He even despoiled the temple of its holy vessels, and carried off the treasures of the nation collected there. Two years later he attempted to carry out the plan of reducing the various religious systems of his empire to one single profession, that of the Grecian polytheism. He polluted the altar of the temple—put a stop to the daily sacrifice— to the great festivals—to the rite of circumcision—burned the copies of the law—and commanded that the temple itself should be converted into an edifice sacred to the Olympian Júpiter.

6. These acts, and the insolent cruelties with which they were accompanied, met with a fierce and desperate resistance from the brave family of the Mac' cabees,[a] or Asmonéans, who, under their heroic leader Judas, first fled to the wilderness, and the caves of the mountians, where they were joined by numerous bands of their exasperated countrymen, who, ere long, began to look upon Judas as an instrument appointed by heaven for their deliverance. Thoroughly acquainted with every impregnable cliff and defile of his mountain land, Judas was successful in every encounter in which he chose to engage with the Syrians :—by rapid assaults he made himself master of many fortified places, and within three years after the pollution of the temple he had driven out of Judea four generals at the head of large and regular armies. He then went up to Jerusalem, and although a fortress in the lower city was still held by a Syrian garrison, he restored the walls and doors of the temple, caused the daily sacrifice to be renewed, and proclaimed a solemn festival of eight days on the joyful occasion.

a. The appellation of Mac' cabees was given them from the initial letters of the text displayed on their standard, which was, Mi Chamoka Baalim, Jahoh! "Who is like unto thee among the gods, O Lord!"—from Exod. xv. 11.

7. The war with Syria continued during the brief reign of the youthful son of Antíochus Epiph'anes, and was extended into the subsequent reign of Demétrius Sóter, (B. C. 162,) who sent two powerful armies into Judea, the first of which was defeated in the defile of Bethóron,[1] and its general slain. Another army was more successful, and Judas himself fell, after having destroyed a multitude of his enemies; but his body was recovered, and he was buried in the tomb of his fathers. "And all Israel mourned him with a great mourning, and sorrowed many days, and said, How is the mighty fallen that saved Israel."

8. After the death of Judas a time of great tribulation followed; the Syrians became masters of the country, and Jonathan, the brother of Judas, the new leader of the patriotic band, was obliged to retire to the mountains, where he maintained himself two years, while the cities were occupied by Syrian garrisons. Eventually, during the changing revolutions in the Syrian empire itself, Jonathan was enabled to establish himself in the priesthood, and under his administration Judea again became a flourishing State. Being at length treacherously murdered by one of the Syrian kings, (B. C. 143,) his brother Simon succeeded to the priesthood, and during the seven years in which he judged Israel, general prosperity prevailed throughout the land. "The husbandmen tilled the field in peace, and the earth gave forth her crops, and the trees of the plain their fruits. The old men sat in the streets; all talked together of their blessings, and the young men put on the glory and the harness of war."

9. The remaining history of the Jews, from the time of Simon down to the formation of Judea into a Roman province, is mostly occupied with domestic commotions, whose details would possess little interest for the general reader. The circumstances which placed Judea under the sway of the Romans will be found detailed in their connection with Roman history.

10. Before the beginning of the "authentic period" of Grecian history, various circumstances, such as the desire of adventure com

II. GRECIAN mercial interests, and, not unfrequently, civil dissension
COLONIES. at home, led to the planting of Grecian colonies on many distant coasts of the Mediterranean. Those of Thrace, Mac'edon, and Asia-Minor, were ever intimately connected with Greece proper, in whose general history theirs is embraced; but the Greek cities

---

1. *Bethóron* was a village about ten miles north-west from Jerusalem.

of Italy, Sicily, and Cyrenáica, were too far removed from the drama that was enacting around the shores of the Æ'gean to be more than occasionally and temporarily affected by the changing fortunes of the parent States. Nevertheless, a brief notice of those distant settlements that eventually rivalled even Athens and Sparta in power and resources, cannot be uninteresting, and it will serve to give the reader more accurate views, than he would otherwise possess, of the extent and importance of the field of Grecian history.

11. At an early period the shores of southern Italy and Sicil were peopled by Greeks · and so numerous and powerful did the Grecian cities in those countries become, that the whole were comprised by Strabo and others under the appellation *Magna* III. MAGNA *Græcia* or "Great Greece"—an appropriate name for a GRÆCIA. region containing many cities far superior in size and population to any in Greece itself. The earliest of these distant Grecian settlements appear to have been made at Cúmæ,[1] and Neap'olis,[2] on the western coast of Italy, about the middle of the eleventh century Nax'os,[3] on the eastern coast of Sicily, was founded about the year 735 B. C.; and in the following year some Corinthians laid the foundation of Syracuse. Géla,[4] on the western coast of the island, and Messána[5] on the strait between Italy and Sicily, were founded

1. *Cúmæ*, a city of Campania, on the western coast of Italy, a short distance north-west from Neapolis, and about a hundred and ten miles south-east from Rome, is supposed to have been founded by a Grecian colony from Euboe'a about the year 1050 B. C. Cumæ was built on a rocky hill washed by the sea; and the same name is still applied to the ruins that lie scattered around its base. Some of the most splendid fictions of Virgil relate to the Cumæan Sibyl, whose cave, hewn out of solid rock, actually existed on the top of the hill of Cumæ. (*Map* No. VIII.)

2. *Neap'olis*, (a Greek word meaning the *new city*,) now called *Naples*, was founded by colony from Cumæ. It is situated on the north side of the Bay of Naples, in the immediate vicinity of Mount Vesuvius, one hundred and eighteen miles south-east from Rome. (*Map* No. VIII.)

3. *Nax'os* was north-east from Mount Ætna, and about equi-distant from Messána and Cat'ana. Nax'os was twice destroyed; first by Dionysius the Elder, and afterwards by the Siculi; after which Tauromenium was built on its site. The modern *Taormina* occupies the site of the ancient city. (*Map* No. VIII.)

4. *Géla* was on the southern coast of Sicily, a short distance from the sea, on a river of the same name, and about sixty miles west from Syracuse. On the site of the ancient city stands the modern *Terra Nuova*. (*Map* No. VIII.)

5. *Messána*, still a city of considerable extent under the name of *Messina*, was situated at the north-eastern extremity of the island of Sicily, on the strait of its own name. It was regarded by the Greeks as the key of the island, but the circumstance of its commanding position always made it a tempting prize to the ambitious and powerful neighboring princes. It underwent a great variety of changes, under the power of the Syracusans, Carthaginians, and Romans. It was treacherously seized by the Mamertini, (see p. 152) who slew the males, and took the wives and children as their property, and called the city Mamertina. Firstly, a portion of the inhabitants called in the aid of the Romans, and thus began the first Punic war. (265 B. C

soon after. Agrigen'tum,[1] on the south-western coast, was founded about a century later.

12. In the meantime the Greek cities Syb'aris, Crotóna,[2] and Taren'tum,[4] had been planted, and had rapidly grown to power and opulence, on the south-eastern coast of Italy. The territorial dominions of Syb'aris and Crotóna extended across the peninsula from sea to sea. The former possessed twenty-five dependent towns, and ruled over four distinct tribes or nations. The territories of Crotóna were still more extensive. These two Grecian States were at the maximum of their power about the year 560 B. C.—the time of the accession of Pisis'tratus at Athens; but they quarrelled with each other, and the result of the fatal contest was the ruin of Syb'aris, 510 B. C. At the time of the invasion of Italy by Pyr'rhus, (see p. 149.) Crotóna was still a considerable city, extending on both sides of the Æsárus, and its walls embracing a circumference of twelve miles. Taren'tum was formed by a colony from Sparta about the year 707,—soon after the first Messénian war. No details of its history during the first two hundred and thirty years of its existence

[1] "The modern city has a most imposing appearance from the sea, forming a fine circular sweep about two miles in length on the west shore of its magnificent harbor, from which it rises in the form of an amphitheatre; and being built of white stone, it strikingly contrasts with the dark fronts that cover the forests in the background." (*Map* No. VIII.)

1. *Agrigen' tum* was situated near the southern shore of Sicily, about midway of the island. Next to Syracuse it was not only one of the largest and most famous cities of Sicily, but of the ancient world; and its ruins are still imposingly grand and magnificent. The modern town of *Girgenti* lies adjacent to the ruins, from which it is separated by the small river Arcagas (*Map* No. VIII.)

2. *Syb' aris* was a city of south-eastern Italy on the Tarentine Gulf. *Crotóna* was about seventy miles south of it. Pythogoras resided at Crotóna during the latter years of his life; and Milo, the most celebrated athlete of antiquity, was a native of that city. The Sybarites were noted for the excess to which they carried the refinements of luxury and sensuality.—— The events which led to the destruction of Syb' aris, about 510 B. C., are thus related. A democratical party, having gained the ascendancy at Syb'aris, expelled five hund ed of the principal citizens, who sought refuge at Crotóna. The latter refusing, by the advice of Pythagoras, to give up the fugitives, a war ensued. Milo led out the Crotoniats, 'en thousand in number, who were met by three hundred thousand Syb'arites; but the former gained a complete victory, and then, marching immediately to Syb'aris, totally destroyed the city. (*Map* No. VIII.)

3. *Taren' tum*, the emporium of the Greek towns of Italy, was an important commercial city near the head of the gulf of the same name. It stood on what was formerly an isthmus, but which is now an island, separating the gulf from an inner bay fifteen or sixteen miles in circumference. The early Tarentines were noted for their military skill and prowess, and for the cultivation of literature and the arts; but their wealth and abundance so enervated their minds and bodies, and corrupted their morals, that even the neighboring barbarians, who had hated and feared, learned eventually to despise them. The Tarentines fell an easy prey to the Romans, after Pyrrhus had withdrawn from Italy. (See p. 150.) The modern town of Toranto, containing a population of about eighteen thousand inhabitants, occupies the site of the ancient city. (*Map* No. VIII.)

are known to us; but in the fourth century B. C. the Tarentines
stand foremost among the Italian Greeks.

13. During the first two centuries after the founding of Nax′os in
Sicily, Grecian settlements were extended over the eastern, southern,
and western sides of the island, while Him′era[1] was the only Grecian town on the northern coast. These two hundred years were a
period of prosperity among the Sicilian Greeks, who did not yet extend their residences over the island, but dwelt chiefly in fortifie
towns, and exercised authority over the surrounding native popula
tion, which gradually became assimilated in manners, language, and
religion, to the higher civilization of the Greeks. During the sixth
century before the Christian era, the Greek cities in Sicily and
southern Italy were among the most powerful and flourishing that
bore the Hellénic name. Géla and Agrigen′tum, on the south side
of Sicily, had then become the most prominent of the independent
Sicilian governments; and at the beginning of the fifth century we
find Gélo, a despot, or self-constituted ruler of the former city, subjecting other towns to his authority, and finally obtaining possession
of Syracuse, which he made the seat of his empire, (485 B. C.)
leaving Géla to be governed by his brother Híero, the first Sicilian
ruler of that name.

14. Gélo strengthened the fortifications and greatly enlarged the
limits of Syracuse, while, to occupy the enlarged space, he dis-,
mantled many of the surrounding towns, and transported their inhabitants to his new capital, which now became, not only the first city
in Sicily, but, according to Herod′otus, superior to any other Hellénic power; for we are told that when, in 481 B. C., the Corinthians
solicited aid from Gélo to resist the invasion of Xerxes, the Syracusans could offer twenty thousand heavy armed soldiers, and, in all, an
army of thirty thousand men, besides furnishing provisions for the
entire Grecian host so long as the war might last; but as Gélo demanded to be constituted commander-in-chief of all the Greeks in
the war against the Persians, the terms were not agreed to.

15. During the invasion of Greece by Xerxes, a formidable Carthaginian force under Hamil′car, said to consist of three hundred
thousand men, landed at Panor′mus,[2] a Carthaginian sea-port on the

---

1. *Him′era* was on the northern coast of Sicily, near the mouth of the river of the same
name, one hundred and ten miles north-west from Syracuse. The modern town of *Termini*,
at the mouth of the river Leonardo, occupies the site of the ancient city. (*Map* No. VIII.)
2. *Panor′mus*, supposed to have been first settled by Phœnicians, was in the north western

northern coast of the island, and proceeded to attack the Greek city
of Him′ era. (480 B. C.) Gélo, at the head of fifty-five thousand
men, marched to the aid of his brethren; and in a general battle
which ensued, the entire Carthaginian force was destroyed, or com
pelled to surrender, Hamil′ car himself being numbered among the
slain. The victory of Him′ era procured for Sicily immunity from
foreign war, while at the same time the defeat of Xerxes at Sal′ amis
dispelled the terrific cloud that overhung the Greeks in that quarter.

16. On the death of Gélo, a year after the battle of Him′ era, the
government fell into the hands of his brother Híero, a man whose
many great and noble qualities were alloyed by insatiable cupidity
and ambition. The power of Híero, not inferior to that of Gélo,
was probably greater than that of any other Grecian ruler of that
period. Híero aided the Greek cities of Italy against the Carthaginian and Tyrrhénian fleets; he founded the city of Ætʹ na,[1] and
added other cities to his government. He died after a reign of ten
years, and was succeeded by his brother Thrasybúlis, whose cruelties
led to his speedy dethronement, which was followed, not only by the
extinction of the Gelónian dynasty at Syracuse, but by an extensive
revolution in the other Sicilian cities, resulting, after many years of
civil dissensions, in the expulsion of the other despots who had relied
for protection on the great despot of Syracuse, and the establishment of governments more or less democratical throughout the
island.

17. The Gelónian dynasty had stripped of their possessions, and
banished, great numbers of citizens, whose places were filled by for
eign mercenaries; but the popular revolution reversed many of these
proceedings, and restored the exiles; although, in the end, adherents
of the expelled dynasty were allowed to settle partly in the territory
of Messána, and partly in Kamarína.[2] After the commotions at
tendant on these changes had subsided, prosperity again dawned on

art of Sicily, and had a good and capacious harbor. It early passed into the hands of the
Carthaginians, and was their stronghold in Magna Græcia. It is now called *Palermo*, and is
the capital city and principal sea-port of Sicily, having a population of about one hundred and
fifty thousand inhabitants. It is built on the south-west side of the Bay of Palermo, in a plain,
which, from its luxuriance, and from its being surrounded by mountains on three sides, has
been termed the "golden shell," *conca d' oro*. (*Map* No. VIII.)

1. *Ætʹ na*, first called *Inessus*, was a small town on the southern declivity of Mount Ætʹ na,
near Catʹ ana. The ancient site, now marked with ruins, bears the name *Castro*. (*Map* No.
VIII.)

2. *Kamarína* was on the southern coast, about fifty miles south-west from Syracuse and
twenty miles south-east from Géla.

Sicily, and the subsequent period of more than fifty years, to the time of the elder Dionysius, has been described as by far the best and happiest portion of Sicilian history.

18. At the time of the breaking out of the Peloponnésian war, 431 B. C., Syracuse was the foremost of the Sicilian cities in power and res)urces. Agrigen' tum was but little inferior to her, while in her foreign commerce and her public monuments the latter was not sur-passed by any Grecian city of that age. In the great Peloponnésian struggle, the Ion' ic cities of Sicily, few in number, very naturally sympathized with Athens, and the Dórian cities with Sparta; and in the fifth year of the war we find the Ion' ic cities soliciting Athens for aid against Syracuse and her allies. Successive expeditions were sent out by Athens, and soon nearly all Sicily was involved in the war, when at length, in 424 B. C., a congress of the Sicilian cities decided upon a general peace among themselves, to the great dissat isfaction of the Athenians, who were already anticipating important conquests on the island.

19. A few years later, (417 B. C.,) a quarrel broke out between the neighboring Sicilian cities Selínus and Eges' ta,[1] the latter of which, although not of Grecian origin, had formerly been in alliance with Athens. Selínus was aided by the Syracusans; and Eges' ta applied to Athens for assistance, making false representations of her own resources, and enlarging upon the dangers to be apprehended from Syracusan aggrandizement as a source of strength to Sparta. The Athenian Nic' ias, most earnestly opposed any farther interven tion in Sicilian affairs; but the counsels of Alcibíades prevailed, and in the summer of 415 B. C., the largest armament that had ever left a Grecian port sailed on the most distant enterprize that Athens had ever undertaken, under the command of three generals, Nic' ias Lam' achus, and Alcibíades; but the latter was recalled soon after the fleet had reached Cat' ana,[2] on the eastern coast of the island.

---

1. *Selinus* was a flourishing city of more than thirty thousand inhabitants, on the southern shore of the western part of the island. Its ruins may still be seen near what is called *Terra di Pollace*. *Eges' ta*, called by the Romans Segesta, was on the northern coast, near the modern *Alcamo*. Selinus and Eges' ta were engaged in almost continual wars with each other. After the Athenian expedition the Egestans called to their assistance the Carthaginians, who took, plundered, and nearly destroyed Selinus; but Eges' ta, under Carthaginian rule, experienced a fate but little better. (*Map No. VIII.*)

2. *Cat' ana*, now *Catánia* was at the southern base of Mount Æt' na, thirty-two miles north from Syracuse. The distance from the city to the summit of the mountain was thirty miles. Catánia has been repeatedly destroyed by earthquakes, and by torrents of liquid fire from the neighboring volcano; but it has risen like the fabled phœnix, more splendid from its ashes.

20. From Cat'ana Nic'ias sailed around the northern coast to Eges'ta, whence he marched the land forces back through the island to Cat'ana, having achieved nothing but the acquisition of a few insignificant towns, while the Syracusans improved the time in making preparations to receive the invaders. At length, about the last of October, Nic'ias sailed with his whole force to Syracuse—defeated the Syracusans in the battle which followed—and then went into winter quarters at Nax'os; but in the spring he returned to his former station at Cat'ana, soon after which he commenced a regular siege of Syracuse.

21. In a battle which was fought on the grounds south of the city, towards the river Anápus, Lam'achus was slain, although the Athenians were victorious. Nic'ias continued to push forward his successes, and Syracuse was on the point of surrendering, when the arrival of the Spartan general Gylip'pus at once changed the fortune of war, and the Athenians were soon shut up in their own lines.

22. At the solicitation of Nic'ias a large reënforcement, commanded by the Athenian general Demosthenes, was sent to his assistance in the spring of 413; but at the same time the Spartans reënforced Gylip'pus, and, in addition, sent out a force to ravage At'tica During the summer many battles, both on land and in the harbor of Syracuse, were fought by the opposing forces, in nearly all of which the Syracusans and their allies were victorious; and, in the end, the entire Athenian force in Sicily, numbering at the time not less than forty thousand men, was destroyed. " Never in Grecian history," says Thucyd'ides, " had ruin so complete and sweeping, or victory so glorious and unexpected, been witnessed."

23. Soon after the termination of the contest between the Athenians and Syracusans, the Carthaginians again sought an opportunity of invading the island, and established themselves over its entire western half; but they were ably resisted by Dionysius the Elder, " tyrant of Syracuse," who was proclaimed chief of the republic about 405 B. C.; and it was owing to his exertions that any part of the island was saved from falling into the hands of the enemy It was at length agreed that the river Him'era[1] should form the limit between the Grecian territories on the east and the Carthagi

and is still a beautiful city. The streets are paved with lava; and houses, palaces, churches, and convents, are built of it. Remains of ancient temples, aqueducts, baths, &c., are numerous. The environs are fruitful, and well cultivated. (Map No. VIII.)

1. The river Him'era here mentioned, now the Salso, falls into the Mediterranean on the southern coast, to the west of Céla. (Map No. VIII.)

nian dependencies on the west; but the peace was soon broken by the Carthaginians, who, amid the civil dissensions of the Greeks, sought every opportunity of extending their dominion over the entire island.

24. Subsequently the aspiring power of Carthage was checked by Timóleon, and afterwards by Agath'ocles. The former, a Corinthian by birth, having made himself master of the almost deserted Syracuse, about the year 340 B. C., restored it to some degree of its former glory. He defeated the Carthaginians in a great battle, and established the affairs of government on so firm a basis that the whole of Sicily continued, many years after his death, in unusual quiet and prosperity. Agath'ocles usurped the sovereignty of Syracuse by the murder of several thousand of its principal citizens in the year 317 B. C. He maintained his power twenty-eight years. Having been defeated by the Carthaginians, and being besieged in Syracuse, with a portion of his army he passed over to Africa, where he sustained himself during four years. In the year 306 he concluded a peace with the Carthaginians. He died by poison, 289 B. C., leaving his influence in Sicily and southern Italy to his son-in-law, the famous Pyr'rhus, king of Epírus. After the death of Agath'ocles, the Carthaginians gained a decided ascendancy in Sicily, when the Romans, alarmed by the movements of so powerful a neighbor, and being invited over to the assistance of a portion of the people of Messána, commenced the first Punic war, (265 B. C.,) and after a struggle of twenty-four years made themselves masters of the whole of Sicily, —nearly a hundred years before the reduction of Greece itself to a Roman province.

25. On the northern coast of Africa, within the district of th modern Barca, the important Grecian colony of Cyrenáica[1] was planted by Lacedæmonian settlers from Thera,[2] an island of the Æ'gæn, about the year 630 B. C. Its chief city, Cyréne, was about ten miles from the sea, having a sheltered port called Apollónia, itself a considerable town. Ovei the Libyan tribes between the borders of Egypt and the Great Desert, the Cyreneans exercised an ascendancy similar to that which Carthage possessed over the tribes farther westward. About the year 550 B. C., one of the neighboring Libyan kings, finding the Greeks rapidly encroaching upon his territories, declared himself

1. Cyrenáica, see p. 70.
[a] Thera, now Santorin, belonged to the cluster called the Sporades. (Map No. III.)

subject to Egypt, when a large Egyptian army marched to his assistance, but the Egyptians experienced so complete a defeat that few of them ever returned to their own country. We find that the next Egyptian king, Amásis, married a Cyrenean.

26. Soon after the defeat of the Egyptians, the tyranny of the Cyrenean king, Agesiláus, led to a revolt among his subjects who being joined by some of the neighboring tribes, founded the city of Bar'ca, about seventy miles to the westward of Cyréne. In the war which followed, a great battle was fought with the allies of Bar'ca in which Agesiláus was defeated, and seven thousand of his men were left dead on the field. The successor of Agesiláus was deposed from the kingly office by the people, who, in imitation of the Athenians, then established a republican government, (543 B. C.,) under the direction of Demónax, a wise legislator of Mantinéa. But the son of the deposed monarch, having obtained assistance from the people of Sámos, regained the throne of Cyréne, about the time that the Persian prince Camby'ses conquered Egypt. Both the Cyrenean and the Barcan prince sent their submission to the great conqueror. Soon after this event the Persian satrap of Egypt sent a large force against Bar'ca, which was taken by perfidy, and great numbers of the inhabitants were carried away into Persian slavery.

27. At a later period, Cyréne and Bar'ca fell under the power of the Carthaginians they subsequently formed a dependency of Egypt; and in the year 76 B. C., they were reduced to the condition of a Roman province. Cyréne was the birth-place of the poet Callim'achus ; of Eratos'thenes the geographer, astronomer, and mathematician ; and of Carnéades the sophist. Cyrenean Jews were present at Jerusalem on the day of pentecost : it was Simon, a Cyrenean Jew, whom the soldiers compelled to bear the Saviour's cross ; and Christian Jews of Cyréne were among the first preachers of Christianity to the Greeks of Antioch. (Matthew, xxvii. 32 : Mark xv 21 · Acts ii. 10 : vi. 9 : xi. 20.)

CHAPTER V

ROMAN HISTORY:

FROM THE FOUNDING OF ROME, 753 B. C., TO THE CONQUESTS OF GREECE AND
CARTHAGE, 146 B. C. = 607 YEARS.

SECTION I.

EARLY ITALY: ROME UNDER THE KINGS: ENDING 510 B. C.

ANALYSIS. 1. ITALY—names and extent of.—2. Mountains, and fertile plains.—3. Climate -
4 Principal States and tribes.—5. Our earliest information of Italy. Etruscan civilization
[The Etruscans. The Tiber.]—6. Southern Italy and Sicily colonized by Greeks. The rise of
Rome, between the Etruscans on the one side and the Greeks on the other.—7. Sources and
character of early Roman history.—8. The Roman legends, down to the founding of Alba.-
[Lavin'ium Latium. Alba.]—9. The Roman legends continued, down to the saving of
Rom'ulus and Remus.—10. To the death of Amu'lius.—11. Auguries for selecting the site and
name of a city.—12. The FOUNDING OF ROME   [Description of Ancient and Modern Rome.]—
13. Stratagem of Romulus to procure wives for his followers. [Sabines.]—14. WAR WITH THE
SABINES. Treachery and fate of Tarpéia.--15. Reconciliation and union of the Sabines and
Romans. Death of Tullius. [Laurentines.]—16. The intervening period, to the death of
Rom'ulus. Death of Rom'ulus.

17. Rule of the senators. Election of NUMA, the 2d king. His institutions, and death.
[Jánus.]—18. Reign of TUL'LIUS HOSTIL'IUS, the 3d king, and first dawn of historic truth.—
19. Legend of the Horátii and Curiátii.—20. Tragic death of Horátia. Submission, treachery,
and removal of the Albans. Death of Tul'lius.—21. The reign of AN'CUS MAR'TIUS, the 4th
king. [Ostia.]—22. TARQUIN THE ELDER, the 5th king. His origin. Unanimously called to
the throne. [Tarquin'ii.]—23. His wars. His public works. His death.—24. SER'VIUS
TUL'LIUS, the 6th king. Legends concerning him. Wars, &c.—25. Division of the people
into centuries. Federal union with the Latins. Administration of Justice, &c.—26. Displeasure of the patricians, and murder of Servius.—27. The reign of TARQUIN THE PROUD, the 7th
king. His reign disturbed by dreams and prodigies.—28. The dispute between Sextus, his
brothers, and Collatinus. How settled. [Ardea Collátia.]—29. The story of Lucretia, and
banishment of the Tarquins.

1. ITALY, known in ancient times by the names *Hespéria, Ausónia,
Satur'nia,* and *Œnótria,* comprises the whole of the central peninsula of southern Europe, extending from the Alps in a   I. ITALY
southern direction nearly seven hundred and seventy miles, with a
breadth varying from about three hundred and eighty miles in northern Italy, to less than eighty near its centre.

2. The mountains of Italy are the Alps on its north-western boundary, and the Apennines, which latter pass through the peninsula nearly
in its centre, and send off numerous branches on both sides.   They
are much less rugged than the Alps, and abound in rich forests and

pasture land   But though for the most part mountainous, Italy has
some plains of considerable extent and extraordinary fertility.   Of
these the most extensive, and the richest, is that of Lombardy in the
north, watered by the river Po and its numerous branches, embracing an area of about two hundred and fifty miles in length, with a
breadth varying from fifty to one hundred and twenty miles, and now
containing a vast number of cities.   The next great plain stretches
along the western coast of central Italy about two hundred miles,
from the river Arno in Tuscany, to Terracína, sixty miles south-east
from Rome.   Although this plain was once celebrated for its fertility
and was highly cultivated and populous, it is now comparatively a
desert, a consequence of the prevalence of *malaria*, which infects
these districts to such an extent as to render them at certain portions
of the year all but uninhabitable.   The third great plain (the Apú-
lian) lies along the eastern coast, towards the southern extremity of
the peninsula, and includes the territory occupied by the ancient
Daúnians Peucétians, and Messápians.   A great portion of this plain
has a sandy and thirsty soil, and is occupied mostly as pasture land
in winter.   The plain of *Naples*, on the western coast, is highly fertile, and densely peopled.

3. The climate of Italy is in general delightful, the excessive
heats of summer being moderated by the influence of the mountains
and the surrounding seas, while the cold of winter is hardly ever
extreme.   In the Neapolitan provinces, which lie in the latitude of
central and southern Pennsylvania and New Jersey, snow is rare, and
the finest fruits are found in the valleys throughout the winter.   At
the very southern extremity of Italy, which is in the latitude of
Richmond, Virginia, the thermometer never falls to the freezing
point.   From a variety of circumstances it appears that the climate
of Italy has undergone a considerable change, and that the winters
are now less cold than formerly; although probably the summer-
heat was much the same in ancient times as at present.

4. The principal States of ancient Italy were Cisal'pine Gaul
Etrúria, Um'bria, Picénum, Látium, Campánia, Sam'nium, Apúlia,
Calábria, Lucánia, and Brutiórum A'ger,—the situation of which,
together with the names of the principal tribes that inhabited them,
may be learned from the map of Ancient Italy accompanying this
volume.   (See Maps Nos. VIII. and X.)

5. The earliest reliable information that we possess of Italy represents the country in the possession of numerous independent tribes

many of which, especially those in the southern part of the peninsula, were, like the early Grecians, of Pelas' gic origin. Of these tribes, the Etrúrians or Etrus' cans,[1] inhabiting the western coasts above the Tiber,[2] were the most important; as it appears that, before the founding of Rome, they had attained to a considerable degree of power and civilization ; and two centuries after that event they were masters of the commerce of the western Mediterranean. Many works of art attributed to them still exist, in the walls of cities, in vast dikes to reclaim lands from the sea, and in subterranean tunnels cut through the sides of hills to let off the lakes which had formed in the craters of extinct volcanoes.

6. It appears that during the height of Etrus' can power in Italy, the southern portions of the peninsula, together with Sicily, first began to be colonized by Grecians, who formed settlements at Cúmæ and Neap' olis, as early as the tenth or eleventh century before the Christian era, and at Taren' tum, Crotóna, Nax' os, and Syracuse, in the latter part of the eighth century; and such eventually became the number of the Grecian colonies that all southern Italy, in connection with Sicily, received the name of Magna Grecia. (See p. 115.) But while the old Etrúrian civilization remained nearly stationary, fettered, as in ancient Egypt, by the sway of a sacerdotal caste, whose privileges descended by inheritance,—and while the Greek colonies were dividing and weakening their power by allowing to every city an independent sovereignty of its own, there arose on the western coast, between the Etrus' cans on the one side and the Greeks on the other, the small commonwealth of Rome, whose power ere long eclipsed that of all its rivals, and whose dominion was destined, eventually, to overshadow the world.

1. The *Etrúrians*, or *Etrus' cans*, were the inhabitants of *Etruria*, a celebrated country of Italy, lying to the north and west of the Tiber. They were farther advanced in civilization than any of their European cotemporaries, except the Greeks, but their origin is involved in obscurity, and of their early history little is known, as their writings have long since perished, and their hieroglyphic inscriptions on brass are utterly unintelligible. (*Maps* Nos. VIII. and X.)

2. The river *Tiber*, called by the ancient Latins *Albula*, and by the Greeks *Thymbris*, the most celebrated, though not the largest river of Italy, rises in the Tuscan Apennines, and has a general southerly course about one hundred and thirty miles until it reaches Rome, when it turns south-west, and enters the Mediterranean by two mouths, seventeen miles from Rome, terminating in a marshy pestiferous tract. Its waters have a yellowish hue, being discolored by the mud with which they are loaded. Anciently the Tiber was capable of receiving vessels of considerable burden at Rome, and small boats to within a short distance of its source, but the entrance of the river from the sea, and its subsequent navigation, have become so difficult, that the harbor of Ostia at its mouth has long been relinquished, and *Civita Vecchia* is now the port of Rome, although at the distance of thirty-six miles north, with which it is connected merely by a road. (*Maps* Nos. VIII. an X.)

7. What historians have related of the founding of Rome, and of the first century, at least, of its existence, has been drawn from numerous traditionary legends, known, from their character, to be mostly fabulous, and has therefore no valid claims to authenticity. Still it is proper to relate, as an introduction to what is better known, the story most accredited by the Romans themselves, and contained in their earliest writings, while at the same time we express the opinion that it has little or no foundation in truth.[a]

8. The Roman legends state that, immediately after the fall of Troy, Æneas, a celebrated Trojan warrior, escaping from his devoted country, after seven years of wanderings arrived on the western coast of Italy, where he established a colony of his countrymen, and built the city of Lavin' ium.[1] From Latínus, a king of the country, whom he had slain in battle, and whose subjects he incorporated with his own followers, the united people were called *Latíni* or *Latins*, and their country *Látium*.[2] After the lapse of thirty years, which were occupied mostly in wars with neighboring tribes, the Latins, now increased to thirty hamlets, removed their capital to Alba,[3] a new city which they built on the Alban Mount, and which continued to be the head of the confederate people during three centuries.

9. The old Roman legends go on to state, that, at an uncertain date, Prócas, king of Alba, left two sons at his death, and that Númitor the elder, being weak and spiritless, suffered Amúlius the younger to wrest the government from him, to murder the only son, and to consecrate the daughter of his brother to the service of the temple, in the character of a vestal virgin. But the attempts of Amúlius to remove all claimants of the throne were fruitless, for Syl' via, the daughter of Númitor, became the mother of twin sons

1. *Lavin' ium*, a city of Látium, was about eighteen miles south of Rome. The modern village of *Practica*, about three miles from the coast, is supposed to occupy the site of the ancient city. (*Maps* Nos. VIII. and X.)

2. Ancient *Látium* extended from the Tiber southward along the coast about fifty miles, to the Circæan promontory. It was afterwards extended farther south to the river Liris, and at still later period to the Vulturnus. The early inhabitants of Látium were the *Latins*, (also general term applied to all the inhabitants of Látium,) Rutulians, Hernicians, and Volscians. (*Maps* Nos. VIII. and X.)

3. *Alba* appears to have been about fifteen miles south-east from Rome, on the eastern shore of the Alban lake, and on the western declivity of the Alban Mount. The modern villa of Palazzuolo is supposed to mark the site of the ancient Alban city. (*Map* No. X.)

a. "The Trojan legend is doubtless a home sprung fable, having not the least historical truth nor even the slightest historical importance."—Niebuhr's Rom. Hist., i. p. 107.

"Niebuhr has shown the early history of Rome to be unworthy of credit, and made it impossible for any one to revive the old belief."—Anthon's Clas. Dict.; article Rome.

Rom' ulus and Rémus, by Mars, the god of war.   Amúlius ordered
that the mother and her babes should be drowned in the Tiber ; but
while Syl' via perished, the infants, placed in a cradle of rushes, floated to the shore, where they were found by a she wolf, which carried
them to her den, and nursed them as her own offspring.

10. After awhile the children were discovered by the wife of a
shepherd, who took them to her cottage on the Palatine hill, where
they grew up with her twelve sons,—and being the stoutest and
bravest of the shepherd lads, they became their leaders in every
wild foray, and finally the heads of rival factions—the followers of
Rom' ulus being called Quinctil' ii, and those of Rémus Fábii.   At
length Rémus having been seized and dragged to Alba as a robber,
the secret of the royal parentage of the youths was made known to
Rom' ulus, who armed a band of his comrades and rescued Rémus
from danger.   The brothers then slew the king Amúlius, and the
people of Alba again became subject to Númitor.

11. Rom' ulus and Rémus next obtained permission from their
grandfather to build a city for themselves and their followers on the
banks of the Tiber ; but as they disputed about the location and
name of the city, each desiring to call it after his own name, they
agreed to settle their disputes by auguries.   Each took his station
at midnight on his chosen hill, Rom' ulus on the Pal' atine, and
Rémus on the Av' entine, and there awaited the omens.   Rémus
had the first augury, and saw six vultures flying from north to south ;
but scarcely were the tidings brought to Rom' ulus when a flock of
twelve vultures flew past the latter.   Each claimed the victory, but
the party of Rom' ulus, being the stronger, confirmed the authority
of their leader.

12. Rom' ulus then proceeded to mark out the limits of the city
by cutting a furrow round the foot of the Pal' atine hill, which he
inclosed, on the line thus drawn, with a wall and ditch. II. FOUNDING
But scarcely had the walls begun to rise above the sur- OF ROME.
face, when Rémus, still resenting the wrong he had suffered, insult-
ingly leaped over the puny rampart, and was immediately slain,
either by Rom' ulus or one of his followers.   His death was regarded as an omen that no one should cross the walls but to his destruction.   Soon the slight defences were completed, and a thousand rude
huts marked the beginning of the " eternal city ROME,'" within whose

1. See description of Rome page 582 and Map. No. X.

limits strangers from every land, exiles, and even criminals, and
fugitives from justice, found an asylum.   The date usually assigned
for the founding of the city is the 753d year before the Christian era.

13. But the Romans, as we must now call the dwellers on the
Pal'atine, were without wives; and the neighboring tribes scorn
fully declined intermarriages with this rude and dangerous horde.
After peaceful measures had failed, Rom'ulus resorted to stratagem
He proclaimed a great festival; and the neighboring people, es
pecially the Lat'ins and Sábines,² came in numbers, with their
wives and daughters, to witness the ceremonies; but while they were
intent on the spectacle, the Roman youths rushed in, and forcibly
bore off the maidens, to become wives of the captors.

14. War followed this outrage, and the forces of three Latin
cities, which had taken up arms without concert, were successively
defeated.   At last the Sábine king, Títus Táti·us, brought a power
III. WAR   ful army against Rome, which Rom'ulus was unable to
WITH THE   resist in the open field, and he therefore retreated to
SÁ'BINES.   the city, while he fortified and garrisoned the Capitoline
hill, over against the Pal'atine on the north, intrusting the command
of it to one of his most faithful officers.   But Tarpéia, the daughter
of the commander, dazzled by the golden bracelets of the Sábines,
agreed to open a gate of the fortress to the enemy on condition that
they should give her what they bore on their left arms—meaning
their golden ornaments.   Accordingly the gate was opened, but the
traitress expiated her crimes by her death; for the Sábines overwhelmed her with their shields as they entered, these also being
carried on their left arms.   To this day Roman peasants believe
that in the heart of the Capitoline hill the fair Tarpéia is still sitting,
bound by a spell, and covered with the gold and jewels of the Sábines.

15. The Sábines next tried in vain to storm the city, and Rom'-
ulus made equally fruitless attempts to recover the fortress which he
ad lost.   While both parties thus maintained their positions, the
Sábine women, now reconciled to their lot, and no longer wishing for
revenge, but for a reconciliation between their parents and husbands.
rushed in between the combatants, and by earnest supplications in

1. The territory of the Sábines lay to the north-east of Rome.   At the time when its limits
were most clearly defined it was separated from Látium on the south by the river Anio, from
Etruria by the Tiber, from Umbria by the river Nar, and from Picenum on the east by the
Apennines.   (Maps Nos. VIII. and X.)

duced them to agree to a suspension of hostilities, which terminated
in a treaty of peace. The Sábines and Romans were henceforth to
form one nation, having a common religion, and Rom'ulus and
Tátius were to reign jointly. Not long after, Tátius was slain by
some Laurentines[1] on the occasion of a national sacrifice at Laviu'-
ium, and henceforward Rom'ulus ruled over both nations.

16. At this point in Roman history, remarks Niebuhr, the old
Roman legend, or poetic lay, is suspended until the death of Rom'-
ulus; while the intervening period has been filled by subsequent writers
with accounts of Etrus'can wars, which find no place in the ancient
legend, and which are probably wholly fictitious. Just before the
death of Rom'ulus, who is said to have ruled thirty-seven years, the
poetic lay is resumed. It relates that, while the king was reviewing
his people, the sun withdrew his light, and Mars, descending in a
whirlwind and tempest, bore away his perfected son in a fiery chariot
to heaven, where he became a god, under the name of Quirínus.[a]
(B. C. 716.)

17. The legend further relates that after the death of Rom'ulus,
the chosen senators, or elders of the people, who were also called
patres, or *fathers*, retained the sovereign power in their   IV. NUMA.
hands during a year; but as the people demanded a king, it was
finally agreed that the Romans should choose one from the Sábine
part of the population. The election resulted in the choice of the
wise and pious Núma Pompil'ius, who had married the daughter of
Tátius. After Núma had assured himself by auguries that the
gods approved of his election, his first care was to regulate the laws
of landed property, by securing the hereditary possession of land to
the greatest possible number of citizens, thereby establishing the
most permanent basis of civil order. He then regulated the services of religion, pretending that he received the rituals of the law
from the goddess Egéria : he also built the temple of Jánus;[2] and

1. The *Laurentines* were the people of *Lauren'tum*, the chief city of *Látium*. Lauren'tum
was eighteen miles south from Rome, on the coast, and near the spot now called *Paterno*.
(*Maps* Nos. VIII. and X.)

2. *Jánus* was an ancient Italian deity, whose origin is traced back to India. He was represented sometimes with two faces looking in opposite directions, and sometimes with four. He
was the god of the year, and also of the day, and had charge of the gates of heaven through

a. Niebuhr deals severely with those writers who, in attempting to deduce historic truth
from this poetical fiction, have made the supposition that, instead of an eclipse, there was
tempest, and that the senators themselves tore Rom'ulus to pieces (See Niebuhr, L. 127 &.
also Schmitz' Rome, p. 90.)

after a quiet and prosperous reign of forty-two years he fell asleep full of days and peaceful honors. (673 B. C.) The legend adds that the goddess Egéria, through grief for his loss, melted away in tears into a fountain.

18. The death of Núma was followed by another interregnum after which the young and warlike Tullus Hostilius was chosen king. A gleam of historic truth falls upon his reign, and the purely poetic age of Roman story here begins to disappear in our confidence that such a king as Túllus Hostilius actually existed, and that during his reign the Albans became united with the Romans. Still, the story of the Alban war, and of subsequent wars during the life of Tullus, retain much of legendary fiction, destitute of historic certainty.

V. TULLUS HOSTILIUS.

19. A tradition of the Alban war, preserved by the early poets, relates, that when the armies of Rome and Alba were drawn up against each other, their leaders agreed to avert the battle by a combat between three twin brothers on the one side, and three on the other, whose mothers happened to be sisters, although belonging to different nations. The Roman brothers were called Horátii, and the Albans Curiátii. Meeting in deadly encounter between the two armies, two of the Horátii fell, but the third, still unwounded, resorted to stratagem, and, pretending to flee, was followed at unequal distances by the wounded Curiátii, when, suddenly turning back, he overcame them in succession.

20. A mournful tragedy followed. At the gate of the city the victor was met by his sister Horátia, who, having been affianced to one of the Curiátii, and now seeing her brother exultingly bearing off the spoils of the slain, and, among the rest, the embroidered cloak of her betrothed, which she herself had woven, gave way to a burst of grief and lamentation, which so incensed her brother that he slew her on the spot. For this act he was condemned to death, but was pardoned by the interference of the people, although they ordered a monument to be raised on the spot where Horátia fell. By the terms of an agreement made before the combat the Albans were to submit to the Romans; but not long after this event they showed evidence of treachery, when, by order of Tullus, their city

which the sun passes; and hence all gates and doors on earth were sacred to him. January the first month in the religious year of the Romans, was named after him. His temples at Rome were numerous, and in time of war the gates of the principal one were open, but in time of peace they were closed to keep wars within.

was levelled to the ground, and the people were removed to the Cælian hill, adjoining the Pal' atine on the east. After a reign of thirty-two years, Tullus and all his family are said to have been killed by lightning. (642 B. C.)

21. We find the name of Ancus Martius, said to have been a grandson of Núma, next on the list of Roman kings. He is rep resented both as a warrior, and a restorer of the ordi- VI. ANCUS nances and rituals of the ceremonial law, which had fallen MARTIUS. into disuse during the reign of his predecessor. He subdued many of the Latin towns—founded the town and port of Ostia'—built the first bridge over the Tiber—and established that principle of the Roman common law, that the State is the original proprietor of all lands in the commonwealth. The middle of his reign is said to have been the era of the legal constitution of the plebeian order, and the assignment of lands to this body out of the conquered territories. He is said to have reigned twenty-four years.

22. The fourth king of Rome was Tarquinius Priscus, or Tarquin the Elder. The accounts of his reign are obscure and conflicting. By some his parents are said to have fled from Corinth to Tarquin' ii,[2] a town of Etruria, where Tarquin was born: by others VII. TARQUIN he is said to have been of Etruscan descent; but Niebuhr THE ELDER. believes him to have been of Latin origin. Having taken up his residence at Rome at the suggestion of his wife Tanaquil, who was celebrated for her skill in auguries, he there became distinguished for his courage, and the splendor in which he lived; and his liberality and wisdom so gained him the favor of the people that, when the throne became vacant, he was called to it by the unanimous voice of the senate and citizens. (617 B. C.)

23. Tarquin is said to have carried on successful wars against the Etrus' cans, Latins, and Sábines, and to have reduced all those people under the Roman dominion; but his reign is chiefly memorable on account of the public works which he commenced for the security and improvement of the city. Among these were the embanking of

1. Os' tia, the early port and harbor of Rome, once a place of great wealth, population, and importance, was situated on the east side of the Tiber, near its mouth, fifteen miles from Rome. Os' tia, which still retains its ancient name, is now a miserable village of scarcely a hundred inhabitants, and is almost uninhabitable, from Malaria; the fever which it engenders carrying off annually nearly all whom necessity confines to this pestilential region during the hot season. The harbor of Os' tia is now merely a shallow pool. (Maps Nos. VIII. and X.)

2. Tarquin' ii, one of the most powerful cities of Etruria, was about forty miles north-west from Rome, on the left bank of the river Marta, several miles from its mouth. The ruins of Tur Aina mark the site of the ancient city. (Maps Nos. VII. and X.)

the Tiber; the sewers, which yet remain, for draining the marshes and lakes in the vicinity of the capital; the porticos around the market-place, the race-course of the circus, and the foundations of the city wa'ls, which were of hewn stone. It is said that Tarquin, after a reign of thirty-eight years, was assassinated at the instigation of the sons of Ancus Martius, who feared that he would secure the succession to his son-in-law Servius Tullius, his own favorite, and the darling of the Roman people. (579 B. C.)

24. Notwithstanding the efforts of the sons of Ancus Martius, the senate and the people decided that Servius should rule over them. The birth of this man is said, in the old legends, to have been very humble, and his infancy to have been attended   VIII. SERVIUS TULLIUS. with marvellous omens, which foretold his future greatness. Of his supposed wars with the revolted Etrus'cans nothing certain is known; but his renown as a law-giver rests on more substantial grounds than his military fame.

25. The first great political act of his reign was the institution of the census, and the division of the people into one hundred and ninety-three *centuries*, whose rights of suffrage and military duties were regulated on the basis of property qualifications. The several Latin communities that had hitherto been allied with the Romans by treaty he now incorporated with them by a federal union; and to render that union more firm and lasting, he induced the confederates to unite in erecting a temple on Mount Aventine to the goddess Diana, and there unitedly to celebrate her worship. He also made wise regulations for the impartial administration of justice, prohibited bondage for debt, and relieved the people from the oppressions with which they already began to be harassed by the higher orders.

26. His legislation was received with displeasure by the patricians; and when it was known that Servius thought of resigning the crown, and establishing a consular form of government, which would have rendered a change of his laws difficult, a conspiracy was formed for securing the throne to Tarquinius, surnamed the Proud, a son of the former king, who had married a daughter of Servius. The old king Servius was murdered by the agents of Tarquin, and his body left exposed in the street, while his wicked daughter Tullia, in her haste to congratulate her husband on his success, drove her chariot over her father's corpse, so that her garments were stained with his blood. (535 B. C.)

27 The reign of Tarquinius Superbus, or the Proud, was distin

guished by a series of tyrannical usurpations, which made his name
odious to all classes; for although he at first gratified his supporters
by diminishing the privileges of the plebeians, or the IX. TARQUIN
common people, he soon made the patricians themselves THE PROUD.
feel the weight of his tyranny. The laws of Servius were swept
away—the equality of civil rights abolished—and even the ordinances
of religion suffered to fall into neglect. But although Tarquin was
tyrant, he exalted the Roman name by his successful wars, and
alliances with the surrounding nations. In the midst of his successes,
however, he was disturbed by the most fearful dreams and appalling
prodigies. He dreamed that the sun changed its course, rising in
the west; and that when the two rams were brought to him for sacrifice, one of them pushed him down with its horns. At one time a
serpent crawled from the altar and seized the flesh which he had
brought for sacrifice : a flock of vultures attacked an eagle's nest in
his garden, threw out the unfledged eaglets upon the ground and
drove the old birds away ; and when he sent to Delphi to consult the
oracle, the responses were dark and fearful.

28. The reverses threatened were brought upon him by the wickedness of Sextus, one of his sons. It is related that while the Romans were besieging Ardea,[1] a Rutulian city, Sextus, with his
brothers Titus and Aruns, and their cousin Collatínus, happened to
be disputing, over their wine, about the good qualities of their wives
when, to settle the dispute, they agreed to visit their homes by surprise, and, seeing with their own eyes how their wives were then employed, thus decide which was the worthiest lady. So they hastily
rode, first to Rome, where they found the wives of the three Tarquins feasting and making merry. They then proceeded to Collátia,[2]
the residence of Collatínus, where, although it was then late at night,
they found his wife Lucretia, with her maids around her, all busy
working at the loom. On their return to the camp all agreed that
Lucretia was the worthiest lady.

29. But a spirit of wicked passion had seized upon Sextus, and a
few days later he went alone to Collátia, and being hospitably lodged
in his kinsman's house, violated the honor of Lucretia. Thereupon

1. *Ardea*, a city of Látium, and the capital of the Rutulians, was about twenty-four miles
south from Rome, and three miles from the sea. Some ruins of the ancient city are still visible,
and bear the name of Ardea. (*Maps* Nos. VIII. and X.)

2. *Collátia*, a town of Látium, was near the south bank of the river Anio, twelve or thirteen
miles east from Rome. Its ruins may still be traced on a hill which has obtained the name of
Castellacio. (*Maps* Nos. VIII. and X.)

she sent in haste for her father, and husband, and other relatives, and having told them of the wicked deed of Sextus, and made them swear that they would avenge it, she drew a knife from her bosom and stabbed herself to the heart. The vow was renewed over the dead body, and Lucius Junius Brutus, who had long concealed patriotic resolutions under the mask of pretended stupidity, and thus saved his life from the jealousy of Tarquin, exhibited the corpse to the people, whom he influenced, by his eloquence, to pronounce sentence of banishment against Tarquin and his family, and to declare that the dignity of king should be abolished forever. (510 B. C.)

SECTION II.

THE ROMAN REPUBLIC, FROM THE ABOLITION OF ROYALTY, 510 B.C.,

TO THE BEGINNING OF THE WARS WITH CARTHAGE:

263 B. C. = 247 YEARS.

ANALYSIS. 1. Royalty abolished. The laws of Servius reëstablished. CONSULS elected.— 2. Aristocratic character of the government. The struggle between the patricians and plebeians begins.—3. Extent of Roman territory.—4. Conspiracy in favor of the Tarquins. ETRUS'-CAN WAR.—5. Conflicting accounts. Legend of the Etrus'can war. [Clusium.]—6. The story of Mutius Scæv'ola.—7. Further account of the Roman legend. The probable truth.—8. Humiliating condition of the plebeians after the Etrus can war.—9. Continued contentions. The office of DICTATOR.—10. Circumstances of the first PLEBEIAN INSURRECTION. [Volscians.]—11. Confusion. Withdrawal of the Plebeians. [Mons Sacer.]—12. The terms of reconciliation. Office and power of the TRIBUNES.—13. League with the Latins and Hernicians.—14. VOLSCIAN AND ÆQUIAN WARS. Contradictory statements. [Æquians. Corioli.] Proposal of Coriolánus.—15. His trial—exile—and war against the Romans.—16. The story of Cincinátus.— 17. The public lands—and the fate of Spurius Cassius.—18. Continued demands of the people. Election and office of THE DECEM'VIRS.—19. The laws of the decem'virs.—20. The decem'-virs are continued in office—their additional laws—and tyranny.—21. The story of Virginia.— 22. Overthrow of the decem'virs, and death of Appius.—23. Plebeian innovations. The office of CENSORS.—24. Rome, as viewed by the surrounding people. Circumstances that led to the WAR WITH VEII. [Situation of Veii.]—25. Destruction of Veii, and extension of Roman territory.

26. GALLIC INVASION. Circumstances of the introduction of the Gauls into Italy. [Cisalpine Gaul.]—27 The Roman ambassadors. Conduct of Brennus.—28. The Romans defeated by the Gauls. General abandonment of Rome. [The Allia. Roman Forum.]—29. Entrance of the Gauls into the city. Massacre of the Senators. Rome plundered and burned.—30 Vain attempts to storm the citadel. The Roman legend of the expulsion of the Gauls. The more probable account. [The Venetians.]—31. The rebuilding of Rome.—32. Renewal of the PLEBEIAN AND PATRICIAN CONTESTS. Philanthropy and subsequent history of Manlius.—33. Continued oppression of the plebeians.—34. Great reforms made by Licinius Stolo and Lucius Sextus. The office of PRÆTOR.—35. Progress of the Roman power. The Samnite confederacy [The Samnites.]—36. FIRST SAMNITE WAR. [Cap'ua.] League with the Samnites. Latin war.—37 SECOND SAMNITE WAR.—Defeat of the Romans, and renewed alliance. [Caudine

1. As narrated at the close of the previous section, royalty was abolished at Rome, after an existence of two hundred and forty years. The whole Roman people took an oath that whoever should express a wish to rule as king should be declared an outlaw. The laws of Servius were reëstablished, and, according to the code which he had proposed, the royal power was intrusted to two consuls,[a] annually elected. The first chosen were Butus and Collatínus.

I. CONSULS

2. From the expulsion of the Tarquins, and the downfall of mon· archy, is dated the commencement of what is called the *Roman Republic.* Yet the government was at this time entirely aristo- cratical; for all political power was in the hands of the nobility, from whom the consuls were chosen, and there was no third party to hold the balance of power between them and the people. Hence arose a struggle between these two divisions of the body politic; and it was not until the balance was properly adjusted by the in· creased privileges of the plebeians, and a more equal distribution of power, that the commonwealth attained that strength and influence which preëminently exalted Rome above the surrounding nations.

3. The territory possessed by Rome under the last of the kings is known, from a treaty made with Carthage in the first year of the Republic, to have extended at least seventy miles along the coast south of the Tiber. Yet all this sea-coast was destined to be lost to Rome by civil dissensions and bad government, before her power was to be firmly established there.

---

a The *consuls* had at first nearly the same power as the kings; and all other magistrates were subject to them, except the tribunes of the people. They summoned the meetings of the senate and of the assemblies of the people—they had the chief direction of the foreign affairs of the government—they levied soldiers, appointed most of the military officers, and, in time of war had supreme command of the armies. In dangerous conjunctures they were armed with absolute power by a decree of the senate that "they should take care that the republic receives no harm." Their badges of office were the *toga prætexta,* or mantle bordered with purple, and an ivory sceptre; and when they appeared in public they were accompanied by twelve officers called *lictors,* each of whom carried a bundle of rods, (*fas'ces,*) with an axe (*securis*) placed in the middle of them;—the former denoting the power of scourging, or of ordinary punishment—and the latter, the power of life and death.

4. The efforts of Tarquin to recover the throne gave rise to a con
spiracy among some of the younger patricians who had shared in
the tyrant's extortions. Among the conspirators were the sons of
Brutus; and the duty of pronouncing their fate devolved upon the
consul their father, who, laying aside parental affection, and acting
the part of the magistrate only, condemned them to death. The
II. ETRUS' CAN cause of the Tarquins was also espoused by the Etrus'-
WAR.   cans, to whom they had fled for protection, and thus a war
was kindled between the two people.

5. The accounts of the events and results of this war are exceed
ingly conflicting. The ancient Roman legend relates that when
Porsenna, king of Clusium,[1] the most powerful of the Etrus'can
princes, led an overwhelming force against Rome, the Romans were
at first repulsed, and fled across a wooden bridge over the Tiber;
and that the army was saved by the valor of Horatius Cócles, who
alone defended the pass against thousands of the enemy, until the
bridge was broken down in the rear, when he plunged into the stream,
and, amid a shower of darts, safely regained the opposite shore.

6. It is farther related, that when Porsenna had reduced Rome
to extremities by famine, a young man, Mutius Scæv' ola, undertook,
with the approbation of the Senate, to assassinate the invading king.
Making his way into the Etrus' can camp, he slew one of the king's
attendants, whom he mistook for Porsenna. Being disarmed, and
threatened with torture, he scornfully thrust his right hand into the
flame, where he held it until it was consumed, to show that the rack
had no terrors for him. The king, admiring such heroism, gave him
his life and liberty, when Scæv' ola warned him, as a token of gratitude, to make peace, for that three hundred young patricians, as brave
as himself, had conspired to destroy him, and that he, Scæv' ola, had
only been chosen by lot to make the first attempt.

7. The Roman legend asserts that Porsenna, alarmed for his life,
offered terms of peace, which were agreed upon. And yet it is known,
from other evidence, that the Romans, about this time, surrendered
their city, and became tributary to the Etrus' cans; and it is probable that when, soon after, Porsenna was defeated in a war with the
Latins, the Romans embraced the opportunity to regain their independence.

8. It was only while the attempts of the Tarquins to regain the

1. Clusium, now Chiusi, was a town of Etruria, situated on the western bank of the river
Clanis, a tributary of the Tiber, about eighty-five miles north-west from Rome. (Map No. VIII.)

throne excited alarm, and the Etrus'can war continued, that the government under the first consuls was administered with justice and
moderation.   When these dangers were over, the patricians again
began to exert their tyranny over the plebeians, and as nearly all
the wealth of the State had been engrossed by the former, the latter
were reduced to a condition differing little from the most abject
slavery.   A decree against a plebeian debtor made not only him,
but his children also, slaves to the creditor, who might imprison,
scourge or otherwise maltreat them.

9. The contentions between the patricians and plebeians were at
length carried to such an extent, that in time of war the latter refused to enlist; and as the consuls, for some cause now unknown
could not be confided in, the plebeians were induced to consent tc
the creation of a *dictator*, who, during six months, had III. OFFICE OF
supreme power, not only over patricians, plebeians, and DICTATOR.
consuls, but also over the laws themselves.   Under a former law of
Valerius the people had the right of appeal from a sentence of the
consul to a general assembly of the citizens; but from the decision
of the dictator there was no appeal, and as he was appointed by the
Senate, this office gave additional power to the patrician order.[a]

10. During a number of years dictators continued to be appointed
in times of great public danger; but they gave only a temporary
calm to the popular dissensions.   It was during a war with the Volscians[1] and Sabines that the long-accumulating resentment of the
plebeians against the patricians first broke forth in open IV. PLEBEIAN
insurrection.   An old man, haggard and in rags, pale INSURRECTION
and famishing, escaping from his creditor's prison, and bearing the
marks of cruel treatment, implored the aid of the people.   A crowd
gathered around him.   He showed them the scars that he had received in war, and he was recognized as a brave captain who had
fought for his country in eight and twenty battles.   His house and
farm-yard having been plundered by the enemy in the Etrus'can war

1. The *Volscians* were the most southern of the tribes that inhabited Latium. Their territory extending along the coast southward from Antium about fifty miles, swarmed with cities
 and with a hardy and warlike race.   (*Maps* Nos. VIII. and X.)

a. The office of *dictator* had existed at Alba and other Latin towns long before this time.
The authority of all the other magistrates, except that of the tribunes, (see p. 138,) ceased as
soon as the dictator was appointed. He had the power of life and death, except perhaps in the case of knights and senators, and from his decision there was no appeal; but for
any abuse of his power he might be called to account after his resignation or the expiration of
his term of office. At first the dictator was taken from the patrician ranks only; but about the
year 356 B. C. it was opened to C. Marcius to the plebeians also. See Niebuhr's Rome, i 270

famine had first compelled him to sell his all, and then to borrow;
and when he could not pay, his creditors had obtained judgment
against him and his two sons, and had put them in chains. (495
B C.)

11. Confusion and uproar spread through the city. All who had
been pledged for debt were clamorous for relief; the people spurned
the summons to enlist in the legions; compulsion was impossible,
and the Senate knew not how to act. At length the promises of the
consuls appeased the tumult; but finally the plebeians, after having
been repeatedly deceived, deserted their officers in the very midst
of war, and marched in a body to Mons Sacer,[1] or the Sacred Mount
within three miles of Rome, where they were joined by a vast mul
titude of their discontented brethren. (493 B. C.)

12. After much negotiation, a reconciliation was finally effected
on the terms that all contracts of insolvent debtors should be can
celled; that those who had incurred slavery for debt should recover
their freedom; that the Valerian law should be enforced, and that
two annual magistrates, (afterwards increased to five,) called *trib*

V. TRIBUNES   *unes*,[a] whose persons were to be inviolable, should be
OF THE   chosen by the people to watch over their rights, and pre-
PEOPLE.   vent any abuses of authority. It will be seen that the
power of the tribunes, so humble in its origin, eventually acquired a
preponderating influence in the State, and laid the foundation of
monarchical supremacy.[b]

13. During the same year that the office of the tribunes was
created, a perpetual league was made with the Latins, (493 B. C.)
and seven years later with the Hernicians, who inhabited the north-
eastern parts of Látium, both on terms of perfect equality in the
contracting parties, and not, as before, on the basis of Roman supe-

---

1. The *Mons Sacer*, or "Sacred Mountain," is a low range of sandstone hills extending
along the right bank of the Anio, near its confluence with the Tiber, about three miles from
Roma. (*Maps* Nos. VIII. and X.)

a. The *tribunes of the people* wore no external marks of distinction; but an officer called
srator attended them, to clear the way and summon people. Their chief power at first consisted in preventing, or arresting, by the word *veto*, "I forbid," any measure which they
thought detrimental to the interests of the people.

b. After the plebeians had withdrawn to the "Sacred Mount," the Senate despatched an
embassy of ten men, headed by Menenius Agrippa, to treat with the insurgents. Agrippa is
said, on this occasion, to have related to the people the since well-known fable of the Belly and
the Members. The latter, provoked at seeing all the fruits of their toil and care applied to
the use of the belly, refused to perform any more labor; in consequence of which the whole
body was in danger of perishing. The people understood the moral of the fable, and were
ready to enter upon a negotiation.

riority. These leagues made with cities that were once subject to
the Romans, show that the Roman power had been greatly dimin
ished by the plebeian and aristocratic contentions in the early years
of the Republic.

14. In the interval between these treaties, occurred important
wars with the Volscians and Æquians.[1] The historical VI. VOLSCIAN
contradictions of this period are so numerous, that little AND ÆQUI-
reliance can be placed on the details of these wars; but AN WARS.
it is evident that the Volscians and Æquians were defeated, and tha
Caius Marcius, a Roman nobleman, acquired the surname of Coriolánus from his bravery at the capture of the Volscian town of Corioli'
and that Lucius Quinctius, called Cincinnátus, acquired great distinction by his conduct of the war against the Æquians. Coriolánus
belonged to the patrician order, and was an enemy of the tribunes;
and it is related that when, during a famine, a Sicilian prince sent a
large supply of corn to relieve the distresses of the citizens, Coriolánus proposed in the Senate that the plebeians should not share in
the subsidy until they had surrendered the privileges which they had
acquired by their recent secession.

15 The rage of the plebeians was excited by this proposition, and
they would have proceeded to violence against Coriolánus, had not
the tribunes summoned him to trial before the assembly of the peo
ple. The senators made the greatest efforts to save him, but the
commons condemned him to exile. Enraged by this treatment, he
went over to the Volscians—was appointed a general in their armies
—and, after defeating the Romans in several engagements, laid siege
to the city, which must have surrendered had not a deputation of
Roman matrons, headed by the wife and the mother of Coriolánus,
prevailed upon him to grant his countrymen terms of peace. It is
said that on his return to the Volscians he lost his life in a popular
tumult; but a tradition relates that he lived to a very advanced age,
and that he was often heard to exclaim, "How miserable is the con
dition of an old man in banishment."

16. It is related that during the war with the Æquians the enemy
had surrounded the Roman consul in a defile, where there was neither
forage for the horses nor food for the men. In this extremity, the

1. The *Æquians* dwelt principally in the upper valley of the Anio, north of that stream, and
between the Sabines and the Marsi. (*Maps* Nos. VIII. and X.)

2. *Corioli* is supposed to have been about twenty-two or twenty-three miles south-east from
Rome. A hill now known by the name of *Monte Giove*, is thought, with some degree of prob
ability, to represent the site of this ancient Volscian city. (*Map* No. X.)

Senate and people chose Cincinnátus dictator, and sending in haste to inform him of his election, the deputies found him at work in his field, dressed in the plain habit of a Roman farmer. After he had put on his toga, or cloak, that he might receive the message of the Senate in a becoming manner, he was saluted as dictator, and con-ducted into the city. He soon raised an army, surrounded the enemy, and took their whole force prisoners, and at the end of sixteen days, having accomplished the deliverance of his country, resigned his power, and returned to the peaceful pursuits of private life.[a]

17. The first acquisitions of territory made by the Romans appear to have been divided among the people at large ; but of late the con quered lands had been suffered to pass, by connivance, occupation, or purchase, chiefly into the hands of the patricians. The complaints of the plebeians on this subject at length induced one of the consuls, Spurius Cassius, to propose a division of recently-conquered lands into small estates, for the poorer classes, who, he maintained, were justly entitled to their proportionate share, as their valor and labors had helped to acquire them. But while this proposition alarmed the Senate and patricians with danger to their property, the motives of Cassius appear to have been distrusted by all classes, for he was charged with aiming at kingly power, and, being convicted, was ig-nominiously beheaded, and his house razed to the ground. (458 B. C.)

18. Still the people continued to demand a share in the conquered lands, now forming the estates of the wealthy, and, as the only way of evading the difficulty, the Senate kept the nation almost constantly involved in war. During thirty years succeeding the death of Cas sius, the history of the Republic is occupied with desultory wars waged against the Æquians and Volscians, and with continued strug-gles between the patricians and plebeians. At length the tribunes succeeded in getting their number increased from five to ten, when the Senate, despairing of being able to divert the people any longer from their purpose, consented to the appointment of ten persons, VII. THE hence called *decem' virs*, who were to compile a body of DECEMVIRS. laws for the commonwealth, and to exercise all the pow ers of government until the laws should be completed. (451 B. C.)

19. After several months' deliberation, this body produced a code

a. It should be remarked here, that the story of Cincinnátus formed the subject of a beauti-ful poem, to the substance of which most writers have given the credit of historical authen-ticity, although Niebuhr has shown that the truth of the legend will not stand the test of criticism. (See Niebuhr, vol. ii. pp. 125–6. and Arnold's Rome, i. pp. 131–5. and notes.)

of laws, engraven on ten tables, which continued, down to the time of the emperors, to be the basis of the civil and penal jurisprudence of the Roman people, though almost concealed from view under the enormous mass of additions piled upon it. The new constitution aimed at establishing the legal equality of all the citizens, and there was a show of dividing the great offices of State equally between patricians and plebeians, but the exact character of the ten tables cannot now be satisfactorily distinguished from two others that were subsequently enacted.

20. After the task of the decemvirs had been completed, all classes united in continuing their office for another year; and an equal number of patricians and plebeians was elected; but the former appear to have sought seats in the government for the purpose of overthrowing the constitution. The decemvirs now threw off the mask, and enacted two additional tables of laws, by which the plebeians were greatly oppressed, for, among the laws attributed to the *twelve* tables, we find that although all classes were liable to imprisonment for debt, yet the pledging of the person affected plebeians only,—that the latter were excluded from the enjoyment of the public lands,—that their intermarriage with patricians was prohibited,—and that consuls could be elected from the patrician order only. Moreover, the decemvirs now refused to lay down the powers of government which had been temporarily granted them, and, secretly supported by the patricians, ruled without control, thus establishing a tyrannical oligarchy.

21. At length a private injury accomplished what wrongs of a more public nature had failed to effect. Appius Claudius, a leading decemvir, had fallen in love with the beautiful Virginia, daughter of Virginius, a patrician officer; but finding her betrothed to another, in order to accomplish his purpose he procured a base dependant to claim her as his slave. As had been concerted, Virginia was brought before the tribunal of Appius himself, who, by an iniquitous decision, ordered her to be surrendered to the claimant. It was then that the distracted father, having no other means of preserving his daughter's honor, stabbed her to the heart in the presence of the court and the assembled people. (448 B. C.)

22 A general indignation against the decemvirs spread through the city; the army took part with the people; the power of the decemvirs was overthrown; and the ancient forms of government were restored; while additional rights were conceded to the commons, by

giving to their votes, in certain cases, the authority of law. Appius, having been impeached, died in prison, probably by his own hand before the day appointed for his trial.

23. Other plebeian innovations followed. After a difficult struggle the marriage law was repealed, (B. C. 445,) and two years later military tribunes, with consular powers, were chosen from the plebeian ranks. One important duty of the consuls had been the taking of the census once in every five years, and a new distribution of the people, at such times, among the different classes or ranks, according to their property, character, and families. But the patricians, unwilling that this power should devolve upon the plebeians, stipulated that these duties of the consular office should be disjoined from the military tribuneship, and conferred upon two new officers of patrician VIII. OFFICE birth, who were denominated *censors;*[a] and thus the OF CENSORS. long-continued efforts of the people to obtain, from their own number, the election of officers with full consular powers, were defeated

24. But while dissensions continued to mark the domestic councils of the Romans with the appearance of divided strength and wasted energies, the state of affairs presented a different aspect to the surrounding people. They saw in Rome only a nation of warriors that had already recovered the strength it had lost by a revolutionary change of government, and that was now marching on to increased dominion without any signs of weakness in the foreign wars it had to maintain. Véii,[1] the wealthiest and most important of the Etruscan cities, had long been a check to the progress of the Romans north of the Tiber, and had often sought occasion to provoke hostilities with IX. WAR the young republic. At length the chief of the people WITH VÉII of Véii put to death the Roman ambassadors; and the Roman Senate, being refused satisfaction for the outrage, formally resolved that Véii should be destroyed.

25. The Etruscan armies that marched to the relief of Véii were

---

1. *Véii,* numerous remains of which still exist, was about twelve miles north from Rome, a place now known by the name of *l'Insola Farnese.* (*Maps* Nos. VIII. and X.)

a. An important duty of the *censors* was that of inspecting the morals of the people. They had the power of inflicting various marks of disgrace upon those who deserved it,—such as excluding a senator from the senate-house—depriving a knight of his public horse if he did not take proper care of it;—and of punishing, in various ways, those who did not cultivate their grounds properly—those who lived too long unmarried—and those who were of dissolute morals. They had charge, also, of the public works, and of letting out the public lands. The office of censor was esteemed highly honorable. In allusion to the severity with which Cato the Elder discharged its duties, he is commonly styled, at the present day "Cato the Censor."

repeatedly defeated by the Roman legions, and the people of Véii were finally compelled to shut themselves up in their city, which was taken by the Roman dictator, Camillus, after a blockade and siege of nearly ten years. (396 B. C.)   The spoil taken from the con·· quered city was given to the army, the captives were sold for the benefit of the State, and the ornaments and images of the gods were transferred to Rome.   The conquerors also wreaked their vengeance on the towns which had aided Véii in the war, and the Roman territory was extended farther north of the Tiber than at any previous period.

26. But while the Romans were enjoying the imaginary security which these successful wars had given them, they were suddenly assailed by a new enemy, which threatened the extinction of the Roman name.   During the recent Etruscan wars, a vast horde of barbarians of the Gallic or Celtic race had crossed the Alps   x. GALLIC from the unknown regions of the north, and had sat down   INVASION. in the plains of Northern Italy, in the country known as Cisalpine Gaul.[1]   Tradition relates that an injured citizen of Clusium, an Etruscan city, went over the mountains to these Gauls, taking with him a quantity of the fruits and wines of Italy, and promised these rude people that if they would leave their own inhospitable country and follow him, the land which produced all these good things should be theirs, for it was inhabited by an unwarlike race; whereupon the whole Gallic people, with their women and children, crossed the Alps, and marched direct to Clusium. (391 B. C.)

27. Certain it is that the people of Clusium sought aid from the Romans, who sent three of the nobility to remonstrate with the Brennus, or chieftain of the Gauls, but as the latter treated them with derision, they forgot their sacred character as ambassadors, and joined the Clusians in a sally against the besiegers.   Immediately Brennus ordered a retreat, that he might not be guilty of shedding the blood of ambassadors, and forthwith demanded satisfaction of the Roman senate; and when this was refused he broke up his camp before Clusium and took up his march for Rome at the head of seventy thousand of his people.

28. Eleven miles from the city, on the banks of the Al' ia,[2] a battle

---

1. *Cisalpine Gav'*, meaning " Gaul this side of the Alps," to distinguish it from ' Gaul beyond the Alps," embraced all that portion of Northern Italy that was watered by the river Po and its numerous tributaries, extending south on the Adriatic coast to the river Rubicon, and on the Tuscan coast to the river Macra. (*Map* No. IX.)

2. The *Al' ia*, now the *Aia*, was a small stream that flowed into the Tiber from the east, about ten miles north-east from Rome. (*Map* No. X.)

was fought, and the Romans, forty thousand in number, were defeat ed. (390 B. C.) Brennus meditated a sudden march to Rome to consummate his victory, but his troops, abandoning themselves to pillage, rioting, and drunkenness, refused to obey the voice of their leader, and thus, the attack being delayed, the existence of the Roman nation was saved. The defeat on the Al'ia had rendered it impossible to defend the city, but a thousand armed Romans took possession of the capitol and the citadel, and laying in a store of provisions determined to maintain their post to the last extremity, while the mass of the population sought refuge in the neighboring towns, bearing with them their riches, and the principal objects of their religious veneration. But while the rest of the people quitted their homes, eighty priests and patricians of the highest rank, deeming it intolerable to survive the republic and the worship of the gods, sat down in the Forum,[1] in their festal robes, awaiting death.

29. Onward came the Gauls in battle array, with horns and trumpets blowing, but finding the walls deserted, they burst open the gates and entered the city, which they found desolate and death-like. They marched cautiously on till they came to the Forum, where, in solemn stillness, sat the aged priests, and chiefs of the senate, looking like beings of another world. The wild barbarians, seized with awe at such a spectacle, doubted whether the gods had not come down to save the city or to avenge it. At length a Gaul went up to one of the priests and gently stroked his white beard, but the old man indignantly repelled the insolence by a stroke of his ivory sceptre He was cut down on the spot, and his death was the signal of a general massacre. Then the plundering commenced : fires broke out in several quarters ; and in a few days the whole city, with the exception of a few houses on the Pal'atine, was burnt to the ground.[2] (390 B. C.)

30. The Gauls made repeated attempts to storm the citadel, but in vain. They attempted to climb up the rocks in the night, but the cackling of the sacred geese in the temple of Juno awoke Marcus Man'lius, who hurled the foremost Gaul headlong down the

1. The Roman *Forum* was a large open space between the Capitoline and Pal'atine hills, surrounded by porticos, shops, &c., where assemblies of the people were generally held, justice administered, and public business transacted. It is now a mere open space strewed for the most part with ruins, which, in the course of centuries, have accumulated to such an extent as to raise the surface from fifteen to twenty feet above its ancient level. See p. 582.

2. Different writers have given the date of the taking of Rome by the Gauls, from 388 to 398 B. C

precipice, and prevented the ascent of those who were mounting after him. At length famine began to be felt by the garrison. But the host of the besiegers was gradually melting away by sickness and want, and Brennus agreed, for a thousand pounds of gold, to quit Rome and its territory. According to the old Roman legend, Camil'lus entered the city with an army while the gold was being weighed, and rudely accosting Brennus, and saying, " It is the custom of us Romans to ransom our country, not with gold, but with iron," ordered the gold to be carried back to the temple, whereupon a battle ensued, and the Gauls were driven from the city. A more probable account, however, relates that the Gauls were suddenly called home to protect their own country from an invasion of the Venetians.[1] According to Polybius this great Gallic invasion took place in the same year that the " peace of Antalcidas" was concluded between the Greeks and Persians. (See p. 89.)

31. The walls and houses of Rome had now to be built anew, and so great did the task appear that the citizens clamored for a removal to Véii; but the persuasion of Camil'lus, and a lucky omen, induced them to remain in their ancient situation. Yet they were not allowed to rebuild their dwellings in peace, for the surrounding nations, the Sábines only excepted, made war upon them; but their attacks were repelled, and one after another they were made to yield to the sway of Rome, which ultimately became the sovereign city of Italy.

32. Soon after the rebuilding of the city the old contests between the patricians and plebeians were renewed, with all their former violence. The cruelties exercised towards helpless credit- XI. PLEBEIAN ors appear to have aroused the sympathies of the patrician AND PATRI-CIAN CON Man'lius, the brave defender of the capitol, for he sold TESTS. the most valuable part of his inheritance, and declared that so long as a single pound remained no Roman should be carried into bondage for debt. Henceforward he was regarded as the patron of the poor but for some hasty words was thrown into prison for slandering the government, and for sedition. Released by the clamors of the multitude, he was afterwards accused of aspiring to kingly authority; and the more common account states that he was convicted of treason. and sentenced to be thrown headlong from the Tarpéian rock, the scene of his former glory. But another account states that, being

1. The *Venetians* were a people of ancient Italy who dwelt north of the mouths of the Po, around the head-waters of the Adriatic. (*Map* No. VIII.)

:n insurrection, and in possession of the capitol, a treacherous slave hurled him down the precipice.[a] (384 B. C.)

33. The plebeians mourned the fate of Man'lius, but his death was a patrician triumph. The oppression of the plebeians now increased, until universal distress prevailed : debtors were every day consigned to slavery, and dragged to private dungeons; the number of free citizens was visibly decreasing; those who remained were ro duced to a state of dependence by their debts, and Rome was on the point of degenerating into a miserable oligarchy, when her decline was arrested by the appearance of two men who changed the fate of their country and of the world.

34. The authors of the great reform in the constitution were Li cinius Stolo and Lucius Sextius. Confining themselves strictly to the paths permitted by the laws, they succeeded, after a struggle of five years against every species of fraud and violence, in obtaining for the plebeians an acknowledgment of their rights, and all possible guarantees for their preservation. (376 to 371 B. C.) The history of the struggle would be too long for insertion here. As on a former occasion, it was only in the last extremity, when the people had taken up arms, and gathered together upon the Aventine, that the patrician senate yielded its sanction to the three bills brought forward by Licinius. The first abolished the military tribuneship, and gained for the plebeians a share in the consulship : the second regulated the shares, divisions, and rents, of the public lands : the third regulated the rate of interest, gave present relief to unfortunate debtors, and secured personal freedom against the rapacity of creditors. To save

XII. OFFICE something from the general wreck of their power, the OF PRÆTOR. patricians stipulated that the judicial functions of the consul should be exercised by a new officer with the title of *Prætor*,[1] chosen from the patrician order; yet within thirty-five years after the passage of the laws of Licinius, not only the prætorship, but the dictatorship also, was opened to the plebeians.

35. The legislation of Licinius freed Rome from internal dissen sions, and gave new development to her strength and warlike'ener

1. The *prætors* were judicial magistrates,—officers answering to the modern chief-justice o chancellor. The modern English forms of judicial proceedings in the trial of causes are mostly taken from those observed by the Roman prætors. At first but one prætor was chosen; after wards, when foreigners became numerous at Rome, another prætor was added to administe justice to them, or between them and the citizens. In later times subordinate judges, called provincia prætors, were appointed to administer justice in the provinces.

a. See Niebuhr, i. 275.

gies. Occasionally the Gauls came down from the north and made inroads upon the Roman territories, but they were invariably driven back with loss; while the Etrus'cans, almost constantly at war with Rome, grew less and less formidable, from repeated defeats. On the south, however, a new and dangerous enemy appeared in the Samnite[1] confederacy, now in the fulness of its strength, and in extent of territory and population far superior to Rome and her allies.

36. Cap'ua,[2] a wealthy city of Campánia, having obtained from Rome the promise of protection against the Samnites, the latter haughtily engaged in the war, and with a larger army than Rome could muster invaded the territory of Campánia, but in two desperate battles were defeated by the Romans. *XIII. FIRST SAMNITE WAR.* Two years later the Samnites proffered terms of peace, which were accepted. (341 B. C.) A league with the Samnites appears to have broken the connection that had long existed between Rome and Látium, and although the latter was willing to submit to a common government, and a complete union as one nation, yet the Romans, rejecting all compromise, haughtily determined either that their city must be a Latin town, or the Latins be subject to Rome. The result of the Latin war was the annexation of all Látium, and of Campánia also, to the territory of the Republic. (338 B. C.)

37. The Samnites were alarmed at these successes, and Roman encroachments soon involved the two people in another war. The Samnites lost several battles, but under their able general Pontius they effectually humbled the pride of Rome. The armies of the two Roman consuls, amounting to twenty thousand men, *XIV. SECOND SAMNITE WAR.* while passing through a narrow defile call the Caudine Forks,[3] were surrounded by the enemy, and in this situation, unable either to fight or to retreat, were obliged to surrender (321 B. C.) The terms of Pontius were that the Roman soldiers should be allowed to return to their homes, after passing under the

1. The *Samnites* dwelt at the distance of about ninety miles south-east from Rome, their territory lying between Apulia on the east and Campánia and Látium on the west. (*See Nos.* VIII. and X.)

2. *Cap'ua,* the capital of Campánia, was about three miles from the left bank of the river Vultur'nus, (now Vulturno,) about one hundred and five miles south-east from Rome. The remains of its ancient amphitheatre, said to have been capable of containing one hundred thousand spectators, and some of its tombs, &c., attest its ancient splendor and magnificence. Two and a half miles from the site of the ancient city, is the modern city of Cap'ua, on the left bank of the Vulturno. (*Map* No. VIII.)

3. The *Caudine Forks* were a narrow pass in the Samnite territory. about thirty-five miles north-east from the Cap'ua. The present valley of *Arpaia,* (or Forchia di Arpaia,) not far from Benevento, is thought to answer to this pass.

yoke; that there shou.d be a renewal of the ancient equal alliance
between Rome and Samnium, and a restoration of all places that
had been dependent upon Samnium before the war. For the fulfilment of these stipulations the consuls gave their oaths in the name
of the republic, and Pontius retained six hundred Roman knights as
hostages.

38. But notwithstanding the recent disaster, and the hard fate
that might be anticipated for the hostages, the Roman senate imme
diately declared the peace null and void, and decreed that those who
had sworn to it should be given up to the Samnites, as persons who
had deceived them. In vain did Pontius demand either that the
whole army should be again placed in his power, or that the terms
of capitulation should be strictly fulfilled; but he showed magnanimity of soul in refusing to accept the consuls and other officers
whom the Romans would have given up to his vengeance. Not long
after, the six hundred hostages were restored, but on what conditions
is unknown.

39. The war, being again renewed, was continued with brief intervals of truce, during a period of thirty years; and although the Sam
XV. THIRD
SAMNITE
WAR. nites were at times aided by Umbrians,[1] Etrus'cans
and Gauls, the desperate valor of the Romans repeatedly
triumphed over all opposition. The last great battle
which occurred fifty-one years from the commencement of the first
Samnite war, and which decided the contest between Rome and
Samnium, has no name in history, and the place where it was
fought is unknown, but its importance is gathered from the common
statement that twenty thousand Samnites were left dead on the field
and four thousand taken prisoners, and that among the latter was
Pontius himself. (B. C. 292.) He was led in chains to grace the
triumph of the Roman general, but the senate tarnished its honor
by ordering the old man to execution. (291 B. C.) One year after
the defeat of Pontius, the Samnites submitted to the terms dictated
by the conquerors. (290 B. C.)

40. The Samnite wars had made the Romans acquainted with the
Grecian cities on the eastern coast, and it was not long before they
XVI. WAR
WITH THE
TARENTINES. found a pretext for war with Taren'tum, the wealthiest
of the Greek towns of Italy. The Tarentines, abandoned
to ease and luxury, had often employed mercenary Gre-

<hr/>

1. Um'bria, the territory of the Umbrians, was east of Etruria on the left bank of the Tiber
and north of the Sabine territory. (Maps Nos. VIII. and X.)

cian troops in their wars with the rude tribes by which they were surrounded, and now, when pressed by the Romans, they again had recourse to foreign aid, and applied for protection to Pyr'rhus, king of Epirus, who has previously been brought under our notice in connection with events in Grecian history. (See p. 106.)

41. Pyr'rhus, ambitious of military fame, accepted the invitation of the Tarentines, and passed over to Taren'tum at the head of an army of nearly thirty thousand men, having among his forces twenty elephants, the first of those animals that had been seen in Italy. In the first battle, which was fought with the consul Lævínus, seven times was Pyr'rhus beaten back, and to his elephants he was finally indebted for his victory. (280 B. C.) The valor and military skill of the Romans astonished Pyr'rhus, who had expected to encounter only a horde of barbarians. As he passed over the field of battle after the fight, and marked the bodies of the Romans who had fallen in their ranks without turning their backs, and observed their countenances, stern even in death, he is said to have exclaimed in admiration: " With what ease I could conquer the world had I the Romans for soldiers, or had they me for their king."

42. Pyr'rhus now tried the arts of negotiation, and for this purpose sent to Rome his friend Cineas, the orator, who is said to have won more towns by his eloquence than Pyr'rhus by his arms; but all his proposals of peace were rejected, and Cineas returned filled with admiration of the Romans, whose city he said, was a temple, and their senate an assembly of kings. The war was renewed, and in a second battle Pyr'rhus gained a dearly-bought victory, for he left the flower of his troops on the field. " One more such victory," he replied to those who congratulated him, "and I am undone " 279 B. C.)

43. It is related that while the armies were facing each other the third time, a letter was brought to Fabricius, the Roman consul and commander, from the physician of Pyr'rhus, offering, for a suitable reward, to poison the king, and that Fabricius thereupon nobly informed Pyr'rhus of the treachery that was plotted against him. When the message was brought to Pyr'rhus, he was astonished at the generosity of his enemy, and exclaimed, " It would be easier to turn the sun from his course than Fabricius from the path of honor." Not to be outdone in magnanimity he released all his prisoners without ransom, and soon after, withdrawing his forces, passed over into Sicily, where his aid had been requested by the

Greek cities against the Carthaginians. (276 B. C. See p 121.) Re-turning to Italy after an absence of three years, he renewed hostili-ties with the Romans, but was defeated in a great battle by the consul Curius Dentatus, after which he left Italy with precipitation, and sought to renew his broken fortunes in the Grecian wars. The de-parture of Pyr' rhus was soon followed by the fall of Taren' tum and the establishment of Roman supremacy over all Italy, from the Rubicon[1] and the Arnus,[2] on the northern frontier of Umbria and Etruria, to the Sicilian straits, and from the Tuscan[2] sea to the Adriat' ic.

44. Sovereigns of all Italy, the Romans now began to extend their influence abroad. Two years after the defeat of Pyr' rhus, Ptol' cmy Philadelphus, king of Egypt, sought the friendship and alliance of Rome by embassy, and the Roman senate honored the proposal by sending ambassadors in return, with rich presents, to Alexandria. An interference with the affairs of Sicily, soon after, brought on a war with Carthage, at this time a powerful republic, superior in strength and resources to the Roman. From this period the Roman annals begin to embrace the histories of surrounding nations, and the circle rapidly enlarges until all the then known world is drawn within the vortex of Roman ambition.

- - ——————— •◆•• ———————

SECTION III.

ANALYSIS. 1. Geographical account of CARTHAGE. [Tunis.]—2. African dominions of Carthage. Foreign possessions. Trade. [Sardinia. Corsica. Balearic Isles. Malta.]—3. Circumstances of Roman interference in the affairs of Sicily.—4. Commencement of the FIRST PUNIC WAR. The Carthaginians driven from Sicily. The Romans take Agrigentum.—5. The Carthaginians ravage Italy. Building of the first Roman fleet. First naval encounter with the

1. The *Rubicon*, which formed in part the boundary between Italy proper and Cisalpine Gaul, is a small stream which falls into the Adriat' ic, eighteen or twenty miles south of Rav-enna. (*Map* No. VIII.)

9 The river *Arnus* (now the *Arno*) was the boundary of Etruria on the north until the time of Augustus. On both its banks stood Florentia, the modern *Florence;* and eight miles from its mouth, on its right bank, stood Pisæ, the modern *Pisa.* (*Map* No. VIII.)

3. The *Tuscan Sea* was that part of the Mediterranean which extended along the coast of Etruria, or Tuscany. (*Map* No. VIII.)

1. Carthage, believed to have been founded by a Phœnician colony from Tyre in the ninth century before the Christian era, was situated on a peninsula of the northern coast of Africa, about twelve miles, according to Livy, north-east from the modern city of Tunis,[1] but, according to some modern writers, only three or four miles. Probably the city extended over a great part of the space between Tunis and Cape Carthage. Its harbor was southward from the city, and was entered from what is now the Gulf of Tunis

I. CARTHAGE.

2. The Carthaginians early assumed and maintained a dominion over the surrounding Libyan tribes. Their territory was bounded on the east by the Grecian Cyrenáica; their trading posts extended westward along the coast to the pillars of Hercules; and among their foreign possessions may be enumerated their depen

[1] Tunis is about four miles from the sea, and three miles south-west from the ruins of ancient Carthage. Among these ruins have been discovered numerous reservoirs or large cisterns, and the remains of a grand aqueduct which brought water to the city from a distance of at least fifty miles. According to Strabo, Tunis, or *Tunes*, existed before the foundation of Carthage. The chief events in the history of Tunis are its numerous sieges and captures. (See pp. 335-510. *Map* No. VIII.)

dencies in south-western Spain, in Sicily, and in Sardinia,¹ Corsica,² the Balearic Isles,³ and Malta.⁴ It is believed that they carried on an extensive caravan trade with the African nations as far as the Niger; and it is known that they entered into a commercial treaty with Rome in the latter part of the sixth century; yet few details of their history are known to us previous to the beginning of the first Carthaginian war with Syracuse, about 480 B. C.

3. At the time to which we have brought down the details of Roman history, the Mamertines, a band of Campanian mercenaries, who had been employed in Sicily by a former king, having established themselves in the island, and obtained possession of Messána, by fraud and injustice, quarrelled among themselves, one party seeking the protection of Carthage, and the other that of Rome. The Greek towns of Sicily were for the most part already in friendly alliance with the Carthaginians, who had long been aiming at the complete possession of the island; and the Romans did not hesitate to avail themselves of the most trifling pretexts to defeat the ambitious designs of their rivals.

4. The first Punic ᵃ war commenced 263 years B. C., eight years

II. FIRST PUNIC WAR. after the surrender of Taren'tum, when the Romans made a descent upon Sicily with a large army under the

---

1. *Sardinia* is a hilly but fertile island of the Mediterranean, about one hundred and thirty miles south-west from the nearest Italian coast. At an early period the Carthaginians formed settlements there, but the shores of the island fell into the hands of the Romans in the interval between the first and second Punic wars, 237 B. C. The inhabitants of the interior bravely defended themselves, and were never completely subdued by the Roman arms. (*Map* No. VIII.)

2. *Corsica* lies directly north of Sardinia, from which it is separated by the strait of Bonifacio, ten miles in width in the narrowest part. Some Greeks from Phócis settled here at an early period, but were driven out by the Carthaginians. The Romans took the island from the .... 231 B. C. (*Map* No. VIII.)

3. The *Balearic Isles* were those now known as *Majorca* and *Minorca*, the former of which is one hundred and ten miles east from the coast of Spain. By some the ancient Ebusus, now *Ivica*, is ranked among the Baleares. The term *Balearic* is derived from the Greek word *ballein*, "to throw,"—alluding to the remarkable skill of the inhabitants in using the sling. At an early date the Phœnicians formed settlements in the Baleares. They were succeeded by the Carthaginians, from whom the Romans, under Q. Metellus, conquered these islands 123 B. C. (*Map* No. IX.)

4. *Malta*, whose ancient name was *Melita*, is an island of the Mediterranean, sixty miles south from Sicily. The Phœnicians early planted a colony here. It fell into the hands of the Carthaginians about four hundred years before the Christian era, and in the second Punic war t was conquered by the Romans, who made it an appendage of their province of Sicily. See also p. 469. (*Map* No. VIII.)

a. The term *Punic* means simply 'Carthaginian." It is a word of Greek origin, *phoinikes*, in its sense of *purple*, which the Greeks applied to Phœnicians and Carthaginians, in allusion to the famous purple or crimson of Tyre, the parent city of Carthage. The Romans, adapting the word to the analogy of the Latin tongue, changed it to *Punicus*, whence the English wor ? *Punic*

command of the consul Claudius. After they had gained possession of Messina, in the second year of the war, Hiero, king of Syracuse, the second of the name, deserted his former allies and joined the Romans, and ere long the Carthaginians were driven from their most important stations in the island, although their superior naval power still enabled them to retain the command of the surrounding seas, and the possession of all the harbors in Sicily. The Carthaginians fortified Agrigentum, a place of great natural strength; yet the Romans besieged the city, which they took by storm, after defeating an immense army that had been sent to its relief. (262 B. C.)

5. But while the Sicilian towns submitted to the Roman arms, a Carthaginian fleet of sixty ships ravaged the coast of Italy; and the Romans saw the necessity of being able to meet the enemy on their own element. Unacquainted with the building of large ships, they must have been obliged to renounce their design had not a Carthaginian ship of war been thrown upon the Italian coast by a storm From the model thus furnished a hundred and thirty ships were built within sixty days after the trees had been felled. The Carthaginians ridiculed the awkwardness and clumsiness of their structure, and thought to destroy the whole fleet in a single encounter; but the Roman commander, having invented an elevated draw-bridge, with grappling irons, for the purpose of close encounter and boarding, boldly attacked the enemy, and took or destroyed forty-five of the Carthaginian vessels in the first battle, while not a single Roman ship was lost. (260 B. C.)

6. After the war had continued eight years with varied success, involving in its ravages not only Sicily, but Sardinia and Corsica also, a Roman armament of three hundred and thirty ships, intrusted to the command of the consuls Regulus and Manlius, was prepared for the great enterprise of carrying the war into Africa. But the Carthaginians met these preparations with equal efforts, and under their two greatest commanders, Hanno and Hamil'car, went out to meet the enemy with three hundred and fifty ships, which carried no less than a hundred and fifty thousand men. In the engagement that followed, the rude force of the Romans, aided by their boarding bridges, overcame all the advantages of naval art and practice. Again the Carthaginians were defeated,—more than thirty of their ships being sunk, and sixty-four, with all their crews, taken. (256 B C.)

7. Regulus proceeded to Africa, and landing on the eastern coast

of the Hermæan promontory[1] took Clyp'ea[2] by storm, conquered
Tunis, received the submission of seventy-four towns, and laid waste
the country to the very gates of Carthage. An embassy sued for
peace in the Roman camp; but the terms offered by Regulus were
little better than destruction itself, and Carthage would probably
have perished thus early, had not foreign aid unexpectedly come to
her assistance. All of a sudden we find Xanthip'pus, a Spartan
general, with a small body of Grecian troops, among the Carthaginians, promising them victory if they would give him the conduct of
the war. A presentiment of deliverance pervaded the people, and
Xanthip'pus, after having arranged and exercised the Carthaginian
army before the city, went out to meet the greatly superior forces of
the Romans, and gained a complete victory over them. (255 B. C.)
Regulus himself was taken prisoner, and, out of the whole Roman
army, only two thousand escaped, and shut themselves up in Clyp'ea.
Of Xanthip'pus nothing is known beyond the events connected with
this Carthaginian victory.

8. A Roman fleet, sent to bring off the garrison of Clyp'ea, gained
a signal success over the Carthaginians near the Hermæan promontory, but on the return voyage, while off the southern coast of Sicily
was nearly destroyed by a tempest. Another fleet that had laid
waste the Libyan coast experienced a similar fate on its return,—a
hundred and fifty ships, and the whole booty, being swallowed up in
the waves. The Romans were discouraged by these disasters, and
for a time abandoned the sea to their enemies, the senate having at
one time decreed that the fleet should not be restored, but limited
to sixty ships for the defence of the Italian coast and the protection
of transports. Still the war was continued on the land, and in Sicily
the Roman consul Metellus gained a great victory over the Carthaginians near Panor'mus, killing twenty thousand of the enemy, and
taking more than a hundred of their elephants. (250 B. C.) This
was the last great battle of the first Punic war, although the contest
was continued in Sicily, mostly by a series of slowly-conducted sieges,
eight years longer.

9. Soon after the defeat at Panor'mus, the Carthaginians sent an
embassy to Rome with proposals of peace. Regulus was taken from

1. The *Hermæan promontory*, or "promontory of Mercury," is the same as the modern *Cape
Bon*, usually called the northern cape of Africa, at a distance of about forty-five miles north-
east from the site of Carthage. (*Map* No. VIII.)

2. *Clyp'ea*, now *Aklib'ia*, was situated on the peninsula which terminates in Cape Bon a
short distance south from the cape. (*Map* No. VI'I.)

his dungeon to accompany the embassy, the Carthaginians trusting that, weary of his long captivity, he would urge the senate to accept the proffered terms; but the inflexible Roman persuaded the senate to reject the proposal and continue the war, assuring his countrymen that the resources of Carthage were already nearly exhausted. Bound by his oath to return as a prisoner if peace were not concluded, he voluntarily went back to his dungeon. It is generally stated that after his return to Carthage he was tortured to death by the exasperated Carthaginians. But although his martyrdom has been sung by Roman poets, and his self-sacrifice extolled by orators, there are strong reasons for believing that he died a natural death.[a]

10. The subsequent events of the first Punic war, down to within a year of its termination, were generally unfortunate to the Romans; but eventually the Carthaginian admiral lost nearly his whole fleet in a naval battle. (241 B. C.) Again the Carthaginians, having exhausted the resources of their treasury, and unable to equip another fleet, sought peace, which was finally concluded on the conditions that Carthage should evacuate Sicily, and the small islands lying between it and Italy, pay three thousand two hundred talents of silver, and restore the Roman prisoners without ransom. (B. C. 240.) Sicily now became a Roman province; Corsica and Sardinia were added two years later; and the sway of Rome was extended over all the important islands which Carthage had possessed in the Mediterranean.

11. Soon after the termination of the first Punic war, Rome found herself at peace with all the world, and the temple of Jánus was shut for the second time since the foundation of the city. But the interval of repose was brief. A war soon broke out with the Illyr'ians,[1] which led the Roman legions, for the first time, across the Adriat'ic. (229 B. C.) The Illyr'ians had committed numerous piracies on the Italian coasts, and when ambassadors were sent to demand reparation, Teu'ta, the Illyr'ian queen, told them that piracy was the national custom of her subjects, and she could not forbid them what was their right and privilege. One of the ambassadors thereupon told her that it was the custom of the

III. ILLYR'-IAN WAR.

1. The *Illyr'ians* were inhabitants of *Illyr'ia* or *Illyr'icum*, a country bordering on the Adriat'ic sea, opposite Italy, and bordered on the south-east by Epirus and Macedonia. (*Map No. VIII.*)

a. Niebuhr, R. iii. p. 275, and 1 iv. 70.

Romans to do away with bad customs; and so incensed was the queen at his boldness that she procured his assassination.

12. The Illyr'ians, after successive defeats, were glad to conclude a peace with the Romans, and to abandon their piracies, both on the Italian and Grecian coasts. (228 B. C.) Several Greek communities showed themselves grateful for the favor; a copy of the treaty was read in the assembly of the Achæan league; and the Corinthians conferred upon the Romans the right of taking part in the Isthmian games. Roman encroachments on the territory of the Gauls next

IV. WAR brought on a war with that fierce people, and a vast swarm WITH THE of the barbarians poured down upon Italy, and advanced GAULS. irresistibly as far as Clusium, a distance of only three days' journey from Rome. (226 B. C.) After four years continuance the war was ended by a great victory gained over the Gauls by Claudius Marcellus, at Clastid'ium,[1] where the noted Gallic leader, Viridomarus, was slain. (222 B. C.)

13. While Rome was thus engaged, events were secretly ripening for another war with Carthage. Hamil'car, the soul of the Carthaginian councils, and the sworn enemy of Rome, had turned his eyes to Spain,[2] with the view of forming a province there which should compensate for the loss of Sicily and Sardinia. "I have three sons," said this veteran warrior, "whom I shall rear like so many lion's whelps against the Romans." When he set out for Spain, where Carthage then had several colonies, he took his son Hannibal, then only nine years of age, to the altar, and made him swear eternal enmity to Rome.

14. In a few years the Carthaginians gained possession of all the south of Spain, and Hamil'car being dead, the youthful Hannibal who proved himself the greatest general of antiquity, was appointed to the command of their armies. The rapid progress of his Spanish conquests alarmed the Romans. When the people of Sagun'tum,[3]

1. *Clastid'ium,* (now *Chiasteggio,*) was in that part of Cisalpine Gaul called Liguria, south f the river Po, and a short distance south-east from the modern *Pavia.* (See Pavia, *Map* No VIII.)

2. *Spain,* (consisting of the present Spain and Portugal,) called by the Greeks *Iberia,* and by the Romans *Hispania,* embraced all the great peninsula in the south-west of Europe. The divisions by which it is best known in ancient history are those of *Tarraconensis, Lusitania,* and *Betica,* which were made during the reign of Augustus, when, for the first time, the country was wholly subdued by the Romans. (*Map* No. XIII.)

3. *Sagun'tum* was built on a hill of black marble in the east of Spain, about four miles from the Mediterranean, and fifteen miles north-east from the modern Valencia. Half way up the hill are still to be seen the ruins of a theatre, forming an exact semi-circle, and capable of accommodating nine thousan' spectators. Other ruins are found in the vicinity The castle or

a Grecian city on the eastern coast, found themselves exposed to his rage, they applied to Rome for aid; but the ambassadors of the latter power, who had been sent to remonstrate with Hannibal, were treated with contempt; and Sagun'tum, after a siege of eight months, was taken. (219 B. C.) Hannibal then crossed the Ibér'us,[1] and invaded the tribes of Catalonia,[2] which were in alliance with Rome. A Roman embassy was then sent to Carthage with the preposterous demand that Hannibal and his army should be delivered up as satisfaction for the trespass upon Roman territory; and when this was refused, the Roman commissioners, according to the prescribed form of their country, made the declaration of war. Both parties were already prepared for the long-anticipated contest. (218 B. C.)

15. The plan of Hannibal, at the opening of the second Punic war, was to carry the war into Italy; while that of the Roman consuls, Publius Scipio and Semprónius, was to confine it to Spain, and to attack Carthage. Hannibal quickly passed over the V. SECOND Pyrenees, and rapidly traversing the lower part of Gaul,[3] PUNIC WAR. though opposed by the warlike tribes through which his march lay, and avoiding the army of Scipio, which had landed at Marseilles,[4] crossed the Alps at the head of nearly thirty thousand men, and had taken Turin[5] by storm before Scipio could return to Italy to oppose

citadel on the top of the hill has been successively occupied by the Sagun' tines, Carthaginians, Romans, Moors, and Spaniards. Along the foot of the hill has been built the modern town of *Murviedro*, now containing a population of about six thousand inhabitants. (*Map* No. XIII.)

1. *Ibérus*, now the *Ebro*, rises in the north of Spain, in the country of the ancient Cantabri, and flows with a south-eastern course into the Mediterranean sea. Before the second Punic war this river formed the boundary between the Roman and Carthaginian territories; and, in the time of Charlemagne, between the Moorish and Christian dominions. (*Map* No. XIII.)

2. *Catalonia* is the name by which the north-eastern part of Spain has long been known, and it is now a province of modern Spain. (*Map* No. XIII.)

3. *Gaul* embraced nearly the same territory as modern France. When first known it was divided among the three great nations of the Belgæ, the Celtæ, and the Aquitani, but the Romans called all the inhabitants *Gauls*, while the Greeks called them *Celts*. The Celts proper inhabited the north-western part of the country, the Belgæ the north-eastern and eastern, and the Aquitani the south-western. The divisions by which Gaul is best known in ancient history are Lugdunensis, Belgica, Aquitania, and Narbonensis,—called the "Four Gauls," which were established by the Romans after the conquest of the country by Julius Cæsar. As far back as we can penetrate into the history of western Europe, the Gallic or Celtic race occupied early all Gaul, together with the two great islands north-west of the country, one of which, (England and Scotland) they called Alb-in, "White Island," and the other (Ireland) they called Er-in "Isle of the West." (*Map* No. XIII.)

4. *Marseilles*, anciently called *Massila*, was originally settled by a Greek colony from Phócis. It is now a large commercial city, and sea port of the Mediterranean, situated in a beautiful plain on the east side of the bay of the Gulf of Lyons. (*Map* No. XIII.)

5. *Turin*, called by the Romans *Augusta Taurinorum*, now a large city of north-western Italy, is situated on the northern or western side of the river Po, eighty miles south-west of Milan. (*Map* No. VIII.)

his progress In a partial encounter on the Ticínus[1] the Roman cavalry was beaten by the Spanish and Numidian horsemen,[2] and Scipio, who had been severely wounded, retreated across the Po[3] to await the arrival of Semprónius and his army. Soon after, the entire Roman army was defeated on the left bank of the Trébia,[4] when the hesitating Gauls at once espoused the cause of the victors (218 B. C.)

16. In the following year Hannibal advanced towards Rome, and Semprónius, falling into an ambuscade near Lake Trasiménus,[5] was slain, and his whole army cut to pieces. (217 B. C.) In another campaign, Hannibal, after passing Rome, and penetrating into southern Italy, having increased his army to fifty thousand men, defeated the consuls Æmilius and Varro in a great battle at Cannæ. (216 B. C.) The Romans, whose numbers exceeded those of the enemy, lost, in killed alone, according to the lowest calculation, more than forty-two thousand men. Among the slain was Æmilius, one of the consuls.

17. The calamity which had befallen Rome at Cannæ shook the allegiance of some of her Italian subjects, and the faith of her allies; many of the Grecian cities, hoping to recover their independence, made terms with the victors; Syracuse deserted the cause of Rome; and Philip of Mac'edon sent an embassy to Italy and formed an alliance with Hannibal. (See p. 109.) But the Romans did not despond. They made the most vigorous preparations to carry on the war in Sicily, Sardinia, Spain, and Africa, as well as in Italy: they formed an alliance with the Grecian States of Ætólia, and thus found sufficient employment for Philip at home, and in the

1. The *Ticínus*, now *Ticino*, enters the Po from the north about twenty miles south-west from Milan. Near its junction with the Po stood the ancient city of *Ticínum*, now called *Pavia*. (*Map* No. VIII.)

2. *Numidia* was a country of northern Africa, adjoining the Carthaginian territory on the west, and embracing the eastern part of the territory of modern Algiers. (*Map* No. IX.)

3. The river Po, the *Erid'anus* or *Padus* of the ancients, rises in the Alps, on the confines of France; and, flowing eastward, receives during its long course to the Adriat'ic, a vast number of tributary streams. It divides the great plain of Lombardy into two nearly equal parts. (*Map* No. VIII.)

4. The *Trébia* is a southern tributary of the Po, which enters that stream near the modern city of *Piacenza*, (anciently called *Placentia*) thirty-five miles south-east from Milan. (*Map* No. VIII.)

5. Lake *Trasiménus*, (now called *Perugia*,) was in Etruria, near the Tiber, eighty miles north from Rome. (*Map* No. VIII.)

6. *Cannæ*, an ancient city of Apulia, was situated near the river Aufidus (now Ofanto) five or six miles from the Adriat'ic. The scene of the great battle between the Romans and Carthaginians is marked by the name of *campo di sangue*, "field of blood;" and spears, heads of lances, and other pieces of armor, still continue to be turned up by the plough. (*Map* No. VIII.)

and reduced him to the humilating necessity of making a separate peace.

18. From the field of Cannæ Hannibal led his forces to Cap'ua, which at once opened its gates to receive him, but his veterans were enervated by the luxuries and debaucheries of that licentious city In the meantime Fabius Maximus had been appointed to the command of the Roman army in Italy, and by a new and cautious system of tactics—by avoiding decisive battles—by watching the motions of the enemy, harassing their march, and intercepting their convoys, he gradually wasted the strength of Hannibal, who at length summoned to his assistance his brother Has'drubal, who had been contending with the Scipios in Spain. Has'drubal crossed the Pyrenees and the Alps with little opposition, but on the banks of the Metaurus[1] he was entrapped by the consuls Livius and Nero,— his whole army was cut to pieces, and he himself was slain. (B. C. 207.) His gory head, thrown into the camp of Hannibal, gave the latter the first intelligence of this great misfortune. Before this event the ancient city of Syracuse had been taken by storm by the Romans, after the siege had been a long time protracted by the mechanical skill of the famous Archimédes.[a]

19. At length the youthful Cornelius Scipio, the son of Publius Scipio, having driven the Carthaginians from Spain, and being elected consul, gained the consent of the senate to carry the war into Africa, although this bold measure was opposed by the age and experience of the great Fabius. Soon after the landing of Scipio near Utica,[2] Massinis'sa, king of the Numidians, who had previously

1. The *Metaurus*, now the *Metro*, was a river of Umbria, which flowed into the Adriat' ic. The battle was fought on the left bank of the river, at a place now occupied by the village of Fo:smbrone. (*Map* No. VIII.)

2. The city of *Utica* stood on the banks of the river Bagrada, (now the *Mejerdah,*) a few miles north-west from Carthage. Its ruins are to be seen at the present day near the port of Farina. (*Map* No. VIII.)

a. *Archimédes*, the most celebrated mathematician among the ancients, was a native of Syracuse. He was highly skilled in astronomy, mechanics, geometry, hydrostatics, and optics, in all of which he produced many extraordinary inventions. His knowledge of the principle of specific gravities enabled him to detect the fraudulent mixture of silver in the golden crown of Hiero, king of Syracuse, by comparing the quantity of water displaced by equal weights of gold and silver. The thought occurred to him upon observing, while he was in the bath, that he displaced a bulk of water equal to his own body. He was so highly excited by the discovery, that he is said to have run naked out of the bath into the street, exclaiming *eureka !* 'I have found it." His acquaintance with the power of the lever is evinced by his famous declaration to Hiero : "Give me where I may stand, and I will move the world." At the time of the siege of Syracuse he is said to have fired the Roman fleet by means of immense reflecting mirrors.

been in alliance with the Carthaginians, went over to the Romans,
and aided in surprising and burning the Carthaginian camp of Has'-
drubal, still another general of that name. Both Tunis and Utica
were next besieged ; the former soon opened its gates to the Romans,
and the Carthaginian senate, in despair, recalled Hannibal, from
Italy for the defence of the city. (202 B. C.)

20. Peace, which Hannibal himself advised, might even now have
been made on terms honorable to Carthage, had not the Carthaginians, elated by the presence of their favorite hero, and confident
of his success, obstinately resisted any concession. Both generals
made preparations for a decisive engagement, and the two armies
met on the plains of Zama;[1] but the forces of Hannibal were mostly
raw troops, while those of Scipio were the disciplined legions that
had so often conquered in Spain. Hannibal showed himself worthy
of his former fame ; but after a hard-fought battle the Romans prevailed, and Carthage lost the army which was her only reliance.
Peace was then concluded on terms dictated by the conqueror. Carthage consented to confine herself to her African possessions, to keep
no elephants in future for purposes of war, to give up all prisoners
and deserters, to reduce her navy to ten small vessels, to undertake
no war without the consent of the Romans, and to pay ten thousand
talents of silver. (202 B. C.) Scipio, on his return home, received
the title of Africanus, and was honored with the most magnificen
triumph that had ever been exhibited at Rome.

21. The second Punic war had brought even greater distress upon
the Roman people than upon the Carthaginians, for during the sixteen years of Hannibal's occupation of Italy the greater part of the
Roman territory had lain waste, and was plundered of its wealth,
and deserted by its people ; and famine had often threatened Rome
itself; while the number of the Roman militia on the rolls had
been reduced by desertion, and the sword of the enemy, from two
hundred and seventy thousand nearly to the half of that number.
Yet in their greatest adversity the Roman people had never given
way to despair, nor shown the smallest humiliation at defeat, nor
manifeste 1 the least design of concession ; and when the pressure of
war was removed, this same unconquerable spirit rapidly raised
Rome to a state of prosperity and greatness which she had never attained before.

1. The city of Zama, the site of which is occupied by the modern village of Zowéria, was
about a hundred miles southwest from Carthage. (Map No. VIII.)

22. The state of the world was now highly favorable for the advancement of a great military republic, like that of Rome, to universal dominion. In the East, the kingdoms formed from the fragments of Alexander's mighty empire were either still engaged in mutual wars or had sunk into the weakness of exhausted energies; the Grecian States were divided among themselves, each being ready to throw itself upon foreign protection to promote its own immediate interests; while in the West the Romans were masters of Spain; their colonies were rapidly encroaching on the Gallic provinces; and they had tributaries among the nations of Northern Africa.

23. The war with Carthage had scarcely ended when an embassy from Athens solicited the protection of the Romans against the power of Philip II. of Mac'edon; and war being unhesitatingly VI. A GRE-declared against Philip, Roman diplomacy was at once CIAN WAR. plunged into the maze of Grecian politics. (B. C. 201.) After a war of four years Philip was defeated in the decisive battle of Cynoceph'alæ, (B. C. 197,) and forced to submit to such terms as the conquerors pleased to dictate; and at the Isthmian games the Greeks received with gratitude the declaration of their freedom under the protection of Rome. When, therefore, a few years later, the Ætólians, dissatisfied with the Roman policy, invited Antíochus of Syria into Europe, and that monarch had made himself master of Eubœ'a, a plausible pretext was again offered for Roman interference: and when the Ætólians had been reduced, Antíochus driven back, and Greece tranquillized upon Roman terms, an Asiatic war was open to the cupidity of the Romans.

24. After a brief struggle, Antíochus, completely overthrown in the general battle of Magnésia,[1] (B. C. 191,) purchased a peace by surrendering to the Romans all those portions of Asia VII. SYRIAN Minor bounded on the east by Bithyn'ia, Galátia, Cap- WAR. padócia, and Cilic'ia,[a] pledging himself not to interfere in the affairs of the Roman allies in Europe—giving up his ships of war and paying fifteen thousand talents of silver. The Romans now erected the conquered provinces, with the exception of a few Greek maritime towns, into a kingdom which they conferred upon Eúmenes, their

---

1. *Magnésia*, (now *Manisa*,) a city of Lydia, was situated on the southern side of the river Hermus, (now *Kodus*,) twenty-eight miles north-east from Smyrna. The modern Manisa is one of the neatest towns of Asia Minor, and contains a population of about thirty thousand inhabitants. There was another Magnésia, now in -uing, fifty miles south-east from Smyrna. ' *Map No. IV.*)

a. See Map of Asia Minor, No. VI.

ally, a petty prince of Per' gamus,[1] while to the Rhodians, also their al ies, they gave the provinces of Lyc' ia and Cária.[a]

25. Soon after the close of the second Punic war, Hannibal, having incurred the enmity of some of his countrymen, retired to Syria, where he joined Antíochus in the war against Rome. A clause in the treaty with the Syrian monarch stipulated that Hannibal should be delivered up to the Romans; but he avoided the danger by seeking refuge at the court of Prúsias, king of Bithyn' ia, where he remained about five years. An embassy was finally sent to de- mand him of Prúsias, who, afraid of giving offence to the Romans, agreed to give him up, but the aged veteran, to avoid falling into the hands of his ungenerous enemies, destroyed himself by poison, in the sixty-fifth year of his age The same year witnessed the death of his great rival and conqueror Scipio. (B. C. 183.)[b] The latter, on his return from carrying on the war against Antíochus, was charged with secreting part of the treasure received from the Syrian king. Scorning to answer the unjust accusation, he went as an exile into a country village of Italy, where he soon after died.

26. The events that led to the overthrow of the Macedónian monarchy, and the reduction of Greece to a Roman province, have VIII. THIRD been related in a former chapter.[c] Already the third PUNIC WAR. Punic war was drawing to a close, and the same year that Greece lost her liberties under Roman dominion, witnessed the destruction of the miserable remains of the once proud republic of Carthage. During the fifty years that had elapsed since the battle of Zama, the conduct of the Carthaginians had not afforded the Ro- mans any cause whatever for complaint, and amicable relations be- tween the two people might still have continued; but the expediency of a war with Carthage was a favorite topic of debate in the Roman senate, and it is said that, of the many speeches which the elder Cato made on this subject, all ended with the sentence, *delenda est Car- thago*, " Carthage must be destroyed."

27 Carthage, still a wealthy, but feeble city, had long been har- assed by the encroachments of Massinis' sa, king of Numid' ia, who

---

l. The *Per' gamus* here mentioned, the most important city of Mysia, was situated in the southern part of that country, in a plain watered by two small rivers which united to form the Caicus. (*Map* No. IV.)

a. See *Map* of Asia Minor, No. VI.

b. Some of the ancients placed the death of Hannibal one or two years later. The dates of Scipio's death vary from 183 t 187

c. See p. 110

appears to have been instigated to hostile acts by the Romans; and
although Massinis' sa had wrested from Carthage a large portion of
her territory, yet the Romans, seeking a pretext for war, called Carthage to account for her conduct, and without waiting to listen to
expostulation or submission, sent an army of more than eighty
thousand men to Sicily, to be there got in readiness for a descent
upon the African coast. (149 B. C.)   At Sicily the Carthaginan
ambassadors were received by the consuls in command of the army, and
required to give up three hundred children of the noblest Carthaginian
families as hostages; and when this demand had been complied with
the army crossed over and landed near Carthage.   The Carthagi
nians were now told that they must deliver up all their arms and
munitions of war ; and, hard as this command was, it was obeyed.[a]
The perfidious Romans next demanded that the Carthaginians should
abandon their city, allow its walls to be demolished, and remove to
a place ten miles inland, where they might build a new city, but
without walls or fortifications.

28. When these terms were made known to the Carthaginian
senate, the people, exasperated to madness, immediately put to death
all the Romans who were in the city, closed the gates, and, for want
of other weapons, collected stones on the battlements to repel the
first attacks of the enemy.   Hasdrubal, who had been banished because he was an enemy of the Romans, was recalled, and unexampled
exertions made for defence : the brass and iron of domestic utensils
were manufactured into weapons of war, and the women cut off their
long hair to be converted into strings for the bowmen and cordage
for the shipping.

29. The Romans had not anticipated such a display of courage
and patriotism, and the war was prolonged until the fourth year
after its commencement.   It was the struggle of despair on the part
of Carthage, and could end only in her destruction.   The city was
finally taken by Scipio Æmiliánus, the adopted son of the great
Africánus, when only five thousand citizens were found within its
walls, fifty thousand having previously surrendered on different occasions, and been carried away into slavery.   Hasdrubal begged his
life, which was granted only that he might adorn the triumph of
the Roman general ; but his wife, reproaching him for his cowardice,
threw herself with her children into the flames of the temple in

a. " Roman commissioners were sent into the city, who carried away two thousand cata
pults, and two hundred thousand suits of armor."

which she had taken refuge.   The walls of Carthage were levelled to the ground, the buildings of the city were burned, a part of the Carthaginian territory was given to the king of Numid'ia, and the rest became a Roman province.   (146 B. C.)   Thus perished the republic of Carthage, after an existence of nearly eight hundred years,—like Greece, the victim of Roman ambition.

We give below a description of Jerusalem, which was omitted by mistake in its pr per place.

Jerusalem, a famous city of southern Palestine, and long the capital of the kingdom of Judah, is situated on a hill in a mountainous country, between two small valleys, in one of which, on the west, the brook Gihon runs with a south-eastern course, to join the brook Kedron in the narrow valley of Jehoshaphat, east of the city. The modern city, built about three hundred years ago, is entirely surrounded by walls, barely two and a-half miles in circuit, and flanked here and there with square towers. The boundaries of the old city varied greatly at different times; and they are so imperfectly marked, the walls having been wholly destroyed, that few facts can be gathered respecting them. The interior of the modern city is divided by two valleys, intersecting each other at right angles, into four hills, on which history sacred and profane, has stamped the imperishable names of Zion, Acra, Bezetha, and Moriah. Mount Zion, on the south-west, the "City of David," is now the Jewish and Armenian quarter: Acra, or the lower city, on the north-west, is the Christian quarter; while the Mosque of Omar, with its sacred enclosure, occupies the hill of Moriah, which was crowned by the *House of the Lord* built by Solomon. West of the Christian quarter of the city is Mount Calvary, the scene of the Saviour's crucifixion; and on the eastern side of the valley of Jehoshaphat is the Mount of Olives, on whose western slope are the gardens of Gethsemane, enclosed by a wall, and still in a sort of ruined cultivation. A little west of Mount Zion, and near the base of Mount Calvary, is the pool of Gihon, near which "Zadok the priest and Nathan the prophet anointed Solomon king over Israel." South of Mount Zion is the valley of Hinnom, watered by the brook Gihon. A short distance up the valley of Jehoshaphat, and issuing from beneath the walls of Mount Moriah, is

> "Siloa's brook, that flow'd
> Fast by the oracles of God."

Jerusalem and its suburbs abound with many interesting localities, well authenticated as the scenes of events connected with the history of the patriarchs, and the sufferings of Christ; but to hundreds of others shown by the monks, minute criticism denies any claims to our respect. Considered as a modern town, the city is of very little importance: its population is about ten thousand, two-thirds of whom are Mohammedans: it has no trade—no industry whatever— nothing to give it commercial importance, except the manufacture, by the monks, of shells, beads, and relics, large quantities of which are shipped from the port of Jaffa, for Italy, Spain, and Portugal.

Jerusalem is generally believed to be identical with the Salem of which Melchisedek was king in the time of Abraham. When the Israelites entered the Holy Land it was in the possession of the Jebusites; and although Joshua took the city, the *citadel* on Mount Zion was held by the Jebusites until they were dislodged by David, who made Jerusalem the metropolis of his kingdom.

CHAPTER VI.

ROMAN HISTORY:

FROM THE CONQUEST OF GREECE AND CARTHAGE, 146 B. C., TO THE
COMMENCEMENT OF THE CHRISTIAN ERA.

ANALYSIS. 1. Situation of SPAIN AFTER THE FALL OF CARTHAGE. [Celtibérians. Lusi‐
ánians.]—2. Character, exploits, and death of Viriáthus.—3. Subsequent history of the Lusitá‐
sians. War with the Numan' tians. [Numan' tia.]—4. SERVILE WAR IN SICILY. Situation of
Sicily. Events of the Servile war.—5. DISSENSIONS OF THE GRACCHI. Corrupt state of society
at Rome.—6. Country and city population.—7. Efforts of the tribunes. Character and efforts
of Tiberius Gracchus. Condition of the public lands.—8. The agrarian laws proposed by
Tiberius.—9. Opposed by the nobles, but finally passed. Triumvirate appointed to enforce
them. Disposition of the treasures of At' talus,—10. Circumstances of the death of Tiberius.—
11. Continued opposition of the aristocracy—tribuneship of Caius Gracchus—and circumstances
of his death.—12. Condition of Rome after the fall of the Gracchi.—13. Profligacy of the Ro‐
man senate, and circumstances of the first JUGURTHINE WAR.—14. Renewal of the war with
Jugurtha. Events of the war, and fate of Jugurtha. [Mauritánia.]—15. GERMANIC INVASION.
[Cimbri and Teu' tones.] Successive Roman defeats. [Danube. Noreja.] 16. Márius, ap‐
pointed to the command, defeats the Teu' tones. [The Rhone. Aix.] 17. The Cimbri. Great‐
ness of the danger with which Rome was threatened.—18. THE SOCIAL WAR.—19. FIRST
MITHRIDATIC WAR. [Pontus. Eu' menes. Per' gamus.]—20. Causes of the Mithridatic war,
and successes of Mithridátes.—CIVIL WAR BETWEEN MA' RIUS AND SYLLA.—22. Triumph of
the Márian faction. Death and character of Márius.—23. Continuance of the civil war.
Events in the East. Sylla master of Rome.—23. Proscription and massacres. Death of Sylla.
—25. The Márian faction in Spain. SERVILE WAR IN ITALY.

26. SECOND AND THIRD MITHRIDATIC WARS. Lucullus. Manil' ius, and the Manil ian
law.—27. Pompey's successes in the East. Reduction of Palestine. Death of Mithridátes.—28
CONSPIRACY OF CATILINE. Situation of Rome at this period. Character and designs of Catiline.
Circumstances that favored his schemes. By whom opposed.—29. Cicero elected consul.
Flight, defeat, and death of Catiline.—30. THE FIRST TRIUMVIRATE. Division of power.—31.
Cæsar's conquests in Gaul, Germany, and Britain. Death of Crassus. Rivalry between Cæsar
and Pompey. [The Rhine. Parthia.]—32. Commencement of the CIVIL WAR BETWEEN CÆSAR
AND POMPEY. Flight of the latter. [Raven' na.]—33. Cæsar's successes. Sole dictator. His
defeat at Dyrrach' ium.—34. Battle of Pharsália. Flight, and death of Pompey. [Pharsália.
Peleu' sium.]—35. Cleopatra. Alexandrine war. Reduction of Pontus. [Pharos.]—36. Cæsar's
clemency. Servility of the senate. The war in Africa, and death of Cato. [Thapsus.]—37
Honors bestowed upon Cæsar. Useful changes—reformation of the calendar.—38. The war in
Spain. [Munda.]—39. Cæsar, dictator for life. His gigantic projects. He is suspected of
aiming at sovereign power.—40. Conspiracy against him. His death.—41. Conduct of Brutus.
Mark Antony's oration. Its effects.—42. Ambition of Antony. Civil war. SECOND TRIUMVI‐
RATE. The proscription that followed.—43. Brutus and Cassius. Their defeat at Philippi.
[Philippi.]—44. Antony in Asia Minor,—at the court of Cleopatra. [Tarsus.] Civil war in
Italy.—45. Antony's return. Reconciliation of the rivals, and division of the empire among
them. [Brundúsium.]—46. The peace is soon broken. Sextius Pompey. Lep' idus. Antony
—47. The war between Octávius and Antony. Battle of Actium, and disgraceful flight of
Antony.—48. Death of Antony and Cleopatra.—49 OCTA' VIUS SOLE MASTER OF THE ROMAN
WORLD. Honors and offices conferred upon him. Character of his government.—50. Success‐
ful wars,—followed by a general peace. Extent of the R. man empire. Birth of the Saviour.

1. After the fall of Carthage and the Grecian republics, which were the closing events of the preceding chapter, the attention of the Roman people was for a time principally directed to Spain

I. SPAIN AFTER THE FALL OF CARTHAGE.

When, near the close of the second Punic war, the Carthaginian dominion in Spain ended, that country was regarded as being under Roman jurisdiction; although, beyond the immediate vicinity of the Roman garrisons, the native tribes, the most prominent of which were the Celtibérians[1] and Lusitánians,[2] long maintained their independence.

2. At the close of the third Punic war, Viriáthus, a Lusitánian prince, whose character resembles that of the Wallace of Scotland, had triumphed over the Roman legions in several engagements, and had already deprived the republic of nearly half of her possessions in the peninsula. During eight years he bade defiance to the most formidable hosts, and foiled the ablest generals of Rome, when the Roman governor Cæ'pio, unable to cope with so great a general treacherously procured his assassination.[a]   (B. C. 140.)

3. Soon after the death of Viriáthus the Lusitánians submitted to a peace, and many of them were removed from their mountain fastnesses to the mild district of Valen'cia,[3] where they completely lost their warlike character; but the Numan'tians[4] rejected with scorn the insidious overtures of their invaders, and continued the war. Two Roman generals, at the head of large armies, were conquered by them, and on both occasions treaties of peace were concluded with the vanquished, in the name of the Roman people, but after-

1. The *Celtibérians*, whose country was sometimes called *Celtibéria*, occupied the greatest part of the interior of Spain around the head waters of the Tagus.

2. The *Lusitánians*, whose country was called *Lusitánia*, dwelt on the Atlantic coast, and when first known, principally between the rivers Douro and Tagus.

3. The modern district or province of *Valencia* extends about two hundred miles along the south-eastern coast of Spain. The city of Valencia, situated near the mouth of the river Guadalaviar, (the ancient Tusia,) is its capital. (*Map* No. XIII.)

4. *Numan'tia*, a celebrated town of the Celtibérians, was situated near the source of the river Douro, and near the site of the modern village of *Chavaler*, and about one hundred and twenty-five miles north-east from Madrid.

a. *Viriáthus*, at first a shepherd, called by the Romans a robber, then a guerilla chief and finally an eminent military hero, aroused the Lusitánians to avenge the wrongs and injuries inflicted upon them by Roman ambition. He was unrivalled in fertility of resources under defeat, skill in the conduct of his troops, and courage in the hour of battle. Accustomed to a free life in the mountains, he never indulged himself with the luxury of a bed: bread and meat were his only food, and water his only beverage; and being robust, hardy, adroit, always cheerful, and dreading no danger, he knew how to avail himself of the wild chivalry of his countrymen, and to keep alive in them the spirit of freedom. During eight years he constantly harassed the Roman armies, and defeated many Roman generals, several of whom lost their lives in battle. His name still lives in the songs and legends of early Spain.

ward; rejected by the Roman senate. Scip'io Æmiliánus, at the head of sixty thousand men, was then sent to conduct the war, and laying siege to Numan'tia, garrisoned by less than ten thousand men, he finally reduced the city, but not until the Numan'tians, worn out by toil and famine, and finally yielding to despair, had destroyed all their women and children, and then, setting fire to their city, had perished, almost to a man, on their own swords, or in the flames. (B. C. 133.) The destruction of Numan'tia was followed by the submission of nearly all the tribes of the peninsula, and Spain henceforth became a Roman province.

4. Two years before the fall of Numan'tia, Sicily had become the theatre of a servile war, which merits attention principally on account of the view it gives of the state of the conquered countries then under the jurisdiction of Rome. The calamities which usually follow in the train of long-continued war had swept away **II. SERVILE** most of the original population of Sicily, and a large **WAR.** portion of the cultivated lands in the island had been added, by conquest, to the Roman public domain, which had been formed into large estates, and let out to speculators, who paid rents for the same into the Roman treasury. In the wars of the Romans, and indeed of most nations at this period, large numbers of the captives taken in war were sold as slaves; and it was by slave labor the estates in Sicily were cultivated. The slaves in Sicily were cruelly treated, and as most of them had once been free, and some of high rank, it is not surprising that they should seek every favorable opportunity to rise against their masters. When once, therefore, a revolt had broken out, it spread rapidly over the whole island. Seventy thousand of the slaves were at one time under arms, and in four successive campaigns four Roman prætorian armies were defeated. The most frightful atrocities were perpetrated on both sides, but the rebellion was finally quelled by the destruction of most of those who had taken part in it. (B. C. 133.)

5. While these events were occuring in the Roman provinces, affairs in the capital, generally known in history as the " dissensions of the Gracchi," were fast ripening for civil war. More **III. DISSEN-** than two hundred years had elapsed since the animosi- **SIONS OF** ties of patricians and plebeians were extinguished by an **THE** equal participation in public honors; but the wealth of **GRACCHI.** conquered provinces, and the numerous lucrative and honorable offices, both civil and military, that had been created, had produced

corruption at home, by giving rise to factions which contended for the greatest share of the spoils, while, apart from these new distinctions had arisen, and the rich and the poor, or the illustrious and the obscure, now formed the great parties in the State.

6. As the nobles availed themselves of the advantages of their station to accumulate wealth and additional honors, the large slave plantations increased in the country to the disparagement of free labor, and the detriment of small landholders, whose numbers were constantly diminishing, while the city gradually became crowded with an idle, indigent, and turbulent populace, attracted thither by the frequent cheap or gratuitous distributions of corn, and by the frequency of the public shows, and made up, in part, of emancipated slaves, who were kept as retainers in the families of their former masters So long as large portions of Italy remained unsettled, there was an outlet for the redundancy of this growing populace; but the entire Italian territory being now occupied, the indigent could no longer be provided for in the country, and the practice of colonizing distant provinces had not yet been adopted.

7. The evils of such a state of society were numerous and formidable, and such as to threaten the stability of the republic. Against the increasing political influence of the aristocracy, the tribunes of the people had long struggled, but rather as factious demagogues than as honest defenders of popular rights. At length Tibérius Grac'chus, a tribune, and grandson of Scipio Africánus one of the noblest and most virtuous among the young men of his time, commenced the work of reform by proposing to enforce the Licinian law, which declared that no individual should possess more than five hundred jugers,[a] (about two hundred and seventy-five acres) of the public domain. This law had been long neglected, so that numbers of the aristocracy now cultivated vast estates, the occupancy of which had perhaps been transmitted from father to son as an inheritance, or disposed of by purchase and sale; and although the republic still retained the fee simple in such lands, and could at any time legally turn out the occupants, it had long ceased to be thought probable that its rights would ever be exercised.

8. The law of Tibérius Grac'chus went even beyond strict legal justice, by proposing that buildings and improvements on the public lands should be paid for out of the public treasury. The impression has generally prevailed that the Agrarian laws proposed by Tibérius

a. A *juger* was nearly five-ninths of our acre.

Grac'chus were a direct and violent infringement of the rights of private property; but the genius and learning of Niebuhr have shown that they effected the distribution of *public* lands only, and not those of private citizens; although there were doubtless instances where, incidentally, they violated private rights.

9. When the senators and nobles, who were the principal land-holders, perceived that their interests were attacked, their exasperation was extreme; and Tibérius, whose virtues had hitherto been acknowledged by all, was denounced as a factious demagogue, a disturber of the public tranquillity, and a traitor to the conservative interests of the republic. When the law of Tibérius was about to be put to the vote in the assemblies of the people, the corrupt nobles engaged Octávius, one of the tribune's colleagues, to forbid the proceedings; but the people deposed him from the tribuneship, and the agrarian law was passed. A permanent triumvirate, or committee of three, consisting of Tibérius Grac'chus, his brother Cáius, and Ap'pius Clau'dius, was then appointed to enforce the law. About the same time a law was passed, providing that the treasures which At'talus, king of Per'gamus, had recently bequeathed to the Roman people, should be distributed among the poorer citizens, to whom lands were to be assigned, in order to afford them the means of purchasing the necessary implements of husbandry.[a]

10. At the expiration of the year of his tribuneship, Tibérius offered himself for reëlection, conscious that unless shielded by the sacredness of the office of tribune, his person would no longer be safe from the resentment of his enemies. After two of the tribes had voted in his favor, the opposing party declared the votes illegal, and the disputes which followed occupied the day. On the following morning the people again assembled to the election, when a rumor was circulated that some of the nobles, accompanied by bands of armed retainers, designed to attack the crowd and take the life of Tibérius. A tumult ensued, and a false report was carried to the senate, then in session, that Tibérius had demanded a crown of the people. The senate seized upon this pretext for violent interference, but when the consul refused to disturb the people in their legal assembly, the senators rose in a body, and, headed by Scip'io Nasíca,

a. In 133 B. C. At'talus Philométer bequeathed his kingdom and all his treasures to the Roman people. At'talus was one of the worst specimens of Eastern despots, and took great delight in dispatching his nearest relatives by poison. The Romans had long looked upon his kingdom as their property, and his will was probably drawn up by Roman dictation.

and accompanied by a crowd of armed dependants, proceeded to the assembly, where a conflict ensued, in which Tibérius and about three hundred of his adherents were slain. (B. C. 132.)

11. Notwithstanding this disgraceful victory, and the persecutions that followed it, the ruling party could not abolish the triumvirate which had been appointed to execute the law of Tibérius. During ten years, however, little was accomplished by the popular party, owing to the powerful opposition of the aristocracy; but after Cáius Grac' chus, a younger brother of Tibérius, had been elected tribune, the cause of the people received a new impulse; an equitable division of the public lands was commenced, and many salutary reforms were made in the administration of the government. But, at length, Cáius being deprived of the tribuneship by false returns and bribery, and his bitter enemy Opim' ius having been elected consul by the aristocratic faction, and afterwards appointed dictator by the senate, the followers of Cáius were driven from the city by armed violence, and three thousand of their number slain. (B. C. 120.) The head of Cáius was thrown at the feet of Opim' ius, who had offered for it a reward of its weight in gold.[a]

12. Thus ended what has been termed the "dissensions of the Gracchi;" and with that noble family perished the freedom of the republic. An odious aristocracy, which derived its authority from wealth, now ruled the State: the tribunes, becoming rich themselves, no longer interposed their authority between the people and their oppressors; while the lower orders, reduced to a state of hopeless subjection, and despairing of liberty, became factious and turbulent, and ere long prepared the way, first for the tyranny of a perpetual dictatorship, and lastly for the establishment of a monarchy on the ruins of the commonwealth.

13 The profligacy and corruption of the senate were manifest in the events that led to the Jugur' thine war, which began to embroil

a. Tibérius and Cáius Grac chus, though of the noblest origin, and of superior natural endowments, are said to have been indebted more to the judicious care of their widowed mother Cornelia, than to nature, for the excellence of their characters. This distinguished Roman matron, the daughter of Scip' io Africánus the Elder, occupies a high rank for the purity and excellence of her private character, as well as for her noble and elevated sentiments. The following anecdote of Cornelia is often cited. A Campánian lady who was at the time on a visit to her, having displayed to Cornelia some very beautiful ornaments which she possessed, desired the latter, in return, to exhibit her own. The Roman mother purposely detained her in conversation until her children returned from school, when, pointing to them, she exclaimed, "There are my ornaments." She bore the untimely death of her sons with great magnanimity, and in honor of her a statue was afterwards erected by the Roman people, bearing for an inscription the words, "*Cornelia, mother of the Gracchi.*"

the republic soon after the fall of the Grac'chi. The Numid'ian king Micip'sa, the son of Massinis'sa, had divided his kingdom, on his death-bed, between his two sons Hiemp'sal and Adher'bal, and his nephew Jugur'tha ; but the latter, resolving to obtain possession of the whole inheritance, soon murdered Hiemp'sal, and compelled Adher'bal to take refuge in Rome. The senate, won by the bribes of the usurper, decreed a division of the kingdom between the two claimants, giving to Jugur'tha the better portion ; but the latter soon declared war against his cousin, and, having gained possession of his person, put him to death. The senate could no longer avoid a declaration of war against Jugur'tha; but he would have escaped by an easy peace, after coming to Rome to plead his own cause, had he not there murdered another relative, whom he suspected of aspiring to the throne of Numid'ia. (B. C 109.)

IV. JUGUR' THINE WAR.

14. Jugur'tha was allowed to return to Africa ; but his briberies of the Roman senators were exposed, and the war against him was begun anew. After he had defeated several armies, Metel'lus drove him from his kingdom, when the Numid'ian formed an alliance with Bac'chus, king of Mauritánia,[1] but their united forces were successively routed by the consul Márius, formerly a lieutenant in the army of Metel'lus, but who, after obtaining the consulship, had been sent to terminate the war. Eventually the Moorish king betrayed Jugur'tha into the hands of the Romans, as the price of his own peace and security, (B. C. 106,) and the captive monarch, after gracing the triumph of Márius, was condemned to be starved to death in prison.

15. Soon after the fall of Jugur'tha, Márius was recalled from his command in Africa to defend the northern provinces of Italy against a threatened invasion from immense hordes of the Cim'bri and Teu'tones,[a] German nations, who, about the year 113, had crossed the Danube[2] and appeared on the east-

V. GERMANIC INVASION

1. *Mauritánia* was an extensive country of Northern Africa, west of Numid'ia, embracing the present Morocco and part of Algiers. (*Map* No. IX.)

2. The *Danube*, the largest river in Europe, except the Volga, rises in the south-western part of Germany, in the Duchy of Baden, only about thirty miles from the Rhine, and after a general south-eastern course of nearly eighteen hundred miles, falls into the Black Sea. (*Map* No. VIII.)

a. The barbarian torrent of the *Cim'bri* and *Teu'tones* appears to have originated beyond the Elbe. The original seat of the Cim'bri was probably the Cimbrian peninsula, so called by the Romans,—the same as the modern Jutland, or Denmark. Opinions differ concerning the Teu'tones, some believing them to have been the collective wanderers of many tribes between the Vistula and the Elbe, while others fix their original seats in northern Scandinavia,—i t in the north of Sweden and Norway.

ern declivities of the Alps, where the Romans guarded the passes
into Italy.   The first year of the appearance of these unknown
tribes, from which is dated the beginning of German history,[a] they
defeated the Roman consul Papir'ius Car'bo, near Noréja,[1] in the
mountains of the present Styr'ia.   Proceeding thence towards south
ern Gaul they demanded a country from the Romans, for which they
promised military assistance in war; but when their request was re
fused they determined to obtain by the sword what was denied them
by treaty.   Four more Roman armies were successively vanquished
by them, the last under the consuls Man'lius and Cæ'pio in the year
105, with the prodigious loss of 80,000 Roman soldiers slain, and
40,000 of their slaves.

16. Fortunately for the Romans, the enemy, after this great victory, turned aside towards the south of France and Spain, while
Márius, who had been appointed to the command of the northern
army, marching over the Alps towards Gaul, formed a defensive
camp on the Rhone.[2]   The Germans, returning, in vain tempted
Márius to battle, after which they divided into two bands, the Cim'-
bri taking up their march for Italy, while the Teu'tones remained
opposed to Márius.   But when the Teu'tones saw that their chal-
lenge for battle was not accepted, they also broke up, and marching
past the Romans, jeeringly asked them "if they had any commissions
to send to their wives."   Márius followed at their side, keeping upon
the heights, but when he had arrived at the present town of Aix,[3] in the
south of France, some accidental skirmishing at the outposts of the
two armies brought on a general battle, which continued two days,
and in which the nation of the Teu'tones was nearly annihilated,
(B. C. 102,)—two hundred thousand of them being either killed or
taken prisoners.

17. In the meantime the consul Catul'lus had been repulsed by
the Cim'bri in northern Italy, and driven south of the Po.   Márius
hastened to his assistance, and their united forces now advanced
across the Po, and defeated the Cim'bri in a great battle on the Rau

---

1. *Noréja*, or *Noreia*, was the capital of the Roman province of *Noricum*. The site of this
city is in the present Austrian province of *Styria*, about sixty miles north-east from Laybach.
(*Map* No. VIII.)

2. The *Rhone* rises in Switzerland, passes through the Lake of Geneva, and after uniting
with the Saone flows south through the south-eastern part of France, and discharges its waters
by four mouths into the Mediterranean.   (*Map* No. XIII.)

3. *Aix*, called by the Romans *Aquæ Sextæ*, is situated in a plain sixteen miles north of Mar
seilles.   (*Map* No. XIII.)

a. Kohlrausch's Germany, p. 43

dian plains.[a] (B. C. 101.) Thus ended the war with the German nations. The danger with which it for a time threatened Rome was compared to that of the great Gallic invasion, nearly three hundred years before. The Romans, in gratitude to their deliverer, now styled Márius the third founder of the city.

18. A still more dangerous war, called the social war, soon after broke out between the Romans and their Italian allies, caused by the unjust treatment of the latter, who, forming part of the commonwealth, and sharing its burdens, had long in vain demanded for themselves the civil and political privileges that were enjoyed by citizens of the metropolis. The war continued three years, and Rome would doubtless have fallen, had she not, soon after the commencement of the struggle, granted the Latin towns, more than fifty in number, all the rights of Roman citizens, and thus secured their fidelity. (90 B. C.)[b] The details of this war are little known, but it is supposed that, during its continuance, more than three hundred thousand Italians lost their lives, and that many flourishing towns were reduced to heaps of ruins. The Romans were eventually compelled to offer the rights of citizenship to all that should lay down their arms; and tranquillity was thus restored to most of Italy, although the Samnites continued to resist until they were destroyed as a nation.

VI. THE SOCIAL WAR.

19. While these domestic dangers were threatening Rome, an important African war had broken out with Mithridátes, king of Pontus.[1] It has been related that in the time of Antíochus the Great, king of Syria, the Romans obtained, by conquest and treaty, the western provinces of Asia Minor, most of which they conferred upon one of their allies, Eúmenes, king of Per'gamus, and that At'talus, a subsequent prince of Per'gamus, gave back these same provinces, by will, to the Roman people. (See p. 161 and p. 169.)

VII. FIRST MITHRIDATIC WAR.

20. The Romans, thus firmly established in Asia Minor, saw with jealousy the increasing power of Mithridátes, who, after reducing the nations on the eastern coasts of the Black Sea, had added to his

1. *Pontus* was a country of Asia Minor, on the south-eastern coast of the Euxine, having Colchis on the east, and Paphlagónia and Galátia on the west.

a. The exact locality is unknown, but it was on a northern branch of the Po, between Vercelli and Verona, probably near the present Milan. Some say near Vercelli, on the west bank of the Sessites.

b. This was done by the celebrated *Lex Julia*, or Julian law, proposed by L. Julius Cæsar.

dominions on the west, Paphlagónia and Cappadocia,[a] which he claimed by inheritance. Nicomédes, king of Bithyn'ia, disputing with him the right to the latter provinces, appealed to the Roman senate, which declared that the disputed districts should be free States, subject to neither Nicomédes nor Mithridátes. The latter then entered into an alliance with Tigránes, king of Arménia,— seized the disputed provinces—drove Nicomédes from his kingdom— defeated two large Roman armies, and, in the year 88, before the end of the social war, had gained possession of all Asia Minor. All the Greek islands of the Ægean, except Rhodes, voluntarily submitted to him, and nearly all the Grecian States, with Athens throwing off the Roman yoke, placed themselves under his protection. Mithridátes had received a Greek education, and was looked upon as a Grecian, which accounts for the readiness with which the Greeks espoused his cause.

21. The Roman senate gave the command of the Mithridatic war to Sylla, a man of great intellectual superiority, but of profligate morals, who had served under Márius against Jugur'tha and the

VIII. CIVIL WAR BE-TWEEN MA'-RIUS AND SYLLA. Cim'bri, and had rendered himself eminent by his services in the social war. The ambitious Márius, though more than twenty years the senior of Sylla, had long regarded the latter as a formidable rival, and now he succeeded in obtaining a decree of the people, by which the command was transferred from Sylla to himself. Sylla, then at the head of an army in the Samnite territory, immediately marched against Rome, and entering the city, broke up the faction of Márius, who, after a series of romantic adventures, escaped to Africa.[b] (88 B. C.)

22. Scarcely had Sylla departed with his army for Greece, to carry on the war against Mithridátes, when a fierce contest arose within

a. See Map of Asia Minor, No. IV.

b. Márius fled first to Ostia, and thence along the sea-coast to Mintur'næ, where he was put on shore, at the mouth of the Liris, and abandoned by the crew of the vessel that carried him. After in vain seeking shelter in the cottage of an old peasant, he was forced to hide himself in the mud of the Pontine marshes; but he was discovered by his vigilant pursuers, dragged out, and thrown into a dungeon at Mintur'næ. No one, however, had the courage to put him to death; and the magistrates of Mintur'næ therefore sent a public slave into the prison to kill him; but as the barbarian approached the hoary warrior his courage failed him, and the Mintur'nians, moved by compassion, put Márius on board a boat and transported him to Africa. Being set down at Carthage, the Roman governor of the district sent to inform him that unless he left Africa he should treat him as a public enemy. "Go and tell him," replied the wanderer "that you have seen the exile Márius sitting on the ruins of Carthage." In the following year during the absence of Sylla, he returned to Italy. For localities of *Pontine Marshes Liris* and *Mintur'næ*, see Map No. X.

the city between the partisans of Sylla and Márius; one of the con
suls, Cinna, espousing the cause of the latter, and the other, Octavius, that of the former.   Cinna recalled the aged Márius; both
parties flew to arms; and all Italy became a prey to the horrors of
civil war.   (B. C. 87.)   The senate and the nobles adhered to Octavius; but Rome was besieged, and compelled to surrender to the
adverse faction.   Then commenced a general massacre of all the opponents of Márius, which was continued five days and nights, until
the streets ran with blood.   Having gratified his revenge by this
bloody victory, Márius declared himself consul, without going through
the formality of an election, and chose Cinna to be his colleague ,
but sixteen days later his life was terminated by a sudden fever, at
the age of seventy-one years.   Márius has the character of having
been one of the most successful generals of Rome; but after having
borne away many honorable offices, and performed many noble ex
ploits, he tarnished his glory by a savage and infamous old age.

23.   During three years after the death of · Márius, Sylla was con
ducting the war in Greece and Asia, while Italy was completely in
the hands of the party of Cinna.   The latter even sent an army to
Asia to attack Sylla, and was preparing to embark himself, when he
was slain in a mutiny of his soldiers.   In the meantime Sylla, having taken Athens by storm, and defeated two armies of Mithridátes,
concluded a peace with that monarch; (84 B. C.,) and having induced
the soldiers sent against him to join his standard, he returned to Italy
at the head of thirty thousand men to take vengeance upon his enemies, who had collected an army of four hundred and fifty cohorts,
numbering one hundred and eighty thousand men,[a] to oppose him.
(B. C. 83.)   But none of the generals of this vast army were equal,
in military talents, to Sylla; their forces gradually deserted them,
and after a short but severe struggle, Sylla became master of Rome.

24.   A dreadful proscription of his enemies followed, far exceeding the atrocities of Márius; for Sylla filled not only Rome, but
all Italy, with massacres, which, in the language of the old writers,
had neither numbers nor bounds.   He caused himself to be appointed
dictator for an unlimited time, (B. C. 81,) reëstablished the government on an aristocratical basis, and after having · ruled nearly three
years, to the astonishment of every one he resigned his power, and
retired to private life.   He died soon after, of · a loathsome disease,

a. " From the time of Márius, the Roman military forces are always counted by cohorts o
small battalions, each containing four hundred and twenty men."—Niebuhr, iv. 195.

at the age of sixty years, leaving, by his own direction, the following
characteristic inscription to be engraved on his tomb. "Here lies
Sylla, who was never outdone in good offices by his friend, nor in
acts of hostility by his enemy." (B. C. 77.)

25. A Márian faction, headed by Sertórius, a man of great mili
tary talents, still existed in Spain, threatening to sever that province
from Rome, and establish a new kingdom there. After Sertórius
had defeated several Roman armies, the youthful Pompey, afterwards surnamed the Great, was sent against him; but he too was
vanquished, and it was not until the insurgents had been deprived of
their able leader by treachery, that the rebellion was quelled, and
Spain tranquillized. (B. C. 70.) During the continuance of the
Spanish war, a formidable revolt of the slaves, headed by Spar'tacus,

IX. SERVILE   a celebrated gladiator, had broken out in Italy. At first
WAR IN   Spar'tacus and his companions formed a desperate band
ITALY.   of robbers and murderers, but their numbers eventually
increased to a hundred and twenty thousand men, and three prætorian and two consular armies were completely defeated by them.
The war lasted upwards of two years, and at one time Rome itself
was in danger; but the rebels, divided among themselves, were finally
overcome, and nearly all exterminated, by the prætor Cras'sus, the
growing rival of Pompey. (B. C. 70.)

26. During the progress of these events in Italy, a second war had
broken out with Mithridátes, (83 B. C.,) but after a continuance of

X. SECOND   two years it had been terminated by treaty. (81 B. C.,
AND THIRD   Seven years later, Mithridátes, who had long been pre-
MITHRIDATIC paring for hostilities, broke the second treaty between
WARS.   him and the Romans by the invasion of Bithyn'ia, and
thus commenced the third Mithridatic war. At first Lucullus, who
was sent against him, was successful, and amassed immense treasures;
but eventually he was defeated, and Mithridátes gained possession
of nearly all Asia Minor. Manil'ius, the tribune, then proposed
that Pompey, who had recently gained great honor by a successful
war against the pirates in the Mediterranean, should be placed over
all the other generals in the Asiatic provinces, retaining at the same
time the command by sea. This was a greater accumulation of
power than had ever been intrusted to any Roman citizen, but the
law was adopted. It was on this ocasion that the orator Cicero
pronounced his famous oration *Pro lege Manilia*, (" for the Manilian
law.") Cæsar also, who was just then rising into eminence, approved

the measure, while the friends of Cras'sus in vain attempted to defeat it.

27. Pompey, then passing with a large army into Asia, (B. C. 66,) in one campaign defeated Mithridátes on the banks of the Euphrates and drove the monarch from his kingdom; and in the following year, after reducing Syria, thus putting an end to the empire of the Seleu'cidæ he found an opportunity of extending Roman interference to the affairs of Palestine. Each of the two claimants to the throne, the brothers Hyrcánus and Aristobúlus, sought his assistance, and as he deci led in favor of the former, the latter prepared to resist the Roman, and shut himself up in Jerusalem. After a siege of three months the city was taken; its walls and fortifications were thrown down; Hyrcánus was appointed to be high-priest, and governor of the country, but was required to pay tribute to the Romans; while Aristobúlus, with his sons and daughters, was taken to Rome to grace the triumph of Pompey. From this time the situation of Judea differed little from that of a Roman province, although for a while later it was governed by native princes; but all of them were more or less subject to Roman authority. About the time of Pompey's conquest of Jerusalem, Mithridátes, driven from one province to another, and finding no protection even among his own relatives, terminated his life by poison. (B. C. 63.) His dominions and vast wealth were variously disposed of by Pompey in the name of the Roman people.

28. While Pompey was winning laurels in Asia, the republic was brought near the brink of destruction by a conspiracy headed by the infamous Catiline. Rome was at this time in a state of complete anarchy; the republic was a mere name; the laws had lost their power; the elections were carried by bribery; and the city populace was a tool in the hands of the nobles in their feuds against one another. In this corrupt state of things Sergius Catiline, a man of patrician rank, and of great abilities, but a monster of wickedness, who had acted a distinguished part in the bloody scenes of Sylla's tyranny, placed himself at the head of a confederacy of profligate young nobles, who hoped, by elevating their leader to the consulship, or by murdering those who opposed them, to make themselves masters of Rome, and to gain possession of the public treasures, and the property of the citizens Many circumstances, favored the audacious schemes of the conspirators. Pompey was abroad—Cras'sus, striving with mad eagerness

for power and riches, counterbanced the growing influence of Catiline, as a means of his own aggrandizement—Cæsar, laboring to revive the party of Márius, and courting the favor of the people by public shows and splendid entertainments, spared Catiline, and perhaps secretly encouraged him, while the only two eminent Romans who boldly determined to uphold their falling country were Cato the younger, and the orator Cicero.

29. While the storm which Catiline had been raising was threatening to burst upon Rome, and every one dreaded the arch-conspirator, but no one had the courage to come forward against him, Cicero offered himself a candidate for the consulship, in opposition to Catiline, and was elected. An attempt of the conspirators to murder Cicero in his own house was frustrated by the watchful vigilance of the consul ; and a fortunate accident disclosed to him all their plans, which he laid before the senate.   Even in the senate-house Catiline boldly confronted Cicero, who there pronounced against him that famous oration which saved Rome by driving Catiline from the city.   Catiline then fled to Etrúria, where he had a large force already under arms, while several of his confederates remained in the city to open the gates to him on his approach ; but they were apprehended, and brought to punishment.   An army was then sent against the insurgents, who were completely defeated ; and most of them, imitating Catiline, fought to the last, and died sword in hand.   (B. C. 63.)   Cicero, to whom the Romans were indebted for the overthrow of the conspiracy, was now hailed as the Father and Deliverer of his country.

30. Soon after the return of Pompey from Asia, the jealousies between him and Cras'sus were renewed ; but Julius Cæsar succeeded in reconciling the rivals, and in uniting them with himself in a secret partnership of power, called the First Triumvirate. (60 B. C.)   These men, by their united influence, were now able to carry all their measures ; and they virtually usurped the powers of the senate, as well as the command of the legions.   Cæsar first obtained the office of consul, (B. C. 59,) and, when the year of his consulship had expired, was made commander of all Gaul, (B. C. 58,) although but a small portion of that country was then under the Roman dominion.   Cras'sus, whose avarice was unbounded, soon after obtained the command of Syria, famed for its luxury and wealth ; while to Pompey were given Africa and Spain, although he left the care of his provinces to others, and still remained in Italy.

XII. THE FIRST TRIUMVIRATE.

31. In the course of eight years Cæsar conquered all Gaul, which consisted of a great number of separate nations—twice passed the Rhine[1] into Germany—and twice passed over into Britain, and subdued the southern part of the island.   Hitherto Britain had been known only by name to the Greeks and Romans; and its first invasion by Cæsar, in the year 55 B. C., is the beginning of its authentic history   The disembarkation of the Romans, somewhere on the eastern coast of Kent,[a] was firmly disputed by the natives; but stern discipline and steady valor overawed them, and they proffered submission.   A second invasion in the ensuing spring was also resisted; but genius and science asserted their usual superiority; and peace, and the withdrawal of the invaders, were purchased by the payment of tribute.   In the meantime Cras'sus had fallen in Parthia,[2] (B. C. 52,) thus leaving but two masters of the Roman world; but Pompey had already become jealous of the greatness of Cæsar's fame, and on the death of Julia, the wife of Pompey and daughter of Cæsar, the last tie that bound these friends was broken, and they became rivals, and enemies.   Pompey had secured most of the senate to his interests; but Cæsar, though absent, had obtained, by the most lavish bribes, numerous and powerful adherents in the very heart of Rome. Among others, Mark Antony and Quintus Cassius, tribunes of the people, favored his interests.

32. When Cæsar requested that he might stand for the consulship in his absence, the senate denied the request.   When or dered to disband his legions and resign his provinces, he immediately promised compliance, if Pompey would do the same; but the senate peremptorily ordered him to disband his

XIII. CIVIL WAR BE-TWEEN CÆSAR AND POMPEY.

1. The *Rhine* rises in Switzerland, only a few miles from the source of the Rhone—passes through Lake Constance—then flows west to the town of Basle, near the borders of France, thence generally north-west to the North Sea or German Ocean. It formed the ancient boundary between Gaul and the German tribes, and was first passed by Julius Cæsar in his invasion of the German nation of the Sicambri.

2. *Parthia* was originally a small extent of country, south-east of the Caspian Sea. After the death of Alexander the Great a separate kingdom was formed there, which gradually extended to the Indus on the east and the Tigris on the west, until it embraced the fairest provinces of the old Persian monarchy.   By the victory over Crassus the Parthians obtained a great increase of power, and during a long time after this event they were almost constantly at war with the Romans.   The Parthian empire was overthrown by the southern Persians 226 years after the Christian era, when the later Persian empire of the *Sassanidæ* was established.   "The mode of fighting adopted by the Parthian cavalry was peculiar, and well calculated to annoy When apparently in full retreat, they would turn round on their steeds and discharge their arrows with the most unerring accuracy; and hence, to borrow the language of an ancient writer it was victory to them if a counterfeit flight threw their pursuers into disorder."

a. The place where Cæsar is believed to have landed is at the town of Deal, near what is called the South Foreland, sixty-six miles south-east from London

army before a specified day, under the penalty of being declared a
public enemy. (B. C. 49.) The tribunes Antony and Cassius fled
to the army of Cæsar then at Raven' na,[1] bearing with them the hos
tile mandate of the senate, and by their harangues inflaming the soldiers against the measures of the senatorial party. Cæsar, confident
of the support of his troops, now passed the Rúbicon in hostile array,
an act deemed equivalent to an open declaration of war against his
country. The senate and Pompey, alarmed at the rapidity of his
movements, and finding their forces daily deserting them, fled across
the Adriat' ic into Greece ; and in sixty days from the passage of the
Rúbicon, Cæsar was master of all Italy.

33. Cæsar soon obtained the surrender of Sicily and Sardinia
after which he passed over to Spain, where Pompey's lieutenants
commanded,—rapidly reduced the whole Peninsula, took Marseilles
by siege on his return through Gaul, and, on his arrival at Rome,
was declared by the remnant of the senate sole dictator ; but after
eleven days he laid aside the office, and took that of consul. Pompey
had already collected a numerous army in the eastern provinces,
and thither Cæsar followed him. Near Dyrrach' ium,[2] in Illyr' i-
cum, he assaulted the intrenched camp of Pompey, but was repulsed with the loss of many standards, and his own camp would
have been taken had not Pompey called off his troops, in apprehension of an ambuscade ; on which Cæsar remarked that "the war
would have been at an end, if Pompey had known how to profit by
victory."

34. Cæsar then boldly advanced into Thes' saly, followed by Pompey
at the head of a superior force. The two armies met on the plains
of Pharsália,[3] where was fought the battle which decided the fate of
the Roman world. (B. C. 48.) Cæsar was completely victorious,

1 Raven' na was originally built on the shore of the Adriat' ic, near the most southern
mouth of the river Po. Augustus constructed a new harbor three miles from the old town,
nd henceforward the new harbor became the principal station of the Roman Adriat' ic fleet :
at such was the accumulation of mud brought down by the streams, that, as Gibbon relates,
e early as the fifth or sixth century after Christ, "the port of Augustus was converted into
pleasant orchards ; and a lonely grove of pines covered the ground where the Roman fleet
once rode at anchor." Raven' na was the capital of Italy during the last years of the Western
empire of the Romans, and it still contains numerous interesting specimens of the architecture
of that period.

2. Dyrrach' ium, which was a Grecian city, at first called Epidamnus, was situated on the
Illyrian coast of Macedonia, north of Apollonia. Its modern name is Durazzo, au unhealthy
village of Turkish Albania.

3. Pharsália was a city situated in the central portion of Thessaly, on a southern tributary
of the Peneus. The name of Pharsa, applied to a few ruins about fifteen miles south-west
from Larissa, marks the site of the ancient city

and Pompey, fleeing in disguise from the field of battle, attended
only by his son Sextus, and a few followers of rank, pursued his
way to Mytiléne, where he took on board his wife Cornelia and
sailed to Egypt, intending to claim the hospitality of the young king
Ptol' emy, whose father he had befriended. Ptol' emy, then at war
with his sister Cleopátra, was encamped with his army near Pelúsium,[1] whither Pompey directed his course, after sending to inform
the king of his approach. In the army of Ptol' emy there was a
Roman, named Septim' ius, who advised the young prince to put
Pompey to death, in order to secure the favor of Cæsar; and just
as Pompey was stepping on shore from a boat that had been sent to
receive him, he was stabbed, in the sight of his wife and son. Soon
after Cæsar arrived at Alexandria in Egypt in pursuit of the fugitives, when the ring and head of Pompey, which were presented to
him, gave him the first information of the fate of his rival. He
shed tears at the sight, and turned away with horror from the spectacle. He afterwards ordered the head to be burned with perfumes,
in the Roman method, and loaded with favors those who had adhered
to Pompey to the last.

35. Cæsar, in his eager pursuit of Pompey, had taken with him
to Alexandria only a small body of troops, and when, captivated by
the charms and beauty of Cleopátra, the Egyptian queen, who ap
plied to him for protection, he decided against the claims of her
brother, the party of the latter conceived the plan of overwhelming
him in Alexandria, so that his situation there was similar to that of
Cortez in Mexico. The royal palace, in which Cæsar had fortified
himself, was set on fire, and the celebrated library established there
by Ptol' emy Philadelphus was burnt to ashes. With difficulty
Cæsar escaped from the city to the island of Pharos,[2] where he
maintained himself until reënforcements arrived. He then overthrew the power of Ptol' emy, who lost his life by drowning, and
after having established Cleopátra on the throne he marched against
Pharnáces, king of Pontus, son of Mithridátes, whose dominions he
reduced with such rapidity that he announced the result to the Ro-

---

1. *Pelúsium* was a frontier city of Egypt, at the entrance of the eastern mouth of the
Nile.

2. *Pharos* was a small island in the bay of Alexandria, at the entrance of the principal harbor, one mile from the shore, with which it was connected by a causeway. The celebrated
"Tower of Pharos" was built on the island in the reign of Ptol' emy Philadelphus, to serve
as a lighthouse. The modern lighthouse tower, which stands on the island, has nothing of the
beauty and grandeur of the old one.

man senate in the well known words, *veni, vidi vici,* " I came, I saw I conquered."

36. On Cæsar's return to Rome, (B. C. 47,) after an absence of nearly two years, he granted a general amnesty to all the followers of Pompey, and by his clemency gained a strong hold on the affec-tions of the people. The servility of the senate knew no bounds, and the whole republic was placed in his hands. Still there was a large and powerful party in Africa and Spain opposed to him, headed by Cato, the sons of Pompey, and other generals. Cæsar, passing over to Africa, defeated his enemies there in the decisive battle of Thapsus,[1] after which the inflexible Cato, who commanded the garrison of Utica, having advised his followers not to continue their resistance, commit-ted suicide. (46 B. C.) He had seen, he said, the republic passing away, and he could live no longer. Cæsar expressed his regret that Cato had deprived him of the pleasure of pardoning him.

37. The war in Africa had been finished in five months. Fresh honors awaited Cæsar at Rome. He enjoyed four triumphs in one month; the senate created him dictator for ten years; he was ap-pointed censor of the public morals, and his statue was placed oppo-site that of Jupiter, in the capitol, and inscribed, " To Cæsar, the demigod." He made many useful changes in the laws, corrected many abuses in the administration of justice, extended the privileges of Roman citizens to whole cities and provinces in different parts of the empire, and reformed the calendar upon principles established by the Egyptian astronomers, by making an intercalation of sixty-seven days between the months of November and December, so that the name of the December month was transferred from the time of the autumnal equinox to that of the winter solstice, where it still re-mains.

38. From the cares of civil government Cæsar was called to Spain, where Cnéus and Sextus, the two sons of Pompey, had raised a large army against him. In the spring of the year 45 he defeated them in a hard-fought battle in the plains of Munda,[2] after having been obliged, in order to encourage his men, to fight in the foremost ranks as a common soldier. Cæsar said that he had often fought for victory, but that in this battle he fought for his life. The elder of Pompey's

---

1. *Thapsus,* now *Demsas,* was a town of little importance on the sea-coast, about one hundred miles south-east from Carthage.

2. *Munda* was a town a short distance from the Mediterranean in the southern part of Spain. The little village of *Monda* in Grenada, twenty-five miles west from Malaga, is supposed to be near the site of the ancient city.

sons was slain in the pursuit after the battle, but Sextus the younger escaped. After a campaign of nine months Cæsar returned to Rome, and enjoyed a triumph for the reduction of Spain, which had terminated the civil war in the Roman provinces.

39. Cæsar was next made dictator for life, with the title of imperator and the powers of sovereignty, although the outward form of the republic was allowed to remain. His ever active mind now planned a series of foreign conquests, and formed vast designs for the improvement of the empire which he had gained. He ordered the laws to be digested into a code, he undertook to drain the great marshes in the vicinity of Rome, to form a capacious harbor at the mouth of the Tiber, to cut across the isthmus of Corinth, to make roads across the Apennines, dig canals, collect public libraries, erect a new theatre, and build a magnificent temple to Mars. But while he was occupied with these gigantic projects the people became suspicious that he courted the title of king; and at his suggestion, as is supposed, Mark Antony offered him a royal diadem during the celebration of the feast of the Lupercalia; but no shout of approbation followed the act, and he was obliged to decline the bauble.[a]

40. A large number of senators, headed by the prætors Cassius and Brutus, regarding Cæsar as an usurper, soon after formed a conspiracy to take his life, and fixed on the fifteenth (the Ides) of March, a day appointed for the meeting of the senate, for the execution of their plot. As soon as Cæsar had taken his seat in the senate-house, the conspirators crowded around him, and as one of them, pretending to urge some request, laid hold of his robe as if in the act of supplication, the others rushed upon him with drawn daggers, and he fell pierced with twenty-three wounds, at the base of Pompey's statue which was sprinkled with his blood.[b]   (B. C. 44.)

41 As soon as the deed of death was consummated, Brutus raised

a. "You all did see, that on the Lupercal,
    I thrice presented him a kingly crown,
    Which he did thrice refuse. Was this ambition?
    Yet Brutus says, he was ambitious;
    And sure, he is an honorable man."
                    Antony's Oration. Shakspeare's Julius Cæsar.
b. "For when the noble Cæsar saw him stab,
    Ingratitude more strong than traitors arms,
    Quite vanquished him: then burst his mighty heart;
    And, in his mantle muffling up his face,
    Even at the base of Pompey's statue,
    Which all the while ran blood, great Cæsar fell."
                            Antony's Oration

his bloody dagger, and congratulated the senate, and Cicero in par ticular, on the recovery of liberty; but the greater part of the sena tors fled in dismay from Rome, or shut themselves up in their houses; and as the conspirators had formed no plans of future action, the minds of the citizens were in the utmost suspense; but tranquillity prevailed until the day appointed by the senate for the funeral Then Mark Antony, who had hitherto urged conciliation, ascended he rostrum to deliver the funeral oration. After he had wrought upon the minds of the people in a most artful manner by enumerating the great exploits and noble deeds of the murdered Cæsar, he lifted up the bloody robe, and showed them the body itself, ' all marred by traitors.' The multitude were seized with such indignation and rage, that while some, tearing up the benches of the senate-house, formed of them a funeral pile and burnt the body of Cæsar, others ran through the streets with drawn weapons and flaming torches, de-nouncing vengeance against the conspirators. Brutus and Cassius, and their adherents, fled from Rome, and prepared to defend them- selves by force of arms.

42. Antony, assisted by Lep'idus, now sought to place himself at the head of the State; but he found a rival in the young Octavius Cæsar, the grandson of Cæsar's sister Julia, and principal heir of the murdered dictator. The senate adhered to the interests of Octavius, and declared Antony a public enemy, and several battles had already been fought between the opposing parties in the north of Italy and Gaul, when the three leaders, Antony, Lep'idus, and Octavius, hav-

XIV. THE SECOND TRI-UMVIRATE. ing met in private conference on a small island of the Rhine, agreed to settle their differences, and take upon themselves the government of the republic for five years— hus forming the Second Triumvirate. (B. C. 43.) A cold-blooded proscription of the enemies of the several parties to the compact fol lowed. Antony yielded his own uncle, and Lep'idus his own brother, while Octavius, to his eternal infamy, consented to the sac rifice of the virtuous Cicero to satisfy the vengeance of his colleagues. Cicero was betrayed to the assassins sent to dispatch him, by one of his own domestics; but, tired of life, he forbade his servants to de- fend him, and yielded himself to his fate without a struggle.

43. Brutus and Cassius, at the head of the republican party had by this time made themselves masters of Macedónia, Greece, and the Asiatic provinces; and Octavius and Antony, as soon as they had settled the government at Rome, set out to meet them. At

Philip'pi,[1] a town in Thrace, two battles were fought, and fortune, rather than talent, gave the victory to the triumvirs. (B. C. 42.) Both Cassius and Brutus, giving way to despair, destroyed themselves; their army was dispersed, and most of the soldiers afterwards entered the service of the victors. Octavius returned with his legions to Italy, while Antony remained as the master of the Eastern provinces.

44 From Greece Antony passed over into Asia Minor, where he caused great distress by the heavy tribute he exacted of the inhabitants. While at Tarsus,[2] in Cilicia, the celebrated Cleopátra came to pay him a visit; and so captivated was the Roman with the charms and beauty of the Egyptian queen, that he accompanied her on her return to Alexandria, where he lived for a time in indolence, dissipation, and luxury, neglectful of the calls of interest, honor, and ambition. In the meantime a civil war had broken out in Italy; for the brother of Antony, aided by Fulvia, the wife of the latter, had taken up arms against Octavius; but it was not until the rebellion had been quelled, and Octavius was everywhere triumphant, that Antony saw the necessity of returning to Italy.

45. On his way he met at Athens his wife Fulvia, whom he blamed as the cause of the recent disasters, treated her with the utmost contempt, and leaving her on her death-bed hastened to fight Augustus. All thought that another fierce struggle for the empire was at hand; but the rivals had a personal interview at Brundúsium,[3] where a reconciliation was effected. To secure the permanence of the peace, Antony married Octavia, the half-sister of Octavius. A new division of the empire was made; Antony was to have the eastern provinces beyond the Ionian sea; Octavius the western, and Lep'idus Africa·

---

1. *Philip'pi*, a city in the western part of Thrace, afterwards included in Macedónia, was about seventy-five miles north-east from the present Cavalli. In addition to the victory gained here by Antony and Octavius, it is rendered more interesting from the circumstance of its being the first place where the Gospel was preached by St. Paul (see Acts, xvi.,) and also from he Epistle addressed by him to the *Philippians*. The ruins of the city still retain the name of *Filibah*, pronounced nearly the same as *Philippi*. (*Map No. V.*)

2 *Tarsus*, the capital of Cilicia, was situated on the river Cydnus about twelve miles from the Mediterranean. It was the birth-place of St. Paul, of Antip'ate, the stoic, and of Athenodórus the philosopher. It is still a village of some six or seven thousand inhabitants, and some remains of its ancient magnificence are still visible. The visit of Cleopátra to Antony — herself attired like Venus, and her attendants like cupids, in a galley covered with gold, whose sails were of purple, the oars of silver, and cordage of silk—is finely described in Shakspeare's play of Antony and Cleopátra, Act II. scene 2. (*Map No. IV.*)

3. *Brundúsium*, now *Brindisi*, one of the most important cities of ancient Italy, and the port whence the intercourse between Italy and Greece and the East was usually carried on, was situated on the coast of Apulia, about three hundred miles south-east from Rome. I once had an excellent harbor, which is now nearly filled up. (*Map No. VII.*)

and soon after, Sextus Pompey, who had long maintained himself in Sicily against the triumvirs, was admitted into the partnership, and assigned Sicily, Sardinia, Corsica, and Achaia.

46. The peace thus concluded was of short duration. Octavius, without any reasonable pretext for hostilities, quarrelled with Sextius Pompey and drove him from his dominions. Pompey fled to Phrygia, where he was slain by one of Antony's lieutenants. Lep' idus and Octavius next quarrelled about the possession of Sicily; but Octavius corrupted the soldiers of Lep' idus, and induced them to desert their general, who was compelled to surrender his province to his rival. Antony, in the meantime, had been engaged in an unsuccessful expedition against the Parthians; after which, returning to Egypt, he once more became enslaved by the charms of Cleopátra, upon whom he conferred several Roman provinces in Asia. When his wife Octavia set out from Rome to visit him he ordered her to return, and afterwards repudiated her, pretending a previous marriage with Cleopatra.

47. After this insult Octavius could no longer keep peace with him and as the war had long been anticipated, the most formidable preparations were made on both sides, and both parties were soon in readiness. Their fleets met off the promontory of Ac' tium,[1] in the Iónian sea, while the hostile armies, drawn up on opposite sides of the strait which enters the Ambracian Gulf, were spectators of the battle (B. C. 31.) While the victory was yet undecided, Cleopátra, who had accompanied Antony with a large force, overcome with anxiety and fear, ordered her galley to remove from the scene of action. A large number of the Egyptian ships, witnessing her flight, withdrew from the battle; and the infatuated Antony, as soon as he saw that Cleopátra had fled, apparently losing his self-possession, hastily followed her in a quick-sailing vessel, and being taken on board the galley of Cleopátra, became the companion of her flight. The fleet of Antony was annihilated, and his land forces, soon after, made terms with the conqueror.

48. Octavius, after first returning to Italy to tranquillize some disturbances there, pursued the fugitives to Egypt. Antony endeavored to impede the march of the victor to Alexandria, but seeing all his efforts fruitless, in a paroxysm of rage he reproached Cleopátra with being the author of his misfortunes, and resolving never to fall alive into the hands of his enemy, he put an end to his own life. When

1. The promontory of *Ac' tium* was a small neck of land at the north-western extremity of Acarnania, at the entrance of the *Ambracian Gulf*, now Gulf of *Arta.*

Cleopátra, who had shut herself up in her palace, found that Octa
vius designed to spare her only to adorn his triumph, she caused a
poisonous viper to be applied to her arm, and thus followed Antony
in death   (B. C. 30.)   Egypt immediately submitted to the sway
of Octavius, and became a province of the Roman empire.

49. The death of Antony had put an end to the Triumvirate; and
Octavius was now left sole master of the Roman world.   While
taking the most effectual measures to secure his power,   XV. OCTA-
he dissembled his real purposes, and talked of restoring   VIUS SOLE
the republic; but it was evident that a free constitution   MASTER OF
could no longer be maintained;—the most eminent citi-   WORLD.
zens besought him to take the government into his own hands, and at
the beginning of the 28th year before the Christian era, the history
of the *Roman Republic* ends.   All the armies had sworn allegiance
to Octavius; he was made pro-consul over the whole Roman empire—
he gave the administration of the provinces to whomsoever he
pleased—and appointed and removed senators at his will.   In the
27th year B. C. the senate conferred upon him the title of AUGUSTUS,
or " The Divine," and of *Imperator*, or " chief governor," for ten
years, and gave his name to the sixth month of the Roman year,
(August) as that of *Julius* Cæsar had been given to the fifth, and
four years later he was made perpetual tribune of the people, which
rendered his person sacred.   Although without the title of a monarch, and discarding the insignia of royalty, his exalted station con
ferred upon him all the powers of sovereignty, which he exercised,
nevertheless, with moderation,—seemingly desirous that the triumvir
Octavius should be forgotten in the mild reign of the emperor Augustus.

50. After a series of successful wars in Asia, Africa, and in Spain,
and the subjugation of Aquitánia, Pannónia, Dalmátia, and Illy'ria,
by the Roman arms, a general peace, with the exception of some
trifling disturbances in the frontier provinces, was established
throughout the vast dominions of the empire, which now extended
on the east from the cataracts of the Nile to the plains of Scythia,
and on the west from the Libyan deserts and the pillars of Hercules
to the German ocean.[a]   The temple of Jánus was now closed[b] for
the third time since the foundation of Rome.   It was at this auspi
cious period that Jesus Christ, the promised Messiah, was born,
and thus, literally, was his advent the herald of " peace on earth,
and good will toward men."

a. (B. C. 10. See Map No. IX.)   b. (B. C. 11.)

PART · II.

MODERN HISTORY

CHAPTER I.

ROMAN HISTORY CONTINUED, FROM THE COMMENCEMENT (
THE CHRISTIAN ERA, TO THE OVERTHROW OF THE WESTERN
EMPIRE OF THE ROMANS, A. D. 1, TO A. D. 476.

SECTION I.

ROMAN HISTORY FROM THE BEGINNING OF THE CHRISTIAN ERA TO THE DEATH
OF DOMITIAN, THE LAST OF THE TWELVE CÆSARS, A. D. 96.

ANALYSIS. 1. EARLIER AND LATER HISTORY OF THE EMPIRE COMPARED.—2. The empire at the end of the first century of the Christian era. The feeling with which we hurry over the closing scenes of Roman history. Importance of the history of the "decline and fall" of the empire. Subjects of the present chapter.

3. JULIUS CÆSAR. Commencement of the Roman empire.—4. The reign of AUGUSTUS. Rebellion of the Germans.—5. Grief of Augustus at the loss of his legions. The danger of invasion averted.—6. The accession of TIBE'RIUS. The selection of future sovereigns.—7. Character of Tiberius, and commencement of his reign.—8. German wars—German'icus.—9. Sejánus, the minister of Tibérius. [Cápreæ.]—10. The death of Sejánus. Death of Tibérius. Crucifixion of the Saviour.—11. CALIG'ULA. His character, and wicked actions.—12. His follies. His extravagance. His death.—13. CLAUDIUS proclaimed emperor. His character.—14. His two wives. His death.—15. Foreign events of the reign of Claudius.—16. NERO. The first five years of his reign. Death of Agrippina, and of Burrhus, Seneca, and Lucan. Conflagration of Rome.—17. Persecution of the Christians. Nero's extravagances.—18. The provinces pillaged by him. His popularity with the rabble. Revolts against him. His death.—19. Foreign events of the reign of Nero. [Druids. The Icéni London.]

20. End of the reign of the Julian family. Brief reign of GALBA.—21. Character, and reign of OTHO.—22. Character, and reign of VITEL'LIUS. Revolt in Syria.—23. Vitel'lius, forced to resist, is finally put to death by the populace.—24. Temporary rule of Domitian. Character, and reign of VESPASIAN.—25. Beginning, and causes of the JEWISH WAR.—26. Situation of Jerusalem, and commencement of the siege by the Roman army. Expectations of Titus.—27. Promises made to the Jews. Their strange infatuation.—28. The horrors of the siege.—29. Dreadful mortality in the city. The fall of Jerusalem.—30. The number of those who perished, and of those made prisoners. Fate of the prisoners. Destruction of the Jewish nation—31. Completion of the conquest of Britain. The enlightened policy of Agric'ola. [Caledonia.]—32. TITUS succeeds Vespasian. His character. Events of his brief reign. [Vesuvius. Herculaneum. Pompeii.]—33. DOMITIAN. His character, and the character of his reign. Persecutions.—34

1. As we enter upon the time of the Roman emperors, Roman history, so highly pleasing and attractive in its early stages, and during the eventful period of the Republic, gradually declines in interest to the general reader ; for the Roman people, whose many virtues and sufferings awakened our warmest sympathies, had now become corrupt and degenerate ; the liberal influences of their popular assemblies, and the freedom of the Roman senate, had given place to arbitrary force ; and although the splendors of the empire continue to dazzle for awhile, henceforward the political history of the Romans is little more than the biographies of individual rulers, and their few advisers and associates in power, who controlled the political destinies of more than a hundred millions of people.

I. EARLIER AND LATER HISTORY OF THE EMPIRE COMPARED.

2. We shall find that, at the end of the first century of the Christian era, the empire, having already attained its full strength and maturity, began to verge towards its decline ; and we are apt to hurry over the closing scenes of Roman history with an instinctive feeling that shrinks from the contemplation of waning glories and national degeneracy. But while the history of the Republican era may exceed in interest that of the " decline and fall " of the empire, yet the latter is of far greater political importance than the former ; for, including the early history of many important sects, and codes, and systems, whose influences still exist, it is the link that connects the past with the present—the Ancient with the Modern world. The theologian and jurist must be familiar with it in order to understand much of the learning and history of their respective departments ; and it deserves the careful preparatory study of every reader of modern European history ; as nearly all the kingdoms of modern Europe have arisen from the fragments into which the empire of the Cæsars was broken. We proceed then, in the present chapter to a brief survey, which is all that our limited space will allow, of first, the overtowering greatness, and, second, the decline, and final overthrow, in all the west of Europe, of that mighty fabric of empire which valor had founded, and enlightened policy had so long sustained, upon the seven hills of Rome.

3. The rule of Julius Cæsar, who is called the first of the twelve

Cæsars, although he was not nominally king, was that of one who pos-
II. JULIUS sessed all the essential attributes of sovereignty; and
CÆSAR. from the battle of Pharsalia, which decided the fate
of the Roman world, might with propriety be dated the commencement of the Roman empire, although its era is usually dated at the
beginning of the twenty-eighth year before the Christian era,—the
time of the general acknowledgment of the sovereignty of Augustus.

4. The reign of Augustus continued until the fourteenth year
III. AUGUS- after the birth of Christ—forty-four years in all, dating
TUS. from the battle of Ac'tium, which made Augustus sole
sovereign of the empire. After the general peace which followed the
early wars and conquests of the emperor, the great prosperity of his
reign was disturbed by a rebellion of the Germans, which had been
provoked by the extortions of Varus, the Roman commander on the
northern frontier. Varus was entrapped in the depths of the German
forests, where nearly his whole army was annihilated, and he himself,
in despair, put an end to his own life. (A. D. 9.) Awful vengeance
was taken upon the Romans who became prisoners, many of them
being sacrificed to the gods of the Germans.

5. The news of the defeat of his general threw Augustus into transports of grief, during which he frequently exclaimed, " Varus, restore
me my legions!" It was thought that the Germans would cross the
Rhine, and that all Gaul would unite with them in the revolt; but
a large Roman army under Tibérius, the son-in-law and heir of
Augustus, was sent to guard the passes of the Rhine, and the danger
was averted.

6. Augustus, having designed Tibérius for his successor, associated
him in his counsels, and conferred upon him so large a share of present
power, that on the death of the emperor, Tibérius easily took his
place, so that the nation scarcely perceived the change
IV TIBÉRIUS. of masters. (A. D. 14.) The policy of Augustus in
selecting, and preparing the way for, the future sovereign, was successfully imitated by nearly all his successors during nearly two centuries, although the emperors continued to be elected, ostensibly at
least, by the authority of the senate, and the consent of the soldiers.

7. Tibérius, a man of reserved character, and of great dissimulation,—suspicious, dark, and revengeful, but possessing a handsome
figure, and in his early years exhibiting great talents and unwearied
industry, having yielded with feigned reluctance to the wishes of the
senate that he would undertake the government, commenced his

reign with the appearance of justice and moderation, but after nine years of dissimulation, his sensual and tyrannical character openly exhibited itself in the vicious indulgence of every base passion, and the perpetration of the most wanton cruelties.

8. The early part of his reign is distinguished by the wars carried on in Germany by his accomplished general and nephew, the virtuous German' icus; but Tibérius, jealous of the glory and fame which German' icus was winning, recalled him from his command, and then sent him as governor to the Eastern provinces, where all his undertakings were thwarted by the secret commands of the emperor, who was supposed to have caused his death to be hastened by poison.

9. The only confidant of Tibérius was his minister Sejánus, whose character bore a great resemblance to that of his sovereign. Secretly aspiring to the empire, he contrived to win the heart of Tibérius by exciting his mistrust towards his own family relatives, most of whom he caused to be poisoned, or condemned to death for suspected treason; but his most successful project was the removal of Tibérius from Rome to the little island of Capreæ,' where the monarch remained during a number of years, indulging his indolence and debaucheries, while Sejánus, ruling at Rome, perpetrated the most shocking cruelties in the name of his master, and put to death the most eminent citizens, scarcely allowing them the useless mockery of a trial.

10. But Sejánus at length fell under the suspicion of the emperor, and the same day witnessed his arrest and execution—a memorable example of the instability of human grandeur. His death was followed by a general massacre of his friends and relations. At length Tibérius himself, after a long career of crime, falling sick, was smothered in bed by one of his officers, at the instigation of the base Calig' ula, the son of German' icus, and adopted heir of the emperor. It was during the reign of Tibérius that Jesus Christ was crucified in Judea, under the prætorship of Pontius Pilate, the Roman governor of that province.

11. Calig' ula, whose real character was unknown to the people,

1. *Capreæ*, now called *Capri*, is a small island, about ten miles in circumference, on the south side of the entrance to the bay of Naples. It is surrounded on all sides but one by lofty and perpendicular cliffs; and in the centre is a secluded vale, remarkable for its beauty and salubrity. The tyrant was led to select this spot for his abode, as well from its difficulty of access, as from the mildness and salubrity of its climate, and the unrivalled magnificence of the prospects which it affords. He is said to have built no less than twelve villas in different parts of the island, and to have named them after the twelve celestial divinities. The ruins of one, them—the villa of Jove—are still to be seen on the summit of a cliff opposite *Sorrento*.

received from them an enthusiastic welcome on his accession to the

v. calig'-　throne, (A. D. 37,) but they soon found him to be a

ula.　greater monster of wickedness and dissimilation than his

predecessor.　A detailed description of his wicked actions, which some have attributed to madness, would afford little pleasure to the reader.　Not satisfied with mere murder, he ordered all the prisoners in Rome, and numbers of the aged and infirm, to be thrown to wild beasts : he claimed divine honors, erected a temple, and instituted a college of priests to superintend his own worship; and finding the senate too backward in adulation, he seriously contemplated the massacre of the entire body.

12. His follies were no less conspicuous than his vices.　For his favorite horse Incitátus he claimed greater respect and reverence than were due to mortals : he built him a stable of marble and a manger of ivory, and frequently invited him to the imperial table ; and it is said that his death alone prevented him from conferring upon the animal the honors of the consulship !　A fortune of eighteen millions sterling, which had been left by Tibérius, was squandered by Calig'ula, in a most senseless manner, in little more than a year, while fresh sums, raised by confiscations, were lavished in the same way.　At length, after a reign of four years, Calig'ula was murdered by his own guards, to the great joy of the senators, who suddenly awoke to the wild hope of restoring the Republic.

13. The illusion soon disappeared, for the spirit of Roman liberty no longer existed.　The Prætorian guards,[a] who had all the power in their own hands, insisting upon being governed by a monarch, proclaimed the imbecile Claudius emperor, at a time when he expected

vi.　nothing but death; and their choice was sanctioned by

claudius.　the senate　Claudius was an uncle of the late emperor and brother of German'icus.　He was so deficient in judgment and reflection as to be deemed intolerably stupid ; he was not destitute of

a. The *Prætorian guards* were gradually instituted by Augustus to protect his person, aw the senate, keep the veterans and legions in check, and prevent or crush the first movements of rebellion. Something similar to them had existed from the earliest times in the body of armed *guides* who accompanied the general in his military expeditions. At first Augustus stationed three cohorts only in the capital: but Tibérius assembled all of them, to the number of ten thousand, at Rome, and assigned them a permanent and well-fortified camp close to the walls of the city, on the broad summit of the Quirinal and Viminal hills. This measure of Tibérius forever riveted the fetters of his country. The Prætorian bands, soon learning their own strength, and the weakness of the civil government, became eventually the real masters Rom 61 . and Niebuhr. v. 75.

good nature, but unfortunately he was made the dupe of abandoned
favorites, for whose crime history has unjustly held him responsible.

14. For a time his wife Messalína, the most dissolute and abandoned of women, ruled him at pleasure; and numbers of the most
worthy citizens were sacrificed to her jealousy, avarice, and revenge;
but finally she was put to death by the emperor for her shameless in
fidelity to him.   Claudius then married his niece Agrippína, then a
widow and the mother of the afterwards infamous Nero.   She was
no less cruel in disposition than Messalína; her ambition was un
bounded, and her avarice insatiable.   After having prevailed upon
Claudius to adopt as his heir and successor her son Nero, to the
exclusion of his own children, she caused the emperor to be poisoned
by his physician. (A. D. 54.) As Agrippína had gained the captain
of the Prætorian guards to her interest, the army proclaimed Nero
emperor, and the senate confirmed their choice.

15. The foreign events of the reign of Claudius were of greater
importance than his domestic administration.   Julius Cæsar had
first carried the Roman arms into Britain in a brief and fruitless invasion; but during the reign of Claudius the Romans began to
think seriously of reducing the whole island under their dominion
At first Claudius sent over his general Plau'tus, (A. D. 43,) who
gained some victories over the rude inhabitants.   Claudius himself
then made a journey into Britain, and received the submission of the
tribes that inhabited the south-eastern parts of the island; but the
other Britons, under their king Carac'tacus, maintained an obstinate
resistance until the Roman army was placed under the command of
Ostórius, who defeated Carac'tacus in a great battle, and sent him
prisoner to Rome. (A. D. 51.)

16. Nero, the successor of Claudius, was a youth of only seventeen
when he ascended the throne. (A. D. 54.) He had been nurtured
in the midst of crimes, and the Roman world looked upon
him with apprehension and dread; but during five years,   VII. NERO.
while he still remained under the influence of his early instructors
Seneca and Burrhus, he disappointed the fears of all by the mildness
of his reign.   At length his mother Agrippína fell under the sus
picion of designing to restore the crown to the still surviving son of
Claudius; and the emperor caused both to be put to death.   After
this he abandoned himself to bloodshed, in which he took a savage
delight   He is accused of having caused the death of his able min

ister Burrhus by poison; Seneca[a] the philosopher, Lucan[b] the poet,
and most of the leading nobles, were condemned on the charge of
treason; and a conflagration in Rome which lasted nine days, and
destroyed the greater part of the city, (A. D. 64,) was generally be
lieved to have been kindled by his orders; and some reported that
in order to enjoy the spectacle, he ascended a high tower, where he
amused himself with singing the Destruction of Troy.

17. In order to remove the suspicions of the people, he caused a
report to be circulated that the Christians were the authors of the
fire; and thousands of that innocent sect were put to death under
circumstances of the greatest barbarity. Sometimes, covered by the
skins of wild beasts, they were exposed to be torn in pieces by de-
vouring dogs; some were crucified: others, wrapped in combustible
garments, which were set on fire, were made to serve as torches to
illuminate the emperoi's gardens by night. Nero often appeared on
the Roman stage in the character of an actor, musician, or gladiator ·
he also visited the principal cities of Greece in succession, where he
obtained a number of victories in the public Grecian games.

18. While he was engaged in these extravagances, the provinces
of the empire were pillaged to support his luxuries and maintain his
almost boundless prodigalities. To the lower classes, who felt nothing of his despotism, he made monthly distributions of corn, to the
encouragement of indolence; and he gratified the populace of Rome
by occasional supplies of wine and meat, and by the magnificent
shows of the circus. Nero was popular with the rabble, which ex-
plains the fact that his atrocities and follies were so long endured
by the Roman people. At length, however, the standard of revolt
was raised in Gaul by Vindex, the Roman governor, and soon after
by Galba in Spain. Vindex perished in the struggle; and Galba

a. *Seneca*, the moral philosopher, was born at Cordova in Spain, in the second or third
year of the Christian era; but at an early age be went to reside at Rome. Messalina,
who hated him, caused him to be banished to Corsica, where he remained eight years; bu-
Agrippina recalled him from banishment, and appointed him, in conjunction with Burrhus,
tutor to Nero. Burrhus, a man of stern virtue, instructed the prince in military science
Seneca taught him philosophy, the fine arts, and elegant accomplishments. Although Seneca
laid down excellent rules of morality for others, his own character is not above reproach.
Being ordered by Nero to be his own executioner, he caused his veins to be opened in a bot
bath; but as, at his age, the blood flowed slowly, he drank a dose of hemlock to accelerate
his death.

b. *Lucan*, a nephew of Seneca, and also a native of Cordova, was an eminent Latin poet,
although he died at the early age of twenty-seven years. Of his many poems, the *Pharsalia*
or war between Cæsar and Pompey, is the only one that has escaped destruction. He incurred
the enmity of Nero by vanquishing him in a poetical contest.

would have been ruined had not the Prætorian guards, under the influence of their commander Otho, renounced their allegiance. With this latter calamity Nero abandoned all hope; and when he learned that the senate had declared him an enemy to the country, too cowardly to kill himself, he sought death by the hands of one of his freedmen, from whom he received a mortal wound. (A. D. 68.)

19. During the greater part of the reign of Nero the empire enjoyed, in general, a profound peace; the only wars of importance being with the Parthians and the Britons. The former were defeated and reduced by Cor'bulo, the greatest general of his time. This virtuous Roman had kept his faith even to Nero; but the only reward which he received from the emperor for his victories, was— death. In Britain, Suetónius Paulínus defeated the inhabitants in several battles, and penetrating into the heart of the country, destroyed the consecrated groves and altars of the druids.[a] Afterwards the Icéni,[b] under the command of their queen Boadic'ea, revolted, burned London,[c] then a flourishing Roman colony, reduced many other settlements, and put to death, in all, seventy thousand Romans. Suetónius avenged their fate in a decisive battle, in which eighty thousand Britons are said to have perished. The heroic Boadic'ea, rather than submit to the victor, put an end to her life by poison. During the reign of Nero also occurred the famous rebellion in Judea, and the beginning of the war which resulted in the destruction of the Jewish nation.

20. With the death of Nero the reign of the Julian family, or the true line of the Cæsars, ended; although six succeeding emperors are included in what are usually styled "the twelve Cæsars." A series of sanguinary wars, arising from disputed succession, followed.

a. The *druids* were the priests or ministers of religion among the ancient Gauls and Britons. Their chief seat was an island of the Irish Sea, now called *Anglesey*, which was taken by Suetónius after a fanatical resistance. This general cut down the groves of the druids, and nearly exterminated both the priests and their religion. The druids believed in the existence of one Supreme Being, a state of future rewards and punishments, the immortality of the soul, and its transmigration through different bodies. They possessed some knowledge of geometry, natural philosophy, and astronomy; they practiced astrology, magic, and sooth-saying; they regarded the mistletoe as the holiest object in nature, and esteemed the oak sacred; they abhorred images; they worshipped fire as the emblem of the sun, and in their sacrifices often immolated human victims. They exercised great authority in the government of the State, appointed the highest officers in the cities, and were the chief administrators of justice. On the introduction of Christianity into Britain, the druidical order gradually ceased.

b. The *Icéni* inhabited the country on the eastern coast of England. Their chief town was a place now called *Caister*, about three miles from Norwich.

c. *London*, anciently *Londinium* was in existence, as a town of the Trinobantes, before the invasion of Julius Cæsar.

At first Galba, then in the seventy-third year of his age, a man of un

VIII. GALBA. blemished personal character, was universally acknowl edged emperor; but he soon lost the attachment of the soldiery by his parsimony, while the influence of injudicious favorites led him into unseasonable severities for the suppression of the enormous vices of the times. Several revolts against his authority rapidly succeeded each other, and finally, Otho, who had been among the foremost to espouse his cause, finding that Galba refused to nominate him for his successor, procured a revolt of the Prætorian guards in his own favor. After a brief struggle in the streets of Rome, Galba was slain, after a reign of only seven months.

21. While the unworthy Otho, a passive instrument in the hands of a licentious soldiery, remained at Rome, with the title of emperor,

IX. OTHO. immersed in pleasures and debaucheries, Vitel' lius, a man more vulgar and vicious than Otho, was proclaimed emperor by the legions under his command on the German frontier A brief but sanguinary struggle followed, and Otho, having sustained a defeat in the north of Italy, fell by his own hand, after a reign of ninety-five days.

22. Vitel' lius, entering Rome in triumph, ordered more than a hundred of the prætorian guards to be put to death; but he en-

X. VITEL'- LIUS. deavored to win the favor of the populace by large donations of provisions, and expensive games and enter tainments. His personal character was cruel and contemptible. Under the most frivolous pretences the wealthy were put to death, and their property seized by the emperor; and in less than four months, as stated by historians, this bloated and pampered ruler, ex pended on the mere luxuries of the table a sum equal to about seven millions sterling. But while wallowing in the indulgence of the most debasing appetites, he was startled by the intelligence that the legions engaged in the Jewish war in Syria had declared their general, Vespasian, emperor, and were already on their march towards Rome.

23. As province after province submitted to Vespasian, and his generals rapidly overcame the little opposition they encountered, Vitel' iius in dismay would have abdicated his authority, but the Prætorian guards, dreading the strict discipline of Vespasian, com pelled the wretched monarch to a farther resistance. Rome how ever easily fell into the hands of the conquerors, and Vitel' lius, having retained the sceptre only eight months, was ignominiously

put to death, and his mangled carcass thrown into the Tiber, amid the execrations of the same fickle multitude that had so recently welcomed his accession to power. (A. D. Dec. 69.)

24. During several months, Domitian, the second son of Vespasian, ruled at Rome in the absence of his father, taking part with the contending factions, committing many acts of cruelty, and already exhibiting the passions and vices which characterized his later years; but at length the arrival of the monarch elect restored tranquillity and diffused universal joy. (A. D. 70.) Vespasian was XI. VESPA-universally known and respected for his virtues, and his SIAN. mild and happy reign restored to the distracted empire some degree of its former prosperity. He improved the discipline of the army, enlarged the senate to its former numbers, and revived its authority, reformed the courts of law, and enriched Rome with many noble buildings, of which the Colosséum still remains, in much of its ancient grandeur—the pride and glory of his reign.

25. Three years before his accession to the throne, Vespasian had been sent into Judea by Nero, (A. D. 67,) at the head of sixty thousand men, to conduct the war against the Jews, who XII. JEWISH had revolted against the Roman power. They had WAR. been driven to rebellion by the exactions and tyranny of Florus the Roman governor, and having once taken up arms they were so strangely infatuated as to believe that, although without a regular army, or munitions of war of any kind, they could resist the united force of the whole Roman empire. The war thus commenced was one of extermination, in which mercy was seldom asked or shown by either party

26. While the war raged around Jerusalem, and city after city was taken, and desolated by the massacre of its inhabitants, there were three hostile factions in Jerusalem, afterwards reduced to two, holding possession of different parts of the city, and wasting their strength in cruel conflicts with each other. When Vespasian depart ed for Rome to assume the royal authority, he left the conduct of the war to his son Titus, who soon after commenced the siege of Je rusalem, during the time of the feast of the passover, when the city was crowded with people from all Judea. Titus expected that al-though Jerusalem was defended by six hundred thousand men, such a multitude gathered within the walls of a poorly-provisioned city, would occasion a famine that would soon make a surrender inevitable.

27. Although the Jews were promised liberty and safety if they

would surrender the city; and Josephus, the future historian of his country, who had been taken prisoner by the Romans, was sent to expostulate with them on the folly of longer resistance; yet they re jected all warnings and counsel with scorn and derision; and although the opposing Jewish factions were embroiled in a civil war, with a strange infatuation both declared their resolution to defend the city to the very last, confident that God would not permit his temple and city to fall before the heathen.

28. The horrors of the siege surpassed all that the pen can describe. When the public granaries had become empty the people were plundered of their scanty stores, so that the famine devoured by houses and by families. At length no table was spread, nor regular meal eaten in Jerusalem. People bartered all their wealth for a measure of corn, and ate it in secret, uncooked, or snatched half baked from the coals. They were often compelled, by torture, to discover their food, or were still more cruelly treated if they had eaten it. Wives would steal the last morsel from their husbands, children from parents, mothers from children; and there were instances of dead infants being eaten by their parents; so that the ancient prophecy, in which Moses had described the punishments of the unbelieving Jews, was fulfilled.[a]

29. At length the dead accumulated so fast that they were left unburied, and were cast off the walls by thousands down into the valleys; and as Titus went his rounds, and saw the putrefying masses, he wept, and, stretching his hands to heaven, called God to witness that this was not his work! By slow degrees one wall after another was battered down; but so desperate was the defence of the Jews that it was three months after the lower city was taken before th Romans gained possession of the temple, and, in its destruction, com pleted the fall of Jerusalem. (A. D. 70.) Titus would have saved the noble edifice, but was unable to restrain the rage of his soldiery, and the Temple was burnt.

30. Josephus computes the number of his countrymen wh perished during the war at more than one million three hundred thousand, with a total of more than a million prisoners. Thousands of the latter were sent to toil in the Egyptian mines; but such were their numbers that they were offered for sale " till no man would buy them," and then they were sent into different provinces as pre

a. Deut. xxviii 56, 57.

sents, where they were consumed by the sword, or by wild beasts in the amphitheatres. With the destruction of the holy city and its famous temple Israel ceased to be a nation, and thus was inflicted the doom which the unbelieving Jews invoked when they cried out, " His blood be on us and on our children."

31. Britain had been only partially subdued prior to the reign of Vespasian, but during the two years after the fall of Jerusalem its conquest was completed by the Roman governor Julius Agric'ola who was justly celebrated for his great merits as a general and a states man. Carrying his victorious arms northward he defeated the Brit tons in every encounter, penetrated the forests of Caledónia,[1] and established a chain of fortresses between the Friths of Clyde and Forth, which marked the utmost permanent extent of the Roman dominion in Britain. The fastnesses of the Scottish highlands were ever too formidable to be overcome by the Roman arms. By an enlightened policy Agric'ola also taught the Britons the arts of peace, introduced laws and government among them, induced them to lay aside their barbarous customs, taught them to value the conveniencies of life, and to adopt the Roman language and manners. The life of Agric'ola has been admirably written by Tac'itus, the historian, to whom the former had given his daughter in marriage.

32. On the death of Vespasian (A. D. 79) his son Titus succeeded to the throne. Previous to his accession the general opinion of the people was unfavorable to Titus, but afterwards his conduct changed, and he is celebrated as a just and humane ruler; and so numerous were his acts of goodness, that his grateful subjects bestowed upon him the honorable title of " benefactor of the human race." During his brief reign of little more than two years, Rome and the provinces were in the enjoyment of peace and prosperity, only disturbed by an eruption of Mount Vesuvius,[2]

XIII. TITUS.

---

1. Ancient Caledónia comprehended that portion of Scotland which lay to the north of the Forth and the Clyde. A frith is a narrow passage of the sea, or the opening of a river into the sea. Agric'ola penetrated north as far as the river Tay. (See Map No. XVL.)

2. Mount Vesuvius, ten miles south-east from the city of Naples, is the only active volcano at present existing on the European continent. Its extreme height is three thousand eight hundred and ninety feet—about two-fifths of that of Æt'na. Its first known eruption occurred on the 24th of August, A D. 79, when Herculáneum and Pompéii were buried under showers of volcanic ashes, sand, stones, and lava, and the elder Pliny lost his life, being suffocated by the sulphurous vapor as he approached to behold the wonderful phenomena. It is related that such was the immense quantity of volcanic ashes thrown out during this eruption, the whole country was involved in pitchy darkness; and that the ashes fell in Egypt, Syria, and various parts of Asia Minor. Since the destruction of Herculáneum and Pompeii there have been nearly fifty authenticated eruptions of Vesuvius.

which caused the destruction of Herculáneum and Pompéii,[1] (A. D. 79,) and by a great fire at Rome, which was followed by a pestilence. (A. D. 80.)

33. Domitian succeeded his brother without opposition, (A. D. 81,) although the perfidy and cruelty of his character were notorious.

XIV.   He began his reign by an affectation of extreme virtue, DOMITIAN. but was unable long to disguise his vices. There was no law but the will of the tyrant, who caused many of the most eminent senators to be put to death without even the form of trial; and when, by his infamous vices, and the openness of his debaucheries, he had sunk, in the eyes of his subjects, to the lowest stage of degradation, he caused himself to be worshipped as a god, and addressed with the reverence due to Deity. Both Jews and Christians were persecuted by him, and thousands of them put to death because they would not worship his statues. This is called in ecclesiastical history the second great persecution of the Christians, that under Nero being the first.

34. It was in the early part of this reign that Agrícola completed the conquest of Britain; but on the whole the reign of Domitian was productive of little honor to the Roman arms, as in Mœ'sia,[3] and Dácia,[4] in Germany,[5] and Pannónia, the Romans were defeated,

---

1. *Herculáneum* was close to the sea, south of Vesuvius, and eight miles south-east from the city of Naples. Little is known of it except its destruction. It was completely buried under a shower of ashes, over which a stream of lava flowed, and afterwards hardened. So changed was the aspect of the whole country, and even the outlines of the coast, that all knowledge of the city, beyond its name, was soon lost, when, in 1713, after a concealment of more than sixteen centuries, accident led to the discovery of its ruins, seventy feet below the surface of the ground.

2. *Pompéii* was fifteen miles south-east from Naples, and was not buried by lava, but by ashes, sand, and stones only, and at a depth of only twelve or fifteen feet above the buildings. It has been excavated much more extensively than Herculáneum—disclosing the city walls, streets, temples, theatres, the forum, baths, monuments, private dwellings, domestic utensils, &c.,—the whole conveying the impression of the actual presence of a Roman town in all the circumstantial reality of its existence two thousand years ago. "The discovery of Pompéii has thrown a strong and steady light on many points connected with the private life and economy of the ancients, that were previously involved in the greatest obscurity."—The small number of skeletons discovered in Herculáneum and Pompéii render it quite certain that most of the inhabitants saved themselves by flight.

3. *Mœ'sia*, extending north to the Danube and eastward to the Euxine, corresponded to the present Turkish provinces of *Ser'via* and *Bulgária*. (*Map* No. IX.)

4. *Dácia* was an extensive frontier province north of the Danube, extending east to the Euxine. It embraced the northern portions of the present Turkey, together with Transylvánia and a part of Hungary. (*Map* No. IX.)

5. The word *Germánia* was employed by the Romans to designate all the country east of the Rhine and north of the Danube as far as the German ocean and the Baltic, and eastward as far as Sarmátia and Dácia. The limits of Germany, as a Roman province, were very indefinite (*Map* No. IX.)

and whole provinces lost.   In Mœ'sia, Domitian himself was several times defeated, yet he wrote to the senate boasting of extraordinary victories, and the servile body decreed him the honors of a triumph. In a similar manner other triumphs were decreed him, which caused Pliny the younger to say that the triumphs of Domitian were always evidence of some advantages gained by the enemies of Rome.

35. At length, after a reign of fifteen years, Domitian was assassinated at the instigation of his wife, who accidentally discovered that her own name was on the fatal list of those whom the emperor designed to put to death.   The soldiers, whose pay he had increased, and with whom he often shared his plunder, lamented his fate; but the senate ordered his name to be struck from the Roman annals, and obliterated from every public monument.

36. The death of Domitian closes the reign of those usually denominated "the twelve Cæsars," only three of whom, Augustus, Vespasian, and Titus, died natural deaths.   Julius Cæsar fell under the daggers of conspirators in the very senate-house of Rome.   Tiberius, at the instigation of Calig'ula, was smothered on a sick bed Calig'ula was murdered in his own palace while attending a theatrical rehearsal: Claudius was poisoned, at the instigation of his own wife, by his favorite physician: Nero, by the aid of his freedman, committed suicide to avoid a public execution: the aged Galba was slain in the Roman forum, in a mutiny of his guards: Otho, on learning the success of his rival Vitel'lius, committed suicide: Vitel'lius was dragged by the populace through the streets of Rome, put to death with tortures, and his mangled carcass thrown into the Tiber; and Domitian was killed in his bed-chamber by those whom he had marked for execution.   The heart sickens not more at the recital of these murders than of the crimes that prompted them; and thus far the history of the Roman emperors is little else than a series of constantly recurring scenes of violence and blood.

37. But as we pass from the city of Rome into the surrounding Roman world, we almost forget the revolting scenes of the capital in view of the still-existing power and majesty of the Roman empire—an empire the greatest the world has ever seen—and still great in the remembrance of the past, and in the influences which it has bequeathed to modern times.   While the emperors were steeped in the grossest sensuality, and Rome was a hot-bed of infamy and crime the numerous provincial governments were generally administered with ability and success; and the glory of the Roman arms was

I*

sustained in repelling the barbarous hordes that pressed upon the frontiers. But national valor cannot compensate for the want of national virtue: the soul that animated the Republic was dead; the spirit of freedom was gone; and national progress was already beginning to give place to national decay.

SECTION II.

ROMAN HISTORY FROM THE DEATH OF DOMITIAN, A. D. 96, TO THE ESTABLISHMENT OF MILITARY DESPOTISM, AFTER THE MURDER OF ALEXANDER SEVE'RUS, A. D. 235 = 139 YEARS

ANALYSIS. 1. NERVA. His character, reign, and death. [Um'bria.]—2. TRAJAN. His character, and character of his reign. Remarkable words attributed to him.—3. His wars and conquests. His death. [Ctes'iphon. Trajan's column.]—4. Persecutions of the Christians during the reign of Trajan. The proverbial goodness of Trajan's character.—5. Accession of ADRIAN. His peaceful policy. General administration of the government. His visit to the provinces.—6. Revolt of the Jews. Results of the Jewish war. Defences in Britain. [Solway Frith. River Tyne.]—7. Doubtful estimate of Adrian's character and reign. His ruling passions.—8. Accession of TITUS ANTONI'NUS.—9. His character, and the character of his reign.—10. MARCUS AURE'LIUS ANTONI'NUS. Verus associated with him.—11. War with the Parthians. With the Germans. Remarkable deliverance of the Roman army.—12. Character of the five preceding reigns. The evils to which an arbitrary government is liable. Illustrated in the annals of the Roman emperors.—13. Accession of COM'MODUS. Beginning of his government.—14. The incident which decided his fluctuating character. His subsequent wickedness.—15. His debaucheries and cruelties. His death.—16. The brief reign of PERTINAX.—17. Disposal of the empire to DID'IUS JULIA'NUS.—18. Dangerous position of the new ruler.—19. His competitors. [Dalmatia.] Successes of SEPTIM'IUS SEVE'RUS, and death of Juliánus.—20. Dissimulation of Severus. He defeats Niger at Issus in Asia. His continued duplicity. Overthrow and death of Albinus. [Lyons.]—21. Subsequent reign of Severus. His last illness and death. [York.]—22. CARACAL'LA and Géta. Death of the latter. Character, reign, and death of Caracal'la. Brief reign of MACRI'NUS.—23. Accession of ELAGABA'LUS.—24. His character and follies. Circumstances of his death.—25. ALEXANDER SEVE'RUS. His attempts to reform abuses. Character of his administration. His death. His successor.

1. Domitian was succeeded by Nerva, who was a native of Um'bria,[1] but whose family originally came from Crete. He was the

I. NERVA.

first Roman emperor of foreign extraction, and was chosen by the senate on account of his virtues. His mild and equitable administration forms a striking contrast to the sanguinary rule of Domitian; but his excessive lenity, which was his greatest fault, encouraged the profligate to persevere in their accustomed

---

1. *Um'bria* was a country of Italy east of Etrúria and north of the Sabine territory The ancient Um'brians were one of the oldest and most numerous nations of Italy. (*Map No. VIII.*

peculations At length the excesses of his own guards convinced him that the government of the empire required greater energy than he possessed, and he therefore wisely adopted the excellent Trajan as his successor, and made him his associate in the sovereignty. Nerva soon after died, (A. D. 98,) in the seventy-second year of his age, having reigned but little more than sixteen months.

2 Trajan, who was by birth a Spaniard, proved to be one of Rome's best sovereigns; and it has been said of him that he was equally great as a ruler, a general, and a man. After he had made a thorough reformation of abuses, he re- **II. TRAJAN.** stored as much of the free Roman constitution as was consistent with a monarchy, and bound himself by a solemn oath to observe the laws; yet while he ruled with equity, he held the reins of power with a strong and steady hand. No emperor but a Trajan could have used safely the remarkable words attributed to him, when, giving a sword to the prefect of the Prætorian guards, he said, " Take this sword and use it; if I have merit, for me; if otherwise, against me."

3. In his wars, Trajan, commanding in person, conquered the Dácians, after which he passed into Asia, subdued Armenia, took Seleúcia and Ctes'iphon,[1] the latter the capital of the Parthian kingdom, and sailing down the Tigris displayed the Roman standards for the first time on the waters of the Persian Gulf, whence he passed into the Arabian peninsula, a great part of which he annexed to the Roman empire. But while he was thus passing from kingdom to kingdom, emulating the glory of Alexander, and dreaming of new conquests, he was seized with a lingering illness, of which he died in Cilicia, in the twentieth year of his reign. (A. D. 117.) His ashes were conveyed to Rome in a golden urn, and deposited under the famous column which he had erected to commemorate his Dácian victories.[a]

---

1. *Ctes'iphon* was a city of Parthia, on the eastern bank of the Tigris, opposite to and three miles distant from Seleúcia.

a. Trajan's column, which is still standing, is the most beautiful mausoleum ever erected to departed greatness. Its height, not including the base, which is now covered with rubbish, is one hundred and fifteen feet ten inches; and the entire column is composed of twenty-four great blocks of marble, so curiously cemented as to seem one entire stone. It is ascended on the inside by one hundred and eighty-five win ling steps. The noblest ornament of this pillar was a bronze statue of Trajan, twenty-five feet in height, representing him in a coat of arms, holding in the left hand a sceptre, and in the right a hollow globe of gold, in which, it has been asserted, the ashes of the emperor were deposited. The column is now surmounted by a statue of St. Peter, which Sixtus V. had the bad taste to substitute in place of that of Trajan. On the external face of the column is a series of bas-reliefs, running in a spiral course up the shaft, representing Trajan's victories, and containing two thousand five hundred human figures.

4. The character of Trajan, otherwise just and amiable, is stained by the approval which he gave to the persecution of Christians in the eastern provinces of the empire; for although he did not directly promote that persecution, he did little to check its progress, and allowed the enemies of the Christians to triumph over them. Still, the goodness of his character was long proverbial, inasmuch as, in later times, the senate, in felicitating the accession of a new emperor were accustomed to wish that he might surpass the prosperity of Augustus and the virtue of Trajan.

5. Whether Trajan, in his last moments, adopted his relative Adrian as his successor, or whether the will attributed to him was forged by the empress Plotína, is a doubtful point in history; but

III. ADRIAN. Adrian succeeded to the throne with the unanimous declaration of the Asiatic armies in his favor, whose choice was immediately ratified by the senate and people. His first care was to make peace with the surrounding nations; and in order to preserve it he at once abandoned all the conquests made by his predecessor, except that of Dacia, and bounded the eastern provinces by the river Euphrates. He diminished the military establisnments, lowered the taxes, reformed the laws, and encouraged literature. He also passed thirteen years in visiting all the provinces of the empire inspecting the administration of government, repressing abuses, and erecting and repairing public edifices.

6. During his reign occurred another war with the Jews, who, incensed at the introduction of Roman idolatry into Jerusalem, were excited to revolt by an impostor who called himself Bar-Cóchab, (*the son of a star*,) and who pretended to be the expected Messiah. Two hundred thousand devoted followers soon flocked to the Jewish standard, and for a time gained important advantages; but Sevérus, afterwards emperor, being sent against them, in a sanguinary war of three years' duration he accomplished the almost total destruction of the Jewish nation. More than five hundred thousand of the misguided Jews are estimated to have fallen by the sword during this period; and those who survived were "scattered abroad among all the nations of the earth."—In Britain, Adrian repaired the frontier fortresses of Agricola as a bulwark against the Caledónians, and erected a second wall, from the Solway Frith[1] to the Tyne,[2] remains of which are still visible

1. Solway Frith, the north-eastern arm of the Irish sea, divides England from Scotland. (Map No. XVI.)

2. The Tyne, an important river in the north of England, enters the sea on the eastern coast the southern extremity of Northumberland county. (Map No. XVI.)

7. Although the general tenor of the reign of Adrian deserved praise for its equity and moderation, yet his character had some dark stains upon it; and the Romans of a later age doubted whether he should be reckoned among the good or the bad princes. He allowed a severe persecution of the Jews and Christians; he was jealous, suspicious, superstitious, and revengeful; and although in general he was a just and able ruler, he was at times an unrelenting and cruel tyrant. · His ruling passions were curiosity and vanity; and as they were attracted by different objects, his character assumed the most opposite phases.

8. Adrian, a short time previous to his death, (A. D. 138,) adopted for his successor, Titus Antonínus, surnamed Pius, on **iv. titus** condition that the latter should associate with him, in **antoni' nus.** the empire, Marcus Aurélius, and the youthful Vérus. Antonínus, immediately after his accession, gave one of his daughters in marriage to Marcus Aurélius, afterwards called Marcus Aurélius Antonínus; but while he associated the worthy Aurélius in the labors of government, he showed no regard for the profligate Vérus.

9. During twenty-two years Antonínus governed the Roman world with wisdom and virtue, exhibiting in his public life a love of religion, peace and justice; and in his private character goodness, amiability, and a cheerful serenity of temper, without affectation or vanity. His regard for the future welfare of Rome is manifest in the favor which he constantly showed to the virtuous Aurélius: the latter, in return, revered the character of his benefactor, loved him as a parent, obeyed him as a sovereign, and, after his death, regulated his own administration by the example and maxims of his predecessor.

10. On the death of Antonínus, (A. D. 161,) the senate, distrusting Vérus on account of his vices, conferred the sover- **v. marcus** eignty upon Marcus Aurélius alone; but the latter im- **aurélius** mediately took Vérus as his colleague, and gave him his **antoni' nus.** daughter in marriage; and notwithstanding the great dissimilarity in the characters of the two emperors, they reigned jointly ten years, until the death of Vérus, (A. D. 171,) without any disagreement, for Vérus, destitute of ambition, was content to leave the weightier affairs of government to his associate.

11. Although Aurélius detested war as the disgrace of humanity and its scourge, yet his reign was less peaceful than that of his predecessor; for the Parthians overran Syria; but they were eventually repulsed, and some of their own cities captured. During five years

Aurélius, in person, conducted a war against the German tribes, without once returning to Rome. During the German war occurred that remarkable deliverance of the emperor and his army from danger, which has been related both by pagan and Christian writers. It is said that the Romans, drawn into a narrow defile, where they could neither fight nor retreat, were on the point of perishing by thirst, when a violent thunder-storm burst upon both armies, and the lightning fired the tents of the barbarians and broke up their camp while the rain relieved the pressing wants of the Romans. Many ancient fathers of the Church ascribed the seasonable shower to the prayers of the Christian soldiers then serving in the imperial army; and we are told by Eusébius that the emperor immediately gave to their division the title of the " Thundering Legion," and henceforth relaxed his severity towards the Christians, whose persecution he had before tolerated.

12. The reigns of Nerva, Trajan, Adrian, and the two Atonines, comprised a happy period in the annals of the Roman empire These monarchs observed the laws, and the ancient forms of civil administration, and probably allowed the Roman people all the freedom they were capable of enjoying. But under an arbitrary government there is no guarantee for the continuance of a wise and equitable administration; for the next monarch may be a profligate sensualist, an imbecile dotard, or a jealous tyrant; and he may abuse, to the destruction of his subjects, that absolute power which others had exerted for their welfare. The uncertain tenure by which the people held their lives and liberties under despotic rule, is fully illustrated in the dark pictures of tyranny which the annals of the Roman emperors exhibit. The golden age of Trajan and the Antonines had been preceded by an age of iron; and it was followed by a period of gloom, of whose public wretchedness, the shortness, and violent termination, of most of the imperial reigns, is sufficient proof.

13. Com'modus, the unworthy son of Aurélius, succeeded to the throne on the death of his father, (A. D. 180,) amidst the acclamations of the senate and the armies. During three years, while he retained his father's counsellors around him, he ruled with equity and moderation; but the weakness of his mind and the timidity of his disposition, together with his natural indolence, rendered him the slave of base attendants; and sensual indulgence and crime, which others had taught him, finally degenerated into a habit and became the ruling passions of his soul.

VI. COM.'-
MODUS.

14. A fatal incident decided his fluctuating character, and suddenly developed his dormant cruelty and thirst for blood. In an attempt to assassinate him, the assailant, aiming a blow at him with a dagger, exclaimed, " the senate sends you this." The menace prevented the deed; but the words sunk deep into the mind of Com'modus, and kindled the utmost fury of his nature. It was found that the conspirators were men of senatorial rank, who had been instigated by the emperor's own sister. Suspicion and distrust, fear and hatred, were henceforth indulged by the emperor towards the whole body of senators: spies and informers were encouraged; neither virtue nor station afforded any security; and when Com'modus had once tasted human blood, he became incapable of pity or remorse. He sacrificed a long list of consular senators to his wanton suspicion, and took especial delight in hunting out and exterminating all who had been connected with the family of the Antonines.

15. The debaucheries of Com'modus exceeded, in extravagance and iniquity, those of any previous Roman emperor. He was averse to every rational and liberal pursuit, and all his sports were mingled with cruelty. He cultivated his physical, to the neglect of his mental powers.; and in shooting with the bow and throwing the javelin, Rome had not his superior. Delighting in exhibiting to the people his superior skill in archery, he at one time caused a hundred lions to be let loose in the amphitheatre; and as they ran raging around the arena, they successively fell by a hundred arrows from the royal hand. He fought in the circus as a common gladiator, and, always victorious, often wantonly slew his antagonists, who were less completely armed than himself. This monster of folly and wickedness was finally slain, (A. D. 193,) partly by poisoning and partly by strangling, at the instigation of his favorite concubine Marcia, who accidentally learned that her own death, and that of several officers of the palace, had been resolved upon by the tyrant.

16. On the death of Com'modus the throne was offered to Per ti nax, a senator of consular rank and strict integrity, who accepted the office with extreme reluctance, fully aware of the dangers which he incurred, and the great weight of responsibility thrown upon him. The virtues of Per'tinax secured to him the love of the senate and the people; but his zeal to correct abuses provoked the anger of the turbulent Prætorian soldiery, who preferred the favor of a tyrant to the stern equality of the laws; and

VII. PER'TI NAX.

after a reign of three months, Per'tinax was slain in the imperial palace by the same guards who had placed him on the throne.

17. Amidst the wild disorder that attended the violent death of the emperor, the Prætorian guards proclaimed that they would dispose of the sovereignty of the Roman world to the highest bidder, and while the body of Per'tinax remained unburied in the streets

VIII. DID'IT'S of Rome, the prize of the empire was purchased by a
JULIA'NUS vain and wealthy old senator, Did'ius Juliánus, who, epairing to the Prætorian camp, outbid all competitors, and actually paid to each of the soldiers, ten thousand in number, more than two hundred pounds sterling, or nearly nine millions of dollars in all.

18. The obsequious senate, overawed by the soldiery, ratified the unworthy negotiation ; but the Prætorians themselves were ashamed of the prince whom their avarice had persuaded them to accept ; the citizens looked upon his elevation with horror, as a lasting insult to the Roman name ; and the armies in the provinces were unanimous in refusing allegiance tó the new ruler, while the emperor, trembling with the dangers of his position, found himself, although on the throne of the world, scorned and despised, without a friend, and even without an adherent.

19. Three competitors soon appeared to contest the throne with Juliánus,—Clódius Albínus, who commanded in Britain,—Pescen'.

IX. SEPTIM'. nius Níger in Syria,—and Septim'ius Sevérus in Dal-
IUS SEVÉRUS. mátia[1] and Pannónia. The latter, by his nearness to Rome, and the rapidity of his marches gained the advance of his rivals, and was hailed emperor by the people : the faithless Prætorians submitted without a blow, and were disbanded; and the senate pronounced a sentence of deposition and death against the terror stricken Juliánus, whose anxious and precarious reign of sixty-five days was terminated by the hands of the common executioner.

20. While Sevérus, employing the most subtle craft and dissimu 'ation, was flattering Albínus in Britain with the hope of being associated with him in the empire, he rapidly passed into Asia, and after several engagements with the forces of Níger completely defeated them on the plains of Issus, where Alexander and Daríus had long before contended for the sovereignty of the world. Such was the

1. *Dalmátia,* anciently a part of Illyr'icum, and now the most southern province of the Austrian empire, comprises a long and narrow territory on the eastern shore of the Adriat'ic. After the division of the Roman provinces under Con'stantine and Theodósius, Dalmátia be same one of the most important parts of the empire.

duplicity of Sevérus, that even in the letter in which he announced the victory to Albínus, he addressed the latter with the most friendly salutations, and expressed the strongest regard for his welfare, while at the same time he intrusted the messengers charged with the letter to desire a private audience, and to plunge their dagger to the heart of his rival. It was only when the infamous plot was detected that Albínus awoke to the reality of his situation, and began to make vigorous preparations for open war. This second contest for empire was decided against Albínus in a most desperate battle near Lyons,[1] in Gaul, (A. D. 197,) where one hundred and fifty thousand Romans are said to have fought on each side. Albínus was overtaken in flight, and slain; and many senators and eminent provincials suffered death for the attachment which they had shown to his cause.

21. After Sevérus had obtained undisputed possession of the empire, he governed with mildness: considering the Roman world as his property, he bestowed his care on the cultivation and improvement of so valuable an acquisition, and after a reign of eighteen years he could boast, with a just pride, that he received the empire oppressed with foreign and domestic wars, and left it established in profound, universal, and honorable peace. In his last illness, Sevérus deeply felt and acknowledged the littleness of human greatness. Born in an African town, fortune and merit had elevated him from an humble station to the first place among mankind; and now, satiated with power, and oppressed with age and infirmities, all his prospects in life were closed. "He had been all things," he said, "and all was of little value." Calling for the urn in which his ashes were to be inclosed, he thus moralized on his decaying greatness. "Little urn, thou shalt soon hold all that will remain of him whom the world could not contain." He died at York,[2] in Britain, (A. D. 211,) having been called into that country to repress an insurrection of the Caledonians.

1. *Lyons*, called by the Romans *Lugdúnum*, is situated at the confluence of the rivers Rhone and Saône. The Roman town was at the foot of a hill on the western bank of the Rhone. Cæsar conquered the place from the Gauls: Augustus made it the capital of a province; and, being enlarged by succeeding emperors, it became one of the principal cities of the Roman world. It is now the principal manufacturing town of France, containing a population of about two hundred thousand inhabitants. (*Map* No. XIII.)

2. *York*, called by the Romans *Ebor'acum*, is situated on the river Ouse, one hundred and seventy miles N. N. west from London. It was the capital of the Roman province, and next to London, the most important city in the island. It was successively the residence of Adrian, Severus, Géta and Caracal'la, Constan'tius Chlórus, Con'stantine the Great, &c. The modern city can still show many vestiges of Roman power and magnificence. Constan'tius Chlórus, the father of Constantine the Great, died here. (*Map* No. XVI.)

22 Sevérus had left the empire to his two sons Caracal'la and
Géta, but the former, whose misconduct had imbittered
X. CARA-
CAL' LA. the last days of his father, soon after his accession slew
his brother in his mother's arms. His character resembled that of
Com'modus in cruelty, but his extortions were carried to a far
greater extent. After the Roman world had endured his tyranny
nearly six years, he was assassinated while in Syria, at the instiga-
XI. MACRI'- tion of Macrínus, the captain of the guards, (A. D. 217,)
NUS. who succeeded to the throne; but after a reign of fourteen months, Macrínus lost his life in the struggle to retain his
power.

23. Bassiánus, a youth of fourteen, and a cousin of Caracal'la,
had been consecrated, according to the rites of the Syrian worship,
to the ministry of high-priest of the sun; and it was a rebellion of
the Eastern troops in his favor that had overthrown the power of
Macrínus. Although these events occurred in distant Syria, yet the
Roman senate and the whole Roman world received with servile
XII. ELAGA- submission the emperors whom the army successively
BA' LUS. offered them. As priest of the sun Bassiánus adopted
the title of Elagabálus,[a] and on his arrival at Rome established
there the Syrian worship, and compelled the grandest personages of
the State and the army to officiate in the temple dedicated to the
Syrian god.

24. The follies, gross licentiousness, boundless prodigality, and
cruelty of this pagan priest and emperor, soon disgusted even the
licentious soldiery, the only support of his throne. He established
a senate of women, the subject of whose deliberations were dress
and etiquette; he even copied the dress and manners of the female
sex, and styling himself empress, publicly invested one of his officers
with the title of husband. His grandmother Moe' sa, foreseeing that
the Roman world would not long endure the yoke of so contemptible
a monster, artfully persuaded him, in a favorable moment of fond-
ness, to adopt for his successor his cousin Alexander Sevérus; yet
soon after, Elagabálus, indignant that the affections of the army
were bestowed upon another, meditated the destruction of Sevérus,
but was himself massacred by the indignant Prætorians, who dragged
his mutilated corpse through the city, and threw it into the Tiber,
while the senate publicly branded his name with infamy. (A. D. 222.)

---

a. A name derived from two Syriac words, *ela* a god, and *gabal* to form: —signifying the
forming, or plastic god,—a proper and even happy epithet for the sun.—Gibbon, i. 83.

25. At the age of seventeen Alexander Sevérus was raised to the throne by the Prætorian guards.   He proved to be a XIII. ALEX-
ANDER SE-
VÉRUS. wise, energetic, and virtuous prince: he relieved the provinces of the oppressive taxes imposed by his prede- cessors, and restored the dignity, freedom, and authority of the senate; but his attempted reformation of the military order served only to inflame the ills it was meant to cure.   His administration of the government was an unavailing struggle against the corruptions of the age; and after many mutinies of his troops his life was at length sacrificed, after a reign of fourteen years, to the fierce discon- tents of the army, whose power had now increased to a height so dangerous as to obliterate the faint image of laws and liberty, and introduce the sway of military despotism.   Max' imin, the instigator of the revolt, was proclaimed emperor.

⚫◆⚫

SECTION III.

ROMAN HISTORY FROM THE ESTABLISHMENT OF MILITARY DESPOTISM, AFTER THE MURDER OF ALEXANDER SEVE'RUS, A. D. 235, TO THE SUBVERSION OF THE WESTERN EMPIRE OF THE ROMANS, A. D. 476 = 241 YEARS.

ANALYSIS. 1. Earliest account of the Thracian MAX' IMIN.—2. His origin. His history down to the death of Alexander Sevérus. [The Goths. Aláni.]—3. Max' imin proclaimed emperor by the army. Commencement of his reign.—4. GOR' DIAN. PUPIE' NUS AND BALBI'- NUS. Death of Max' imin. The SECOND GOR' DIAN.—5. German and Persian wars.—6. Sápor, the Persian king. Death of Gor' dian, and accession of PHILIP THE ARABIAN.—7. Insurrections and rebellions. DE' CIUS proclaimed emperor, and death of Philip. [Veróna.]—8. War with the Goths, and death of Décius. Reign of GALLUS ÆMILIA' NUS. Accession of VALE' RIAN.— 9. Worthy character of Valérian. Ravages of the barbarians. Spain, Gaul, and Britain. The Persans. [The Franks. The Aleman' ni. Lombardy.]—10. Valérian taken prisoner. His treatment. GALLIE' NUS.—11. Odenátus, prince of Palmyra. He routs the Persians. [Palmyra.]—12. Numerous competitors for the throne.—13. Death of Galliénus, and accession of CLAUDIUS. [Milan.]—14. Character, reign, and death of Claudius. [Sir' mium.]—15. QUIN TILIUS.—16. The reign of AURE' LIAN. His wars. Zenóbia. Character of Aurélian. His death. [Tíbur. Byzan' tium.]—17. An interregnum. Election of TACITUS. His reign and death. [Bos' porus.]—18. FLO' RIAN. The reign, and death, of PROBUS. [Sarmatia ' an'- dale.]—19. Reign of CA' RUS. His character, and death. NUME' RIAN AND CARI' NUS.—20. Su- perstition, and retreat, of the Roman army in Persia. Character of Carínus, and death of Numérian.—21. Carínus marches against Dioclétian. His death. DIOCLE' TIAN acknowledged emperor. His treatment of the vanquished. 22. The reign of Dioclétian, an important epoch. [Copts and Abyssinians.]—23. Division of the imperial authority.—24. The rule of MAXIM' IAN. [Nicomédia.] Of his colleague Constan' tius. Countries ruled by Dioclétian, and his colleague Galérius.—25. Important events of the reign of Dioclétian. The insurrection in Britain.—26. Revolt in Egypt and northern Africa. [Busíris and Cop' tos. The Moors. 27. The war with Persia. [Antioch

Kurdistan.]--27. Persecut on of the Christians. Dioclétian's edict against them.—29. Results, and effects of this persecution.—30. Dioclétian and Maxim' ian lay down the sceptre, and retire to private life. GALE' RIUS AND CONSTAN' TIUS acknowledged sovereigns. Discord and confusion.—31. Death of Constan' tius. CON' STANTINE proclaimed emperor. Six competitors for the throne. Death of Galérius.—32. Conversion of Con' stantine, and triumph of Christianity. —33. Most important events in the reign of Con' stantine. The choice of a new capital.—34. Removal of the seat of government to Byzan' tium, and the changes that followed. Con' stantine divides the empire among his three sons and two nephews. His death.—35. Sixteen years of civil wars. CONSTAN' TIUS II. becomes sole emperor. His reign of twenty-four years. His death. [The Saxons.]—36. JULIAN THE APOSTATE. His character. Hostility to the Christians. —37. His efforts against Christianity. The result.—38. His attempt to rebuild Jerusalem.—39. Causes of the suspension of the work.—40. Julian's invasion of Persia. His death.—31. The brief reign of Jo' VIAN.—42. VALENTIN' IAN elected emperor. Associates his brother VA' LENS with him. Final division of the empire. The two capitals.- Rome.

43. BARBARIAN INROADS. Picts and Scots.—44. Death of Valentin' ian, and westward progress of the Huns. The Vis' igoths are allowed to settle in Thrace.—45. The Os' trogoths cross the Danube in arms. The two divisions raise the standard of war. Death of Valens. [Adrianóple.]—46. GRA' TIAN emperor of the West. THEODO' SIUS emperor of the East. The Goths. Many of them settle in Thrace, Phrygia, &c.—47. Death of Grátian. VALENTIN' IAN II. His death. Theodósius sole emperor. Death of Theodósius. Division of the empire between HONO' RIUS AND ARCA' DIUS.—48. Civil wars. AL' ARIC THE GOTH ravages Greece, and then passes into Italy. [Julian Alps.]—49. Honórius is relieved by Stil' icho. [As' ta Pollen'. tia.] Rome saved by Stil' icho.—50. Raven' na becomes the capital of Italy. Deluge of barbarians. [Raven' na. Van' dals. Suévi. Burgun' dians.]—51. Italy delivered by Stil' icho. [Florence.]—52. Stil' icho put to death. Massacre of the Goths, and revolt of the Gothic soldiers.—53. Rome besieged by Al' aric. His terms of ransom.—54. The terms finally agreed upon. Rejected by Honórius. [Tuscany.] Al' aric returns and reduces Rome.—55. Pillage of Rome. Al' aric abandons Rome. His death and burial.—56. The Goths withdraw from Italy. The Vis' igoths in Spain and Gaul. Saxons establish themselves in England.—57. The Van' dals in Spain and Africa. VALENTIN' IAN III. CONQUESTS OF AT' TILA. [Andalusia. The Huns. Chalons. Venetian Republic.]—58. Extinction of the empire of the Huns. Situation of the Roman world at this period. Rome pillaged by the VAN' DALS, A. D. 455.—59 AVI' TUS. MAJO' RIAN.—60. SEVE' RUS. Van' dal invasions. Expedition against Carthage.—61. Revolutionary changes. Demands of the barbarians, and SUBVERSION OF THE WESTERN EMPIRE. [Her' uli.]

1. ' Thirty-two years before the murder of Alexander Sevérus, the emperor Septim' ius Sevérus, returning from his Asiatic expedition, halted in Thrace to celebrate with military games the birthday of his-younger son Géta   Among the crowd that flocked to behold their sovereign was a young barbarian of gigantic stature, who earnestly solicited, in his rude dialect, that he might be allowed to contend for the prize of wrestling. As the pride of

1. MAX' IMIN.

discipline would have been disgraced in the overthrow of a Roman soldier by a Thrácian peasant, he was matched with the stoutest followers of the camp, sixteen of whom he successively laid on the ground.   His victory was rewarded by some trifling gifts, and a permission to enlist in the troops.   The next day th a happy barbarian was distinguished above a crowd of recruits, dancing and exulting after the fashion of his country.   As soon as as he perceived that he had attracted the emperor's notice, he ran up to his horse.

and followed him on foot, without the least appearance of fatigue, in a long and rapid career. "Thracian," said Sevérus, with astonishment, "art thou disposed to wrestle after thy race?" "Most willingly, sir," replied the unwearied youth, and almost in a breadth overthrew seven of the strongest soldiers in the army. A gold collar was the prize of his matchless vigor and activity, and he was immediately appointed to serve in the horse-guards, who always attended on the person of the sovereign.'[a]

2. Max'imin, for that was the name of the Thracian, was descended from a mixed race of barbarians,—his father being a Goth,[1] and his mother of the nation of the Aláni.[2] Under the reign of the first Sevérus and his son Caracal'la he held the rank of centurion; but he declined to serve under Macrínus and Elagabálus. On the accession of Alexander he returned to court, and was promoted to various military offices honorable to himself and useful to the nation, but, elated by the applause of the soldiers, who bestowed on him the names of Ajax and Hercules, and prompted by ambition, he conspired against his benefactor, and excited that mutiny in which the latter lost his life.

3. Declaring himself the friend and advocate of the military order,

---

1. The *Goths*, a powerful northern nation, who acted an important part in the overthrow of the Roman empire, were probably a Scythian tribe, and came originally from Asia, whence they passed north into Scandinavia. When first known to the Romans, a large division of their nation lived on the northern shores of the Euxine. About the middle of the third century of our era they crossed the Dnies'ter, and devastated Dácia and Thrace. The emperor Décius lost his life in opposing them; after which his successor Gal'lus induced them by money, to withdraw to their old seats on the Dnies'ter. (See p. 215.) Soon after this period the Goths appear in two grand divisions;—the Os'trogoths, or Eastern Goths, passing the Euxine into Asia Minor, and ravaging Bythin'ia;—and the Vis'igoths, or Western Goths, gradually pressing upon the Roman provinces along the Danube. About the year 375, the Huns, coming from the East, fell upon the Os'trogoths, and drove them upon the Vis'igoths, who were then living north of the Danube. A vast multitude of the latter were permitted by the emperor Válens to settle in Mœ'sia, and on the waste lands of Thrace; but being soon after joined by their Eastern brethren, they raised the standard of war, carried their ravages to the very gates of Constantinople, and killed Válens in battle. (See p. 228.) It was Al'aric, king of the Vis'igoths, who plundered Rome in the beginning of the fifth century. (See p. 231.) The Vis'igoths afterwards passed into Spain, where they founded a dynasty which reigned nearly three centuries, and was finally conquered by the Moors, A. D. 711. In the meantime the Os'trogoths had been following in the path of their brethren, and in the year 493 their great king Theod'oric defeated Odoácer, and seated himself on the throne of Italy. (See p. 239.) The Gothic kingdom lasted only till the year 554, when it was overthrown by Nar'ses, the general of Justin'ian (See p. 241.) From this period the Goths no longer occupy a prominent place in history, except in Spain.

2. The *Aláni*, likewise a Scythian race, when first known occupied the country between the Volga and the Don. Being conquered, eventually, by the Huns, most of the Aláni united with their conquerors, and proceeded with them to invade the limits of the Gothic empire of Italy.

a. Gibbon, I. 96.

Max'imin was unanimously proclaimed emperor by the applauding legions, who, now composed mostly of peasants and barbarians of the frontiers, knowing no country but their camp, and no science but that of war, and discarding the authority of the senate, looked upon themselves as the sole depositaries of power, as they were, in reality, the real masters of the Roman world. Max'imin commenced his reign by a sanguinary butchery of the friends of the late monarch; but his avarice and cruelty soon provoked a civil war, and raised up against him several competitors for the throne.

4. At first the aged and virtuous Gor'dian, pro-consul of Africa, II GOR'DIAN. was declared sovereign by the legions in that part of the Roman world, but he persisted in refusing the dangerous honor until menaces compelled him to accept the imperial title. At Rome the news of his election was received with universal joy, and confirmed by the senate; but two months after his accession he perished in a struggle with the Roman governor of Mauritánia, who still adhered to Max'imin. Two senators of consular dignity, Pu-

III. PUPIÉ-NUS AND BALBI'NUS. piénus, (sometimes called Max'imus) and Balbínus, were then declared emperors by the senate; and soon after, Max'imin, while on his march from Pannónia to Rome, was slain in his tent by his own guards. (A. D. 238.) Only a few IV. SECOND GOR'DIAN. days later both Pupiénus and Balbínus were slain in a mutiny of the troops. The youthful Gor'dian, grandson of the former Gor'dian, was then declared emperor.

5. During these rapid changes in the sovereignty of the Roman world, the empire was involved in numerous foreign wars, which gradually wasted its strength and resources, and hastened its downfall. On the north, the German nations, and other barbarian tribes, almost constantly harassed the frontier provinces; while in the east the Persians, after overthrowing the Parthian empire, and establishing the second or later Persian empire under the dynasty of the Sassan'idæ, (A. D. 226,) commenced a long series of destructive ars against the Romans, with the constant object of driving the latter from Asia.

6. At the time of the accession of the second Gor'dian to the sovereignty of the Roman empire, Sápor, the second prince of the Sas'sanid dynasty, was driving the Romans from several of their Asiatic provinces. The efforts of Gor'dian, who went in person to protect the provinces of Syria, were partially successful but while

the youthful conqueror was pursuing his advantages, he was supported
in the affections of his army by Philip the Arabian, the   V. PHILIP
prefect or commander of the Prætorian guards, who caused   THE
his monarch and benefactor to be slain, (A. D. 244.)   ARABIAN.

7. It is not surprising that the generals of Philip were disposed
to imitate the example of their master, and that insurrections and
rebellions were frequent during his reign. At length a rebellion
having broken out in Pannónia, Décius was sent to suppress it, when he himself was proclaimed emperor by   VI. DÉCIUS.
the fickle troops, and compelled, by the threat of instant death, to
submit to their dictation. Philip immediately marched against Décius, but was defeated and slain near Veróna.[1] (A. D. 249.)

8. Several monarchs now succeeded each other in rapid succession.
Décius soon fell in battle with the Goths, (A. D. 251,) large numbers of whom during his reign first crossed the Danube, and desolated the Roman provinces in that quarter. Gal'lus, a   VII. GAL
general of Décius, being raised to the throne, concluded   LUS.
a dishonorable peace with the barbarians, and renewed a violent persecution of the Christians, which had been commenced by Décius
As new swarms of the barbarians crossed the Danube, the pusillani
mous emperor seemed about to abandon the defence of   VIII. ÆMILI
the monarchy, when Æmiliánus, governor of Pannónia   A'NUS.
and Mœ'sia, unexpectedly attacked the enemy and drove them back
into their own territories. His troops, elated by the victory, proclaimed their general emperor on the field of battle ; and Gal'lus
was soon after slain by his own soldiers. In three months   IX. VALÉ-
a similar fate befel Æmiliánus, when Valérian, governor   RIAN.
of Gaul, then about sixty years of age, a man of learning, wisdom,
and virtue, was advanced to the sovereignty, not by the clamors of
the army only, but by the unanimous voice of the Roman world.

9. Valérian possessed abilities that might have rendered his admin
istration happy and illustrious, had he lived in times more peaceful,
and more favorable for the display and appreciation of virtue ; but
his reign had not only a most deplorable end, but was marked, throughout, with nothing but confusion and calamities. At this time the
Goths, who had already formed a powerful nation on the lower Dan-

---

.. *Veróna*, a large and flourishing Roman city of Cisalpine Gaul, still retains its ancient name.
It is situated on both sides of the river Adige, sixty-four miles west from Venice. The great glory
of Verona is its amphitheatre, one of the noblest existing monuments of the ancient Romans,
and, excepting the Colosséum at Rome, the largest extant edifice of its class. It is supposed
to have been capable of accommodating twenty thousand spectators. *Maj No.* XVII.)

ube and the northern coasts of the Black Sea, ravaged the Roman do
minions on their borders, and penetrating into the interior of Greece,
or Acháia, destroyed Ar' gos, Corinth, and Athens, by fire and by
the sword: the Franks,[1] who had formed a kingdom on the lower
Rhine, began to be formidable: the Aleman' ni[2] broke through their
boundaries, and advanced into the plains of Lom' bardy[3]: Spain,
Gaul, and Britain, were virtually torn away from the empire, and
overned by independent chiefs; while in the East, the Persians,
under their monarch Sápor, fell like a mountain torrent upon Syria
and Cappadócia, and almost effaced the Roman power from Asia.

10. Valérian in person led the Roman army against the Persians,
but, penetrating beyond the Euphrátes, he was surrounded and taken
prisoner by Sápor, who is accused of treating his royal captive with
wanton and unrelenting cruelty,—using him as a stepping-stone when
he mounted on horseback, and at last causing him, after nine years
of captivity, to be flayed alive, and his skin to be stuffed in the form
x. GALLIÉ. of the living emperor—dyed in scarlet in mockery of
NUS. his imperial dignity, and preserved as a trophy in a
temple of Persia. Galliénus, the unworthy son of Valérian, receiving the news of his father's captivity with secret joy and open indifference, immediately succeeded to the throne. (A. D. 259.)

11. At the time when nearly every Roman town in Asia had sub
mitted to Sápor, Odenátus, prince of Palmyra,[4] who was attached

1. The *Franks*, or "Freemen," were a confederation of the rudest of the Germanic tribes,
and were first known to the Romans as inhabiting the numerous islets formed by the mouth of
the Rhine; but they afterwards crossed into Gaul, and, in the latter part of n.e fifth century,
under their leader Clovis, laid the foundation of the French monarchy. (See also p. 255.)

2. The *Aleman' ni*, or "all men," that is, men of all tribes, were also a German confederacy,
situated on the northern borders of Switzerland. They were finally overthrown by Clovis, after
which they were dispersed over Gaul, Switzerland, and northern Italy.

3. *Lom' bardy* embraced most of the great plain of northern Italy watered by the Po and its
tributaries.

4. *Palmyra*, "The ancient "Tadmor in the wilderness" built by king Solomon, (2. Chron.
viii. 4,) was situated in an oasis of the Syrian desert, about one hundred and forty miles
north-east from Damascus. The first notice we have of it in Roman history is at the com
mencement of the wars with the Parthians, when it was permitted to maintain a state of independence and neutrality between the contending parties. Being on the caravan route from the
coast of Syria to the regions of Mesopotámia, Persia, and India, it was long the principal emporium of commerce between the Eastern and Western worlds—a city of merchants and factors, whose wealth is still attested by the number and magnificence of its ruins. After the
victories of Trajan had established the unquestionable preponderance of the Roman arms, it
became allied to the empire as a free State, and was greatly favored by Adrian and the Anto
nines, during whose reigns it attained its greatest splendor. Odenátus maintained its glory
and for his defeat of the Persians the Roman senate conferred on him the title of Augustus,
and associated him with Galliénus in the empire; but his queen and successor, the
famous Zenóbia, broke the alliance with the imbecile Galliénus, annexed Egypt to her do

to the Roman interest, desirous at least to secure the forbearance of the conqueror, sent Sápor a magnificent present of camels and merchandise, accompanied with a respectful, but not servile, epistle; but the haughty monarch ordered the gifts to be thrown into the Euphrátes, and returned for an answer that if Odenátus hoped to mitigate his punishment he must, prostrate himself before the throne of Sápor with his hands tied behind his back. The Palmyrean prince reading his fate in the angry message of Sápor, resolved to meet the Persian in arms. Hastily collecting a little army from the villages of Syria, and the tents of the desert, he fell upon and routed the Persian host, seized the camp, the women, and the treasures of Sápor, and in a short time restored to the Romans most of the provinces of which they had been despoiled.

12. The indolence and inconstancy of Galliénus soon raised up a host of competitors for the throne, generally reckoned thirty in all, although the number of actual pretenders did not exceed nineteen. Among these was Odenátus the Palmyrean, to whom the Roman senate had intrusted the command of the Eastern provinces, after associating him with Galliénus. Of all these competitors, several of whom were models of virtue, two only were of noble birth, and not one enjoyed a life of peace, or died a natural death. As one after another was cut off by the arms of a rival, or by domestic treachery, armies and provinces were involved in their fall. During the deplorable reigns of Valérian and Galliénus, the contentions of the imperial rivals, and the arms of barbarians, brought the empire to the very brink of ruin.

13. Galliénus, after a reign of nine years, was murdered while he was besieging one of his rivals in Mediolánum;[1] (Milan, A. D. 268;) but before his death he had appointed Marcus Aurélius Claudius, a general of great reputation, to succeed him, and the choice was confirmed by the joyful acclamations of the army and the people.

XI. CLAUDIUS.

minions, and assumed the title of "Augusta, Queen of the East." The emperor Aurélian marched against the ill-fated Palmyra with an irresistible force; the walls of the city were razed to the ground; and the seat of commerce, of arts, and of Zenóbia, gradually sunk into an obscure town, a trifling fortress, and, at length, a miserable Arab village.

1. *Mediolánum*, now Milan, was a city of Cisalpine Gaul, one hundred and fifty miles west from Venice, situated in a beautiful plain between two small streams the Olona and Lambra, which unite at San Angelo and form a northern tributary of the Po. Mediolánum was annexed to the Roman dominions by Scipio Nasica, 191 B. C. A good specimen of ancient Roman architecture may still be seen at Milan, being a range of sixteen beautiful Corinthian columns, with their architrave, before the church at San Lorenzo. (*Map No. VIII.*)

14 A succession of better princes now restored for awhile the decaying energies of the empire. Claudius merited the confidence which had been placed in his wisdom, valor, and virtue; and his early death was a great misfortune to the Roman world. After having overthrown and nearly destroyed an army of three hundred and twenty thousand Goths and Van' dals, who had invaded the empire by the way of the Bos' porus, Claudius was cut off by a pestilence at Sir' mium,[1] as he was making preparations to march against the famous Zenóbia, the "Queen of the East," and the widow and successor of Odenátus.

15. Quintil' ius, the brother of Claudius, was proclaimed emperor by the acclamations of the troops; but when he learned that the great army of the Danube had invested Aurélian with imperial power, he sunk into despair, and terminated his life after a reign of seventeen days.

XII. QUIN-
TIL' IUS.

16. The reign of Aurélian, which lasted only four years and nine months, was filled with memorable achievements. After a bloody conflict, he put an end, by treaty, to the Gothic war of twenty years' duration; he chastised and drove back the Aleman' ni, who had traced a line of devastation from the Danube to the Po; he recovered Gaul, Spain, and Britain; and passing into Asia at the head of a large army, he destroyed the proud monarchy which Zenóbia had erected there, and led that unfortunate, but heroic princess, captive to Rome. Being presented with an elegant villa at Tibur,[2] the Syrian queen insensibly sunk into a Roman matron, and her daughters married into the noblest families of the empire. With great courage and superior military talents, Aurélian possessed many private virtues; but their influence was impaired by the sternness and severity of his character. He fell in a conspiracy of his officers near Byzan' tium,[3] while preparing to carry on a war with Persia. (A. D. March, 275.)

XIII. AURÉ-
LIAN.

1. *Sir' mium* was an important city in the south-eastern part of Pannonia, on the northern ide of the river Save. Its ruins may be seen near the town of *Mitrovitz*, in Austrian Slavonia.

2. *Tibur*, now *Tivoli*, (teé-vo-le) was situated at the cascades of the A' nio, now the Teverone, eighteen miles north-east from Rome. Its ancient inhabitants were called the *Tiburtins.* The declivities in the vicinity of Tibur were anciently interspersed with splendid villas, the favorite residences of the refined and luxurious citizens of Rome, among which may be mentioned those of Sallust, Mæcénas, Tibul' lus, Várus, At' ticus, Cassius, Brutus, &c. Here Virgil and Horace elaborated their immortal works. Although the temples and theatres of ancient Tibur have crumbled into dust, its orchards, its gardens, and its cool recesses, still bloom and flourish in unfading beauty. (*Map* No. X.)

3. *Byzan' tium*, now Constantinople; a celebrated city of Thrace on the western shore of the Thracian Bos' porus. is supposed to have been founded by a Dorian colony from Mag' ara, led

17. On the death of Aurélian, a generous and unlooked-for disinterestedness was exhibited by the army, which modestly referred the appointment of a successor to the senate. For six months the senate persisted in declining an honor it had so long been unaccustomed to enjoy; and during this period the Roman world remained without a sovereign, without a usurper, and without a sedition   At length the senate yielded to the continual request of the egions, and elected to the imperial dignity Marcus XIV. TACITUS. Claudius Tacitus, a wealthy and virtuous senator, who had already passed his seventy-fifth year. Tacitus, after enacting some wise laws, and restoring to the senate its ancient privileges, proceeded to join the army, which had remained assembled on the Bos'porus[1] for the invasion of Persia; but the hardships of a military life, and the cares of government, proved too much for his constitution, and he died in Cappadócia, after a reign of little more than six months. (A. D. Sept., 275.)

18. Flórian, a brother of Tacitus, showed himself unworthy to reign, by assuming the government without even con- XV. FLO- sulting the senate. His own soldiers soon after put him RIAN. to death, while in the meantime the Syrian army proclaimed their leader, Próbus, emperor. The latter proved to be an XVI. PRO- excellent sovereign and a great general; and in the wars BUS. which he carried on with the Franks, Aleman'ni, Sarmátians,[2] Goths, and Van'dals,[3] he gained greater advantages than any of his predecessors. In the several battles which he fought, four hundred thousand of the barbarians fell; and seventy cities opened their gates to

by *Byzas* a Thracian prince, about the middle of the seventh century before the Christian era. It was destroyed by the Persians in the reign of Darius: it resisted successfully the arms of Philip of Mac'edon: during the reign of Philip II. it placed itself under Roman sway: it was destroyed, and afterwards rebuilt, by Septim'ius Sevérus; and in the year 328 A. D., Con'stantine made it the capital of the Roman empire. On the subjugation of the western empire by the barbarians, A. D. 476, it continued to be the capital of the eastern empire. It was taken by the crusaders in the year 1204; and in 1453 it fell into the hands of the Turks, when the last remnant of the Roman empire was finally suppressed. (*Map* No. III.)

1. The *Bos'porus*, (corrupted by modern orthography to Bos'phorus,) is the strait which connects the Euxine or Black Sea, with the Propon'tis or Sea of Marmóra. The length of this remarkable channel is about seventeen miles, with a width varying from half a mile to two miles. (*Map* No. VII.)

2. Ancient *Sarmátia* extended from the Baltic Sea and the Vis'tula to the Caspian Sea and the Volga. European Sarmátia embraced Poland, Lithuánia, Prussia, and a part of Russia. Asiatic Sarmátia comprised the country between the Caspian Sea and the river Don.

3. The *Van'dals* were a people of Germany, and are supposed to have been of Gothic origin. They formed one of the three divisions of the great Slavonian race;—viz., Va.dals, An and Slavonians proper. The Slavonian language is the stem from which have issued the Russian Polish, Bohemia, &c.

him. After he had secured a general peace by his victories, he employed his armies in useful public works; but the soldiers disdained such employment, and while they were engaged in draining a marsh near Sir' mium, in the hot days of summer, they broke out into a furious mutiny, and in their sudden rage slew their emperor. (A. D. 282.)

19. The legions next raised Cárus, prefect of the Prætorian guards, to the throne. He was full of warlike ambition and the desire of military glory, and seems to have held a middle rank between good and bad princes. He signalized the beginning of his reign by a memorable defeat of the Sarmátians in Illyr'icum, sixteen thousand of whom he slew in battle. He then marched against Persia, and had already carried his victorious arms beyond the Tigris, when he was killed in his tent, as was generally believed by lightning. (A. D. 283.) Numérian, one of the sons of Cárus, who had accompanied his father in his eastern expedition, and Carínus his elder brother, who had been left to govern Rome, were immediately acknowledged emperors by the troops.

XVII. CA′RUS.

XVIII. NUMÉRIAN AND CARI′NUS.

20. On the death of Cárus, the eastern army, superstitiously regarding places or persons struck by lightning as singularly devoted to the wrath of heaven, refused to advance any farther; and the Persians beheld with wonder the unexpected retreat of a victorious army.—While Carínus remained at Rome, immersed in pleasures and acting the part of a second Com′modus, the virtuous Numérian perished by assassination. The army of the latter then chose for his successor Dioclétian, the commander of the domestic body guards of the late emperor. (A. D. Dec., 285.)

21. Carínus, being determined to dispute the succession, marched with a large army against Dioclétian, whom he was on the point of defeating in a desperate battle on the plains of Margus, a small city of Mœ′sia, when he was slain by one of his own officers in revenge for some private wrong. The army of Carínus then acknowledged Dioclétian as emperor. He used his victory with mildness, and, contrary to the common practice, respected the lives and fortunes of his late adversaries, and even continued in their stations many of the officers of Cárinus.

XIX. DIOCLÉ-TIAN.

22. The reign of Dioclétian is an important epoch in Roman history, as it was one of long duration and general prosperity, and is

the beginning of the division of the Roman world into the Eastern and Western empire. The accession of Dioclétian also marks a new chronological era, called the "era of Dioclétian," or, "the era of martyrs," which was long recognized in the Christian church, and is still used by the Copts and Abyssinians.[1]

23. The natural tendency of the eastern parts of the empire to become separated from the western, together with the difficulties of ruling singly over so many provinces of different nations and diverse interests, led Dioclétian to form the plan of dividing the imperial authority, and governing the empire from two centres, although the whole was still to remain one. He therefore first took as a colleague his friend and fellow soldier Maxim'ian; but still the weight of the public administration appearing too heavy, the two sovereigns took each a subordinate colleague, to whose name the title of Cæsar was prefixed.

24. Maxim'ian made Milan his capital, while Dioclétian held his court at Nicomédia,[2] in Asia Minor. Maxim'ian ruled over Italy and Africa proper; while his subordinate colleague, Constan'tius, administered the government of Gaul, Spain, Britain, and Mauritánia. Dioclétian reserved, for his personal supervision, nearly all the empire east of the Adriat'ic, except Pannónia and Moe'sia, which he conferred upon his subordinate colleague Galérius. Each of the four rulers was sovereign within his own jurisdiction; but each was prepared to assist his colleagues with counsel and with arms; while Dioclétian was regarded as the father and head of the empire.

xx. MAXIM'-IAN.

25. The most important events of the reign of Dioclétian were the insurrection of Caraúsius in Britain, a revolt in Egypt and throughout northern Africa, the war against the Persians, and a long-continued persecution of the Christians. During seven years, Caraúsius, the commander of the northern Roman fleet, ruled over Britain, and diffused beyond the columns of Hercules the terror of his name. He was murdered by his first minister Alec'tus; but the latter, soon after, was defeated and slain in battle by Constan'tius; and after a separation of ten years, Britain was reunited with the empire.

26. The suppression of a formidable revolt in Egypt was accom-

1. The *Copts* are Christians—descendants of the ancient Egyptians, as distinguished from the Arabians and other inhabitants of modern Egypt. The *Abyssinians* inhabitants of Abyssinia, in eastern Africa, profess Christianity, but it has little influence over their conduct.

2. *Nicomédia* was in Bithyn'ia, at the eastern extremity of the Propon'tis, or Sea of Marmora. The modern *Is-Mid* occupies the site of the ancient city.

plished by Dioclétian himself, who took a terrible vengeance upon Alexandria, and utterly destroyed the proud cities of Busíris and Cop' tos.[1] In the meantime a confederacy of five Moorish[2] nations attacked all the Roman provinces of Africa, from the Nile westward to Mount Atlas, but the barbarians were vanquished by the arms of Maxim' ian.

27. Next commenced the war with Persia, which was carried on by Galérius, although Dioclétian, taking his station at An' tioch,[3] prepared and directed the military operations. In the first campaign the Roman army received a total overthrow on the very ground rendered memorable by the defeat and death of Crassus. In a second campaign Galérius gained a complete victory by a night attack ; and by the peace which followed, the eastern boundary of the Roman world was extended beyond the Tigris, so as to embrace the greater part of Cardúchia, the modern Kurdistan'.[4]

28. The triumphs of Dioclétian are sullied by a general persecution of the Christians (the tenth and last), which he is said to have commenced at the instigation of Galérius, aided by the artifices of the priesthood. (A. D. 303.) The famous edict of Dioclétian against the Christians excluded them from all offices, ordered their churches to be pulled down, and their sacred books to be burned, and led to a general and indiscriminate massacre of all such as professed the name of Jesus.

1. Four cities of Egypt bore the name of *Busíris*. The one destroyed by Dioclétian was in the Thebáis, or southern Egypt,—generally called Upper Egypt. *Cop' tos* was likewise in Upper Egypt, east of the Nile. Its favorable situation for commerce caused it again to arise after its destruction by Dioclétian.

2. The *Moors*, whose name is derived from a Greek word (*Maures*) signifying "dark," "obscure," are natives of the northern coast of Africa, or, more properly, of the Roman *Mauritánia*. The Moors were originally from Asia, and are a people distinct from the native Arabs, Berbers, &c. The modern Moors are descendants of the ancient Mauritánians, intermixed with their Arab conquerors, and with the remains of the Van' dals who once ruled over the country.

3. *An' tioch*, once eminent for its beauty and greatness, was situated in northern Syria, on the left bank of the Oron' tes, (now the Aaazy,) twenty miles from its entrance into the Mediterranean. An' tioch was the capital of the Macedónian kingdom of Syria; and about the year 65 B. C. the conquests of Pompey brought it, with the whole of Syria, under the control of the Romans. It was long the centre of an extensive commerce, the residence of the governor of Syria, the frequent resort of the Roman emperors, and, next to Rome, the most celebrated city of the empire for the amusements of the circus and the theatre. Paul and Bárnabas planted there the doctrines of Christianity ; and "the disciples were called Christians first in An' tioch."—Acts, xi. 26. (*Map* No. VII.)

4. *Kurdistan'*, comprised chiefly within the basin of the Tigris, is claimed partly by Turkey and partly by Persia. It is the country of the *Kurds*, in whose character the love of theft and brigandage is a marked feature; but, at the same time, when visited by travellers they exercise the most generous hospitality and often force handsome presents on their departing guests.

29. During ten years the persecution continued with scarcely mitigated horrors ; and such multitudes of Christians suffered death that
at last the imperial murderers boasted that they had extinguished
the Christian name and religion, and restored the worship of the
gods to its former purity and splendor.   In spite, however, of the
efforts of tyranny, the Christian Church survived, and in a few years
reigned triumphant in the very metropolis of heathen idolatry.

30. After a reign of twenty years, Dioclétian, in the presence of
a large concourse of citizens and soldiers who had assembled at
Nicomédia to witness the spectacle, voluntarily laid down the sceptre,
and retired to private life ; and on the same day Maxim' ian, accord
ing to previous agreement, performed a similar ceremony
at Milan.   (May 1st, 305.)   Galérius and Constan' tius
were thereupon acknowledged sovereigns ; and two subordinates, or Cæsars, were appointed to complete the
system of imperial government which Dioclétian had established.
But this balance-of-power system needed the firm and dexterous
hand of its founder to sustain it ; and the abdication of Dioclétian
was followed by eighteen years of discord and confusion.

31. One year after the abdication of the sovereigns, Constan' tius
died at York, in Britain, when his soldiers proclaimed his son Con'-
stantine emperor.   In a short time the empire was divided between six sovereigns ; but Con'stantine lived to
see them destroyed in various ways ; and, eighteen years after his
accession, having overcome in battle Licin' ius, the last of his rivals,
he was thus left sole master of the Roman world, whose dominions
extended from the wall of Scotland to Kurdistan', and from the Red
Sea to Mount Atlas in Africa.   Galérius had already died of a
loathsome disease, which was considered by many as a punishment from
Heaven for his persecution of the Christians

32. Con' stantine has been styled the first Christian emperor.
During one of his campaigns (A. D. 312) he is said to have seen a
miraculous vision of a luminous cross in the Heavens, on which was
inscribed the following words in Greek, " *By this conquer.*"   Certain
it is that from this period Con' stantine showed the Christians marks
of positive favor, and caused the cross to be employed as the imperial
standard . in his last battle with Licin' ius it was the emblem of the
cross that was opposed to the symbols of paganism ; and as the latter
went down in a night of blood, the triumph of Christianity over the
Roman world was deemed complete.

33. The most important events in the reign of Con'stantine, after he had restored the outward unity of the empire, were his wars with the Sarmátians and Goths, whom he severely chastised, his domestic difficulties, in which he showed little of the character of a Christian; and the establishment, at Byzan'tium, of the new capital of the Roman empire; afterwards called *Constantinople*, from its founder. The motives which led Con'stantine to the choice of a new capital, on a spot which seemed formed by nature to be the metropolis of a great empire, were those of policy and interest, mingled with feelings of revenge for insults which he had received at Rome, where he was execrated for abandoning the religion of his forefathers.

34. The removal of the seat of government was followed by an entire change in the forms of civil and military administration. The military despotism of the former emperors now gave place to the despotism of a court, surrounded by all the forms and ceremonies, the pride, pomp, and circumstances, of Eastern greatness: all magistrates were accurately divided into new classes, and a uniform system of taxation was established, although the amount of tribute was imposed by the absolute authority of the monarch. Finally Con'-stantine, as he approached the end of his life, went back to the system of Dioclétian, and divided the empire among his three sons Con'stantine, Constan'tius, and Con'stans, and his two nephews, Dalmátius and Hannibaliánus. After a reign of thirty-one years Con'stantine the First died at Nicomédia, at the age of sixty-three years. (A. D. 337.)

35. The division of sovereign power among so many rulers involved the empire in frequent insurrections and civil wars, until XXIII. CON- sixteen years from the death of Con'stantine, Constan'STAN'TIUS II. tius, or Constan'tius II., after having seen all his rivals overcome, and several usurpers vanquished, was left in the sole possession of the empire. During his reign of twenty-four years he was engaged in frequent wars with the Franks, Saxons,[1] Aleman'ni, and Sarmátians, while the Persians continued to harass the Eastern

1. The *Saxons* were a people of Germany, whose original seats appear to have been on the neck of the Cimbric peninsula, (now Denmark,) between the Elbe and the Baltic, and embracing the present Sleswick and Holstein. (Map No. XVII,) The early Saxons were a nation of fishermen and pirates; and it appears that after they had, extended their depredations to the coasts of Britain and eastern and southern Gaul, numerous auxiliaries from the shores of the Baltic joined them, and, gradually coalescing with them into a national body, accepted the name and the laws of the Saxons. In the early part of the fifth century, the Saxons were converted .ö Christianity by the Roman missionaries· and half a century later they had obtained a permanent establishment in Britain.

provinces. While Constan'tius was sustaining a doubtful war in the East, his cousin Júlian, whom he had appointed to the command of the Western provinces, with the title of Cæsar, was proclaimed emperor by his victorious legions in Gaul. Preparations for civil war were made on both sides; but the Roman world was saved from the calamities of the struggle by the sudden death of Constan'tius. (A. D. 361.)

36. Júlian, commonly called the Apostate, on account of his relaps ing from Christianity into paganism, possessed many ami· able and shining qualities, and his application to business was intense. He reformed numerous abuses of his prede- cessor, but, in the great object of his ambition, the restoration of ancient paganism, although he had issued an edict of universal toler- ation, he showed a marked hostility to the Christians, subjecting them to many disabilities and humiliations, and allowing their ene- mies to treat them with excessive rigor.

XXIV.

JU'LIAN THE APOSTATE.

37. Trained in the most celebrated schools of Grecian philosophy at Athens, Júlian was an able writer and an artful sophist, and, employ- ing the weapons of argument and ridicule against the Christians, he strenuously labored to degrade Christianity, and bring contempt upon its followers. In this effort he was partially successful; but ere long the sophisms of the "apostate emperor" were ably refuted by St. Cyril and others, and the result of the controversy was highly favorable to the increase and spread of the new religion.

38. Not relying upon the weapons of argument and ridicule alone, Júlian aimed what he thought would be a deadly blow to Christi- anity, by ordering the temple of Jerusalem to be rebuilt, hoping thus to falsify the language of prophecy and the truth of Revela- tion. But although the Jews were invited from all the provinces of the empire to assemble once more on the holy mountain of their fathers, and every effort was made to secure the success of the under taking, both by the emperor and the Jews themselves, the work did not prosper, and was finally abandoned in despair.

39 Most writers, both Christians and pagans, declare that the work was frustrated in consequence of balls of fire that burst from the earth and alarmed the workmen who were employed in digging the foundations. Whether these phenomena, so gravely and abun dantly attested, were supernatural or otherwise, does not affect the authenticity of the prophecy that pronounced desolation upon Jeru salem. The most powerful monarch of the earth, stimulated by

pride, passion, and interest, and aided by a zealous people, attempted to erect a building in one of his cities, but found all his efforts vain, because "the finger of God was there."[a]

40. During the same year in which Julian attempted the rebuilding of the temple, he set out with a large army for the conquest of Persia. The Persian monarch made overtures of peace through his ambassadors; but Julian dismissed them with the declaration that he intended speedily to visit the court of Persia. He marched with great rapidity into the heart of the country, overcoming all obstacles, but being led astray in the desert by treacherous guides, his army was reduced to great distress by want of provisions, and he was forced to commence a retreat. At length Julian himself, in a skirmish which proved favorable to the Romans, was mortally wounded by a Persian javelin. He died the same night, spending his last moments, like Socrates, in philosophical discourse with his friends. (A. D. 363.)

41. In the death of Julian, the race of the great Con' stantine was extinct; and the empire was left without a master and without an heir. In this situation of affairs, Jovian, who had held some important offices under Con' stantine, was proclaimed emperor by the army, which was still surrounded by the Persian hosts. The first care of Jovian was to conclude a dishonorable peace, by which five provinces beyond the Tigris, the whole of Mesopatámia, and several fortified cities in other districts, were surrendered to the Persians. On his arrival at An' tioch, Jovian revoked the edicts of his predecessor against the Christians. Soon after while on his way to Constantinople, he was found dead in his bed, having been accidentally suffocated, as was supposed, by th fumes of burning charcoal. (Feb. A. D. 364.)

xxv.
JO' VIAN.

42. After an interval of ten days, Valentin' ian, the commander of the body guard at the time of Jovian's death, was elected emperor. One month later he associated with himself, as a colleague in the empire, his brother Válens upon whom he conferred the government of the Eastern

XXVI. VAL-
ENTIN' IAN
AND
VA' LENS.

<hr>

a. The probable explanation of the remarkable incidents attending the attempt of Julian to rebuild the temple, is, that the numerous subterranean excavations, reservoirs, &c., beneath and around the ruins of the temple, which had been neglected during a period of three hundred years, had become filled with inflammable air, which, taking fire from the torches of the work men, repelled, by terrific explosions, those who attempted to explore the ruins. From a similar cause terrible accidents sometimes occur in deeply-excavated mines.—*See Milman's Notes on Gibbon.* *Gibbon,* vol. ii. p. 447.

provinces, from the lower Danube to the confines of Persia; while he reserved for himself the extensive territory reaching from the extremity of Greece to the wall of Scotland, and from the latter to the foot of Mount Atlas. This was the final division of the Roman world into the Eastern and Western. Empire. The capital of the former was established at Constantinople, and of the latter at Milan. The city of Rome had long been falling into neglect and insignificance.

43. Soon after the period at which we have now arrived, the inroads of the barbarian tribes upon the northern and eastern frontiers of the empire became more vexatious and formidable than ever. The Picts and Scots' ravaged Britain; the Saxons began their piracies in the Northern seas; the German tribes of the Aleman'ni harassed Gaul; and the Goths crossed the Danube into Thrace; but during the twelve years of Valentin'ian's reign, his firmness and vigilance repulsed the barbarians at every point, while his genius directed and sustained the feeble counsels of his brother Válens.

    XXVII.
    BARBARIAN
    INROADS.

44. About the time of the death of Valentin'ian, (A. D. 375) Válens was informed that the power of the Goths, long the enemies of Rome, had been subverted by the Huns, a fierce and warlike race of savages, till then unknown, who coming from the East, and crossing the Don and the sea of Azof, had driven before them the European nations that dwelt north of the Danube. The Vis'igoths first solicited from the Roman government protection against their ruthless invaders; and a vast multitude of these barbarians, whose numbers amounted to near a million of persons, of both sexes, and all ages, were permitted to settle on the waste lands of Thrace.

45. In the meantime the Os'trogoths, pressed forward by the unrelenting Huns, appeared on the banks of the Danube, and solicited the same indulgence that had been shown to their countrymen; and when their request was denied they crossed the stream with arms in their hands, and established a hostile camp on the territories of the empire. The two divisions of the Gothic nation now united their forces under their able general Frit'igern, and raising the standard

---

1. The *Picts* were a Caledonian race, famed for their marauding expeditions into the country south of them. The *Scots* were also a Caledonian race, who are believed to have come, originally, from Spain into Ireland, whence they passed over into Scotland. The genuine descendants of the ancient Scotch are believed to be the Gaels, or Highlanders, who speak the Erse or Gaelic language, which differs but little from the Irish.

of war devastated Thrace, Mac' odon, and Thes' saly, and carried
their ravages to the very gates of Constantinople. In a decisive battle
fought near Adrianóple[1] the Romans were defeated, and Válens himself was slain. (A. D. 378.)

46. Grátian, the son of Valentin' ian, and his successor in the
Western empire, was already on his march to the aid of

XXVIII.
GRA' TIAN
AND
THEODO' SIUS

Válens, when he heard the tidings of the defeat and
death of his unfortunate colleague. Too weak to avenge
his fate, and conscious of his inability to sustain alone
the sinking weight of the empire, he chose as his associate Theodó
sius, afterwards called the Great, assigned to him the government of
the East, and then returned to his own provinces. Theodósius, by
his prudence, rather than his valor, delivered his provinces from the
scourge of barbarian warfare. The Goths, after the death of their
great leader Frit' igern, were distracted by a multiplicity of counsels;
and while some of them, falling back into their forests, carried their
conquests to the unknown regions of the North, others were allowed
to settle in Thrace, Phrygia, and Lydia, where, in the bosom of despotism, they cherished their native freedom, manners, and language, and
lent to the Roman arms assistance at once precarious and dangerous.

47. Five years after the accession of Theodósius, Grátian perished
in an attempt to quell a revolt of Max' imus, governor

XXIX. VAL-
ENTIN' IAN II.

of Britain, who had been joined by the legions of Gaul.
Valentin' ian II., who succeeded Grátian, was driven from Italy by
the usurper, and forced to take refuge in the court of Theodósius;
but the latter, marching into Italy, defeated and slew Max' imus, and
restored the royal exile to his throne. (A. D 388.) The murder
of Valentin' ian by the Gaul Abrogas' tes, and the revolt which he
excited, (A. D. 392,) again called for the interference of Theodósius
in the affairs of the West. His arms soon triumphed over all opposition; and the whole empire again came, for the last time, into the

XXX. HONO'-
RIUS AND
ARCA' DIUS.

hands of one individual. (A. D. 894.) Theodósius died
four months after his victory, having previously bestowed
upon his youngest son, Honórius, the throne of Milan, and
upon the oldest, Arcádius, that of Constantinople.

1. Adrianóple, one of the most important cities of Thrace, stood on the left bank of the river
Hebrus, now the Maritza, in one of the richest and finest plains of the world, one hundred and
thirty-four miles north-west from Constantinople. It was founded by and named after the emperor Adrian, although in early times a small Thracian village existed there, called Uskadama.
It is now the second city in the Turkish empire, containing a population o not less than one
hundred thousand souls. (Map No. VII.)

48. The civil wars that followed the accession of the new emperor were soon interrupted by the more important events of new barbarian invasions.   Scarcely had Theodósius expired, when the Gothic
nation, guided by the bold and artful genius of Al'aric, XXXI. AL'A-
who had learned his lessons of war in the school of RIC THE
Frit'igern, was again in arms.   After nearly all Greece GOTH.
had been ravaged by the invader, Stil'icho, the able general of
Honórius, came to its assistance ; but Al'aric evaded him by passing
into Epirus, and soon after, crossing the Júlian Alps,[1] advanced
toward Milan. (A. D. 403.)

49. Honórius fled from his capital, but was overtaken by the
speed of the Gothic cavalry, and obliged to shut himself up in the
little fortified town of As'ta,[2] where he was soon surrounded and
besieged by the enemy. Stil'icho hastened to the relief of his sovereign, and suddenly falling upon the Goths in their camp at Pollen'-
tia,[3] routed them with great slaughter, released many thousand prisoners, retook the magnificent spoils of Corinth, Athens, Argos, and
Sparta; and made captive the wife of Al'aric. The Gothic chief,
undaunted by this sudden reverse, hastily collected his shattered
army, and breaking through the unguarded passes of the Apennines,
spread desolation nearly to the walls of Rome. The city was saved
by the diligence of Stil'icho ; but the withdrawal of the barbarians
from Italy was purchased by a large ransom.

50. The recent danger to which Honórius had been exposed at
Milan, induced the unwarlike emperor to seek a more secure retreat
in the fortress of Raven'na,[4] which, from this time to the middle of

---

1. Augustus divided the Alpine chain, which extends from the Gulf of Genoa to the Adriat'-
ic, in a crescent form, into seven portions ; of which the Júlian range, terminating in Illyr'-
icum, is the most eastern.

2. As'ta (now Asti) was on the north side of the river Tanárus, (now Tanáro) in Ligúria,
twenty-eight miles south-east from Turin.

3. "The vestiges of Pollen'tia are twenty-five miles to the south-east of Turin." (Gibbon, ii.
221.) "The modern village of Pollenza stands near the site of the ancient city."—Cramer's
Italy, . 28.

4. Raven'na was situated on the coast of the Adriat'ic, a short distance below the mouths
of the Po. Although originally founded on the sea-shore, in the midst of marshes, in the days
of Strabo the marshes had greatly increased, seaward, owing to the accumulation of mud
brought dow by the Po and other rivers. In the latter times of the republic it was the great
naval station of the Romans on the Adriat'ic. Augustus constructed a new harbor three miles
from the old town, but in no very long time this was filled up also, and, "as early as the fifth or
sixth century of the Christian era, the port of Augustus was converted into pleasant gardens ;
and a lonely grove of pines covered the ground where the Roman fleet once rode at anchor."
(Gibbon, ii. 294.) But this very circumstance, though it lessened the naval importance, increased the strength of the place, and the shallowness of the water was a barrier against large
ships of the enemy. The only means of access inland was by a long and narrow causeway

the eighth century, was considered as the seat of government and the capital of Italy. The fears of Honórius were not without foundation; for scarcely had Al'aric departed, when another deluge of barbarians, consisting of Vandals,[1] Suévi,[2] Burgun'dians,[3] Goths, and Aláni, and numbering not less than two hundred thousand fighting men, under the command of Radagáisus, poured down upon Italy.

51. The Roman troops were now called in from the provinces for the defence of Italy, whose safety was again intrusted to the counsels and the sword of Stil'icho. The barbarians passed, without resistance, the Alps, the Po, and the Apennines, and were allowed by the wary Stil'icho to lay siege to Florence,[4] when, securing all the passes, he in turn blockaded the besiegers, who, gradually wasted by famine, were finally compelled to surrender at discretion. (A. D. 406.) The triumph of the Roman arms was disgraced by the execution of Radagáisus; and one-third of the vast host that had accompanied him into Italy were sold as slaves.

several miles in extent, over an otherwise impassable morass; and this avenue might be easily guarded or destroyed on the approach of a hostile army. Being otherwise fortified, it was a place of great strength and safety; and during the last years of the Western empire was the capital of Italy, and successively the residence of Honórius, Valentin'ian, Odoäcer, Theod'oric, and the succeeding Gothic monarchs. It is now a place of about sixteen thousand inhabitants, and is chiefly deserving of notice for its numerous architectural remains. (*Map* No. VIII.)

1. *Van'dals*, see p. 219.

2. The *Suévi* were a people of eastern Germany who finally settled in and gave their name to the modern *Suabia*.

3. The *Burgun'dians*—dwellers in *burgs* or towns—a name given to them by the more nomade tribes of Germany, were a numerous and warlike people of the Gothic or Van'dal race, who can be traced back to the banks of the Elbe. Driven southward by the Gep'idæ, they pressed upon the Aleman'ni, with whom they were in almost continual war. They were granted by Honórius, the Roman emperor, the territory extending from the Lake of Geneva to the junction of the Rhine with the Moselle, as a reward for having sent him the head of the usurper Jovinus. A part of Switzerland and a large portion of eastern France belonged to their new kingdom, which, as early as the year 470, was known by the name of Burgundy. Their seat of government was sometimes at Lyons, and sometimes at Geneva. Continually endeavoring to extend their limits, they were at last completely subdued, in a war with the Franks, by the son of Clovis, after Clovis himself had taken Lyons. Their name was for a long time retained by the powerful dukedom, afterwards province of Burgundy, now divided into several *departments*.

4. *Florence*, (anciently *Florentia*,) is a city of central Italy on the river Arno, (anciently Arnus,) one hundred and eighty-seven miles north-west from Rome. It owes its first distinction to Sylla, who planted in it a Roman colony. In the reign of Tibérius it was one of the principal cities of Italy. In 541 it was almost wholly destroyed by Totila, king of the Goths, but was restored by Charlemagne, after which it was, for a long time, the chief city of one of the most famous of the Italian republics. It is now the capital of the grand-duchy of *Tuscany*, which comprises the northern part of ancient Etrúria. With a population of one hundred thousand, it bears the aspect of a city filled with nobles and their domestics—a city of bridges, churches, and palaces. It has produced more celebrated men than any other city of Italy, or perhaps of Europe, among whom may be specified Dan'te, Pétrarch, Boccácio, Lorenzo de Medici, Galiléo Michael An'gelo, Macc'hiavelli,—the Popes Leo X and XI., and Clement VII., VIII., and XII

52. Two years after the great victory of Stil'icho, that minister whose genius might have delayed the fall of the empire, was treacherously murdered by the orders of the jealous and unworthy Honórius. The monarch had soon reason to repent of his guilty rashness. Adopting the counsels of his new ministers, he ordered a massacre of the families of the barbarians throughout Italy. Thirty thousand Gothic soldiers in the Roman pay immediately revolted, and invited Al'aric to avenge the slaughter of his countrymen.

53. Again Al'aric entered Italy, and without attempting the hopeless siege of Raven'na marched direct to Rome, which, during a period of more than six hundred years, had not been violated by the presence of a foreign enemy. After the siege had been protracted until the rigors of famine had been experienced in all their horror, and thousands were dying daily in their houses or in the streets for want of sustenance, the Romans sought to purchase the withdrawal of their invaders. The terms of Al'aric were, at first, *all* the gold and silver in the city, *all* the rich and precious movables, and *all* the slaves of barbarian origin. When the ministers of the senate asked, in a modest and suppliant tone, "If such, O King, are your demands, what do you intend to leave us?" "YOUR LIVES," replied the haughty conqueror.

54. The stern demands of Al'aric were, however, somewhat relaxed, and Rome was allowed to purchase a temporary safety by paying an enormous ransom of gold and silver and merchandize. Al'aric retired to winter quarters in Tuscany,[1] but as Honórius and his ministers, enjoying the security of the marshes and fortifications of Raven'na, refused to ratify the treaty that had been concluded by the Romans, the Goth turned again upon Rome, and, cutting off the supplies, compelled the city to surrender. (A. D. 409.) He then conferred the sovereignty of the empire upon At'talus, prefect of the city, but soon deposed him and attempted to renew his negotiations with Honórius. The latter refused to treat, when the king of the Goths, no longer dissembling his appetite for plunder and revenge, appeared a third time before the walls of Rome; treason opened the gates to him, and the city of Romulus was abandoned to the licentious fury of the tribes of Germany and Scythia.

---

1. *Tuscany*, after the fall of the Western empire, successively belonged to the Goths and Lombards. Charlemagne added it to his dominions, but under his successors it became independent. In the twelfth and thirteenth centuries it was divided among the famous republics of Florence, Pisa, and Sienna: in 1531 these were reunited into a duchy which, in 1737 fell into the hands of the house of Austria. In 1801 Napoleon erected it into the kingdom of Etruria; in 1808 it was incorporated with the French empire; and in 1814 it reverted to Austria.

55. The piety of the Goths spared the churches and religious houses, for Al'aric himself, and many of his countrymen, professed the name of Christians; but Rome was pillaged of her wealth, and a terrible slaughter was made of her citizens. Still Al'aric was unwilling that Rome should be totally ruined; and at the end of six days he abandoned the city, and took the road to southern Italy. As he was preparing to invade Sicily, with the ulterior design of subjugating Africa, his conquests were terminated by a premature death. (A. D. 410.) His body was interred in the bed of a small rivulet,[a] and the captives who prepared his grave were murdered, that the Romans might never learn the place of his sepulture.

56 After the death of Al'aric, the Goths gradually withdrew from Italy, and, a few years later, that branch of the nation called Vis'igoths established its supremacy in Spain and the east of Gaul. Toward the middle of the same century, the Britons, finally abandoned by the Romans, and unable to resist the barbarous inroads of the Picts and Scots, applied for assistance to the Angles[1] and Saxons, warlike tribes from the coasts of the Baltic. The latter, after driving back the Picts and Scots, turned their arms against the Britons, and after a long struggle finally established themselves in the island.

57. During these events in the north and west, the Van'dals, a Gothic tribe which had aided in the reduction of Spain, and whose name, with a slight change, has been given to the fertile province of Andalusia,[2] passed the straits of Gibraltar under the guidance of their chief Gen'-

XXXII.
VALENTIN'-
IAN III.

seric, and, in the course of ten years, completed, in the capture of Carthage, the conquest of the Roman provinces of northern Africa. (A. D. 439.) Honórius was already dead, and had been succeeded by Valentin'ian III., a youth

XXXIII.
CONQUESTS
OF AT'TILA.

only six years of age. In the meantime At'tila, justly called the "scourge of God" for the chastisement of the human race, had become the leader of the Hunnish[3] hordes. He rapidly extended his dominion over all the tribes of Germany and Scythia, made war upon Persia, defeated Theodosius,

1. *Angles.* From them the English have derived their name.

2. *Andalúsia*, so called from the *Van'dals*, comprised the four Moorish kingdoms of Sevhia, Cor'dova, Jáen, and Granáda. It is the most southern division of Spain. Trajan and the Senecas were natives of this province. (*Map* No. XIII.)

3. The *Huns*, when first known, in the century before the Christian era, dwelt on the western borders of the Caspian sea. The power of the Huns fell with At'tila, and the nation was soon after dispersed. The present *Hungarians* are descended from the Huns, intermingled with Turkish, Slavonic, and German races.

a. The *Basentinus*, a small stream that washes the walls of Consentia, now Cosenza. .. .,

the emperor of the East, in three bloody battles, and after ravaging Thrace, Macedónia, and Greece, pursued his desolating march west ward into Gaul, but was defeated by the Romans and their Gothic allies in the bloody battle of Chálons.[1] (A. D. 451.) The next year the Huns poured like a torrent upon Italy, and spread their ravages over all Lombardy. This visitation was the origin of the Venetian republic,[2] which was founded by the fugitives who fled at the terror of the name of At' tila.

58. The death of the Hunnic chief soon after this inroad, the civil wars among his followers, and the final extinction of the empire of the Huns, might have afforded the Romans an opportunity of escap ing from the ruin which impended over them, if they had not been lost to all feelings of national honor. But they had admitted numerous bands of barbarians in their midst as confederates and allies; and these, courted by one faction, and opposed by another, became, ere long, the actual rulers of the country. The provinces were pillaged, the throne was shaken, and often overturned by seditions; and two years after the death of At' tila, Rome itself was taken and pillaged by a horde of Van' dals from Africa, conducted by the famous Gen' seric, who had been invited across the Mediterranean to avenge the insults which a Roman princess[a] had received from her own husband. (A. D. 455.)

ᴠᴀɴᴅᴀʟs.

XXXIV. THE VAN' DALS.

1. *Chálons* (shah-long) is a city of France, on the river Marne, a branch of the Seine, ninety-five miles east from Paris, and twenty-seven miles south-east from Rheims. It is situated in the middle of extensive meadows, which were formerly known as the Catalaunian fields, (*Gibbon*, iii. 340.) In the battle of Chálons the nations from the Caspian sea to the Atlantic fought together; and the number of the barbarians slain has been variously estimated at from one hun_red and sixty-two thousand to three hundred thousand. (*Map* No. XIII.)

2. The origin of *Venice* dates from the invasion of Italy by the Huns, A. D. 452. The city is built on a cluster of numerous small islands in a shallow but extensive lagoon, in the north-western part of the Adriat' ic, north of the Po and the Adige, about four miles from the main land. It is divided into two principal portions by a wide canal, crossed by the principal bridge in the city, the celebrated *Rialto*. Venice is traversed by narrow lanes instead of streets, seldom more than five or six feet in width; but the grand thoroughfares are the canals; and gondolas, or canal boats, are the universal substitute for carriages.

Venice gradually became a wealthy and powerful independent commercial city, maintaining its freedom against Charlemagne and his successors, and yielding a merely nominal alleg'ance to the Greek emperors of Constantinople. Towards the middle of the fifteenth century the republic was mistress of several populous provinces in Lom' bardy,—of Crete and Cyprus—of the greater part of southern Greece, and most of the isles of the Ægean sea; and it continued to engross the principal trade in Eastern products, till the discovery of a route to India by the Cape of Good-Hope turned this traffic into a new channel. From this period Venice rapidly declined. Stripped of independence and wealth, she now enjoys only a precarious existence, and is slowly sinking into the waves from which she arose. (*Map* No. VIII.)

a. Eudox' ia, the widow of Valentin' ian III., had been compelled to marry Max' imus, the murderer, and successor in the empire, of her late husband, and it was she who invited the Van' dal chief to avenge her wrongs.

59. After the withdrawal of the Van'dals, which occurred the year of the death of Valentin'ian I II., Av'itus, a Gaul, was installed
xxxv. Emperor by the influence of the gentle and humane
Av' ITUS. Theod'oric, king of the Vis'igoths; but he was soon de-
MAJO' RIAN. posed by Ric'imer, the Gothic commander of the barbarian allies of the Romans. (A. D. 456.) The wise and beneficent Majórian was then advanced to the throne by Ric'imer; but his virtues were not appreciated by his subjects; and a sedition of the troops compelled him to lay down the sceptre after a reign of four years (A. D. 431.)

60. Ric'imer then advanced one of his own creatures, Sevérus, to
xxxvi. the nominal sovereignty; but he retained all the powers
SEVÉRUS. of state in his own hands. Annually the Van'dals from Africa, having now the control of the Mediterranean, sent out from Carthage, their seat of empire, piratical vessels or fleets, which spread desolation and terror over the Italian coasts, and entered at will nearly every port in the Roman dominions. At length application for assistance was made to Leo, then sovereign of the Eastern empire, and a large armament was sent from Constantinople to Carthage. But the aged Gen'seric eluded the immediate danger by a truce with his enemies, and, in the obscurity of night, destroyed by fire almost the entire fleet of the unsuspecting Romans.

61. Amid the frequent revolutionary changes that were occurring in the sovereignty of the Western empire,[a] Roman freedom and dignity were lost in the influence of the confederate barbarians, who formed both the defence and the terror of Italy. As the power of the Romans themselves declined, their barbarian allies augmented their demands and increased their insolence, until they finally insisted, with arms in their hands, that a third part of the lands of Italy should be divided among them. Under their leader Odoácer, a chief of the barbarian tribe of the Her'uli,[1] they overcame the little re-

1. Of all the barbarians who threw themselves on the ruins of the Roman empire, it is mos difficult to trace the origin of the Her'uli. Their names, the only remains of their language are Gothic; and it is believed that they came originally from Scandinávia. They were a fierce people, who disdained the use of armor: their bravery was like madness: in war they showed no pity for age, nor respect for sex or condition. Among themselves there was the same ferocity: the sick and the aged were put to death at their own request, during a solemn festival; and the widow hung herself upon the tree which shadowed her husband's tomb. The Her'uli, though brave and formidable, were few in number, claiming to be mostly of royal blood; and they seem not so much a nation, as a confederacy of princes and nobles, bound by an oath to live and die together with their arms in their hands. (Gibbon, liii. 8; and Note, 495-6.)

a. The remaining sovereigns of the Western empire, down to the time of its subversion, were Anthémius, Olyb'rius, Glycérus, Népos, and Augus'tulus.

sistance that was offered them; and the conqueror, abolishing the imperial titles of Cæsar and Augustus, proclaimed him-
self king of Italy. (A. D. 476.) The Western em- XXXVII. SUB-
pire of the Romans was subverted : Roman glory had THE WEST-
passed away: Roman·liberty·existed only in the remem- ERN EMPIRE.
brance of the past : the rude warriors of Germany and Scythia pos
sessed the city of Romulus ; and a barbarian occupied the palace of
the Cæsars.

CHAPTER II.

HISTORY OF THE MIDDLE AGES:

EXTENDING FROM THE OVERTHROW OF THE WESTERN EMPIRE OF THE ROMANS
A. D. 476, TO THE DISCOVERY OF AMERICA, A. D. 1492 = 1016 YEARS.

SECTION I.

GENERAL HISTORY, FROM THE OVERTHROW OF THE WESTERN EMPIRE OF THE
ROMANS, TO THE BEGINNING OF THE TENTH CENTURY: = 424 YEARS.

ANALYSIS. 1. INTRODUCTORY. The period embraced in the Middle Ages.—2. Unin-
structive character of its early history. At what period its useful history begins.—3. Extent
of the barbarian irruptions. The Eastern Roman empire. Remainder of the Roman world.—
4. The possessions of the conquerors toward the close of the sixth century. The changes
wrought by them. Plan of the present chapter.

5. THE MONARCHY OF THE HER'ULI. Its overthrow.—6. MONARCHY OF THE OS'TROGOTHS,
Theod'oric. Treatment of his Roman and barbarian subjects.—7. General prosperity of his reign.
Extent of his empire. The Os'trogoth and Vis'igoth nations again divided.—8. The successors
of Theod'oric. The emperor of the East.—9. THE ERA OF JUSTIN'IAN. State of the kingdom.
Persian war.—10. Justin'ian's armies. Absence of military spirit among the people.—11. Af-
rican war. First expedition of Belisárius, and overthrow of the kingdom of the Van'dals.
Fate of Gel'imer. His Van'dal subjects.—12. Sicily subdued. Belisárius advances into Italy.
Besieged in Rome.—13. The Gothic king Vit'iges surrenders. Final reduction of Italy by
Nar'ses.—14. Second war with Persia. Barbarian invasion repelled by Belisárius. Mournful
fate of Belisárius. Death and character of Justin'ian.—15. His reign, why memorable. Its
brightest ornament. Remark of Gibbon. History of the "Pandects and Code."—16. Subse-
quent history of the Eastern empire. Invasion of Italy by the Lombards.—17. THE LOMBARD
MONARCHY. Its extent and character.—18. Period of general repose throughout Western
Europe. Events in the East.—19. The darkness that rests upon European history at this
period. Remark of Sismondi. The dawning light from Arabia.

20. THE SARACEN EMPIRE. History of the Arabians.—21. Ancient religion of the Arabs. Religious toleration in Arabia. [Judaism. The Magian idolatry.]—22. Mahomet begins to preach a
new religion.—23. The declared medium of divine communication with him. Declared origin of
the Koran.—24. The materials of the Koran. Chief points of Moslem faith. Punishment of the
wicked. The Moslem paradise. Effects of the predestinarian doctrine of Mahomet. Practical part
of the new religion. Miracles attributed to Mahomet. [Mecca.]—25. Beginning of Mahomet's
preaching. The Hegira.—26. Mahomet at Medina. [Medina.] Progress of the new religion through
out all Arabia. [Mussulman.]—27. The apostasy that followed Mahomet's death. Restoration of
religious unity.—28. Saracen conquests in Persia and Syria. [Saracens. Bozrah.]—29. Conquest of all Syria. [Emes'sa. Baalbec. Yermouk. Aleppo.]—30. Conquest of Persia, and
expiration of the dynasty of the Sassan'idæ. [Cadésiah. Review of Persian History.]—31.
Conquest of Egypt. Destruction of the Alexandrian library.—32. Death of Omar. Caliphate
of Othman.—33. Military events of the reign of Othman. [Rhodes. Tripoli.] Othman's successors. Conquest of Carthage, and all northern Africa.—34. Introduction of the Saracens into
Spain.—35. Defeat of Roderic, and final conquest of Spain. [Guadaléte. Guadalquiver. Meri-
da.]—36. Saracen encroachments in Gaul. Inroad of Abdelrahman. [The Pyrenees.]—37. Over

throw of the Saracen hosts by Charles Martel. Importance of this victory. [Tours. Poictiers.] —38. The Eastern Saracens at this period. [Hindostan.] Termination of the civil power of the central caliphate.—39. The power that next prominently occupies the field of history.

40. MONARCHY OF THE FRANKS: Its origin. [Tournay. Cambray. Terouane. Cologne.] Clovis. Extent of his monarchy. [Soissons. Paris.]—41. Religious character of Clovis. His barbarities.—42. The descendants of Clovis. Royal murders. Regents. Charles Martel. Pepin, the first monarch of the Carlovingian dynasty. [Papal authority.]—43. The reign, and the character, of Pepin. His division of the kingdom.—44. First acts of the reign of Charlemagne. [The Loire.] The Saxons. Motives that led Charlemagne to declare war against them. [The Elbe.]—45. His first irruption into their territory. [Weser.] History of Witikind. Saxon rebellion. Changes produced by these Saxon wars.—46. Causes of the war with the Lombards. Overthrow of the Lombard kingdom. [Geneva. Pavia.]—47. Charlemagne's expedition into Spain. [Catalonia. Pampeluna. Saragossa. Roncesvalles.]—48. Additional conquests. Charlemagne crowned emperor at Rome.—49. Importance of this event. General character of the reign of Charlemagne. [Aix-la-Chapelle.] His private life. His cruelties. Concluding estimate.—50. Causes that led to the division of the empire of Charlemagne.—51. Invasion of the Northmen.—52. Ravages of the Hungarians. The Saracens on the Mediterranean coasts. Changes, and increasing confusion, in European society. The island of Britain.

53. ENGLISH HISTORY. Saxon conquests. Saxon Heptarchy.—54. Introduction and spread of Christianity.—55. Union of the Saxon kingdoms. Reign of Egbert, and ravages of the Northmen.—56. The successors of Egbert. Accession of Alfred. State of the kingdom.—57. Alfred withdraws from public life—lives as a peasant—visits the Danish camp.—58. Defeats the Danes, and overthrows the Danish power. Defence of the kingdom.—59. Limited sovereignty of Alfred. Danish invasion under Hastings. The Danes withdraw. Alfred's power at the time of his death.—60. Institutions, character, and laws, of Alfred.

1. The "Middle Ages," to which it is impossible to fix accurate limits, may be considered as embracing that dark and gloomy period of about a thousand years, extending from the fall of the Western empire of the Romans nearly to the close of the fifteenth century, at which point we detect the dawn of modern civilization, and enter upon the clearly-marked outlines of modern history.[a]

1. INTRODUCTORY.

2. The history of Europe during several centuries after the overthrow of the Western Roman empire offers little real instruction to repay the labor of wading through the intricate and bloody annals of a barbarous age. The fall of the Roman empire had carried away with it ancient civilization; and during many generations, the elements of society which had been disruptured by the surges of barbarian power, continued to be widely agitated, like the waves of the ocean, long after the fury of the storm has passed. It is only when the victors and the vanquished, inhabitants of the same country had become fused into one people, and a new order of things, new bonds of society, and new institutions began to be developed, that the useful history of the Middle Ages begins.

3. We must bear in mind that it was not Italy alone that was

a. "The ten centuries, from the fifth to the fifteenth, seem, in a general point of view, to constitute the period of the Middle Ages."—*Hallam.*

affected by the tide of barbarian conquest; but that the storm spread likewise over Gaul, Spain, Britain, and Northern Africa; while the feeble empire which had Constantinople for its centre, alone escaped the general ruin. Here the majesty of Rome was still faintly represented by the imaginary successors of Augustus, who continued until the time of the crusades to exercise a partial sovereignty over the East, from the Danube to the Nile and the Tigris. The remainder of the Roman world exhibited one scene of general ruin; for wherever the barbarians marched in successive hordes, their route was marked with blood: cities and villages were repeatedly plundered, and often destroyed; fertile and populous provinces were converted into deserts; and pestilence and famine, following in the train of war, completed the desolation.

4. When at length, toward the close of the sixth century, the frenzy of conquest was over, and a partial calm was restored, the Saxons, from the shores of the Baltic, were found to be in possession of the southern and more fertile provinces of Britain: the Franks or Freemen, a confederation of Germanic tribes, were masters of Gaul: the Huns, from the borders of the Caspian Sea, occupied Pannónia; the Goths and the Lombards, the former originally from northern Asia, and the latter of Scandinavian origin, had established themselves in Italy and the adjacent provinces; and the Gothic tribes, after driving the Van'dals from Spain, had succeeded to the sovereignty of the peninsula. A total change had come over the state of Europe: scarcely any vestiges of Roman civilization remained; but new nations, new manners, new languages, and new names of countries were everywhere introduced; and new forms of government, new institutions, and new laws began to spring up out of the chaos occasioned by the general wreck of the nations of the Roman world. In the present chapter we shall pass rapidly over the history of the Middle Ages; aiming only to present the reader such a general outline, or framework, of its annals, as will aid in the earch we shall subsequently make for the seeds of order, and the first rudiments of policy, laws, and civilization, of Modern Europe.

5. After Odoácer, the chief of the tribe of the Her'uli, had conquered Italy, he divided one third of the ample estates of the nobles

II. THE MON-
ARCHY OF
THE HER'ULI.

among his followers; but although he retained the government in his own hands, he allowed the ancient forms of administration to remain; the senate continued to sit, as usual; and after seven years the consulship was restored; while

none of the municipal or provincial authorities were changed.
Odoácer made some attempts to restore agriculture in the provinces;
but still Italy presented a sad prospect of misery and desolation.
After a duration of fourteen years, the feeble monarchy of the
Her'uli was overthrown by the Os'tro goth king, Theod'oric, who
disregarding his plighted faith, caused his royal captive, Odoácer, to
be assassinated at the close of a conciliatory banquet. (A. D. 493.)

6. Theod'oric, the first of the Os'trogoth kings of Italy, had
been brought up as a hostage at the court of Constantinople. At
times the friend, the ally, and the enemy of the imbecile
monarchs of the Eastern empire, he restored peace to
Italy, and a degree of prosperity unusual under the
sway of the barbarian conquerors. Like Odoácer, he indulged his Roman subjects in the retention of their ancient laws
language, and magistrates; and employed them chiefly in the administration of government; while to his rude Gothic followers he
confided the defence of the State; and by giving them lands which
they were to hold on the tenure of military service, he endeavored
to unite in them the domestic habits of the cultivator, with the exercises and discipline of the soldier.

III. MON-
ARCHY OF
THE OS'TRO-
GOTHS.

7. Theod'oric encouraged improvements in agriculture, revived
the spirit of commerce and manufactures, and greatly increased the
population of his kingdom, which, at the close of his reign, embraced
nearly a million of the barbarians, many of whom, however, were
soldiers of fortune and adventurers who had flocked from all the surrounding barbarous nations to share the riches and glory which
Theod'oric had won. Theod'oric reigned thirty-three years; and
at the time of his death his kingdom occupied not only Sicily and
Italy, but also Lower Gaul, and the old Roman provinces between
the head of the Adriat'ic and the Danube. If he had had a son to
whom he might have transmitted his dominions, his Gothic successors would probably have had the honor of restoring the empire of
the West; but on his death, (A. D. 526) the two nations of the Os'-
trogoths and the Vis'igoths were again divided; and the reign of
the Great Theod'oric passed like a brilliant meteor, leaving no permanent impression of its glory.

8. Seven Os'trogoth kings succeeded Theod'oric on the throne
of Italy during a period of twenty-seven years. Nearly all met
with a violent death, and were constantly engaged in a war with
Justin'ian, emperor of the East, who finally succeeded in reducing

Italy under his dominion. The reign of that monarch is the most brilliant period in the history of the Eastern empire; and as it follows immediately after the career of Theod'oric in the West, and embraces all that is interesting in the history of the period which it occupies, we pass here to a brief survey of its annals.

9. The year after the death of Theod'oric, Justin'ian succeeded IV. THE his uncle Justin on the throne of the Eastern empire. ERA OF His reign is often alluded to in history as the "Era of JUSTIN'IAN. Jus'tinian." On his accession he found the kingdom torn by domestic factions; hordes of barbarians menaced the frontiers, and often advanced from the Danube three hundred miles into the country; and during the first five years of his reign he waged an expensive and unprofitable war with the Persians. The conclusion of this war, by the purchase of a peace at a costly price, enabled Justin'ian, who was extremely ambitious of military fame, to turn his arms to the conquest of distant provinces.

10. Justin'ian never led his armies in person; and his troops consisted chiefly of barbarian mercenaries—Scythians, Persians, Her'uli, Van'dals, and Goths, and a small number of Thracians: the citizens of the empire had long been forbidden, under preceding emperors, to carry arms,—a short-sighted policy which Justin'ian's timidity and jealousy led him to adopt: and so little of military spirit remained among the people, that they were not only incapable of fighting in the open field, but formed a very inadequate defence for the ramparts of their cities. Under these circumstances, with but a small body of regular troops, and without an active militia from which to recruit his armies, the military successes of Justin'ian are among the difficult problems of the age.

11. Africa, still ruled by the Van'dals, first attracted the military ambition of Justin'ian, although his designs of conquest were concealed under the pretence of restoring to the Van'dal throne its legitimate successor, of the race of the renowned Gen'seric. The first expedition, under the command of Belisárius, the greatest general of his age, numbering only ten thousand foot soldiers and five thousand horsemen, landed, in September 533, about five days' journey to the south of Carthage. The Africans, who were still called Romans, long oppressed by their Van'dal conquerors, hailed Belisárius as a deliverer; and Gel'imer, the Van'dal king, who ruled over eight or nine millions of subjects, and who could muster eighty thou-

sand warriors' of his own nation, found himself suddenly alone with his Van'dals in the midst of a hostile population. Twice Gel'imer was routed in battle; and before the end of November Africa was conquered, and the kingdom of the Van'dals destroyed. Gel'imor himself, having capitulated, was removed to Galátia, where ample possessions were given him, and where he was allowed to grow old in peace, surrounded by his friends and kindred, and a few faithful followers. The bravest of the Van'dals enlisted in the armies of Jus tin'ian; and ere long the remainder of the Van'dal nation in Africa, being involved in the convulsions that followed, entirely disappeared

12. Justin'ian next projected the conquest of the Gothic empire of Italy, and its dependencies; and in the year 535 Belisárius land ed in Sicily at the head of a small aimy of seven thousand five hun dred men. In the first campaign he subdued that island: in the second year he advanced into southern Italy, where the old Roman population welcomed him with joy, and the Goths found themselves as unfavorably situated as the Van'dals had been in Africa; but, deposing their weak prince, they raised Vit'iges to the throne, who was a great general and a worthy rival of Belisárius. The latter gained possession of Rome, (Dec. 536,) where for more than a year he was besieged by the Goths; and although he made good his de fence, almost the entire population of the city in the meantime per ished by famine.

13. Vit'iges himself was next besieged in Raven'na, and was finally forced to surrender the place, and yield himself prisoner. (Dec. 539.) He was deeply indebted to the generosity of Justin'ian, who allowed him to pass his days in affluence in Constantinople The jealousy of Justin ian, however, having recalled Belisárius from Italy, in a few years the Goths recovered their sway; but it was over a country almost deserted of its inhabitants. At length, in the year 552, Justin'ian formed in Italy an army of thirty thousand men, which he placed under the command of the eunuch Nar'ses, wh unexpectedly proved to be an able general. In the following year the last of the Os'trogoth kings was slain in battle, and the empire of Justin'ian was extended over the deserted wastes of the once fer tile and populous Italy. (A. D. 554.)

14. In the East, Justin'ian was involved in a second war with Chosroes, or Nashirvan, the most celebrated Persian monarch of the

---

1. Gibbon, iii. 63, says one hundred and sixty thousand; and Sismondi, Fall of the Roman Empire, i. 221, has the same number. See the correction in Milman's Notes to Gibbon.

Sassanid dynasty. Hostilities were carried on during sixteen years (A. D. 540—556) with unrelenting obstinacy on both sides; but after a prodigious waste of human life, the frontiers of the two empires remained nearly the same as they were before the war. When Justin'ian was nearly eighty years of age he was again obliged to have recourse to the services of his old general Belisárius, not less aged than himself, to repel an invasion of the barbarians who had advanced to the very gates of Constantinople. At the head of a small band of veterans, who in happier years had shared his toils, he drove back the enemy; but the applauses of the people again excited the jealousy and fears of the ungrateful monarch, who, charging his faithful servant with aspiring to the empire, caused his eyes to be torn out, and his whole fortune to be confiscated; and it is said that the general who had conquered two kingdoms, was to be seen blind, and l·d by a child, going about with a wooden cup in his hand to solicit charity. Justin'ian died at the age of eighty-three, after a reign of more than thirty-eight years. (Nov. 565.) The character of Justin'ian was a compound of good and bad qualities; for although personally inclined to justice, he often overlooked, through weakness, the injustice of others, and was in a great measure ruled during the first half of his reign by his wife Theodóra, an unprincipled woman, under whose orders many acts of oppression and cruelty were committed.

15. The reign of Justin'ian forms a memorable epoch in the history of the world. He was the last Byzantine emperor who, by his dominion over the whole of Italy, reunited in some measure the two principal portions of the empire of the Cæsars. But his extensive conquests were not his chief glory: the brightest ornament of his reign, which has immortalized his memory, is his famous compilation of the Roman laws, known as the "Pandects and Code of Justin'ian." "The vain titles of the victories of Justin'ian," says Gibbon, "are crumbled into dust: but the name of the legislator is inscribed on a fair and everlasting monument." To a commission of ten eminent lawyers, at the head of which was Tribónian, Justin'ian assigned the task of reducing into a uniform and consistent code, the vast mass of the laws of the Roman empire; and after this had been completed, to another commission of seventeen, at the head of which also was Tribónian, was assigned the more difficult work of searching out the scattered monuments of ancient jurisprudence,—of collecting and putting in order whatever was useful in

the books of former jurisconsults, and of extracting the true spirit of the laws from questions, disputes, conjectures, and judicial decisions of the Roman civilians. This celebrated work, containing the immense store of the wisdom of antiquity, after being lost during several centuries of the Dark Ages, was accidentally brought to light, in the middle of the twelfth century, when it contributed greatly to the revival of civilization; and the digest which Gibbon has made f it is now received as the text book on civil Law in some of the universities of Europe.[a]

16. The history of the Eastern or Greek empire, during several centuries after Justin'ian, is so extremely complicated, and its annals so obscure and devoid of interest, that we pass them by, for subjects of greater importance. Three years after the death of Justin'ian, Italy underwent another revolution. In the year 568, the whole Lombard nation, comprising the fiercest and bravest of the Germanic tribes, led by their king Alboin, and aided by twenty thousand Saxons, descended from the eastern Alps, and at once took possession of northern Italy, which, from them, is called Lombardy. The Lombard monarchy, thus established, lasted, under twenty-one kings, during a period of little more than two centuries.

17. As the Lombards advanced into the country, the inhabitants shut themselves up in the walled cities, many of which, after enduring sieges, and experiencing the most dreadful calamities, were compelled to surrender; but the Lombard dominion never embraced the whole peninsula. The islands in the upper end of the Adriat'ic, embracing the Venetian League, the country immediately surrounding Raven'na, together with Rome, Naples, and a few other cities, remained under the jurisdiction of the Eastern or Greek emperors, or were at times independent of foreign rule. The Lombards were ruder and fiercer than the Goths who preceded them; and they at first proved to the Italians far harder task-masters than any of the previous invaders; but he change from a wandering life exerted an influence favorable to their civilization; and their laws, considered as those of a barbarous people, exhibited a considerable degree of wisdom and equality.

V. THE LOMBARD MONARCHY.

18. The period at which we have now arrived, towards the close of the sixth century, exhibits the first interval of partial repose that had fallen upon Western Europe since the downfall of the Roman empire. Some degree of quiet was now settling upon Italy under

a. Notes to Gibbon, iii. 151.

the rule of the Lombard kings: the Goths were consolidating their power in Spain: a stable monarchy was gradually rising in France, from the union of the Gallic tribes; and the Saxons had firmly es tablished themselves in the south of Britain.   The only events in .the East that attract our notice consist of a series of wars between the Greek emperors and the Persians, during which period, if we are to rely upon doubtful narratives which wear the air of fables, at one time all the Asiatic provinces of the Eastern empire were conquered by the Persians; and subsequently, the whole of Persia, to th frontiers of India, was conquered by the monarchs of the Eastern empire.   Eventually the two empires appear to have become equally exhausted; and when peace was restored (A. D. 628) the ancient boundaries were recognized by both parties.

19. But while a degree of comparative repose was settling upon Europe, a night of darkness, owing to the absence of all reliable documents, rests upon its history, down to the time of Charlemagne. "A century and a half passed away," says Sismondi, "during which we possess nothing concerning the whole empire of the West, except dates and conjectures."[a]   This obscurity lasts until a new and unex-pected light breaks in from Arabia; when a nation of shepherds and robbers appears as the depository of letters which had been allowed to escape from the guardianship of every civilized people.

20. Turning from the darkness which shrouds European history in the seventh century, we next proceed to trace the remarkable rise and establishment of the power of the Saracens.   In the parched, sandy, and, in great part, desert Arabia, a country nearly four times the extent of France, the hardy Arab, of an original and unmixed race, had dwelt from time immemorial, in a constant struggle with nature, and enjoying all the wild freedom of the rudest patriarchal state.   The descendants of Ishmael—the "wild man of the desert"—have always been free, and such they will ever remain; an effect, at once, of their local position and, as many believe, the fulfilment of prophecy; and although a few of the frontier cities of Arabia have been at times temporarily subjected by the surrounding nations, Arabia, as a country, is the only land in all antiquity that never bowed to the yoke of a foreign conqueror.

VI. THE SARACEN. EMPIRE.

21. The ancient religion of the Arabs was Sabaism, or star-worship, which assumed a great variety of-forms, and was corrupted by adora tion of a vast number of images, which were supposed to have some

a. Sismondi, Fall of the Roman Empire, i. 258.

mysterious affinity to the heavenly bodies. The Arabs had seven temples dedicated to the seven planets: some tribes exclusively revered the moon, others the dog star: Judaism[a] was embraced by a few tribes, Christianity by some, and the Mágian idolatry[1] of Persia by others. So completely free was Arabia, each sect or tribe being independent, that absolute toleration necessarily existed; and numerous refugee sects that fled from the persecution of the Roman emperors, found in the wild wastes of that country a quiet asylum.

22. About the beginning of the seventh century, Mahom'et or Moham'med, an Arabian impostor, descended from the Sabæan priests of Mecca, where was the chief temple of the Sabæan idolatry, began to preach a new religion to his countrymen. He represented to them the incoherence and grossness of their religious rites, and called upon them to abandon their frail idols, and to acknowledge and adore the One true God,—the invisible, all good, and allpowerful ruler of the universe. Acknowledging the authenticity both of the Jewish scriptures and the Christian revelation, he professed to restore the true and primitive faith, as it had been in the days of the patriarchs and the prophets, from Adam to the Messiah.

23. Like Numa of old, Mahom'et sought to give to the doctrines which he taught the sanction of inspired origin and miraculous approval; and as the nymph Egéria was the ministering goddess of the former, so the angel Gabriel was the declared medium of divine communication with the latter. During a period of twenty-three

---

1. The *Mágian idolatry* consisted of the religious belief and worship presided over by the Mágian priesthood, who comprised, originally, one of the six tribes into which the nation of the Medes was divided. The *Mági*, or "wise men," had not only religion, but the higher branches of all learning also, in their charge; and they practised different sorts of divination, astrology, and enchantment, for the purpose of disclosing the future, influencing the present, and calling the past to their aid. So famous were they that their name has been applied to all orders of magicians and enchanters. Zoroas'ter, who is supposed to have lived about the seventh century before Christ, reformed the Mágian religion, and remodelled the priesthood; and by some he is considered the founder of the order.

The Mágian priests taught that the gods are the spiritual essences of fire, earth, and water,—that there are two antagonistic powers in nature, the one accomplishing good designs, the other evil;—that each of these shall subdue and be subdued by turns, for six thousand years, but that, at last, through the intervention of the still higher and Supreme Being, the evil principle shall perish, and men shall live in happiness, neither needing food, nor yielding a shadow.

The great influence of the Magi is well illustrated in the book of Daniel, where Nebuchadnezzar invoked the aid of the different classes of their order—magicians, astrologers, sorcerers, Chaldeans, and soothsayers. In the time of the Saviour, the Mágian system was not extinct, as we have evidence of in the allusion made to Simon Magus, who boasted himself to be "some great one." (Acts, viii. 9—xiii. 6 &c.)

a. By the term *Judaism* is meant the religious rites and doctrines of the Jews, as enjoined in the law of Moses.

years occasional revelations, as circumstances required, are said to have been made to the Prophet, who was consequently never at a loss for authority to justify his conduct to his followers, or for authoritative counsel in any emergency. These revelations, carefully treasured up in the memories of the faithful, or committed to writing by amanuenses, (for the Moslems boast that the founder of their religion could neither read nor write,) were collected together two years after the death of the Prophet, and published as the *Koran*, or Moham'medan Bible.

24. The materials of the Koran are borrowed chiefly from the Jewish and Christian Scriptures, and from the legends, traditions, and fables of Arabian and Persian mythology. The two great points of Moslem faith are embraced in the declaration—"There is but one God, and Mahom'et is his prophet." The other prominent points of the Moslem creed are the belief in absolute predestination,—the existence and purity of angels,—the resurrection of the body,—a general judgment, and the final salvation of all the disciples of the Prophet, whatever be their sins. Wicked Moslems are to expiate their crimes during different periods of suffering, not to exceed seven thousand years; but infidel contemners of the Koran are to be doomed to an eternity of woe. A minute and appalling description is given of the place and mode of torment,—a vast receptacle, full of smoke and darkness, dragged forward with roaring noise and fury by seventy thousand angels, through the opposite extremes of heat and cold, while the unhappy objects of wrath are tormented by the hissing of numerous reptiles, and the scourges of hideous demons, whose pastime is cruelty and pain. The Moslem paradise is all that an Arab imagination can paint of sensual felicity;—groves, rivulets, flowers, perfumes, and fruits of every variety to charm the senses; while, to every other conceivable delight, seventy-two damsels of immortal youth and dazzling beauty are assigned to minister to the enjoyment of the humblest of the faithful. The promise to every faithful follower of the Prophet, of an unlimited indulgence of the corporeal propensities, constitutes a fundamental principle of the Moham'medan religion. The predestinarian doctrine of Mahom'et led his followers towards fatalism, and exercised a marked influence upon their lives, and especially upon their warlike character; for as it taught them that the hour of death is determined beforehand, it inspired them with an indifference to danger, and gave a permanent security to their bravery. Mahom'et promised to those

of his followers who fell in battle an immediate admission to the joys of paradise. The practical part of the new religion consisted of prayer five times a day, and frequent ablutions of the whole body, alms, fastings, and the pilgrimage to Mecca.[1] Tradition asserts that Mahom' et confirmed by miracles the truth of his religion; and a mysterious hint in the Koran has been converted, by the traditionists, into a circumstantial legend of a nocturnal journey through the seven heavens, in which Mahom' et conversed familiarly with Adam, Moses and the prophets, and even with Deity himself.

25. It was in the year 609, when Mahom' et was already forty years old, that he began to preach his new doctrine at Mecca. His first proselytes were made in his own family; but by the people his pretensions were long treated with ridicule; and at the end of thirteen years he was obliged to flee from Mecca to save his life. (A. D. 622.) This celebrated flight, called the Hegíra, is the grand era of the Moham' medan religion.

26. Repairing to Yatreb, the name of which he changed to Medína,[2] (or Medinet el Nebbi, the city of the Prophet,) he was there received by a large band of converts with every demonstration of joy; and soon the whole city acknowledged him as its leader and prophet. Mahomet now declared that the empire of his religion was to be established by the sword: every day added to the number of his proselytes, who, formed into warlike and predatory bands, scoured the desert in quest of plunder; and after experiencing many successes and several defeats, Mahom' et, in the seventh year of the Hegíra, with scarcely a shadow of opposition, made himself master of Mecca, whose inhabitants swore allegiance to him as their temporal and spiritual prince. The conquest or voluntary submission of the rest of Arabia soon followed, and at the period of Mahom' et's last pilgrimage to Mecca, in the tenth year of the Hegíra, and the year of his death, a hundred and fourteen thousand Mussulmen[2] marched under his banner. (A. D. 632.)

---

1. *Mecca*, the birth-place of Mahom' et, and the great centre of attraction to all pilgrims of the Moham' medan faith, is in western Arabia, about forty miles east from the Red Sea. Formerly the concourse of pilgrims to the "holy city" was immense; but the taste for pilgrimages is now rapidly declining throughout the Moham' medan world.

2. *Medina* is situated in western Arabia, one hundred miles north-east from its port of Yembe on the Red Sea, and two hundred and sixty miles north from Mecca. It is surrounded by a wall about forty feet high, flanked by thirty towers. It is now chiefly important as being in possession of the tomb containing the remains of the prophet.

The word *Mussulman*, which is used to designate a follower of Mahom' et, signifies, in Turkish language, "a true believer."

27. Mahom'et died without having formed any organized govern ment for the empire which he had so speedily established; and al though religious enthusiasm supplied; to his immediate followers, the place of legislation, the Arabs of the desert soon began to relapse into their ancient idolatries. The union of the military chiefs of the Prophet alone saved the tottering fabric of Moslem faith from dis solution. Abubekr, the first believer in Mahom'et's mission, was declared lieutenant or caliph; and the victories of ' his general Khaled, surnamed " the sword of God, over the apostate tribes in a few months restored religious unity to Arabia.

28. But the spirit of the Saracens' needed employment; and pre parations were made to invade the Byzantine and Persian empires, both of which, from the long and desolating wars that had raged between them, had sunk into the most deplorable weakness. Khaled advanced into Persia and conquered several cities near the ruins of Babylon, when he was recalled, and sent to join Abu Obeidah, who had marched upon Syria. Palmyra submitted : the governor of Boz rah* turned both traitor and Mussulman, and opened the gates of the city to the invaders; Damascus was attacked, besieged, and finally one part of the city was carried by storm at the moment that an other portion had capitulated. (Aug. 3d, 634.) Abubekr died the very day the city was taken, and Omar succeeded to the Caliphate.

29. The fall of Emes'sa,* and Baalbec* or Heliop'olis, soon fol-

1. The word *Saracen*, from *sara*, " a desert," means an Arabian.

2. *Bozrah*, was fifty miles south from Damascus, and eighty miles north-east from Jerusalem. Though now almost deserted, the whole town and its environs are covered with pillars and other ruins of the finest workmanship. It is frequently mentioned in Scripture. In Jeremiah, xlix. 13, we read, " For I have sworn by myself, saith the Lord, that Bozrah shall become a desolation, a reproach, a waste, and a curse." (*Map* No. VI.)

3. *Emes'sa*, now *Hems*, a city of Syria, was on the eastern bank of the Oron'tes, now the Aazy, eighty-five miles north-east from Damascus. It was the birth-place of the Roman em peror Elagabalus. (*Map* No. VI.)

4. *Baalbec*, or Heliop'olis,—the former a Syrian and the latter a Greek word—both mean ing the " city of the sun," was a large and splendid city of Syria, forty miles north-west from Da mascus, and about thirty-five miles from the Mediterranean. The remains of ancient architec ural grandeur in Baalbec are more extensive than in any other city of Syria, Palmyra excepted It is believed that Baal-Ath, built by Solomon in Lebanon, (2. Chron. viii. 6,) was identical with Baal-Bec. While under the Roman power it was famed for its wealth and splendor; and the terms of its surrender to the Saracens sufficiently attest its great resources at that period :— two thousand ounces of gold, four thousand ounces of silver, two thousand silken vests, and one thousand swords, besides those of the garrison, being the price demanded and paid to pre serve it from plunder. Although repeatedly sacked and dismantled, yet the changes that have taken place in the channels of commerce are the principal causes of its decay ; and, judging from its decline during the last century,—from five thousand inhabitants to less than two hun dred,—probably the day is not far distant when, like many other Eastern cities, it will cease to be inhabited. (*Map* No. VI.)

lowed that of Damascus.   Herac' lius, the Byzantine emperor, made
one great effort to save Syria, but on the banks of the Yermouk' his
best generals were defeated by Khaled with a loss of seventy thousand
soldiers, who were left dead on the field.   (Nov. 636.)   Jerusalem,
after a siege of four months, capitulated to Omar, who caused the
ground on which had stood the temple of Solomon to be cleared of
its rubbish, and prepared for the foundation of a mosque, which still
bears the name of the Caliph.   The reduction of Aleppo' and An
tioch, six years after the first Saracen invasion, completed the con·
quest of Syria.   (A. D. 638.)

3C   In the meantime the conquest of Persia had been followed
up by other Saracen generals.   In the same year that witnessed the
battle of Yermouk, the Persians and Saracens fought on the plains
of Cadésiah' one of the bloodiest battles on record.   Seven thousand
five hundred Saracens and one hundred thousand Persians are said
to have fallen.   The fate of Persia was determined, although the
Persian monarch kept together some time longer the wrecks of his
empire, but he was finally slain in the year 651, and with him ex·
pired the second Persian dynasty, that of the Sassan' idæ.'

31. Soon after the battle of Cadésiah, Omar intrusted to his lieu

1. The *Yermouk*, the Hieromax of the Greeks, is a river that empties into the Jordan from
the east, seventy-five miles south-west from Damascus. (*Map* No. VI.)

2. *Aleppo*, in northern Syria, is one hundred and ninety-six miles north-east from Damascus,
and fifty-five miles east from Antioch.   It is surrounded by massive walls thirty-feet high and
twenty broad.   It was once a place of considerable trade, communicating with Persia and
India by way of Bagdad, and with Arabia and Egypt by way of Damascus; but the discovery
of a passage to India by way of the Cape of Good Hope struck a deadly blow at its greatness,
and it is now little more than a shadow of its former self.

3. *Cadésiah* was on the borders of the Syrian desert, south-west from Babylon.

4. The overthrow of the last of the great Persian dynasties is an appropriate point for a brief
review of Persian history.

It has been stated that, after the overthrow of the Persian monarchy by Alexander the Great,
Asia continued to be a theatre of wars waged by his ambitious successors, until Seleucus,
about the year 307 before our era, established himself securely in possession of the countries
between the Euphrates, the Indus, and the Oxus, and thus founded the empire of the *Seleucidæ*.
This empire continued undisturbed until the year 250 B. C., when the Parthians, under *Arsaces*,
revolted, and established the Parthian empire of the *Arsac' idæ*.   The Parthian empire at
tained its highest grandeur in the reign of its sixth monarch, Mithridátes I., who carried his
arms even farther than Alexander himself.   The descendants of Arsáces ruled until A. D. 229,
a period of 480 years, when the last prince of that family was defeated and taken prisoner by
Ar' deshir Bab' igan, a revolted Persian noble of the family of Sassan, who thus became the
founder of the dynasty of the *Sassan' idæ*.   The period of nearly five centuries between the
death of Alexander the Great and the reign of Ar' deshir, is nearly a blank in Eastern history;
and what little is known of it is obtained from the pages of Roman writers.   No connected
authentic account of this period can be given.   The dynasty of the Sassan' idæ continued until
the overthrow of the Persian hosts on the plains of Cadésiah, when the religion of Zoroaster
gave place to the triumph of the Mussulman faith.

L *

tenant the conquest of Egypt, then forming a part of the Byzantine
or Greek empire. Peleu'sium,[1] after a month's siege, opened to the
Saracens the entrance to the country (638); the Coptic inhabitants
of Upper Egypt joined the invaders against the Greeks; Memphis,
after a siege of seven months, capitulated; Alexandria made a
longer and desperate resistance, but at length, at the close of the
year 640, the city was surrendered, a success which had cost the besiegers twenty-three thousand lives. When Amru asked Omar what
disposition he should make of the famous Alexandrian library, the
caliph replied, " If these writings agree with the Koran, they are useless, and need not be preserved; if they disagree, they are pernicious,
and should be destroyed." The sentence was executed with blind
obedience, and this vast store of ancient learning fell a sacrifice to
the blind fanaticism of an ignorant barbarian.[a]

32. Four years after the conquest of Egypt, the dagger of an as
sassin put an end to the life and reign of Omar. (Nov. 6th, 644.)
Othman, the early secretary of Mahom'et, succeeded to the caliphate,
but his extreme age rendered him poorly capable of supporting the
burden laid upon him. Various sects of Moslem believers began to
arise among the people: contentions broke out in the armies; and
Othman, after a reign of eleven years, was poniarded on his throne,
while he covered his heart with the Koran. (June 18th, 655.)

33. The conquest of Cyprus and Rhodes,[2] and the subjugation of
the African coast as far westward as Tripoli,[3] were the principal

1. _Pelusium_, an important city of Egypt, was at the entrance of the Pelusiac, or most east
ern branch of the Nile. It was surrounded by marshes; and the name of the city was derived
from a Greek word signifying _mud_. Near its ruins stands a dilapidated castle named _Tineh_,
the Arabic term for _mire_.

2. _Rhodes_, a celebrated island in the Mediterranean, is off the south-west coast of Asia
Minor, ten miles south from Cape Volpe, the nearest point of the main land. Its greatest
length is forty-five miles; greatest breadth eighteen. The city of Rhodes, one of the best built
and most magnificent cities of the ancient world, was at the north-eastern extremity of the
island. The celebrated colossus of Rhodes,—a brazen statue of Apollo, about one hundred
and five feet in height, and of the most admirable proportions,—has been deservedly reckoned
one of the seven wonders of the world; but the assertion that it stood with a foot on each side
the entrance to the port, and that the largest vessels, under full sail, passed between its legs, is
an absurd fiction, for which there is not the shadow of authority in any ancient writer. The
story originated with one Blaise de Vigenere, in the 16th century. (_Map_ No. IV.)

3. _Tripoli_, a maritime city of northern Africa, is west of the ancient Barca and Cyrenaica,
and about two hundred and seventy miles south from Sicily.

a. Sismondi, ii. p. 18, distrusts the common account of the loss of the Alexandrian library.
Gibbon, vol. iii. p. 439, says, " For my own part, I am strongly tempted to deny both the fact
and the consequences." But since Gibbon wrote, several new Mohammedan authorities have
been adduced to support the common version of the story. See Note to Gibbon, iii. 523; also
Crichton's Arabia, i. 355.

military events that distinguished the reign of Othman; but the political feuds and civil wars that distracted the reign of his successors, Ali and Moawíyah, suspended the progress of the western conquests of the Saracens nearly twenty years.[a] Gradually, however, the Saracens extended their dominion over all northern Africa; and in the year 689 one of their generals penetrated to the Atlantic coast; but Carthage, repeatedly succored from Constantinople, held out nine years longer, when being taken by storm, it was finally and utterly destroyed.   From this epoch northern Africa became a section of the great Moham'medan empire. All the Moorish tribes, resembling the roving Arabs in their customs, and born under a similar climate, being ultimately reduced to submission, adopted the language, name, and religion, of their conquerors; and at the present day they can with difficulty be distinguished from the Saracens.

34. Scarcely had the conquest of Africa been completed, when a Vis'igothic noble, irritated by the treatment which he had received from his sovereign, the tyrant Roderic, secretly despatched a messenger to Musa, the governor of Africa, and invited the Saracens into Spain.   A daring Saracen, named Taric, first crossed the straits in the month of July, 710, on a predatory incursion; and in the following spring he passed over again at the head of seven thousand men and took possession of Mount Calpe, whose modern name of Gibraltar (Gibel-al-Taric, or Hill of Taric), still preserves the name of the Saracen hero.

35 When Roderic was informed of the descent of the Saracens, he sent his lieutenant against them, with orders to bind the presumptuous strangers and cast them into the sea.   But his lieutenant was defeated, and soon afterward, Roderic himself also, who had collected, on the banks of the Guadaléte,[1] his whole army, of a hundred thousand men.   Roderic, a usurper and tyrant, was hated and despised by numbers of his people; and during the battle, which continued seven days, a portion of his forces, as had been previously

---

[1] The *Guadaléte* is a stream that enters the harbor of Cadiz, about sixty miles north-west from Gibraltar. The battle appears to have been fought on the plains of the modern Xeres de la Frontera, about ten miles north-west from Cadiz. (*Map* No. XIII.)

[a] Mahom'et had promised forgiveness of sins to the first army which should besiege the Byzantine capital; and no sooner had Moawiyah destroyed his rivals and established his throne, than he sought to expiate the guilt of civil blood by shedding that of the infidels; but during every summer for seven years (668--675) a Mussulman army in vain attacked the walls of Constantinople, and the tide of conquest was turned aside to seek another channel for its entrance into Europe.

arranged, deserted to the Saracens. The Goths were finally routed
with immense slaughter, and Roderic avoided a soldier's death only
to perish more ignobly in the waters of the Guadalquiver:[1] but the
victory of the Saracens was purchased at the expense of sixteen
thousand lives. Most of the Spanish towns now submitted without
opposition; Mer'ida,[2] the capital, after a desperate resistance, capitulated with honor; and before the end of the year 713 the whole
of Spain, except a solitary corner in the northern part of the penin
sula, was conquered. The same country, in a more savage state, had
resisted, for two hundred years, the arms of the Romans; and it re
quired nearly eight hundred years to regain it from the sway of the
Moors and Saracens.

36. After the conquest of Spain, Mussulman ambition began to
look beyond the Pyrenees:[3] the disunited Gallic tribes of the
Southern provinces soon began to negotiate and to submit; and in a
few years the south of France, from the mouth of the Garonne to
that of the Rhone,[4] assumed the manners and religion of Arabia.
But these narrow limits were scorned by the spirit of Abdelrahman,
the Saracen governor of Spain, who, in the year 732, entered Gaul
at the head of a host of Moors and Saracens, in the hope of adding
to the faith of the Koran whatever yet remained unsubdued of France
or of Europe. An invasion so formidable had not been witnessed
since the days of At'tila; and Abdelrahman marked his route with
fire and sword; for he spared neither the country nor the inhabit
ants.

37. Everything was swept away by the overpowering torrent, until
Abdelrahman had penetrated to the very centre of France, and

1. The river *Guadalquiver* (in English gau-d'l-quiv'-er 'n Spanish gwad-al-ke-veer'), on
which stands the cities Seville and Cor'dova, enters the Atlantic about fifteen miles north from
Cadiz. Its ancient name was *Bœtis :* its present appellation, *Wady-al-kebir*, signifying "the
great river," is Arabic. (*Map* No. XIII.)

2. *Mer'ida*, the *Augusta Emer'ita* of the Romans, whence its modern name, was founded
by Augustus Cæsar 25 B. C. It is in the south-western part of Spain, on the north bank of the
Guadiana, and in the province of Estremadura. It is now a decayed town; but the architec
tural remains of the power and magnificence of its Roman masters render it an object of great
interest. It remained in the hands of the Saracens from 713 to 1228, when it opened its gates to
Alphonso IX., after his signal victory over the Moors; and from this period downward, it has
been attached to the kingdoms of Castile and Leon. (*Map* No. XIII.)

3. The *Pyrenees* mountains, which separate Spain from France, extend from the Atlantic to
the Mediterranean, a distance of about two hundred and seventy miles, with an average breadth
of about thirty-eight miles. (*Map* No. XIII.)

4. For the territory thus embraced under the Saracen sway, see *Map* No. XIII. The Garonne,
rising near the Spanish border, runs a north-westerly course. From its union with the Dor
dogne, forty-five miles from its entrance into the Bay of Biscay, it is called the *Gironde*—from
which the noted "department of the Gironde" takes its name.

pitched his camp between Tours[1] and Poietiers.[2] His progress had not been unwatched by the confederacy of the Franks, which, torn asunder by intrigues, and the revolts of discontented chiefs, now united to oppose the common enemy of all Christendom. At the head of the confederacy was Charles Martel, who, collecting his forces, met Abdelrahman on the plains of Poictiers, and, after six days' skirmishing, engaged on the seventh in that fearful battle that was to decide the fate of Europe. In the light skirmishing the archers of the East maintained the advantage; but in the close onset of the deadly strife, the German auxiliaries of Charles, grasp- ing their ponderous swords with "stout hearts and iron hands" stood to the shock like walls of stone, and beat down the light armed Arabs with terrific slaughter. Abdelrahman, and, as was reported by the monkish historians of the period, three hundred and seventy- five thousand[a] of his followers, were slain. The Arabs never re- sumed the conquest of Gaul, although twenty-seven years elapsed before they were wholly driven beyond the Pyrenees. Europe to this day owes its civil and religious freedom to the victory gained over the Saracens before Poictiers, by Charles, the *Hammer*[b] which shattered the Saracen forces.

38. About the time of the conquest of Spain, the Saracens made a second unsuccessful attempt to reduce the Byzantine capital; but farther east they were more successful, and extended their do- minion and their religion into Hindostan',[3] and the frozen regions

1. *Tours* is situated between the rivers Cher and Loire, near the point of their confluence, one hundred and twenty-seven miles south-west from Paris. Tours was anciently the capital of the *Turones*, conquered by Cæsar 55 B. C. After many vicissitudes it fell into the hands of the Plantagenets, and formed part of the English dominions till 1204, when it was annexed to the French crown. (*Map* No. XIII.)

2. *Poictiers*, or *Poitiers*, (anciently called *Limonum*, and afterward *Pictavi*,) sixty miles south-west from Tours, is the capital of the department of Vienne. It is one of the most ancient towns of Gaul; and the vestiges of a Roman palace, an aqueduct, and an amphithe- atre, are still visible. Besides the celebrated defeat of the Saracens in 732, Poictiers is mem- orable for the signal victory obtained in its vicinity Sept. 19th, 1356, by an English army commanded by Edward the Black Prince, over a vastly superior French force commanded by king John. (See p. 300. *Map* No. XIII.)

3. *Hindostan'*, a vast triangular country beyond the Indus, and south of the Himalaya mountains—the country of the Hindoos—has no authentic early history, although there is evi- dence to show that it was one of the early seats of Eastern civilization. The incursion of Al exander (325 B. C.) first made Hindostan' known to the European world. In the early part of the 11th century it was repeatedly invaded by the Moham' medans of Affghanistan, who, in

a. This was probably the whole number of the Mussulman force, not the number slain. See Nichton's Arabia, i. 409, Note.

b. Charles wielded a huge mace; and the epithet of "le martel," or "the Hammer" is ex pressive of the resistless force with which he dealt his blows.

of Tartary.　But the animosities of contending sects, domestic broils, revolts, assassinations, and civil wars, had long been weakening the central power which held together the unwieldy Saracen empire; and before the close of the eighth century, the civil power of the central caliphate had broken into fragments, although the spiritual power of the religion of the Prophet still maintained its ascendancy in all the regions that had once adopted the Moslem faith.

39.　We have thus briefly traced the history of the rise and establishment of the civil power and the religion of the Saracens, and their progress until effectually checked by the arms of the Franks and their confederates on the plains of Poictiers.　The power which thus obtrudes upon our view, as the bulwark and defence of Christendom, is the one that next prominently occupies the field of History, while that of the Saracens, weakened and distracted by its divisions, declines in historical interest and importance.

40.　The origin of the monarchy of the Franks is generally traced

VII.
MONARCHY
OF THE
FRANKS. back nearly two centuries and a half prior to the defeat of the Saracens by Charles Martel, about the era of the downfall of the Western empire of the Romans.　It is said that the Germanic tribes of the Franks or Freemen, occupied, at this early period, four cities in north-eastern or Belgic Gaul, viz. :—Tournai,[1] Cambray,[2] Terouané,[3] and Cologne,[4] which were governed by four separate kings, all of whom ascribed their origin to Merovæus, a half fabulous hero, whose rule is dated back a century and a half earlier.　Of the four kings of the Franks,

---

1193, made Delhi their capital.　In 1225 the country was conquered by Baber, the fifth in descent from "Timour the Tartar;" and with him began a race of Mogul princes.　Arungzebe, who died in 1707, was the greatest of the Mogul sovereigns.　The discovery of a passage to India, by way of the Cape of Good Hope, opened the country to a new and more formidable race of conquerors.　The Portuguese, the Dutch, and the French, obtained possession of portions of the Indian territory; but in the end they were overpowered by the English, who have established beyond the Indus a great Asiatic empire.

1.　*Tournay*, a town of Belgium, on the river Scheldt, (skelt) forty-five miles south-west from Brussels, and one hundred and thirty north-east from Paris, is the *Civ' itas Nerviórum* taken by Julius Cæsar.　It has since belonged to an almost infinite number of masters.　(*Map* No. XV.)

2.　*Cambray* on the Scheldt, (skelt) is thirty-three miles south from Tournay.　It was a city of considerable importance under the Romans, and has been the scene of many important events in modern history.　It was long famous for its manufacture of fine linens and lawns; whence all similar fabrics are called, in English, *cambrics*.　(*Map* No. XV.)

3.　*Terouané* (tĕ r-oo-an') appears to have been west from Brussels, near Dunkirk.

4.　*Cologne* is in the present Prussia, on the left bank of the Rhine, one hundred and twelve miles east from Brussels.　A Roman colony was planted in Cologne by Agrippina, the daughter of German'icus, who was born there.　Hence it obtained the name of *Agrippina Colónia* : afterwards it was called *Colónia*, or "the colony," whence the term *Cologne*.　(*Map* No. XVII.)

the ambitious Clovis,[a] who ruled over the tribe at Tournai was the most powerful. Being joined by the tribe at Cambray, he made war upon the last remains of the Roman power in Gaul; enlarged his territory by conquest, and established his capital at Soissons.[1] (A. D. 484.) At a later period he transferred the seat of sovereignty to Paris;[2] (A. D. 494) and at the time of his death, in 511, nearly the half of modern France, embracing that portion north of the Loire was comprised in the monarchy of which he is the reputed founder.[b]

41. Clovis, like many of the barbarian chiefs of that period, was a nominal convert to Christianity; and being the first of his nation who embraced the orthodox faith, he received from the Gaulish clergy the title of *most Christian king*, which has been retained by his successors to the present day. But his religion, a matter of mere form, seems to have exerted no influence in restraining the natural ferocity and blood thirstiness of his disposition, as all the rival monarchs or chieftains whom he could conquer or entrap were sacrificed to his jealousy and ambition. He put to death with his own hand most of his relations, and then, pretending to repent of his barbarity, he offered his protection to all who had escaped the massacre, hoping thus to discover if any survived, that he might rid himself of them also.

42. The descendants of Clovis, who are called Merovingians, from their supposed founder, reigned over the Franks for nearly two centuries and a half; but the repulsive annals of this long and barbarous period are one tissue of perfidy and crime. It was usually the first act of a monarch, on ascending the throne, to put to death his brothers, uncles, and nephews; and thus consanguinity generally led to the most deadly and fatal enmity. These murders so thinned the race of Clovis as often to produce the reign of kings under age;

1. *Soissons*, (sooah-song) now a fortified town on the river Aisne, sixty-eight miles north-east from Paris,—anciently *Noviodunum*,—was a city of the *Suessones*, in Belgic Gaul, which submitted to Julius Cæsar. Here Clovis extinguished the last remains of the Western empire by his victory over the Roman general Syagrius. The town then became the capital of the Franks, and, afterwards, of a kingdom of its own name, in the sixth and seventh centuries. (*Map* No. XIII.)

2. *Paris*, the metropolis of France, is situated on the river Seine, (sane) one hundred and ten miles from its mouth, and two hundred and ten miles south-east from London. When Gaul was invaded by Julius Cæsar, Paris, then called *Lutetia*, was the chief town of the Belgic tribe of the *Parisii*,—whence the city derives its modern name. It was at Lutetia that Julian the Apostate was saluted emperor by his soldiers. (*Map* No. XIII.)

a. The Roman corruption of Chlodwig, or, in modern German, Ludwig: in modern French Louis.—*Sismondi*, i. 175, Note.

b. See *Neustria*, Note, p. 272.

and eventually the custom was established of electing regents or guardians for them, who, by exercising the royal functions during the minority of their wards, acquired a power above that of the monarch himself At the time of the Saracen invasion of France, Charles Martel the guardian of the nominal sovereign, governed France with the humble title of mayor or duke.   His son Pepin succeeded him, and during the minority of his royal ward, the imbecile Childeric III., wielded the power, without assuming the name and honors of oyalty.; but at length, in 752, he threw off the mask, obtained a decree of pope Zachary in his favor, dethroned the last of the Merovingian kings, and caused himself to be crowned in the presence of the assembled nation, the first monarch of the Carlovingian dynasty. It was upon this occasion that the popes first exercised the authority of enthroning and dethroning kings.[1]

43. Of the reign and the character of Pepin we know little, except that he exhibited a profound deference for the priesthood, and was engaged in a long struggle with the former German allies of the Franks ; and that at the time of his death, in 768, there was no portion of Gaul that was not subject to the French monarchy.   He divided his kingdom between his two sons, Charles the elder, usually called Charlemagne, and Carloman the younger ; to the former of whom he bequeathed the western portion of the empire, and to the latter, the eastern ; but as Carloman died soon after, Charles stripped

1. The frequent allusions made in history to papal authority and papal supremacy, render necessary some explanation of the growth of the papal power.

The word *pope* comes from the Greek word *papa*, and signifies *father*. In the early times of Christianity this appellation was given to all Christian priests ; but during many centuries past it has been appropriated to the Bishop of Rome, whom the Roman Catholics look upon as the common father of all Christians.

Roman Catholics believe that Jesus Christ constituted St. Peter the chief pastor to watch over his whole flock here on earth—that he is to have successors to the end of time—and that the bishops of Rome, elected by the *cardinals* or chief of the Romish clergy, are his legitimate successors, popes, or fathers of the church, who have power and jurisdiction over all Christians, in order to preserve unity and purity of faith, doctrine, and worship.

During a long period after the introduction of Christianity into Rome, the bishops of Rome were merely *fathers of the Church*, and possessed no temporal power. It was customary however, to consult the pope in temporal matters ; and the powerful Pepin found no difficulty in obtaining a papal decision in favor of dethroning the imbecile Childeric, and inducing the pope to come to Paris to officiate at his coronation. Soon after, in 755, Pepin invested the pope with the exarchate of Raven'na ; and it is at this point—the union of temporal and spiritual jurisdiction—that the proper history of the papacy begins. Charlemagne and succeeding princes added other provinces to the papal government : but a long struggle for supremacy followed, between the popes and the German emperors ; and under the pontificate of Gregory VII., towards the close of the eleventh century, the claims of the Roman pontiffs to supremacy over all the sovereigns of the earth, were boldly asserted as the basis of the political system of the papacy.

his brother's widow and children or their inheritance, which he added to his own dominions.

44. The first acts of the reign of Charlemagne showed the warrior eager for conquest; for, advancing with an army beyond the Loire,[1] he compelled the Aquitánians, who had been subdued by Pepin, but had since revolted, to submit to his authority. His next enemies were the Saxons, who bounded his dominions on the north-east, and whose territories extended along the German ocean from the Elbe[2] to the Rhine. While all the other German tribes had adopted Christianity, the Saxons still sacrificed to the gods of their fathers; and it was both the desire of chastising their repeated aggressions, and the merit to be derived from their conversion to Christianity, that led Charlemagne to declare war against these fierce barbarians. (A. D. 772.)

45. His first irruption into the Saxon territory was successful, for he destroyed the pagan idols, received hostages, and on the banks of the Weser[3] concluded an advantageous peace. But the free spirit of the Saxons was not quelled: again and again they rose in insurrection, headed by the famous Witikind, a hero worthy of being the rival of Charlemagne; and the war continued, with occasional interruption, during a period of thirty-two years. At length, however, peace was granted to Witikind, who received baptism, Charlemagne himself acting as sponsor; and Saxony submitted to the Frankish institutions, as well as to those of Christianity. A few years later the Saxon youth, who had taken no share in the previous conflicts, arose in rebellion, but they were eventually subjugated, (A. D. 804,) when ten thousand of their number were transported into the country of the Franks, where they were gradually merged into the nation of their conquerors. It was in the midst of the ravages of these Saxon wars that the north of Germany passed from barbarism to civilization; for monasteries, churches, and bishoprics, immediately sprung up in the path of the conquerors; and although

1 The *Loire*, (looar) (anciently *Liger*), is the principal river of France, through the central par. of which it flows, in a W. direction to the Atlantic. Its basin comprises nearly one-fourth part of the kingdom. The Loire was the northern boundary of the county of the *Aquitánians*. The early seat of the empire of Charlemagne was therefore north of the Loire. (*Map No. XIII.*)

2. The *Elbe*, (anciently *Al' bis*,) rising in the mountains of Bohemia, flows north-west through central Europe, and enters the German ocean, or North sea, at the southern extremity of Denmark. This stream was the easternmost extent of the Germanic expeditions of the Romans. (*Map No. XVII.*)

3. The *Weser*, (anciently *Visur' gis*,) a river of Germany, enters the north sea between the Elbe on the east and the Ems on the west. (*Map No. XVII.*)

the religion which they planted was superficial and corrupt, they at least diffused some respect for the arts of civilized life.

46. Soon after the commencement of the Saxon wars, Charlemagne found another, but less formidable enemy, in the Lombards of Italy. The Lombard king had given protection to the widow of Carloman, the deceased brother of Charlemagne, and had required pope Adrian to anoint her sons as kings of the Franks; and upon Adrian's refusal, he threatened to carry war into his little territory of a few square miles around Rome. The pope demanded aid from Charlemagne, who, assembling his warriors at Geneva,[1] crossed the Alps into Italy and compelled the Lombard king, Desidérius, to shut himself up in his capital at Pávia,[2] which, after a siege of six months, surrendered. Desidérius became prisoner, and was sent to end his days in a monastery, while Charlemagne, placing the iron crown of the Lombards upon his head, caused himself to be proclaimed king of Italy. (774.)

47. A few years after the overthrow of the kingdom of the Lombards, Charlemagne carried his conquering arms into Spain, whither he had been invited by the viceroy of Catalónia,[3] to aid him against the Moham'medans. (677–8.) Pampelúna[4] and Saragos'sa[5] were dismantled, and the Arab princes of that region swore fealty to the conqueror, but on the return of Charlemagne across the Pyrenees, his rear guard was attacked in the famous pass of Roncesvalles,[6] and

---

1. *Geneva*, described by Cæsar as being "the frontier town of the Allobrógians," retains its ancient name. It is on the Rhone, at the south-western extremity of the Lake of Geneva, (anciently *Leman' nus*), and is the most populous city of Switzerland. In the year 426 it was taken by the Burgun'dians, and became their capital. It afterwards belonged, successively, to the Os'trogoths and Franks, and also to the second kingdom of Bur'gundy. On the fall of the latter it was governed by its own bishops; but at the time of the Reformation the bishops were expelled, and Geneva became a republic. (*Maps* No. XIV. and XVII.)

2. *Pávia*, (anciently *Ticinum*,) is situated on the Ticino (anciently Ticinus,) north of the Po, and twenty miles south from Milan. Pávia has sustained many sieges, but is principally distinguished for the great battle fought in its vicinity Feb. 24th, 1525. See p. 327. (*Map* No. XVII.)

3. *Catalónia* was the north-western province of Spain. It was successively subject to the Romans, Goths, and Moors; but in the 8th and 9th centuries, in connection with the adjoining French province of Rous'sillon, it became an independent State, subject to the counts or earl of Barcelona. (*Map* No. XIII.)

4. *Pampelúna*, a fortified city of Spain, supposed to have been built by Pompey after the defeat of Sertórius, (see p. 176,) is a short distance south of the Pyrenees, and forty miles from the Bay of Biscay. It was the capital of the kingdom, now province, of Navarre. (*Map* No. XIII.)

5. *Saragos'sa*, (anciently *Cæsar Augusta*) situated in a fine plain on the Ebro, (anciently *Ibérus*,) is eighty-seven miles south-east from Pampelúna. It is a very ancient city, and is said to have been founded by the Phœnicians or Carthaginians. Julius Cæsar greatly enlarged it, and Augustus gave it the name of Cæsar Augusta, with the privileges of a free colony (*Map* No. XIII.)

6. *Roncesvalles* (*Ron'-sa-val*) is about twenty miles north-east from Pampelúna. (*Map* No. XIII.)

entirely cut to pieces. Poesy and fable have combined to render memorable a defeat of which history has preserved no details.

48. After Charlemagne had extended his empire over France, Germany, and Italy, minor conquests easily followed; and many of the other surrounding nations, or rather tribes, fell under his power or solicited his protection. Thus the dominion of the Franks penetrated into Hungary, and advanced upon the Danube as far as the frontiers of the Greek empire. A conspiracy in Rome having forced the pope to seek the protection of Charlemagne, in the year 800 the latter visited Rome in person to punish the evil doers. While he was there attending services in St. Peter's Church, at the Christmas festival, the gratified pontiff placed upon his head a crown of gold, and, in the formula observed for the Roman emperors, and amid the acclamations of the people, saluted him by the titles of Emperor and Augustus. This act was considered as indicating the revival of the Empire of the West, after an interruption of about three centuries.

49. Charlemagne, a king of the German Franks, was thus seated on the throne of the Cæsars. Nor was the circumstance of his receiving the imperial crown unimportant, as by the act he declared himself the representative of the ancient Roman civilization, and not of the barbarism of its destroyers. In Italy, Charlemagne sought teachers for the purpose of establishing public schools throughout his dominions: he encouraged literature, and attempted to revive commerce; and his capital of Aix-la-Chapelle[1] he so adorned with sumptuous edifices, palaces, churches, bridges, and monuments of art, as to give it the appearance of a Roman city. By the wisdom of his laws, and the energy which he displayed in executing them, he established order and regularity, and gave protection to all parts of his empire. But with all the greatness of Charlemagne, his private life was not free from the stain of licentiousness; and where his ambition led him he was unsparing of blood. He caused four thousand five hundred imprisoned Saxons to be beheaded in one day, as a terrible example to their countrymen, and as an act of retribution for an army which he had lost; and as a right of conquest he denounced the penalty of death against those who refused baptism, or who even eat flesh during Lent. Still his long reign is a brilliant

1. *Aix-la-Chapelle* (*a-la-shappel'*) the favorite residence of Charlemagne, is an old and well-built city of Prussian Germany, west of the Rhine, and seventy-eight miles east from Brussels. (*Map*, No. XIII. and XVII.)

period in the history of the middle ages ;—the more interesting, from the preceding chaos of disorder, and the disgraces and miseries which followed it;—resembling the course of a meteor that leaves the darkness still more dreary as it disappears.

50 The posterity of Charlemagne were unequal to the task of preserving the empire which he had formed, and it speedily fell asunder by its own weight. To the mutual antipathies of different races,—the German on the one side, including the Franks, knit together by their old Teutonic tongue,—and the nation of mingled Gallic, Roman, and Barbarian origin, on the other, which afterwards assumed the name of Franks, and gave to their own country the appellation France,—was added the rivalry of the Carlovingian princes; and about thirty years after the death of Charlemagne (A. D. 814), at the close of a period of anarchy and civil war, the empire was divided among his descendants, and out of it were constituted the separate kingdoms,—France, Germany, and Italy (A. D. 843.)[a]

51. The motive that led the Carlovingian princes to put an end to their unnatural wars with each other, was the repeated invasion of the coasts of France and Germany by piratical adventurers from the north, called Northmen or Danes, a branch of the great Teutonic race, who, issuing from all the shores of the Baltic, annually ravaged the coasts of their more civilized neighbors,—and, by hasty incursions, even pillaged the cities far in the interior. During more than a century these Northern pirates continued to devastate the shores of Western Europe, particularly infesting the coasts of Britain, Ireland, and France.

52. In the meantime central Europe became a prey to the Hungarians, a warlike Tartarian tribe, whose untamed ferocity recalled the memory of At'tila. The Saracens also, masters of the Mediterranean, kept the coasts of Italy in constant alarm, and twice insulted and ravaged the territory of Rome. Amid the tumult and confusion thus occasioned, European society was undergoing a change, from the absolutism of imperial authority to the establishment of numerous dukedoms, having little more than a nominal dependence upon the reigning princes. Power was transferred from the palace of the king to the castle of the baron ; and for a time European history,—that of France in particular—is occupied with the annals of an intriguing, factious, aspiring nobility, rather than

a. By the treaty of Verdun, Aug. 11th, 843.

with those of monarchs and the people. From the confusion inci dent to such a state of society we turn to the neighboring island of Britain, where, a few years after the dissolution of the empire of Charlemagne, the immortal Alfred arose, drove back the tide of bar barian conquest, and laid the foundation of those laws and institutions which have rendered England the most enlightened and most powerful of the nations of Europe.

53. We have mentioned that, towards the close of the sixth century, the Saxon tribes from the shores of the Baltic had made themselves masters of the southern and more fertile provinces of Britain. After having extirpated the ancient British population, or driven it into Cornwall and Wales on the western side of the island, the kindred tribes of the Angles and Saxons, under the common name of Anglo Saxons, established in England seven independent kingdoms, which are known in history as the Saxon Heptarchy. The intricate details, so far as we can learn them, of the history of these kingdoms, are uninteresting and unimportant; and from the period of the first inroads of the Saxons down to the time of the coronation of Alfred the Great in 872, the chronicles of Britain present us with the names of numerous kings, the dates of many battles, and frequent revolutions attended with unimportant results;—the history of all which is in great part conjectural, and gives us little insight into individual or national character.

VIII.
ENGLISH
HISTORY.

54. It appears that about the year 597 Christianity was first introduced into England by the monk Augustine, accompanied by forty missionaries, who had been sent out by pope Gregory for the con version of the Britons. The new faith, such as it pleased the church to promulgate, being received cordially by the kings, descended from them to their subjects, and was established without persecution, and without the shedding of the blood of a single martyr. The religious zeal of the Anglo Saxons greatly exceeded that of the nations of the continent; and it is recorded that, during the Heptarchy, ten kings and eleven queens laid aside the crown to devote themselves to a monastic life.

55. In the year 827 the several kingdoms of the Saxon Heptarchy were united in one great State by Egbert, prince of the West Saxons, an ambitious warrior, who exhibits some points of comparison with his illustrious cotemporary Charlemagne, at whose court he had spent twelve years of his early life. The Saxon union, under the firm administration of Egbert, promised future tranquillity to the in

habitants of Britain; but scarcely had a regular government been established when the piratical Scandinavians, known in France under the name of Normans, and in England by that of Danes, landed in the southern part of the island, and after a bloody battle with Egbert at Charmouth in Dorsetshire, made good their retreat to their ships, carrying off all the portable wealth of the district. (A. D. 833.) This was the beginning of the ravages of the Northmen in England; and they continued to plunder the coasts for nearly two centuries.

56. From the death of Egbert in 838, to the accession of Alfred the Great in 871, the throne of England was occupied by four Saxon princes;[a] and the whole of this period, like the corresponding one in French history, is filled with the disastrous invasions of the Danes.[b] In the course of a single year nine sanguinary battles were fought between the Saxons and their invaders; and in the last of these battles king Ethelred received a wound which caused his death (871–2.) His brother Alfred, then only twenty-two years of age, succeeded to the throne. He had served with distinction in the numerous bloody battles fought by his brother; but on his accession he found nearly half the kingdom in the possession of the Danes; and within six years the almost innumerable swarms of these invaders struck such terror into the English, that Alfred, who strove to assemble an army, found himself suddenly deserted by all his warriors.

57. Obliged to relinquish the ensigns of royalty, and to seek shelter from the pursuit of his enemies, he disguised himself under the habit of a peasant, and for some time lived in the cottage of a goatherd, known only to his host, and regarded by his hostess as an inferior, and occasionally intrusted by her with the menial duties of the household. It is said that, as he was one day trimming his arrows by the fire-side, she desired him to watch some cakes that were baking, and that when, forgetting his trust, he suffered them to burn, she severely upbraided him for his neglect. Afterwards, retiring with a few faithful followers to the marshes of Somersetshire, he built there a fortress, whence he made occasional successful sallies upon the Danes, who knew not from what quarter the blow came. While his very existence was unsuspected by the enemy, under the

a. Ethelwolf, Ethelbald, Ethelbert, and Ethelred.
b. As the term *Normans* was at a later period exclusively appropriated to that branch of the Scandinavians which settled in Normandy, we shall follow the English writers and apply the term *Danes* to those barbarians of the same family who so long ravaged the English coast. It should not be forgotten by the reader that the Saxons also were of Scandinavian origin

disguise of a harper he visited their camp, where his musical skill obtained for him a welcome reception, and an introduction to the tent of the Danish prince, Guthrum.   Here he spent three days, witnessed the supine security of the enemy, thoroughly examined the camp and its approaches, and then went to meet his countrymen, for whom he had appointed a gathering in Selwood forest.[a]

58. The Saxons, inspired with new life and courage at the sight of their beloved prince, whom they had supposed dead, fell upon the unsuspecting Danes, and cut nearly all of them to pieces.   (A. D. 878.) Guthrum, and the small band of followers who escaped, were soon besieged in a fortress, where they accepted the terms of peace that were offered them.   Guthrum embraced Christianity; the greater part of the Danes settled peaceably on the lands that were assigned them, where they soon intermingled with the Saxons; while the more turbulent spirits went to join new swarms of their countrymen in their ravages upon the French and German coasts.   The shores of England were unvisited, during several years, by the enemy, and Alfred employed the interval of repose in organizing the future defence of his kingdom.   In early life he had visited Italy, and seen the Greek and Roman galleys, which were greatly superior to the Danish unarmed vessels, that were fitted only for transport. Alfred now formed a navy; and his vessels never met those of the Danes without the certain destruction of the latter.

59. The Danes, however, who had settled in England, still occupied the greater part of the country, so that the acknowledged sovereignty of Alfred did not extend over any of the countries northward of the city of London,—and fifteen years after the defeat of Guthrum, Hastings, another celebrated Danish chief, threatened to deprive the English king of the limited possessions which he still retained.   After having plundered all the northern provinces of France, Hastings appeared on the coast of Kent with three hundred and thirty sail, and spreading his forces over the country, committed the most dreadful ravages.   (A. D. 893.)   The Danes in the northern parts of England joined him; but they were everywhere defeated, and eventually Hastings withdrew to his own country, taking back with him the most warlike portion of the Danish population, from the English channel to the frontiers of Scotland, after which the whole of England no longer hesitated to acknowledge the authority of Alfred, although his power over the Danish population in the northern

a. At Brixton, on the borders of the forest, in Wiltshire.   Wiltshire is east of Somerset.

part of the kingdom was still little more than nominal. He died after a reign of twenty-nine years and a-half, having deservedly attained the appellation of Alfred the GREAT, and the title of founder of the English monarchy. (A. D. 901.)

60. To Alfred the English ascribe the origin of many of those institutions which lie at the foundation of their nation's prosperity and renown. As the founder of the English navy, he planted the seeds of the maritime power of England : with him arose the grandeur and prosperity of London, the place of the assembling of the national parliament or body of prelates, earls, barons, and burghers, or deputies from the English burghs, or associations of freemen : he made a collection of the Saxon laws, to which he added others framed or sanctioned by himself; he reformed the Saxon division of the country into counties and shires ; divided the citizens into corporations of tens and hundreds, with a regular system of inspection and police, in which equals exercised a supervision over equals ; and in the mode which he adopted of settling controversies, we trace the first indications of the glory of the English judiciary—the trial by jury. The cultivation of letters, which had been interrupted at the first invasion of the then barbarous Saxons, was revived by Alfred, who was, himself, the most learned man in the kingdom : he founded schools at Oxford—the germ of the celebrated university of that name ; and he set aside a considerable portion of his revenues for the payment of the salaries of teachers. The character of Alfred is almost unrivalled in the annals of any age or nation ; and in the details of his private life we cannot discover a vice, or even a fault, to stain or sully the spotlessness of his reputation.

SECTION II.

GENERAL HISTORY, DURING THE TENTH, ELEVENTH, TWELFTH, AND THIR-
TEENTH CENTURIES : A. D. 900 TO 1300 = 400 YEARS.

I. COMPLETE DISSOLUTION OF THE BONDS OF SOCIETY.

ANALYSIS. 1. Causes of the CONFUSION OF HISTORIC MATERIALS at this period.—2. STATE OF THE SARACEN WORLD. [Bagdad. Cor'dova. Khorassan'.]—3. THE BYZANTINE EMPIRE. Turkish invasions and conquests. [Georgia.]—4. The divisions of the Carlovingian empire. CONDITION OF ITALY. Berenger duke of Friuli. Prince of Burgundy. Hugh count of Provence. Surrender of the kingdom to Otho. [Friuli. Switzerland. Provence.]—5. Italy under the German emperors. Guelfs and Ghibellines. Dukes, marquises, counts, and prelates

Petty Italian republics.—6. Condition of Germany. Its six dukedoms. [Saxony. Thurin'gia. Franconia. Bavaria. Suabia. Lorraine.] Encroachments of the dukes. Reign of Conrad Henry I. of Saxony. Powers of the Saxon rulers.—7. Condition of France. Charles the Simple. Other princes. Deposition of Charles. [Transjurane Burgundy. Provence. Brittany.]—8. Settlement of the Northmen in France. [Normandy.] Importance of this event.—9. The counts of Paris. Hugh Capet. [Rheims.] Situation of France for two hundred and forty years after the accession of Hugh Capet.

II. THE FEUDAL SYSTEM; CHIVALRY; AND THE CRUSADES.

1. Europe in the central period of the Middle Ages. Origin of the Feudal System. Its duration and importance.—2. Partition of lands by the barbarians who overthrew the Roman empire. Conditions of the allotment. Gradations of the system.—3. Nature of the estates thus obtained. Crown lands—how disposed of. The word *feud.*—4. The feudal system in France. Charlemagne's efforts to check its progress. Effects upon the nobility. Growth of the power of the nobles after the overthrow of royal authority. Their petty sovereignties.—5. Condition of the allodial proprietors. They are forced to become feudal tenants.—6. Legal qualities and results that grew out of the feudal system. Reliefs, fines, escheats, aids, wardship and marriage.—7. The feudal government in its best state. Its influence on the character of society. General ignorance at this period. Sentiments of independence in the nobility.

8. Rise of Chivalry. Our first notices of it. Its origin.—9. Its rapid spread, and its good effects.—10. Its spirit based on noble impulses. Extract from Hallam: From James. Customs and peculiarities of chivalry. Who were members of the institution.—11. The profession of arms among the Germans. Education of a knight. The practice of knight-errantry.—12. Extent of chivalry in the 11th century. Its spirit led to the crusades.

Origin of the Crusades.—13. Pilgrimages to Jerusalem. General expectation of the approaching end of the world.—14. Extortion and outrage practiced upon the pilgrims. Horror and indignation excited thereby in Europe. The preaching of Peter the Hermit. [Amiens.]—15. The councils of Placentia and Clermont. [Placentia and Clermont.] Gathering of the crusaders for the First Crusade.—16. Conduct and fate of the foremost bands of the crusaders. The genuine army of the crusade. [Bouillon.]—17. Conduct of Alexius, emperor of Constantinople. His proposals spurned by the crusaders.—18. Number of the crusaders collected in Asia Minor. First encounter with the Turks. [Nice. Bithyn'ia. Roum.] The march to Syria. [Dorylæ'um.]—19. The siege and capture of Antioch. The Persian and Turkish hosts defeated before the town.—20. Civil wars among the Turks. The caliph of Egypt takes Jerusalem. Proposal to unite his forces with the Christians rejected.—21. March of the crusaders to Jerusalem. [Mt. Lib'anus. Trip'oli. Tyre. Acre. Cæsarea.] Transports of the Christians on the first view of the city. Attack, and repulse.—22. Capture of Jerusalem. Acts of veneration and worship. Reception given to Peter the Hermit. His ultimate fate.—23. The new government of Jerusalem. Minor Christian States. Defenceless state of Jerusalem under Godfrey. Continued pilgrimages. Orders of knighthood established at Jerusalem. The noted valor of the knights.

24. Continued yearly emigration of pilgrim warriors to the Holy Land. Six principal crusades. Their general character.—25. The Second Crusade. The leading army under Conrad. The army of French and Germans.—26. Jerusalem taken by Saladin. The Third Crusade. Fate of the German emperor. Successes of the French and English. Return of Philip. Richard concludes a truce with Saladin. [Ascalon.]—27. The Fourth Crusade, led by Boniface. The crusaders take Zara, and conquer Constantinople. No benefit to Palestine. [Montserrat. Zara.]—28. The Fifth Crusade. Partial successes, and final ruin, of the expedition. [Damietta.] Expedition of the German emperor, Frederic II. Treaty with the sultan, by which Jerusalem is yielded to the Christians. Jerusalem again taken by the sultan, but restored.

29. Cotemporary events in northern Asia. Tartar Conquests in Asia and in Europe. [China. Russia. Kiev. Moscow.] Alarm of the Christian nations of Europe. Recall of the conquering hordes.—30. The Corasmins. They overrun Syria and take Jerusalem, but are finally expelled by the united Turks and Christians.—31. The Sixth Crusade, led by Louis IX., who attacks Egypt. The second crusade of Louis. Attack upon Carthage. Result of the expedition.—32. Acre, the last stronghold of the Christians in Syria, taken by the Turks, 1291. Results of the Crusades.

M

III. ENGLISH HISTORY.

1. Our last reference to the history of England. The present continuation. 2. Condition of ENGLAND AFTER THE DEATH OF ALFRED. England during the reign of Ethelred II. Massacre of the Danes. Effects of this impolitic measure. Canute. Recall of Ethelred. Edmund Ironside. Canute sole monarch.—3. His conciliatory policy. His vast possessions. Character of his administration of the government.—4. Harold and Hardicanute. The reign of Edward the Confessor. Events that disturbed his reign. Accession of Harold. The NORMAN CONQUEST. [Sussex. Hastings.]—5. Gradual conquest of all England. William's treatment of his conquered subjects.—6. The feudal system in England. The Doomsday Book. Saxons and Normans.—7. Reigns of William Rufus, and Henry I.—8. Usurpation and reign of Stephen. Henry II. [Plantagenet.]—9. Henry's extensive possessions. REDUCTION OF IRELAND. [History of Ireland.] The troubles of Henry's reign. -10. Reign of Richard, the Lion Hearted.—11. Reign of John, surnamed Lackland. Loss of his continental possessions. Quarrels with the pope:—with the barons. Magna Charta. Civil war, and death of John.—12. The long reign of Henry III. His difficulties with the barons. First germs of popular representation. 13. The reign of Edward I. SUBJUGATION OF WALES. [History of Wales.]—14. Relations between England and Scotland. The princess Margaret.—15. Baliol and Bruce. Beginning of the SCOTTISH WARS. Submission of Baliol. [Dunbar.]—16. William Wallace recovers Scotland, but is defeated at Falkirk. [Stirling. Falkirk.] Fate of Wallace.—17. Robert Bruce crowned king of Scotland. Edward II. defeated by him. [Scone. Bannockburn.]

18. Northern nations of Europe during this period. Wars between the Moors and Christians in the Spanish peninsula. Final overthrow of the Saracen power in the peninsula.

1. COMPLETE DISSOLUTION OF THE BONDS OF SOCIETY.—1. The tenth century brings us to the central period of what has been denominated the Middle Ages. The history of the known world presents

I. CONFUSION OF HISTORIC MATERIALS. a greater confusion and discordance of materials at this than at any preceding epoch; for at this time we have neither a great empire, like the Grecian, the Persian, or the Roman; nor any great simultaneous movement, like the mighty tide of the barbarian invasions, to serve as the starting and the returning point for our researches, and to give, by its prominence, a sort of unity to cotemporaneous history; but on every side we see States falling into dissolution; the masses breaking into fragments; dukes, counts, and lords, renouncing their allegiance to kings and emperors; cities, towns, and castles, declaring their independence, and, amid a general dissolution of the bonds of society, we find almost universal anarchy prevailing.

2. In the East, the empire of the caliphs, the mighty colossus of Mussulman dominion, was broken; the Saracens were no longer ob-

II. THE SARACEN WORLD. jects of terror to all their neighbors, and the frequent revolutions of the throne of Bagdad,[1] the central seat of the religion of the prophet, had ceased to have any

---

1. Bagdad, a famous city of Asiatic Turkey,—long the chief seat of Moslem power in Asia, —the capital of the Eastern caliphate, and of the scientific world during the "Dark Ages," is situated on the river Tigris, sixty-eight miles north of the ruins of Babylon.

Bagdad was founded by the caliph Al-Mansour, A. D. 763, and is said to have been prime.

influence on the rest of the world.   About the middle of the eighth century, the Moors of Spain had separated themselves from their Eastern brethren, and made Cor'dova[1] the seat of their dominion, and little more than two centuries and a half later, (A. D. 1031) the division of the Western Caliphate into a great number of small principalities, which were weakened by civil dissensions, contributed to the enlargement of the Christian kingdoms in the northern part of the peninsula.   Soon after the defection of the Moors of Spain, an independent Saracen monarchy had arisen in Africa proper: this was followed by the establishment of new dynasties in Egypt, Khorassan',[2] and Persia; and eventually, in the tenth century, we find the Caliphate divided into a great number of petty States, whose annals, gathered from oriental writers, furnish, amid a labyrinth of almost unknown names and countries, little more than the chronology of princes, with the civil wars, parricides, and fratricides of each reign.   Such was the condition of that vast population, comprising many nations and languages, which still adhered, although under different forms, and with many departures from the originals, to the general principles of the moslem faith.

3. The Byzantine empire still continued to exist, but in weakness and corruption.   "From the age of Justin'ian," says Gibbon, " it

pally formed out of the ruins of Ctes'iphon. It was greatly enlarged and adorned by the grandson of its founder, the famous Haroun-al-Raschid. It continued to flourish, and to be the principal seat of learning and the arts till 1258, when Hoolaku, grandson of Gengis Khan, reduced the city after a siege of two months, and gave it up to plunder and massacre. It is said that the number of the slain in the city alone amounted to eight hundred thousand.   Since that event Bagdad has witnessed various other sieges and revolutions. It was burnt and plundered by the ferocious Timour A. D. 1401, who erected a pyramid of human heads on its ruins.   In 1637 it incurred the vengeance of Amurath IV., the Turkish sultan, who barbarously massacred a large portion of the inhabitants.   Since that period the once illustrious city now numbering less than a hundred thousand inhabitants, has been degraded to the seat of a Turk ish pashalic.   The rich merchants and the beautiful princesses of the Arabian Tales have all disappeared; but it retains the tomb of the charming Zobeide, the most beloved of the wives of Haroun-al-Raschid, and can still boast of its numerous gardens and well stocked bazaars.

1. Cor'dova, a city of Andalusia in Spain, is situated on the Guadalquiver, one hundred and eighty-five miles south-west from Madrid.   It is supposed to have been founded by the Romans, under whom it attained to great distinction as a rich and populous city, and a seat of learning.   In 572 it was taken by the Goths, and in 711 by the Moors, under whom it afterwards became the splendid capital of the "Caliphate of the West;" but with the extinction of the Western caliphate, A. D. 1031, the power and the glory of Cor'dova passed away. Cor'dova continued to be a separate Moorish kingdom until the year A. D. 1236, when was taken and almost wholly destroyed by the impolitic zeal of Ferdinand III. of Castile.   It has never since recovered its previous prosperity; and its population has diminished since the 11th century, from five hundred thousand to less than forty thousand.   (Map No. XIII.)

2. Khorassan', (the " region of the sun,") is a province of Modern Persia, at the south-eastern extremity of the Caspian Sea, inhabited by Persians proper, Turkmans and Kurds.   The religion is still Moham'medan

was sinking below its former level: the powers of destruction were
more active than those of improvement; and the calamities of war were imbittered by the more permanent
evils of civil and ecclesiastical tyranny."[a]   It was daily
becoming more and more separated from Western Europe; its relations, both of peace and war, being chiefly with the Saracens, who
in the period of their conquests, overran all Asia Minor, and were
forming permanent establishments within sight of Constantinople
Toward the close of the tenth century, however, a brief display of
vigor in the Byzantine princes, Niceph'orus, Zimisus, and Basil II.
repelled the Saracens, and extended the Asiatic boundaries of the
empire as far south as Antioch, and eastward to the eastern limits
of Arménia; but twenty-five years after the death of Basil (1025),
his effeminate successors were suddenly assaulted by the Turks or
Turcomans, a new race of Tartar barbarians of the Mussulman faith,
whose original seats were beyond the Caspian Sea, along the northern
boundaries of China.   During the first invasion of the Turks, under
their leader Togrul, (1050) one hundred and thirty thousand
Christians were sacrificed to the religion of the prophet.   His successor, Alp Arslan, the "valiant lion," reduced Georgia[1] and Arménia, and defeated and took captive the Byzantine emperor Románus
Diog'enes; and succeeding princes of the Turkish throne gathered
the fruits of a lasting conquest of all the provinces beyond the Bos'-
porus and Hellespont.

III. THE
BYZANTINE
EMPIRE.

4. Turning to the West, to examine the condition of the three
great divisions of the empire of the Carlovingians—Italy, Germany,
and Gaul,—we find there but the wrecks of former greatness. In
Italy, the dukes, the governors of provinces, and the leaders of
armies, were possessed of far greater power than the
reigning monarch.   Having for a long period perpetu-
ated their dignities in their families, they had become
in fact petty tyrants over their limited domains; ever jealous of th
royal authority, and dreading the loss of their privileges, they con

IV. CONDI-
TION OF
ITALY.

---

1. *Georgia* is between the Caspian and the Black Sea, having Circassia on the north and Arménia on the south. This country was annexed to the Roman empire by Pompey, in the year
65 B. C. During the 6th and 7th centuries it was a theatre of contest between the Greek empire and the Persians. In the 8th century a prince of the Jewish family of the Bagrat'ides established there a monarchy which, with few interruptions, continued in his line down to the
commencement of the 19th century. In 1801 the emperor Paul of Russia declared himself, at
the request of the Georgian prince, sovereign of Georgia.

a. Gibbon, iv. 4.

spired against their sovereign as often as he showed an inclinatior to rescue the people from the oppressive exactions of their masters. In the early part of the tenth century they arose against Berenger duke of Friúli,[1] who had been proclaimed king, and offered the crown to the prince of Bur'gundy, who during two years united the government of Italy to that of Switzerland.[2] (923–925.) Soon abandoning him, the turbulent nobles elevated to the throne Hugh, count of Provence;[3] and finally Italy, exhausted by the animosities and struggles of the aristocracy, made a voluntary surrender of the kingdom to Otho the Great, the Saxon prince of Germany, who, in the year 962, was crowned at Milan with the iron crown of Lom'-bardy, and at Rome with the golden crown of the empire.

5. During several succeeding centuries the German emperors were nominally recognized as sovereigns of the greater part of Italy; but as they seldom crossed the Alps, their authority was soon reduced to a mere shadow The pretensions of the court of Rome were op-posed to those of the German princes; and during the quarrels that arose between the Guelfs and Ghibellines,[4]—the former the adherents of Rome, and the latter of Germany—Italy was thrown into the greatest confusion. While some portions were under the immediate jurisdiction of the German emperor, a large number of the dukes, marquises, counts, and prelates, residing in their castles which they

1. *Friúli* is an Italian province at the head of the Adriat' ic, and at the north-eastern ex tremity of Italy.

2. *Switzerland*, anciently called Helvétia, is an inland and mountainous country of Europe having the German States on the north and east, Italy on the south, and France on he west Julius Cæsar reduced the Helvétians to submission 15 years B. C.; after which the Romans founded in it several flourishing cities, which were afterwards destroyed by the barbarians. In the beginning of the 5th century the Burgun' dians overran the western part of Switzerland and fixed their seats around the lake of Geneva, and on the banks of the Rhone and the Saone Fifty years later the Aleman' ni overran the eastern part of Switzerland, and a great part of Germany, overwhelming the monuments of Roman power, and blotting out the Christianity which Rome had planted. At the close of the fifth century the Aleman' ni were overthrown by Clovis;—the first Burgun' dian empire fell A. D. 535; and for a long period afterward Hel-vétia formed a part of the French monarchy. The partition of the dominions of Charlemagne threw Switzerland into the German part of the empire. In the year 1307 the three forest cantons, Uri, Schwytz, and Unterwalden, entered into a confederacy against the tyranny of the Austrian house of Hapsburg, then at the head of the German empire. Other cantons from time to time joined the league, or were conquered from Austria; but it was not till the time of Napoleon that all the present existing cantons were brought into the confederacy. (*Maps* No. XIV. and XVII.)

3. *Provence*, see p. 271.

4. These party names, obscure in origin, were imported from Germany. In the wars of Frederic Barbarossa, (the Redbeard,) the *Guelfs* were the champions of liberty: in the crusades which the popes directed against that prince's unfortunate descendants they were merely the partisans of the Church. The name soon ceased to signify principles, and merely served the same purpose as a watchword, or the color of a standard.

had strongly fortified against the depredating inroads of the Normans, Saracens, and Hungarians, exercised an almost independent authority within their limited domains; while a number of petty republics, the most important of which were Venice, Pisa, and Genoa, fortifying their cities, and electing their own magistrates, set the authority of the pope, the nobles, and the emperor, equally at defiance. Such was the confused state of Italy in the central period of the Middle Ages.

6. Germany, at the beginning of the tenth century, under the rule of a minor, Louis IV., the last of the Carlovingian family, was harassed by frequent invasions of the Hungarians; while the six dukedoms into which the country was divided, viz.: Saxóny,[1] Thurin'gia,[2] Franconia,[3] Bavária,[4] Suábia,[5] and Lorraine,[6] appeared like so many distinct nations, ready to declare war against each other. The dukes, originally regarded as ministers and representatives of their king, had long been encroaching on the royal prerogatives, and by degrees had arrogated to themselves such an increase of power, that the dignities temporarily conferred upon them became hereditary in their families. They next seized the royal revenues, and made themselves masters of the people

CONDITION OF GERMANY.

---

1. *Saxony*, the most powerful of the ancient duchies of Germany, embraced, at the period of its greatest development, the whole extent of northern Germany between the mouths of the Rhine and the Oder. (*Map* No. XVII.)

2. *Thurin'gia* was in the central part of Germany, west of Prussian Saxony. In the 13th century it was subdivided among many petty princes, and incorporated with other States, after which the name fell gradually into disuse. It is still preserved, in a limited sense, in the *Thurin'gian forest*, a hilly and woody tract in the interior of Germany, on the northern confines of Bavaria. (*Map* No. XVII.)

3. *Franconia* was situated on both sides of the river Maine, and is now included mostly within the limits of Bavaria. (*Map* No. XVII.)

4. *Bavaria*—comprising most of the Vindelicia and Nor'icum of the Romans, is a country in the southern part of Germany. It was anciently a duchy—afterwards an electorate—and has now the rank of a kingdom. (*Map* No. XVII.)

5. *Suabia*, of which Ulm was the capital, was in the south-western part of Germany, west of Bavaria, and north of Switzerland. It is now included in Baden, Wurtemburg, and Bavaria. (*Map* No. XVII.)

6. *Lorraine*, (German *Lotharingia*,) so called from Lothaire II., to whom this part of the country fell in the division of the empire between him and his brothers Louis II. and Charles, in the year 854, eleven years after the treaty of Verdun, (see p. 260,) was divided into Upper and Lower Lorraine, and extended from the confines of Switzerland, westward of the Rhine to its mouths, and the mouths of the Scheldt. (Skelt.) A part of the Lower Lorraine was afterwards embraced in the French province of Lorraine, (see *Map* No. XIII.,) and is now comprised in the departments of the Meuse, the Vosges, the Moselle, and the Meurthe. Lorraine was for centuries a subject of dispute between France and Germany.

The relative position of the six German dukedoms was therefore as follows:—Saxony occupied the northern portions of Germany; Thurin'gia and Franconia the centre; Bavaria the south-eastern; Suabia the south-western; and Lorraine the north-western. (*Maps* No. XIII. and XVII.)

and their lands. On the death of Louis IV., (A. D. 911,) they set aside the legitimate claimant, and elected for their sovereign one of their own number, Conrad, duke of Francónia. His reign of seven years was passed almost wholly in the field, checking the incursions of the Hungarians, or quelling the insurrections of the other dukedoms against his authority. On his death (A. D. 918), Henry I., surnamed the Fowler, duke of Saxony, was elected to the throne which his family retained little more than a century. (Until 1024. The Saxon rulers of Germany, however, were not, like Charlemagne, the sovereigns of a vast empire; but rather the chiefs of a confederacy of princes, reckoned of superior authority in matters of national concern, while the nobles still managed their provincial administration mostly in their own way. The history of the little more than nominal sovereigns of Germany, therefore, during this period, contains but little of the history of the German people.

7. In France, the royal authority, at the beginning of the tenth century, exercised an influence still more feeble than in Germany, and was little more than an empty honor. Charles the Simple, whose name bespeaks his character, was the nominal sovereign; but four other princes in Gaul, besides himself, bore the title of king,—those of Lorraine, Transjurane-Búrgundy,[1] Provence,[2] and Brittany;[3]—while in other parts of the country, powerful dukes and counts governed their dominions with absolute independence. At length, in the year 920, an assembly of nobles formally deposed Charles, but he continued his nominal reign nearly three years longer, while the people and the nobility were scarcely conscious of his existence.

VI. CONDITION OF FRANCE.

1 *Transjurane-Bur'gundy*, is that portion of Bur'gundy that was embraced in Switzerland-beyond the *Jura*, or western Alps.

2. *Provence* was in the south-eastern part of France, on the Mediterranean, bounded on the east by Italy, north by Dauphiny, and west by Languedoc. Greek colonies were founded here at an early period, (see Marseilles, p. 157,) and the Romans, having conquered the country (B. C. 124,) gave it the name of *Provincia*, (the province,) whence its later name was derived. After the three-fold division of the empire of Louis le Debonnaire, the son and successor of Charlemagne, by the treaty of Verdun in 843, (see p. 260,) Provence fell to Lothaire; but it afterwards became a separate kingdom, under the name of the kingdom of Arles. In 1246 't passed to the house of Anjou by marriage; and in 1481 Louis XI. united it to the dominions of the French crown. (*Map* No. XIII.)

3 *Brittany*, or Bretagne, was one of the largest provinces of France, occupying the peninsula at the north-western extremity of the kingdom, and joined on the east by Poitou, Anjou, Maine, and Normandy. It now forms the five departments, Finisterre, Cotes du Nord, (coast-of-nor) Morbihan, Ille and Vilaine, and Lower Loire. Brittany is supposed to have derived its name from the Britons, who, expelled from England by the Anglo Saxons, took refuge here in the fifth century. It formed one of the duchies of France till it was united to the crown by Francis I. in 1532. (*Map* No. XIII.)

8. The only really important event of French history during the tenth century was the final settlement of the Northmen in that part of Neustria,[1] which received from them the name of Normandy.[2] In the year 911, during the reign of Charles the Simple, the Norman chief Rollo, who had made himself the terror of the West, ascended the Seine with a formidable fleet, and laid siege to Paris. After the purchase of a brief truce, Charles made him the tempting offer, to cede to him a vast province of France, in which he might establish himself on condition that he would abstain from ravaging the rest of the kingdom, acknowledge the sovereignty of the crown of France and, together with his followers, make a public profession of Christianity. The terms were accepted : a region that had been completely laid waste by the ravages of the Normans was now assigned to them for an inheritance ; and these ruthless warriors, abandoning a life of pillage and robbery, were soon converted, by the wise regulations of their chiefs, into peaceful tillers of the soil, and the best and bravest of the citizens of France. This remarkable event put an end to the war of Norman devastation, which, during a whole century, had depopulated western Germany, Gaul, and England.

9. Of the independent aristocracy of France, after the death of Charles the Simple, the most powerful were the counts of Paris, who during the last few reigns of the Carlovingian princes, exercised little less than regal authority. At length, in the year 987, on the death of Louis V., the fifth monarch after Charles the Simple, Hugh Capet, count of Paris, was proclaimed king by his assembled vassals, and anointed and crowned in the cathedral of Rheims,[3] by the archbishop of that city. The rest of France took no part in this election, and several provinces refused to acknowledge the successors of Hugh Capet, for three or four generations. The aristocracy still monopo

1. *Neustria.* On the death of Clovis A. D. 511, (see p. 255,) his four sons divided the Merovingian kingdom, embracing northern Gaul and Germany, into two parts, calling the eastern *Austrasia,* and the western *Neustria,*—the latter term being derived from the negative particle *e* "not," and *Austria :—Austrasia,* meaning the Eastern; and *Neustria* the Western monarchy *Neustria* embraced that portion of modern France north of the Loire and west of the Meuse .Map No. XIII.)

2. *Normandy* was an ancient province of France, adjoining Brittany on the north-east. (See *Map No. XIII.*) It became annexed to England through the accession of William, duke of Normandy, to the English throne, A. D. 1066. (See p. 290.) Philip Augustus wrested it from John, and united it to France, in 1203.

3. *Rheims,* a city of France ninety-five miles north-east from Paris, was a place of considerable importance under the Romans, who called it *Durocortorum.* It became a bishopric before the irruption of the Franks, and received many privileges from the Merovingian kings Map No. XIII.)

lised all the prerogatives of royalty; and the power of the nobles alone flourished or subsisted in the State.   The period of two hundred and forty years,—from the accession of Hugh Capet to that of Louis IX., or Saint Louis,—is described by Sismondi as " a long interregnum, during which the authority of king was extinct, although the name continued to exist."

II. The Feudal System, Chivalry, and the Crusades.—1. A glance at the state of Southern and Western Europe in the central period of the Middle Ages will show that, with the waning power, and final overthrow, of the Carlovingian dynasty, a new order of things had arisen; that kingdoms were broken into as many separate principalities as they contained powerful counts or barons; that regularly-constituted authority no longer existed; and that a numerous class of nobles, superior to all restraint, and involved in petty feuds with each other, oppressed their fellow subjects, and humbled or insulted their sovereigns, to whom they tendered an allegiance merely nominal.   The rude beginnings of this state of society may be traced back to the germinating of the first seeds of order after the spread of barbarism over the Roman world; its growth was checked under the first Carlovingians, who reduced the nobles to the lowest degradation; but with the decline of royal authority in France, Germany, and Italy, it started into new life and vigor, and, towards the end of the tenth century, became organised under the name of the *Feudal System*.   It maintained itself until I. THE about the end of the thirteenth century; and during the FEUDAL period of its existence is the prominent object that en- SYSTEM. gages the attention of the historian of the Middle Ages.   The unity of this portion of history will best be preserved by a brief historical outline of the system itself, and of the relations and events that grew out of it.

2 The people who overturned the empire of the Romans, made a partition of the conquered lands between themselves and the original possessors; but in what manner or by what principles the division was made cannot now be determined with certainty; nor can the exact condition in which the Roman provincials were left be ascertained, as the records of none of the barbarous nations of Europe extend back to this remote period.   It is, however, evident that the chiefs, or leaders of the conquering invaders, in order to maintain their acquisitions, annexed, to the apportionment of lands among

their followers, the condition that every freeman who received a share should appear in arms, when called upon, against the enemies of the community; and military service was probably at first the only condition of the allotment. The immediate grantees of lands from the leading chief, or king, were probably the most noted warriors who served under him; and these divided their ample estates among their more immediate followers or dependents, to be held of themselves by a similar tenure; so that the system extended, through several gradations, from the monarchs down through all the subordinates in authority. Each was bound to resort to the standard of his immediate grantor, and thence to that of his sovereign, with a band of armed followers proportioned, in numbers, to the extent of the territory which he had received.

3. The primary division of lands among the conquerors, was probably *allodial;* that is, they were to descend by inheritance from father to son; but in addition to the lands thus distributed among the nation, others were reserved to the crown for its support and dignity; and the greater portion of the latter, frequently extending to entire counties and dukedoms, were granted out, sometimes as hereditary estates, sometimes for life, sometimes for a term of years, and on various conditions, to favored subjects, and especially to the provincial governors, who made under-grants of them to their vassals or tenants. On the failure of the tenant to perform the stipulated conditions, whether of military service, or of certain rents and payments, the lands reverted to the grantors; and as the word *feud* signifies " an estate in trust," hence the propriety of calling this the *Feudal System.*

4. In a very imperfect state this system existed in France in the time of Charlemagne; but that monarch, jealous of the ascendancy which the nobles had already acquired, checked it by every means in his power,—by suffering many of the larger grants of dukedoms, counties, &c., to expire without renewal,—by removing the administration of justice from the hands of local officers into the hands of his own itinerant judges,—by elevating the ecclesiastical authority as a counterpoise to that of the nobility,—and by the creation of a standing army, which left the monarch in a measure independent of the military support of the great landholders. Thus the nobles, desisting from the use of arms, and abandoning the task of defending the kingdom, soon became unable to defend themselves; but when in the ninth and tenth centuries the royal authority was entire

ly prostrated, when the provinces were subject to frequent inroads of .the Normans and Hungarians, and government ceased to afford protection to any class of society, the proprietors of large estates found in their wealth a means of defence and security not within the reach of the great mass of the people. They converted their places of abode into impregnable castles, and covered their persons with kı ightly armor, jointed so as to allow a free movement of every par of the body; and this protection, added to the increased physical strength acquired by constant military exercises, gave them an im portance in war over hundreds of the plebeians by whom they were surrounded. In the confusion of the times, the governors of provinces, under the various titles of dukes, counts, and barons, usurped their governments as little sovereignties, and transmitted them by inheritance, subject only to the feudal superiority of the king.

5. Meanwhile the small allodial proprietors, or holders of lands in their own right, exposed to the depredating inroads of barbarians, or, more frequently, to the rapacity of the petty feudal lords, sunk into a condition much worse than that of the feudal tenantry. Exposed to a system of general rapine, without law to redress their injuries, and without the royal power to support their rights, they saw no safety but in making a compromise with oppression, and were reduced to the necessity of subjecting themselves, in return for protection, to the feudal lords of the country. During the tenth and eleventh centuries a large proportion of the allodial lands in France Germany, and Italy, were surrendered by their owners, and received back again upon feudal tenures; and it appears that the few who re tained their lands in their own right universally attached themselves to some lord, although in these cases it was the privilege of the freemen to choose their own superiors.

6. Such was the state of the great mass of European society when the feudal system had reached its maturity, in the tenth and eleventh centuries. Among the legal incidents and results that grew out of the feudal relation of service on the one side and protection on the other, were those of *reliefs*, or money paid to the lord by each vassal on taking a fief, or feudal estate, by inheritance; *fines*, on a change of tenancy; *escheats*, or forfeiture of the estate to the lord on account of the vassals delinquency, or for want of heirs; *aids*, or sums of money exacted by the lord on various occasions, such as the knighting of his eldest son, the marriage of his eldest daughter, or for the redemption of his person from prison; *wardship*, or the

privilege of guardianship of the tenant by the lord during the mi
nority of the former, with the use of the profits of his estate; *marriage*, or the right of a lord to tender a husband to his female wards
while under age, or to demand the forfeiture of the value of the
marriage. These feudal servitudes, which were unknown in the time
of Charlemagne, distinguish the maturity of the system, and show
the gradual encroachments of the strong upon the weak.

7. The feudal government, in its best state, was a system of op
pression, which destroyed all feelings of brotherhood and equality
between man and man: it was admirably calculated, when the nobles
were united, for defence against the assaults of any foreign power ;
but it possessed the feeblest bonds of political union, and contained
innumerable sources of anarchy, in the interminable feuds of rival
chieftains. It exerted a fatal influence on the character of society
in general ; while individual man, in the person of the lord or baron,
was doubtless improved by it; and the great mass of the population
of Europe, during the three or four centuries in which it was under
the thraldom of this system, was sunk in the most profound ignorance. Literature and science, confined almost wholly to the cloister,
could receive no favor in the midst of turbulence, oppression, and
rapine : judges and kings often could not write their own names :
many of the clergy did not understand the liturgy which they daily
recited : the Christianity of the times, " a dim taper which had need
of snuffing," degenerated into an illiberal superstition ; and everything combined to fix upon this period the distinctive epithet of the
DARK AGES. Still the sentiment of independence—the pride and
consciousness of power—and the feelings of personal consequence
and dignity with which the feudal state of society inspired the nobles,
contributed to let in those first rays of light and order which dispelled barbarism and anarchy, and introduced the virtues of a better
age.

8. In the midst of confusion and crime, while property was held
by the sword, and cruelty and injustive reigned supreme,
II. CHIVALRY.
the spirit of *chivalry* arose to turn back the tide of oppression, and to plant, in the very midst of barbarism, the seeds of
the most noble and the most generous principles. The precise time
at which chivalry was recognized as a military institution, with out
ward forms and ceremonials, cannot now be ascertained; but the
first notices we have of it trace it to that age when the disorders in
the feudal system had attained their utmost point of excess, towards

the close of the tenth century. It was then that some noble barons, filled with charitable zeal and religious enthusiasm, and moved with compassion for the wretchedness which they saw around them, combined together, under the solemnity of religious sanctions, with the holy purpose of protecting the weak from the oppression of the powerful, and of defending the right cause against the wrong.

9. The spirit and the institution of chivalry spread rapidly; treachery and hypocrisy became detestable; while courtesy, magnanimity, courage, and hospitality, became the virtues of the age; and the knights, who were ever ready to draw their swords, at whatever odds, in defence of innocence, received the adoration of the populace, and, in public opinion, were exalted even above kings themselves. The meed of praise and esteem gave fresh vigor and purity to the cause of chivalry; and under the influence of its spirit great deeds were done by the fraternity of valiant knights who had enrolled themselves as its champions. "The baron forsook his castle, and the peasant his hut, to maintain the honor of a family, or preserve the sacredness of a vow: it was this sentiment which made the poor serf patient in his toils, and serene in his sorrows: it enabled his master to brave all physical evils, and enjoy a sort of spiritual romance: it bound the peasant to his master, and the master to his king; and it was the principle of chivalry, above all others, that was needed to counteract the miseries of an infant state of civilization."[a]

10. Though in the practical exemplifications of chivalry there was often much of error, yet its spirit was based upon the most generous impulses of human nature. "To speak the truth, to succor the helpless and oppressed, and never to turn back from an enemy," was the first vow of the aspirant to the honors of chivalry. In an age of darkness and degradation, chivalry developed the character of woman, and, causing her virtues to be appreciated and honored, made her the equal companion of man, and the object of his devotion "The love of God and the ladies," says Hallam, "was enjoined as a single duty. He who was faithful and true to his mistress, was held sure of salvation in the theology of castles, though not of cloisters."[b] In the language of another modern writer, "chivalry gave purity to enthusiasm, crushed barbarous selfishness, taught the heart to expand like a flower to the sunshine, beautified glory with generosity, and smoothed even the rugged brow of war." A description of the

a. Introduction to Froissar.'s Chronicles.　　　b. Hallam's Middle Ages, p. 51ᵈ
a. James's Chrivalry and the Crusades, p. 31.

various customs and peculiarities of chivalry, as they grew up by de
grees into a regular institution, would be requisite to a full develop
ment of the character of the age, but we can only glance at these
topics here.   As chivalry was a military institution, its members
were taken wholly from the military class, which comprised none but
the descendants of the northern conquerors of the soil; for, with few
exceptions, the original inhabitants of the western Roman empire
had been reduced to the condition of serfs, or vassals, of their barbarian lords.

11. The initiation of the German youth to the profession of arms
had been, from the earliest ages, an occasion of solemnity; and when
the spirit of chivalry had established the order of knighthood, as
the concentration of all that was noble and valiant in a warlike age,
it became the highest object of every young man's ambition one day
to be a knight.   A long and tedious education, consisting of instruction in all manly and military exercises, and in the first principles of
religion, honor and courtesy, was requisite as a preparation for this
honor.   Next, the candidate for knighthood, after undergoing his
preparatory fasts and vigils, passed through the ceremonies which
made him a knight.   Armed and caparisoned he then sallied forth
in quest of adventure, displayed his powers at tournaments, and
often visited foreign countries, both for the purpose of jousting with
other knights, and for instruction in every sort of chivalrous knowledge.   It cannot be denied, however, that the practice of knight-
errantry, or that of wandering about armed, as the avowed champions of the right cause against the wrong, gave to the evil-minded
a very convenient cloak for the basest purposes, and that every adventure, whether just or not in its purpose, was too liable to be esteemed honorable in proportion as it was perilous.   But these were
abuses of chivalry, and perversions of its early spirit.

12. During the eleventh century we find that chivalry, although
probably first appearing in Gaul, had spread to all the surrounding
nations.   In Spain, the wars between the Christians and the Moors
exhibited a chivalric spirit unknown to former times: about this
period the institution of knighthood appears to have been introduced
among the Saxons of England; and it was first made known to the
Italians, in the beginning of the eleventh century, by a band of
knights from Normandy, whose religious zeal prompted them, as
they were returning from a pilgrimage to the Holy Land, to undertake the relief of a small town besieged by the Saracens.   As the

feudal system spread over Europe, chivalry followed in its path Its spirit, combined with religious enthusiasm, led to the crusades, and it was during the progress of those holy wars, which we now proceed to describe, that it attained its chief power and influence.

13. Pilgrimages to Jerusalem, and other hallowed localities in Palestine, had been common in the early ages of the church; and towards the close of the tenth century they had increased to a perfect inundation, in consequence of the terror that arose from the almost universal expectation then enter-tained, of the approaching end of the world.[a] III. ORIGIN OF THE CRUSADES. The idea originated in the interpretation given to the twelfth chapter of the Apocalypse, where it was announced that, after the lapse of a thousand years, Satan would be let loose to deceive the nations, and to gather them together to battle against the holy city, but that, after a little season, the army of the Deceiver should be destroyed by fire from heaven. But the dreaded epoch, the year 1000, passed by; yet the current of pilgrimage still continued to flow towards the East; for fanati cism had taken too strong hold of the minds of the people to be easily diverted from its course.

14. After Palestine had fallen into the possession of the Turks, about the middle of the seventh century, (see p. 249,) the pilgrims to Jerusalem were subjected to every species of extortion and out-rage from this wild race of Saracen conquerors; and the returning Christians spread through all the countries of Europe indignation and horror by the pathetic tales which they related, of the injuries and insults which they had suffered from the infidels. Among others, Peter the Hermit, a native of Amiens,[1] returning from a pil-grimage to Palestine, where he had spent much time in conferring with the Christians about the means of their deliverance, complained in loud terms of these grievances, and began to preach, in glowing language, the duty of the Christian world to unite in expelling the infidels from the patrimony of the Saviour.

15. The pope, Urban II., one of the most eloquent men of the age, engaged zealously in the project, and at two general councils,

---

1. *Amiens* is a fortified city of France in the ancient province of Picardy, seventy-two miles north from Paris. (*Map* No. XIII.)

a. The archives of European countries contain a great number of charters of the tenth century, beginning with these words: *Appropinquante fine mundi,*—"As the end of the world is approaching."—Sismondi's Roman Empire, ii. 256.

held at Placen' tia,[1] and Clermont,[2] and attended by a numer us train of bishops and ecclesiastics, and by thousands of the laity, the multitude, harangued by the zealous enthusiasts of the cause, caught the spirit of those who addressed them, and pledged themselves, and all they possessed, to the crusade against the infidel possessors of the Holy Land. The flame of enthusiasm spread so rapidly throughout Christian Europe, that although the council of Clermont was held in November of the year 1095, yet in the following spring large bands

IV. THE FIRST CRUSADE

of the crusaders, gathered chiefly from the refuse and dregs of the people, and consisting of men, women, and children—of all ages and professions—and of many and distinct languages,—were in motion toward Palestine.

16. Walter the Penniless, leading the way, was followed by Peter the Hermit; but the ignorant hordes which they directed, marching without order and discipline, and pillaging the countries which they traversed, were nearly all cut off before they reached Constantinople; and the few who passed over into Asia Minor fell an easy prey to the swords of the Turks. Immense bands that followed these hosts, mingling the motives of plunder, licentiousness and vice, with a foul spirit of fanatical cruelty, which proclaimed the duty of exter minating all, whether Jews or Pagans, who rejected the Saviour, were utterly destroyed by the enraged natives of southern Germany and Hungary, through whose dominions they attempted to pass. The loss of the crusaders in this first adventure is estimated at three hundred thousand men.[a] But while these undisciplined and barbarous multitudes were hurrying to destruction, the flower of the chivalry of Europe was collecting—the genuine army of the crusade— under six as distinguished chiefs as knighthood could boast, headed by Godfrey of Bouillon,[3] one of the most celebrated generals of the age. In six separate bands they proceeded to Constantinople, some

1. *Placen' tia*, now *Piazenza*, was a city of northern Italy, near the junction of the Trebia with the Po, thirty-seven miles south-east from Milan. When colonized by the Romans, 218 . C., it was a strong and important city; and it afforded them a secure retreat after the unfor tunate battles of Ticinus and Treb' bia. (*Map* No. XVII.)

2. *Clermont*, a city of France, in the ancient province of Auvergne, is eighty-two miles west from Lyons, and two hundred and eight south from Paris. (*Map* No. XIII.)

3. *Bouillon* was a small, woody, and mountainous district, nine miles wide and eighteen long, now included in the duchy of Luxembourg, on the borders of France and Belgium The town of Bouillon is fifty-miles north-west from the city of Luxembourg. Bouillon, when in the possession of Godfrey, was a dukedom. In order to supply himself with funds for his expedition to the Holy Land, Godfrey, who was likewise duke of Lower Lorraine, (note p. 270,) mortgaged Bouillon to the bishop. (*Map* No. XIII.)

a Gibbon, iv. 16–125.

by way of Italy and the Adriat'ic, and others by way of the Danube
but their conduct, unlike that of the first crusaders, was in general
remarkable for its strict discipline, order, and moderation.

17. Alex'ius, the Greek emperor of Constantinople, had before
craved, in abject terms, assistance against the infidel Turks; but
now, when the Turks, occupied with other interests, no longer menaced his frontier, his conduct changed, and alarmed by the vast
swarms of crusaders who crossed his dominions, he strove, by treach
ery and dissimulation, and even by hostile annoyances, to diminish
their numbers, and thwart their designs, and to wring from their
chiefs acts of homage to his own person. With some of the chiefs,
the crafty Greek succeeded; but others spurned his proposals with
indignation, and at the hazard of war resolved to maintain their in
dependent position; and when at length the several detachments of
the army of the crusaders passed into Asia, they left behind them
in their treacherous auxiliaries, the Christians of the Byzantine empire, worse enemies than they had to encounter in the Turks.

18. It is said that after the crusaders had united their forces in
Asia Minor, and had been joined by the remains of the multitude that
had followed Peter the Hermit, the number of their fighting men,
without including those who did not carry arms, was six hundred
thousand, and that, of these, the number of knights alone was two
hundred thousand.[a] At Nice,[1] in Bithyn'ia,[2] the capital of the
Sultany of Róum,[3] they first encountered the Turks, and after a siege
of two months compelled the city to surrender, in spite of the efforts
of the Sultan, Soliman, for its relief. (A. D. 1097.) From Nice
they set out for Syria; and after having gained a victory over Soliman near Dorilæ'um,[4] in a march of five hundred miles they trav
ersed Lesser Asia, through a wasted land and deserted towns, without
finding a friend or an enemy.

19. The siege of Antioch, unparalleled for its difficulties and the

---

.. *Nice*, called by the Romans *Nicæ a*, was the capital of Bithyn'ia. The Tuikish town of
Is-nik occup'es the site of the Bithyn'ian city. (*Map* No. IV.)

2. *Bithyn'ia* was a country of Asia Minor, having the Euxine on the north, and the Propontis and Mysia on the west. (*Map* No. IV.)

3. *Róum* (meaning *the kingdom of the Romans*), was the name given by Soliman sultan of
the Turks, to the present *Natólis*, (the western part of Asia Minor,) when he invaded and
became master of it in the 11th century.

4. *Dorilæ'um* was a city of Phrygia, on the confines of Bithyn'ia. The plain of Dorilæ'um
is often mentioned in history as the place where the armies of the Eastern empire assembled
in their wars against the Turks. (*Map* No. IV.)

a. James's History of the Crusades, p. 111

losses on both sides, was the next obstacle to the onward march of the crusaders, now reduced to half the number that had been collected at the capture of Nice; but when the enterprise seemed hopeless, the town was betrayed into their hands by a Syrian renegado, (June 1098.) A few days later, the victors themselves, suffering the extremity of privation and famine, were encompassed by a splendid Turkish and Persian army of three hundred thousand men; yet the Christians collecting the relics of their strength, and urged on by a belief of miraculous interposition in their favor, sallied from the town, and in a single memorable day annihilated or dispersed the host of their enemies.

20. While the siege of Antioch was progressing, the Turkish princes consumed their time and resources in civil wars beyond the Tigris; and the caliph of Egypt, embracing the opportunity of weakness and discord to recover his ancient possessions, besieged and took Jerusalem. The Egyptian monarch offered to join his arms to those of the Christians, for the purpose of subduing all Palestine; but it was evident that he purposed to enjoy the fruits of victory without participation; and the answer of the crusading chiefs was firm and uniform: "the usurper of Jerusalem, of whatever nation, was their enemy, and they would conquer the holy city with the sword of Christ, and keep it with the same."

21. With an army reduced to less than fifty thousand armed men, the crusaders, in the month of May, 1099, proceeded from Antioch towards Jerusalem. Marching between Mount Lib' anus[1] and the sea-shore, they obtained by treaty a free passage through the petty Turkish principalities of Trip' oli,[2] Sidon, Tyre,[3] Acre,[4] and Cæsaréa,[5]

1. To the four chains of mountains running parallel to the sea-coast through northern Syria or Palestine, the name *Lit' anus* has been applied. To a chain farther east the Greeks gave the name *Anti-Lib' anus*. (*Map* No. VI.)

2. *Trip' oli*, at this day one of the neatest towns of Syria, is a seaport, seventy-five miles north-west from Damascus. It was one of the most flourishing seats of ancient literature, and contained an extensive library, numbering, it is said, one hundred thousand volumes, which was destroyed by the crusaders in the year 1106. On this occasion the crusaders displayed the same fanatical zeal of which the Saracens have been accused, though some think unjustly, in the case of the Alexandrian library. A priest having visited an apartment in the library in which were several copies of the Koran, reported that it contained none but impious works of Mahomet; and the whole was forthwith committed to the flames. (*Map* No. VI.)

3. *Tyre* and *Sidon*, see p. 61, and *Map* No. VI.

4. *Acre* is a town of Syria on the coast of the Mediterranean, at the north-eastern limit of the bay of Acre. Mount Carmel terminates on the south-western side of the bay. This town is rendered famous in modern history by its determined and successful resistance to the arms of Napoleon in 1799. See p. 471. (*Map* No. VI.)

5. *Cæsaréa* was an ancient Roman town on the sea-coast of Palestine, thirty miles south-west from Acre. It was a flourishing city till A. D. 635, when it fell into the hands of the Saracens

which promised to remain, for the time, neutral, and to follow the example of the capital. When at length the holy city broke upon the view of the Christian host, a sudden enthusiasm of joy filled every bosom; past dangers, fatigues, and privations, were forgotten; the name Jerusalem was echoed by every tongue; and while some shouted to the sky, some knelt and prayed, some wept aloud, and some cast themselves down and kissed the earth in silence. But to the excess of rejoicing succeeded the extreme of wrath at seeing the city in the hands of the infidels; and in the first ebullition of rage, a simultaneous attack was commenced on the town; but a vigorous repulse taught the necessity of more judicious methods of assault.

22. Passing over the details of the siege which followed, it is sufficient to state, that, within forty days, Jerusalem was taken by a desperate assault, and that the blood of seventy thousand Moslems washed the pavements of the captured city; for the soldiers of the cross believed that they were doing God good service in exterminat ing the blasphemous strangers; and that all mercy to the infidels was an injury to religion. When the bloody strife was over, the leaders and soldiers, washing the marks of gore from their persons, and casting off their armor, in the guise of penitents and amid the loud anthems of the clergy, ascended the Hill of Calvary[1] on their knees, and proceeding to the holy sepulchre, with tears of joy kissed the stone which had covered the Saviour, and then offered up their prayers to the mild Teacher of that beautiful religion whose principles are "peace and good will to men." Peter the Hermit, whose preaching had excited the crusade, had followed the army through all its perils; and when he entered the city with the conquerors, the Christians of Jerusalem recognized the poor pilgrim who had first spoken to them words of hope, and promised them deliverance from the oppression of their Turkish masters. The reception which he now met with from the enthusiastic multitude, who in the fervor of their gratitude attributed all to him, and casting themselves at his feet, invoked the blessings of heaven on their benefactor, more than a thousand fold repaid the Hermit for all the anxiety, the toils, and dangers, which he had endured. The ultimate fate of this extraor dinary individual is unknown.

In 1101 it fell into the hands of the crusaders, when it sunk to rise no more. Cæsarea was the place where Peter converted Cornelius and his house, (Acts, x. 1,) and where Paul made his memorable speeches to Felix and Agrippa. (Acts, xxiv., xxv., xxvi.)

1. *Hill of Calvary.* See description of Jerusalem p. 164, and *Map* No VII.)

23. Jerusalem was now delivered from the hands of the infidels the great object of the expedition was accomplished; and the feudal institutions of Europe were introduced into Palestine in all their purity. Godfrey of Bouillon was chosen the first sovereign of Jerusalem; and the Christian kingdom thus established continued to exist nearly a century. Several minor States were established in the East by the crusaders, but as they seldom united cordially for mutual defence, and were continually assailed by powerful enemies, one of them were of long duration. Even during the sovereignty of Godfrey, the kingdom of Jerusalem, owing to the return of many of the crusaders, and their losses in battle, was left for a time to be supported by an army of less than three thousand men. But the spirit of pilgrimage was still rife; and it is estimated that, between the first and second crusade, five hundred thousand people set out from Europe for Syria, in armed bands of several thousand men each; and although the greater portion of them perished by the way, the few who reached their destination proved exceedingly serviceable in supporting the Christian cause, and in re-peopleing the devastated lands of Palestine. The period between the first and second crusade is remarkable for the rise, at Jerusalem, of the two most distinguished orders of knighthood—the Hospitallers, and the Red-Cross Knights, or Templars. The valor of both orders became noted: the Hospitallers ever burned a light during the night, that they might always be prepared against the enemy; and it is said that any Templar, on hearing the cry " to arms," would have been ashamed to ask the number of the enemy. The only question was, " where are they?"

24. During nearly two centuries after the council of Clermont, each returning year witnessed a new emigration of pilgrim warriors for the defence of the Holy Land, although but six principal crusades followed the first great movement; and all these were excited by some recent or impending calamity to Palestine. A detailed account of these several crusades would only exhibit the perpetual recurrence of the same causes and effects; and would appear but so many faint and unsuccessful copies of the original. Avoiding detail, we shall therefore speak of them only in general terms.

25. Forty-eight years after the conquest of Jerusalem, the loss of the principal Christian fortresses in Palestine led to a second crusade, which was undertaken by Conrad III., emperor of Germany, and Louis VII., king of France (A. D. 1147.) The Pope Eugenius abetted the design, and com

V. THE SECOND CRUSADE.

missioned the eloquent St. Bernard to preach the cross through France and Germany. A vast army under Conrad took the lead in the expedition; but not a tenth part ever reached the Syrian boundaries. The army of French and Germans was but little more fortunate; and the poor remains of these mighty hosts, still led by the emperors of France and Germany, after reaching Jerusalem, joined the Christian arms in a fruitless siege of Damascus, which was the termination of the second crusade.

26. Forty years after the second crusade, Jerusalem was taken b Saladin, the Sultan of Egypt, whose authority was acknowledged also by the greater part of Syria and Persia. (A. D. 1187.) The loss of the holy city filled all Europe with consternation; and new expeditions were fitted out for its recovery. France, Germany, and England, joined in the crusade; and the armies of each country were headed by their respective sovereigns, Philip Augustus, Frederic Barbarossa, and Richard I., surnamed the lion-hearted. Frederic, after defeating the Saracens in a pitched battle on the plains of Asia Minor, lost his life by imprudently bathing in the river Orontes;[a] and his army was reduced to a small body when it reached Antioch. The French and English, more successful than the Germans, besieged and took Acre, after a siege of twenty-two months (July, A. D. 1191); but as Richard and Philip quarrelled, owing to the latter's jealousy of the superior military prowess of the former, Philip returned home in disgust · and Richard, after defeating Saladin in a great battle near Ascalon, and penetrating within sight of Jerusalem, concluded a three years truce with his rival, and then set sail for his own dominions. (A. D Oct. 1192.)

VI. THE THIRD CRUSADE.

27. The fourth crusade[b] was undertaken at the beginning of th. thirteenth century, (A. D. 1202,) at the instigation of pope Innocent III. No great sovereign joined in the enterprise; but the most powerful barons of France

VII. THE FOURTH CRUSADE

1. *Ascalon*, a very ancient city of the Philistines, was a sea-port town of the Mediterranean. forty-five miles south-west from Jerusalem. Its ruins present a strange mixture of Syrian, Greek, Gothic, and Roman remains. There is not a single inhabitant within the old walls, which are still standing. The prophecy of Zechariah, "Ascalon shall not be inhabited," and that of Ezekiel, "It shall be a desolation," are now actually fulfilled. (*Map* No. VI.)

a. Some authorities say the Cydnus. See James's Chivalry and the Crusades, p. 239.

b. Several important expeditions that were made to the Holy Land a short time previous to this, and that were promoted by the exhortations of pope Celestine III., are represented by some writers as the fourth crusade. In this way some writers enumerate nine distinct crusades some more, while others describe only six

took the cross, and gave the command to Boniface, marquis of Montserrat.[1] They hired the Venetians to transport them to Palestine, and agreed to recapture for them the city of Zara,[2] in Dalmátia; and this object was accomplished, while the pope in vain launched the thunders of the church at the refractory crusaders. Instead of sailing to Palestine, the expedition was then directed against the Greek empire, under the pretence of dethroning a usurper; and the result was the conquest of Constantinople by the Latins, and the founding of a new Latin or Roman empire on the ruins of the Byzantine. (A. D. April 1204.) The new empire existed during a period of fifty-seven years, when the Greeks partially recovered their authority. The fourth crusade ended without producing any benefit to Palestine.

28. The fifth crusade, undertaken fourteen years after the fall of the Byzantine empire, was at first conducted by Andrew, monarch of Hungary. The Christian army, after spending some time in the vicinity of Acre, sailed to Egypt;

VIII. THE
FIFTH
CRUSADE.

but after some successes, among which was the taking of Damietta,[3] ultimate ruin was the issue of the expedition. A few years later, (A. D. 1228), Frederic II., emperor of Germany, then arrayed in open hostility with the pope, led a formidable army to Palestine, and after he had advanced some distance from Acre towards Jerusalem concluded a treaty with the sultan Melek Kamel, whereby the holy city and the greater part of Palestine were yielded to the Christians After the return of Frederic to Europe, new bands of crusaders proceeded to Palestine: the sultan Kamel retook Jerusalem, but the Christians again obtained it by treaty.

29. While these events had been passing in Palestine a new dynasty had arisen in the north of Asia, which for a time threatened a complete revolution of all the known countries of the world. In the early part of the thirteenth century Gengis Khan, the son of a petty Mongol prince, had raised himself to be the lord of all the pastoral nations throughout the vast plains of Tartary. After desolating China,[4] and adding its five

IX. TARTAR
CONQUESTS.

1. *Montserrat* was an Italian marquisate in western Lombardy, now included in Piedmont The marquises of Montserrat, rising from small beginnings in the course of the tenth century and gradually extending their territories, acted, during the twelfth and thirteenth centuries one of the most brilliant parts alloted to any reigning house in Europe.

2. *Zara*, still the capital of Dalmátia, is a seaport on the eastern coast of the Adriatic, one hundred and fifty miles south-east from Venice.

3. *Damietta* is on the Damietta, or principal eastern branch of the Nile, six miles from its mouth

4. *China*, a vast country of eastern Asia, may be almost said to have no history of any im

northern provinces to his empire, at the head of seven hundred thousand warriors[a] he invaded and overran the dominions of the sultan
of Persia.   His successor Octai directed his resistless arms westward, under the conduct of his general Baton, who, in the course of
six years, led his warriors, in a conquering march, from east to west,
over a fourth part of the circumference of the globe.   The inun-
dating torrent, passing north of the territories of the Byzantine empire, left them unharmed; but it rolled with all its fury upon the
more barbarous nations of Europe.   A great part of Russia[1] was
desolated; and both Kiev[2] and Moscow,[3] the ancient and modern
capital, were reduced to ashes: the Tartars penetrated into the heart
of Poland,[4] and as far as the borders of Germany, whence they
turned to the south and spread over the plains of Hungary.   Already
the remote nations of the Baltic trembled at the approach of these
barbarian warriors; and Germany, France, England, and Italy, were
on the point of arming in the common defence of christendom, when
Baton and the five hundred thousand warriors who still accompanied
him were recalled to Asia by the death of their sovereign.   (A. D.
1245.)

30. Among the many tribes and nations that had been driven from
their original seats by the great Tartar inundation, were the Corasmins, embracing numerous hordes of Tartar origin, that had attached
themselves to the fortunes of the sultan of Persia.   They now precipitated themselves upon Syria and Palestine, and massacred indis-

terest to the general reader, it has so few revolutions or political changes to record. The
authentic history of the Chinese begins with the compilations of Confucius, who was born
B. C. 550. From that period the annals of the empire have been carefully noted and preserved
in an unbroken line to the present day—forming a series of more than five hundred volumes
of uninteresting chronological details.

1. *Russia*, the largest, and one of the most powerful empires, either of ancient or modern
times, extends from Behring's straits and the Pacific on the east, to the Gulf of Bothnia on the
west,—a distance of nearly six thousand miles, with an average breadth of about fifteen hundred miles. In this immense empire about *forty* distinct languages are in use, having attached
to them a great number of different dialects. In the year 1535 the extent of the Russian dominions was estimated at thirty-seven thousand German square miles; but in the year 1850 it
had increased to ten times that amount. (For early history of Russia see p. 309.)

2. *Kiev*, or *Kiow*, the capital of the modern Russian province of the same name, is on the
Dnieper, two hundred and twenty miles north of Odes' sa, the nearest port on the Black Sea.
Kiev was the former residence of the grand dukes of Russia—the earliest seat of the Christian
religion in Russia—and for a considerable period the capital of the empire. (*Map* No. XVII.)

3. *Moscow*, still one of the capitals of the Russian empire, and the grand entrepôt of its internal commerce, is situated on the navigable river Moskwa, a branch of the Volga, four hundred miles south-east from St. Petersburg. It was founded in the year 1147. (*Map* No. XII.)

4. *Poland*, see p. 311.

a. Gibbon, iv 251.

criminately Turks, Jews, and Christians who opposed them. Jeru salem was taken; and it is said every soul in it was put to the sword; but at length the Turks and Christians, uniting their forces, utterly defeated the Corasmins, and thus delivered Palestine from one of the most terrible scourges that had ever been inflicted on it.

31. The ravages of the Corasmins in Palestine called forth the sixth crusade, which was led by Louis IX., king of France, commonly called St. Louis. He began by an attack on Egypt; but after some successes he was de fiated, made prisoner when enfeebled by disease, and forced to purchase his liberty by the payment of an immense ransom. (A. D 1250.) Twenty years later St. Louis embarked on a second crusade—the last of those great movements for the redemption of the Holy Land. The fleet of Louis being driven by a storm into Sar dinia, here a change of plans took place, and it was resolved to attack the Moors of Africa. The French landed near Carthage, and took the city; but a pestilence soon carried off Louis and the greater portion of his army, when the expedition was abandoned.

X. THE SIXTH CRUSADE.

32. From this time the fate of the Eastern Christians grew daily more certain; and in the year 1291 a Turkish army of two hundred thousand men appeared before the walls of Acre, the last strong hold of the crusaders in Palestine. After a tedious siege the city was taken; and thus the last vestige of the Christian power in Syria was swept away. The crusades had occupied a period of nearly two centuries, and had led two millions of Europeans to find their graves in Eastern lands; and yet none of the objects of these expeditions had been accomplished;—a sad commentary upon the folly and fanaticism of the age. The effects of these holy wars upon the state of European society will be referred to in a subsequent chapter.[a]

III ENGLISH HISTORY.—1. Our last reference to the history of England was to that period rendered brilliant by the reign of Alfred the Great, the real founder of the English monarchy; and we now proceed to give a brief but connected outline of the continuation of English history during the central period of the Middle Ages, which has just passed in review before us.

I. ENGLAND AFTER THE DEATH OF ALFRED.

2. After the death of Alfred, in the first year of the tenth century, (A. D. 901,) England, still a prey to the ravages of the Danes,

a. See Part II. ch. ix. of the University Edition

and intestine disorder, relapsed into confusion and barbarism; and under a succession of eight sovereigns,[a] from the time of Alfred, its history presents little that is important to the modern reader. During the reign of Ethelred II., the last of these rulers, the Danes and Norwegians, led by Sweyn king of Denmark,[1] acquired possession of the greater portion of the kingdom; and on several occasions Ethelred purchased a momentary respite from their rav ages by large bribes, which only increased their avidity, and insured their return. At length the weak and cruel monarch ordered the massacre of all the Danes in the Saxon territories. (A. D. 1002.) The execution of the barbarous mandate occasioned the renewal of hostilities: the English nobles, in contempt of their sovereign, of fered the crown to Sweyn; while Ethelred fled for refuge to the court of Richard, duke of Normandy, whose sister he had married. On the death of Sweyn, in the year 1014, the Danish army in Eng land chose his son Canute to succeed him; while the Saxon chiefs, with their wonted inconstancy, recalled Ethelred. On the death of the latter, his son Edmund, surnamed Ironside, from his hardihood and valor, was chosen king by the English; but by his death, (A. D. 1016,) after a few months, Canute, in accordance with a previous treaty, was left in undisturbed possession of the whole of England.

3. Canute, surnamed the Great, proved to be the most powerful monarch of the age. By marrying Emma, the widow of Ethelred, he conciliated the vanquished Britons, and disarmed the hostility of the duke of Normandy; while the earl of Godwin, the most powerful of the English barons, was gained to his interests, by receiving the hand of the king's daughter. In the year 1025 he subdued Sweden, and Norway[2] two years later, and on his death (Nov. 1036) he left his vast possessions of Denmark, Sweden, Norway, and Eng land, to be divided among his children His administration of the government of England was at first harsh, but he gradually emerged from his original barbarism, embraced Christianity, encouraged liter ature, and adopted some wise institutions for the benefit of his Anglo Saxon subjects.

4. After the death of Canute, two of his sons, Harold and Hardi canute, reigned in succession over England; after which, in 1041,

---

1. *Denmark, Sweden,* and *Norway;*—see p. 308.
2. *Sweden* and *Norway.* See *Denmark,* p. 308.

a. Edward I. the Elder, 901. Athelstan, 925. Edmund I., 941. Edred, 946. Edwy, 955. Edgar, 959. Edward II., the Martyr, 975. Ethelred II., 978 the crown returned to the ancient Saxon family, in the person of Edward the Confessor, a younger son of Ethelred. The mild character of Edward endeared him to his Saxon subjects, notwithstanding the partiality which he showed to his Norman favorites; but his reign of twenty-five years was weak and inglorious, and it was disturbed by the rebellion of the earl of Godwin, by occasional hostilities with the Welsh and Scotch, and by intrigues for the succession. On his death, (1066,) Harold, son of Godwin, took possession of the throne; but scarcely had he overcome his brother Tostig, who disputed the supremacy with him, when he found a more formidable competitor in William, duke of Normandy, to whom the late king had either bequeathed or purposed the succession. On the 25th of September, 1066, Harold gained a great victory over his brother; but three days later, William landed in Sussex,[1] at the head of sixty thousand men, and on the fourteenth of October fought

'1. NORMAN CONQUESTS. with Harold the bloody battle of Hastings,[2] which terminated the Saxon dynasty, and put William the Norman in possession of the throne of England. Harold was killed in battle; the English army was nearly destroyed, and a fourth part of the Normans slain. The victory gave to William the title of the Conqueror; and the subjugation of the realm by him is termed, in English history, the Norman conquest.

5. This conquest, however, was gradual, for the immediate results of the battle of Hastings gave to William less than a fourth part of the kingdom; and his wars for the subjugation of the West, the North, and the East, were protracted during a period of seven years. William treated the English as rebels for appearing in the field against him, and distributed their lands among his Norman followers. To this distribution, the titles and revenues of many of the English nobility owe their origin.[a] The northern Saxons made a vigorous resistance, and William treated them with a severity in proportion to the valor and pertinacity of their defence—laying waste the country with fire and sword, until, in some countries, the danger of rebellion was removed by a total dearth of inhabitants.

---

[1] is a southern county of England, on the English channel, west of Kent.

[2] Hastings, now a town of ten thousand inhabitants, is fifty-four miles south-east from London. It is pleasantly situated in a vale, surrounded on every side, except toward the sea by hills and cliffs. On a hill east of the town are still to be seen banks and trenches, supposed to have been the work of the Normans at the time of the invasion. (Map No. XVI.)

a. See Notes, *Warwick, Richmond, &c.,* p. 306.

6. The foundations of the feudal system had existed in England before the conquest; but the distribution of the conquered lands among the Norman followers of William, gave that prince the opportunity of fully establishing the system as it then existed, in its maturity, on the continent. Preparatory to the introduction of the feudal tenures, William caused a survey to be made of all the lands in the kingdom,—the particulars of which were inserted in what is called the Doomsday Book, or Book of Judgment, which is still in being. Under the iron rule of the conqueror the Anglo Saxons became vassals of their Norman lords; the name *Saxon* was made a term of reproach; and the Saxon language was regarded as barbarous; while the Norman-French idiom was employed in all the acts of administration.

7. On the death of William, in the year 1087, his second son, William Rufus, took possession of the throne, to the prejudice of his elder brother Robert, then absent in Normandy. His reign, and that of his brother and successor, Henry I., are distinguished by few events of importance; but both plundered the kingdom: an ancient Saxon chronicle says that the former was " loathed by nearly all his people, and odious to God;" and of the latter it is said that "justice was in his hands a source of revenue, and judicial murder a frequent instrument of extortion."

8. Henry had married a Saxon princess; and to his daughter Matilda, by this marriage, he designed to leave the crown; but his nephew Stephen defeated his intentions by immediately seizing the vacant throne on the death of Henry. (1135.) A long civil war that followed was terminated by a general council of the kingdom which adopted Henry Plantagenet,[1] Matilda's son, as the successor of Stephen. One year later the boisterous life and wretched reign of Stephen were brought to a close, when Henry II., the first of the Plantagenet dynasty, ascended the throne of England. (A. D. 1154.)

9. By inheritance and marriage, Henry possessed, in addition to the duchy of Normandy, the fairest provinces of north-western

[1. *Plantagenet* is the surname of the kings of England from Henry II. to Richard III. inclusive. Antiquarians are much at a loss to account for the origin of this name; and the best derivation they can find for it is, that Fulk, the first earl of Anjou of that name, being stung with remorse for some wicked action, went in pilgrimage to Jerusalem as a work of atonement; where, being soundly scourged with broom twigs, which grew plentifully on the spot, he ever after took the surname of *Plantagenet*, or *broomstalk*, which was retained by his noble posterity. (Encyclopedia.)

France; and these, in connection with his English dominions, ren
III. REDUC- dered him one of the most powerful monarchs in chris
TION OF tendom. He also reduced Ireland[1] to a state of subjec
IRELAND. tion, and formally annexed it to the English crown, al·
though the complete conquest of that country was not effected until
nearly four centuries later. By a wise and impartial administration
of the government, Henry gained the affections of his people; but he
was long engaged in a kind of spiritual warfare with the pope, and
the close of his life was clouded by domestic misfortunes. His sons,
instigated by their mother, and aided by Louis VII., king of France,
repeatedly rebelled against him; and he finally died of a broken
heart, after a long reign of thirty-five years. (A. D. 1189.)

10. Henry was succeeded by his eldest son Richard, surnamed
the Lion-hearted, who immediately on his accession, after plundering
his subjects of an immense sum of money, embarked on a crusade
to the Holy Land. After filling the world with his renown, being
wrecked in his homeward voyage, and travelling in disguise through
Germany, he was seized and imprisoned, and only obtained his lib
erty by an immense ransom, which was paid by his subjects. The

1. *Ireland* is a large island west of England, from which it is separated by the Irish Sea and
St. George's Channel. Its divisions, best known in history, are the four great provinces, Ulster
in the north, Leinster in the east, Connaught in the west, and Munster in the south.
Irish historians speak of Greek, Phœnician, Scotch, Spanish, and Gaulic colonies in Ireland,
before the Christian era; for which, however, there is no historical foundation. The oldest
authentic Irish records were written between the tenth and twelfth centuries; but some of
them go back, with some consistency, as far as the Christian era. The early inhabitants of
Ireland were evidently more barbarous than even those of Britain. In the fifth century Christi
anity was introduced among them by St. Patrick, a native of North Britain, who in his youth
had been carried a captive into Ireland; but the new faith did not flourish until a century or
two later; and it appears that, even then, the learning of the Irish clergy did not extend beyond the walls of the monasteries. In the ninth and tenth centuries the Danes made themselves masters of the greater part of the coasts of the island, while the interior, divided among
a number of barbarous and hostile chiefs, was agitated by internal wars, which no sense of
common dangers could interrupt. In the early part of the eleventh century, Brian Boru, king
of Munster, united the greater part of the island under his sceptre, and expelled the Danes;
but soon after his death, A. D. 1014, the kingdom was again divided; and sanguinary war
continued to rage between opposing princes until the invasion by Henry II. of England, in the
year 1169. So early as 1155 Henry had projected the conquest of Ireland, and had obtained
from pope Adrian IV. full permission to invade and subdue the Irish, for the purpose of reforming them. The grant was accompanied by a stipulation for the payment to St. Peter, of a
penny annually from every house in Ireland,—this being the price for which the independence
of the Irish people was coolly bartered away. Henry, however, conquered only the four
counties Dublin, Meath, Louth, and Kildare, being a part of Leinster, on the eastern coast
In 1315 Edward Bruce, brother of the king of Scotland, being invited over by the Irish, landed
in Ireland, and caused himself to be proclaimed king; but not being well supported, he was
finally defeated and killed in the battle of Dundalk, in the year 1318, after which the Scotch
forces were withdrawn. It was not until the time of Cromwell that English supremacy was
fully established in every part of the island. (*Map* No. XVL)

reign of this famous knight is chiefly signalized by his deeds in Palestine, and is of little importance in English history.

11. Richard was succeeded by his profligate brother John, surnamed Lackland. (A. D. 1199.) In a long struggle with Philip Augustus of France, John lost most of his continental possessions: by stripping the church of its treasures he made the pope his enemy; and after a vain attempt to brave the storm of his vengeance, he made a cowardly submission, swore allegiance to the pope, and agreed to hold his kingdom tributary to the holy see. The barons, provoked by the tyranny and vices of their sovereign, next took up arms against him: they received with indignation the pope's declaration in favor of his vassal,—took possession of London,—and finally compelled the king to yield to their demands, and to sign the *Magna Charta*, or Great Charter of rights and liberties, which laid the first permanent foundation of British freedom.[a] John attempted to annul the conditions imposed, and, being absolved by the pope from the oath which he had taken to the barons, he collected an army of mercenary soldiers from Germany, and proceeded to lay waste the kingdom; but the barons proffered the crown to Louis, the eldest son of the French monarch, who came over with a large army to enforce his claims, when the sudden death of John arrested impending dangers, and prevented England from becoming a province of France.

12. On the death of John, his eldest son, Henry III., then in the tenth year of his age, was acknowledged king by the nobility and the people. Henry was a weak and fickle sovereign; and during his long reign of more than half a century, the country was agitated by internal commotions, caused by the king's prodigality, favoritism, oppressive exactions, and continual violation of the people's rights in direct opposition to the principles of the Great Charter. Again the barons resisted, and called a parliament, when the king was virtually deposed. (A. D. 1258.) An attempt to regain his authority led to all the horrors of civil war. In another parliament, called by the barons, (A. D. 1265,) and embracing delegates from the counties, cities, and boroughs, we find the first germs of popular representation in England; and although, eventually, the baronial party, whose tyranny was found scarcely less than that of the king, was overthrown, yet their incautious innovation had already laid the basis of the future House of Commons.

a. The Great Charter was signed on the 19th of June, 1215, at Runnymede, on the Thames, between Staines and Windsor.

13. Henry was succeeded by his son, Edward I., who, at the time of his father's death, was absent on the last crusade to the Holy Land. (A. D. 1272.) The active and splendid reign of this prince, who left behind him the character of a great statesman and commander, was mostly occupied with the attempt to unite the whole of Great Britain under one sovereignty. When Llewellyn, prince of

IV. SUBJU-
GATION OF
WALES.

Wales,[1] refused to perform the customary homage to the English crown, Edward declared war against him, overran the country, and subdued it, after a brave resistance (1277—1283.)

14. The remainder of Edward's reign was filled with attempts to subjugate Scotland, to which country the English monarch laid claim as lord paramount, by the rights of fealty and succession. A Scotch king, taken prisoner by Henry II., had been compelled, as the price of his release, to do homage for his crown; and the same had been demanded of later princes, in return for lands which they held in England. By the death of Alexander III. of Scotland, in the year 1283, the crown devolved on his grand daughter the princess Margaret, who was a niece of Edward I. of England. This lady was soon after affianced to Edward's only son, the prince of Wales; and thus the prospect of uniting the crowns of the two kingdoms seemed near at hand, when the frail bond of union was suddenly destroyed by the untimely death of the princess.

15. The two principal Scotch competitors for the crown were now John Baliol and Robert Bruce, who agreed to submit their claims to the decision of Edward. The latter decided in favor of Baliol, on condition of his becoming a vassal of the English king. (A. D. 1292.)

---

1. *Wales*, anciently called *Cambria*, a principality in the west of Great Britain, having on the north and west the Irish Sea, and on the south and south-west Bristol Channel, is about one hundred and fifty miles in length from north to south, and from fifty to eighty in breadth. The Welsh are descendants of the ancient Britons, who, being driven out of England by the Anglo Saxons, took refuge in the mountain fastnesses of Wales, or fled to the continent of Europe, where they gave their name to Brittany. In the ninth century Wales was divided into three sovereignties, North Wales, South Wales, and the intermediate district called Powis,—the reigning princes of which were held together by some loose ties of confederacy. In the year 933 the English king Athelstan compelled the Welsh principalities to become his tributaries; and upon the treaty then concluded with them, founded on the feudal relation of lord and vassal, the Normans based their claim of lordship paramount over all Wales. During the eleventh and twelfth centuries, South Wales was the scene of frequent contests between the Welsh and Normans. When Edward I. claimed feudal homage of Llewellyn, the duty of fealty was acknowledged by the latter; but he was unwilling, by going to London, to place himself in the power of a monarch who had recently violated a solemn treaty with him; and hence arose a war which resulted in the death of Llewellyn, and the subjugation of his country. A. D 1282-5. (*Map* No. XVI.)

The impatient temper of Baliol could not brook the humiliating acts of vassalage required of him; and when war broke out between France and England, he refused military aid to the latter, and concluded a treaty of alliance with the French monarch. (A. D. 1292.) War between England and Scotland followed; and Baliol, after a brief resistance, being defeated in the great battle of Dunbar,[1] was forced to make submission to Edward in terms of abject supplication. The victor returned to London, carrying with him not only the Scottish crown and sceptre, but also the sacred stone on which the Scottish monarchs were placed when they received the royal inauguration. (A. D. 1296.)

v. SCOTTISH WARS.

16 Scarcely, however, had Edward crossed the frontiers, when the Scots reasserted their independence, and under the brave Sir William Wallace, a man of obscure birth, but worthy to be ranked among the foremost of patriots, defeated the English at Stirling,[2] and recovered the whole of Scotland as rapidly as it had been lost. Again Edward advanced, at the head of a gallant muster of all the English chivalry, and the Scots were defeated at Falkirk[3] (A. D. 1298.) The adherents of Wallace mutinied against him; and a few years later the hero of Scotland was treacherously betrayed into the hands of Edward, and being condemned for the pretended crime of treason, was infamously executed, to the lasting dishonor of the English king. (A. D. 1305.)

17. The cause of Scottish freedom was revived by Robert Bruce, grandson of the Bruce who had been competitor for the throne against Baliol. In the spring of the year 1306 he was crowned king at Scone[4] by the revolted barons. In the following year, led-

1. *Dunbar* is a seaport of Scotland, twenty-seven miles north-east from Edinburgh. The ancient castle of Dunbar, the scene of many warlike exploits, stood on a lofty rock, the base of which was washed by the sea. It was taken by Edward I. in 1296;—four times it received within its walls the unfortunate Queen Mary;—and it was in the vicinity of Dunbar that Cromwell defeated the Scots under General Leslie, in 1650. (*Map* No. XVI.)

2. *Stirling* is a river port and fortress of Scotland, on the Forth, thirty miles north-west from Edinburgh. Its fine old castle is placed on a basaltic rock, rising abruptly three hundred feet from the river's edge. (*Map* No. XVI.)

3. *Falkirk* is an ancient town of Scotland, twenty-two miles north-west from Edinburgh, and three miles south of the Frith of Forth. In the valley, a little north of the town, the Scotch, under Wallace, were defeated on the 22d of July, 1298. In this battle fell Sir John Stewart, the commander of the Scottish archers, and Sir John the Grahame, the bosom friend of Wallace. The tomb of Grahame, which the gratitude of his countrymen has thrice renewed, is to be seen in the churchyard of Falkirk. On a moor, half a mile south-west from the town, Charles Stuart, the Pretender, gained a victory over the royal army in 1746. (*Map* No. XVI. *r.*)

4. *Scone*, now a small village of Scotland, is a little above Perth, on the river Tay, eighteen miles west from Dundee, and thirty-five north-west from Edinburgh. It was formerly the resi-

ward, assembling a mighty army, to render resistance hopeless, took the field against him, but he died on his march, and the expedition was abandoned by his son and successor, Edward II., in opposition to the dying injunctions of his father. (A. D. 13C7.) Still the war continued, and the Scotch were generally successful; but after seven years Edward himself marched against the rebels at the head of more than a hundred thousand men; but being met by Bruce at the head of little more than a third of that number, he experienced a total defeat in the battle of Bannockburn,[1] which established the in dependence of Scotland. (A. D. June 24th, 1314.)

18. The northern nations of Europe, during the tenth, eleventh, twelfth, and thirteenth centuries, were much less advanced in civilization than those which sprung from the wrecks of the Roman empire; and their obscure annals offer little to our notice but the germs of rude king. doms in the early stages of formation. In the south-west of Europe, the wars between the Moors and Christians of the Spanish peninsula had already continued during a period of more than five centuries, with ever-varying results; but the overthrow of the Western cali phate of Cordova, in the year 1030, followed by the dismemberment of the Moham'medan empire of Spain, into several independent States, (A. D. 1238,) struck a fatal blow at the Saracen dominion. But, unfortunately, the Christian provinces also were little united, and it was not uncommon for the Christian princes to form alliances with the Moors against one another. The founding of the Moorish kingdom of Granada, in 1238, for a time delayed the fall of the Moslems; but the Christians gradually extended their power, until, near the close of the fifteenth century, Granada yielded to the tor rent that had long been setting against it, and with its fall the su premacy of the Christian faith and power was acknowledged through out the peninsula.[a]

łuuee of the Scottish kings—the place of their coronation—and has been the scene of many istorical events. The remains of its ancient palace are incorporated with the mansion of the earl of Mansfield. (Map No. XVL)

1. *Bannockburn*, the name of which is inseparably connected with one of the most mem orable events in British history, is three miles south-west from Stirling. About one mile west from the village James III. was defeated in 1488, by his rebellious subjects and his son James IV., and, after being wounded in the engagement, was assassinated at a mill in the vicinity *Map* No. XVI.)

a. See next Section, pp. 317-18. and Notes.

SECTION III

GENERAL HISTORY DURING THE FOURTEENTH AND FIFTEENTH CENTURIES.

I. ENGLAND AND FRANCE DURING THE FOURTEENTH AND FIFTEENTH CENTURIES.

ANALYSIS. 1. Continuation of the histories of France and England.—2. Defeat of Edward II. in the battle of Bannockburn. Edward offends the barons. [Gascony.] The Great Charter confirmed, and annual parliaments ordained.—3. Rebellion of the barons, and death of Edward II. Reign of Edward III. Invasion of Scotland. [Halidon Hill.]

FRENCH AND ENGLISH WARS.—4. Edward disputes the succession to the throne of France Invasion of France, and battle of Cressy. [Cressy.] Defeat of the Scots, and capture of Calais. [Durham. Calais.]—5. Renewal of the war with France, and victory of Poictiers. (1356.) Anarchy in France. Treaty of Bretigny. The conquered territory. [Bretigny. Aquitaine. Bordeaux.]—6. Renewal of the war with France in 1368. Relative condition of the two powers. The French recover their provinces. [Bayonne. Brest, and Cherbourg.]—7. Death of Edward III. of England, and Charles V. of France. The distractions that followed in both kingdoms. [Orleans. Lancaster. Gloucester.] Wat Tyler's insurrection. [Blackheath.]—8. Character of Richard II. He is deposed, and succeeded by Henry IV. (1399.) The legal claimant. Origin of the contentions between the houses of York and Lancaster.—9. Insurrection against Henry. [Shrewsbury.]—10. Accession of Henry V., and happy change in his character. He invades France, and defeats the French in the battle of Agincourt.—11. Civil war in France, and return of Henry. The treaty with the Burgundian faction. Opposition of the Orleans party. [The States General. The dauphin.]—12. The infant king of the English, Henry VI., and the French king Charles VII. Joan of Arc. Her declared mission.—13. Successes of the French, and fate of Joan.—14. The English gradually lose all their continental possessions, except Calais. Tranquillity in France.

15. Unpopularity of the reigning English family. Popular insurrection. Beginning of the WARS OF THE TWO ROSES. [St. Albans.]—16. Sanguinary character of the strife. First period of the war closes with the accession of Edward IV., of the house of York.—17. The French king. The reign of Edward IV. The earl of Warwick. Overthrow of the Lancastrians. The fate of Margaret, her son, and the late king Henry IV. [Warwick. Tewkesbury.]—18. The cotemporary reign of Louis XI. of France. The relations of Edward and Louis.—19. Fate of Edward V., and accession of Richard III. Defeat and death of Richard, and end of the "Wars of the Two Roses." [Richmond. Bosworth.]

20. REIGN OF HENRY VII. The impostors Simnel and Warbeck. [Dublin.]—21. Treaties with France and Scotland. The Scottish marriage.—22. Why the reign of Henry VII. is an important epoch in English history.

II. OTHER NATIONS AT THE CLOSE OF THE FIFTEENTH CENTURY.

1 DENMARK, SWEDEN AND NORWAY. Union of Calmar. [Calmar.]

2. The RUSSIAN EMPIRE. Its early history. [Dnieper. Novogorod.] Divisions of the kingdom in the eleventh century.—3. Tartar invasions. The reign of John III. duke of Moscow. Russia at the end of the fifteenth century.—4. Founding of the OTTOMAN EMPIRE, on the ruins of the Eastern or Greek empire. [Emir.] The Turkish empire at the close of the fourteenth century. The sultan Bajazet overthrown by Tamerlane.—5. The TARTAR EMPIRE OF TAMERLANE. Defeat of the Turks. Turks and Christians unite against the Tartars. Death of Tamerlane. [Samarcand. Angora.]—6. Taking of Constantinople by the Turks, and extinction of the Eastern empire.

7. POLAND. Commencement and early history of Poland. Extent of the kingdom at the close of the fifteenth century. [Poland. Lithuania. Teutonic knights. Moldavia.]—8. The GERMAN EMPIRE at the close of the fifteenth century. Elective monarchs.—9. Causes that render the history of Germany exceedingly complicated. The three powerful States of Germany about the middle of the fourteenth century. [Luxemburg. Bohemia. Moravia. Silesia.

III. DISCOVERIES.

I. ENGLAND AND FRANCE DURING THE FOURTEENTH AND FIFTEENTH CENTURIES.—1. France and England occupy the most prominent place in the history of European nations during the closing period of the Middle Ages; and as their annals, during most of this period are so intimately connected that the history of one nation is in great part the history of both, the unity of the subject will best be preserved, and repetition avoided, by treating both in connection.

2. The reign of Edward II. of England, whose defeat by the Scots in the famous battle of Bannockburn has already been mentioned, although inglorious to himself, and disastrous to the British arms, was not, on the whole, unfavorable to the progress of constitutional liberty. The unbounded favoritism of Edward to Gaveston a handsome youth of Gascony,[1] whom the king elevated in wealth and dignities above all the nobles in England, roused the resentment of the barons; and the result was the banishment of the favorite, and a reformation of abuses in full parliament. (A. D. 1313.) The Great Charter, so often violated, was again confirmed; and the important provision was added, that there should be an annual assembling of parliament, for protection of the people, when "aggrieved by the king's ministers against right."

3. But other favorites supplied the place of Gaveston: the nobles rebelled against their sovereign: his faithless queen Isabella, sister of the king of France, took part with the malcontents, and

1. *Gascony*, before the French Revolution, was a province of France, situated between the Garonne, the sea, and the Pyrenees. The Gascons are a people of much spirit; but their exaggeration in describing their exploits has made the term *gasconade* proverbial. (*Map* No. XIII.)

Edward was deposed, imprisoned, and afterwards murdered. (A D. 1327.) Edward III., crowned at fourteen years of age, unable to endure the presence of a mother stained with the foulest crimes, caused her to be imprisoned for life, and her paramour, Mortimer, to be executed. He then applied himself to redress the grievances which had proceeded from the late abuses of authority; after which he invaded Scotland, and defeated the Scots at Halidon Hill; but on his withdrawal from the country, the Scottish arms again triumphed.

4 On the death, in the year 1328, of Charles IV. of France, the last of the male descendants of Philip the Fair, the crown of that kingdom became the object of contest between Edward III. of England, the son of Philip's daughter Isabella, and Philip of Valois, son of the brother of Philip. After war had continued several years between the two nations, with only occasional intervals of truce, in the year 1346 Edward, in person, invaded France, and, supported by his heroic son Edward, called the Black Prince, then only fifteen years of age, gained a great victory over the French in the famous battle of Cressy[2]—slaying more of the enemy than the total number of his own army. (Aug. 26th, 1346.) A few weeks after the battle of Cressy, the Scots, who had seized the opportunity of Edward's absence to invade England, were defeated in the battle of Durham,[3] and their king David Bruce taken prisoner. (Oct. 17, 1346.) To crown the honors of the campaign, the important seaport of Calais,[4] in France, surrendered to Edward, after a vigorous siege; and this important acquisition was retained by the English more than two centuries.

I. FRENCH AND ENGLISH WARS.

1. *Halidon Hill* is an eminence north of the river Tweed, not far from Berwick.

2. *Cressy*, or *Crecy*, is a small village, in the former province of Picardy, ninety-five miles north-west from Paris. It is believed that cannon, but of very rude construction, were first employed by the English in this battle. (*Map* No. XIII.)

3. *Durham*, the capital of the county of the same name, is an important city in the north of England, two hundred and thirty miles north-west from London. The field on which the battle was fought, some distance north of Durham, on the road to Newcastle, (Oct. 17th, 1346,) was called *Neville's Cross*. (*Map* No. XVI.)

4. *Calais* (Eng. Cal-is, Fr. Kah-la',) a seaport of France, on the Straits of Dover, in the former province of Picardy, is fifty miles north of Cressy. In 1558 Calais was retaken by surprise by the duke of Guise. In 1596 it was again taken by the English under the archduke Albert, but in 1598 was restored to France by the treaty of Nervins.

The obstinate resistance which Calais made to Edward III. in 1347, is said to have so much incensed the conqueror that he determined to put to death six principal burgesses of the town, who, to save their fellow citizens, had magnanimously placed themselves at his disposal; but that he was turned from his purpose only by the tears and entreaties of his queen Philippa. It is believed, however, that Froissart alone, among his cotemporaries, relates this story; and doubts may very reasonably be entertained of its truth. (*Map* No. XIII.)

5. After a truce of eight years, during which occurred the death of the French monarch, Philip of Valois, and the accession of his son John to the throne of France, war was again renewed, but was speedily terminated by a great victory, which the Black Prince obtained over king John in the battle of Poictiers. (Sept. 1356.) The French monarch, although taken prisoner, and conveyed in triumph to London, was treated with great moderation and kindness; but his captivity produced in France the most horrible anarchy, which was carried to the utmost extreme by a revolt of peasants, or serfs, against their lords, in most of the provinces surrounding the capital.[a] At length, while king John was still a prisoner, the two nations concluded a treaty at Bretigny,[1] (A. D. 1360,) which provided that king John should be restored to liberty, and that the English monarch should renounce his claim to the throne of France, and to the possession of Normandy and other provinces in the north; but that the whole south-west of France, embracing more than a third of the kingdom, and extending from the Rhone nearly to the Loire, should be guaranteed to England. The territory obtained from France was erected into the principality of Aquitaine,[2] the government of which was intrusted to the Black Prince, who, during several years, kept his court at Bordeaux.[3]

6. The treaty with France was never fully ratified; and in the year 1368 war between the two countries was commenced anew, the blame of the rupture being thrown by each nation upon the other. In the interval since the late treaty a great change had taken place in the condition of the rival powers: king Edward was now declining in age; and his son the Black Prince was enfeebled by disease; and the ceded French provinces were eager to return to their native king; while, on the other hand, France had recovered from her great losses, and the wise and popular Charles V. occupied the throne, in the place of the rash and intemperate John. France gradually recovered

1. *Bretigny* is a small hamlet six miles south-east from Chartres, and fifty miles south-west from Paris, in the former province of Orleans.

2. *Aquitaine (Aquitania)* was the name of the Roman province in Gaul south of the Loire. Since the time of the Romans it has been sometimes a kingdom and sometimes a duchy. Before the revolution, what remained of this ancient province passed under the name of Guienne. Bordeaux was its capital. (*Map* No. XIII.)

3. *Bordeaux*, called by the Romans *Burdigala*, an important commercial city and seaport of France, is on the west bank of the Garonne, fifty-five miles from its mouth, and three hundred and seven miles south-west from Paris. Montesquieu and Montaigne, Edward the Black Prince, pope Clement V., and Richard II. of England, were natives of this city. (*Map* No. XIII.)

a. Feb. 1358. This revolt was called *La Jacquerie*, from Jacques Ben Homme, the leader of the rebels.

most of her provinces without obtaining a single victory, although the keys of the country—Bordeaux, Bayonne,[1] Calais, Brest, and Cherbourg[2]—were still left in the hands of the English.

7. On the death of Edward (A. D. 1377) the crown fell to the son of the Black Prince, Richard II., then only eleven years of age. Three years later, Charles V., by his death, left the crown of France to his son Charles VI., a youth of only twelve years. Both kingdoms suffered from the distractions attending a regal minority:—in France the people were plundered by the exactions of the regents, and the kingdom harassed by the factious struggles for power between the dukes of Bur'gundy and Orleans;[3] and in England similar results attended the contests for the regency between the king's uncles, the dukes of Lancaster,[4] York,[5] and Gloucester.[6] In the year 1381 the injustice of parliamentary taxation occasioned a famous revolt of

1. *Bayonne* is on the south side of the Adour, four miles from its mouth, near the south western extremity of France. Bayonne is strongly fortified, and, although often besieged, has never been taken. The military weapon called the *bayonet* takes its name from this city, where it is said to have been first invented, and brought into use at the siege of Bayonne, during the war between Francis I. and Charles V. (*Map* No. XIII.)

2. *Brest* and *Cherbourg* are small but strongly-fortified seaport towns in the north-west of France. Cherbourg was the last town in Normandy retained by the English. (*Map* No. XIII.)

3. *Bur'gundy* and *Orleans.* An account of Bur'gundy has already been given. *Orleans*, a city of France, and formerly capital of the province of the same name, is situated on the Loire, sixty-eight miles south-west from Paris. Orleans occupied the site of the ancient Genabum, the emporium of the Cornutes, which was taken and burned by Cæsar. (*Cæsar* B. VII. 12.) It subsequently rose to great eminence, and was unsuccessfully besieged by At'tila and Odoácer. It became the capital of the first kingdom of Bur'gundy under the first race of French kings. Philip of Valois erected it into a duchy and peerage in favor of his son; and Orleans has since continued to give the title of *duke* to a prince of the blood royal. Charles VI. conferred the title of "duke of Orleans" on his younger brother, who became the founder of the Valois-Orleans line. Louis XIV. conferred it on his younger brother Philip, the founder of the Bourbon dynasty of the house of Orleans. Louis Philip was the first and only ruling prince of the Bourbon-Orleans dynasty. (*Map* No. XIII.)

4. *Lancaster*, which has given its name to the "dukes of Lancaster," is a seaport town on the coast of the Irish Sea, forty-six miles from Liverpool, and two hundred and five miles north-west from London. Lancaster is supposed, from the urns, altars, and other antiquities found there, to have been a Roman station. The first earl of Lancaster was created in 1266. In 1351 Henry, earl of Derby, was made duke of Lancaster: John Gaunt, fourth son of Edward III., married Blanch, the duke's daughter, and, by virtue of this alliance, succeeded to the title. His son Henry of Bolingbroke became duke of Lancaster on his father's death in 1398, and finally Henry IV., king of England in 1399, from which time to the present this duchy has been associated with the regal dignity. (*Map* No. XVI.)

5. *York*, See Note, p. 209. (*Map* No. XVI.)

6. *Gloucester* is on the east bank of the Severn, ninety-three miles north-west from London. It was founded by the Romans A. D. 44; and Roman coins and antiquities are frequently dug up on the supposed site of the old encampment. Richard II. created his uncles dukes of York and Gloucester; and since that time the ducal title has remained the highest title of English nobility. The duke of Lancaster was the only one who really possessed a duchy (the county of Lancaster) subject to his government, and that was reunited to the crown in 1461. (*Map* No. XVI.)

the lower classes headed by the Blacksmith Wat Tyler, similar to the insurrection of the French peasants which raged in 1358. In both nations these events mark the advance of the serfs, in their progress toward emancipation, to that stage in which their hopes are roused, and their wrongs still unredressed. The serfs of England demanded equal laws, and the abolition of bondage: to the number of sixty thousand they assembled at Blackheath,[1]—obtained possession of London, and put to death the chancellor and primate, as evil counsellors of the crown, and cruel oppressors of the people; but the fall of their leader struck terror into the insurgents, and the revolt was easily extinguished, while the honor of the crown was sullied by a revocation of the promised charters of enfranchisement and pardon. More than fifteen hundred of the mutineers perished by the hand of the hangman.

8. It was not till the age of twenty-three that Richard escaped from the tutelage of his uncles; and then his indolence, dissipation, and prodigality, brought him into contempt; and during his absence in Ireland a successful revolution elevated his cousin, Henry of Lancaster, surnamed Bolingbroke, to the throne. (A. D. 1399.) The parliament confirmed the deposition of Richard, who was soon after privately assassinated in prison.[a] The accession of Henry IV. to the throne met with no opposition, although he was not the legal claimant, the hereditary right being in Edward Mortimer, who was descended from the second son of Edward III., whereas Henry was descended from the third son. The claim of Mortimer was at a later period vested by marriage in the family of the duke of York, descended from the fourth son of Edward; and hence began the contentions between the houses of York and Lancaster.

9. The discontented friends of Henry proved his most dangerous enemies.; for the Percys, who had enthroned him, dissatisfied with his administration, took up arms and involved the country in civil war;[b] but in the great battle of Shrewsbury[2] (July 21, 1403) the

1. *Blackheath* is an elevated moory tract in the vicinity of the British metropolis, south-west of the city. The greater portion is in the parish of Greenwich.

2. *Shrewsbury* is situated on the Severn, one hundred and thirty-eight miles north-west from London. William the Conqueror gave the town and surrounding country to Roger de Montgomery, who built here a strong baronial castle; but in 1102 the castle and property were forfeited to the crown. Shrewsbury, from its situation close to Wales, was the scene of many border frays between the Welsh and English. In the battle of July 1403, the fall of the famous Lord Percy, surnamed Hotspur, by an unknown hand, decided the victory in the king's favor (*Map* No. XVI.)

a. Read Shakspeare's "King Richard II."

b. Read Shakspeare's "First Part of King Henry IV

insurgents were defeated, although the insurrection was still kept up a number of years, chiefly by the successful valor of Owen Glendower, the Welsh ally of the Percys.

10. Henry IV. was succeeded by his son Henry V. in the year 1413. The previous turbulent and dissipated character of the new sovereign had given little promise of a happy reign; but immediately after his accession he dismissed the former companions of his vices,—took into his confidence the wise ministers of his father,— and, laying aside his youthful pleasures, devoted all his energies to the tranquillizing of the kingdom, and the wise government of the people.[u] Taking advantage of the disorders of France, and the temporary insanity of its sovereign Charles VI., he revived the English claim to the throne of that kingdom, and at the head of thirty thousand men passed over into Normandy to support his pretensions. After his army had been wasted by a contagious disease, which reduced it to eleven thousand men, he met and defeated the French army of fifty thousand in the battle of Agincourt,[1]—slaying ten thousand of the enemy and taking fourteen thousand prisoners, among whom were many of the most eminent barons and princes of the realm. (Oct. 24, 1415.)

11. The Orleans and Burgundian factions which had temporarily laid aside their contentions to oppose the invader, renewed them on the departure of Henry, and soon involved the kingdom in the horrors of civil war. In the midst of these evils Henry returned to follow up his victory, and fought his way to Paris, when the Burgundian faction tendered him the crown of France, with the promise of its aid to support his claim. A treaty was soon concluded with the queen of the insane king and the duke of Bur'gundy, by which it was agreed that Henry should marry Catherine, the daughter of Charles, and succeed to the throne on the death of her father; while in the meantime he was to govern the kingdom as regent. (May 1420.) The States General[2] of the kingdom assented to the treaty and the western and northern provinces owned the sway of England but the central and south-eastern districts adhered to the cause of

---

1. *Agincourt* is a small village of France in the former province of Artois, one hundred and en miles north from Paris. (*Map* No. XIII.)

2. By the *States General* is meant the great council or general parliament of the nation, composed of representatives from the nobility, the clergy, and the municipalities. The *country districts* sent no representatives. (See University Edition, p. 824.)

a. Happily portrayed in Shakspeare's "Second Pai of King Henry IV." Act v., Scene ii and v.

the dauphin,[1] afterwards Charles VII., the only surviving son of his father, and the head of the Orleans party. Henry V. did not live to wear the crown of France; and the helpless Charles survived him only two months. (Died A. D. 1422.)

12. The English king left a son, Henry VI., then only nine months old, to inherit his kingdom. France, however, was now openly divided between the rival monarchs—its native sovereign Charles VII., and the English king, in the person of the infant Henry. In the war which followed, the prospects of the English were gradually improving, when they received a fatal check from the extraordinary appearance of a heroine, the famous Joan of Arc, whom the credulity of the age believed to have been divinely commissioned for the salvation of the French nation. Moved by a sort of religious phrensy, this obscure country girl was enabled to inspire her sovereign, the priests, the nobles, and the army, with the truth of her holy mission, which was, to drive the English from Orleans, which they were then besieging, and to open the way for the crowning of Charles at Rheims, then in the hands of the enemy.

13. Superstition revived the hopes of the French, and inspired the English with manifold terrors—the harbingers of certain defeat: in a short period all the promises of the maiden were fulfilled, and in accordance with her predictions she had the happiness to see Charles VII. crowned in the cathedral. Her mission ended, she wished to retire to the humble station from which Providence had called her, but being retained with the army, she afterwards fell into the hands of the English, who inhumanly condemned and executed her for the imaginary crime of sorcery.

14. In the death of Joan of Arc the English indeed destroyed the cause of their late reverses; but nothing could stay the new impulse which her wonderful successes had given to the French nation. In the year 1137 Charles gained possession of his capital, after twenty years exclusion from it; the Burgundian faction had previously become reconciled to him, and thenceforward the war lost its serious character, while the struggle of the English grew more and more feeble, until, in 1453, Calais was the only town of the continent remaining in their hands. From this period until the death of

1. *Dauphin* is the title of the eldest son of the king of France. In 1349 Hambert II. transferred his estate, the province of *Dauphiny*, to Philip of Valois, on condition that the eldest son of the king of France should, in future, be called the *dauphin*, and govern this territory. The dauphin, however, retains only the title, the estates having long been united with the crown lands.

Charles VII., in 1461, France enjoyed domestic tranquillity, while civil wars of the fiercest violence were raging in England.

15. The hereditary claim of the house of York to the English throne has already been mentioned. (p. 302.) Henry was a weak prince, and subject to occasional fits of idiocy; but his wife, Margaret of Anjou,[1] a woman of great spirit and ambition, possessing the allurements, but without the virtues, of her sex, ruled in his name. The haughtiness of the queen, the dishonor brought on the English arms by the loss of France, and the imbecility and insignificance of Henry, when contrasted with the popular virtues of Richard duke of York, rendered the reigning family unpopular with the nation; and when Richard advanced his pretensions to the crown, a powerful party rallied to his support. A formidable rising of the people in the year 1450, under a leader who is known in history under the nickname of Jack Cade, first manifested the gathering discontent. Five years later civil war between the York- II. THE WARS OF THE TWO ROSES. ists and Lancastrians broke out in different parts of the kingdom; and in the first battle, at St. Albans,[2] King Henry was taken prisoner. The Yorkists wore, as the symbol of their party, a white rose, and the Lancastrians a red rose; and the contests which marked their struggle for power are usually called the "wars of the two roses."

16. We have not room to enter into details of the sanguinary strife that followed. "In my remembrance," says a cotemporary writer,[a] "eighty princes of the blood royal of England perished in these convulsions; seven or eight battles were fought in the course of thirty years; and their own country was desolated by the English as cruelly as the former generation had wasted France." After many vicissitudes of fortune, in which Henry was twice defeated and taken prisoner, and Richard and his second son were slain, at the close of the first period of the war the white rose triumphed, and Edward IV., eldest son of the late duke of York, became king of England. (A. D. 1461.)

17. Charles VII. of France died the same year, and was succeed-

---

1. *Anjou* was an ancient province of France, on both sides of the Loire, north of Poitou. In the year 946 Louis IX. of France bestowed this province on his younger brother Charles, with the title of count of Anjou; but in 1328 it fell to the crown, at the accession of Philip VI. Subsequently different princes of the blood bore the title of Anjou; and Margaret, who became queen of England, was the daughter of René of Anjou. (*Map* No. XIII.)

2. *St. Albans* is a small town twenty miles north-west from London.

a. Philip de Comines.

ed on the throne by his son Louis XI. The reign of Edward IV of England was a reign of terror. Once he was deposed, and Henry reinstated, by the great power and influence of the earl of Warwick,[1] to whom the people gave the name of *king-maker*. But Warwick afterwards fell in battle; and in the year 1471 the heroic Margaret and her son were defeated and taken prisoners, and the power of the Lancastrians was overthrown in the desperate battle of Tewkesbury,[2] which concluded this sanguinary war. Margaret was at first imprisoned, but afterwards ransomed by the king of France: her son was assassinated: Henry VI. breathed his last, as a prisoner, in the Tower of London; and Edward was finally established on the throne.

18. The reign of Edward IV. was throughout cotemporary with that of Louis XI. of France, a prince of a tyrannical, superstitious, crafty, and cruel nature, but who possessed such a fund of comic humor, and such oddities of thoughts and manner, as to throw his atrocious cruelties into the shade. The relations of these two princes with each other were in a high degree dishonorable to both. Edward, by threatening war upon France, obtained from Louis the secret payment of exorbitant pensions for himself and his ministers; and the latter were with much reason charged with being the hired agents of the French king. Both these princes died in 1483, and both were succeeded by minors.

19. Edward V., at the age of twelve years, succeeded his father as king of England; but after a nominal reign of little more than two months, the young king and his brother the duke of York were murdered in the Tower, at the instigation of their uncle the duke of Gloucester, who caused himself to be proclaimed king, with the title of Richard III. But the whole nation was alienated by the crimes of Richard: the claims of the Lancastrian family were revived by Henry Tudor, earl of Richmond;[3] and at the decisive battle of Bos-

1. The earldom of *Warwick* dates from the time of William the Conqueror, whc bestowed the town and castle of that name, with the title of earl, on Henry de Newburg, one of his followers. The town of Warwick, capital of the county of the same name, is on the river Avon, eighty-two miles north-west from London. (*Map* No. XVI.)

2 *Tewkesbury* is on the river Avon, near its confluence with the Severn, thirty-three miles south-west from Warwick, and ninety miles north-west from London. The field on which the battle was fought, in the immediate vicinity of the town, is still called the "Bloody Meadow."

3. *Richmond*, which gave a title to the dukes of that name, is in the north of England, forty-one miles north-west from York. Its castle was founded by the first earl of Richmond, who received from William the Conqueror the forfeited estates of the earl of Mercia, and built Richmond castle to protect his family and property. The title and property, after being possessed by different persons allied to the blood royal, were at length vested in the crown by the accession of Henry, earl of Richmond, to the throne, with the title of Henry VII. (*Map* No. XVI.)

worth field,[1] Richard was defeated and slain (1485). The crown which Richard wore in the action was immediately placed on the head of the earl of Richmond, who was proclaimed king, with the title of Henry VII. His marriage soon after with the princess Elizabeth heiress of the house of York, united the rival claims of York and Lancaster in the Tudor family, and put an end to the civil contests which, for more than half a century, had deluged England with blood

20. The early part of the reign of Henry VII. was disturbed b two singular enterprises,—the attempt made in Ireland, by Lambert Simnel, to counterfeit the person of the young earl of Warwick, nephew of Edward IV., and the

III. REIGN OF HENRY VII.

only remaining male heir of the house of York; and the similar attempt of Perkin Warbeck to counterfeit the young duke of York, one of the princes who had been murdered in the Tower at the instigation of Richard III Both impostors, claiming the right to the throne, received their principal support in Ireland; but the former, after being crowned at Dublin,[2] and afterwards defeated in battle, (1487,) ended his days as a menial in the king's household,— while the latter, after throwing himself upon the king's mercy, being detected in subsequent plots, expiated his crime on the scaffold.

21. The most important of the foreign relations of Henry were a treaty with France, which stipulated that no rebel subjects of either power should be harbored or aided by the other; and a treaty of peace with Scotland, by which Margaret, eldest daughter of Henry, was given in marriage to the Scottish king, James IV., a marriage from which have sprung all the sovereigns who have reigned in Great Britain since the time of Elizabeth The reply of Henry to his counsellors who objected to the Scottish marriage, that the kingdom of England might by that connection fall to the king of Scotland, shows a great degree of sagacity, that has been verified by the result. " Scotland would then," said Henry, " become an accession to Eng land, not England to Scotland, for the greater would draw the less it is a safer union for England than one with France."

22. The reign of Henry VII. may justly be considered an im portant era in English history. It began in revolution, at the close

1. *Bosworth* is a small town ninety-five miles north-west from London. In the battle-field, in the vicinity of this town, is an eminence called Crown Hill, where Lord Stanley is said to have placed Richard's crown on the head of Richmond's head. (*Map* No. XVI.)

2. *Dublin*, the capital of Ireland, is on the eastern sea-coast of the island, at the mouth of the river Liffey, two hundred and ninety-two miles north-west from London. It was called by the Danes *Divelin*, or *Dubhlin*, " the black pool," from its vicinity to the mu ldy swamps at the mouth of the river. I has a population of two hundred and fifty thousand. (*Map* No. XVI)

of the long and bloody wars between the houses of York and Lan caster · it effected a change in descents: it marks the decline of the feudal system, the waning power of the baronial aristocracy, and a corresponding increase of royal prerogatives: it was cotemporary with that greatest of events in Modern History, the discovery of America,—with the advance in knowledge and civilization that dawned upon the closing period of the Middle Ages; with the consolidation of the great European monarchies into nearly the shape and extent which they retain at the present day; and with the growth of the " balance of power" system, which neutralized the efforts of princes at universal dominion. A general survey of the condition of the prin cipal States of Europe at this period will better enable us to com prehend the relations of their subsequent history.

II. OTHER NATIONS AT THE CLOSE OF THE FIFTEENTH CENTURY.—
1. Of the States of Northern Europe—Denmark,[1] Sweden, and Nor-

L. DENMARK, way,—constituting the ancient Scandinavia, merit our
SWEDEN, AND first attention. After these kingdoms had long been
NORWAY. agitated by internal dissensions, they were finally, by
the treaty of Calmar,[2] (1397,) united into a single monarchy, near

1. *Denmark* embraces the whole of the peninsula north of Germany, early known as the *Cimbric Chersonese*, and afterwards as *Jutland*. Its earliest known inhabitants were the *Cimbri*. (See p. 171.) The famous but mysterious Odin, the Mars as well as the Mohammed of Scandinavian history, is said to have emigrated, with a band of followers, from the banks of the Tan'ais to Scandinavia about the middle of the first century before the Christian era, and to have established his authority, and the Scythian religion, over Denmark, Norway, and Sweden. Skiold, son of Odin, is said to have ruled over Denmark ; but his history, and that of his posterity for many generations, are involved in fable. Hengist and Horsa, the two Saxon chiefs who conquered England in the fifth century, reckoned Odin, (or Wodin in their dialect,) as their ancestor. Gorm the Old, son of Hardicanute I., (*Horda-knut,*) united all the Danish States under his sceptre in the year 863. His grandson Sweyn, subdued a part of Norway in the year 1000, and a part of England in 1014. His son Canute completed the conquest of England in 1016, and also subdued a part of Scotland. Canute embraced the Christian religion, and introduced it into Denmark ; upon which a great change took place in the character of the people. At his death, in 1036, he left the crowns of Denmark and England to his son Hardi canute II. In 1385, Margaret, daughter of the Danish prince Waldemar and wife of Haquin king of Norway, styled the Semir'amis of the North, ascended the throne of Norway and Denmark. In 1389 she was chosen by the Swedes as their sovereign ; and in 1397 the treaty of Calmar united the three crowns—it was supposed forever. In 1448, the princes of the family of Skiold having become extinct, the Danes promoted Christian I., count of Oldenburg, to the throne. He was the founder of the royal Danish family which has ever since kept possession of the throne. In 1523 the Swedes emancipated themselves from the cruel and tyrannical yoke of Christian II., king of Denmark. In their struggle for independence they were led by the famous Gustavus Vasa, who was raised to the throne of Sweden by the unani mous suffrages of his fellow cit'izens. Norway remained connected with Denmark till 1814, when the allied powers gave it to Sweden, as indemnity for Finland. (*Map* No. XIV.)

2. *Calmar*, rendered famous by the treaty of 1397, is a seaport town on the small island of Quarnholm, which is in the narrow strait that separates the island of Oland from the south eastern coast of Sweden. (*Map* No. XIV.)

the close of the fourteenth century, through the influence of Margaret of Denmark, whose extraordinary talents and address have rendered her name illustrious as the "Semir'amis of the North." But the union of Calmar, although forming an important epoch in Scandinavian history, was never firmly consolidated; and after having been renewed several times, was at length irreparably broken by Sweden, which, in the early part of the sixteenth century, (1521,) under the conduct of the heroic Gustavus Vasa, recovered its ancient independence.

2. East and south-east of the Scandinavian kingdoms were the numerous Sclavonic tribes, which were gradually gathered into the empire of Russia. The original cradle of that mighty empire which dates back to the time of Rurick, a chief-　　II. RUSSIAN EMPIRE. tain cotemporary with Alfred the Great, was a narrow territory extending from Kiev, along the banks of the Dnieper,[1] north to Novogorod.[2] Darkness for a long time rested upon early Russian history, but it has been in great part dispelled by the genius and research of Karamsin, and it is now known that as early as the tenth century the Russian empire had attained an extent and importance, as great, comparatively, among the powers of Europe, as it boasts at the present day. About the middle of the eleventh century the system of dividing the kingdom among the children of successive monarchs began to prevail, and the result was ruinous in the extreme, occasioning innumerable intestine wars, and a gradual decline of the strength and consideration of the empire.

3. Toward the middle of the thirteenth century the Tartar hordes of Northern Asia, falling upon the feeble and disunited Russian States, found them an easy prey; and during a period of two hundred and fifty years, Russia, under the Tartar yoke, suffered the direst atrocities of savage cruelty and despotism. At length, about the year 1480 John III., duke of Moscow, the true restorer of his

1. *Dnieper*, the *Borysthenes* of the ancients, still frequently called by its ancient name, is a large river of European Russia. It rises near Smolensko, runs south, and falls into the Black Sea, north-east of the mouths of the Danube. (*Map* No. XVII.)

2. *Novogorod*, or Novgorod, called also *Veliki*, or "the Great," formerly the most important city in the Russian empire, is situated on the river Volkhof, near its exit from Lake Ilmen, one hundred miles south-east from St. Petersburgh, and three hundred and five north-west from Moscow. The Volkhof runs north to Lake Ladoga. So impregnable was Novgorod once deemed as to give rise to the proverb,

　　Quis contra Deos et magnam Novogordiam?
　　"Who can resist the Gods and Great Novgorod?"

From Novgorod to Kiev is a distance of nearly six hundred miles.

country's glory, succeeded in abolishing the ruinous system by which the regal power had been frittered away, while at the same time he threw off the yoke of the Moguls, and repulsed their last invasion of his country. Under the reign of this wise and powerful prince, the many petty principalities which had long divided the sovereignty were consolidated, and, at the end of the century, Russia, although scarcely emerged from its primitive barbarian darkness, was one of the great powers of Europe.

4. South of the country inhabited by the Russians, we look in vain, at the close of the fifteenth century, for the once III. OTTOMAN famed Greek empire of Justinian, or, as sometimes called, EMPIRE. the Eastern empire of the Romans. The account which we have given of the crusades represents the Turks, a race of Tartar origin, as spread over the greater part of Asia Minor. About the beginning of the fourteenth century, a Turkish emir,[a] called Ottoman, succeeded in uniting several of the petty Turkish States of the peninsula, and thus laid the foundation of the Ottoman empire. About the year 1358 the Ottoman Turks first obtained a foothold in Europe ; and at the close of the fourteenth century their empire extended from the Euphrates to the Danube, and embraced, or held as tributary, ancient Greece, Thes'saly, Macedónia, and Thrace, while the Roman world was contracted to the city of Constantinople, and even that was besieged by the Turks, and closely pressed by the calamities of war and famine. The city would have yielded to the efforts of Bajazet, the Turkish sultan ; but almost in the moment of victory the latter was overthrown by the famous Timour, or Tamerlane, the new Tartar conqueror of Asia.

5 About the year 1370, Tamerlane, a remote descendant of the Great Gengis Khan, (p. 286,) had fixed the capital of his new dominions at Samarcand,[1] from which central point of his power he

---

. *Samarcand*, anciently called *Marakanda*, now a city of Independent Tartary, in Pozharn, was the capital of the Persian satrapy of Sogdiana. (See *Map* No. IV.) Alexander is thought to have pillaged it. It was taken from the sultan Mahomet, by Gengis Khan, in 1220; and under Timour or Tamerlane, it became the capital of one of the largest empires in the world and the centre of Asiatic learning and civilization, at the same time that it rose to high distinction on account of its extensive commerce with all parts of Asia. Samarcand is now in a

-a. *Emir*, an Arabic word, meaning a leader, or commander, was a title first given to the caliphs ; but when they assumed the title of sultan, that of emir was applied to their children At length it was bestowed upon all who were thought to be descendants of Mahomet in the line of his daughter Fatimah.

made thirty-five victorious campaigns,—conquering all Persia, North
ern Asia, and Hindostan,—and before his death he had
placed the crowns of twenty-seven kingdoms on his
head. In the year 1402 he fought a bloody and decisive
battle with the Turkish sultan Bajazet, ôn the plains of Angòra,' in
Asia Minor, in which the Turk sustained a total defeat, and fell into
the hands of the conqueror. Tamerlane would have carried his
son quests into Europe; but the lord of myriads of Tartar horsemen
was not master of a single galley; and the two passages of the Bosporus and the Hellespont were guarded, the one by the Christians,
the other by the Turks, who on this occasion forgot their animosities
to act with union and firmness in the common cause. Two years
later Tamerlane died, at the age of sixty-nine, while on his march
for the invasion of China

iv. TARTAR EMPIRE OF TAMERLANE.

6. The Ottoman empire not only soon recovered from the blow
which Tamerlane had inflicted upon it, but in the year 1453, during
the reign of Mahomet II., effected the final conquest of Constantinople. On the 29th of May of that year the city was carried by
assault, and given up to the unrestrained pillage of the Turkish
soldiers: the last of the Greek emperors fell in the first onset: the
inhabitants were carried into slavery; and Constantinople was left
without a prince or a people, until the sultan established his own
residence, and that of his successors, on the commanding spot which
had been chosen by Constantine. The few remnants of the Greek
or Roman power were soon merged in the Ottoman dominion; and
at the close of the fifteenth century the Turkish empire was firmly
established in Europe.

7. While at the close of the fifteenth century the three Scandinavian kingdoms of the North, and Russia, formed, as it
were, separate worlds, having no connection with the
rest of Europe, Poland,² the ancient Sarmatia, supplying the connect

v. POLAND.

decayed condition: gardens, fields, and plantations, occupy the place of its numerous streets
and mosques; and we search in vain for its ancient palaces, whose beauty is so highly eulo-
gized by Arab historians.

1. *Angora*, a town of Natolia in Asia Minor, (see Note, *Rosm*, p. 231,) is the same as the
ancient *Ancyra*, which, in the time of Nero, was the capital of Galatia. Here St. Paul preached
to the Galatians.

2. *The Poles* were a Sclavonic tribe (a branch of the Sarmatians), who, in the seventh century, passed up the Dnieper, and thence to the Niemen and the Vistula. About the middle of
the tenth century they embraced Christianity, and toward the end of the same century were
first called *Poles*, that is, *Sclavonians of the plain* The numerous principalities into which

ing link between the Sclavonian and German tribes had risen to a considerable degree of eminence and power. The history of Poland commences with the tenth century; but the prosperity of the kingdom began with the reign of Casimir the Great. (1333–1370.) In the year 1386 Lithuania[1] was added to Poland; and about the middle of the following century the Polish sovereign, Wladislas, was present d with the crown of Hungary, which he had nobly defended against the Turks. But Hungary soon reverted again to the German empire. After long wars with the Teutonic knights,[2] who, since the crusades, had firmly established their order in the Prussian part of the Germanic empire, the knights were everywhere defeated during the reign of Casimir IV., (1444–1492,) who added a large part of Prussia to the Polish territories. The Turkish province of Moldavia[3] also became tributary to Poland; and at the close of the fifteenth century this kingdom had extended its power from the Baltic to the Euxine, along the whole frontier of European civilization, thus forming an effectual barrier to the Western States of Europe against barbarian invasion.

8. The German empire, at the close of the fifteenth century, comprised a great number of States lying between France and Poland, extending even west of the Rhine, and embracing the whole of cen-

the Poles were divided were first united into one kingdom in 1025, under king Boleslaus I.; but Poland was afterwards subdivided among the family of the Piasts until 1305, when Wladislas, king of Cracow, united with hiss sovereignty the two principal remaining divisions, Great and Little Poland. From 1370 to 1382 Hungary was united with Poland. The union with Lithuania in 1386, occasioned by the marriage of the grand duke of Lithuania with the queen of Poland, was more permanent. After the Lithuania nobility, in 1569, united with Great and Little Poland, in one diet, Poland became the most powerful State in the North. Although Poland has ceased to constitute an independent and single State—its detached fragments having become Austrian, Prussian, or Russian provinces—still the country is distinctly separated from those which surround it, by national character, language, and manners. The present Poland possessing the name without the privileges of a kingdom, and reduced to a territory extending two hundred miles north and south, and two hundred east and west, is, substantially, a part of the Russian empire. (Map No. XVII.)

1. The greater part of *Lithuania*, once forming the north-eastern d vision of Poland, has been united to Russia. It is comprised in the present governments of Mohilew, Witepsk Minsk, Wilna, and Grodno. (*Map* No. XVII.)

2. The *Teutonic Knights* composed a religious order founded in 1190 by Frederic, duke of Suabia, during a crusade in the Holy Land, and intended to be confined to Germans of noble rank. The original object of the association was to defend the Christian religion against the infidels, and to take care of the sick in the Holy Land. By degrees the order made several conquests, and acquired great riches; and at the beginning of the fifteenth century it possessed a large extent of territory extending from the Oder to the Gulf of Finland. The war with the Poles greatly abridged its power, and finally the order was abolished by Napoleon, in his war with Austria, April 24th, 1809.

3. *Moldavia*, nominally a Turkish province, but in reality under the protection of Russia, embraces the north-eastern part of the ancient Dacia. (*Maps* Nos. IX. and XVII.)

tral Europe. The Carlovingian sovereigns of Germany were hereditary monarchs; but as early as the year 887 the great
vassals of the crown deposed their emperor, and elected
another sovereign, and from that remote period the emperors of Germany have continued to be elective.

9. Owing to the great number of the Germanic States, which were
of different grades, from large principalities down to free cities and
the estates of earls or counts—the frequent changes of territory
among them, by marriages, alliances, and conquests,—the weakness
of the federal tie by which they were united—and their conflicting
interests, and frequent wars with each other and with the emperor,—
the history of Germany is exceedingly complicated, and generally
devoid of great points of interest. Many of the States had their
own sovereigns, subordinate to their common emperor. About the
middle of the fourteenth century there were three powerful States in
Germany, which had absorbed nearly all the rest. These were 1st,
Luxemburg,[1] which possessed Bohemia,[2] Moravia,[3] and part of Silesia,[4] and Lusatia:[5] 2d, *Bavaria*, which had acquired Brandenburg,[6]
Holland,[7] and the Tyrol:[8] and 3d, *Austria*,[9] which, in addition to a

1. The Grand Duchy of *Luxemburg* was divided in the year 1839, between Holland and Belgium. The *town* of Luxemburg, one hundred and eighty-five miles north-east from Paris,
containing one of the strongest fortresses in Europe, belongs, with a portion of the surrounding country, to Holland. (*Map* No. XV.)

2. *Bohemia*, having Silesia and Saxony on the north, Moravia and the arch-duchy of Austria
on the south-east, and Bavaria on the west, forms an important portion of the Austrian empire.
(*Map* No. XVII.)

3. *Moravia*, an important province of Austria, lies east of Bohemia. In 1783 a portion of
Silesia was incorporated with it. Moravia is the country anciently occupied by the *Quadi* and
Marcomanni, who waged fierce wars against the Romans. (*Map* No. XVII.)

4. *Silesia* is north-east of Bohemia and Moravia, embracing the country on both sides of the
Oder. (*Map* No XVII.)

5. *Lusatia* was a tract of country having Brandenburg on the north, Silesia on the east, Bohemia and Bavaria on the south, and Meissen on the west. It is now embraced in the eastern part of the kingdom of Saxony, east of Dresden, the southern part of Brandenburg, and
the north-western part of Silesia. It was divided into Upper and Lower Lusatia, the former
being the southern portion of the territory. (*Map* No. XVII.)

6. *Brandenburg*, the most important of the Prussian States, lies between Mecklenburg and
Pomerania on the north, and West Prussian Saxony and the kingdom of Saxony on the south.
It includes Berlin, the capital of the Prussian empire. (*Map* No. XVII.)

7. *Holland* has the Prussian German States on the south-east, Belgium on the south, and
the sea on the west. (*Maps* Nos. XV. and XVII.)

8. The *Tyrol*, (comprising the ancient Rhœtia with a part of Noricum, see *Map* No. IX.,)
is a province of the Austrian empire, east of Switzerland, and having Bavaria on the north,
and Lombardy on the south. The Tyrolese, although warmly attached to liberty, have always
been steadfast adherents of Austria. (*Map* No. XVII.)

9. The arch-duchy of *Austria*, the nucleus and centre of the Austrian empire, lies on both
sides of the Danube, having Bohemia and Moravia on the north, and Styria and Carinthia on
the south. In the time of Charlemagne, about the year 800, the margravate of Austria was

large number of hereditary States, possessed much of the Suabian territory. (See *Suabia*, p. 270.)

10. In the year 1438 the German princes elected an emperor from the house of Austria; and, ever since, an Austrian prince, with scarcely any intermission, has occupied the throne of Germany. Near the close of the fifteenth century the German States, then under the reign of Maximilian of the house of Austria, made an important change in their condition, by which the private wars and feuds, which the laws then authorized, and the right to carry on which against each other the petty States regarded as the bulwark of their liberty, were made to give place to regular courts of justice for the settlement of national controversies. In the year 1495, at a general diet held at Worms,[1] the plan of a Perpetual Public Peace was subscribed to by the several States: oppression. rapine, and violence, were made to yield to the authority of *law*, and the public tranquillity was thus, for the first time in Germany, established on a firm basis.

11. For a considerable period previous to the beginning of the fourteenth century, Switzerland, the *Helvetia* of the Romans, had formed an integral part of the Germanic empire; but in the year 1307 the house of Austria, under the usurping emperor Albert, endeavored to extend his sway over the rude mountaineers of that inhospitable land. The tyranny of Austria provoked the league of Rutuli;[2] the famous episode of the hero William Tell[3] gave a new impulse to the cause of freedom; and in

VII. SWIT-
ZERLAND.

formed south of the Danube, by a body of militia which protected the south-east of Germany from the Incursions of the Asiatic tribes. In 1156 its territory was extended north of the Danube, and made a duchy. In 1438 the ruling dynasty of Austria obtained the electoral crown of the German emperors, and in 1453 Austria was raised to an arch-duchy. In 1526 it acquired Bohemia and Hungary, and attained the rank of a European monarchy. (*Map* No. XVII.)

1. *Worms* is on the west bank of the Rhine, forty-two miles south-west from Frankfort (*Map* No. XVI.)

2. *Rutuli* was a meadow slope under the Salzburg mountain, in the canton of Uri, and on the west bank of the Lake of Lucerne, where the confederates were wont to assemble at dead of night, to consult for the salvation of their country. (*Map* No. XIV.)

3. The story of *William Tell*, one of the confederates of Rutuli, is, briefly, as follows. Gessler the Austrian governor had carried his insolence so far as to cause his hat to be placed upon a pole, as a symbol of the sovereign power of Austria, and to order that all who passed should uncover their heads and bow before it. Tell, having passed the hat without making obeisance, was summoned before Gessler, who, knowing that he was a good archer, commanded him to shoot, from a great distance, an apple placed on the head of his own son,—promising him his life if he succeeded. Tell hit the apple, but, accidentally dropping a concealed arrow, was asked by the tyrant why he had brought two arrows with him? "Had I shot my child," replied the archer, "the second shaft was for thee:—and, to sure, I should not have

the year 1308 the united cantons of Uri, Schwytz, and Unterwalden,[1] struck their first blow for liberty, and expelled their oppressors from the country.   In 1315 the Swiss gained a great victory over the Austrians at Morgarten,[2] and another at Sempach[3] in 1386; but they were regarded as belonging to the Germanic empire until about the close of the fifteenth century, when, in the famous Suabian war, army after army of the Austrians was defeated, and the emperor Maximilian himself compelled to effect a disgraceful retreat.   This was he last war of the early Swiss confederates in the cause of freedom; and the peace concluded with Maximilian in 1499 established the independence of Switzerland.

12. The condition of Italy during the central period of the Middle Ages has already been described.   (See II.)   At the close of that period Italy still formed, nominally, a part of the Germanic empire; but the authority of the German emperors had silently declined during the preceding centuries, until at length it was reduced to the mere ceremony of coronation, and the exercise of a few honorary and feudal rights over the Lombard vassals of the crown.   In the twelfth and thirteenth centuries, numerous republics had sprung up in Italy; and, animated by the spirit of liberty, they for a time enjoyed an unusual degree of prosperity; but eventually, torn to pieces by contending factions, and a prey to mutual and incessant hostilities, they fell under the tyranny of one despot after another, until, in the early part of the fifteenth century, Florence, Genoa,[4] and Venice, were the only im-

VIII. ITALIAN HISTORY.

missed my mark a second time." Gessler, in a rage not unmixed with terror, declared tha although he had promised Tell his life, he should pass it in a dungeon; and taking his captive bound, started in a boat to cross the Lake of Lucerne, to his fortress. But a violent storm arising, Tell was set at liberty, and the helm committed to his hands. He guided the boat successfully to the shore, when, seizing his bow, by a daring leap he sprung upon a rock, leaving the barque to wrestle with the billows. Gessler escaped the storm, but only to fall by the unerring arrow of Tell. The death of Gessler was a signal for a general rising of the Swiss cantons

1. *Uri, Schwytz, Unterwalden,* see *Map* No. XIV.

2. *Morgarten,* the narrow pass in which the battle was fought, is on the eastern shore of the small Lake of Egeri, in the canton of Schwytz, seventeen miles east from Lucerne. (*Map* No. XIV.)

3. *Sempach* is a small town on the east bank of the small lake of the same name, seven miles northwest from Lucerne. (*Map* No. XIV.)

4. *Genoa,* a maritime city of northern Italy, is at the head of the gulf of the same name, seventy-five miles south-east from Turin. After the downfall of the empire of Charlemagne, Genoa erected itself into a republic. In 1174 it possessed an extensive territory in north-western Italy, nearly all of Provence, and the island of Corsica. Genoa carried on long wars with Pisa and Venice,—that with the latter being one of the most memorable in the Italian annals of the Middle Ages.

portai t States that had escaped the general catastrophe. Nearly all the numerous free towns and republics of Lombardy had been conquered by the duchy of Milan, which acknowledged a direct dependence on the German emperor.

13. The Florentines, who greatly enriched themselves by their commerce and manufactures, maintained their republican form of government, from about the close of the twelfth century, during a period of nearly two hundred and fifty years. The Genoese and Venetians, whose commercial interests thwarted each other, both in the Levant[1] and the Mediterranean, quarreled repeatedly; but eventually the Venetians gained the superiority, and retained the command of the sea in their own hands. Of all the Italian republics, Genoa was the most agitated by internal dissensions; and the Genoese, volatile and inconstant, underwent frequent voluntary changes of masters. At the close of the fifteenth century Genoa was a dependency of the duchy of Milan, although subsequently it recovered once more its ancient state of independence.

14. Venice, to whose origin we have already alluded, was the earliest, and, for a long time, the most considerable, commercial city of modern Europe. At a very early period the Venetians began to trade with Constantinople and other eastern cities; the crusades, to which their shipping contributed, increased their wealth, and extended their commerce and possessions; and toward the end of the fifteenth century, besides several rich provinces in Lombardy, the republic was mistress of Crete and Cyprus, of the greater part of the Morea,[2] or Southern Greece, and of most of the isles in the Ægean Sea. The additional powers that at this time shared the dominion of Italy, were the popes, and the kings of Naples; but the temporal domains of the former were small, and those of the latter soon passed into other hands; for the continual wars which all the Italian States waged with each other had already encouraged foreign powers to form plans of conquest over them. In the year 1500 Ferdinand of Spain deprived France of Naples; and from this time the Spaniards who were already masters of Sicily and Sardinia, became, for more than a hundred years, the predominating power in Italy.

1. The *Levant* is a term applied to designate the eastern coasts of the Mediterranean, from southern Greece to Egypt. In the Middle Ages the trade with these countries was almost exclusively in the hands of the Italians, who gave to them the general appellation of *Levant* or eastern countries. (Italian, *Levante*: French, *Levant.*)

2. *Morea*, the ancient *Peloponnesus*, or southern Greece, is said to derive its modern name from its resemblance to a mulberry leaf. (Greek, *morea*, a mulberry tree.)

15. Turning to Spain, we behold there, in the beginning of the fifteenth century, the three Christian States of Navarre,[1] Aragon,[2] Castile[3] and Leon[4] united, and the Moorish kingdom of Granada.[5] Frequent dissensions among the Christian States had long prevented unity of action among them, but in the year 1474 Ferdinand V. ascended the throne of Aragon; and, as he had previously married Isabella, a princess of Castile, the two most powerful Christian States were thus united. The plan of expelling the Moors from Spain had long been agitated; and in 1481 the war, for that purpose was commenced by Ferdinand and Isabella Ten years, however, were spent in the sanguinary strife, before the

IX. SPAIN.

1. *Navarre* is in the northern part of Spain, having France and the Pyrenees on the north, Aragon on the east, Old Castile on the south, and the Basque provinces (Biscay, Guipuzcoa, and Alava) on the west. A portion of ancient Navarre extended north of the Pyrenees, and afterwards formed the French province of Bearn. (See *Map* No. XIII.) During many centuries Navarre was an independent kingdom, but in 1284 it became united, by intermarriage, with that of France. In 1329 it again obtained a sovereign of its own. Although still claimed by France, in 1512 Ferdinand of Aragon united all the country south of the Pyrenees to the crown of Spain. In 1590 Henry IV., grandson of Henry king of Navarre, ascended the throne of France; and from that time to the reign of Charles X., the French monarchs, (with the exception of Napoleon,) assumed the title of "king of France and Navarre;" but only the small portion of Navarre north of the Pyrenees remained annexed to the French monarchy. Spanish Navarre is still governed by its separate laws, and has, nominally at least, the same constitution which it enjoyed when it was a separate monarchy; but its sovereignty is vested in the Spanish crown. (*Map* No. XIII.)

2. *Aragon* was bounded on the north by the Pyrenees, east by Catalonia, south by Valencia, and west by Castile and Navarre. While a separate kingdom it was the most powerful of the peninsular States, and comprised, in 1479, under the sovereignty of Ferdinand, exclusive of Aragon proper, Navarre, Catalonia, Valencia, and Sardinia. (*Map* No. XIII.)

3. *Castile* is the central and largest division of modern Spain. The northern portion being that first recovered from the Saracens, is called Old Castile, and comprises the modern provinces of Burgos, Soria, Segovia, and Avila: the southern portion, called New Castile, comprises the provinces of Madrid, Guadalaxara, Cuenca, Toledo, and La Mancha. After the expulsion of the Saracens, and various vicissitudes, the sovereignty of Castile was vested by marriage in Sancho III. king of Navarre, whose son Ferdinand was made king of Castile in 1034. Three years later he was crowned king of Leon. The crowns of Castile and Leon were repeatedly separated and united, till, by the marriage of Isabella, who held both crowns, with Ferdinand, king of Aragon, in 1497, the three kingdoms were consolidated into one. (*Map* No. XIII.)

4. The kingdom of *Leon* was bounded north by Asturias, east by Old Castile, south by Estremadura, and west by Galicia and Portugal. During the eighth century, this district, after the expulsion of the Moors, was formed into a kingdom, called after its capital, and connected with Asturias. It was first added to Castile in 1037, in the reign of Ferdinand I. king of Castile, who was king of Leon in right of his wife; but it continued in an unsettled state till 1230, when it was finally united, by inheritance, to the dominions of Ferdinand III. king of Castile (*Map* No. XIII)

5. *Granada*, consisting of the south-eastern part of ancient Andalusia, (Note p. 232,) is on the Mediterranean coast, in the south-eastern part of Spain. On the breaking up of the African empire in Spain, in the year 1238, Mohammed ben Alhamar founded the Moorish kingdom of Granada, making the city of Granada his capital. Granada remained in the possession of the Moors two hundred and fifty years, which comprise the season of its prosperity In 1492 it surrendered to Ferdinand the Catholic, being the last foothold of Saracen power in Spain. (*Map* No. XIII.)

Christians were enabl:d to besiege Granada, the Moorish capital; but the capitulation of that city in January, 1492, put an end to the Saracen dominion in the Spanish peninsula, after it had existed there during a period of eight hundred years. In the year 1512 Ferdinand invaded and conquered Navarre; and thus the whole of Spain was united under the same government.

16. Toward the close of the eleventh century, the frontier province of Portugal,[1] which had been conquered by the Christians from the Moors, was formed into an earldom tributary to Leon and Castile; but in the twelfth century it was erected into an independent kingdom, and in the early part of the thirteenth it had reached its present limits. The history of Portugal is devoid of general interest, until the period of those voyages and discoveries of which the Portuguese were the early promoters and which have shed immortal lustre on the Portuguese name

III. Discoveries.—1. A brief account of the discoveries of the fifteenth century will close the present chapter. From the subversion of the Roman empire, until the revival of letters which succeeded the Dark Ages, no advance was made in the art of navigation; and even the little geographical knowledge that had been acquired

---

1 *Portugal*, anciently called *Lusitania*, (Note p. 106,) was taken possession of by the Romans about two hundred years before the Christian era; previously to which the Phœnicians, Carthaginians, and Greeks, traded to its shores, and probably planted colonies there. In the fifth century it was inundated by the Germanic tribes, and in 712 was conquered by the Saracens Soon after, the Spaniards of Castile and Leon, aided by the native inhabitants, wrested northern Portugal, between the Minho and the Douro, from the Moors, and placed counts or governers over this region. About the close of the eleventh century Henry, a Burgundian prince came into Spain to seek his fortune by his sword, in the wars against the Moors. Alphonso VI. king of Castile and Leon, gave to the chivalric stranger the hand of his daughter in marriage, and also the earldom of the Christian provinces of Portugal. In 1139 the Portuguese sarl, Alphonso I., having gained a brilliant victory over the Moors, his soldiers proclaimed him king on the field of battle; and Portugal became an independent kingdom. Its power now rapidly increased: it maintained its independence against the claims of Castile and Leon; and Alphonso extended his dominions to the borders of Algarve, in the south. In 1249 Alphonso III. conquered Algarve, and thus, in the final overthrow of the Moorish power in Portugal, extended the kingdom to its present limits.

The language of Portugal is merely a dialect of the Spanish; but the two people regard each other with a deep-rooted national antipathy. The character attributed to the Portuguese is not very flattering. "Strip a Spaniard of all his virtues, and you make a good Portuguese of him," says the Spanish proverb. "I have heard it more truly said," says Dr. Southey "add hypocrisy to a Spaniard's vices, and you have the Portuguese character. The two nations differ, perhaps purposely, in many of their habits. Almost every man in Spain smokes; the Portuguese never smoke, but most of them take snuff. None of the Spaniards will use a wheelbarrow: none of the Portuguese will carry a burden: the one says, ' it is only fit for beasts to draw carriages;' the other, that ' it is fit only for beasts to carry burdens.' " (*Map* No. XIII.)

was nearly lost during that gloomy period. Upon the returning dawn of civilization, however, commerce again revived; and the Italian States, of which Venice, Pisa,[1] and Genoa, took the lead, soon became distinguished for their enterprising commercial spirit. The discovery of the magnetic needle gave a new impulse to navigation, as it enabled the mariner to direct his bark with increased boldness and confidence farther from the coast, out of sight of whose landmarks he before seldom dared venture; while the invention of the art of printing disseminated more widely the knowledge of new discoveries in geography and navigation. In the fourteenth century the Canary[2] islands, believed to be the *Fortunate islands* of the ancients, were accidentally rediscovered by the crew of a French ship driven thither by a storm. But the career of modern discovery was prosecuted with the greatest ardor by the Portuguese. Under the patronage of prince Henry, son of king John the First, Cape Bojador, before considered an impassable limit on the African coast, was doubled; the Cape de Verd[3] and Azore[4] islands were discovered; and the greatest part of the African coast, from Cape Blanco to Cape de Verd, was explored. (1419—1430.)

2. The grand idea which actuated prince Henry, was, by circumnavigating Africa, to open an easier and less expensive route to the Indies, and thus to deprive the Italians of the commerce of those fertile regions, and turn it at once upon his own country. Although prince Henry died before he had accomplished the great object of his ambition, the fame of the discoveries patronized by him had rendered his name illustrious and the learned, the curious, and the

1. *Pisa,* the capital of one of the most celebrated republics of Italy, and now the capital of the province of its own name in the grand duchy of Tuscany, is on the river Arno, about eight miles from its entrance into the Mediterranean, and thirteen miles north-east from Leghorn. In the tenth century Pisa took the lead among the commercial republics of Italy, and in the eleventh century its fleet of galleys maintained a superiority in the Mediterranean. In the thirteenth century a struggle with Genoa commenced, which, after many vicissitudes, ended in the total ruin of the Pisans. Pisa subsequently became the prey of various petty tyrants, and was finally united to Florence in 1406.

2. The *Canaries* are a group of fourteen islands belonging to Spain. The peak of Teneriffe, a half extinct volcano, on one of the more distant islands, is about two hundred and fifty miles from the north-west coast of Africa, and eight hundred miles south-west from the straits of Gibraltar.

3. The *Cape de Verd* islands, belonging to Portugal, are off the west coast of Africa, about three hundred and twenty miles west from Cape de Verd.

4. The *Azores* (az-ōres') are about eight hundred miles west from Portugal. The name is said to be derived from the vast number of hawks, (called by the Portuguese *açor,*) by which they were frequented. At the time of their discovery they were uninhabited, and covered with forest and underwood.

adventurous, repaired to Lisbon[1] to increase their knowledge by the
discoveries of the Portuguese, and to join in their enterprises. Among
them Christopher Columbus, a native of Genoa, arrived there about
the year 1470. He had already made himself familiar with the
navigation of the Mediterranean, and had visited Iceland;[2] and he
now accompanied the Portuguese in their expeditions to the coast of
Guinea[3] and the African islands. But while others were seeking a
passage to India by the slow and tedious process of sailing around
the southern extremity of Africa, the bold and daring mind of Columbus conceived the project of reaching the desired land by a western route, directly across the Atlantic. The spherical figure of the
earth was then known, and Columbus doubted not that our globe
might be circumnavigated.

3. Of the gradual maturing and development of the theory of Columbus,—of the poverty and toil which he endured, and the ridicule
humiliation, and disappointments which he encountered, as he wandered from court to court, soliciting the patronage which ignorance,
bigotry, prejudice, and pedantic pride, so long denied him,—and of his
final triumph, in the discovery of a new continent, equal to the old
world in magnitude, and separated by vast oceans from all the earth
before known to civilized man,—our limits forbid us to enter into
details, and it would likewise be superfluous, as these events have already been familiarized to American readers by the chaste and glowing narrative of their countryman Irving. In the year 1492, the
genius of Columbus, more than realizing the dreams of Plato's
famous Atlantis,[4] revealed to the civilized world another hemisphere,

1. *Lisbon*, the capital and principal seaport of Portugal, is situated on the right bank, and
near the mouth, of the Tagus. The Moors captured the city in the year 716, and, with some
slight exceptions, it remained in their power till, in 1145, Alphonso I. made it the capital of
his kingdom. (*Map* No. XIII.)

2. *Iceland* is a large island in the Northern Ocean, on the confines of the polar circle. It
was discovered by a Norwegian pirate in the year 861, and was soon after settled by Norwegians. In the year 928 the inhabitants formed themselves into a republic, which existed nearly
our hundred years; after which Iceland again became subject to Norway. On the annexation
of that kingdom to Denmark, Iceland was transferred with it.

3. *Guinea* is a name applied by European geographers to designate that portion of the African coast extending from about eleven degrees north of the equator, to seventeen degrees
south.

4. *Atlantis* was a celebrated island supposed to have existed at a very early period in the
Atlantic Ocean, and to have been, eventually, sunk beneath its waves. Plato is the first who
gives an account of it, and he obtained his information from the priests of Egypt. The statement which he furnishes is substantially as follows:

"In the Atlantic Ocean, over against the pillars of Hercules, lay a very large and fertile
island, whose surface was variegated by mountains and valleys, its coasts indented with many
navigable rivers, and its fields well cultivated. In its vicinity were other islands from which

and first opened a communication between Europe and America that
will never cease while the waters of the ocean continue to roll between them.   Five years after the discovery of America, Vasco de
Gama, a Portuguese admiral, doubled the Cape of Good Hope, and
had the glory of carrying his national flag as far as India.   These
were the closing maritime enterprises of the fifteenth century: they
opened to the Old World new scenes of human existence: new na
tions, new races, and new continents, rapidly crowded upon the
vision; and imagination tired in contemplating the future wonders
that the genius of discovery was about to develop.

there was a passage to a large continent lying beyond.   The island of Atlantis was thickly settled and very powerful: its kings extended their sway over Africa as far as Egypt, and over
Europe until they were checked by the Athenians, who, opposing themselves to the invaders,
became the conquerors.   But at length that Atlantic island, by a flood and earthquake, was
suddenly destroyed, and for a long time afterwards the sea thereabouts was full of rocks and
shoals."

A dispute arose among the ancient philosophers whether Plato's statement was based upon
reality, or was a mere creation of fancy. Posidonius thought it worthy of belief: Pliny remains undecided.   Among modern writers, Rudbeck labors to prove that Sweden was the
Atlantis of the ancients: Bailly places it in the farthest regions of the north, believing that the
Atlantides were the far-famed Hyperboreans; while others connect *America*, with its Mexican
and Peruvian remains of a remote civilization, with the legend of the lost Atlantis.   In connection with this view they point to the peculiar conformation of our continent along the
shores of the Gulf of Mexico, where everything indicates the sinking, at a remote period, of a
large tract of land, the place of which is now occupied by the waters of the Gulf.   And may
not the mountain tops of this sunken land still appear to view as the islards of the West Indian
group; and may not the large continent lying beyond Atlantis and the adjacent islands have
been none other than America?

o*   21

CHAPTER III.

EUROPEAN HISTORY DURING THE SIXTEENTH CENTURY

I. INTRODUCTORY.

ANALYSIS   I. The unity of ancient history. How broken, in the history of the Middle Ages. Still less unity in modern history. How, only, confusion can be avoided.—2. Approximation towards a knowledge of universal history. Future plan of the work. What must not be overlooked, and what alone we can hope to accomplish.—3. State of Europe at the beginning of the sixteenth century. Condition of Persia. Mogul empire in Hindostan. China. Egypt. The New World. Where, only, we look for historic unity.

II. THE AGE OF HENRY VIII., AND CHARLES V.

1. Rise of the STATES-SYSTEM OF EUROPE. Growing intricacy of the relations between States.—2. Causes of the first development of the States-system.—3. The Great power of Austria under Charles V.—4. Ferdinand, the brother of Charles. Philip II., son of Charles.—5. Beginning of THE RIVALRY BETWEEN FRANCIS I. AND CHARLES V. The favor of HENRY VIII. OF ENGLAND courted by both.—6. Favorable position of Henry at the time of his accession.—7. Efforts of Charles and Francis to win his favor. The result.—8. Efforts of Francis to recover Navarre. The Italian war that followed. Francis defeated, and made prisoner, in the battle of Pavia. [House of Bourbon.]—9. Imprisonment, and release, of Francis.—10. A general league against Charles V.—11. Operations of the duke of Bourbon in Italy. Pillage of Rome, and death of Bourbon.—12. Captivity of the pope. The French army in Italy. The peace of Cambray.—13. The domestic relations of Henry VIII.—14. The rise, power, and fall, of Wolsey.

15. THE REFORMATION. The maxim of religious freedom. Papal power and pretensions at this period. Persecution of reformers. [Wickliffe. Council of Constance. The Albigenses.] Effect of advancing civilization on papal power. Avarice of pope Leo. X. Indulgences. Martin Luther. [Wittemberg.]—16. Luther's first opposition to the Church of Rome. His gradual progress in rejecting the doctrines and rites of popery. His writings declared heretical. He burns the papal bull of condemnation.—17. Declaration of the Sorbonne. [Sorbonne.] The diet of Worms. Henry VIII. joins in opposing Luther.—18. Circumstances in Luther's favor. Decrees of the diet of Spires. Protest of the Reformers. [Spires.]—19. The diet of Augsburg, 1530. [Augsburg.]—Melancthon. Result of the diet. League of the Protestants. Henry VIII. and Francis I. favor the Protestant cause.—20. Invasion of Hungary by the Turks. Crusade of Charles V. against the Moors. [Algiers.] Renewal of the war by the French monarch. [Savoy.] Invasion of France by Charles.—21. Brief truce, and renewal of the war. [Nice.] The Parties to this war, and its results. [Cerisoles. Boulogne.]—22. War carried on by Charles against his Protestant German subjects. Revolt of Maurice of Saxony.—23. Surprise and mortification of Charles, and final treaty of Augsburg. [Passau.]

24. Circumstances which led to the ABDICATION AND RETIREMENT OF CHARLES V. [St. Just.]—25. The emperor in his retirement.—26. The Protestant States of Europe. Character of the Reformation in England. Religious intolerance of Henry. Character of Henry's government.—27. Brief reign of Edward VI. Reign of Mary. Character of her reign. War with France. [St. Quentin.] Death of Mary, and accession of Elizabeth, 1588.

III. THE AGE OF ELIZABETH.

1. The claims of Elizabeth not recognized by the Catholic States. MARY OF SCOTLAND.—2. Progress of Protestant principles in England. Philip II. Effect of the rivalry between France and Spain.—3. Death of Henry II. of France. Francis II. and Charles IX. Mary proceeds to

Scotland. Principal events of her reign. She throws herself on the protection of Elizabeth.—
4. The attempts to establish the Inquisition on the continent. Circumstances which led to
the CIVIL AND RELIGIOUS WAR IN FRANCE. [Havre-de-Grace.]—5. Character of this war.
Atrocities committed on both sides. [Guienne. Dauphiny.]—6. Battle of Dreux. Capture
of the opposing generals, and conclusion of the war by the treaty of Amboise. [Amboise.]—
7. Renewal of the war. The "Lame Peace." Treachery of the Catholics. Peace of St.
Germain. [St. Germain.]—8. Designs of the French Court. Preparations for the destruction
of the Protestants.—9. MASSACRE OF ST. BARTHOLOMEW.—10. General massacre throughout
the kingdom. Noble conduct of some officers. The princes of Navarre and Condé. 11. The
joy excited by the massacre. Commemoration and defence of it. 12. The real causes which
induced it. Character of the age. Servetus. Melancthon. 13. The Spanish Inquisition.
Philip II. Intolerance. 14. Renewal of the civil war. The feelings of Charles,—his sickness
and death.

15. The duke of Alva's administration of THE NETHERLANDS. The "Pacification of Ghent,"
and expulsion of the Spaniards. [Ghent.] 16. Causes that led to the "union of Utrecht."
[Utrecht.] The States-general of 1580. [Antwerp.] Continuance of the war by Philip.—17.
The remaining history and fate of Mary of Scotland.—18. Resentment of the Catholics. Complaints, and projects of Philip.—19. Vast preparations of Philip against England, and sailing
of THE SPANISH ARMADA. Preparations for resistance.—20. Disasters, and final destruction
of the fleet. Important results. Decline of the Spanish power.—21. History of France during
the remainder of the sixteenth century. Charles IX., Henry III., and Henry IV. Termination of the religious wars by the EDICT OF NANTES.—History of England after the defeat of
the Spanish Armada. Irish insurrection of 1598.—CHARACTER OF ELIZABETH.

IV. COTEMPORARY HISTORY.

1. Prominent events of the sixteenth century not included in European history. The POR-
TUGUESE COLONIAL EMPIRE. Union of Portugal with Spain. The Hollanders. [Ormus,
Goa.]—2. SPANISH COLONIAL EMPIRE. Services of Cortez, and the treatment which he re-
ceived.—3. The conquests of Pizarro. The Spanish empire in America at the close of the
sixteenth century. Influence of the precious metals upon Spain.—4. THE MOGUL EMPIRE IN
INDIA.—5. THE PERSIAN EMPIRE. The reign of Ismael.—6. The reign of Tamasp. His three
sons. The youthful Abbas becomes ruler of the empire.—7. General character of his reign.
His character as a parent and relative. 8. Remaining history of Persia.

I. INTRODUCTORY.—1. In the history of ancient Europe, two predominating nations,—first the Greeks, and afterwards the Romans,
occupy the field; preserving, in the mind of the reader, a general
unity of action and of interest. In the history of the Middle Ages
this unity is broken by the forcible dismemberment of the Roman
empire, by the confusion that followed the inroads of the barbarians,
and that attended their first attempt at social organization, and by
the introduction of a broader field of inquiry, embracing countries
and nations previously unknown. In Modern History, subsequent
to the fifteenth century, there is still less apparent unity, if we consider the increased extent of the field to be explored, and the still
greater variety of nations, governments, and institutions, submitted
to our view; and to avoid inextricable confusion, and dry summaries
of unintelligible events, we are under the necessity, in a brief compend like the present, of selecting and developing the *principal
points* of historic interest, and of rendering all other matters subordinate to the main design.

2. But while it would be in vain to attempt, within the limits of a work like the present, to give a separate history of every nation, the reader should not lose sight of any,—that, as opportunities occur, he may have a place in the general framework of history for the stores which subsequent reading may accumulate. It was in accordance with these views, that, near the close of the preceding chapter, we took a general survey of the nations of Europe; and although a few of the European kingdoms will still continue to claim our chief attention in the subsequent part of this history, we must not shut our eyes to the fact that they embraced, during this period, but a small portion of the population of the globe; and that a History, strictly *universal*, would comprise the cotemporary annals of more than *i* hundred different nations. The extent of the field of modern history is indeed vast; in it we can select only a few verdant spots, with which alone we can hope to make the reader familiar; while the riches of many an unexplored region must be left to repay the labor of future researches.

3. At the opening of the sixteenth century, Great Britain, Scotland, France, Spain, Portugal, Germany, Poland, Prussia, and Turkey, were distinct and independent nations; Hungary and Bohemia were temporarily united under one sovereignty; Denmark, Sweden, and Norway, still feebly united by the union of Calmar, were soon to be divided again; the Netherlands, known as the dominions of the House of Burgundy, had become a dependence of the Austrian division of the Germanic empire; and Italy, comprising the Papal States, and a number of petty republics and dukedoms, was fast becoming the prey of surrounding sovereigns. In the *East*, Persia, after having been for centuries the theatre of perpetual civil wars, revolutions, and changes of no interest to foreigners, again emerged from obscurity at the beginning of the sixteenth century, and, toward the end of that period, under the Shah Abbas, surnamed the Great, established an empire embracing Persia Proper, Media, Mesopotamia, Syria, and Farther Armenia. About the same time a Tartar or Mogul empire was established in Hindostan by a descendant of the great conqueror Tamerlane. China was at this time, as it had long been, a great empire, although but little known. Egypt, under the successors of the victorious Saracens, still preserved the semblance of sovereignty, until, in 1517, the Turks reduced it to the condition of a province of the Ottoman empire. Such were the principal States, kingdoms, and nations, of the Old World, whose

annals find a place on the page of *universal* history; and, turning
to the West, beyond the wide ocean whose mysteries had been so recently unveiled by the Genoese navigator, we find the germs of civilized nations already starting into being;—and History must enlarge
its volume to take in a mere abstract of the annals that now begin
to press forward for admission to its pages.   Amidst this perplexing
profusion of the materials of history, we turn back to the localities
already familiar to the reader, and seek for historic unity where only
it can be found,—in those principles, and events, that have exerted
a world-wide influence on the progress of civilization, and the des
tinies of the human race.

II. THE AGE OF HENRY VIII. AND CHARLES V.—1. About the
period of the beginning of the sixteenth century a new era opens in
European history, in the rise of what has sometimes been called "the
States-system of Europe;" for it was now that the re-   I. THE STATES-
ciprocal influences of the European States on each other SYSTEM OF
began to be exerted on a large scale, and that the weaker EUROPE.
States first conceived the idea of a balance-of-power system that
should protect them against their more powerful neighbors.   Hence
the increasing extent and intricacy of the relations that began to
grow up between States, by treaties of alliance, embassies, negotiations, and guarantees; and the more general combination of powers
in the wars that arose out of the ambition of some princes, and the
attempts of others to preserve the political equilibrium.

2. The inordinate growth of the power of the house of Austria,
in the early part of the sixteenth century, first developed the de
fensive and conservative system to which we have alluded; and for
a long time the principal object of all the wars and alliances of
Europe was to humble the ambition of some one nation, whose preponderance seemed to threaten the liberty and independence of the
rest.

3 It has been stated that the marriage of Maximilian of Austria,
with Mary of Bur'gundy, secured to the house of Austria the whole
of Bur'gundy, and the "Low Countries," corresponding to the
modern Netherlands.   In the year 1506, Charles, known in history
as Charles V., a grandson of Maximilian and Mary of Austria, and
also of Ferdinand and Isabella of Spain, inherited the Low Countries:
on the death of Ferdinand, in 1516, he became heir to the whole
Spanish succession, which comprehended Spain, Naples, Sicily, and

Sardinia, together with Spanish America. To these vast possessions
were added his patrimonial dominions in Austria; and in 1519 the
imperial dignity of the Germanic empire was conferred upon him by
the choice of the electors, when he was only in his nineteenth year.

4. Charles soon resigned to his brother Ferdinand his hereditary
Austrian States; but the two brothers, acting in concert for the advancement of their reciprocal interests, were regarded but as one
power by the alarmed sovereigns of Europe, who began to suspect
that the Austrian princes aimed at universal monarchy; and their
jealousy was increased when Ferdinand, by marriage, secured the addition of Hungary and Bohemia to his dominions; and, at a later
period, Charles, in a similar manner, obtained for his son, afterwards
Philip II. of Spain, the future sovereignty of Portugal.

5. When the imperial throne of Germany became vacant by the
death of Maximilian, Francis I. of France and Charles
V. were competitors for the crown; and on the success
of the latter, the mutual claims of the two princes
on each other's dominions, especially in Italy and the
Low Countries, soon made them declared enemies.
France then took the lead in attempting to regulate the balance of
power against the house of Austria; and the favor of
Henry VIII. of England was courted by the rival monarchs, as the prince most likely to secure the victory to
whomsoever he should give the weight of his influence.

*IL. THE RI-
VALRY BE-
TWEEN FRAN-
CIS I. AND
CHARLES V.*

*III. HENRY
VIII. OF
ENGLAND.*

6. In year 1509 Henry VIII., then at the age of eighteen, had
succeeded his father Henry VII. on the throne of England,—receiving at the same time a rich treasury and a flourishing kingdom,
and uniting in his person the opposing claims of the houses of York
and Lancaster. The real power of the English monarch was at this
time greater than at any previous period; and Henry VIII. might
have been the arbiter of Europe, in the rivalries and wars between
Francis I. and Charles V., had not his actions been the result of
passion, vanity, caprice, or resentment, rather than of enlightened
policy.

7. Each of the rival princes sedulously endeavored to enlist the
English monarch in his favor: both gave a pension to his prime
minister, cardinal Wolsey; and each had an interview with the
king—Francis meeting him at Calais, and Charles visiting him in
England,—but the latter won Henry through the influence of Wolsey whose egregious vanity he duped by encouraging his hopes of

promotion to the papal crown. Moreover, Henry was, at the beginning, ill-disposed towards the king of France, who virtually governed Scotland through the influence of the regent Albany; and, by an alliance with Charles, he hoped to recover a part of those domains which his ancestors had formerly possessed in France. Charles also gained the aid of the pope, Leo X.; but, on the other hand, Francis was supported by the Swiss, the Genoese, and the Venetians.

8. In the year 1520 Francis seized the opportunity of an insurrection in Spain to attempt the recovery of Navarre, which had been united to the French crown by marriage alliance in 1490, and conquered by Ferdinand of Spain in 1512. Navarre was won and lost in the course of a few months, and the war was then transferred to Italy. In two successive years the French governor of Milan was driven from Lombardy: the Duke of Bourbon,[1] constable of France, the best general of Francis, who had received repeated affronts from the king, his master, deserted to Charles, and was by him invested with the chief command of his forces; and in the year 1525 Francis himself was defeated by his rebellious subject in the battle of Pavia, and taken prisoner, but not until his horse had been killed under him, and his armor, which is still preserved, had been indented by numerous bullets and lances. In the battle of Pavia the French army was almost totally destroyed. In a single line Francis conveyed the sad intelligence to his mother. "Madam all is lost but honor."

9. Francis was conveyed a prisoner to Madrid; and it was only at the expiration of a year that he obtained his release, when a fever, occasioned by despondency, had already threatened to put an end at once to his life, and the advantages which Charles hoped to derive from his captivity. Francis had already prepared to abdicate the throne in favor of his son the dauphin, when Charles decided to

---

1. The house of *Bourbon* derives its name from the small village of Bourbon in the former province of Bourbonnais, now in the department of Allier, thirteen miles west from Moulins, and one hundred and sixty-five miles south from Paris. (*Map* No. XIII.) In early times this town had lords of its own, who bore the title of barons. Aimer, who lived in the early part of the tenth century, is the first of these barons of whom history gives any account. The male princes of this line having become extinct, Beatrix, duchess of Bourbon, married Robert, second son of St. Louis; and their son Louis, duke of Bourbon, who died in 1341, became the founder of the house of Bourbon. Two branches of this house took their origin from the two sons of Louis. The elder line became extinct at the death of the constable of Bourbon, who defeated Francis at Pavia, and was himself killed in 1527, in the assault of the city of Rome. From the other line have sprung several branches,—first, the royal branch, and that of Condé; since which the former has undergone several subdivisions, giving sovereigns to France, to Spain, the two Sicilies, and Lucca and Parma.

release the captive monarch, after exacting from him a stipulation to surrender Bur'gundy, to renounce his pretensions to Milan and Naples, and to ally himself, by marriage, with the family of his enemy But Francis, before his release, had secretly protested, in the presence of his chancellor, against the validity of a treaty extorted from him while a prisoner; and, once at liberty, it was not difficult for him to elude it. His joy at his release was unbounded. Being escorted to the frontiers of France, and having passed a small stream that divides the two kingdoms, he mounted a Turkish horse, and putting him at full speed, and waving his hand over his head, exclaimed aloud, several times, "I am yet a king!" (March 18, 1526.)

10. The liberation of Francis was the signal for a general league against Charles V. The Italian States, which, since the battle of Pavia, had been in the power of the Spanish and German armies, now regarded the French as liberators; the pope put himself at the head of the league; the Swiss joined it; and Henry VIII., alarmed at the increasing power of Charles, entered into a treaty with Francis, so that the very reverses of the French monarch, by exciting the jealousy of other States against his rival, rendered him much stronger in alliances than before.

11. During these events, the rebel Duke of Bourbon remained in Italy, quartering his mercenary troops on the unfortunate inhabitants of Milan; but when the Italians declared against the emperor, all Italy was delivered up to pillage. To obtain the greater plunder, Bourbon marched upon Rome, followed not only by his own soldiers, but by an additional force of fourteen thousand brigands from Germany. Pope Clement, terrified by the greatness of the danger which menaced the States of the Holy See, discharged his best troops, and shut himself up in the castle of St. Angelo. Rome was attacked, and carried by storm, although Bourbon fell in the assault; the pillage was universal, neither convents nor churches being spared; from seven to eight thousand Romans were massacred the first day and not all the ravages of the Goths and Huns surpassed those of the army of the first prince in christendom.

12. The pillage of Rome, and the captivity of the pope, excited great indignation throughout Europe; and the hypocritical Charles, instead of sending orders for his liberation, ordered prayers for his deliverance to be offered in all the Spanish churches. At this favorable moment Francis sent an army into Italy, which penetrated to the very walls of Naples; but here his prosperity ended; and the

impolicy of the French king, in disgusting and alienating his most faithful allies, lost for him all the advantages which he had gained. Both the rival monarchs now desired peace, but both strove to dissemble their real sentiments : although Charles had been generally fortunate in the contest, yet all his revenues were expended ; and he desired a respite from the cares of war to enable him to crush the Reformation, which had already made considerable progress in his German dominions. A peace was therefore concluded at Cambray, in August 1529, which was as glorious to Charles as it was disgraceful to France and her monarch. The former remained supreme master of Italy ; the pope submitted ; the Venetians were shorn of their conquests ; and Henry VIII. reaped nothing but the emperor's enmity for his interference.

13. The conduct of Henry VIII. in his domestic relations reflects disgrace upon his name, and is a dark stain upon his character. He was first married to Catherine of Aragon, daughter of Ferdinand and Isabella of Spain, and aunt of Charles V. of Germany, a woman much older than himself, but who acquired and retained an ascendancy over his affections for nearly twenty years. For divorcing her, and marrying Anne Boleyn, he was excommunicated by the pope,—a measure which induced him to break of all allegiance to the Holy See, and declare himself supreme head of the English church. Three years after his second marriage, a new passion for Jane Seymour, one of the queen's maids of honor, effaced from his memory all the virtues and graces of Anne Boleyn ; and seventeen days saw the latter pass from the throne to the scaffold. The marriage ceremony with the lady Jane was performed on the day following the execution. Her death followed, in little more than a year. In 1540 Henry married Anne of Cleves, on the recommendation of his minister Cromwell ; but his dislike to his new wife hastened the fall of that minister, who was unjustly condemned and executed on a charge of treason. Soon after, Henry procured a divorce from Anne, and married Catherine Howard, niece of the duke of Norfolk ; but on a charge of dissolute conduct Catherine was brought to the scaffold. In 1543 the king married Catherine Parr, who alone, of all his wives, survived him ; and even she, before the king's death, came near being brought to the block on a charge of heresy.

14. Soon after the accession of Henry, the celebrated Wolsey appeared on the theatre of English politics. Successfully courting the favor of the monarch, he soon obtained the first place in the royal

favor, and became uncontrolled minister.   Numerous ecclesiastical
dignities were conferred upon him : in 1518, the pope, to ingratiate
himself with Henry, created Wolsey cardinal. Courted by the emperors of France and Germany, he received pensions from both ;
and ere long his revenues nearly equalled those of the crown, part
of which he expended in pomp and ostentation, and part in laudable
munificence for the advancement of learning.   When Henry, seized
with a passion for Anne Boleyn, one of the queen's maids of honor,
formed the design of getting rid of Catherine, and of making the
new favorite his wife, Wolsey was suspected of abetting the delays
of the court of Rome, which had been appealed to by Henry for a
divorce. The displeasure of the king was excited against his minister ; and, in the course of three years, Wolsey, repeatedly accused
of treason, and gradually stripped of all his possessions, died of a
broken heart.   (1530.)   In his last moments he is said to have
exclaimed, in the bitterness of humiliation and remorse, "Had I
but served my God as diligently as I have served my king, he
would not have given me over in my gray hairs."

15. During the stirring and eventful period of the early rivalries
of Francis I. and Charles V.—a period full of great
IV. THE RE-
FORMATION.   events, of conquests and reverses, all arising out of the
selfish views of individual monarchs, but none of them
causing any lasting change or progress in human affairs, the subject
of the *Reformation of the Church* began to agitate all classes, and
to give fresh life to the public mind in Europe.   The immoralities
and crimes of such popes as Alexander VI., and the corrupt lives
of great numbers of the clergy, had, even before the sixteenth century, become the scandal of the church.[1]   Added to this, the popes,
as the divinely appointed head of the church, had long claimed for
themselves the right to both spiritual and temporal authority over
all the kingdoms of the world : they avowed, and their adherents
proclaimed, the doctrine of papal *infallibility*, or "entire exemp-
tion from liability to err, in matters of religious doctrine and belief ; " and, although bold men in every age had protested against
papal pretensions, yet the great mass of the people, the clergy, the

---

1. The corrupt state of the church, in the age prior to the Reformation, is candidly acknowledged by the learned Italian cardinal, Robert Bellarmine, the great champion of the
Roman Catholic Church, who died in 1621. He says: " For some years before the Lutheran
and Calvinistic heresies were published, there was not any severity in ecclesiastical judicato-
ries, any discipline with regard to morals, any knowledge of sacred literature, any reverence
for divine things : there was almost not any religion remaining."

nobility, and the monarchs, still regarded the pope as the supreme
authority in matters of religion. The memory and opinions of
Wickliffe[1] the reformer had been solemnly condemned by the
council of Constance[2] thirty years after his death : John Huss, and
Jerome of Prague, with many others of less celebrity, had been
publicly burned for professing heretical opinions ; and the creed
of the unfortunate Albigenses[3] had been extinguished in blood.
Yet, in the progress of society, the power and authority of the
popes declined ; and the spirit of religious inquiry daily grew more
rife. At this time an enormous extension was given to the traffic
in indulgences, which, in the theory of the church, are remissions
of temporal punishment or penance only. This traffic was carried
on chiefly by the mendicant monks,—the pope, Alexander VI., having been the first to declare officially that they released from purgatory.[4] Even temporal sovereigns, with that singular blending

1. *Wickliffe*, born in England about the year 1324—called the "morning star of the Reformation"—was an eminent divine and ecclesiastical reformer. He vigorously defended secular
authority against papal encroachments, and attacked the abuses of the church. The pope insisted on his being brought to trial as a heretic; but he was effectually protected by his patron,
the duke of Lancaster. He died in 1384.

2. *Constance*, a city highly interesting from its historical associations, is on the river Rhine,
at the point where the river unites the upper part of the Lake of Constance with the lower.

The great object of the celebrated *Council of Constance*, which continued in session from
1414 to 1418, was to remove the divisions in the church, settle controversies, and vindicate
the authority of general councils, to which the Roman pontiff was declared to be amenable.
When, in 1411, Sigismund ascended the throne of Germany, there were three popes, each of
whom had anathematized the two others. To put an end to these disorders, and stop the
influence of John Huss, a native of Bohemia, who had adopted and zealously propagated
some of the doctrines of Wickliffe, Sigismund summoned a general council. The alleged
heresies of Wickliffe and Huss were condemned ; and the latter, notwithstanding the assurances of safety given him by the German emperor, was burnt at the stake, July 6th, 1415.
His friend and companion, Jerome of Prague, met with the same fate, May 30th, 1416. After
the ecclesiastical dignitaries supposed they had sufficiently checked the progress of heresies
by these executions, they proceeded to depose the three popes, or anti-popes, John XXIII.,
Gregory XII., and Benedict XIII. They next elected Martin V., and thus put an end to a
schism that had lasted forty years.

3. *Albigenses* is a name given to several heretical sects in the south of France, who, while
they cherished certain superstitious beliefs of their own, opposed the dominion of the Roman
hierarchy, and aimed to restore the simplicity of primitive Christianity. In 1209 they were
first attacked, in a cruel and desolating war, by the army of the cross, called together by
pope Innocent III.—the first war which the church waged against heretics within her own
dominions. In 1229 Louis VIII. of France fell in a campaign against the heretics. It is said
that hundreds of thousands fell, on both sides, in this war; but the Albigenses were subdued,
and the inquisition was called in to extirpate any remaining germs of heresy. The name of
the Albigenses disappeared about the middle of the thirteenth century ; but fugitives of their
party formed, in the mountains of Piedmont and Lombardy, what is called the French Church,
which was continued to the times of the Hussites and the Reformation. But the Albigenses
are not to be confounded with the Waldenses, who were a distinct party, of a purer faith.

4. *Ranke's* Hist. of the Popes, p. 24. *Mosheim*, iii. 83, translation. For the *form* of Papal
Letters of Indulgence, see Robertson's Charles V., Harper's edition, p. 128.

of worldly greed and religious zeal which was characteristic of the age, sought to make a gain of this traffic; and in the year 1500 the imperial government of Germany restricted the papal legates to a third of the produce of indulgences, reserving the other two-thirds to itself, to be devoted to the war against the Turks. Even under the papal rule of Leo X.,—enlightened, kindly, and genial as he was, and a munificent patron of learning and the arts,—indulgences were sold by thousands among the credulous German peasantry. Martin Luther, a man of high reputation for sanctity and learning, and then professor of theology at Wittemberg[1] on the Elbe, first called in question the efficacy of these indulgences; and his word, like a talisman, broke the spell of papal supremacy.

16. In 1517 Luther first read in public his famous theses, or propositions, in which he bitterly inveighed against the traffic in indulgences, and challenged all the learned men of the day to contest them with him in a public disputation. Luther did not at once form the resolution to separate from the papal church; but the pressure of circumstances, and the warmth of controversy with his adversaries, impelled him from one step to another; and as he enlarged his observation and reading, and discovered new abuses and errors, he began to entertain doubts of the pope's divine authority—rejected the doctrine of his infallibility—gradually abolished the practice of mass, auricular confession, and the worship of images—denied the doctrine of purgatory, and opposed the fastings of the church, monastic vows, and the celibacy of the clergy. In 1520 the pope declared the writings of Luther heretical; and Luther in return solemnly burned, on the public square of Wittemberg, the papal bull of condemnation, and the volumes of the canon law of the papal church.

17. In 1521 the council of the Sorbonne, in Paris, under the influence of the French monarch, declared, "that flames, and not reasoning, ought to be employed against the arrogance of Luther;" and in the same year the diet of Worms, at which Charles V. himself presided, pronounced the imperial ban of excommunication against Luther, his adherents, and protectors, condemned his writings to be burned, and commanded him to be seized and brought

1. *Wittemberg*, a town of Prussian Saxony, on the Elbe, is fifty miles south-west from Berlin. (*Map* No. XVII.) It derives its chief interest from its having been the cradle of the Reformation,—Luther and Melancthon having both been professors in its university, and their remains being deposited in its cathedral. A noble bronze statue of the great reformer was erected in the market-place in 1821.

to punishment. The king of England, Henry VIII., who made pretensions to theological learning, wrote a volume against Luther; and the pope was so pleased with this token of Henry's religious zeal, that he conferred upon him the title of "*defender of the faith*," an appellation still retained by the sovereigns of England.

18. But notwithstanding this opposition from high quarters, the age was rife for changes: the art of printing rapidly spread the tenets of the reformers; and many of the German princes espoused the cause of Luther, and gave him protection. But Charles V., after the peace of Cambray, had determined to arrest the farther progress of the Reformation; and for this purpose he proceeded to Germany, where he assembled a diet of the empire at Spires,[1] March, 1529; and here the majority of the States, which were Catholic, decreed that the edicts of the diet of Worms should be retained, and that all those who had been gained over to the new doctrine should abstain from farther innovations. The reformers, including nearly half the German princes, entered a decided *protest* against these proceedings, on which account they were distinguished as Protestants,—an appellation since applied indiscriminately to all the sects, of whatever denomination, that have withdrawn from the Romish church. Impartial history, in passing judgment upon Luther, the great light of the Reformation, is compelled to admit that, with all his really grand qualities, he was not without serious defects of character. He was of a dogmatic temper: he sometimes treated with harshness his brother reformers who differed from him; and his paradoxical statements of the new doctrines occasionally gave his opponents an advantage over him. Nor was religious freedom—general freedom of thought, aimed at by Luther, or, so far as known, by any of the early reformers, although it was, indeed, the natural tendency of the Reformation. That Luther was tolerant, *for the times*, is true; but it was an intolerant age; and few, if any, rose wholly superior to its baneful influences.[2]

19. In the year 1530 Charles assembled another diet of the empire at Augsburg,[3] to try the great cause of the Reformation, hoping to be able to effect a reconciliation between the opposing parties, although he was urged by the pope to have recourse at once to the

1. *Spires*, one of the most ancient cities of Germany, is in Rhenish Bavaria, on the west bank of the Rhine, twenty-two miles south of Worms.

2. See University edition, pp. 794–7.

3. *Augsburg* is a city of Bavaria, between and near the confluence of the rivers Wertach and Lech, branches of the Danube, thirty-five miles northwest from Munich.

most rigorous measures against the stubborn enemies of the Catholic faith.   The learned and peaceable Melancthon presented to the diet the articles of the Lutheran creed, since known by the name of the confession of Augsburg; but no reconciliation of opposing opinions could be effected; and the Protestants were commanded to renounce their errors, upon pain of being put under the ban of the empire.   Charles was preparing to employ violence, when the Protestant princes of Germany concluded a defensive league (Dec. 1530), and having obtained promises of aid from the kings of France, England, and Denmark, held themselves ready for combat.   At this time Henry VIII., although abhorring all connection with the Lutherans, was fast approaching a rupture with the pope, who stood in the way of the king's contemplated divorce from his first wife Catherine, and his marriage with the afterwards unfortunate Anne Boleyn; and Francis, although he burned heretics in France, did not hesitate to league himself with the reformers of Germany, in order to weaken the power of his rival.

20. In addition to these obstacles to the purpose of Charles, at this moment the Turkish sultan, Solyman the Magnificent, invaded Hungary, at the head of three hundred thousand men; and Charles, fearing the consequences of a religious war at this juncture, hastened to offer to the Protestants all the toleration they demanded, until the next diet.   After the Turks had been defeated, and driven back upon their own territories, Charles thought it his duty, as the greatest monarch, and the protector of entire Christendom, to make a crusade against the piratical Moors of Northern Africa, who, under their leader Barbarossa, held Tunis and Algiers,[1] and were in close alliance with the Turkish sultan.   In the summer of 1535 he landed at Tunis at the head of thirty thousand men, defeated the Moors in battle, and, to his inexpressible joy, was enabled to set at liberty twenty-two thousand Christian captives, whom the Moors had reduced to slavery.   On his return from this expedition he found the king of France preparing for war against him; and the hostilities which immediately broke out between the rival monarchs delayed the decisive rupture between the Catholics and Protestants of Germany for a period of twelve years.   In the summer of 1535 Francis invaded Savoy,[2] and threatened Milan; and

1. *Algiers*, or Algeria, a country of northern Africa, having the city Algiers for its capital, comprises the *Numidia* proper of the ancients.   It formed part of the Roman empire.
2. *Savoy*, now included in the kingdom of Sardinia, is in north-western Italy, south of the Lake of Geneva, and bordering on France and Switzerland.   (*Map* No. XIII.)

in the following year Charles V. entered the south of France with a large force; but the French marshal, Montmorency, who commanded there, acting the part of the Roman Fabius, avoided a general battle, laid waste the country, and finally compelled the emperor to retreat in disgrace, with the wreck of a ruined army.

21. In 1538 the rival monarchs, having exhausted all their pecuniary resources, concluded, at Nice,[1] a truce of ten years, through the mediation of the pope; but in 1542 war was again renewed,— the king of Scotland and the sultan of Turkey, together with the Protestant princes of Germany, Denmark, and Sweden, uniting with France, and the king of England taking part with the emperor Charles V. In vain Francis and Solyman, uniting their fleets, bombarded the castle of Nice; and the odious spectacle of the crescent and the cross united, alienated all the Christian world from the king of France. (1543.) The French, however, gained the brilliant victory of Cerisoles[2] against the allies, (April, 1544,) but Henry VIII., crossing over to France, captured Boulogne.[3] (Sept., 1544.) Already Charles had penetrated within thirteen leagues of Paris, when he formed a separate treaty with Francis, at Cressy. A short time later a peace was proclaimed between Francis and Henry, both of whom died in the same year, 1547.

22. At the time of the death of the king of France and the king of England, Charles V. was engaged in a war with his Protestant German subjects, having now determined, in concert with the pope, to adopt decisive measures for putting down the Reformation in his dominions. At the commencement of the war, the Protestant German States, although abandoned by France, Denmark, and England, leagued together for the common defence; but Maurice of Saxony, one of the leading Protestant princes, deserted to the emperor, and the isolated members of the league were soon overthrown. The rule of Charles now became highly tyrannical; and Catholics and Protestants equally declaimed against him. At length Maurice, to whom Charles was chiefly indebted for his recent victories, being secretly dissatisfied with the conduct of the emperor, formed a bold plan for establishing religious freedom, and

1. *Nice* is a seaport of north-western Italy, ninety-five miles south-west from Genoa. (*Map* No. XIII.)

2. *Cerisoles* is a small village of Piedmont, near Carignan, in north-western Italy.

3. *Boulogne* is a seaport town of France on the English Channel, near the Straits of Dover, twenty miles south-west from Calais. (*Map* No. XIII.)

German liberties, but concealed his projects until the most favorable moment for putting them into execution. Having concluded a secret treaty with Henry II. of France, the son and successor of Francis, in 1552 he suddenly proclaimed war against the emperor, issuing at the same time a manifesto of grievances.

23. Charles, taken completely by surprise, narrowly escaped being made prisoner; and after having had the mortification of seeing all his projects overthrown by the man whom he had most trusted, he was compelled to sign the convention of Passau[1] with the Protestants. Three years later, the bad success of the war which he carried on against France changed this convention into the definite peace of Augsburg, (Sept., 1555,) by which the free exercise of religion was secured to the Protestants throughout Germany, although neither party was allowed to seek proselytes at the expense of the other. Such was the first victory of religious liberty under the banner of the Reformation. The spirit that had been awakened, pursued, from this time, a determined course, and all the efforts of princes were not able to arrest its progress.

24. The treaty of Augsburg was to Charles V. the handwriting on the wall which showed him that the end of the mighty power which he had wielded was fast approaching. So offended was the pope at the sanction which Charles had given to the principles of religious toleration, that he became the avowed enemy of the house of Austria, and entered into a close alliance with the young king of France. Charles saw, from afar, the storm that was approaching, and, abandoned as he was by fortune, afflicted by disease, and opposed in his declining years by a rival in the full vigor of life, he wisely resolved not to forfeit his fame by vainly struggling to retain a power which he was no longer able to wield; and, in imitation of Diocletian, to the surprise of the world he abdicated his throne, and, having resigned his German empire to his brother Ferdinand, and his kingdoms of Spain, the Netherlands, and Italy, to his son Philip, he retired to end his days in the solitude of the monastery of St. Just.[2]

25. The ex-emperor divided the hours of his retirement between pious meditation and mechanical inventions, taking little interest in the affairs of the world around him. It is related of him that,

V. ABDICATION AND RETIREMENT OF CHARLES V.

---

1. _Passau_ is a fortified frontier city of eastern Bavaria, on the southern bank of the Danube.
2. The monastery of _St. Just_ is in the province of Estremadura in Spain, near the town of Placencia, about one hundred and twenty miles south-west from Madrid. (_Map_ No. XIII.).

for amusement, he once endeavored to make two watches go exactly alike. Several times he thought he had succeeded; but all in vain—the one went too fast, the other too slow. At length he exclaimed: "Behold, not even two watches can I bring to agree with each other! and yet, fool that I was, I thought that I should be able to govern, like the works of a watch, so many nations all living under different skies, in different climes, and speaking different languages." Finally, shortly before his death, he caused a solemn rehearsal to be made of his own funeral obsequies—a too faithful picture of that eclipsed glory which he had survived. He died in the year 1558, being at the time in the fifty-sixth year of his age.

26. During the reign of Charles V., England, Sweden, and Denmark, had followed the example of Germany in separating from the church of Rome. The Reformation in England, however, was, at this early period, a political rather than a moral and religious change, accomplished by the king and the aristocracy with little regard to the dictates of conscience or the convictions of reason, and retaining in part the Catholic hierarchy. By a decree of parliament (1534) the king was acknowledged as the protector and supreme head of the Church of England; the monasteries were suppressed, and their property, amounting to more than a million of dollars, was given to the crown. Nothing would induce the king to renounce the title, which he had received from the pope, of "defender of the faith;" and, with equal intolerance, he persecuted both Catholics and Protestants,—the former for having denied his supremacy, and the latter as heretics. But while Henry VIII. merely withdrew his kingdom from the authority of the pope, the true principles of the Reformation were spreading among the people. The government of Henry was administered with numerous violations, both of the chartered privileges of Englishmen, and of those still more sacred rights which national law has established; and yet we meet, in cotemporary authorities, with no expressions of abhorrence at his tyranny; but the monarch is often mentioned, after his death, in language of eulogy. Although he had few qualities that deserve esteem, he had many which a nation is pleased to behold in a sovereign.

27. On the death of Henry VIII., in 1547, and the accession of his son Edward[a] VI., then in the tenth year of his age, the Prot-

a. Son of Henry VIII. and Jane Seymour.

~stant religion prevailed in England; but this amiable prince died at the early age of fifteen; and after a rash attempt of a few of the nobility to seat Lady Jane Grey, niece to Henry VIII., on the throne, the sceptre passed to the hands of Edward's sister Mary,[a] (1553,) called the "Bloody Mary," an intolerant Catholic and cruel persecutor of the Protestants. In her reign, of only five years' duration, more than eight hundred miserable victims were burnt at the stake,—martyrs to their religious opinions. Mary married Philip II. of Spain, the son and successor of Charles V., who induced her in 1557 to unite with him in the war against France. Among the events of this war, the most remarkable are the victory of St. Quentin,[1] gained by the Spaniards, and the conquest of Calais by the French, under the duke of Guise, the last possession of the English in France. (1558.) In the same year occurred the death of Mary, about a month later than the death of Charles V. Mary was succeeded by her sister Elizabeth, the daughter of Anne Boleyn, under whose reign the Protestant religion became firmly established in England.

III. The Age of Elizabeth.—1. As the marriage of Henry VIII. with Anne Boleyn had not been sanctioned by the Romish Church, the claims of Elizabeth were not recognized by the Catholic States of Europe; and the youthful Mary,[b] queen of Scotland, and grand niece of Henry VIII., and next heir to the crown if the illegitimacy of England could be established, was regarded by them as the rightful claimant of the throne. Mary, who had been educated in France, in the Catholic faith, and had been married when very young to the dauphin, was persuaded by the king of France, and her maternal uncles, the Guises, to assume the arms and title of Queen of England; a false step, which laid the foundation of all her subsequent misfortunes.

I. MARY OF SCOTLAND.

2. Elizabeth endeavored to promote Protestant principles, as the best safeguard of her throne; and in the year 1559 the parliament formally abolished the papal supremacy, and established the Church of England in its present form. On the other side, Philip II. was the champion of the Catholics; and hence England now became the counterpoise to Spain, as France had been during the reign of

1. *St. Quentin*, formerly a place of great strength, is a town of France, in the former province of Picardy, eighty miles north-east from Paris.

a. Daughter of Henry's first wife Catherine.

b. Daughter of James V., who was son of James IV. and Margaret of England. See p. 307.

Charles V., while the ancient rivalry between France and Spain prevented these Catholic powers from cordially uniting to check the progress of the Reformation.

3. On the death of Henry II. of France, by a mortal wound received at a tournament, (1559,) the feeble Francis II., the husband of Mary of Scotland, ascended the throne, but died the following year, (Dec., 1560,) and was succeeded by his brother Charles IX., then at the age of only ten years. Mary then left France for her native dominions; but she found there the Romish church overthrown, and Protestantism erected in its stead. The marriage of the queen to the young Henry Stuart, Lord Darnley, in spite of the remonstrances of Elizabeth, led to the first open breach between Mary and her Protestant subjects. Darnley, jealous of the ascendency which an Italian, David Rizzio, Mary's private secretary, had acquired over her, headed a band of conspirators who murdered the favorite before the eyes of the queen. Soon after, the house which Darnley inhabited was blown up by powder; Darnley was buried under its ruins; and three months later Mary married the earl of Bothwell, the principal author of the crime. An insurrection of the Protestant lords followed these proceedings; Mary was forced to dismiss Bothwell, and resign the crown to her infant son James VI., but subsequently endeavoring to resume her authority, and being defeated by the regent Murray, her own brother, she fled into England, and threw herself upon the protection of Elizabeth, her deadly enemy. (1568.) Elizabeth retained the unfortunate Mary a prisoner, gave the guardianship of her young son to whom she pleased, and, through her influence over the Protestant nobility of Scotland, was enabled to govern that country mostly at her will.

4. During these events in Scotland Elizabeth was carrying on a secret war against the attempts of Philip II. to establish the inquisition in the Netherlands, and also against a similar design of the Catholic party in France, which ruled that country during the minority of the sovereign. In both these countries the attempts of the Catholic rulers provoked a desperate resistance. In France, banishment or death had become the penalty of heresy, when in January, 1562, an edict was issued by the government, through the influence of the queen regent, granting **II. CIVIL AND RELIGIOUS WAR IN FRANCE.** tolerance to the Huguenots, as the French Protestants were called, and allowing them to assemble for worship *outside* the walls of towns. The powerful family of Guises were

indignant at the countenance thus given to heresy; and as the duke of Guise was passing through a small village, his followers fell upon the Protestants who were assembled outside the walls in prayer, and killed sixty of their number. This atrocity was the signal for a general rising; the prince of Condé, the leader of the Protestant party, took possession of Orleans, and made that town the head-quarters of the Huguenots, as the capital was of the Catholics, while at the same time the aid of Philip of Spain was openly proffered to the Guises, and Condé concluded a treaty with Elizabeth, to whom he delivered Havre-de-Grace[1] in return for a corps of six thousand men.

5. At the opening of this civil and religious war, the greatest enthusiasm prevailed on both sides,—in the opposing armies prayers were heard in common, morning and evening,—there was no gambling, no profane language, nor dissipation; but, under an exterior of sanctity, feelings of the most vindictive hate were nourished, and the direst cruelties were openly perpetrated in the name of religion. The Catholic governor of Guienne[2] went through his province with hangmen, marking his route by the victims whom he hung on the trees by the road-side. On the other hand, a Protestant baron in Dauphiny[3] precipitated his prisoners from the top of a tower on pikes;—both parties made retaliatory reprisals, each spilling blood upon scaffolds of its own erection.

6. The first great battle was fought at Dreux,[4] the prince of Condé commanding the army of the Protestants, and the constable Montmorency that of the Catholics; but while the latter won the field, each of the two generals became prisoner to the opposite party. The duke of Guise, who was next in command to Montmorency, treated his captive rival with the utmost generosity: they shared the same tent—the same bed; and while Condé, from the strangeness of his position, remained wakeful, Guise, he declared, enjoyed the most profound sleep. The admiral Coligni succeeded

1. *Havre-de-Grace*, now called *Havre*, is a fortified town, and the principal commercial seaport, on the western coast of France, at the mouth of the river Seine, one hundred and nine miles north-west from Paris. (*Map* No. XIII.)

2. The province of *Guienne* was in the south-west part of the kingdom, on both sides of the Garonne. (*Map* No. XIII.)

3. The province of *Dauphiny*, of which Grenoble was the capital, was in the south-eastern part of France, having Burgundy on the north, Italy on the east, Provence on the south, and the Rhine on the west. (*Map* No. XIII.)

4. *Dreux*, the ancient seat of the counts of Dreux, is a town of France, forty-fives miles a little south of west from Paris. (*Map* No. XIII.)

to the command of the defeated Huguenots; and Orleans, their principal post, was only saved by the assassination of the duke of Guise, whom a Protestant, from behind, wounded by the discharge of a pistol. The capture or death of the chiefs on both sides, Coligni excepted, brought about an accommodation; and in March, 1563, the treaty of Amboise[1] was declared, granting to the Protestants full liberty of worship within the towns of which they then were in possession.

7. The treaty of Amboise was scarcely concluded when its terms began to be modified by the court, so that, as a cotemporary writer observes, "edicts took more from the Protestants in peace than force could take from them in war." The Protestant leaders, Condé and Coligni, tried in vain to get possession of the young king; and a battle was fought in the very suburbs of Paris, in which the aged Montmorency was slain. (1567.) A "Lame Peace," concluded in the following year, confirmed that of Amboise; but the wary Protestant leaders saw in it only a trap to ensnare them as soon as their army should be disbanded. The mask was soon thrown off by an attempt of the court to seize the two chiefs: the Huguenots were defeated in four battles; Condé was slain, and Coligni severely wounded; but in 1570 the peace of St. Germain[2] was concluded; and amnesty and liberty of worship were again granted to the Protestants.

8. The young king, Charles IX., now in his twentieth year, seems to have been desirous to enforce the terms of the peace, and restore quiet and prosperity to his distracted kingdom; but the plotting of his mother Catherine and the Guises soon involved the country in new perils. A marriage was planned between young Henry of Navarre, a Protestant (afterward Henry IV.), and the king's sister Margaret,—a marriage which Charles, no doubt, sincerely hoped would be a bond of union between the two parties. The Protestant leaders having been invited to Paris with assurances of safety, the nuptials were there celebrated with the greatest magnificence; and amid the festivities which followed, the plan of a massacre of the Protestants was matured by Catherine and the dukes of Guise and Anjou,—the latter brother to the king. An attempt, shortly previous, to assassinate Coligni, had failed; but

---

1. *Amboise* is a town and castle on the Loire, in the former province of Touraine.
2. *St. Germain* is a town of France, on a hill near the south bank of the Seine, six miles north of Versailles, and nine miles north-west from Paris.

he was severely wounded. Under the pretext of a bloody conspiracy among the Huguenot chiefs to destroy the royal family and extirpate Catholicism, Catherine finally persuaded the vacillating king, who was at first appalled by the enormity of the deed, to give orders for the massacre, and, as he gave the royal assent, he exclaimed, with an oath, " Kill all—all—all—so that not one be left to reproach me !"

9. About three o'clock in the morning of St. Bartholomew's day, Sunday, the 24th of August, 1572, the young duke of Guise and his band of cut-throats commenced the bloody work by breaking into the apartment of the aged Coligni, and slaying him while engaged in prayer: at the appointed signal, bells were rung throughout the city, and the adherents of the Guise faction, with the sign of the cross in their caps to distinguish them, rushed forth to the massacre of their brethren. The Huguenots, struck dumb by surprise and terror, made no resistance; and the carnival of blood involved alike manhood, infancy, and old age, in indiscriminate slaughter. The massacre lasted, in Paris, three days and nights, without any apparent diminution of the fury of the murderers.

10. Charles commanded the massacre to be renewed in every important town throughout the kingdom ; and not less than thirty thousand Protestants are believed to have fallen victims to the monarch's order.[1] A few commanders, and provincial magistrates, however, refused to obey the edict. One wrote back to the king " that he commanded soldiers, not assassins :" and the public executioner of Lyons, when ordered to put the imprisoned Huguenots to death, replied : " I am not an assassin : I work only as justice commands me." But the soldiers of the garrison were found

1. It is impossible to arrive at any correct estimate of the numbers slain, either in Paris or in the provinces. The numbers given for Paris, by twenty-one French and Italian authorities, range from one thousand to ten thousand ; and for France, from two thousand to one hundred thousand. De Thou, who at the time was president of the French parliament, and an apologist of the massacre,—who wrote a history of his own times in Latin, and with whom Montfaucon and Popelinière agree,—places the numbers for all France at twenty thousand : Davila, who wrote a history of the civil wars in Italian, says forty thousand. Sully, who passed through the scenes of the massacre in Paris while yet a boy twelve years of age, and who was afterward the eminent minister of Henry IV., places the estimate at seventy thousand ; while others, who seem to have made merely random guesses, go as high as one hundred thousand. From all that can be gathered from the very great number of contemporary writers, we think thirty thousand a moderate estimate. Viewed in the light of history,—and especially in the light of recent investigations into French and Italian archives,—the estimate of Dr. Lingard, the Roman Catholic historian of England, who differs so greatly from the Roman Catholic writers of France as to reduce the numbers so low as sixteen hundred, is manifestly absurd. But whatever be the number of the slain, the *character* of the deed is little affected thereby.

ready to do the bloody work. The prince of Navarre, who had espoused the king's sister, and his companion the young prince of Condé, were spared only on the condition of becoming Catholics; but both yielded in appearance only.

11. A circumstance as horrible as the massacre was the joy it excited in so many quarters. The pretence that the massacre was to crush a plot which the Huguenots had prepared, was probably believed by few, if any. Philip II. of Spain, thinking Protestantism subdued, and secretly rejoicing in this weakening of the French nation, sent to congratulate the court of France: Charles had two medals struck to commemorate the event: three days after the massacre, the bishop of Paris ordered a solemn procession to thank God for "this happy beginning in the extirpation of heresy;" and the annual procession was continued for twenty years, until Henry IV. entered Paris. When the news reached Rome, the cannon of St. Angelo were fired, the bells were rung, and the pope, Gregory XIII., went in state to the church of St. Louis, and returned public thanks to heaven;[1] and, three years later, the chaplain of Charles wrote a labored defence of the massacre, which he dedicated "to the eternal memory and immortality of the soul of the late Charles IX."

12. This foul blot on the page of history has, as we believe, been erroneously attributed to a long premeditated plot, instigated by religious frenzy. But while fanaticism alone urged on a few, priests and laymen alike, it was jealousy and ambition that filled the breast of Catherine; envy, and hatred of merit and virtues which were a standing reproach to him, that inflamed the licentious duke of Anjou; revenge, which hurried on the duke of Guise; and jealousy of the industrious and thrifty Huguenots, mingled with an eagerness for plunder, that drove the degraded masses into this mighty vortex of crime.[2] But it stamps the character of the age

---

1. Original authorities state that a medal, No. 27 of the series of Gregory XIII., was struck at Rome to commemorate the event, and that three frescoes were painted in the Vatican by the celebrated Florentine artist, George Vasari, to illustrate scenes in the plot and the massacre. But recent Catholic writers assert that the rejoicings at Rome were over rebels cut off in the midst of their rebellion, and not over heretics murdered for their religion. See *Dublin Review* for Oct., 1865. *Ranke's Hist. of the Popes.* See *White's Recent Hist. of the Massacre of St. Bartholomew,* p. 466.

2. That the motive of *plunder* had much to do with the extent t which the massacre was carried, is very clearly stated by Salviati, the papal nuncio, who, writing to Rome in the midst of the carnage, says: "The whole city is in arms; the houses of the Huguenots have been forced with great loss of lives, and sacked by the populace with incredible avidity. Many a man to-night will have his horses and his carriage, and will eat and drink off plate, who had never dreamt of it in his life before!"

as intolerant, that such an act was boldly defended by many on religious grounds, and by many others as a great act of state policy. But the age was, emphatically, one of persecution for opinion's sake; and as to their principle on this subject, Protestants and Catholics differed but little. In many instances, in France, the Protestants, when they had the power, exhibited the same spirit of persecution as the Catholics. In 1563 the Protestant synod of Orleans, while claiming absolute liberty for themselves, denied it to those whom they called " atheists, libertines, and anabaptists." In 1553 Servetus, in Switzerland, who had denied the doctrine of the Trinity, was brought to the stake through the instrumentality of Calvin, one of the apostles of the Reformation,—one of the charges against him (though not, to be sure, a principal one) being that he " had denied that Judea was a beautiful, rich, and fertile country; and affirmed, on the authority of travellers, that it was poor, barren, and disagreeable." And not only did the mild Melancthon approve the act, but it was approved generally, by the Protestant divines of Germany and Switzerland.

13. On the other hand, in 1568 the Spanish inquisition solemnly condemned all the inhabitants of the Netherlands to death as heretics,—a few persons only being excepted by name; and Philip II. publicly ratified the sentence, and ordered it to be carried into execution, without regard to sex, age, or condition. At that day it was the current opinion that but one religion could be tolerated in a state, and there were many and able professed advocates of intolerance, both on religious and political grounds. Says that eminent scholar and critic, Justus Lipsius, who wrote near the close of the sixteenth century,—" In matters of religion no favor or indulgence is admissible: the true mercy is to be merciless: to save many, we must not shrink from getting rid of a few." Such were the teachings of an intolerant age, and mournful indeed is the picture of it which history holds up to our view; but yet it would be exceedingly unfair in us to judge the men of those times by our nineteenth century standard.

14. The crime from which so much was expected produced neither peace nor advantage; and the civil war was renewed with greater force than ever: mere abhorrence of the massacre caused many Catholics to turn Huguenots; and although the latter were at first paralyzed by the blow, the former were stung by remorse and shame. Charles himself seemed stricken already by avenging fate. As the

accounts of the murders of old men, women, and children, were successively brought to him, while the massacre continued, he drew aside M. Ambroise, his first surgeon, to whom he was much attached, although he was a Protestant, and said to him, "Ambroise, I know not what has come over me these two or three days, but I find my mind and body in disorder; I see everything as if I had a fever; every moment, as well waking as sleeping, the hideous and bloody faces of the killed appear before me; I wish the weak and innocent had not been included." From that time a continued fever preyed upon him, and, eighteen months later, carried him to the grave, (May, 1574,) but not until he had been compelled to grant the Huguenots a peace, after seeing that his grand and sweeping crime had but enfeebled the Catholic party, instead of insuring its triumph.

15. At the time of the massacre of St. Bartholomew, civil war was raging in the Netherlands. During the six years of the administration of the duke of Alva, Philip's governor in that country, the land was desolated by the insatiate cruelty of one of the greatest monsters of wickedness the world has ever seen; and it is the recorded boast of Alva himself that, during his brief administration, he caused eighteen thousand of the inhabitants to perish by the hands of the executioner. At length, in 1572, a general rising against the Spanish power was organized, the prince of Orange being at the head of the revolters. After a war of varied fortunes on both sides, in 1576 the States-general, or congress, of most of the Batavian and Belgic provinces, met, and assumed the reins of government in the name of the king, and soon after concluded a union between the States, which is known as the *Pacification of Ghent*.[1] The expulsion, from the country, of Spanish soldiers and other foreigners was decreed; Alva's sanguinary decrees and edicts against heresy were repealed, and religious toleration guaranteed.

16. Ere long, however, the confederacy thus formed fell to pieces, owing to jealousies between the Catholic and Protestant States; and it became evident that freedom could be attained only by a closer union of the provinces, resting on an entire separation from Spain. Acting on this belief, in January, 1579, the prince

---

1. *Ghent* is a city of Belgium, thirty miles north-west from Brussels. It belonged, successively, to the counts of Flanders and the dukes of Bur'gundy; but the citizens enjoyed a great degree of independence. It was the birth-place of the emperor Charles V. (*Map* No. XV.)

of Orange convoked an assembly of deputies at Utrecht,[1] where was signed the famous act called the *Union of Utrecht*, the real basis or fundamental compact of the Republic of the United Provinces. Early in the following year, 1850, the States-general assembled at Antwerp,[2] and, in spite of all the opposition of the Catholic deputies, the authority of Spain was renounced forever, and the " United Provinces" declared a free and independent State. Philip, however, still waged a vindictive war against them, while they received important aid from Elizabeth of England, a circumstance which led Philip to declare war against the latter country.

17. The destinies of the unhappy queen of Scotland had long been implicated with the designs of the Catholics of Europe against the power and throne of Elizabeth. About the time of the massacre of St. Bartholomew, the infamous duke of Alva, the Spanish governor of the Netherlands, had formed a project of uniting with the English Catholics and Mary in a confederacy against Elizabeth; and Mary was charged with countenancing the design; but although parliament applied for her immediate trial, Elizabeth was satisfied with increasing the rigor and strictness of her confinement. Mary was subsequently, and repeatedly, charged with being cognizant of similar plans; but her participation in any of them is exceedingly doubtful. At length, however, an act of parliament was passed authorizing her trial; and after an investigation, in which law and justice were little regarded, she was condemned to death. Elizabeth, after some delay and hesitation, signed the warrant for her execution, which, she said, she designed to keep by her, to be used only in case of the attempt of Mary to escape; but her council, having obtained possession of it from her private secretary, hastily despatched it to those who had charge of the prisoner, and the unhappy Mary was beheaded, after having been in captivity nineteen years. (1587.)

18. The execution of the queen of Scots inflamed the resentment of the Catholics throughout Europe, and gave additional vigor to the preparations of Philip II. for an invasion of England, a project which he had long had in contemplation, and by which he hoped to destroy the power of the great supporter of the Protestant cause.

---

1. *Utrecht* is a city of Holland, on the old Rhine, twenty miles south-east from Amsterdam.
2. *Antwerp* is a maritime city of Belgium, on the north bank of the Scheldt, twenty-six miles north from Brussels. In the sixteenth century Antwerp enjoyed a more extensive foreign trade than any other city in Europe. (*Map* No. XV.)

With justice, perhaps, Philip complained of the depredations which the English, under their great admiral Sir Francis Drake, had for many years committed on the Spanish possessions in South America, and more than once on the coasts of Spain itself; and now a vast armament was prepared to sweep the English from the seas, ravage their coasts, burn their towns, and dethrone their Protestant queen.

19. In May, 1588, the Spanish fleet of one hundred and thirty ships, some the largest that had ever plowed the deep, carrying, exclusive of eight thousand sailors, no less than twenty thousand of the bravest troops in the Spanish armies, a large invading force in those days, sailed from the harbor of Lisbon for the English coast. The pope had blessed the expedition, and offered the sovereignty of England as the conqueror's prize; and the Catholics throughout Europe were so confident of success that they had named the armament "The Invincible Armada." The queen of England beheld the preparations, and heard the vauntings of her enemies, with a resolution worthy of the occasion and the cause. She visited the seaports in person, superintended the preparations for defence, and on horseback addressed the troops; and such was the enthusiasm which she everywhere inspired, that even her Catholic subjects joined their countrymen, heart and hand, against foreign domination. Lord Howard of Effingham was appointed admiral of the fleet; Drake, Hawkins, and Frobisher, the most renowned seamen in Europe, served under him; while an army of forty-five thousand men was organized for the defence of the coast and the capital.

V. THE SPANISH ARMADA.

20. After the Armada had sailed from Lisbon it suffered considerably from a storm off the French coast: in passing through the English Channel it was seriously harassed, during several days, by the lighter English vessels; and while at anchor off Calais, the English sent a number of fire-ships into the midst of the fleet, destroyed several vessels, and threw the others into such confusion that the Spanish admiral no longer thought of victory, but only of escape. As the south wind blew, he was unable to retrace his course, and therefore resolved to return by coasting the northern shores of Scotland and Ireland. But his disasters were not ended: many of his vessels were driven, by a storm, on the coasts of Norway and Scotland: off the Irish coast a second storm was experienced, with almost equal loss; and only a few shattered vessels of this mighty armament returned to Spain, to bring intelligence of the

calamities that had overwhelmed the rest. The defeat of the armada was regarded as the triumph of the Protestant cause; it exerted a favorable influence on the welfare of the United Provinces, and virtually secured their independence; and it raised the courage of the Huguenots in France and completely destroyed the decisive influence which Spain had long maintained in the affairs of Europe. Henceforth the naval power and the commerce of Spain declined; and the king, at his death in 1598, bequeathed a vast debt to a nation whose resources, notwithstanding her rich mines of gold and silver in the New World, were already exhausted.

21. The internal history of France, since the massacre of St. Bartholomew and the death of Charles IX., is filled with deplorable civil wars during most of the remaining portion of the sixteenth century. Charles was succeeded by his brother Henry III., who endeavored to play the opposing Catholic and Protestant parties against each other; but being obliged, at length, by the violence of the *Catholic league*, to throw himself on the protection of the Protestants, he was assassinated by James Clement, a fanatic monk, just as he was on the point of driving his enemies from Paris. (Aug. 1589.) In the death of Henry III., the house of Valois became extinct, and the throne passed by right of inheritance to the house of Bourbon, in the person of the Protestant Henry of Navarre, who now became king of France, with the title of Henry IV. He was at first opposed by the Catholic league; but after a struggle of four years, in which he received some aid from Elizabeth of England, he abjured the Protestant faith, and thus became king of a united people. (1593–4.) To the Huguenots, however,

VI. THE
EDICT OF
NANTES.
he atoned for his compulsory desertion, by issuing, in 1598, the celebrated Edict of Nantes,[1] which terminated the religious wars that had distracted France during thirty-six years. The Edict of Nantes secured to the Protestants the free exercise of their religion, and an equal claim with the Catholics to all offices and dignities. The parliament made considerable opposition to the registering of this edict, and the king was obliged to use menaces, as well as persuasion, to overcome their obstinacy.

22. The history of England, after the defeat of the Spanish Armada, offers few events of interest during the remainder of the reign of Elizabeth. A general insurrection, however, broke out in Ire-

1. *Nantes* is a celebrated commercial city and seaport of France, about thirty-four miles from the mouth of the Loire, and two hundred and ten south-west from Paris.

land in 1598, the design of which was to effect the entire expulsion
of the English from the island ; but although the insurgents were
supplied with troops and ammunition by the Spanish monarch, and
the pope held out ample indulgences in favor of those who should
enlist to combat the English heretics, yet the rebels ultimately failed
in their enterprise, after a sanguinary war which lasted six years.

23. The splendor of Elizabeth's reign is a theme on which English historians love to dwell. At this time England held the balance
of power in Christendom, a position that was owing, in
no small degree, to the personal character of the sovereign. No monarch of England ever surpassed Elizabeth
in firmness, penetration, and address; and none ever conducted the
government with more uniform success. Yet her political maxims
were arbitrary in the extreme ; and she had little regard for the
liberties of her people, or the privileges of parliament—believing
that her subjects were entitled to no other rights than their ancestors had enjoyed. The principles of the English constitution were
not yet developed. Elizabeth died in the year 1603, being then in
the seventieth year of her age, and the forty-fifth of her reign.

VII. CHARAC-
TER OF
ELIZABETH.

IV. COTEMPORARY HISTORY.—1. If we pass from European history to that of other portions of the world in the sixteenth century,
the most prominent events that attract our notice are the establishment of the Portuguese in Southern Asia, and of the Spaniards in
Mexico and South America,—the rise of a Mogul empire in India,
and of a new dynasty in Persia. After the fleet of De Gama had
doubled the Cape of Good Hope, the enterprises of the Portuguese
were directed to the securing of the commerce of the Indian seas ;
but, soon after, under the viceroyalty of the illustrious Albuquerque,
they formed numerous settlements and established forts and trading
houses throughout all the coasts. In the year 1507
Albuquerque took possession of Ormus,[1] then the most
splendid and polished city of Asia, situated at the entrance of the Persian Gulf ; and when the king of Persia,
to whom it had long belonged, demanded tribute from the Portuguese, the viceroy, pointing to his cannons and balls, replied :
" There is the coin with which the king of Portugal pays tribute."
The attempts of the Venetians and Mohammedans to expel the

I. THE POR-
TUGUESE
COLONIAL
EMPIRE.

---

1. *Ormus*, anciently called *Ozyris*, is a rocky island at the mouth of the Persian Gulf. It
would scarcely be worth notice were it not for its former celebrity and importance.

intruders were ineffectual, and in 1510, Goa,[1] the chief of the Portuguese establishments, was made the capital of the Portuguese
empire in India. The Portuguese introduced themselves into China
also; and when their colonial empire was at its greatest extent, it
embraced the coasts of Africa from Guinea to the Red Sea, and
extended over all Southern and Eastern Asia; although throughout
this vast extent of country, they had little more than a chain of
factories and forts. On the union of Portugal with Spain (1580),
the Portuguese East India possessions followed the fate of the
mother country, and passed into the unskilful hands of the Spaniards
(1582); but when the intolerable cruelty of the Spanish government
had driven the Dutch to revolt, the latter extended their commerce
to the Indies, and, at the close of the century, had possession of
nearly all that had formed the colonial empire of the Portuguese.

2. The Spaniards were more successful in making and retaining
conquests in the New World. Soon after the discovery
of America they extended their settlements over the　II. SPANISH
COLONIAL
islands of the West Indies, which were depopulated by　EMPIRE.
the excessive and unhealthy labor imposed by them upon the natives. In 1519 the adventurer Cortez landed with a small force
on the eastern coast of Mexico; and in the course of two years the
wealthy and populous kingdom of the Montezumas was reduced to
a province of Spain. Yet, after all his services to his country,
Cortez, like Columbus, was persecuted at home. It was with difficulty that he could gain an audience from the emperor, Charles V.
When one day he pushed through the crowd which surrounded the
coach of the emperor, and placed his foot on the step of the door,
Charles asked who this man was. "It is he," replied Cortez, "who
has given you more kingdoms than your ancestors left you cities."

3. After Mexico, the Spaniards sought other countries to conquer
and depopulate. In 1532 Pizarro, a soldier of fortune, taking with
him a force of only two hundred and fifty foot soldiers, sixty horsemen, and twelve small cannon, invaded Peru, the greatest, the best
governed, and most civilized nation of the New World. Pizarro
and his companions marked their route with blood; but wherever
they directed their course they conquered in the name of Charles

---

1. *Goa* (the old town) is on an island of the same name on the south-western coast of Hindostan, two hundred and fifty miles south-east from Bombay. The old city, now almost deserted except by priests, is "a city of churches; and the wealth of provinces seems to have
been expended in their erection." New Goa, built on the sea-shore about five miles from the
old town, is a well-built city, with a population of about twenty thousand.

V.; and before the close of the century the Spanish empire in
America embraced the islands of the West Indies, all Mexico and
Peru, and the coasts of nearly all South America.   The enormous
quantity of the precious metals which Spain drew from her American possessions contributed to make her, for awhile, the preponderating power in Europe ; but an inordinate thirst for the gold
and silver of America led the Spaniards to neglect agriculture and
manufactures.   The Spanish colonies increased but slowly in population ; the capital itself was ruined ; and before the close of the
sixteenth century the best days of Spain were over.

4. During the three hundred years previous to 1525, India, or
Hindostan, was governed by Affghan princes, whose seat
of government was Delhi.   In 1525, Baber, the fifth in   III. THE
descent from Tamerlane, and sovereign of a little prin-   MOGUL EM-
                                                              PIRE IN
cipality between Kashgar[1] and Samarcand, entered Hin-   INDIA.
dostan at the head of a large army, defeated and killed the last
Affghan sovereign, and seated himself on the throne of Delhi.[2]
With him began the race of Mogul princes, as they are called by
Europeans, although their native tongue was Turkish.   In the next
century the Mogul empire was consolidated under Aurungzebe,
who, by murdering his relatives, and shutting his father up in his
harem, was enabled to ascend the throne of Hindostan in 1659.
But notwithstanding the means by which he had obtained sovereign
authority, he governed with much wisdom, consulted the welfare of
his people, watched over the preservation of justice, and the purity
of manners, and, by a wise administration, sought to confirm his
own power.   After his death, in 1707, the Mogul empire began to
decline ; and even under Aurungzebe it was much inferior, in extent and resources, to the empire now held by Britain in the same
country.

5. We have already alluded to the revival of the Persian empire
at the beginning of the sixteenth century.   At that period we find
the youthful Ismael, who traced his descent to the Skeik   IV. THE
Suffee, a holy person who lived in the time of Tamer-   PERSIAN
                                                              EMP.RE.
lane, heading a band of adherents against a neighboring
prince, and, in the course of four years, reducing all Persia to his

---

1. *Kashgar*, the most western town of any importance in the Chinese empire, is about four
hundred and fifty miles east from Samarcand.

2. *Delhi* is a city of northern Hindostan, about eight hundred and thirty miles north-west
from Calcutta.   It appears that no less than seven successive cities have stood on the ground
occupied by Delhi and its ruins.

sway. For fifteen years fortune smiled on his arms; but he was at length defeated by Selim, the sultan of Constantinople. The latter, however, reaped no real advantage from his dearly-bought victory; and when Ismael died he left a name on which the Persians dwell with enthusiasm, as the restorer of their country, and the founder of one of the most brilliant of the Mohammedan dynasties—called the *Suffeean*, or *Suffavean*, from the holy sheik Suffee.

6. Tamasp succeeded his father Ismael, when only ten years of age. His reign was long and prosperous. Anthony Jenkinson, one of the earliest adventurers to Persia, visited the court of Tamasp as an envoy from queen Elizabeth; but the intolerance of the Mohammedan soon drove the Christian away. The three sons of Tamasp in succession made an effort for the crown; but their short reigns merit little notice. At length, in 1582, the youthful Abbas, a grandson of Tamasp, was proclaimed king by some of the discontented nobles, and forced to appear in arms against his father Mohammed, who was deserted by his army, and is not mentioned again in history. But Abbas did not long remain a tool in the hands of others, for, seizing the reins of power, he soon rose to distinction, defeated the Turks in many battles, in 1622 took Ormuz from the Portuguese, and became supreme ruler of a mighty empire. During his reign commenced an amicable intercourse between the English and Persian nations, which continued for many years.

7. Abbas was, in many respects, an enlightened prince; his foreign policy was generally liberal, and he extended toleration to other religions: he spent his revenues in improvements: caravanseras, bridges, aqueducts, bazaars, mosques, and colleges, arose in every quarter; and Ispahan[1] the capital was splendidly embellished. But as a parent, and relative, the character of Abbas appears in a most revolting light.

8. Abbas was succeeded by a series of imbecile tyrants, during whose reigns the Affghans repeatedly laid waste the country, and destroyed the lives of a million of people. The most noted of the Persian monarchs since the death of Abbas have been the famous Nadir Shah, Mehemet Khan, Futteh Ali Shah, and Abbas Mirza, the latter of whom ascended the throne in 1835.

---

1. *Ispahan*, formerly the capital of Persia, is situated between the Caspian Sea and the Persian Gulf, two hundred and eleven miles soutn of Teheran, the modern capital.

CHAPTER IV.

THE SEVENTEENTH CENTURY.

I. THE THIRTY YEARS' WAR.

ANALYSIS. 1. German history from 1558 to 1618. The events that led to the "Thirty Years' War." Extent of that war.—2. Ferdinand succeeds Matthias as emperor of Germany, but is deposed in Bohemia. Frederic the elector-palatine. THE PALATINE PERIOD OF THE WAR. [Prague.]—3. Mansfeldt is unable to cope with the imperial generals. Protestant alliance with the Danes, and opening of the DANISH PERIOD OF THE WAR. Defeat of the Danish king by Tilly. [Lutter. Göttingen. Brunswick.]—4. The Danes are driven from Hungary, and most of Denmark is conquered. Ambitious views of Ferdinand. Siege of Stralsund. Treaty of Lubec. [Stralsund. Lubec.]—5. The hopes of a general peace. Tyranny of Ferdinand, and revolt of the Protestants. Interposition of Gustavus Adolphus, and opening of the SWEDISH PERIOD OF THE WAR —6. Intrigues of Richelieu,—leading to the invasion of Germany by the Swedes in 1630. [Rochelle.]—7. Contempt in which the Swedes were held by the Germans. [Pomerania.] Character of the opposing forces. The military system of Gustavus.—8. Early successes of the Swedes. Magdeburg plundered and burned by the imperialists. [Magdeburg.]—9. Compensation for the loss of Magdeberg. [Leipsic.] Gustavus overruns Germany. Death of Tilly.—10. Successes of Wallenstein. [Nuremburg. Dresden.] Death of Gustavus. [Lutzen.]—11. Close of the Swedish period of the war, and death of Wallenstein. The FRENCH PERIOD OF THE WAR.—12. Circumstances of the leaguing of the French with the Protestants. The Rhine becomes the chief seat of the war.—13. The remainder of the Thirty Years' War. Death of Ferdinand. Death of Louis XIII. and Richelieu. Treaty of Westphalia [Westphalia.] Condition of Germany.—14. Chief articles of the treaty of Westphalia.

II. ENGLISH HISTORY :—THE ENGLISH REVOLUTION.

1. England during the period of the Thirty Years' War. UNION OF ENGLAND AND SCOTLAND 1603.—2. The character of JAMES I., and the character of his reign.—3. His successor CHARLES I. His misfortunes.—4. Difficulties that immediately followed his accession. The second and third parliament. Dissolution of the latter.—5. The interval until the assembling of another parliament. Conduct of the English clergy, and persecution of the puritans. SCOTCH REBELLION. March of the Covenanters into England. Fourth and fifth parliament.—6. Opening acts of THE LONG PARLIAMENT. Impeachment of Strafford and Laud. Remarks.—7. Continued encroachments of Parliament. Irish rebellion. Impeachment of five members of the Commons.—8. The king erects his standard at Nottingham, and opens the CIVIL WAR—1642. [Nottingham.] Strength of the opposing parties.—9. The battles of Edghill and Newbery. [Edghill. Newbery.]—10. THE SCOTCH LEAGUE.—11. Campaigns of 1644 and 1645. [Marston-Moor. Naseby.] The king a prisoner.—12. Civil and religious dissensions. OLIVER CROMWELL.—13. The reaction in favor of the king arrested by Cromwell. TRIAL AND EXECUTION OF CHARLES I. 1649.—14. Remarks upon this measure. Character of Charles.—15. ABOLITION OF MONARCHY. Cromwell's military successes. [Worcester.]—16. WAR WITH HOLLAND Navigation act. Naval battle.—17. Continuance of the war, and defeat of the British. [Goodwin Sands.] Bravado of Tromp.—18. Defeat of the Dutch in the English Channel. The final conflict, and death of Tromp. Peace with Holland.—19. Controversy between Cromwell and Parliament. THE PROTECTORATE.—20. Continued dissensions and parliamentary opposition to Cromwell. The army. War with Spain.—21. Character of Cromwell's administration. Attempt to invest him with the dignity of king.—22. Remainder of Cromwell's life. His death.—23. Richard. His abdication. Anarchy. RESTORATION OF MONARCHY, 1660. 24. First impressions produced by Charles II. His character. The parliament of 1661.—25. Manners and

morals of the nation.—21. Increasing discontent. War with Holland. The capital threatened. [Dunkirk. Cha ham.]—27. The plague of 1665. The great fire of 1666.—28. Treaty of Breda. [Breda. New Netherlands. Acadia and Nova Scotia.] Another war with Holland. Treaty of Nimeguen. [Orange. Nimeguen.]—29. The professions and the secret designs of Charles. His intrigues with the French monarch. His growing unpopularity. Popish plot. Russell and Sidney. Absolute power of the king. His death.—30. JAMES II. His general policy. The approaching crisis.—31. Arbitrary and unpopular measures of the king. [Windsor.]—32 Monmouth's rebellion. The inhuman Jeffries.—33. Events of the REVOLUTION OF 1688.—34. Settlement of the crown on William and Mary. Declaration of rights.—35. Scotch and Irish rebellion. [Killecrankie.] Events that led to a general European war. French history towards the close of the century. Death of William, 1702.

III. FRENCH HISTORY :—WARS OF LOUIS XIV.

1. The ADMINISTRATION OF CARDINAL RICHELIEU, 1624—42.—2. MAZARIN'S ADMINISTRATION, 1642—61. Treaty of Westphalia, and war of the Fronde.—3. Continuance of the war between France and Spain. Condé and Turenne. England joins France in the war. [Arras. Valenciennes. Flanders.]—4. Both France and Spain desirous of peace. Treaty of the Pyrenees, 1659. [Bidassoa. Gravelines. Roussillon. Franche-Comté.]—5. LOUIS assumes the administration of government. [Louvre. Invalides. Versailles. Languedoc.]—6. Ambitious projects of Louis. His invasion of the Spanish Netherlands. [Brabant.]—7. Capture of Franche-Comte. Triple alliance against Louis. Treaty of Aix-la-Chapelle. [Aix-la-Chapelle.] —8. Designs of Louis against Holland.—9. The bayonet. Comparative strength of the French and Dutch forces.—10. Invasion of Holland. [Amsterdam.] The inhabitants think of abandoning their country. Prince William of Orange effects a general league against the French monarch. (1674.)—11. The war in the Spanish Netherlands. Turenne and Condé. Duquesne. —12. Peace of Nimeguen, 1678. Remarks of Voltaire.—13. Great prosperity and increasing ascendancy of France. The greatest glories of the reign of Louis.—14. Madame de Maintenon. Revocation of the Edict of Nantes.—15. General league, and war, against Louis, 1686—8. His activity in meeting his enemies.—16. Successes of the French commanders. Battle of La Hogue. [Beachy Head. Namur. La Hogue.]—17. Campaign of 1693. Peace of Ryswick, 1697. State of France at the close of the seventeenth century. [Nerwinden. Ryswick. Strasburg.]

IV. COTEMPORARY HISTORY.

1. Increasing extent of the field of history.—2. DENMARK, SWEDEN, AND NORWAY. Gustavus Adolphus, and his successors.—3. POLAND, during the seventeenth century. The reign of John Sobieski, 1674—97. His victories over the Turks. [Kotzim].—4. Siege of Vienna by the Turks and Hungarians. [Vienna.]—5. Its deliverance by Sobieski, 1683.—6. Complete discomfiture of the Turks. Ingratitude of Austria, and decline of Poland.—7. RUSSIA, at the commencement of the seventeenth century. Peter the Great. His efforts for improving the condition of his people and country. [Azof. Dwina. Volga. St. Petersburg.]—8. His travels, &c. Political acts of his reign.—9. TURKEY from the early part of the sixteenth to the latter part of the seventeenth century. Decline of her power at the close of the century. [Zenta. Carlowitz. Transylvania. Sclavonia. Podolia. Ukraine.]—10. ITALY during the seventeenth century. Effects of the Reformation. Of the Spanish rule in Italy.—11. The low state of morals. General suffering and degradation.—12. The SPANISH PENINSULA during the seventeenth century. Expulsion of the Moors, 1610.—13. Revolt of Portugal, 1640. Independence of Holland, 1648. Treaty of Westphalia, 1648.—14. THE ASIATIC NATIONS during the seventeenth century. Persia. China.—15. The great Mogul empire of Asia. Aurungzebe.—16. COLONIAL ESTABLISHMENTS. Dutch colonies. [Surinam. Moluccas. Ceylon.] Colonial policy of the Dutch.—17. Spanish colonial empire.—18. Materials and character of Spanish colonial history.—19. French colonization in the New World. In the Old. [Madagascar. Pondicherry.] —20. English colonial possessions. The London East India Company. [Java. Madras. Bombay. Calcutta.]—21. English colonization in America. History of the British American colonies during the seventeenth century. The early colonists of New England.—22. Instructive and interesting character of early American history. Omission of a separate compend of American history in this work.

I. The Thirty Years' War.—1. From the death of Charles V. in the year 1558, to the year 1618, there were no events in German history that exercised any important influence on the politics of Europe. At the latter period, however, the German emperor, Matthias, succeeded in procuring the subordinate crown of Bohemia for his cousin Ferdinand, a bigoted Catholic; a circumstance which increased the hostile feelings that had long existed between the Roman Catholic and Protestant parties in Bohemia; but when Ferdinand banished the new faith from his dominion, and destroyed the Protestant churches, his impolitic conduct led to an open revolt of his Protestant subjects. (1618.) This was the commencement of a thirty years' war—the last conflict sustained by the Reformation—a war indeterminate in its objects, but one which, before its close, involved, in its complicated relations, nearly all the states of continental Europe.

2. While this petty war was raging on the narrow theatre of the Bohemian territory, Matthias died; and Ferdinand, to the great alarm of the Protestant party throughout Germany, was elected emperor of all the German States, under the title of Ferdinand II. (1619); but at the very moment of his election he received the intelligence of his deposition in Bohemia, which had just been made public among the people. The Bohemians now chose Frederic, the elector-palatine, son-in-law of the British monarch James I., for their sovereign; but Frederic was unequal to the crisis, and being besieged in his own capital, he lost the battle of Prague[1] by his negligence or cowardice. Ferdinand, assisted by a Spanish force under Spinola, and by the Catholic league of Germany, now overran Bohemia, and compelled Frederic to seek refuge in Holland, where he dwelt without a kingdom, and without courage to reconquer it,—maintained at the expense of his father-in-law, the king of England. The punishment inflicted upon Bohemia was severe in the extreme: twenty-seven of the Protestant leaders were condemned to death;—by degrees all Protestant clergyman were banished from the country;—and, finally, it was declared that no subject who did not adhere to the Roman Catholic church would be tolerated. Thirty thousand families, driven away by this cruel

I. PALATINE PERIOD OF THE WAR.

---

1. *Prague*, the capital city of Bohemia, is situated on both sides of the Moldau, a branch of the Elbe. one hundred and fifty-two miles north-west of Vienna, and seventy-two miles south east from Dresden. Jerome, the friend of the great Bohemian reformer John Huss, was a native of this city, and was thence surnamed. "of Prague." (*Map* No. XVII.)

edict, took refuge in the Protestant States of Saxoi y and Branden
burg   Thus closed the Palatine period of the thirty years' war.

3. After the flight of Frederic, his general Mansfeldt still deter
mined to maintain the Protestant cause against the emperor Ferdi
nand; but he found himself unable to cope with the imperial gen
erals, Tilly and Wallenstein. The Protestant towns of Lower Saxony,
foreseeing the fate to which they might be subjected, next took up
arms, and having entered into an alliance with Christian IV. of Denmark, made him captain general of the confederated
army. (1625.)   Thus opened the Danish period of the
war.   With a body of twenty-five thousand men, consisting of Danes, Germans, Scotch, and English, the Danish king crossed
the Elbe, where he was joined by seven thousand Saxons; but, after
some successes, he was defeated by Tilly near the castle of Lutter,[1]
on the road from Göttingen[2] to Brunswick,[3] with the loss of four
thousand men, besides a vast number of prisoners. (Aug. 26th, 1626.)

II. DANISH PERIOD OF THE WAR.

4. In the following year, 1627, the Danes were driven from Germany by Wallenstein, the imperial commander, who had now in
creased his forces to one hundred thousand men. Not content with
driving Christian from Germany, Wallenstein pursued him into
Denmark; and soon the whole of the peninsula, with the exception
of one fortress, was conquered, and the king was obliged to take
refuge in his islands.   The ambitious views of Ferdinand now aimed
at the extirpation of the Lutheran heresy throughout his own empire,
and the reëstablishment of the Catholic faith throughout the entire
north, by the subjugation of Norway and Sweden, in addition to
Denmark.   As a preliminary step towards the accomplishment
of this gigantic undertaking, Wallenstein was first to secure the
dominion of the Baltic and the North Sea.   Assisted by a Spanish
fleet, he took possession of several ports on the Baltic; but the citizens of Stralsund,[4] aided by five thousand Swedish and Scottish
troops, defended their walls with such determined courage and perseverance, that Wallenstein was forced to abandon the siege, after a

1. *Lutter*, "near Barenberg, in Hanover," south-west from Brunswick. This battle was
fought Aug. 20th, 1626.
2. *Göttingen*, in the kingdom of Hanover, is fifty-six miles south-west from Brunswick. It is
especially noted for its university, which, down to 1831, was fully entitled to its appellation
"the queen of German universities." (*Map* No. XVII.)
3. *Brunswick*, the early seat of the dukes of that name, is a city of Germany, situated on the
Ocker, a branch of the Weser, thirty-seven miles a little south of east from Hanover. (*Map*
No. XVII.)
4. *Stralsund* is a strongly-fortified Prussian town, on the narrow strait of the Baltic which
separates the island of Rugen from the continent. (*Map* No. XVII.)

ions of twelve thousand men. This signal discomfiture induced the emperor to consent to treat for peace with Denmark; and by the treaty of Lubec,[1] Christian was restored to his dominions, on the condition of abandoning his German allies. (May, 1629.) Thus terminated the Danish period of the thirty years' war.

5. It had been hoped that the treaty of Lubec would prove the forerunner of a general pacification; and the subjects, the allies, and the enemies of Ferdinand, now united in imploring him to put an end to a civil war which had been waged with a ferocity hitherto unknown since the ages of Gothic barbarism. But, the Protestants being subdued, and no enemy left to oppose the emperor, the Roman Catholics thought the moment too favorable to be neglected, and Ferdinand was urged on by them to exercise the most intolerable tyranny over his Protestant subjects. The last beam of hope from the emperor's clemency was extinguished, and the Protestants only awaited the arrival of a leader to throw off a yoke which had become insupportable. A deliverer was found in Gustavus Adolphus, the Protestant king of Sweden. The circumstances that led to his interposition,—the opening of the Swedish period of the war—show how tangled has often been the web of European politics.

III. SWEDISH PERIOD OF THE WAR.

6. Cardinal Richelieu, the able minister of Louis XIII. of France, after having humbled the Huguenots by the capture of Rochelle,[2] their last stronghold, directed his great powers to the abasement of the house of Austria. With this view he was instrumental in depriving Ferdinand of his ablest general, Wallenstein, whose dismissal from power was successfully urged by an assembly of the German States in the summer of 1630. Richelieu had previously

1. *Lubec*, the capital of the "Hanseatic towns," is situated on the river Trave, about twelve miles from its entrance into the Baltic, and thirty-six miles north-east from Hamburg. The surrounding territory subject to Lubec consists of a district of about eighty square miles. (*Map No. XVII.*)

2. *Rochelle* is a town and seaport of France on the Atlantic coast, in the former province of Saintonge, seventy-six miles south-east from Nantes. During the religious wars, and especially after the massacre of St. Bartholomew, Rochelle was a stronghold of the Protestants. Invested by the Catholic forces in 1572, it withstood a long siege, terminated by a treaty. The numerous infractions of that treaty, in the reign of Louis XIII., and under the ministry of Richelieu, led to a second siege, which commenced in August, 1627, and was as violent as the former, and longer and more decisive. After six months of heroic resistance, the famous engineer, Metezeau, was directed to bar the entrance to the harbor by an immense dyke, extending nearly five thousand feet into the sea, the remains of which are still visible at low water. The result was soon fatally apparent. Famine quickly decimated the ranks of the besieged; and after a resistance of fourteen months and eighteen days, Rochelle was compelled to capitulate. Richelieu made a triumphant entry into the city; the fortifications were demolished, and the Protestants were deprived of their last place of refuge. (*Map No. XIII.*)

offered his successful mediation in negotiating a six years' armistice
between the hostile States of Sweden and Poland, with the view of
leaving Gustavus Adolphus, the Swedish king, at liberty to turn his
arms against the German emperor. All the inducements that an
artful diplomatist could urge were brought to bear upon Gustavus, a
prince ardent in the Protestant faith, and already a sufferer from
the insolence and rapacity of Wallenstein; and the result was a dec-
aration of war against the German emperor, and an invasion of his
territory by the Swedes, in the summer of 1630.

7. When Ferdinand was informed that the Swedish monarch had
landed in Pomerania[1] at the head of only fifteen thousand men, he
treated the affair with much indifference; and the Roman Catholic
party throughout the empire styled Gustavus, in contempt, the petty
snow king, who, they said, would speedily melt beneath the rays of
the imperial sun. But while the German armies were a motley of
all creeds and nations, bound together only by the ties of a common
warfare and pillage, the Swedes formed a phalanx of hardy and well
disciplined warriors, strengthened by the confidence that God was on
their side; and to Him they offered up their prayers twice a day,
each regiment having its own chaplain. Besides this, Gustavus had
introduced a new system of military tactics into his army; and by
the novelty and boldness of his positions, and the impetuosity of his
movements, he completely disconcerted the adherents of the old German routine.

8. Although some of the Protestant princes of Germany, through
fear of their emperor, or from jealousy of foreign dominion, hesitated about joining the new ally of their cause, yet the onset of the
Swedes was irresistible: they rapidly made themselves masters of all
Pomerania, and took Frankfort under the eye of the imperial gen
eral Tilly; but they were unable to relieve Magdeburg,[2] which Tilly
plundered and burned, amid scenes of the most revolting atrocity—
an act which rendered his name infamous among all classes of the
German population.

9. The unfortunate loss of Magdeburg was speedily compensated

1. *Pomerania* is a large province of Prussia, extending east from Mecklenburg about two
hundred miles along the southern coast of the Baltic. Gustavus landed on the islands Wollen
and Usedom, south-east of Stralsund. The first towns reduced by him were Wolgast and
Stettin. (*Map* No. XVIL)

2. *Magdeburg* is a strongly-fortified city, and the capital of Prussian Saxony, situated on the
Elbe, seventy-four miles south-west from Berlin. Magdeburg has suffered numerous sieges, but
its fortifications are now so extensive that it is said it would require fifty thousand men to be-
vest it. It was plundered and burned by Tilly May 19th, 1531. (*Map* No. XVIL)

by formidable accessions of strength received from France and England, and by a great victory gained by Gustavus over Tilly in the vicinity of Leipsic.[1] (Sept. 7th, 1631.) Gustavus now rapidly traversed Germany from the Elbe to the Rhine, pursuing his victorious career to the borders of Switzerland : all northern and western Germany, together with Bohemia, was in the hands of the Protestants ; and early in the following year Tilly himself was slain on the banks of the river Lech, a southern tributary of the Danube, in Bavaria.

10. Ferdinand now saw no alternative, in his sinking fortunes, but to call the great and proud Wallenstein from retirement. His restoration at once gave a new direction to the war. He quickly seized Prague, and restored Bohemia to his sovereign ; and Gustavus was now obliged to retire within the walls of Nuremberg[2] until he could rally his troops, which were scattered over Germany. After a tedious blockade of Nuremberg, in which both parties lost thirty thousand soldiers by famine and the sword, Wallenstein made a sudden movement towards Dresden ;[3] but the advance of Gustavus thwarted his plans and brought on that fatal action in which the Swedish hero lost his life. On the 16th of November, 1632, the two armies met at Lutzen ;[4] but scarcely had the battle commenced when Gustavus, throwing himself before the enemy's ranks, fell pierced by two balls. After a desperate engagement the Protestants triumphed ; but the glory of their victory was dearly bought by the death of their leader.

1. *Leipsic* is a celebrated commercial city of the kingdom of Saxony, sixty miles north-west from Dresden. It is a manufacturing town of considerable importance, and is the greatest book emporium in the world. In Oct. 1813, Leipsic was the scene of a most tremendous conflict between Napoleon and the allies, in which the French, greatly inferior in numbers, were repulsed with a heavy loss. (*Map* No. XVII)

2. *Nuremberg* is a city of Bavaria, ninety-three miles north-west from Munich. It is surrounded by feudal walls and turrets, and these are inclosed by a ditch one hundred feet wide and fifty feet deep, lined throughout with masonry. Nuremberg is celebrated in the history of the Reformation, having early embraced its doctrines. (*Map* No. XVII.)

3. *Dresden,* the capital of the kingdom of Saxony, is situated on the Elbe, one hundred miles south-east from Berlin, and two hundred and thirty north-west from Vienna. Population mostly Protestant. It has a great number of literary and scientific institutions, and establishments devoted to education. Dresden and its environs have been the scene of some of the most important conflicts in modern warfare, particularly on the 26th and 27th of August, 1813, when Napoleon defeated the allies under its walls. (*Map* No. XVII.)

4. *Lutzen* is a small town of Prussian Saxony, twelve miles south-west from Leipsic. It would be unworthy of notice were it not that its environs have been the scene of two of the most memorable conflicts of modern times,—the first, which occurred Nov. 16th, 1632, and in which the Swedish monarch Gustavus Adolphus fell ; and the second, which took place on nearly the same ground, May 2d, 1813, and in which the French, under Napoleon, defeated the allies, who were encouraged by the presence of the emperor Alexander and the king of Prussia. (*Map* No. XVII.)

11. Thus terminated the Swedish period of the "Thirty years war;" for although the Swedes still determined to support the Protestant cause in Germany, the animating spirit of the war had fled, and they were unable, alone, to accomplish anything effectual. A little more than a year after the fall of Gustavus, Wallenstein, being accused of treason to his master and the Catholic cause, was assassinated by the command of the emperor Ferdinand. (Feb. 1634.) We come now to what has been called the French period, embracing the closing scenes of this war.

IV. FRENCH PERIOD OF THE WAR.

12. The French minister, Richelieu, had long observed, with secret satisfaction, the misfortunes of the house of Austria, and of the German empire generally; and now he offered the aid of France to the Swedes and the German Protestants, with Holland and the duke of Savoy as allies, on the condition of extending the French frontier over a portion of the German territory; and thus the persecutor of the Huguenots was leagued with the Protestant powers of Europe against its Roman Catholic princes;—"a clear proof," says a writer of French history, "that his principles were politic, not bigoted." In a short time French armies were sent into Italy, Germany, and the Netherlands; and from this moment the provinces along the Rhine became the chief seat of the war, being pillaged and devastated as those along the Oder, Elbe, and Weser, had been previously.

13. From the moment of the active interference of France, the power of the German imperialists declined; and the remainder of this "Thirty years' war," which was marked by an unusual degree of ferocity on both sides, presents a continuation of gloomy and disheartening scenes, in which Richelieu had the advantage, not from military but diplomatic superiority. Ferdinand died in the year 1637, without living to witness the termination of the civil and domestic war in which he had been engaged from the commencement of his reign. The French monarch Louis XIII., and his minister Richelieu, the great fomentors and leaders of the war, died in 1642, after which the negotiations for peace, which had been begun as early as 1636, were the more easily concluded; and in October 1648, the treaty of Westphalia[1] closed the sad scene of the long and sanguinary

1. *Westphalia* is a province embracing all the northern portion of the Prussian dominions west of the Weser. The "peace of Westphalia" was concluded in 1648, at Munster and Osnaburg,—both then in Westphalia, but the latter now in Hanover. In 1641 preliminaries were agreed upon at Hamburg: in 1644 actual negotiations were commenced at Osnaburg, between the ambassadors of Austria, the German empire, and Sweden; and at Munster between those of the emperor, France, Spain, and other powers; but the articles adopted in both formed one

" Thirty years' war." Peace found the German States in a sadly-depressed condition; the scene that was everywhere presented was a wide waste of ruin; and two-thirds of the population had perished, although not so much by the sword as by contagion, plague, famine, and the other attendant horrors that follow in the train of war.

14. The chief articles of the treaty of Westphalia were, 1st, the confirmation of the religious peace of Passau, and the consequent establishment of the independence of the Protestant German powers: 2d, the dismemberment of many of the German States for the purpose of indemnifying others for their losses; and the sanction of the complete sovereignty of each of the German States within its own territory: 3d, the extension of the eastern limits of France: 4th, the grant, to Sweden, of a considerable territory on the Baltic coast, together with a subsidy of five millions of dollars; and 5th, the acknowledgment of the independence of the Netherlands by Spain, and of the Swiss cantons by the German empire.

II. ENGLISH HISTORY :—THE ENGLISH REVOLUTION.—While the " Thirty years' war" was progressing on the continent, leading to the final triumph of religious liberty there, England was convulsed by domestic dissensions, which eventually led to a civil war, and the temporary overthrow of the monarchy. On the death of Elizabeth in 1603, James VI. of Scotland, the son of the   *I. UNION OF ENGLAND AND SCOTLAND.* unfortunate Mary, succeeded to the throne of England, with the title of James I. England and Scotland were thus united under one sovereign; and henceforth the two countries received the common designation of " Great Britain."

2. The character of James, the first English monarch of the Stuart family, was not calculated to win the affections of his   *II. JAMES I.* subjects. He was as arbitrary as his predecessors of the Tudor race; and, although excelling in the learning of the times, he was signally deficient in all those noble qualities of a sovereign which command respect and enforce obedience. His imprudence in surrounding himself with Scotch favorites irritated the English: the Scotch saw with no greater satisfaction his attempts to subject them to the worship of the English church: some disappointed Roman Catholics formed a conspiracy, which was fortunately detected, to destroy by gunpowder the king and assembled parliament; and the

treaty. After terms had been settled between the parties at Osnaburg, the ministers repaired to Munster, where the final treaty was concluded, Oct. 24th, 1648. (*Map No.* XVII.)

R

puritans, aiming at farther reforms in the church and in the state, were committed to prison for even petitioning for some changes, not in the least inconsistent with the established hierarchy.   James strenuously maintained the " Divine right of kings;" and his entire reign was a continued struggle of the house of commons to restore and to fortify, their own liberties, and those of the people.

3. In 1625 James was succeeded on the throne by his son Charles III.   I., then in the twenty-fifth year of his age.   Had Charles CHARLES I. lived a hundred years earlier, or had not the reformatory spirit of the age introduced great and important changes in the minds of men on the subject of the royal prerogative and the liber ties of the people, he might have reigned with great popularity; for his stern and serious deportment, his disinclination to all licentious- ness, and a deep regard for religion, were highly suitable to the char- acter of the English people at this period ; but it was the misfortune of Charles to be destitute of that political prudence which should have taught him to yield to the necessities of the times.

4. The accession of Charles was immediately followed by difficul- ties with his parliament, which had no confidence in the king, and which he suddenly dissolved, because it refused to vote the supplies demanded by him, and showed an inclination to impeach his favorite minister Buckingham.   The second parliament proceeded with the impeachment of the minister, (1626,) and the king retaliated by im- prisoning two members of the house on the charge of " words spoken by them in derogation of his majesty's honor ;" but the exasperation of the Commons soon obtained their release.   The third parliament, called in 1628, waiving all minor contests, demanded the king's sanc- tion to a " Petition of Right," which set forth the rights of the Eng lish people as guaranteed to them by the Great Charter, and by various laws and statutes of the realm.   Charles, after many evasions, reluctantly signed the Petition; but in a few months he flagrantly violated the obligations it had imposed upon him, and in a fit of in- dignation dissolved parliament, resolving never again to call another. (1629—39.)

5. During an interval of about ten years, and until the assembling of another parliament, no opposition, except such as public opinion interposed, was made to the full enjoyment of the unrestrained pre- rogatives of the king.   Monopolies were now revived to a ruinous extent, and the benefits of them were sold to the highest bidder ; ille gal duties were sustained by servile judges; unheard-of fines were

imposed; and no expedient was omitted that might tend to bring money into the royal treasury, and thus enable the king to rule without the aid of parliament. The English clergy, at the head of whom was archbishop Laud, one of the chief advisers of the king, usurped, by degrees, the civil powers of government; and the puri tans were so rigorously persecuted that great numbers of them sought an asylum in America. In 1637 the attempts of Charles to introduce the Episcopal form of worship into Scotland, drove the Scotch presbyterians to open rebellion; and a *covenant* to defend the re ligion, the laws, and the liberties of their country against every danger, was immediately framed and subscribed IV. SCOTCH REBELLION. by them. The covenanters, having received arms and money from the French minister Richelieu, marched into England, but the English army refused 'to fight against their brethren, when the king, finding himself beset with difficulties on every side, was obliged to place himself at the discretion of a fourth parliament. (April 1640.) This parliament, not fully complying with the king's wishes, was abruptly dissolved after a month's session; but public opinion soon compelled the king to summon another, which assembled in November of the same year.

6. The new parliament, called the Long Parliament, from the ex traordinary length of its session, first applied itself dili V. THE LONG PARLIAMENT. gently to the correction of abuses and a redress of griev ances. Future parliaments were declared to be triennial; many of the recent acts for taxing the people were declared illegal, and monopolies of every kind were abolished—the king yielding to all the demands that were made upon him. Not satisfied with these concessions, the commons impeached the earl of Strafford, the king's first minister, and favorite general, accusing him of exercising pow ers beyond what the crown had ever lawfully enjoyed, and of a sys tematic hostility to the fundamental laws and constitution of the realm. By the unconstitutional expedient of a bill of attainder, Strafford was declared guilty; and the king had the weakness to sign his condemnation. (1641.) Archbishop Laud was brought to trial and executed four years later. The severity of the punishment of Strafford, and the magnanimity displayed by him on his trial, have half redeemed his forfeit-fame, and misled a generous posterity; but he died justly, although the means taken to accomplish his condem nation, by a departure from the ordinary course of judicial proceed ings, established a precedent dangerous to civil liberty.

7. With a strong hand parliament now virtually took possession of the government; it declared itself indissoluble without its own consent, and continued to encroach on the prerogatives of the king until scarcely the shadow of his former power was left him. A rebellion which broke out in Ireland was maliciously charged upon the king as its author; and Charles, to refute the unworthy suspicion, intrusted the management of Irish affairs to parliament, which the latter interpreted into a transference to them of the whole military power of the kingdom. At length Charles, irritated by a threatening remonstrance on the state of the kingdom, caused five members of the Commons to be impeached; and went in person to the House to seize them,—a fatal act of indiscretion which was declared a breach of privilege of parliament, for which Charles found it necessary to atone by a humiliating message.

8. The difficulties between the king and parliament, and their respective supporters, at length reached such a crisis, that in January 1642 the king left London, attended by most of his nobility, and, repairing to Nottingham,[1] erected there the royal standard, resolving to stake his claims on the hazards of war. The adherents of parliament were not unprepared for the contest. On the side of the king were ranged most of the nobility of the kingdom, together with the Roman Catholics—all forming the high church and monarchy party; while parliament had on its side the numerous presbyterian dissenters, and all ultra religious and political reformers;—parliament held the seaports, the fleet, the great cities, the capital, and the eastern, middle, and southern counties; while the royalists had the ascendancy in the north and west.

VI. CIVIL WAR.

9. From 1642 until 1647 the war was carried on with various success. In the battle of Edghill,[2] fought in October 1642, nothing was decided, although five thousand men were left dead on the field. The battle of Newbury,[3] fought in the following year, (Sept

1. *Nottingham* is a city one hundred and eight miles north-west from London. It was the chief place of rendezvous for the troops of Edward IV. and Richard III. during the wars of the Roses. Soon after Charles I. raised his standard here in 1642, the inhabitants, who were attached to the republican cause, compelled him to abandon the town and castle to the parliamentary forces. (*Map* No. XVI.)

2. *Edghill* is a small town in the county of Warwick, seventy-two miles north-west from London. (*Map* No. XVI.)

3. *Newbury* is a town in Berks county, England, on the Kennett, a southern branch of the Thames, fifty-three miles south-west from London. The vicinity of this town is celebrated for two battles fought during the civil wars between the royalist and parliamentary forces,—Charles I. commanding his army in person on both occasions. The first was fought Sept 20th, 1643; the second, Oct 27th, 1644 but neither had any decided result. (*Map* No. XVI.)

20th, 1643,) was equally indecisive; but it was attended with such loss on both sides that it put an end to the campaign, by obliging both parties to retire into winter quarters.

10. Both king and parliament now began to look for assistance to other nations; and while some Irish Roman Catholics   VII. THE joined the royal army, the parliament entered into a   SCOTCH "Solemn League and Covenant" with the Scotch people,   LEAGUE. by which the parties to it bound themselves to aid in the extirpation of popery and prelacy, and to promote the establishment of a church government conformed to that of Scotland. The Scots, rejoicing at the prospect thus held out of extending their mode of religion over England, sent an army of twenty thousand men, at the beginning of 1644, to coöperate with the forces of parliament.

11. The campaign of 1644 was unfortunate to the royal cause, the Irish forces being dispersed by Sir Thomas Fairfax, and the royalists experiencing a severe defeat at Marston Moor,[1] (2d July,) on which occasion fifty thousand British combatants engaged in mutual slaughter. In Scotland the royal cause was for a time sustained by the marquis of Montrose; but the gallant Scot was at length overwhelmed by superior numbers; and in the following year, June 14th, 1645, the battle of Naseby,[2] gained by the parliamentary forces, decided the contest against the king, although the useless obstinacy of the royalists protracted the war till the beginning of 1647.[a] After the defeat at Naseby, the king, relying on the faith of uncertain promises, threw himself into the hands of his Scotch subjects; but the latter, treating him as a prisoner, delivered him up to the commissioners of parliament.

12. The war was now at an end, but civil and religious dissensions raged with greater fury than ever. The late enemies of the king were divided into two factions, the Presbyterians and the Independents, the former having a majority in the parliament, and the latter forming a majority of the army. At the head of the Independent party was Oliver Cromwell, a general of the   VIII. OLIVER army, and a man of talent and address, who appears al-   CROMWELL

1. *Marston Moor* is a small village of Yorkshire, England, seven miles west of the city of York. (*Map* No. XVI.)

2. *Naseby* is a decayed market town of England, eleven and a-half miles north-west from London. It is twenty-nine miles north east of the locality of the battle of Edghill. The battle of Naseby was fought north of the town, in the plain that separated Naseby from Harborough. *Map* No. XVI.)

a. "Some of the castles of North Wales the last that surrendered, held out till April 1647."— Hallam's Const. Hist. Note p. 351.)

ready to have formed the design of obtaining supreme power. By his orders the king was taken from the commissioners of parliament, and placed in the custody of the army. A proposition of parliament to disband the army gave Cromwell an opportunity to heighten the disaffection of the soldiers; and, placing himself at their head, he entered London, purged parliament of the members obnoxious to him, and imprisoned all who disputed his authority.

13. While parliament was suffering under the military domination of Cromwell, a general reaction began to take place in favor of the king. The Scots, ashamed of the reproach of having sold their sovereign, now took up arms in his favor; but Cromwell marched against them at the head of an inferior force, and after defeating them entered Scotland, the government of which he settled entirely to his satisfaction. Parliament also entered into a negotiation with the king, with the view of restoring him to power; but Cromwell surrounded the House of Commons with his soldiers, and excluding all but his own partisans, caused a vote to be passed declaring it treason in a king to levy war against his parliament. Under the influence of Cromwell, proposals were now made for bringing the king to trial;

IX. TRIAL
AND EXECU-
TION OF
CHARLES I.

and when the few remaining members of the House of Lords refused their sanction to the measure, the Commons voted that the concurrence of the Lords was unnecessary, and that the people were the origin of all just power. The Commons then named a court of justice, composed mostly of the principal officers of the army, to try the king; and on the charge of having been the cause of all the bloodshed during the continuance of the war, he was condemned to death. He was allowed only three days to prepare for execution; and on the 30th of January, 1649, the misguided and unhappy monarch was beheaded, being, at the time, in the forty-ninth year of his age, and the twenty fourth of his reign.

14. "The execution of Charles the First," says Hallam, "has been mentioned in later ages by a few with unlimited praise, by some with faint and ambiguous censure, by most with vehement reprobation." Viewing the case in all its aspects, we can find no justification for the deed; for no considerations of public necessity required it; and it was, moreover, the act of a small minority of parliament that had usurped, under the protection of a military force, a power which all England declared illegal. Lingard asserts that "the men who hurried Charles to the scaffold were a small faction of bold and

ambitious spirits, who had the address to guide the passions and fanaticism of their followers, and were enabled, through them, to control the
real sentiments of the nation." The arbitrary principles of Charles,
which he had imbibed in the lessons of early youth,—his passionate
temper, and want of sincerity, indeed rendered him unfit for the
difficult station of a constitutional king; but, on the other hand, he
was deserving of esteem for the correctness of his moral principles·
and in private life he would not have been an unamiable man.

15. A few days after the death of Charles, the monarchical form
of government was formally abolished; the House of   X. ABOLI-
Lords fell by a vote of the Commons at the same time;   TION OF
the mere shadow of a parliament, known by the appella-   MONARCHY.
tion of the *Rump*, and supported by an army of fifty thousand men
under the controlling influence of Oliver Cromwell, took into its
hands all the powers of government; and the former title of the
"English Monarchy" gave place to that of the *Commonwealth of
England*. The royalists being still in considerable force in Ireland,
Cromwell repaired thither with an army, and speedily reduced the
country to submission· after which he marched into Scotland at the
head of sixteen thousand men, and, in the battle of Dunbar, (Sept.
13th, 1650,) defeated the royal covenanters, who had proclaimed
Charles II., son of the late king, as their sovereign. In the following year he pursued the Scotch army into England, and completely
annihilated it in the desperate battle of Worcester.[1] (Sept. 13th,
1651.)

16. Cromwell had formed the project of a coalition with Holland,
which was to make the two republics one and indivisible;   XI. WAR
but national antipathies could not be overcome; and in-   WITH
stead of the proposed coalition there ensued a fierce and   HOLLAND.
bloody war. Under pretence of providing for the interests of commerce,
the British parliament passed the celebrated navigation act, which
prohibited all nations from importing into England, in their ships,
any commodity which was not the growth and manufacture of their
own country;—a blow aimed directly at the Dutch, who were the
general factors and carriers of Europe. Ships were seized and reprisals made; and in the month of May, 1652, the war broke out by

---

1. *Worcester*, the capital of Worcester county, England, is on the eastern bank of the river
Severn, one hundred miles north-west from London. Worcester is of great, but uncertain,
antiquity, and is one of the best built towns in the kingdom. It is principally celebrated in
history for its giving name to the decisive victory obtained there by Cromwell on the 13th
Sept. 1351. (*Map No. XVI.*)

a casual encounter of the hostile fleets of the two nations, in the straits of Dover,—the Dutch admiral Van Tromp commanding the one squadron, and the heroic Blake the other. After five hours' fighting, the Dutch were defeated, with the loss of one ship sunk and another taken.

17. The States-general of Holland were seriously alarmed at the prospect of a naval war with England, but the English parliament would listen to neither reason nor remonstrance; and in a short time the fleets of the two nations were at sea again. Several actions took place with various success, but on the 29th of November a determined battle was fought off the Goodwin sands,[1] between the Dutch fleet commanded by Van Tromp and De Ruyter, and the English squadron under Blake. Blake was wounded and defeated; five English ships were taken, or destroyed; and night saved the fleet from destruction. After this victory, Tromp, in bravado, placed a broom at his mast head, to intimate that he would sweep the English ships from the seas.

18. Great preparations were made in England to remove this disgrace; and in the month of February following (1653) eighty sail, under Blake, assisted by Dean and Monk, met, in the English Channel, the Dutch fleet of seventy-six vessels, commanded by Van Tromp, who was seconded by De Ruyter. Three days of desperate fighting ended in the defeat of the Dutch, although Tromp acquired little less honor than his rival, by the masterly retreat which he conducted. In June several battles were fought; and in July occurred the last of these bloody and obstinate conflicts for naval superiority. Tromp issued forth once more, determined to conquer or die, and soon met the enemy commanded by Monk; but as he was animating his sailors, with his sword drawn, he was shot through the heart with a musket ball. This event alone decided the action, and the defeat which the Dutch sustained was the most decisive of the whole war. Peace was soon concluded on terms advantageous to England; and Cromwell, as protector, signed the treaty of pacification, (April 1654,) after having vainly endeavored to establish a union of government, privileges, and interests, between the two republics.

19. While the war with Holland was progressing, a controversy

---

1. The *Goodwin sands* are famous and very dangerous sand banks, about four miles from the eastern coast of Kent, a few miles north-east from Dover. They are believed to have once formed part of the Kentish land, and to have been submerged about the end of the reign of Will. I. Rufus. The channel between them and the main land is called 'the Downs," a celebrated roadstead for ships, which affords excellent anchorage. (*Map* No. XVI.)

had arisen between Cromwell and the army on the one hand, and the Long Parliament on the other. Each wished to rule supreme, but eventually Cromwell forcibly dissolved the parliament, (April 1653,) and soon after summoned another, composed wholly of members of his own selection. The latter, however, commonly called *Barebone's* parliament, from the name of one of its leading members, at once commenced such a thorough reformation in every department of the state, as to alarm Cromwell and his associates; and it was re solved that these troublesome legislators should be sent back to their respective parishes. A majority of the members voluntarily sur rendered their power into the hands of Cromwell, who put an end to the opposition of the rest by turning them out of doors. (Dec 12th, 1653.) Four days later a new scheme of govern ment, called "The Protectorate," was adopted, by which the supreme powers of state were vested in a lord pro tector, a council, and a parliament; and Cromwell was solemnly in stalled for life in the office of "Lord Protector of the commonwealth of England, Scotland, and Ireland."

XII. THE PROTECTO- RATE.

20. The parliament summoned by Cromwell to meet in September of the following year, suspecting that the Protector aimed at kingly authority, commenced its session (1654) by an inquiry into the right by which he held his power; upon which Cromwell plainly informed the members that he would send them to their homes if they did not acknowledge the authority by which they had been assembled. About three hundred members signed a paper recognizing Cromwell's scheme of government; while the remainder, amounting to a hundred and sixty resolutely refused compliance, and were excluded from their seats; but although parliament was in some degree purged by the operation, it did not exhibit the subserviency which Cromwell had hoped to find in it. On the introduction of a bill declaring the Pro tectorate hereditary in the family of Cromwell, a very large majority voted against it. The spirit which characterized the remainder of the session showed Cromwell that he had not gained the confidence of the nation; and an angry dissolution, early in the following year, (Feb. 1655,) increased the general discontent. Soon after, a conspiracy of the royalists broke out, but was easily suppressed; and even in the army, among the republicans themselves, several officers allowed their fidelity to be corrupted, and took a share in counsels that were intended to restore the commonwealth to its original vigor and puri ty. During the same year (1655), a war with Spain broke out; the

Island of Jamaica, in the West Indies, was conquered; the treasure-ships of the Spaniards were captured on their passage to Europe; and some naval victories were obtained.

21. In his civil and domestic administration, which was conducted with ability, but without any regular plan, Cromwell displayed a general regard for justice and clemency; and irregularities were never sanctioned, unless the necessity of thus sustaining his usurped authority seemed to require it. Such indeed were the order and tranquillity which he preserved—such his skilful management of persons and parties, and such, moreover, the change in the feelings of many of the Independents themselves, since the death of the late monarch, that in the parliament of 1656 a motion was made, and carried by a considerable majority, for investing the Protector with the dignity of king. Although exceedingly desirous to accept the proffered honor, he saw that the army, composed mostly of stern and inflexible republicans, could never be reconciled to a measure that implied an open contradiction of all their past professions, and an abandonment of their principles; and he was at last obliged to re fuse that crown which had been solemnly proffered to him by the representatives of the nation.

22. After this event, the domestic affairs of the country kept Cromwell in perpetual uneasiness. The royalists renewed their con-spiracies against him; and a majority in parliament now opposed all his favorite measures; a mutiny of the army was apprehended; and even the daughters of the Protector became estranged from him. Over-whelmed with difficulties, possessing the confidence of no party, hav-ing lost all composure of mind, and in constant dread of assassina-tion, his health gradually declined, and he expired on the 13th of September, 1658, the anniversary of his great victories, and a day which he had always considered the most fortunate for him.

23. On the death of Cromwell, his eldest son, Richard, succeeded him in the protectorate, in accordance, as was supposed, with the dying wish of his father, and with the approbation of the council. But Richard, being of a quiet, unambitious temper, and alarmed at the dangers by which he was surrounded, soon signed his own abdica-tion, and retired to private life. A state of anarchy followed, and XIII. RESTO- contending factions, in the army and the parliament, for RATION OF a time filled the country with bloody dissensions, when MONARCHY. General Monk, who commanded the army in Scotland, marched into England and declared in favor of the restoration of

royalty. This declaration, freeing the nation from tne state of suspense in which it had long been held, was received with almost universal joy : the House of Lords hastened to reinstate itself in its ancient authority; and on the 18th of May, 1660, Charles the Second, son of the late king, was proclaimed sovereign of England, by the united acclamations of the army, the people, and the two houses of parliament.

24. The accession of Charles II. to the throne of his ancestors was at first hailed as the harbinger of real liberty, and the promise of a firm and tranquil government, although no terms were required of him for the security of the people against his abuse of their confidence. As he possessed a handsome person, and was open and affable in his manners, and engaging in conversation, the first impressions produced by him were favorable ; but he was soon found to be excessively indolent, profligate, and worthless, and to entertain notions as arbitrary as those which had distinguished the reign of his father. The parliament, called in 1661, composed mostly of men who had fought for royalty and the church, gave back to the crown its ancient prerogatives, of which the Long Parliament had despoiled it—endeavored to enforce the doctrine of passive obedience, by compelling all officers of trust to swear that they held resistance to the king's authority to be in all cases unlawful,—and passed an act of religious uniformity, by which two thousand Presbyterian ministers were deprived of their livings, and the gaols filled with a crowd of dissenters. Episcopacy was established by law; and the church, grateful for the protection which she received from the government, made the doctrine of non-resistance her favorite theme, which she taught without any qualification, and followed out to all its extreme consequences.

25. While these changes were in progress, the manners and morals of the nation were sinking into an excess of profligacy, encouraged by the dissolute conduct of the king in private life. Under the austere rule of the puritans, vice and immorality were sternly repressed ; but when the check was withdrawn, they broke forth with ungovernable violence. The cavaliers, as the partisans of the late king were called, in general affected a profligacy of manners, as their distinction from the fanatical and canting party, as they denominated the puritans ; the prevailing immorality pervaded all ranks and professions; the philosophy and poetry of the times pandered to the general licentiousness ; and the public revenues were wasted on the

vilest associates of the king's debauchery. The court of Charles was a school of vice, in which the restraints of decency were laughed to scorn ; and at no other period of English history were the immoralities of licentiousness practiced with more ostenation, or with less disgrace.

26. While Charles was losing the favor of all parties and classes by his neglect of public business, and his wasteful profligacy, the general discontent was heightened by his marriage with Catherine, a Portuguese princess, and by the sale of Dunkirk[1] to France ; but still greater clamors arose, when, in 1664, the king provoked a war with Holland, by sending out a squadron which seized the Dutch settlements on the coast of Africa, and the Cape Verde Islands. The House of Commons readily voted supplies to carry on the war with vigor ; but such was the extravagance, dishonesty, and incapacity of those to whom Charles had intrusted its management, that, after a few indecisive naval battles, it was found necessary to abandon all thoughts of offensive war ; and even then the sailors mutinied in the ports from actual hunger, and a Dutch fleet, sailing up the Thames, burned the ships at Chatham,[2] on the very day when the king was feasting with the ladies of his seraglio. The capital was threatened with the miseries of a blockade, and for the first time the roar of foreign guns was heard by the citizens of London.

27. In the summer of 1665, while the ignominious war with Holland was raging, the plague visited England, but was confined principally to London, where its frightful ravages surpassed in horror anything that had ever been known in the island. But few recovered from the disease, and death followed within two or three days, and sometimes within a few hours, from the first symptoms. During one week in September more than ten thousand died ; and the whole number of victims was more than a hundred thousand. In the following year a fire, such as had not been known in Europe since the

---

1. *Dunkirk*, the most northern seaport of France, is situated on the straits of Dover, in the ormer province of French Flanders, opposite, and forty-seven miles east from, the English town of Dover. Dunkirk is said to have been founded by Baldwin, count of Flanders, in 960: in 1388 it was burned by the English ; and in the sixteenth and seventeenth centuries alternately belonged to them and to the Spaniards and French. Charles II. sold it to Louis XIV. for two hundred thousand pounds sterling. Louis, aware of its importance, fortified it at great expense, but was compelled, by the treaty of Utrecht, in 1713, to consent to the demolition of its fortifications, and even to the shutting up of its port. (*Map* No. XIII.)

2. *Chatham* is a celebrated naval and military depôt, on the river Medway, twenty-eight miles south-east from London. It was anciently called Cetcham, or the village of cottages. Many Roman remains have been found in its vicinity. It is this town which gives the title of earl to the Pitt family. (*Map* No. XVI.

conflagration of Rome under Nero, laid in ruins two-thirds of the metropolis,—consuming more than thirteen thousand dwellings, and leaving destitute two hundred thousand people.

28. After the war with Holland had continued two years, Charles was forced, by the voice of parliament and the bad success of his arms. to conclude the treaty of Breda,[1] (July 1667,) by which the Dutch possessions of New Netherlands,[2] in America, were confirmed to England, while the latter surrendered to France Acadia and Nova Scotia.[3] In 1672, however, Charles was induced by the French monarch, Louis XIV., to join him in another war against the Dutch. The combined armies of the two kingdoms soon reduced the republic to the brink of destruction; but the prince of Orange,[4] being promoted to the chief command of the Dutch forces, soon roused the courage of his dismayed countrymen : the dykes were opened, laying the whole country, except the cities, under water ; and the invaders were forced to save themselves from destruction by a precipitate retreat. At length, in 1674, Charles was compelled, by the discontents of his people and parliament, who were opposed to the war, to conclude a separate treaty of peace with Holland. France continued the war, but Holland was now aided by Spain and Sweden, while in 1676 the marriage of the prince of Orange with the Lady Mary, daughter of the duke of York, the brother of Charles, induced England to espouse the cause of the republic, and led to the treaty of Nimeguen[5]

1. *Breda* is a strongly-fortified town of Holland—province of North Brabant, on the river Merk, thirty miles north-east from Antwerp. Breda is a well-built town, entirely surrounded by a marsh that may be laid under water. It was taken from the Spaniards by prince Maurice in 1590, by means of a stratagem suggested by the master of a boat who sometimes supplied the garrison with fuel. With singular address he contrived to introduce into the town, under a cargo of turf, seventy chosen soldiers, who, having attacked the garrison in the night, opened the gates to their comrades. It was retaken by the Spaniards under the marquis Spinola in 1625, but was finally ceded to Holland by the treaty of Westphalia in 1648. (*Map No. XV.*)

2. *New Netherlands*, the present New York, had been conquered by the English in 1664, while England and Holland were at peace ; and the treaty of Breda confirmed England in the possession of the country.

3. The French possessions in America, embracing New Brunswick, Nova Scotia, and the adjacent islands, were at first called *Acadia*. A fleet sent out by Cromwell in 1654 soon reduced Acadia, but it was restored by the treaty of Breda in 1667.

4. The family of *Orange* derive their title from the little principality of Orange, twelve miles in length and nine in breadth, of which the city of Orange, a town of south-eastern France, was the capital. Orange, known to the Romans by the name of *Araussio*, is situated on the small river Meyne, five miles east of the Rhone, and twelve miles north of Avignon. From the eleventh to the sixteenth century Orange had its own princes. In 1531 it passed, by marriage, to the count of Nassau. It continued in this family till the death, in 1702, of William Henry of Nassau-Orange (William III. of England), when the succession became the subject of a long contest ; and it was not till the peace of Utrecht in 1715 that this little territory was finally ceded to France. (*Map No. XIII.*)

5. *Nimeguen*, or *Nymegen*, is a town of Holland, province of Guelderland on the south side

in 1678, by which the Dutch provinces obtained honorable and advantageous terms.

29. Although Charles professed adherence to the principles of the Reformation, yet his great and secret designs were the establishment of papacy, and arbitrary power, in England. To enable him to accomplish these objects, he actually received, from the king of France, a secret pension of two hundred thousand pounds per annum, for which he stipulated, in return, to employ the whole strength of England, by land and sea, in support of the claims of Louis to the vast monarchy of Spain. But the popularity with which Charles had commenced his reign had long been expended; there was a prevailing discontent among the people,—an anxiety for public liberty, which was thought to be endangered,—and a general hatred of the Roman Catholic Religion, which was increased by the circumstance that the king's brother, and heir presumptive, was known to be a bigoted Roman Catholic. Parliament became intractable, and successfully opposed many of the favorite measures of the king; and at length in 1678 a pretended Popish Plot for the massacre of the Protestants threw the whole nation into a blaze. One Titus Oates, an infamous impostor, was the discoverer of this pretended plot; and in the midst of the ferment which it occasioned, many innocent Catholics lost their lives. At a later period, however, a regular project for raising the nation in arms against the government was detected; and the leaders, among whom were Lord Russell and Algernon Sidney, being unjustly accused of participation in the *Rye House* plot for the assassination of the king, were beheaded, in defiance of law and justice. (1683.) From this time until his death Charles ruled with almost absolute power, without the aid of a parliament. He died suddenly in 1685. His brother, the duke of York, immediately succeeded to the throne, with the title of James II.

30. The reign of James was short and inglorious, distinguished
XIV.   by nothing but a series of absurd efforts to render him-
JAMES II.   self independent of parliament, and to establish the
Roman Catholic religion in England, although he at first made the strongest professions of a resolution to maintain the established government, both in church and state. It soon became evident that a crisis was approaching, and that the great conflict between the pre

of the Waal, fifty-three miles south-east from Amsterdam. It is known in history from the treaty concluded there August 10th, 1678, and from its capture by the French on the 8th of Sept. 1794, after a severe action in which the allies were defeated. (*Map No. XV.*)

rogatives of the crown and the privileges of parliament was about to be brought to a final issue.

31. In the first exercise of his authority James showed the insincerity of his professions by levying taxes without the authority of parliament: in violation of the laws, and in contempt of the national feeling, he went openly to mass: he established a court of ecclesiastical commission with unlimited power over the Episcopal church he suspended the penal laws, by which a conformity had been required to the established church; and although any communication with the pope had been declared treason, he sent an embassy to Rome, and in return received a nuncio from his Holiness, and with much ceremony gave him a public and solemn reception at Windsor.[1] In this open manner the king attacked the principles and prejudices of his Protestant subjects, foolishly confident of his ability to reëstablish the Roman Catholic religion, although the Roman Catholics in England did not comprise, at this time, the one-hundredth part of the nation.

32. An important event of this reign was the rebellion of the duke of Monmouth, a natural son of Charles II., who hoped, through the growing discontents of the people at the tyranny of James, to gain possession of the throne; but after some partial successes he was defeated, made prisoner, and beheaded. After the rebellion had been suppressed, many of the unfortunate prisoners were hung by the king's officers, without any form of trial; and when, after some interval, the inhuman Jeffries was sent to preside in the courts before which the prisoners were arraigned, the rigors of law were made to equal, if not to exceed, the ravages of military tyranny. The juries were so awed by the menaces of the judge that they gave their verdict as he dictated, with precipitation: neither age, sex, nor station, was spared; the innocent were often involved with the guilty; and the king himself applauded the conduct of Jeffries, whom he afterwards rewarded for his services with a peerage, and invested with the dignity of chancellor.

1. *Windsor* is a small town on the south side of the Thames, twenty miles south-west from London. It is celebrated for Windsor castle, the principal country seat of the sovereigns of England, and one of the most magnificent royal residences in Europe. The castle, placed on the summit of a lofty eminence rising abruptly from the river, appears to have been founded by William the Conqueror, and it has been enlarged or embellished by most of his successors. On the north and east sides of the castle is the Little Park, a fine expanse of lawn, comprising nearly five hundred acres: on the south side is the Great Park, comprising three thousand eight hundred acres; while near by is Windsor forest, a tract fifty-six miles in circumference, laid out by William the Conqueror for the purpose of hunting (*Map* No. XVI.)

33 As the king evinced, in all his measures, a settled purpose of invading every branch of the constitution, many of the nobility and great men of the kingdom, foreseeing no peaceable redress of their grievances, finally sent an invitation to William, prince of Orange, the stadtholder of the United Dutch Provinces, who had married the king's eldest daughter, and requested him to come over and aid them

XV REVOLU-
TION OF
1688.
by his arms, in the recovery of their laws and liberties. About the middle of November, 1688, William landed in England at the head of an army of fourteen thousand men, and was everywhere received with the highest favor. James was abandoned by the army and the people, and even by his own children; and in a moment of despair he formed the resolution of leaving the kingdom, and soon after found means to escape privately to France. These events are usually denominated " the Revolution of 1688."

34. In a convention-parliament which met soon after the flight of James, it was declared that the king's withdrawal was an abdication of the government, and that the throne was thereby vacant ; and af-ter a variety of propositions, a bill was passed, settling the crown on William and Mary, the prince and princess of Orange ; the succession to the princess Anne, the next eldest daughter of the late king. and to her posterity after that of the princess of Orange. To this settlement of the crown a declaration of rights was annexed, by which the subjects of controversy that had existed for many years, and particularly during the last four reigns, between the king and the people, were finally determined ; and the royal prerogative was more narrowly circumscribed, and more exactly defined, than in any former period of English history.

35. While the accession of William and Mary was peaceably ac-quiesced in by the English people, some of the Highland clans of Scotland, and the Catholics of Ireland, testified their adherence to the late king by taking up arms in his favor. The former gained the attle of Killiecrankie[1] in the summer of 1689; but the death of heir leader, the viscount Dundee, who fell in the moment of victory, ended all the hopes of James in Scotland. In the meantime Louis XIV. of France openly espoused the cause of the fallen monarch, and

1. *Killiecrankie* is a celebrated pass, half a mile in length, through the Grampian hills in Scotland, in the county of Perth, sixty miles northwest from Edinburgh. In the battle of 1689 fought at the northern extremity of this pass, Mackay commanded the revolutionary forces and the famous Graham of Claverhouse, Viscount Dundee, the troops of James II. (Map No. XVI.)

furnished him with a fleet, with which, in the spring of 1689, James landed in Ireland, where a bloody war raged until the autumn of 1691, when the whole country was again subjected to the power of England. The course taken by the French monarch led to a declaration of war against France in May 1689. The war thus commenced involved, in its progress, most of the continental powers, nearly all of which were united in a confederacy with William for the purpose of putting a stop to the encroachments of Louis. An account of this war will be more properly given in connection with the history of France, which country, under the influence of the genius and ambition of Louis XIV., acquires, in the latter part of the seventeenth century, a commanding importance in the history of Europe. King William died in the spring of 1702, having retained, until his death, the chief direction of the affairs of Holland, under the title of stadtholder; thus presenting the singular spectacle of a monarchy and a republic at the same time governed by the same individual.

III. FRENCH HISTORY:—WARS OF LOUIS XIV —1. During the administration of Cardinal Richelieu, (1624 - 42,) the able minister of the feeble Louis XIII., France was ruled with a rod of iron. " He made," says Montesqueu, " his sovereign play the second part in the monarchy, and the first in Europe; he degraded the king, but he rendered the reign illustrious." He humbled the nobility, the Huguenots, and the house of Austria; but he also encouraged literature and the arts, and promoted commerce, which had been ruined by two centuries of domestic war. He freed France from a state of anarchy, but he established in its place a pure despotism. No minister was ever more successful in carrying out his plans than Richelieu; but his successes were bought at the expense of every virtue; and as a man he merits execration. He died in December 1642, and Louis survived him but a few months, leaving, as his successor, his son Louis, then a child of only six years of age.

I. ADMINISTRATION OF CARDINAL RICHELIEU.

2. During the minority of Louis XIV., Cardinal Mazarin, an Italian, ruled the kingdom as prime minister, under the regency of the queen mother, Anne of Austria. Under Mazarin was concluded the treaty of Westphalia, which terminated the thirty years' war; and during the early part of his administration occurred the civil war of the *Fronde*,' in which the

II. MAZARIN'S ADMINISTRATION

‡ "War of the *Fronde*"—so called because the first outbreak in Paris was commenced by

magistracy of Paris, supported by the citizens, rose against the arbitrary powers of the government, and promulgated a plan for the reformation of abuses; but when the young nobility affected to abet and adopt its principles, they perverted the cause of freedom to their own selfish interests; and the vain struggle for constitutional liberty degenerated into the most ridiculous of rebellions.

3. Though the treaty of Westphalia (1648) had terminated the ' Thirty years' war" among the parties originally engaged in it,[a] yet France and Spain still continued the contest in which they had at first only a secondary share.   The civil disturbances of the *Fronde* occurring at this time, greatly favored the Spaniards, who recovered, principally on the borders of the Low Countries, many places which they had previously lost to the French; and by means of the great military talents of Condé, a French general who had been exiled during the late troubles, and who now fought on the side of the Spaniards, the latter hoped to bring the war to a triumphant issue. The French, however, found in marshal Turenne a general who was more than a rival for Condé: he defeated the latter in the siege of Arras,[1] and compelled the Spaniards to retreat, but was himself compelled to abandon Valenciennes.[2]   At this time Mazarin, by flattering the passions of Cromwell, induced England to take part in the contest: six thousand English joined the French army in Flanders;[3] and Dunkirk, taken from the Spaniards, was given to England, according to treaty, as a reward for her assistance.

4. But France, though victorious, was anxious for peace, as the finances of the kingdom were in disorder, and the death of Cromwell had rendered the alliance with England of little benefit; while

troops of urchins with their *slings—fronde* being the French word for "a sling." In derision, the insurgents were first called *frondeurs*, or "slingers,"—an insinuation that their force was trifling, and their aim merely mischief.

1. *Arras* is a city of northern France, in the former province of Artois, thirty-three miles south-east from Agincourt. Robespierre, of infamous memory, and Damiens, the assassin of Louis XV., were natives of Arras.

2. *Valenciennes* is a town of north-eastern France, on the Scheldt, (skelt), near the Belg'a frontier. (*Map* No. XV.)

3. In 863 Charles the Bold established the county of *Flanders*, which extended from the straits of Dover nearly to the mouths of the Scheldt. At different times Flanders fell under the dominion of Bur'gundy, Spain, &c. Towards the beginning of the eighteenth century it was divided into French, Austrian, and Dutch Flanders. French Flanders comprised the French province of that name. (See *Map* No. XIII.) Adjoining this territory, on the east, was Austrian Flanders; and adjoining the latter, on the east, was Dutch Flanders. Dutch and Austrian Flanders are now comprised in East and West Flanders, the two north-western provinces of Belgium (see *Map* No. XV.,) although the Dutch portion embraced only a small part of East Flanders.

a. See p. 314.

Spain, engaged in war with the Netherlands and Portugal, gladly acceded to the offers of reconciliation with her most powerful enemy. On the banks of the Bidassoa[1] the treaty, usually known as the treaty of the Pyrenees, was concluded, (Nov. 1659,) and the infanta Maria Theresa, eldest daughter of Philip of Spain, was given in marriage to the French monarch; although, to prevent the possible union of two such powerful kingdoms, Louis was compelled to renounce all claim to the Spanish crown, either for himself or his successors. By the treaty of the Pyrenees, Condé was pardoned and again received into favor; the limits of France were extended on the English Channel to Gravelines;[2] while on the south-west the Pyrenees became its boundary, by the acquisition of Roussillon.[3] Thus France assumed almost its present form; its subsequent acquisitions being Franche-Comté[4] and French Flanders.

5. About a year after the conclusion of the treaty of the Pyrenees, Mazarin died, (March 1661,) and Louis, summoning his council, and expressing his determination to take the government wholly into his own hands, strictly commanded the chancellor, and secretaries of state, to sign no paper but at his express bidding. To the stern, economical, and orderly Colbert, he intrusted the management of the treasury; and in a brief period the purchase of Dunkirk from England, the establishment of numerous manufactures, the building of the Louvre,[5] the Invalides,[6] and the

ILL.
LOUIS XIV

1. The *Bidassoa*, which rises in the Spanish territory, and falls into the Bay of Biscay, forms, in the latter part of its course, the boundary between France and Spain. A short distance from its mouth it forms the small Isle of the Pheasants, where the peace of the Pyrenees was concluded in 1659. The Bidassoa was the scene of important operations in the peninsular war of 1813.

2. *Gravelines* is a small town twelve miles east from Calais. (*Map* No. XIII.)

3. *Roussillon*, a province of France before the French Revolution, was bounded on the south and east by the Pyrenees and the Mediterranean. The counts of Roussillon governed this district for a long period. The last count bequeathed it to Alphonso of Aragon in 1173. In 1462 it was ceded to Louis XI. of France, but in 1493 it was restored to the king of Aragon, and in 1659 was finally surrendered to France by the treaty of the Pyrenees. (*Map* No. XIII.)

4. *Franche-Comté*, called also *Upper Bur'gundy*, had Bur'gundy Proper, or Lower Burgundy, on the south and west. Besancon was its capital. In the division of the States of the emperor Maximilian, Franche-Comté fell to Spain; but Louis XIV. conquered it in 1674, and it was ceded to France by the peace of Nimeguen, in 1678. (*Map* No. XIII.)

5. The palace of the *Louvre*, one of the finest regal structures in Europe, has not been the residence of a French monarch since the minority of Louis XV., and is now converted into a national museum and picture gallery. The pictures are deposited on the first floor of a splendid range of rooms above a quarter of a mile in length, and facing the river.

6. The *Hotel des Invalides* (in'-va-leed) is a hospital intended for the support of disabled officers and soldiers who have been in active service upwards of thirty years. It covers a space of nearly seven acres, and is one of the grandest national institutions of France.

palace of Versailles,[1] and the commencement of the canal of Languedoc,[2] attested the miracles that mere economy can work in finance.

6. Arousing himself from the thraldom of love intrigues, Louis
now began to awake to projects of ambition. The splendor of his
court dazzled the nobility: his personal qualities won him the affection
of his people: he breathed a new spirit into the administration; and
foreign potentates, like the proud nobles of his court, seemed to
quail before his power. He repudiated the stipulations of the
treaty of the Pyrenees, on the ground that the dower which he was
to receive with his wife had not been paid; and on the death of his
father-in-law, Philip IV. of Spain, by which event the crown devolved
upon a sickly infant, by a second marriage, he laid immediate claim
to the Spanish Netherlands in right of his wife,—alleging, in support of the claim, an ancient custom of the province of Brabant,[3] by
which females of a first marriage were to inherit in preference to sons
of a second. The French monarch, after securing the neutrality of
Austria, poured his legions over the Belgian frontier, and with great
rapidity reduced most of the fortresses as far as the Scheldt. The
captured towns were immediately fortified by the celebrated engineer
Vauban, and garrisoned by the best troops of France. (1667-8.)

7. These successes encouraged Louis to turn his arms towards
another quarter; and Franche-Comté, a part of the old Burgundy,
but still retained by the Spaniards, was conquered before Spain was
aware of the danger. (Feb. 1668.) The Hollanders, alarmed at
the approach of the French, became reconciled to Spain, and a
Triple Alliance was formed between Holland, Sweden, and England,
three Protestant powers, for the purpose of defending Catholic

1. *Versailles* is nine miles south-west from Paris. The palace of Versailles, of prodigious
size and magnificence, has not been occupied by the court since 1789. It was much out of re
pair, when Louis Philippe transformed it into what may be called a national museum, intended
to illustrate the history of France, and to exhibit the progress of the country in arts, arms, and
civilization. (*Map* No. XIII.)

2. The canal of *Languedoc*, commencing at Cette, fourteen miles south-west of Montpellier
and extending to Toulouse on the Garonne, a distance of one hundred and forty-eight miles,
thus connects the Mediterranean and the Atlantic. (*Map* No. XIII.)

3. *Brabant*, first erected into a duchy in the seventh century, included the Dutch province of
North Brabant, and the Belgic provinces of South Brabant and Antwerp. Having passed, by
marriage, into the possession of the house of Burgundy, it afterwards descended to Charles V
In the seventeenth century the republic of Holland took possession of the northern part, (now
North Brabant,) which was thence called *Dutch* Brabant, while the remainder was known as
Austrian Brabant. Both repeatedly fell into the hands of the French, but in 1815 were in
cluded in the kingdom of the Netherlands. Since the revolution of 1830 North Brabant has
been included in Holland, and the other provinces, or Austrian Brabant, in Belgium. (*Map*
No. XV.)

Spain against Catholic France. Louis receded before this menacing league, and by restoring Franche-Comté, which he knew could at any time easily be regained, while he retained most of his Flemish conquests, concluded the treaty of Aix-la-Chapelle,[1] (1668,) which merely suspended the war until the French king was better prepared to carry it on with success.

8. The great object of Louis was now revenge against Holland, the originator of the triple alliance. Knowing the profligate habits of Charles II., he purchased with ready money the alliance of England; he also bought the neutrality of Sweden, and the neighboring princes of Germany, while in the meantime he created a navy of a hundred vessels, built five naval arsenals, and increased his army to a hundred thousand men.

9. For the first time the bayonet, so terrible a weapon in French hands, was affixed to the end of the musket; and the hundred thousand soldiers who composed the French army, armed as the French were, might well strike terror into the rulers of Holland, who could raise, at most, an army of only thirty thousand men.

10. In the spring of 1672 the French armies, avoiding the Spanish Netherlands, passed through the country betwixt the Meuse and the Rhine,[2] crossed the latter river in June, and rapidly advanced to within a few leagues of Amsterdam,[3] when the Dutch, by opening the dykes, let in the sea and saved the metropolis. But even Amsterdam meditated submission; one project of the inhabitants being to embark, like the Athenians, on board their fleet, sail for their East India settlements, and abandon their country to the modern Xerxes who had come to destroy their liberties. While Amsterdam was secure for the present behind its rampart of waters, and the French armies were wintering triumphantly in the conquered provinces, the envoys of the Dutch roused Europe against the ambition of Louis

1. *Aix-la-Chapelle* (a-lah-shahpel') is an old and well-built city of the Prussian States, near the eastern confines of Belgium, eighty miles east of Brussels. It was the favorite residence of Charlemagne, and for some time the capital of his empire. Two celebrated treaties have been concluded in this city; the first, May 2d, 1668, between France and Spain; and the second, Oct. 18th, 1748, between the different powers engaged in the wars of the Austrian succession. Here also was held the celebrated congress of the allied powers in 1818. (*Map* No XVII.)

2. The *Meuse* and the *Rhine* : —see *Map* No. XV.

3. *Amsterdam*, a famous maritime and commercial city of Holland, is on the south bank of the Y., an inlet or arm of the Zuyder Zee. Being situated in a marsh, its buildings are all founded on piles, driven from forty to fifty feet in a soil consisting of alluvial deposits, peat, clay, and sand. The State-House, a magnificent building of freestone, is erected on a foundation of thirteen thousand six hundred and fifty-nine piles. Numerous canals divide the city into about a hundred islands. (*Map* No. XV.)

Prince William of Orange, a general of only twenty-two years of age, being placed at the head of the Republic, soon succeeded in detaching England from the unnatural alliance which she had formed with her ancient enemy: Spain and Austria, awaking to their interests, prepared to send troops to aid the Dutch; and by 1674 nearly all Europe was leagued against the French monarch.

11. Louis was now obliged to abandon Holland; but, in the Spanish Netherlands, his great generals, Condé and Turenne, turning upon the allied armies, for a while kept all Europe at bay. In the following year, (1675,) Turenne was killed by a cannon ball as he was about to enter Germany; and although Louis created six new marshals, the whole were not equal to the one he had lost. Soon after, Condé retired, disabled by age and infirmity; and with the loss of her great generals the valor of France, on the land, for a while slumbered. But at this time there appeared a seaman of talent and heroism, named Duquesne, who, being sent to succor Messina, which had revolted against Spain, defeated the fleet of De Ruyter in a terrible naval battle within sight of Mount Ætna. The Dutch admiral himself was among the slain. In the second battle, in 1677, Duquesne almost annihilated the Dutch fleet. Under a grateful monarch this man might have become high admiral of France; but Louis was growing bigoted with his years, and his faithful servant was reproached for being a Protestant. "When I fought for your majesty," replied the blunt sailor, "I never thought of what might be your religion." His son, driven into exile for adhering to the reformed faith, carried away with him the bones of his father, determined not to leave them in an ungrateful country.

12. In the meantime conferences took place at Nimeguen: the allies wished peace; and France and Holland, the original parties in the war, were equally exhausted. At length, in August 1678, the treaty was signed, Louis retaining most of his conquests in the Spanish Netherlands,—all French Flanders in fact, as well as Franche-Comté pain, from whom these possessions were obtained, assented to the treaty; for the imbecile monarch of that country knew not what towns belonged to him, nor where was the frontier line of what he still retained of the Spanish Netherlands. "Here may be seen," says Voltaire, "how little do events correspond to projects. Holland, against which the war had been undertaken, and which had nearly perished, lost nothing nay, even gained a barrier; while the

other powers, that had armed to defend and guarantee her indepen
dence, all lost something."

13. The years which followed the peace of Nimeguen were the
most prosperous for France; and formed the zenith of the reign of
Louis XIV. All Europe had been armed against him, and success
had more or less crowned all his enterprises. He assumed to himself the title of *Great ;* and one of his dukes even kept a burning
lamp before the statue of the monarch, as before an altar; the least
insult offered by foreign courts to his representatives, or neglect of
etiquette, was sure to bring down signal vengeance. In the years
1682 and 1683 Algiers was bombarded, then a new mode of warfare:
in 1684 Genoa experienced the same fate because it refused to allow
the French monarch to establish a depot within its territory. Even
the pope was humbled before the " Grand Monarch ;" some of the
German princes were expelled from their territories; and in time
of peace French maurauding parties devastated the Spanish provinces.
Louis increased his navy to two hundred and thirty vessels; and
toward the end of his reign his armies amounted to four hundred
and fifty thousand men. But the greatest glories of the reign of
Louis were those connected with literature and the arts. Men of
letters now, for the first time, began to exert a great influence on the
mind of the French nation; and the familiar names of Molière, Ra-
cine, Boileau, La Fontaine, Bossuet, Massillon, and Fénélon, adorned
the age of Louis, and shed on the land the brightness of their fame.
In the next century the writings of these men, and of their success
ors, determined the fate of the great monarchy which Louis had built
up.

14. The queen of France being dead, towards the year 1685 Louis
secretly married Madame Scarron, the widow of the celebrated
comic writer, on whom he conferred the title of Madame De Maintenon. This woman, who had been educated a Calvinist, and had
abjured her religion, would have made all Protestants do the same;
and it was chiefly through her influence, and that of the royal confessor La Chaise, that the king, naturally bigoted, became a bitter
persecutor of his Protestant subjects. In 1685 he revoked the edict
of Nantes, which had given tolerance to all religions, forbade all exercise of the Protestant worship, and banished from the kingdom,
within fifteen days, all Protestant ecclesiastics who would not recant.
Afterwards he closed the ports against the fugitives, sent to the gal
leys those who attempted to escape, and confiscated their property

France lost by these cruel measures two hundred thousand—some say five hundred thousand—of her best subjects; and the bigotry of Louis gave a greater blow to the industry and wealth of his king-dom than the unlimited expenses of his pride and ambition.

15. The cruelties of Louis to the Protestants roused the hearts of the Germans, Dutch, and English, against him, and accelerated a general war. In 1686 a league was formed at Augsburg by all the German princes to restrain the encroachments of Louis: Holland joined it,—Spain also, excited by jealousy of a domineering neighbor; Sweden, Denmark, and Savoy, were afterwards gained; and the revolution of 1688, by which William of Holland ascended the throne of England, placed the latter country at the head of the confederacy. But Louis was not daunted by the power of the league: anticipating his enemies, he was first in the field, sending an army against Germany in 1688, which ravaged the Palatinate[1] with fire and sword. He also sent an army into Flanders, one into Italy, and a third to check the Spaniards in Catalonia; while at the same time he sent a fleet and an army to Ireland, to aid James II. in re-covering the throne of England.

16. After the first campaign, in which Louis profited little, he gave the command of his armies to new generals of approved talent, and instantly the fortune of the war changed. In 1690 Savoy was overrun by the French marshal Catinat, and Flanders by marshal Luxembourg: the combined squadrons of England and Holland were defeated by the French admiral Tourville, off Beachy Head;[2] and a descent was made on the coast of England. In 1692 the fortress of Namur[3] was taken by the French, in spite of all the efforts of William and the allies to relieve it; but during the progress of the siege the French were defeated in a terrible naval battle off Cape La Hogue;[4] a battle that decided the fate of the Stuarts, and marks the era of England's dominion over the seas.

1. The *Palatinate*, by which is generally understood the *Lower Palatinate*, or Palatinate on the Rhine, was a country of Germany, on both sides of the Rhine, embracing about sixteen hundred square miles, and now divided among Prussia, Bavaria, Baden, Hesse Darmstadt Nassau, &c. That part of it west of the Rhine, and belonging to Bavaria, is still called "The Palatinate." The Upper Palatinate, embracing a somewhat larger territory, was in Bavaria, and bordered on Bohemia. Amberg was its capital. (*Map* No. XVII.)

2. *Beachy Head* is a bold promontory on the southern coast of England, eighteen miles south-west from Hastings. (*Map* No. XVI.)

3 *Namur* is a strongly-fortified town of Belgium, at the junction of the Sambre and Meuse, thirty-five miles south-east from Brussels. (*Map* No. XV.)

4. Cape *La Hogue* is a prominent headland of France, on the English Channel, sixteen miles north-west of Cherbourg. (*Map* No. XIII.)

17. The campaign of 1693 was fortunate for the French, who gained the bloody battle of Nerwinden[1] over king William—defeated the duke of Savoy in a general action at Marscilles—made progress against the Spaniards in Catalonia—and gained some advantages at sea. But after this year Louis no longer visited his armies in person ; and succeeding campaigns became less fruitful of important and decisive results. France had been exhausted by the enormous exertions of her monarch, and all parties were anxious to terminate a war in which much blood had been shed, much treasure expended and no permanent acquisitions made. Conferences for peace commenced in 1696 ; and in the beginning of 1697 the plenipotentiaries of the several powers assembled at Ryswick,[2] a small town in Holland. In the treaty, which was signed in September, England gained only the recognition of the monarch of her choice ; while the French king's renunciation of the Spanish succession, which had been one important object of the war, was not even mentioned. Although in the treaty Louis appeared to make concessions, yet he kept the new frontier that he had chosen in Flanders, whilst the possession of Strasburg[3] extended the French limits to the Rhine. Louis had baffled the most powerful European league ; and although the commerce of the kingdom was destroyed, and the country exhausted of men and money, while a dreadful famine was ravaging what war had spared, yet at the close of the seventeenth century France still preserved, over surrounding nations, the ascendency that Richelieu had planned, and that Louis XIV. had proudly won.

IV. COTEMPORARY HISTORY.—1. Besides France, England, Germany, and the countries connected with them in wars and alliances, the strictly *universal* history of this period embraces a range more extended than that of any previous century. On the continent the histories of the leading powers become more and more intermingled

---

1. *Nerwinden* is a small village of Belgium, about thirty-three miles south-east from Brussels.

2. *Ryswick* is a small town in the west of Holland, two miles south-east from Hague, and thirty-five south-west from Amsterdam. The peace of Ryswick terminated what is known in American history as "King William's War,"—a war between the French and the English American colonies, attended with numerous inroads of the Indians, who were in alliance with the French. (*Map* No. XV.)

3. *Strasburg* is an ancient fortified city on the west bank of the Rhine, in the former province of Alsace. It is principally noted for its cathedral, said to have been originally founded by Clovis, in 504. The modern building, however, was begun in 1015, but not finished till the fifteenth century. Its spire reaches to the extraordinary height of four hundred and sixty-six feet—about seven feet higher than St. Peter's in Rome, and about five feet higher than the great pyramid of Cheops. (*Map*, Nos. XIII. and XVII.)

the Northern States are seen growing in importance, and beginning
to take part in European politics; while, abroad, colonies are planted
that are soon to assume the rank of independent and powerful nations

2. It was not until after the Reformation that the three Scandinavian States, Denmark, Sweden, and Norway, came into
contact with the Southern nations of Christendom, nor
until the commencement of the "Thirty Years' War,'
in the early part of the seventeenth century, that they
took any active part in the concerns of their southern neighbors,
when, under the conduct of the heroic Gustavus Adolphus, Sweden
and her allies warred so manfully in the cause of religious freedom
Under Gustavus, the glory and power of Sweden attained their
greatest height; and although the successes of the Swedish arms
continued under Christina, Charles X., and Charles XI., Swedish
history offers little further that is interesting to the general student
until the accession of Charles XII. in 1697, the extraordinary
events of whose career belong to the next century.

I. DENMARK, SWEDEN, AND NORWAY

3. The history of Poland, during most of the seventeenth century, is of less interest to the general reader than that of
Sweden, being filled with accounts of unimportant do
mestic contentions among the nobility, and of foreign wars with
Sweden, Russia, and Turkey, while the mass of the people, in the
lowest state of degradation, were slaves, in the fullest extent of the
term, and not supposed to have any legal existence. The greatest
of the monarchs of Poland was John Sobieski, elected to the throne
in 1674, the fame of whose victories over the Turks threw a transient
splendor on the waning destinies of his ill-fated country. His first
great achievement was the victory of Kotzim,[1] gained, with a comparative y small force, over an army of eighty thousand Mussulmen,
strongly intrenched on the banks of the Dniester, leaving forty thousand of the enemy dead in the precincts of the camp. (Nov. 1673.)
All Europe was electrified with this extraordinary triumph, the greatest that had been won for three centuries over the infidels.

II. POLAND.

4. Other victories of the Polish hero, scarcely less important, are
recorded in the annals of Poland; but what has immortalized the
name of John Sobieski is the deliverance of Vienna[2] in 1683. A

1. *Kotzim* is now an important fortress of south-western Russia, situated on the right bank
of the Dniester, in the province of Bessarabia. The Turks strongly fortified it in 1718, but it
was successively taken by the Russians in 1730, 1769, and 1738. (*Map* No. XVII.)

. 2. *Vienna*, the capital of the Austrian empire, is on the southern bank of the Danube, three
hundred and thirty miles south-east from Berlin and eight hun lred miles north-west from

revolt of the Hungarians from the dominion of Austria, and an alliance formed between them and the Turks, had brought an army of nearly three hundred thousand men against the Austrian capital, which was defended by its citizens, and a garrison of little more than eleven thousand men. After an active siege of more than two months, Vienna was reduced to the last extremity. In the meantime the Austrian emperor, who had left his capital to make what defence it could against the immense hosts of Turks that poured down upon it, had solicited the aid of the Polish king; and Sobieski was not long in making his appearance at the head of a small, but resolute army of eighteen thousand veterans. The combined Polish and Austrian forces, when all assembled, amounted to only seventy thousand men, whom the Turks outnumbered more than three to one; but Sobieski, whose name alone was a terror to the infidels, was at once the Agamemnon and Achilles of the Christian host.

5. Sunday the 12th of September, 1683, was the important day that was to decide whether the Turkish crescent or the cross, was to wave on the turrets of Vienna. At five o'clock in the afternoon Sobieski had drawn up his forces in the plain fronting the Mussulmen camp, and ordering the advance, he exclaimed aloud, " Not to us, O Lord, but to thee be the glory." Whole bands of Tartar troops broke and fled when they heard the name of the Polish hero repeated from one end to the other of the Ottoman lines. At the same moment an eclipse of the moon added to the consternation of the superstitious Moslems, who beheld with dread the crescent waning in the heavens. With a furious charge the Polish infantry seized an eminence that commanded the grand Vizier's position when Kara Mustapha, taken by surprise at this unexpected attack, fell at once from the heights of confidence to the depths of despair Charge upon charge was rapidly hurled upon the already wavering Moslems, whose rout soon became general. In vain the vizier tried to rally the broken hosts. " Can you not aid me?" said he to the

---

Constantinople. Population about three hundred and seventy thousand. In Roman history Vienna is known as *Vindabona*, (see *Map* No. VIII.,) and is remarkable as being the place where Marcus Aurelius died. After the time of Charlemagne, margraves or dukes held Vienna till the middle of the thirteenth century soon after which it came into the possession of the house of Hapsburg. In 1484 it was taken by the Hungarians, whose king, Matthias, made it the seat of his court. Since the time of Maximilian it has been the usual residence of the arch-dukes of Austria, and the emperors of Germany. About two miles from the city is Schönbrunn, the favorite summer residence of the emperor. It was twice occupied by Napoleon: the treaty of Schönbrunn was signed in it in 1808, and here the duke of Reichstadt, son of Napoleon, died in 1832. (*Map* No. XVII.)

cham of the Tartars, who passed him among the fugitives. " I know
the king of Poland," was the reply ; " and I tell you, that with such
an enemy we have no safety but in flight. Look at the sky ; see if
God is not against us."

6. So sudden and general was the panic among the Turks, that at
six o'clock Sobieski entered the camp where a hundred and twenty
thousand tents were still found standing ; the innumerable multitude
of the Orientals had disappeared ; but their spoils, their horses,
their camels, their splendor, loaded the ground. The cause of Christianity—of civilization—had prevailed ; the wave of Mussulman
power had retired, never to return. But Sobieski received little
thanks from a jealous monarch for rescuing him and his country
from irretrievable ruin ; and Poland—unhappy Poland ! had saved
a serpent from death, which afterward turned and stung her for the
kindness. Sobieski died in 1696, in the midst of the ruin that was
fast overwhelming his country through the dissensions and clamors
of a turbulent nobility, and just in time to save his withered laurels
from being torn from his brow by the rude hand of rebellion. With
him the greatness of his native land may be said to have ended.

7. *Russia*, at the commencement of the seventeenth century, was
immersed in extreme ignorance and barbarism ; and al-
III. RUSSIA.
though a glimmering of light dawned upon her during
the reign of Alexis, who died in 1677, yet the great epoch in the
history of Russia is the reign of Peter the Great, whose genius first
opened to its people the advantages of civilization. In 1689, this
prince, then only seventeen years of age, became sole monarch of
Russia. The vigorous development of his mind was a subject of
universal wonder and admiration. Full of energy and activity, he
found nothing too arduous to be attempted, and he commenced at
once the vast project of changing the whole system of the government, and of reforming the manners of the people. His first exertions were directed to the remodelling and disciplining of the army
and the improvement of his resources ; and from the model of a small
yacht on the river which runs through Moscow, he constructed the
first Russian navy. In 1694 he took from the Turks the advantageous port of Azof,[1] which opened to his subjects the commerce of

1. The *sea of Azof*, the *Palus Mæotis* of the ancients, communicates by the narrow strait of
Yenicale, (an. *Cimmerian Bosporus*,) with the north-western angle of the Black Sea. The
port of Azof is at the mouth of the Don, at the north-eastern extremity of the sea of Azof
The town, anciently called *Tanais*, as it, in the middle ages, *Tana*, once had an extensive trade
but is now fast falling into decay.

the Black Sea. This acquisition enlarged his views, and he commenced a system of internal improvements, which had for its object, by connecting the waters of the Dwina,[1] the Volga,[2] and the Don, to open a water communication between the Baltic, Black, and Caspian Seas. A few years later he laid, near the shores of the Gulf of Finland, the foundations of St. Petersburg,[3] a city which he designed to be the emporium of Northern commerce and the capital of his dominions.

8. Being convinced of the superiority of the natives of Western Europe over his own barbarous subjects, in 1697 he sent out to Italy, Holland, and Germany, two or three hundred young men, to learn the arts of those countries, particularly ship-building and navigation; and in the following year he himself left his dominions, as a private individual, to procure knowledge by his own observation and experience. He visited Amsterdam, where he entered himself as a common carpenter in one of the principal dockyards, laboring and living like the other workmen, and demanding the same pay: he also went to England, where he examined the principal naval arsenals; and after a year's absence returned home, greatly improved in mechanical science, and accompanied by numerous artisans whom he had engaged to aid him in the great design of instructing his subjects in the arts of more civilized nations. The chief political acts of the reign of this truly great man belong to the history of the next century.

9. In the sixteenth century *Turkey*, during the reign of Solyman the Magnificent, the cotemporary of the emperor Charles V., had become the most powerful empire in the world,   IV. TURKEY. reaching from the confines of Austria on the west, to the banks of the Euphrates on the east, and extending over Egypt on the south. Other able princes, who succeeded Solyman, with Mussulman pride held all the rest of the world in scorn, and the Ottoman arms continued to maintain their ascendency over those of Christendom until the latter part of the seventeenth century, when, in 1683, the famous Sobieski, king of Poland, totally defeated the army em-

1. The *Dwina* here mentioned rises near the sources of the Volga, and empties into the Gulf of Riga, in the Baltic, nine miles below Riga. Another river of the same name falls into the White Sea, thirty-five miles below Archangel.

2. The *Volga*, or *Wolga*, the largest river of Europe, has its sources in central Russia, and its mouth in the Caspian Sea. It is the great artery of Russia, and the grand route of the internal traffic of that empire; but it is said that its waters are decreasing in depth, and that sandbanks are becoming serious obstacles to its navigation.

3. *St. Petersburg*, the modern capital of Russia, and one of the largest and finest cities of Europe, is situated at the mouth of the river Neva, at its entrance into the Gulf of Finland

ployed in the siege of Vienna. This event marks the era of the decline of the Ottoman power. A powerful league formed between Austria, Russia, Poland, and Venice, followed upon the defeat of the Ottoman forces at Vienna, and in 1687 the Turks were finally driven out of Hungary, and dispossessed of the greater portion of Southern Greece. In 1697, while this war continued, they sustained a total defeat by the famous Prince Eugene, in the battle of Zenta,[1] in which they lost thirty thousand men. The treaty of Carlowitz[2] in 1699, completed the humiliation of the Porte;[a] Transylvania,[3] Sclavonia,[4] and Hungary, being preserved to the emperor of Austria, Podolia,[5] with other portions of the Ukraine,[6] remaining in the possession of Poland, while Russia retained her conquests on the Black Sea. Morea, or Southern Greece, was ceded to Venice.

10. The political history of *Italy*, during the seventeenth century, is of trifling importance, but the social condition of its

v. ITALY.

people merits a passing notice. The Reformation had destroyed the political influence of the pope, who was reduced to the rank of a petty sovereign over the small territory embraced in the " States of the Church ;" while Spain, mistress of the fairest provinces of the peninsula, as well as of its two large and beautiful islands, inflicted upon the country numerous evils which made the people at once poor and miserable. The effects of Spanish rule are faithfully characterized by a Milanese writer, who forcibly depicts the wretchedness of the fertile and once populous valley of Lombardy. " The Spaniards," he remarks, " possessed central Lombardy for a hundred and seventy-two years. They found in its chief city

1. *Zenta* is a small town of Southern Hungary, on the Theiss, a northern branch of the Danube, two hundred and forty miles south-east from Vienna. (In history the name of this town is variously spelled Zenta, Zentha, Zeuta, and Zeutha.) (*Map* No. XVII.)

2. *Carlowitz* is a town of Austrian Sclavonia, on the southern bank of the Danube, about fifty miles south of Zenta. (*Map* No. XVII.)

3. *Transylvania* is the most eastern province of the Austrian empire, lying east of Hungary and north of the Turkish province of Wallachia. It is divided principally among three distinct races,—the Magyar, the Szekler or Siculi, and the Saxon. (*Map* No. XVII.)

4. *Sclavonia*, a province of the Austrian empire, usually regarded as forming a part of Hungary, has Hungary on the north, and the Turkish provinces of Bosnia and Servia on the south. (*Map* No. XVII.)

5. *Podolia*, now a province of south-western Russia, lies along the eastern bank of the Dniester. It was long governed by its own princes; but, in 1569, it was united to Poland. It has belonged to Russia since 1793. (*Map* No. XVII.)

6. The *Ukraine*, (a word signifying " *the frontier*,") was an extensive country in the south-eastern part of Russian Poland, now forming the Russian provinces of Podolia, Kiev, Charkow, and Poltava. Kiev, on the Dnieper, was the chief town. (*Map* No. XVII.)

a. *Porte*—the Ottoman court, so called from the gate of the sultan's palace where justice is administered; as the Sublime Porte. L. *porta*, Fr. *porte*, " a door or gate."

three hundred thousand souls: they left in it scarcely a third of that number. They found in it seventy woollen manufactories: they left in it no more than five. They found agriculture skilful and flourishing: before the province was wrested from them they had passed laws which made emigration a capital crime." The Spanish governors of the provinces looked upon the conquered countries as estates calculated to fill their own and the royal coffers; and not only was the nation drained of its treasure, but of its blood also. The flower of the people, draughted by thousands into the Spanish armies, perished in the wars of France, Germany, and the Netherlands.

11. But numerous as were the evils which flowed from the administrative oppression of the Spaniards, they were light when compared with the fearful corruption in morals that pervaded the whole system of society. An insidious licentiousness, under the garb of gallantry, had been introduced by the Spaniards, while the spirit of the people, kindled into frenzy by Castilian fancies about knightly honor, but no longer ennobled by personal courage, or manly self-respect, made Italy, for many generations, infamous as the scene of poisonings and assassinations. Risings and revolutions of the people were frequent; during nearly the whole period of the seventeenth century the coasts were continually infested by Turkish and Algerine corsairs; the fields were ravaged; houses, villages, and whole towns were burned; and thousands were carried away into slavery; while, in the interior, robbers were scarcely less destructive, large troops of whom plundered, or exacted ransoms, and more than once resisted successfully battalions of regular soldiers. Such is the mournful picture presented by Italy, the land of Roman greatness and renown, during the seventeenth century.

12. The principal events, to which we have not already alluded, that mark the history of the Spanish peninsula during the seventeenth century, are the expulsion of the Moors, the revolt of Portugal, and the acknowledgment of the independence of Holland. Twice during the sixteenth century, the Moors, or Moriscos, had risen against their Christian masters; they had been dispersed, from Granada, among the other Spanish provinces, and compelled, against their will, to receive Christian baptism. Tranquillity could scarcely be hoped from so arbitrary a measure; and the Moriscos, thirsting for revenge, entered into a correspondence with the African princes, whom they urged to invade the peninsula, promising to rise on the

VI.
SPANISH
PENINSULA

first signal. This circumstance becoming known, the expulsion of the whole body was decreed, and the cruel mandate was carried into execution, although not without open resistance in several of the provinces. (1610.) In all, no fewer than six hundred thousand of the most ingenious and industrious portion of the community were forcibly driven from their homes, while large numbers, by making a profession of Christianity, were permitted to remain. This was a blow no less fatal to the prosperity of Spain, than the revocation of the edict of Nantes was to a sister kingdom.

13. Portugal had been united to Spain in 1580, partly by conquest, and partly in accordance with the wishes of a portion of its nobility; but the union failed to give satisfaction to the people of the former country. Finding themselves ground to the dust by intolerable taxes and forced loans, their complaints disregarded, their persons insulted, and their prosperity at an end, in 1640 they organized a general revolt, and the sway of Spain over Portugal was forever broken, by the election, to the throne, of the duke of Braganza,[1] with the title of John IV. To complete the humiliation of Spain, eight years later, in the treaty of Munster,[2] she was compelled to acknowledge the independence of Holland, after having maintained against her a warfare of eighty years' duration, only interrupted by a brief truce of twelve years from 1609 to 1621; and even during this period, hostilities did not cease in the Indies. The disasters that were befalling Roman Catholic Spain were fast overwhelming that proud monarchy with disgrace and ruin, while the new Republic of Holland was taking its place, as a free and independent State, among the most powerful nations of Europe. The treaty of Westphalia, signed the same year, 1648, secured to Holland internal tranquillity, by reconciling the conflicting interests of her own people, and guaranteeing the enjoyment of civil and religious liberty,—one of the noble aims and results of Christian civilization.

14. The history of the Asiatic nations in the seventeenth century, merits but little notice. During this period a series of imbecile tyrants ruled over Persia. Their reigns were generally peaceful, but the higher classes were enervated

VII.
ASIATIC
NATIONS.

1. *Braganza* is a town at the north-eastern extremity of Portugal. In 1442 it was erected into a duchy, and in 1640, John, eighth duke of Braganza, ascended the Portuguese throne under the title of John IV. His descendants continue to enjoy the crown of Portugal, and have also acquired that of Brazil. The town and surrounding district of Braganza still belong to the king of Portugal as the duke of Braganza. (*Map* No. XIII.)

2. *Munster*, a town of Westphalia, is ninety-five miles north-east from Aix-la-chapelle. The treaty of Munster was a part of that of Westphalia. See Westphalia, p. 300. (*Map* No. XV, &c.)

by luxury, and the martial spirit of the people suffered so much from inaction, that early in the following century the Affghans, a warlike people on the confines of India, invaded the kingdom, and placed the royal diadem on the head of their chief Mahmoud. In 1644 an important revolution was terminated in China, by which the Manchoos, a race sprung from the expelled Mongols and the eastern Tartars, established themselves firmly in the empire, after a war of twenty-seven years' duration. Happily for the country, Shunchy the first emperor of the Manchoo-Tartar dynasty, showed himself a generous and enlightened monarch; and his son and successor Kang-hy, who had the singular fortune to reign sixty years, was one of the most illustrious sovereigns that ever ruled the country,—the Chinese historians ascribing to him almost every virtue that can adorn a throne.

15. In the early part of the seventeenth century the great Mogul empire of Asia, having northern Hindostan for the seat of its central power, and the Persian dominions for its western limits, gradually declined in greatness until, in 1659, the famous Aurungzebe succeeded to the throne, by the imprisonment of his father. Under this prince, who ruled with the most tyrannical cruelty, establishing Mohammedanism throughout his dominions by a rigorous persecution of the Hindoos, and the destruction of their temples, the Mogul empire was extended and consolidated; but on his death, in 1707, it experienced a rapid decline, and was soon broken into fragments.

16. The seventeenth century marks the era of the establishment of the principal Dutch, Spanish, French, and English colonies in the New World, and on the coasts of Asia and Africa. Near the close of the preceding century the Dutch had founded the colony of Surinam[1] in South America, and in 1607 they gained a footing in the East Indies by capturing, from the Portuguese, the Moluccas[2] or Spice Islands, which they continued to hold against all competitors. A few years later they founded New Amsterdam, now New York. In 1619 they founded Batavia,

VIII. COLONIAL ESTABLISHMENTS.

. *Surinam*, or Dutch Guiana, is on the north-eastern coast of South America, having French Guiana on the east, and English Guiana on the west.

2. The *Moluccas*, of which Amboyna is the principal, are a cluster of small islands north of Australia or New Holland, and between Celebes and New Guinea. They are distinguished chiefly for the production of spices, particularly nutmegs and cloves. When in 1511 the Portuguese discovered these islands, the Arabians were already settled there. The Portuguese had almost the entire monopoly of the spice trade till the beginning of the seventeenth century, when the Dutch took the islands from them. Since 1796 the Moluccas have been twice conquered by the English, but by the peace of Paris in 1815 they were restored to the Dutch.

in the island of Java;—about the same time they wrested the Japanese trade from the Portuguese. In 1650 they seized and colonized the Cape of Good Hope, which had previously been claimed by the English, and six years later they expelled the Portuguese from the island of Ceylon.[1] The Dutch adopted, in their colonial regulations, a more exclusive system of policy than other nations; and this, together with their harsh treatment of the natives, was the principal ause of the final ruin of their empire in the Indies.

17. The numerous colonies founded by Spain in the New World during the previous century had now become consolidated into one vast empire, embracing most of the islands of the West Indies, together with the extensive realms of Mexico and Peru, over which the Spanish monarch ruled with the most absolute despotism. The immense wealth derived from these possessions excited the envy and cupidity of all Europe; and frequently, during the wars of the seventeenth century, the Spanish fleets, laden with the gold and silver of the New World, fell into the hands of the Dutch, French, or English cruisers; while bands of pirates, or Buccaneers, who had their coverts among the small islands of the West Indies, often plundered the coasts, and roamed at will, the terror of the Spanish seas.

18. The materials for a history of the Spanish possessions in the New World, during nearly three centuries, are exceedingly meagre and uninteresting, treating of little but the same unvarying rule of arbitrary and avaricious viceroys or governors, of commercial restrictions the most odious and oppressive, and of the miseries of an aboriginal population, the most abject that could possibly be conceived.

19. The French colonization, in the New World, during the seventeenth century, embraces only the founding of Quebec, and a few other feeble settlements in the Canadas; and, at the very close of the century, the landing of two hundred emigrants, and the erection of a rude fort, in Lower Louisiana. Nor was anything importar accomplished by the French, during this period, in the newly discovered regions of the Old World. About the middle of the century they attempted to make Madagascar[2] one of their colonies, a scheme

1. *Ceylon* is a large island belonging to Great Britain, near the southern extremity of Hindostan. The cinnamon tree, which was found only in Ceylon and Cochin-China, is its most valuable production. Extensive ruins of cities, canals, aqueducts, bridges, temples, &c., show that Ceylon was, at a remote period, a rich, populous, and comparatively civilized country. After Holland had been erected into the Batavian republic in 1795, the English took possession of Ceylon, and at the peace of Amiens, in 1802, it was formally ceded to them.

2. *Madagascar* is a large island off the eastern coast of South Africa, from which it is sepa

which proved futile on account of the extreme unhealthiness of the island. In 1672 the French purchased the town of Pondicherry,[1] in Hindostan, from its native sovereign, and established there a colony with every reasonable prospect of success; but the place was several times taken from them by the Dutch and the English, until, finally, it was restored at the treaty of Paris in 1815, and is now the principal French settlement on the Asiatic continent.

2℄ In the latter part of the sixteenth century the English began to turn their attention to the commerce of the East Indies; and in the year 1600 a company of London merchants, known as the London East India Company, obtained a charter from queen Elizabeth, giving to them the exclusive right of trading with those distant countries. During the seventeenth century the London company made little progress in effecting settlements in the Indies; and at the close of that period, a small part of the island of Java,[2] Fort St. George at Madras,[3] the island of Bombay,[4] and Fort William erected at Calcutta[5] in 1699,

rated by Mozambique Channel. Soon after the peace of 1815 the French formed several small colonies on the eastern coast of the island; and from 1818 to 1825 the English missionaries had some success in converting the natives; but since the latter period the missionaries have been forbidden to approach the island, and Madagascar may now be reckoned among the barbarous countries of eastern Africa.

1. *Pondicherry* is a town of Hindostan, on the south-eastern coast, eighty miles south-west from Madras. Population about fifty-five thousand. The French possessions in India, comprising Pondicherry, Chandernagore, Karical in the Carnatic, Mahé in Malibar, and Yanaon in Orissa, with the territory attached to each, have a total population of about one hundred and sixty-six thousand, of whom one thousand are whites.

2. *Java* is a large island of the Asiatic archipelago, south of Borneo, belonging principally to the Dutch, and the centre, as well as the most valuable, of their possessions in the East. Area, a little less than that of the State of New York. Population between five and six millions. The Portuguese reached Java in 1511, and the Dutch in 1595. The latter founded Batavia in 619. In 1811 Java was taken by a British force, and held till 1816, when, in pursuance of the treaty of Paris, it was restored to the Dutch.

3 *Madras* is a large city on the south-eastern coast of Hindostan, eight hundred and seventy miles south-west from Calcutta. Population upwards of four hundred thousand. Madras is badly situated, has no harbor, and is almost wholly unapproachable by sea. It was the first acquisition made in India by the British, who obtained it by grant from the rajah of Bijnagur, in 1639, with permission to erect a fort there. The fort was besieged in 1702 by one of Aurungzebe's generals; and in 1744 by the French, to whom it surrendered after a bombardment of three days. It was restored to the English at the peace of Aix-la-Chapelle, and successfully sustained a memorable siege by the French under Lally in 1758-9; since which it has experienced no hostile attack. Madras is the capital of the British presidency of the same name, which embraces the whole of South Hindostan, extending about five hundred miles north from Cape Comorin.

4. *Bombay* is built on an island of the same name, on the western coast of Hindostan, ten hundred and fifty miles south-west from Calcutta. Population about two hundred and forty thousand. In 1531 Bombay was obtained by the Portuguese from a Hindoo chief: by them it was ceded to Charles II, in 1661, as part of queen Catherine's dowry; and in 1663 it was transferred, by the king, to the East India Company, at an annual rent of ten pounds sterling. Soon after it realized to the company a revenue of three thousand pounds a year. Bombay is the capital of the presidency of the same name.

5. *Calcutta*, the capital of the British dominions in the East, is situated on the eastern side

the whole inhabited by only a few hundred Europeans, formed the extent of their East India possessions. Such was the feeble beginning, and slow progress, of an association of merchants that "now rules over an empire containing a hundred millions of subjects, raises a tribute of more than three millions annually, possesses an army of more than two hundred thousand men, has princes for its servants, and emperors pensioners on its bounty."

21. The first successful attempt at American colonization by the English was the settlement of Jamestown, in Virginia, in the year 1607. This was followed by the settlement of Plymouth in New England, in 1620, by a band of Puritans, who had resolved to seek, in the wilderness of America, that freedom of worship which their native country denied them. During the same century the English formed settlements in all the Atlantic States from Maine to Georgia, the latter only excepted, which was not colonized until the year 1733; the Dutch, who had settled New Amsterdam, now New York, were conquered by the English in 1644; and at the same time the Swedes, who had settled Delaware, and had subsequently been reduced by the Dutch, shared the fate of their masters. The history of the British American colonies, during the seventeenth century is marked no less by the struggles of the colonists against the natural difficulties of their situation, and by the Indian wars in which they were often involved, than by their noble resistance to the arbitrary and oppressive rule of the mother country. The early colonists, those of New England especially, had left their homes on the other side of the Atlantic, to seek, in the wilds of America, an asylum where they might enjoy unmolested their religious faith and worship; and they brought with them to the land of their adoption, that spirit of independence, and those principles of freedom, which laid the foundation of American liberty.

22. The early history of these colonies is full of instruction to all,—in its lessons of patient endurance, and unyielding perseverance, exalted heroism, individual piety, and public virtue; but to American citizens it possesses a peculiar interest, as the history of the development and growth of those principles of free government which suc-

of the river Hoogly, the most western arm of the Ganges, about one hundred miles from its entrance into the Bay of Bengal. Resident population about two hundred and thirty thousand. The English first made a settlement here in 1690, when Calcutta was but a small village, inhabited chiefly by husbandmen. In 1756 a Bengal chief dispossessed the English of their settlement, but it was retaken by Colonel Clive in the following year, since which it has been quietly retained by the British, and risen to its present degree of importance.

ceeding time has perfected to the happiness and glory of our country, and the advancement of the cause of freedom throughout the world. In a work of general history like the present we cannot hope to do such a subject justice; and instead of attempting here a brief and separate compend of our early annals, it will be more satisfactory and useful to refer the student to some of the numerous standard works on American history which are at all times accessible to him, and with some one of which it is presumable every *American* youth will early make himself familiar, before he enters upon the study of the general history of nations.

CHAPTER V.

THE EIGHTEENTH CENTURY.

WAR OF THE SPANISH SUCCESSION, AND CLOSE OF THE REIGN OF LOUIS XIV.

ANALYSIS. 1. Pride and ambition of Louis XIV. Events that led to the " war of the Spanish Succession." ENGLAND, GERMANY, AND HOLLAND, DECLARE WAR AGAINST FRANCE, 702.—2. Causes that induced England to engage in the war. The opposing powers. Death of king William. Queen Anne.—3. Opening of the campaign by Austria and England. The French generals.—4. The CAMPAIGN OF 1702. Naval events. [Cadiz. Vigo Bay.] EVENTS OF 1703.—5. EVENTS OF 1704. [Blenheim. Gibraltar.]—6. EVENTS OF 1705 AND 1706. French losses. [Ramillies. Mons. Barcelona. Madrid.]—7. Overtures of peace. CAMPAIGN OF 1707. [Almanza. Toulon.] EVENTS OF 1708. [Oudenarde. Brussels.]—8. Sufferings of the French in the year 1709. Haughtiness of the monarch.—9. Louis in vain seeks peace with Holland. Battle of Malplaquet. [Malplaquet.] Successes of Louis in Spain. His domestic misfortunes.—10. Death of the Austrian emperor. Importance of that event. Decline of the war.—11. TREATY OF UTRECHT, April 11th, 1713. [Minorca. Newfoundland. Hudson's Bay territory. St. Christopher. Radstadt. Lisle. Alsace.]—12. Death of Louis XIV. CHARACTER OF THE REIGN OF LOUIS XIV.

II. PETER THE GREAT OF RUSSIA, AND CHARLES XII. OF SWEDEN.

1. THE NORTH AND EAST OF EUROPE during the war of the Spanish succession. Beginning of the reign of the Russian monarch.—2. Leading object with the Czar. He is induced to engage in a war with Sweden. His allies. [Livonia. Riga.]—3. Sweden. Reported character of Charles XII. The Swedish council, and declarations of Charles. Change in the king's character.—4. BEGINNING OF HOSTILITIES AGAINST SWEDEN, in the year 1700. [Sleswick. Holstein. Narva.] Charles humbles Denmark. [Copenhagen.]—5. The Polish king. Charles marches against Narva —6. Signal DEFEAT OF THE RUSSIANS AT NARVA. Remark of the Czar. Superstition of the Russians.—7. The course pursued by Peter. Resolution of Charles. —8. VICTORIES OF CHARLES IN THE YEAR 1702. [Courland. Warsaw. Cracow.] The Polish king deposed. [Pultusk.] Charles declines the sovereignty of Poland.—9. Increase of his power and influence. [Borysthenes.] His views, and plans, for the future.—10. Policy, and gradual successes, of the Czar. [Neva. Ingria.]—11. MARCH OF CHARLES INTO RUSSIA, 1707-8. [Smolensko.]—12. Passage of the Desna. [Desna.] Misfortunes of Charles.—13. Situation of the Swedish army in the winter of 1708-9 Advance of Charles in the Spring. [Pultowa.]—14. Flight and BATTLE OF PULTOWA. Escape of Charles. [Bender. Campbell's description of the catastrophe at Pultowa.]—15. Important effects of the battle of Pultowa.—16. Warlike views still entertained by Charles. He enlists THE TURKS in his favor. Treaty between the Russians and Turks. [Pruth.]—17. Lengthened stay of Charles in Turkey. RETURN OF CHARLES.—18. Situation of Sweden on his return. Warlike projects of Charles. EVENTS OF 1715. [Stockholm.] Siege of Stralsund. Irruption into Norway. Project of a union with Russia. DEATH OF CHARLES, 1718. [Frederickshall.]—19. Change in Swedish affairs. Peace with Russia. [Nystad.]—20. CHARACTER OF CHARLES THE TWELFTH. [Dr. Johnson's description of him]—21. DEATH AND CHARACTER OF PETER THE GREAT.

III. SPANISH WARS, AND WARS OF THE AUSTRIAN SUCCESSION.

1. Effects of the treaty of Utrecht. EUROPEAN ALLIANCE for guaranteeing the fulfilment of the treaty Spain finally compelled to accede to it.—2. WAR BETWEEN ENGLAND AND SPAIN

1739. Its causes.—3. CAUSES OF THE WAR OF THE AUSTRIAN SUCCESSION. [Pragmatic
sanction.]—4. Claims, and designs, upon the Austrian dominions. The position of England.—5.
Plan of THE COALITION AGAINST AUSTRIA. Invasion of Austria, 1741. The diet of Frank-
fort. [Frankfort.] Maria Theresa and the Hungarians. EVENTS OF 1742 AND 1743. [Munich.
Dottingen]—6. Successes and rev~ses of Frederic of Prussia, 1744. The Austrian general.—7.
Death of Charles Albert, 1745. Successes of Marshal Saxe. [Fontenoy.] Treaty between
Prussia and Austria. Francis I.—8. Events in Italy in 1745. [Piedmont.] Events of the IN-
VASION OF ENGLAND, 1745-6. [Edinburgh. Preston-pans. Culloden.] Cruelties of the Eng
lish.—9. EVENTS IN AMERICA, 1745-6. [Cape Breton.]—10. EVENTS OF 1747-7. TREATY OF
AIX-LA-CHAPELLE, Oct. 1748. In what respect the result was favorable to all parties.

IV THE SEVEN YEARS' WAR :—1756—63.

1. THE EIGHT YEARS OF PEACE that followed the treaty of Aix-la-Chapelle. CAUSES THAT
THREATENED ANOTHER WAR.—2. East-India colonial difficulties between France and England
—3. North American difficulties. BEGINNING OF HOSTILITIES IN 1754. Braddock's defeat,
1755.—4. The connected interests of all the European States. The relations between Prussia
and Austria. EUROPEAN ALLIANCES growing out of them.—5. The threatened danger to
Prussia.—6. FIRST CAMPAIGN OF FREDERIC, 1756.—7. Declarations of war by France and
England, 1756. The first campaign.—8. The opposing forces, 1757. Victory of Frederic at
Prague, and defeat at Kolin. [Kolin.] General invasion of Prussia. Defeat of the English in
Germany.—9. Dangerous situation of Frederic. [Berlin.] Recall of the Russian army.
Frederic advances into Saxony.—10. Great victory of Frederic at Rossbach. [Rossbach.]—11.
Results of the battle. Frederic's treatment of the wounded and prisoners.—12. The English
and Hanoverians resume their arms. Affairs in Silesia. Victory of Frederic at Lissa. [Lissa.]
Anecdote of Frederic.—13. Results of the campaign of 1757.—14. Successes of the duke of
Brunswick, 1758. Frederic in Silesia—escapes from the Austrians at Olmutz, and marches
against the Russians. [Olmutz.]—15. Battle of Zorndorf. [Zorndorf.] Anecdotes. Action
of Hochkirchen. [Hochkirchen.] Results of the campaign.—16. Losses of the French in India
and America.—17. Opening of the campaign of 1759. Defeat of Frederic at Kunersdorf.
[Kunersdorf.] His loss in Bohemia. Result, to the Austrians.—18. The campaign of the duke
of Brunswick. The results on the ocean and in the colonies.—19. Losses of Frederic in the
campaign of 1760. He defeats the enemy at Liegnitz and Torgau. [Liegnitz. Torgau.]—20.
The campaign in Germany.—21. Alliance between France and Spain. Losses of Spain and
France. [Cuba. Manilla. Belleisle. Guadaloupe.]—22. The campaign of 1761. Coldness
of England, and change in the Russian councils.—23. General PEACE OF 1763. The results, to
England—to France—to Prussia. [Honduras.] The MILITARY CHARACTER OF FREDERIC.

V. STATE OF EUROPE. THE AMERICAN REVOLUTION.

1. GENERAL PEACE IN EUROPE. Results of the "Seven Years' War." Efforts of Frederic
for the good of his people.—2. FRANCE during the closing years of the reign of Louis XV.
Accession of Louis XVI.—3. Condition of RUSSIA. Her war with Turkey and Poland. [Mol-
davia and Wallachia.] DISMEMBERMENT OF POLAND, 1773.—4. STATE OF PARTIES IN EN -1 AND.
Taxation. Resignation of the earl of Bute.—5. The Grenville ministry. The case of Mr
Wilkes.—6 The subject of AMERICAN TAXATION. The Stamp Act.—7. Misfortunes of England
in her attempts to coerce the Americans.—8. OPENING OF THE WAR WITH THE COLONIES.—9.
EUROPEAN RELATIONS OF ENGLAND. Aid extended to the Americans.—10. Capture of Burgoyne, 1777, and ALLIANCE BETWEEN FRANCE AND THE AMERICAN STATES.—11. Beginning of the WAR BETWEEN FRANCE AND ENGLAND.—12. War in the West Indies. [Do-
minica. St. Lucia.]—13. Hostilities in the East Indies, and overthrow of the French power
there.—14. WAR BETWEEN SPAIN AND ENGLAND. Events of 1779. [St. Vincents. Grenada.]
—15. Successes of Admiral Rodney, 1780. English merchant fleet captured by the Spaniards.
—16. The English claim of the right of search. ARMED NEUTRALITY AGAINST ENGLAND.
Principles of the Neutrality. General concurrence in them.—17. RUPTURE BETWEEN ENGLAND
AND HOLLAND.—18. Capture of St. Eustatia by the English. [St. Eustatia.]—19. The Spaniards
conquer West Florida. The French and English in the West Indies. [Tobago.] Naval battle
off the coast of Holland. [Dogger Bank.]—20. Results of the war between England and

her American colonies. Continuance of the war in Europe. Siege of Gibraltar, 1781, and destruction of the Spanish works.—21. Minorca taken by Spain, 1782. Losses of the English in the West Indies. [Bahamas.] Naval victory of the English. [Carribee islands.]—22. Continued siege of Gibraltar. Preparations for an assault.—23. The assault.—24. Generous conduct of the British seamen. Results of the assault.—25. The WAR IN THE EAST INDIES. Account of Hyder Ali. [Mysore. Seringapatam.]—26. Successes of Hyder Ali and his son Tippoo Saib, in 1780. Events of 1781-2.—27. Tippoo concludes a treaty with the English, 1783. Renewal of the war, 1790. Defeat and death of Tippoo, 1799.—28. TREATY OF 1782. GENERAL TREATY OF 1783, between England, France, and Spain. Its terms.—29. Remarks upon the war of the Revolution.

VI. THE FRENCH REVOLUTION.

1. The DEMOCRATIC SPIRIT of the American Revolution :—its influence upon French society. 2. State of France at the time of the death of Louis XV.—3. LOUIS XVI. His character.—4. FINANCIAL DIFFICULTIES. Efforts of Turgot and Neckar, and the opposition which they encountered.—5. The system of Calonne, and its results.—6. Brienne calls THE STATES-GENERAL —7. Removal of Brienne, and restoration of Neckar. The policy of the court.—8. The general agitation throughout France. The evils to be complained of. The clergy and the nobility. The philosophic party. The calling of the States-general—a revolutionary measure. Demands of the Commons. Results of the elections.—9. New difficulty at the opening of the States-general. Its final settlement.—10. Effect of the triumph of the *third estate.* REVOLUTIONARY STATE OF PARIS. Attack upon the Bastile, 1789.—11. Louis throws himself, for support, upon the popular party.—12. The effect. Revolutionary movements throughout France. GREAT POLITICAL CHANGES.—13. Two months of quiet. FAMINE, AND MOBS, in Paris. The mob at Versailles, and return of the Assembly and royal family to Paris.—14. Formation of a NEW CONSTITUTION. MARSHALLING OF PARTIES. The Jacobin club.—15. Its character. Its leaders. Mirabeau. His character, and death.—16. THE EMIGRANT NOBILITY. [Coblentz.] ATTEMPTED ESCAPE OF THE ROYAL FAMILY, 1791. The king swears to support the new constitution. Dissolution of the "Constituent Assembly."—17. The "Legislative Assembly." Chief parties in it. Growing influence of the Jacobins.—18. First acts of the legislative assembly. Object of the Girondists. Demands of the Austrian emperor. WAR DECLARED AGAINST AUSTRIA, 1792. Real causes of the war.—19. Collection of forces, and invasion of France. The effects produced in France.—20. MASSACRE OF THE 10TH OF AUGUST. Acts of the Assembly. Flight of La Fayette. Dumouriez.—21. MASSACRES OF SEPTEMBER.—22. Victories of the French. [Jemappes. Marseilles Hymn.]—23. Decree of the National Convention TRIAL AND EXECUTION OF LOUIS XVI.

[1793.] 24. FALL OF THE GIRONDISTS.—25. Rule of the Jacobins.—26. THE REIGN OF TERROR. Execution of the queen. TRIUMPH OF INFIDELITY.—27. Divisions among the Jacobin leaders. FALL OF THE DANTONISTS.—28. WAR AGAINST EUROPE.—29. Defection of Dumouriez.—30. Fate of Custine.—31. War on the Spanish frontier. In other quarters.—32. INSURRECTION OF LA VENDEE. Victory of the Vendeans at Saumur, and defeat at Nantes. [Saumur.] Repeated defeats of the Republicans. [Torfou.]—33. Cruelties of the Republicans. The Vendeans cross into Brittany. [Cholet. Chateau Gonthier.]—34. Closing scenes of the Vendean war. [Granville. Mans. Savenay. The Vendean leaders.]—35. INSURRECTIONS IN THE SOUTH OF FRANCE. Marseilles and Lyons.—36. Siege of Toulon. Napoleon Bonaparte. —37. Results of the campaign of 1793.

[1794.] 38. Progress of the Revolution after the fall of Danton.—39. FALL OF ROBESPIERRE, AND END OF THE REIGN OF TERROR.—40. Military condition of France.—41. THE ENGLISH VICTORIOUS AT SEA, AND THE FRENCH ON THE LAND. [Biscay.]—42. SECOND PARTITION OF POLAND.—43. THIRD PARTITION OF POLAND.

[1795.] 44. DISSOLUTION OF THE FIRST COALITION AGAINST FRANCE. Austria, England, and Russia.—45. Internal condition of France. THE NEW CONSTITUTION.—46. INSURRECTION IN PARIS, suppressed by Napoleon.—47. Military events of 1795.

[1796.] 48. INVASION OF GERMANY by Jordan and Moreau.—49. THE ARMY OF ITALY. Victories of Napoleon. [Montenotte. Millessimo. Lodi. Arcole. Mantua.]—50. DISTURBANCES IN ENGLAND. Spain. English supremacy at sea. French invasion of Ireland.

[1797.] 51. NAPOLEON'S AUSTRIAN CAMPAIGN. TREATY OF CAMPO FORMIO. [Campo For-

I WAR OF THE SPANISH SUCCESSION, AND CLOSE OF THE REIGN OF
LOUIS XIV.—1. The war which ended in the treaty of Ryswick had
not humbled the pride of Louis XIV., whose ambition soon involved
Europe in another war, known in history as the "War of the Spanish
succession." The immediate events that led to the war were the
following. On the death of Charles the Second of Spain, in the
year 1700, the two claimants of the Spanish throne were the arch-
duke Charles of Austria, and Philip of Anjou, nephew of the French
monarch. Both these princes endeavored, by their emissaries, to
obtain from Charles, then on a sick bed, a declaration in favor of their
respective pretensions; but although the Spanish monarch was strongly in favor of the claims of the arch-duke his kinsman,
the gold and the promises of Louis prevailed with the
Spanish nobles to induce their sovereign to assign by
will, to the duke of Anjou, the undivided sovereignty of
the Spanish dominions. The arch-duke resolved to support his claims by the sword, while the possible and not
improbable union of the crowns of France and Spain in
the person of Philip, after the death of Louis, was looked upon by
England, Germany, and Holland, as an event highly dangerous to the
safety of those nations; and on the 15th of May, 1702, these three
powers declared war against France, in support of the claims of the
arch-duke to the Spanish succession.

I. ENGLAND,
GERMANY,
AND HOL-
LAND DE-
CLARE WAR
AGAINST
FRANCE,
1702.

2. It was, doubtless, of very little importance to England, whether
an Austrian or a French prince became monarch of Spain; but
when, on the death of the exiled James II., his son was acknowledged king of England by the French court, the act was regarded
as an insult and a defiance to Great Britain; the national animosity
was aroused, and king William engaged strenuously in the work of
forming a league against the ambition of France. England, Holland,
and Austria, were the leading powers of the coalition, while France
was aided by Bavaria alone. Already William was preparing to

take the field in person at the head of the allies, when a fall from his horse occasioned a fever, which terminated his life in May 1702. Queen Anne, who next ascended the throne of Great Britain, declared her resolution to adhere to the policy of her predecessor.

3. The emperor of Austria began the war by pouring into Italy a large army under the command of Prince Eugene, a Frenchman by birth, who had early entered the Austrian service, where he had gained distinction in the wars of the Turks. At the same time the English duke of Marlborough, intrusted with the chief command of tne Dutch and English forces, entered on the campaign in Flanders. To these generals was at first opposed marshal Villars; but the complaints of the elector of Bavaria against him induced that able general to resign his command. Marsin, Tallard, and Villeroy, succeeded him; but the French generals, brought up under the despotic authority of Louis, who required in his officers the quality of submission as well as the talent for command, were unable to cope with Marlborough and Eugene, who had been bred in a school that encouraged the development of talent, by allowing a greater independence of character.

4. The campaign of 1702 passed without any remarkable results.

II. THE CAMPAIGN OF 1702. Marlborough took a few towns in Flanders, and Eugene in northern Italy, but on the Rhine the French gained some successes: at sea a combined Dutch and English fleet failed in an attack on Cadiz,[1] but succeeded in capturing and destroying, in Vigo Bay, a French and Spanish fleet that had taken shelter there, laden with the treasures of Spanish America.

III. EVENTS OF 1703. In the spring of 1703 the French succeeded in breaking through the lines of the allies on the Rhine, thus transferring the seat of the war to the Danube, and making a threatening demonstration against Vienna itself.

5. In the spring of 1704 Marlborough, abandoning Flanders,

IV. EVENTS OF 1704. marched to the relief of the Austrian emperor, and having joined prince Eugene, on the 13th of August, near the small village of Blenheim,[2] he won a decisive victory over the French and Bavarians. Each army numbered about eighty

---

1 Cadiz is an important city and seaport of Andalusia, in southern Spain, sixty miles north-west from Gibraltar. It is a very ancient city, having been founded by the Carthaginians. (Map No. XIII.)

2. Vigo Bay is on the western coast of Spain, a little north of Portugal.

3. Blenheim is a small village of western Bavaria, on the Danube, thirty-three miles northeast from Ulm. (Map No. XVII)

thousand men, and the vanquished lost thirty thousand in killed, wounded, and taken, while all their camp equipage, baggage, and artillery, became the prize of the conquerors. The loss of the latter was about five thousand killed and eight thousand wounded. The results of this battle obliged the French to evacuate Germany altogether, abandon Bavaria, and retire behind the Rhine. In the meantime the war continued in northern Italy; Portugal joined the coalition; the arch-duke Charles of Austria, aided by an English force, landed in the Spanish peninsula; and an English and Dutch fleet, commanded by Sir George Rooke, stormed the important fortress of Gibraltar,[1] of which England has ever since retained the possession.

6. The year 1705 passed away with varied success, the French obtaining many advantages in Italy, while the allies were generally victorious in Spain and on the ocean. In 1706 a French force again penetrated into Germany; but the main army, of about eighty thousand men, commanded by marshal Villeroy, advancing into the Spanish Netherlands, was met by an inferior force under the duke of Marlborough, and utterly routed in the decisive battle of Ramillies.[2] (May 23d, 1706.) The consequences of the battle were the loss, to France, of all the Spanish Netherlands, except the fortified towns of Mons[3] and Namur. In

v. events of 1705-6.

---

1. *Gibraltar*, the Calpe of the Greeks, formed, with Abyla on the African coast, the "Pillars of Hercules." The fortress stands on the west side of a mountainous promontory or rock, projecting south into the sea about three miles, and being from one-half to three-quarters of a mile in breadth. The southern extremity of the rock is called Europa Point. The north side of the promontory, fronting the long narrow isthmus which connects it with the main land, is perpendicular, and wholly inaccessible. The east and south sides are steep and rugged, and extremely difficult of access, so as to render any attack upon them, even if they were not fortified, next to impossible, so that it is only on the west side, fronting the bay, where the rock declines to the sea, and the town is built, that it can be attacked with the faintest prospect of success. Here the fortifications are of extraordinary extent and strength. The principal batteries are so constructed as to prevent any mischief from the explosion of shells. Vast galleries have been excavated in the solid rock, and mounted with heavy cannon; and communications have been established between the different batteries by passages cut in the rock to protect the troops from the enemy's fire.

At Gibraltar, the Arabians first landed in Spain, in the year 711. It was taken from them in 1302: in 1333 they retook it, but were finally deprived of it in 1462 by Henry IV. of Spain. August 4th 1704 the British captured it, since which time it has been repeatedly besieged and assaulted, but without success. In 1720 Spain offered two millions sterling for the place, but in vain. The last attempt made for its recovery was by France and Spain combined, in 1779, during the war with England which grew out of the American Revolution. Eighty thousand barrels of gunpowder were provided for the occasion, and more than one hundred thousand men were employed, by land and sea, against the fortress. (*Map* No. XIII.)

2. *Ramillies* is a small village of Belgium, twenty-eight miles south-east from Brussels. (*Map* No. XV.)

3. *Mons* is a fortified town of Belgium, thirty-two miles south-west from Brussels. (*Map* No. XV.)

other quarters the campaign was equally disastrous to Louis. Barcelona[1] surrendered to the English; even Madrid[2] submitted to the allies; and prince Eugene, breaking through the French lines at Turin, drove the enemy from Italy.

7. Louis now made overtures of peace; but the allies, hoping to reduce him lower, would not listen to them. The campaign of 1707 in a measure revived his sinking fortunes. On the plain of Almanza he French won a victory over the allies, as complete as any that had been obtained during the war. (April 1707.) This victory established Philip of Anjou on the throne of Spain. In the same year prince Eugene was foiled in an attempt on the port of Toulon.[4] In the following year, however, (1708,) Marlborough and Eugene defeated a powerful French army near the village of Oudenarde,[5] in Flanders, and recovered Ghent and Bruges,[6] which, a short time before, had been surprised by the French. Again the frontier of France lay completely open.

VI. CAMPAIGN OF 1707.

VII. EVENTS OF 1708.

8. The year 1709 commenced with one of the most rigorous winters ever known. Olives and vines, and many fruit trees perished; the sown grain was destroyed, and everything portended a general famine. The French populace began to

VIII. 1709.

1. *Barcelona*, the capital of Catalonia, is a city and seaport of Spain, on the Mediterranean, three hundred and fifteen miles north-east from Madrid. It is supposed to have been founded by the Carthaginians about two hundred years before the Christian era, and to have been named from its founder Hamilcar *Barcino*. (*Map* No. XIII.)

2. *Madrid*, the modern capital of Spain, is in the centre of the kingdom, and occupies the site of the ancient *Mantua Carpetanorum*, a fortified town belonging to the Carpetani. It was afterwards called *Majoritum*, and was taken and sacked by the Moors, who gave it its present name. (*Map* No. XIII.)

3. *Almanza* is a town of Spain in the northern part of the province of Murcia, ninety-three miles north-west from Carthagena. In the battle fought in the neighborhood of this town April 25th, 1707, the French were commanded by the duke of Berwick. The allies, in the interest of the arch-duke Charles, lost five thousand men killed on the field, and nearly ten thousand taken prisoners. (*Map* No. XIII.)

4. *Toulon*, the first naval port in France, is on the Mediterranean coast, thirty-two miles south-east from Marseilles. The town is strongly fortified, and has an excellent harbor. It is wholly indebted for its importance as a great naval port, and strong military position, to Louis XIV., who expended vast sums on its fortifications, and on the arsenal and harbor. (*Map* No. XIII.)

5. *Oudenarde* is a town of Belgium thirty-three miles west from Brussels. In the battle of July 11th, 1708, the dukes of Brunswick and Vendome commanded the French army. (*Map* No. XV.)

6. *Bruges* is a town of Belgium, seven miles from the sea, and sixty miles north-west from Brussels. At a very early period Bruges was a prosperous seat of manufacturing and commercial industry. Throughout the fourteenth and fifteenth centuries it was the central emporium of the whole commercial world, and, as the leading city of the Hanseatic confederacy, had resident consuls and ministers from every kingdom in Europe. (*Map* No. XV.)

clamor from present sufferings, and the dismal prospect before them, but when the French parliament proposed to appoint deputies to visit the provinces, buy corn, and watch over the public peace, the haughty monarch reprimanded them, and told them they had as little to do with corn as with taxation. The magistrates were silent, and desisted from farther interference with the claims of the royal prerogative.

9 With the finances in disorder, commerce ruined, and agricul ture at a stand, Louis sought peace with Holland; but the States slighting his envoys and his offers, repaid him all his past insults and pride, and he was compelled to resume the war, or submit to conces sions degrading to himself and the nation. Again the chief command of the French armies was given to marshal Villars, who fought with the allies the battle of Malplaquet[1] (Sept. 11th, 1709); but although the latter lost the greatest number of men, the French lost the honor of the day by being driven from the position which they had chosen. The situation of Louis became desperate, when again the successes of his arms in Spain restored him to security and confi dence; but domestic misfortune fell upon him, and humbled his pride more than all his military reverses had done. Most of the near relatives of the king were cut off by sudden death,—since at tributed to the small pox, but then ascribed to the agency of poison.

10. While these clouds were lowering upon France and her mon arch, an unexpected event changed the situations and views of all parties. Early in 1711, the death of the emperor of Austria without issue, and the succession of the arch-duke Charles, the claimant of the Spanish crown, to the sovereignty of Austria, threatened a union of the crowns of Spain and Austria in the person of one individual,— an event looked upon with as much dread as the union of France and Spain in the person of Philip of Anjou. From this period the war languished; and when, by a change in English politics, Marlborough, who had supported, so nobly, the glory of England, was disgraced, and deprived of his command, the influence and support which Eng land had given to the war were taken away.

11. Conferences opened at Utrecht in the early part of 1712, and on the 11th of April, 1713, the terms of a general peace were assented

1. *Malplaquet* (mal-plah'-ka) is a small town of France, near the border of Belgium, forty. three miles south-west from Brussels. In the battle fought here Sept. 11th, 1700—the bloodiest in the "War of the Spanish succession"—the allies were commanded by Marlborough and Eugene. The French army numbered seventy thousand; the allies eighty thousand. The allies lost twenty thousand in killed, and the French about ten thousand. (*Map* No. XV.)

to by all the belligerents except Austria. England was gratified
by the demolition of the port of Dunkirk, in the cession

IX. TREATY
OF
UTRECHT,
1713.

of Gibraltar and Minorca,[1] together with Newfoundland,[2]
Hudson's Bay Territory,[3] and the island of St. Christopher.[4] Spain remained to Philip V. of Anjou, on his
renouncing forever all right of succession to the crown of France.
The treaty of Radstadt,[5] concluded in 1714 between France and
Austria, completed that of Utrecht, and terminated the war, the
Austrian emperor receiving Naples, Milan, and Sardinia, together
with Spanish Flanders, in lieu of Spain,—the Spanish monarchy
thus losing its possessions in Italy and the Netherlands. Louis retained the fortress of Lisle[6] and French Flanders, while the Rhine was
acknowledged the frontier on the side of Alsace.[7]

12. The treaties of Utrecht and Radstadt were the closing political acts of the reign of Louis XIV., who breathed his last

X.. CHARAC-
TER OF THE
REIGN OF
LOUIS XIV.

in September 1715, after a reign of seventy-seven years,
or fifty-four from the expiration of the regency. Louis
was the most despotic monarch that ever reigned over a
civilized people. In the condition of France at the time of his accession, despotism was perhaps the only remedy against anarchy,
and it marks an overmastering spirit that the will of the monarch
alone was able to bend all minds to his purposes. The nobility
stood submissive before the throne,—the people, in silence and suffering, far beneath it. But the reign of Louis has shown that des
potism is not compatible with modern civilization, for everything
was frozen under its chilling touch ; and although letters flourished

1. *Minorca.* See Balearic Isles, p. 152.

2. *Newfoundland,* a large island of North America, off the Gulf of St. Lawrence, is celebrated
for its fisheries. Since the peace of Utrecht, in 1713, it has remained in the possession of
England.

3. *Hudson's Bay Territory* embraced a large but indefinite extent of country, mostly on the
west side of Hudson's Bay. The Hudson's Bay Company has long monopolized nearly all the
fur trade of British North America.

4. *St. Christopher's* is an island of the West Indies, nearly two hundred miles south-east from
Porto Rico. It was discovered and named by Columbus, but was first settled by the English
in 1623.

5. *Radstadt* is a small Austrian town one hundred and forty-five miles south-west from
Vienna. (*Map No.* XVII.)

6. *Lisle* is a strongly-fortified city of France, near the Belgian frontier, one hundred and
twenty-four miles north-east from Paris. Lisle is supposed to have been founded in 640. It
successively belonged to the counts of Flanders, the kings of France, and the dukes of Bur
gundy. (*Map No.* XIII.)

7 *Alsace* was an eastern province of France, on the Rhine. In ancient times it was a Ger
man duchy, and the inhabitants still speak German. Strasburg is the chief city. (*Map No.*
XIII.)

among the favored few, there was no prosperity, no learning, no life among the people; and had the progress of science, and the development of intellect, been checked by the strong arm of authority, France would have needed nothing more to reduce her to a state of oriental simplicity and degradation.

II. PETER THE GREAT OF RUSSIA, AND CHARLES XII. OF SWEDEN.— 1. While the "war of the Spanish succession" engaged the attention of the south and west of Europe, casting a shadow of gloom on the declining years of Louis XIV., the northern and eastern divisions of Christendom were occupied *I. THE NORTH AND EAST OF EUROPE.* with the rivalry of two of the most extraordinary men that the world has ever known—Peter the Great of Russia, and Charles XII. of Sweden. In the preceding chapter we noticed the auspicious events which marked the beginning of the reign of the Russian monarch, just at the close of the seventeenth century, and which promised to his kingdom a rapid augmentation of power, and the opening of a new era in civilization. The results remain to be developed in the present chapter.

2. It was a leading object of the Czar,[a] to make Russia a great commercial nation; and for the success of his plans a free and uninterrupted communication with the ocean, by way of the Baltic Sea, was deemed of the greatest importance; but Sweden possessed the entire eastern coast of the Baltic, together with the gulfs of Finland and Livonia,[1] thus hemming in the Czar in the only quarter where his ardent wishes might, otherwise, be accomplished. During his travels he had been rudely refused admission into the citadel of Riga,[2] which had once belonged to Russia; and this circumstance afforded him a sufficient pretext for engaging in a war with Sweden for the recovery of that valuable seaport. The kings of Denmark and Poland, both of whom had suffered from the Swedish arms, were easily induced to form an alliance with the Czar for dividing between themselves the possessions wrested from their predecessors.

3. Sweden was at this time (1700) governed by Charles XII., a prince only eighteen years of age who was reported by the ministers

1. *Finland* and *Livonia* are the two eastern gulfs of the Baltic. St. Petersburg, at the eastern extremity of the former, and Riga, near the head of the latter, are now the two most important cities and ports in the Russian dominions.

2. *Riga* is a strongly-fortified c' v of Russia, situated on the river Dwina, nine miles from its entrance into the Gulf of Livonia. Population, seventy thousand.

a. The title given by the Russians to their king, and pronounced *Tzar.*

of foreign courts to be of a haughty and indolent disposition, and who had thus far shown no inclination for public business, nor evinced any ardor for military pursuits. But Charles was neither known to others nor did he know himself until the storm that suddenly arose in the north gave him an opportunity of displaying his concealed talents. While the Swedish council, alarmed by the dangers which threatened the country, were debating in his presence the terms of an accommodation with their enemies, the young prince suddenly arose, and with a grave and determined air declared that his resolution was fixed,—" that he would never enter upon an unjust war, but that he would attack any power that evinced hostile intentions, and that, in the present instance, he hoped to conquer the first enemy and to strike terror into the rest." From that moment Charles renounced his former indolent habits and frivolous amusements, and, placing before himself the characters of Alexander and Cæsar, resolved to imitate those heroes in everything but their vices. The vain and trifling boy suddenly became the stern, vigilant, and ambitious soldier of fortune.

4. Almost simultaneously, early in the year 1700, the Czar and his allies began hostilities by invading the Swedish terri-tories. The Danes fell upon Sleswick,[1] a city of Hol-stein, friendly to Sweden; the king of Poland invested Riga; while the Czar, with eighty thousand men, laid siege to Narva.[2] Attacked by so many foes at once, Charles placed himself at the head of his armies, and directed his first efforts against the Danes, whom he compelled to purchase the safety of Copenhagen,[3] their capital, by the payment of four hundred thousand dollars, and soon after to sign a peace, by which Charles was indemnified for all the expenses of the war. Thus the youthful Swede, by his vigorous conduct, humbled a powerful adversary in a campaign of six weeks,

II. BEGIN-NING OF HOSTILITIES AGAINST SWEDEN.

1. *Sleswick*, now included in the duchy of the same name, is a city and seaport town of Den mark, seventy miles north-west from Hamburg. Holstein is the southern duchy or province of Denmark, extending to the Elbe, and having the duchy of Sleswick on the north. At the period above-mentioned the city of Sleswick was included in the territories of the duke of Holstein, who, having married a sister of Charles XII., and being oppressed by the king of Denmark his master, had fled to Stockholm to implore assistance. (*Map* No. XVII.)

2. *Narva* is a small town of Russia on the river Narova, eight miles from its entrance into the Gulf of Livonia, and eighty-one miles south-west from St. Petersburg.

3. *Copenhagen*, the capital of Denmark, is a well-fortified city, built principally on the eastern coast of the island of Zealand, and partly also on the contiguous small island of Amak, the channel between them forming the port. It was founded in 1168. Its environs are celebrated for their beauty. (*Map* No. XIV.)

and rendered his own name, at the age of eighteen, the terror of the North, and the admiration of Europe.

5. In the meantime the king of Poland, who had laid siege to Riga, being thwarted by the activity of its veteran commander, the same who had refused the Czar permission to enter the citadel availed himself of a plausible pretext for withdrawing his forces Charles was now left at liberty to turn his attention to the most powerful of the confederates, the Russian monarch, who, at the head of eighty thousand men and one hundred and fifty pieces of cannon, had been engaged ten weeks in besieging the town of Narva, which was defended by a garrison of scarcely one thousand soldiers.

6. In the month of November Charles landed on the coast with only twenty thousand men, and proceeded rapidly towards the town, at the head of less than one-half of his actual force, driving before him more than thirty thousand Russians who had been sent out to impede his march. III. DEFEAT OF THE RUSSIANS AT NARVA. Scarcely allowing his weary troops a moment's repose, and without waiting for the remainder of his little army, Charles resolved to attack the enemy in their intrenchments: in three hours the camp was forced on all sides: eighteen thousand Russians were killed, besides a great number drowned in attempting to cross the river; and on the next day thirty thousand who had surrendered were dismissed to their homes. (Nov. 30th. Dec. 1st, 1700.) This extraordinary victory did not cost the Swedes over six hundred men. When the Czar, who was absent from Narva at the time, heard of this disaster, he was not disheartened, but attributing the result to the right cause, the ignorance and barbarism of his subjects, he said:—" I know very well that the Swedes will have the advantage of us for a considerable time; but they will at length teach us to become conquerors." The ignorant Russians, unable to account for a victory gained by human means, over such disparity of numbers, imagined the Swedes to be magicians and sorcerers; and a form of prayer, composed by a Russian bishop, was read in their churches, imploring St. Nicholas, the patron of Muscovy, to be their champion in future, and to drive the troop of Northern wizards away from their frontiers.

7. But Peter, disregarding both St. Nicholas and the priests, pursued steadily the course which he had marked out, and, withdrawing to his own dominions, occupied his time in equipping a fleet, in recruiting and disciplining a new army, in carrying out his project of uniting the Baltic, Caspian, and Euxine seas, and in introducing nu-

T

marous.improvements for civilizing his barbarous subjects. Charles,
on the contrary, neglectful of the welfare of his own country, and of
the proceedings of the Czar, had resolved never to return home until
he had driven from the throne of Poland the newly-elected sovereign,
and ally of Peter, Augustus of Saxony.

8. Having wintered at Narva, Charles next drove the Poles and
Saxons from Riga, defeated his enemies on the western bank of the

IV VICTORIES
OF CHARLES
IN THE YEAR
1702.

Dwina, overran Courland[1] and Lithuania, entered Warsaw[2] without opposition, and at length, in July 1702,
defeated Augustus in a bloody battle fought on a vast
plain between Warsaw and Cracow.[3] A second victory
gained by Charles at Pultusk[4] in the following year (May 1st, 1703)
completed the humiliation of Augustus, who was formally deposed
by the Polish diet, while the crown was soon after given to Stanislaus
Leczinski, who had been nominated by the king of Sweden. (January
1704.) Charles, at the head of a victorious army, might easily have
assumed the sovereignty of Poland, to which he was advised by his
ministers, but he declared that he felt more pleasure in bestowing
thrones upon others than in winning them for himself.

9. Charles soon reduced the Saxon States, the hereditary dominions of the unfortunate Augustus; his ships were masters of the
Baltic; Denmark, restrained by the late treaty, was prevented from
offering any active interference with his plans; the German emperor,
engaged in the War of the Spanish succession, was afraid of offend-
ing him; and a detachment of thirty thousand Swedes kept the
Russians in check towards the east: so that the whole region from

1. *Courland* is a province of Russia, on the Baltic coast, north of the ancient Lithuania.
(See Lithuania, p. 312.)

2. *Warsaw*, the capital of Poland, is on the west bank of the Vistula, six hundred and fifty
miles southwest from St. Petersburg, and three hundred and thirty-three miles east from Berlin
the Prussian capital. Population, about one hundred and forty thousand. In 1795, in the third
partition of Poland, Warsaw was assigned to Prussia: in 1806 it was made the capital of the
grand-duchy of Poland; and in 1815 it became the capital of the new kingdom of Poland, if it
was united to the crown of Russia, but with a separate constitution and administration.
Warsaw was the principal seat of the ill-fated Polish revolution of 1831. See p. 527. (Map
No. XVII.)

3. *Cracow* is on the north bank of the Vistula, one hundred and sixty miles south-west from
Warsaw, and two hundred north-east from Vienna. Previously to the seventeenth century
Cracow was the metropolis of the kingdom of Poland. Most of the Polish kings, and many
other illustrious men, have been buried in the cathedral of Cracow. Among others it contains
the tombs of Casimir the Great, of John Sobieski the deliverer of Poland, and of the "last of
the Poles," Kosciusko and Poniatowski. About a mile west of the city is an artificial mound
of earth, one hundred and fifty feet in height, erected to the memory of Kosciusko. (Map No.
XVII.)

4. *Pultusk* is forty miles north of Warsaw on the western bank of a small tributary of the
Vistula. (Map No XVII.)

the German Ocean almost to the mouth of the Borysthenes,[1] and even to the gates of Moscow, was held in awe by the sword of the conqueror.   All Europe was filled with astonishment at the arbitrary manner in which he had deposed the king of Poland; while in the meantime Charles himself was indulging in the most extravagant views of future conquests and glory.   One year he thought sufficient for the conquest of Russia : the pope of Rome was next to feel his vengeance, for having dared to oppose the concession of religious liberty to the German Protestants, in whose behalf Charles had interested himself; and the youthful hero had even despatched officers privately into Egypt and Asia, to take plans of the towns, and ex amine into the resources, of those countries.

10. The Czar, in the meantime, had not been an idle spectator of the progress of the Swedish conqueror.   By keeping large bodies of his troops actively engaged on the Swedish frontiers, he gradually accustomed them to the presence of the enemy, over whom he gained several little advantages; and having driven the Swedes from both banks of the Neva,[2] in the year 1701 he laid the foundations of St. Petersburg, in the heart of his new conquests, and by his judicious measures protected the rising city from the attacks of the Swedish generals.   During the year 1704 he gained possession of all Ingria ;[3] the next year he entered Poland at the head of sixty thousand men; but the advance of Charles from Saxony soon obliged him to retire again towards the Russian territories.

11. In the autumn of 1707, Charles began his march eastward with the avowed object of the conquest of Russia, driving the Russians back to the eastern banks of the Dnieper, then the dividing line between Russia and Poland.   The Czar, seeing his own dominions threatened with war, V. MARCH OF CHARLES INTO RUSSIA. which must put a stop to the vast plans which he had formed for the improvement of his people, now offered terms of peace, but Charles intoxicated with success, only replied, " I will treat at Moscow." Peter, resolving not to act the part of another Darius, wisely determined to check the career of the invaders by breaking up the roads

---

1. *Borysthenes*, see Dnieper, p. 309.

2. The *Neva* is the stream by which Lake Ladoga discharges its surplus waters into the Gulf of Finland.   St. Petersburg is built at its entrance into the Gulf.

3. *Ingria* was a province extending about one hundred and thirty miles along the southern bank of the Neva and the southern shore of the Gulf of Finland.   In 1617 the Swedes took it from the Russians; but in 1700 the latter reconquered a part of it, and in 1703 built St Petersburg within its limits

and desolating the country; and Charles, after crossing the Dnieper and penetrating almost to Smolensko,[1] found it impracticable to continue his march in the direction of the Russian capital. (1708.) His army, exposed to the risk of famine, and the incessant attacks of the enemy, was slowly wasting away; yet, instead of falling back upon Poland, he adopted the extraordinary resolution of passing into the Ukraine, whither he had been invited by Mazeppa, a Pole by birth, and chief of the Cossacks, but who had resolved to throw off his allegiance to the Czar, his master.

12. A march of twelve days, amid almost incredible and unparalleled hardships, brought the Swedes to the river Desna,[2] where Charles expected to meet his new ally with a body of thirty thousand men; but, instead of this, he was compelled to force the passage of the stream against a Russian army. The Czar, having been informed of the treason of Mazeppa, had disconcerted his schemes by the punishment of his associates; and the unfortunate chief appeared in the Swedish army rather as a fugitive than as a powerful prince bringing succors to his ally. Charles soon after learned of a still greater misfortune that had befallen him, the loss of a large convoy and reënforcement expected from Poland.

13. In the midst of one of the severest winters ever known in Europe, (1708–9) the small Swedish army, now reduced to less than twenty thousand men, found itself in the midst of a hostile and almost desolate country, cut off from all resources, and threatened with an attack from nearly a hundred thousand Russians, who were gradually concentrating upon their victims. Yet the iron heart of the Swede did not a moment relent at the sufferings of his soldiers, although in one day he beheld two thousand of them drop dead before him, from the effects of cold and hunger; nor had he relinquished the design of penetrating to Moscow. On the opening of spring he advanced to the town and fortress of Pultowa,[3] in the hope of seizing the magazines of the Czar, and opening a passage into the heart of the Russian territory.

14. Toward the end of May Charles invested Pultowa, but while

<hr />

1. *Smolensko* is a Russian town on the eastern bank of the Dnieper, two hundred and thirty miles south-west from Moscow. (*Map* No. XVII.)

2. The *Desna* is an eastern tributary of the Dnieper, which enters that river a little above Kiev. (*Map* No. XVII.)

3. *Pultowa* is a fortified town of Russia, on the river Worskla, an eastern tributary of the Dnieper, two hundred miles south-east from Kiev, and four hundred and fifty south-west from Moscow. In commemoration of the victory of Pultowa the Russians have erected a column in the city, and an obelisk on the field of battle.

he was pressing the siege with great vigor, on the 15th of June the Czar appeared before the place with an army seventy thousand strong, and, in spite of the exertions of the Swedes, succeeded in throwing a strong reënforcement into the place. When Charles discovered the manœuvre by which this had been effected, he could not forbear saying, " I see well that we have taught the Muscovites the art of war " On the eighth of July a general action was brought on between the two armies, the Czar commanding his troops in person, while Charles, unable to walk, owing to a severe wound he had some days before received in the heel, was carried about the field in a litter, with a pistol in one hand and his drawn sword in the other. The desperate charge of the Swedes broke the Russian cavalry, but the Russian infantry acted with great steadiness, and restored the honor of the day. The Czar received a musket ball through his hat; his favorite general, Menzi koff, had three horses killed under him; and the litter in which Charles was carried was shattered in pieces by a cannon ball. But neither the courage nor the discipline of the Swedes could avail against the overwhelming numbers of their antagonists; and after a dreadful battle of two hours' duration the Swedish army was irretrievably ruined. Charles escaped with about three hundred horsemen to the Turkish town of Bender,[1] abandoning all his treasures to his rival, including the rich spoils of Poland and Saxony.[a]

15. Thus in one day the king of Sweden lost the fruits of nearly a hundred victories, and nine years of successful warfare. Nearly

VI. BATTLE OF PULTOWA.

---

1. *Bender* is now a Russian town, on the Dniester, in the province of Bessarabia, about fifty-eight miles from the Black Sea. In 1770 the Russians took this town by storm, and reduced it to ashes. Four years later it was restored to Turkey, but was reconquered by the Russians in 1809, and was finally ceded to them, with the province of Bessarabia, by the treaty of Bucharest, in 1812. (*Map* No. XVII.)

a. The catastrophe of Pultowa is thus powerfully described by Campbell:

> " Oh! learn the fate that bleeding thousands bore,
> Led by their Charles to Dnieper's sandy shore.
> Faint from his wounds, and shivering in the blast,
> The Swedish soldier sank and groaned his last.
> File after file the stormy showers benumb,
> Freeze every standard sheet, and hush the drum;
> Horseman and horse confessed the bitter pang,
> And arms and warrior fell with hollow clang:
> Yet, ere he sank in Nature's last repose,
> Ere life's warm current to the fountain froze,
> The dying man to Sweden turned his eye,
> Thought of his home, and closed it with a sigh.
> Imperial pride looked sullen on his plight,
> And Charles beheld nor shuddered at the sight.

all Europe felt the effects of the battle of Pultowa: the Saxons
called for revenge on a prince who had pillaged and plundered their
country : Augustus returned to Poland at the head of a Saxon army,
while Stanislaus, knowing it was vain to resist, was unwilling to shed
blood in a useless struggle : Denmark, Russia, and Poland, entered
into a league against Sweden, and but for the interference of the German emperor and the maritime powers, the Swedish monarchy would
have been rent in pieces.

16. Although Charles was now an exile from his country, relying
for his support, upon the generosity of the Turkish sultan, yet he still en.
tertained the romantic project of dethroning the Czar, and marching
back to Sweden at the head of a victorious army. He endeavored to raise
the Turks against his enemies; and his prospects grew

VII. THE
TURKS. bright or dark according as the wavering policy of the
Turkish divan was swayed by his intrigues, or by the
gold of Russia. At one time the vizier promised to conduct him to
Moscow at the head of two hundred thousand men : war was declared
against Russia; and the forces of the two nations were assembled on
the banks of the Pruth.[1] (July 1711.) Here the Russian army,
surrounded by a greatly superior Turkish force, lost, in four days'
fighting, more than sixteen thousand men, when by the resolute sa.
gacity of the empress Catherine, who accompanied her husband
during the campaign, a secret treaty was concluded with the Turkish
commander; and Peter was rescued from the same fate that had befallen his antagonist at Pultowa.

17. The Swedish monarch continued to linger in Turkey until
1714, still flattering himself that he should yet lead an Ottoman
army into Russia. Being at length dismissed by the sultan, and
ordered to depart, he still resolved to remain ; and arming his secre.
taries, valets, cooks, and grooms, in addition to his three hundred
guards, he bade defiance to a Turkish army of twenty-six thousand
men. After a fierce resistance, in which many of his attendants
were slain, he was captured, the Turks being careful not to endanger
his life. Another revolution in the Turkish divan revived the hopes
of Charles, and prolonged his stay ; but when he learned that the
Swedish senate intended to create a regent in his absence, and

---

1. The *Pruth*, rising in Gallicia, forms the boundary between Bessarabia and Moldavia, and
enters the Danube about fifty miles from the Black Sea. By the treaty of Adrianople in 1829,
it was stipulated that the Pruth should continue to form the boundary between the Russian
and Turkish territories. (*Map No.* XVII.)

make peace with Denmark and Russia, his indignation at such proceedings induced him to return home. He was honorably escorted to the Turkish frontiers; but although orders had been given that he should be treated in the Austrian and German dominions with all due honor, he chose to travel in the disguise of a courier, and toward the close of November 1714 reached Stralsund, the capital of Swedish Pomerania.

VIII. RETURN OF CHARLES.

18. At the time of the return of Charles, Sweden was in a truly deplorable condition,—surrounded by enemies—without money, trade, or credit—her foreign provinces lost, and one hundred and fifty thousand of her best soldiers slaves in Turkey and Siberia, or locked up in the fortresses of Denmark and Poland. Yet Charles, instead of seeking that peace which his kingdom so much needed, immediately issued orders for renewing the war with redoubled vigor. During the year 1715, the Danish and Russian fleets swept the Baltic, and threatened Stockholm;[1] and Stralsund, though defended by Charles with his accustomed bravery, was compelled to surrender after a siege of two months. On the night before the surrender Charles made his escape in a small boat, safely passing the batteries and fleets of the allies. In the following year he made an irruption into Norway, but his army was driven back greatly diminished in numbers. His attention was next occupied with the scheme of his favorite minister, Baron Gertz, for uniting the kings of Sweden and Russia in strict amity, and then dictating the law to Europe. The plot embraced the restoration of Stanislaus to the throne of Poland, and Charles was to have the command of a combined Swedish and Russian army of invasion, for establishing the Pretender (son of James II.) on the throne of England. The Czar seemed not averse to the project, and a conference of the ministers of the two nations had already been appointed for making the final arrangements, when the death of the king of Sweden rendered abortive a revolution that might have thrown all Europe into a state of political combustion. In the autumn of 1718 Charles had invaded Norway a second time, and laid siege to Frederickshall;[2] but while engaged in viewing the works

IX. EVENTS OF 1715.

X. DEATH OF CHARLES.

1 *Stockholm*, the capital city, and principal commercial emporium of Sweden, is built partly on a number of islands and partly on the main land, at the junction of the Lake Mælar with the Baltic, four hundred and forty miles a little south of west from St. Petersburg. It was founded in the thirteenth century, but was not recognized as the capital till the seventeenth, previously to which Upsala had been the seat of the court. (*Map No. XIV.*)

2. *Frederickshall* is a maritime town of Norway, near the north-east angle of the Skaggerrack, fifty-seven miles south-east from Christiana. The town spreads irregularly around a pen

in the midst of a tremendous fire from the enemy, he was struck dead by a ball from the Danish batteries. (Dec. 1718.)

19. The death of Charles produced an entire change in the affairs of Sweden. The late king's sister was declared queen by the volun tary choice of the States of the kingdom; but the last reign had taught them a severe lesson, and they compelled their new sovereign to take a solemn oath that she would never attempt the establish ment of arbitrary power. The project of a union with Russia was at once abandoned, and the new government united its forces to those of England against the Czar. For a while the Russian fleet desolat ed the coasts of Sweden, but in 1721 peace was established between the two powers by the treaty of Nystad.[1] Russia gained thereby a large accession of territory on the shores of the Baltic, and dominion over the Gulf of Finland, which Peter had purchased as a highway of commerce to the ocean, with the toils and perils of twenty years of warfare.

20. Charles the Twelfth, at the time of his death, was little more

XL. HIS CHARACTER.

than thirty-six years of age, one-half of which had been spent amid the turmoil of arms, or wasted in foreign exile. War was his ruling passion; but the only ob ject of his conquests seemed to be the satisfaction of bestowing their fruits upon others, without any apparent wish to enlarge his own do minions. After all his achievements, nought but the memory of his renown survives him; for all the acts of his reign sprung from a misdirected ambition, and not one of them was conducive to the per manent welfare of his country. "He was rather an extraordinary than a great man," says Voltaire, "and more worthy to be admired than imitated. His life ought to be a lesson to kings, how much a pacific and happy government is preferable to so much glory."[a]

---

pendicular rock four hundred feet in height, on which is the strong fortress of Frederickstein, at the siege of which Charles XII. was killed.

It was doubted for awhile whether the king met his death by a ball from the fortress, or from an assassin in the rear; but there seem to be no good grounds for supposing that treachery had anything to do with the matter. Dr. Johnson has availed himself of the suspicion in his ad mirable description of the character of the Swedish warrior. The hat, clothes, buff-belt, boots, &c., which Charles wore when he was shot, are still preserved in the arsenal of Stockholm.

1. *Nystad* is a town of Finland, on the eastern coast of the Baltic, one hundred and fifty as north-east from Stockholm.

a. The following is Dr. Johnson's description of the character of Charles XII.

"On what foundation stands the warrior's pride,
How just his hopes, let Swedish Charles decide.
A frame of adamant, a soul of fire,
No dangers fright him, and no labors tire;

21. The Czar Peter, or, as he is usually called in history, Peter the Great, died in 1725, seven years after the death of his great rival the king of Sweden. Through a life of restless activity he labored for the improvement and prosperity of his country; and while Charles left behind him nothing but ruins, Peter the Great may truly be regarded as the founder of an empire. The ruler of a barbarous people, he early saw the advantages of civilization, and by the measures he adopted for reforming his empire he truly merited the epithet of GREAT. Yet it has been truly said of him that although he civilized his subjects, he himself remained a barbarian; for the sternness, or rather the ferocity, of his disposition, spared neither age nor sex, nor his dearest connexions. So conscious was he of his frailties that he was accustomed to say, " I can reform my people, but I cannot reform myself." He never learned the lessons of humanity; and his sublime but uncultivated genius continually wandered without a guide. It is a high and just eulogium of his character to say that " his virtues were his own, and his defects those of education and country."

XII. DEATH AND CHARACTER OF PETER THE GREAT.

O'er love, o'er fear, extends his wide domain,
Unconquered lord of pleasure and of pain;
No joys to him pacific sceptres yield,
War sounds the trump, he rushes to the field;
Behold surrounded kings their powers combine,
And one capitulate, and one resign;
Peace courts his hand, but spreads her charms in vain;
'Think nothing gained,' he cries ' till naught remain;
On Moscow's walls, till Gothic standards fly,
And all be mine beneath the polar sky.'
The march begins in military state,
And nations on his eye suspended wait;
Stern famine guards the solitary coast,
And winter barricades the realms of frost:
He comes; nor want, nor cold, his course delay;
Hide, blushing Glory, hide Pultowa's day.
The vanquished hero leaves his broken bands,
And shows his miseries in distant lands;
Condemned a needy supplicant to wait
While ladies interpose, and slaves debate.
But did not chance at length her error mend?
Did no subverted empire mark his end?
Did rival monarchs give the fatal wound?
Or hostile millions press him to the ground?
His fall was destined to a barren strand,
A petty fortress, and a dubious hand:
He left the name, at which the world grew pale,
To paint a moral, or adorn a tale."

III. Spanish Wars, and Wars of the Austrian Succession.—
1. The treaty of Utrecht in 1713, which closed the war of the Spanish

I. European Alliance. succession, had given pacification to southern and western Europe, by defining the territorial limits of the belligerents in such a manner as to preserve that balance of power on which the peace of Europe depended. The intriguing efforts of Spain in contravention of that portion of the treaty by which Philip V. renounced forever all right of succession to the crown of France, induced England and Holland, in 1717, to unite with France in forming a Triple Alliance guaranteeing the fulfilment of the treaty; but during the same year a Spanish fleet, entering the Mediterranean, quickly reduced the island of Sardinia, which had been assigned to Austria; and in the following year another fleet and army captured Sicily, which had been adjudged to the duke of Savoy. These acts of aggression roused the resentment of Austria; and by her accession to the terms of the Triple Alliance, the Quadruple Alliance was formed, for the purpose of putting a check to the ambition of Spain. A British squadron, under admiral Byng, sailed into the Mediterranean and destroyed the Spanish fleet, whilst an Austrian force passed into Sicily to contest with the Spanish army the sovereignty of that island. The successes of the allies soon compelled even Spain to accede to the terms of the Alliance for preserving the peace of Europe.

2. In 1739, however, the general peace was interrupted by a war

II. War between England and Spain. between England and Spain, growing out of the commercial and colonial difficulties of the two nations. For a long time Spain, claiming the right of sovereignty over the seas adjacent to her American possessions, which had been confirmed by successive treaties, had distressed and insulted the commerce of Great Britain by illegal seizures made under the pretext of the right of search for contraband goods; while Britain on the other hand, secretly encouraged a contraband traffic, little to her honor, and deeply injurious to Spain. War was first declared by England: the vessels of each nation in the ports of the other were confiscated; and powerful armaments were fitted out by the one to seize, and by the other to defend, the Spanish American possessions, while pirates from Biscay harassed the home trade of England.

3. While this war continued with various success, a general European war broke out, called the " war of the Austrian succession," presenting a scene of the greatest confusion, and, eclipsing, by its im

portance, the petty conflicts on the American seas. Charles VI., emperor of Austria, the famous competitor of Philip for the throne of Spain, died in the autumn of 1740; and as he had no male issue he left his dominions to his eldest daughter, Maria Theresa, queen of Hungary, in accordance with a solemn ordinance called the Pragmatic Sanction,' which had been confirmed by all the leading States of Europe. This sanction, however, did not secure his daughter, after his death, from the attacks of a host of enemies, who hoped to make good their pretensions, by force of arms, to different portions of her estates.

III. CAUSES OF THE WAR OF THE AUSTRIAN SUCCESSION.

4. The elector of Bavaria declared himself, by virtue of his descent from the eldest daughter of Ferdinand I., the proper heir of the hereditary Austrian provinces: the elector of Saxony, who was also Augustus III., king of Poland, made the same claims by virtue of a preceding marriage with the house of Saxony: Spain was anxious to appropriate to herself some of the Italian principalities, and virtually laid claim to the whole Austrian succession, while Frederick II., the young king of Prussia, marched suddenly into Silesia, and took possession of that country. France, swayed by hereditary hatred of Austria, sought a dismemberment of that empire; while England offered her aid to Maria Theresa, the daughter of her ancient ally, to preserve the integrity of the Austrian dominions.

5. The plan of the coalition against the Austrian queen embraced the elevation of Charles Albert, the electoral prince of Bavaria, to the sovereignty of all the German States; and accordingly, in the summer of 1741, two French armies crossed the Rhine, and being joined by the Bavarian forces, seized Prague, made several other important conquests, threatened Vienna, and compelled Maria Theresa to flee from her capital. In a diet held at Frankfort,² in Frebruary 1742, the imperial crown, through the influence of France and Prussia, was given to Charles Albert In the meantime Maria Theresa, crushed in

IV. COALITION AGAINST AUSTRIA.

1. *Pragmatic Sanction* There are four ordinances with this title mentioned in history: 1st, that of Charles VII. of France, in 1438, on which rest the liberties of the Gallican church; 2d, the decree of the German diet in 1439, sanctioning the former: 3d, the ordinance of the German emperor Charles VI. in 1740, by which he endeavored to secure the succession to his female descendants, and which led to the war of the Austrian succession: and 4th, the ordinance by which Charles III. of Spain, in 1759, ceded the throne of Naples to his third son and his posterity.

2. *Frankfort*, or *Frankfort-on-the-Mayn*, is a celebrated commercial city of Germany, on the north bank of the Mayn, eighteen miles north-east from its confluence with the Rhine at Mayence. There is also a *Frankfort-on-the-Oder*, ninety-five miles north-east from Dresden. (*Map* No. XVII.)

everything but energy of spirit 'by 'the vast array against her, pre
sented herself, with her infant son, in the diet of the Hungarian
nobles, and haying first sworn to protect their independence, de
manded their aid in tones that her beauty and her tears rendered
more persuasive.   The swords of the Hungarians flashed in the air
as their acclamations replied, " We will die for our sovereign Maria
Theresa !"   On the very day that Charles Albert was crowned at
Frankfort, Munich,' his own capital, fell into the hands of the Aus
trian general; and while Bavaria was plundered, the new emperor
was compelled to live in retirement far from his own dominions. In
another, quarter fortune was not equally favorable to
V. EVENTS
OF 1742–3.   Austria ; and Maria Theresa was compelled to purchase
peace of the Prussians by the surrender of Silesia.
(June 1741.) This loss was compensated, however, by a successful
blockade of Prague, then in the hands of the French, who were a:
length forced to a disastrous retreat, while England began to take a
more active part in the war against France.   The losses of France were
great on the ocean ; and in 1743 George II. of England, advancing into
Germany at the head of a powerful army, defeated the French at Dettingen,' and compelled them to retreat across the Rhine.   (June 1743.)

6. The year 1744 is distinguished by the renewal of hostilities on
the part of Frederick, who, having formed an alliance
VI. 1744.   with the king of France, entered Bohemia at the head
of seventy thousand soldiers, and in the beginning of September sat
down before Prague, which soon surrendered, and with it a garrison
of eighteen thousand men.   But misfortunes rapidly succeeded this
brilliant beginning of the campaign; the illness of Louis XV., king
of France, prevented the promised diversion on the side of the Rhine ;
and Frederick was eventually compelled to retreat to his own dominions, with the loss of twenty thousand men.   The king of Prussia
acknowledged, in his own memoirs, that no general committed greater
faults during the campaign than he did himself: and that the conduct
of his opponent, the Austrian general, marshal Traun, was a model
of perfection, which every military man would do well to study.

7. The death of Charles Albert, early in January 1745, removed
all reasonable grounds for continuing the war ; but the
VII. 1745.   national animosity between England and France prevent

l. *Munich* is a large German city, the capital of Bavaria, on the Isar, a southern branch of
the Danube, two hundred and twenty miles west from Vienna. It is called the " Athens of
south Germany." (*Map* No. XVII.)

2. *Dettingen* is a small village of Bavaria, on the Mayn, sixteen miles south east of Frankfort

ed the restoration of peace. During the same year, the celebrated French general, marshal Saxe, obtained the victory of Fontenoy[1] over the Austrians, and their Dutch and English allies commanded by the duke of Cumberland, and conquered the Austrian Netherlands and Dutch Flanders. The king of Prussia conducted a successful campaign in Silesia and Saxony, and in December concluded with Austria the treaty of Dresden, which confirmed him in the possession of Silesia. In the meantime the German States had elected for their emperor Francis I., the husband of Maria Theresa, and in the treaty of Dresden he was formally acknowledged by Frederick.

8. In Italy the combined armies of France, Spain, and Naples, obtained important advantages over the Austrians and Sardinians; and at the close of the campaign they held possession of all Lombardy and Piedmont.[2] During the same year, while the king of England was warring with the French in the Netherlands, his own dominions were invaded. The loss of the English at Fontenoy seemed to present to Charles Edward, grandson of James II., commonly called the Young Pretender, a fit opportunity for attempting the restoration of his family to the throne of England. Being furnished by the French monarch with a supply of money and arms, at the head of a small force he landed, in July, on the coast of Scotland, and being joined by many of the Highland clans, on the 16th of September he was enabled to take possession of Edinburgh,[3] and a few days later defeated the royal forces at Preston Pans.[4] In November he entered

VIII. INVA-
SION OF
ENGLAND,
1745-6.

1. *Fontenoy* is a village of Belgium, in the province of Hainault (à-nó), forty-three miles south-west from Brussels. The battle was fought April 30th, 1745. Voltaire's account of it, in his ".Age of Louis XV.," is extremely interesting. (*Map* No. XV.)

2. *Piedmont*, (*pied-de-monte*, "foot of the mountain,") the principal province of the Sardinia monarchy, has the Swiss canton of Valais and the Sardinian province of Savoy, on the north, and Savoy and France on the west. Capital, Turin. In 1802 Napoleon incorporated it with France, but it was restored in 1814.

3. *Edinburgh*, the metropolis of Scotland, county of Mid Lothian, is two miles south of the Frith of Forth, and three hundred and thirty-seven miles north-west from the city of London. It is principally built on three parallel ridges running east and west. At the western extremity of the central ridge, which is terminated by a precipitous rock four hundred and thirty-four feet above the level of the sea, is the castle; and a mile distant, at the eastern extremity of the ridge, is the palace of Holyrood, one hundred and eight feet above the same level. The palace has a peculiar interest from the circumstance that the apartments occupied by the unfortunate Queen Mary have been carefully preserved in the state in which she left them. Connected with the palace, on the north, are the ruins of the abbey of Holyrood. Edinburgh is highly celebrated for its literary and educational institutions. (*Map* No. XVI.)

4. *Preston Pans* is a small seaport town of Scotland, on the south shore of the Frith of Forth seven and a-half miles east of Edinburgh. It derives its name from its having, for a length oned period, had a number of salt works or *pans* for the production of salt by the evaporation of sea-water. (*Map* No. XVI.)

England. and advanced to within a hundred miles of London, but was then compelled to retreat into Scotland, where, after having defeated the royal forces a second time, his cause was utterly ruined by the decisive battle of Culloden.[1] (April 1746.) To the disgrace of the English, the surrounding country was given up to pillage and devastation. After a variety of adventures Charles reached France in safety; but numbers of his unfortunate adherents perished on the scaffold, or by military execution, while multitudes were transported to the American plantations.

9. During the year 1745 the important French fortress of Louisburg, on the island of Cape Breton,[2] was captured by

IX. EVENTS IN AMERICA.

the British and their colonial allies, an event which revived the spirits of the English, and roused France to a great vindictive effort for the recovery of Louisburg, and the devastation of the whole American coast from Nova Scotia to Georgia. Accordingly a powerful naval armament was sent out to America in 1746; but it was so enfeebled by storms and shipwrecks, and dispirited by the loss of its commander, that nothing was accomplished by it.

10. During the years 1746 and 1747 hostilities were carried on

x. 1746-7.

with various success by the French and the Spaniards on one side, and the English, Dutch, and Austrians, on the other. By sea the French lost almost their last ship; but no important naval battles were fought, as the English navy had scarcely a rival. On the continent, northern Italy and the Netherlands were the chief seats of the war. The French were driven from the former, and the Austrians and their allies from the latter.

XI. TREATY OF AIX-LA-CHAPELLE, 1748.

France made frequent overtures of peace, and in October 1748 the treaty of Aix-la-Chapelle was concluded between all the belligerents, on the basis of a restitution of all conquests made during the war, and a mutual release of prisoners without ransom. The treaty left unsettled the conflicting claims

1. *Culloden*, or *Culloden Moor*, is a heath in Scotland, four miles east of Inverness, and one hundred and fifteen miles north-west from Edinburgh. The battle of Culloden, fought April 27th, 1746, terminated the attempts of the Stuart family to recover the throne of England. (*Map* No. XVL.)

2. The island of *Cape Breton*, called by the French *Isle Royale*, is on the south-eastern border of the Gulf of St. Lawrence. *Louisburg*, once called the "Gibraltar of America," was a strongly-fortified town, having one of the best harbors in the world. After its capture by general Wolfe in 1758, (see p. 430,) its walls were demolished, and the materials of its buildings were carried away for the construction of Halifax, and other towns on the coast. Only a few fishermen's huts are now found within the environs of the city, and so complete is the ruin that it is with difficulty the outlines of the fortifications, and of the principal buildings, can be traced.

of the English and Spaniards to the trade of the American seas
but France recognized the Hanoverian succession to the English
throne, and henceforth abandoned the cause of the Pretender. Neither
France nor England obtained any recompense for the enormous ex
penditure of blood and treasure which the war occasioned; but in
one aspect the result was favorable to all parties, as, by preserving
the unity of the Austrian dominion, it maintained the due balance
of power in continental Europe.

IV. The Seven Years' War :—1756-63.[a]—1. The treaty of
Aix-la-Chapelle proved to be little better than a suspension of arms. A period of eight years of nominal
peace that followed did not produce, in the different
States of Europe, the desired feeling of united firmness and security
but all seemed unsettled, and in dread of new commotions. Two
causes, of a nature entirely distinct, united to involve all
Christendom in a general war. The first was the long
standing colonial rivalry between France and England;
and the second, the ambition of the Great Frederick of Prussia, and
the jealousy with which the court of Austria regarded the increase
of the Prussian monarchy.

I. EIGHT YEARS OF PEACE.

II. CAUSES OF ANOTHER WAR.

2. Immediately after the peace of Aix-la-Chapelle, difficulties
arose between France and England respecting their colonial possess
ions in India. Several years previous to the breaking out of the
European war, the forces of the English and French East India
companies, having taken part, as auxiliaries, in the wars between the
native princes of the country, had been engaged in a course of hos
tilities at a time when no war existed between the two nations.

3. More serious causes of quarrel arose in North America. The
French possessed Canada and Louisiana, one commanding the mouth
of the St. Lawrence, the other that of the Mississippi; while the in
tervening territory was occupied by the English colonists. The
limits of the American colonial possessions of the two nations had
been left undefined at the treaty of Aix-la-Chapelle, and hence dis
putes arose among the colonists, who did not always arrange their
controversies by peaceful discussion. The French made settlements
at the head of the Bay of Fundy in Nova Scotia, claiming the ter

a That part of the war waged in America between France and England is better known in
American history as the "French and Indian war." Although hostilities began, in the colonies,
in 1754, no formal declaration of war was made by either France or England until the breaking
out of the general European war in 1756.

ritory as a part of New Brunswick; while, by extending a frontier line of posts along the Ohio river, they aimed at confining the British colonies to the Atlantic coast, and cutting them off from the rest of the continent. In 1754 the English Colonial authorities began hostilities on the Ohio, without waiting for the formality of a declaration of war: in the following year the French forts at the head of the Bay of Fundy were reduced by colonel Monckton; but the English general, Braddock, who was sent against Fort Du Quesne, on the Ohio, was defeated with a heavy loss, and his army was saved from total destruction only by the courage and conduct of major Washington, who commanded the provincial troops.

III. BEGIN-
NING OF
HOSTILITIES
IN 1754.

4. These colonial difficulties were the prominent causes of enmity between France and England; but such were now the bonds of interest and alliance that united the different European States, that the quarrel betwixt any two led almost inevitably to a general war. A cause of war entirely distinct from the foregoing was found in the relations existing between Prussia and Austria. Maria Theresa was still dissatisfied with the loss of Silesia, and Frederick, too, clearsighted not to see that a third struggle with her was inevitable, abandoned the lukewarm aid of France, and formed an alliance with England, (Jan. 1756,) an event which altogether changed the existing relations between the different States of Europe. Prussia was thus separated from her old ally France, and England from Austria, while France and Austria, nations that had been enemies for three hundred years, found themselves placed in so close political proximity that an alliance between them became indispensable to the safety of each. Augustus III., king of Poland and also elector of Saxony, allied himself with Austria for the purpose of ruining Prussia; the empress Elizabeth of Russia, entertaining a personal hatred of Frederick, who had made her the object of his political satires, joined the coalition against him, while the latter could regard Sweden in no other light than that of an enemy in the event of a general war.

IV.
EUROPEAN
ALLIANCE.

5. Thus Austria, Russia, France, Sweden, and Poland, had all united against one of the smaller kingdoms, which was deprived of all foreign resources, with the exception of England; and the latter, in a continental war, could give her ally but little effective aid. Austria looked with confidence upon the recovery of Silesia; the partition of Prussia was already planned, and the day of the Prus

sian monarchy appeared to be already numbered; but in this most
unequal contest the superiority of Frederick as a general, and the
discipline of his troops, enabled Prussia to come out of the war with
increased power and glory.

6. Frederick without waiting for the storm that was about to
burst upon him, marched forth to meet it, to the surprise
of his enemies, who were scarcely aware that he was
arming.   In the month of August, 1756, he entered
Saxony at the head of seventy thousand men, blockaded
the Saxon army, and cut off its supplies, defeated an army of Austrians that advanced to the relief of their allies, and finally compelled the Saxon forces, now reduced to fourteen thousand men, to
surrender themselves prisoners, (Oct. 1756,) many of whom he forced
to enter the Prussian service.   Thus the result of the first campaign
of Frederick was the conquest of all Saxony.

V. FIRST CAMPAIGN OF FREDERICK, 1756.

7. It was not till the month of May and June 1756, that England
and France issued their declarations of war against each other, although hostilities had for some time previously been carried on between their colonies.   France commenced the war by an expedition
against the island of Minorca, then in possession of the English;
and that important fortress surrendered, although admiral Byng had
been sent out with a squadron for the relief of the place.   In
America the English had planned, early in the season, the reduction
of Crown Point, Niagara, and Fort Du Quesne, but not a single object of the campaign was either accomplished or attempted.

8. At the beginning of the campaign of 1757 it was estimated
that the armies of the enemies of Frederick, on foot, and
preparing to march against him, exceeded seven hundred
thousand men, while the force which he and his English allies could
bring into the field amounted to but little more than one third of
that number.   Frederick, having succeeded in deceiving the Austrians as to his real intentions, began the campaign by invading Bohemia, where, at the head of sixty-eight thousand men, he fought and
won the celebrated and sanguinary battle of Prague, (May 6,)
against an army of seventy-five thousand Austrians.   Dearly, however, was the victory purchased, as twelve thousand five hundred
Prussians lay dead or wounded on the field of battle.   Seeking to
follow up his advantage, in the following month Frederick experienced a severe check, being defeated by the greatly superior force

VI. 1757.

of marshal Daun at Kolin,[1] in consequence of which the Prussians were forced to raise the siege of Prague, and evacuate Bohemia. The Austrians and their allies, after this unexpected victory, resumed operations with increased activity : a Russian army of one hundred and twenty thousand men invaded Prussia on the east; seventeen thousand Swedes entered Pomerania; and two powerful French armies crossed the Rhine to attack the English and Hanoverian allies of Prussia commanded by the duke of Cumberland. The latter, being defeated, was compelled to sign a disgraceful convention by which his army of thirty-eight thousand men was reduced to a state of inactivity.

9. The loss of his English allies at this juncture was a most grievous blow to the king of Prussia. While he held the Austrians at bay in Lusatia, Saxony, whence the Prussians drew their supplies, was opened to the French; the Russians were advancing from the east, and already the Swedes were near the gates of Berlin,[2] when the sudden recall of the Russian army, owing to the serious illness of the Russian empress, illumined the troubled path of Frederick with a glimmering of hope, which promised to lead him on to better fortune. After having in vain tried to give battle to the Austrians, he suddenly broke up his camp. and by rapid marches advanced into Saxony, to drive the French out of that country.

10. Early in November, Frederick, at the head of only twenty thousand men, came up with the enemy, whose united forces amounted to seventy thousand. After some manœuvring he threw his little army into the low village of Rossback,[3] the heights around which, covered with batteries, served at once to defend his position, and conceal his movements. Here the French and their allies, anticipating a certain victory, determined to surround him, and thus, by making him prisoner, at once put an end to the war. To accomplish this object they advanced by forced marches, with sound of trumpet ; anxious to see if Frederick would have the courage to make a stand

1. *Kolin* is a small town of Bohemia, thirty-seven miles a little south of east from Prague. The battle of Kolin, fought June 18th, 1757, was the first which Frederick lost in the Seven Years' War. (*Map* No. XVII.)

2. *Berlin*, the capital of the Prussian States, and the ordinary residence of the monarch, is on the river Spree, a branch of the Elbe, in the province of Brandenburg, one hundred and sixty miles south-east from Hamburg. Berlin is one of the finest cities in Europe, and is called the Athens of the north of Germany. (*Map* No. XVII.)

3. *Rossback* is near the western bank of the river Saale, in Prussian Saxony, about twenty miles south-west from Leipsic, and consequently near the battle-fields of Leipsic, Jena, and Lutzen. The banks of the Saale are fully immortalized by carnage. (*Map* No. XVII.)

against them. The morning of the 5th of November Fredcriak spent in reconnoitering the enemy, and learned their plans for envel oping him ; but he kept his forces perfectly quiet until the afternoon without allowing a single gun to be fired, when, giving his orders, and suddenly concentrating the greater part of his troops to one point, he hurled them, column after column, in one irresistible tor rent upon the foe Never before had the French encountered such rapidity of action : they were completely overwhelmed and routed before they could even form into line ; and in less than half an hour the action was decided. "It was the most inconceivable and com plete route and discomfiture," says Voltaire, "of which history makes any mention. The defeats of Agincourt, Cressy, and Poitiers, were not so humiliating."

11. The French fled precipitately from the field of battle, and never stopped until they had reached the middle States of Germany while many only paused when they had placed the Rhine between themselves and the victors. Seven thousand prisoners, and three hundred and twenty officers of every rank, including eleven generals, fell into the hands of the king, while the loss of the Prussians amounted to only five hundred in killed and wounded. Frederick caused the wounded among the prisoners to be treated with the greatest humanity and attention. The officers of distinction, who were taken prisoners, he invited to sup with him. He told them he regretted he could not offer them a more splendid entertainment " but gentlemen," said he, " I did not expect you so soon, nor in so large numbers."

12. The victory of Rossback had recovered Saxony, and, what was equally important, it gave an opportunity to the English and Hanoverian troops to resume their arms, which they did on the ground of the alleged infraction of the convention by the French general. Still the affairs of Prussia were gloomy in the extreme, for during the absence of Frederick from Silesia, that province had been overrun by the Austrians, and the Prussians had been defeated in several battles. Frederick returned thither in December with thirty thousand men, and on the 5th of that month was met, on the vast plain of Lissa,[1] by the Austrian force of ninety thousand men

---

[1.] The *Lissa* here mentioned is a small town of Silesia, fourteen miles west of Breslau the capital of the province, and about one hundred and seventy-five miles south-east from Berlin. The battle was fought in the plain between Lissa and Breslau. There is another and larger town of Lissa in Posen, fifty-five miles north-west from Breslau. (*Map No.* XVII.)

exactly one month after the battle of Rossback.   Here Frederick
had recourse to those means by which he had often been enabled to
double his power by the celerity of his manœuvres.   Having succeeded in masking the movements of his troops, by taking possession of
some heights near the field of battle, and causing a false attack to
be made on the Austrian right, he fell suddenly upon their left and
routed it before the right could be brought to its support.   The consequent disorder was communicated to the whole Austrian army, and
in the course of three hours Frederick gained a most complete victory.   The Austrians lost seven thousand four hundred men in killed
and wounded, twenty-one thousand prisoners, and one hundred and
seventeen cannon, while the total Prussian loss was less than five
thousand men.   In this extraordinary battle superior genius triumphed over superior numbers.   When Frederick was told of the
many insulting things that the Austrians had said of him and his
little army, " I pardon them readily," said he, " the follies they may
have uttered, in consideration of those they have just committed."

13. The campaign of 1757 was the most eventful of all those
waged by Frederick; but although he had been forced to risk his
fate in eight battles, and more than a hundred partial actions, his
numerous enemies failed in their object.   The battles of Rossback
and Lissa inspired the English people with the greatest enthusiasm
for the Prussian army, and the result was a fresh subsidiary treaty
entered into with Frederick, by which England agreed to furnish him
an annual subsidy of six hundred and seventy thousand pounds, and
to send an army into Germany.   Mr. Pitt, recently appointed prime
minister, entered fully into the views of supporting Frederick, declaring that " the American colonies of the French were to be conquered through Germany."

14. The campaign of 1758 was opened by Ferdinand, duke of
　　　　　　　Brunswick, who, by the influence of the king of Prussia,
vii. 1758.　had been appointed commander of the English and
Hanoverian troops in Germany.   At the head of thirty thousand
men he drove a French army of eighty thousand beyond the Rhine,
and in a brief campaign of three months, from January to April,
took eleven thousand prisoners.   Frederick commenced the campaign
in March, by reducing the last remaining fortress in Silesia: then
he penetrated to Olmutz,[1] in Moravia, but failed in the siege of that

---

1. *Olmutz*, the former capital of Moravia, and one of the strongest fortresses of the Austrian
empire, is on the small river March or Morava, one hundred and five miles north-east from

place. Here the Austrians completely surrounded him in the very heart of their country, but he effected a retreat as honorable as a victory, and suddenly directed his march against the Russians who were committing the most shocking ravages in the province of Bran denburg, sparing neither age nor sex.

15. At the head of thirty thousand men, Frederick met the enemy, numbering fifty thousand, on the 24th of August, near the small village of Zorndorf,[1] where one of the most sanguinary battles of the Seven Years' War was fought, continuing from nine o'clock in the morning until ten at night. On the evening of this sanguinary day nineteen thousand Russians and eleven thousand Prussians lay dead and wounded on the field of battle; but the victory was claimed for the latter The Prussian king in person led the last attacks, and so much was he exposed to the fire of the Russians that all his aids, and the pages who attended him, were either killed, wounded, or taken prisoners. The able Austrian general, count Daun, who had often fought Fred- erick, and sometimes with success, had written to the general of the Russians, "not to risk a battle with a wily enemy, whose cunning and resources he was not yet acquainted with;" but as the courier who carried this dispatch fell into the hands of the Prussians, Fred- erick himself answered the letter in the following words :—"You had reason to advise the Russian general to be on his guard against a crafty and designing enemy, whom you were better acquainted with than he was ; for he has given battle, and has been beaten." At a later period in this campaign count Daun surprised and routed the right wing of Frederick's troops at Hochkirchen,[2] in Saxony, when nothing but the admirable perfection of the Prussian discipline saved the army from utter destruction. But this reverse could not damp the spirits of Frederick : he drove the Austrians a second time from Silesia ; and then compelled Daun to abandon the sieges of Dresden and Leipsic, and retreat into Bohemia. At the end of the campaign Frederick found himself in possession of the same countries as in the preceding year, while, in addition, northern and central Germany had been recovered from the French.

16. In the meantime the war had been carried on in other quarters

Vienna. It was taken by the Swedes in the thirty years' war, was besieged unsuccessfully by Frederick the Great in 1758, and Lafayette was confined there in 1794. (*Map* No. XVII.)

1. *Zorndorf* is a small village of Brandenburg, about twenty miles north-east from Frank fort on the Oder, and about the same distance south-east from Custrim. (*Map* No. XVII.)

2. *Hochkirchen* is a small village in the present kingdom of Saxony, (formerly in Lusatia,) thirty-seven miles east from Dresden. It is a short distance south-east from Bautzen which was the chief town of Upper Lusatia. (*Map* No. XVII.)

between the French and the English. In India the French were
generally successful, as they not only preserved their possessions, but
wrested several fortresses from their rivals, but they were deprived
of all their settlements on the coast of Africa, while in North
America they abandoned Fort du Quesne to the English, and were
obliged to surrender the important fortress of Louisburg, after a vigorous siege conducted by generals Amherst and Wolfe.

17. The campaign of 1759 commenced under favorable auspices
for the Prussians, as they succeeded early in the season
VIII. 1759. in destroying the Russian magazines in Poland, and
broke up the Austrian armies in Bohemia; but in August Frederick
himself suffered a greater loss, in the battle of Kunersdorf,[1] than
any he had yet experienced. At the head of only forty-eight thousand men he attacked the combined Russian and Austrian force of
ninety-six thousand, defended by strong intrenchments, but he was
defeated with the loss of more than eighteen thousand men in killed
and wounded. The Russian and Austrian loss was nearly sixteen
thousand; in allusion to which, the Russian general, writing to the
empress an account of the battle, said: "Your majesty must not be
surprised at the greatness of our loss. It is the custom of the king
of Prussia to sell his defeats very dear." At a later period of the
campaign Frederick rashly exposed fourteen thousand of his troops
in the defiles of Bohemia, where they were surrounded by the Austrians, and, after a valiant resistance, compelled to surrender, when
only three thousand of the number remained unwounded. Yet, after
all the reverses which the Prussians sustained, the only permanent
acquisition made by the Austrians was Dresden, for Frederick's vigor
and rapidity of movement rendered even their victories fruitless.

18. The campaign of Ferdinand of Brunswick against the French
during this year, was more successful than that of the king of Prussia.
On the 1st of August he attacked the French army of seventy thousand men near Minden,[2] and obtained a complete victory, which
lone prevented the French from gaining possession of the king of
England's Hanoverian dominions. On the ocean and in the colonies
the results of the year 1759 were highly favorable to the English.
The French fleets were destroyed; the English gained a decided

1. *Kunersdorf* is a small village of the province of Brandenburg, a short distance south of
Frankfort-on-the-Oder, and on the eastern bank of the river, fifty-five miles south-east from
Berlin. The battle fought near this town is sometimes called the battle of Frankfort.
2. *Minden* is a Prussian town in Westphalia, on the west bank of the Weser, near the Hanoverian frontier, thirty-five miles south-west from Hanover. (*Map No.* Y VII.)

preponderance in India; while the conquest of Canada was achieved by the gallant Wolfe, who fell in the moment of victory before the walls of Quebec.

19. After a winter spent in futile attempts at negotiation, the most vigorous preparations were made by all parties for the campaign of 1760. It opened with a continuation IX. 1760. of misfortunes to Prussia,—with the loss of nearly nine thousand men surrounded and taken prisoners by the Austrians,—with an unsuccessful attempt on Dresden by Frederick himself, and the surrender of an important fortress in Silesia. For the space of a year Frederick had met with almost continual reverses, but, still undaunted and undismayed, his transcendent talents never shone to greater advantage than when brought into action by the rigors of fortune. At the very moment when he was surrounded with overwhelming forces of Russians and Austrians, to the number of one hundred and seventy-five thousand men, and his ruin seemed inevitable, his genius saved him, and converted what appeared the certainty of defeat into a series of brilliant victories. While his enemies were preparing to attack him in his camp, he suddenly fell upon one of their divisions at Liegnitz[1] and almost annihilated it before the others were aware that he had changed his position. (Aug. 16th.) In November he attacked the intrenched camp of marshal Daun at Torgou,[2] having previously declared to his generals his determination to finish the war by a decided victory, or perish, with his whole army, in the attempt. The battle was perhaps the bloodiest fought during the whole war, but the impetuosity of the Prussians was irresistible, and the result recovered to Frederick all Saxony, except Dresden, and compelled the Austrians, Russians, and Swedes, to evacuate the Prussian dominions.

20. The campaign of Ferdinand of Brunswick against the French in northern and western Germany was marked by a great number of skirmishes which fatigued both parties, and in which towns and villages were taken and retaken; but when it is considered that the hostile armies numbered nearly two hundred thousand men, we are surprised to find that no memorable events occurred.

21. During the year 1760 France and Spain formed an intimate alliance, known by the name of the *Family Compact*, by which the enemy of either was to be considered the enemy of both, and neither was

1. *Liegnitz* is a town of Silesia, on the Katsbach, forty-six miles a little north of west from Breslau. (*Map* No. XVII.)

2. *Torgou* is a town of Prussian Saxony, on the west bank of the Elbe, sixty-six miles south-west from Berlin. (*Map* No. XVII.)

to make peace without consent of the other.   This was an unfortunate
act for Spain, whose colonies of Cuba[1] and Manilla,[2] with her ships
of war and commerce, soon fell into the hands of England.   The
English were also successful against the French ; and the latter, before the close of the war, were divested of all their possessions of
importance in the East Indies, while Belleisle,[3] on the very coast of
France, was captured, and in the West Indies, Martinico, Guadaloupe,[4] and other islands, were added to the list of British conquests.

22. The campaign of 1761 was carried on languidly by all parties.
The king of Prussia, exhausted even by his victories, was forced to
act on the defensive, while the English government, after
the accession of George III. to the throne, (Oct. 1760,)
had shown, under the counsels of Lord Bute, an ardent desire for
peace, even if it were to be obtained by the sacrifice of the Prussian
monarch.   An event which happened early in 1762 greatly improved
the aspect of Prussian affairs, and more than compensated Frederick
for the growing coldness of England towards him.   This was the
death of Frederick's implacable enemy, Elizabeth, empress of Russia,
and the accession of her nephew, the unfortunate Peter the Third,
who was a warm admirer and most sedulous imitator of the king of
Prussia.   The Russian armies withdrew from their former Austrian
allies, and ranged themselves under the Prussian standards : Sweden
concluded a peace with Prussia ; and even Austria consented to a
cessation of hostilities in Silesia and Saxony.

x. 1761.

23. In November 1763 the preliminary articles of peace were
signed at Paris between England, France, and Spain,
while Prussia and Austria, deserted by their allies, were
left to continue the war ; but they also soon agreed to
suspend hostilities, and in the month of February 1763 peace was
concluded between all the belligerents.   France ceded to England,
Canada and Cape Breton, while Spain purchased the restoration of
the conquests which had been made from her, by the cession of
Florida to England, by giving the latter permission to cut logwood

*XI. PEACE
OF 1763.*

---

1. *Cuba*, the largest of the West India islands, and the mistress of the Gulf of Mexico, still
belongs to Spain.
2. *Manilla*, a fortified seaport city of Luzon, one of the Philippine islands, is the capital of
the Spanish settlements in the East.
3. *Belleisle* is an island west of France, on the coast of Brittany, thirty miles south-west from
Vannes. (*Map* No. XIII.)
4. *Martinique* and *Guadaloupe* belong to the Windward group of the West Indies. Both
have frequently changed hands between the French and the English, but both were restored
to France in 1815. Martinique was the birth-place of the empress Josephine.

in the bay of Honduras,[1] and by a renunciation of all claim to the Newfoundland fisheries. But important as these results were to England, they were so much less advantageous than her position might have commanded, that it was said of her, " she made war like a lion, and peace like a lamb." Of France it was said by Voltaire. that " by her alliance with Austria she had lost in six years more men and money than all the wars she had ever sustained against that power had cost her." By the terms of the treaty between Prussia and Austria, prisoners were exchanged, and a restitution of all conquests was made; but Frederick still held the much-contested Silesia, a small territory, which had cost the contending parties more than a million of men. The glory of the war remained chiefly with Frederick, who, at the head of his veteran phalanx, moving among the masses of Austria, France, and Russia, and confronting all, still preserved, through an unexampled series of victories and reverses, the character of *Great*. No general ever surpassed him in regularity and rapidity of manœuvres, in well ordered marches, and in the facility of concentrating masses on the weak side of an enemy. " Bonaparte effected wonders with ample means; but when reduced to play the forlorn game of Frederick against united Europe, the great French captain fell,—the Prussian lived and died a king."

XII. MILITARY CHARACTER OF FREDERICK.

V. STATE OF EUROPE. THE AMERICAN REVOLUTION.—1. The peace of 1763 gave general tranquillity to Europe, which continued until the breaking out of the war between England and her American colonies, called the " War of the American Revolution." The result of the " Seven Years' War was that Prussia and Austria became the principal continental powers; France, by her subserviency to Austria, her ancient enemy, lost the political ascendency which she had previously sustained, and Britain although abandoning her influence in the European system, and maintaining intimate relations with Portugal and Holland only, had obtained complete maritime supremacy. Frederick of Prussia exerted himself successfully to repair the desolation made in his dominions by the ravages of war; he gave corn, for planting, to the destitute, procured laborers from other countries, remitted the taxes for a season, and during the four and twenty years of his

I. GENERAL PEACE IN EUROPE.

1. *Honduras* is a settlement adjoining the bay of the same name, on the eastern coast of Yucatan. In 1798 it was transferred to England, in accordance with a previous treaty.

reign after the peace, he appropriated for the encouragement of agriculture, commerce, and manufactures, no less than twenty-four millions of dollars; and this sum he had saved, by his simple and frugal life, from the amount set apart for the maintenance of his court.

2. In the meantime France, during the last years of the reign of the dissolute Louis XV., was declining in power, and sinking into disgrace. While the finances were in a state of utter confusion, and universal misery pervaded the land, there was the same splendor in the court, and the same profusion in expenditure, that marked the conclusion of the reign of Louis XIV. Both monarchs were doomed to see their children perish by an unaccountable decay; and on the death of Louis XV. in 1774, it was his youthful grandson, already married to an Austrian princess, who was elevated to the throne. As evidence of the heartlessness that often surrounds a court, it is related that no sooner had Louis XV. breathed his last, than the array of sedulous courtiers deserted the apartments of the deceased monarch, and rushed forth in a tumultuous crowd to do homage to the rising power of Louis XVI. The first act of this pious prince and of his queen was to fall on their knees and exclaim, " Our God! guide and protect us : we are too young to reign."

II. FRANCE.

3. While the power and greatness of France were declining, Russia was gradually acquiring a preponderating influence in Eastern Europe. In 1768 a war broke out between her and Turkey, which resulted in a series of defeats and losses to the latter. During this war Russia had taken possession of Moldavia and Wallachia,[1] which she was extremely desirous of retaining; but Austria opposed it, lest Russia should become too powerful; and as the latter was at the same time engaged in a contest with a confederacy of Polish patriots under the pretence of attempting to restore tranquillity to Poland, it was thought best that she should retain a portion of the Polish territory instead of the conquered Turkish provinces. But even this would destroy the balance between the three great eastern powers of Christendom; and, to restore the equilibrium, Prussia and Austria must have a share also; and thus was accomplished

III. RUSSIA.

IV. DISMEMBERMENT OF POLAND.

---

1. *Moldavia* and *Wallachia* are two contiguous provinces of Turkey, embracing the ancient Dacia. (*Map* No. IX.) They are in reality under the protection of Russia. Wallachia lies along the northern bank of the Danube, and Moldavia immediately west of the river Pruth (*Map* No. XVII.)

the iniquitous measure of a dismemberment of Poland, and the di
vision of a large portion of her territory between Russia, Prussia,
and Austria.　(1773.)

4. At the time of the conclusion of the peace of 1763 a strong fee'
ing of animosity existed between the two great parties in
England,—the whigs and the tories,—the latter of whom
had been taken into favor and rewarded with the chief
offices of government soon after the accession of George the Third.
A long and expensive war had increased the national debt, and rendered additional taxes necessary, while the bulk of the nation very
naturally thinking that conquests and riches ought to go hand in
hand, were induced to believe that administration arbitrary and oppressive which loaded them with new taxes immediately after the
great successes which had attended the British arms.　The indiscretion of the ministry, in levying the taxes upon certain important articles of domestic manufacture, threw the kingdom into an almost
universal ferment, and compelled the resignation of the earl of Bute,
who was at the head of the tory administration.

V. STATE OF PARTIES IN ENGLAND.

5. The earl of Bute was succeeded by Mr. Grenville, and as he also
was a tory, and was considered but the passive instrument of the late
minister, he inherited all the unpopularity of his predecessor.　One
of his first acts was the arrest and prosecution of Mr. Wilkes, a
member of parliament, who, in a paper called the North Briton, had
asserted that the king's speech at the opening of parliament, which
he affected to consider as the minister's, contained a falsehood.　On
a hearing before the judges of the common pleas, it was decided
that the commitment of Mr. Wilkes was illegal, and that his privi
leges, as member of parliament, had been infringed by the ministry
Mr. Wilkes was subsequently outlawed by the Commons, on his fail
ing to appear to answer the charges against him; but this extrem
severity only increased the agitation, and imbittered the feelings of
the opposing parties.　At a later period, on a legal trial, the out
awry of Mr. Wilkes was reversed, and he was repeatedly chosen
member of the Commons, although the house as often rejected him.

6. The augmentation of the revenue being at this time the chief
object of the administration, in 1764 Mr. Grenville introduced into parliament a project for taxing the American colonies; and early in 1675 the "Stamp Act" was
passed—an act ordering that all legal writings, together with pam
phlets, newspapers, &c., in the colonies, should be executed on

VI. AMERICAN TAXATION.

stamped paper, for which a duty should be paid to the crown. The colonies resisted every project for taxing them, on the ground that they were not represented in the British parliament, and that taxation and representation were inseparable; and a large party in England, consisting mostly of whigs, united with them in maintaining this doctrine. The stamp act was soon repealed, but the minis try still avowed the right of the mother country to tax her colonial possessions, and this doctrine, still persisted in, laid the foundation for that contest which at length terminated in the independence of the American colonies.

7. Misfortunes seemed to attend almost every scheme undertaken by England for coercing the Americans into obedience. A bill was passed for depriving the people of New England of the benefits of the Newfoundland fisheries; and it was thought that this act would throw into the hands of British merchants the profits which were formerly divided with the colonies; but the Americans refused to supply the British fishermen with provisions, and many of the ships were obliged to abandon, for a time, the business on which they came, and return in quest of supplies. Added to this, a most violent and unprecedented storm swept over the fishing banks; the sea arose thirty feet above its ordinary level, and upwards of seven hundred English fishing boats were lost, with all the people in them, and many ships foundered with their whole crews. When, at the commencement of the war, an immense quantity of provisions was prepared in England for the use of the British army in America, the transports remained for a long time wind-bound; then contrary winds detained them so long near the English coasts that nearly twenty thousand head of live stock perished; a storm afterwards drove many of the ships to the West Indies, and others were captured by American privateers, so that only a few reached the harbor of Boston, with their cargoes greatly damaged. The universal distress produced throughout the British nation by the refusal of the Americans to purchase British goods, completed the catalogue of evils which followed in the train of ministerial measures, and, by exciting the most violent altercations between opposing parties, seemed to threaten England herself with the horrors of civil war.

8. Passing by the arguments that were used for and against tax ation—the acts exhibiting the rash confidence and perseverance of the ministers and the crown—the determined opposition of the colonies—the changes in the English ministry, and the dissensions be

tween opposing parties in England—we come to the decisive open
ing of the war with the British American colonies by the
skirmish at Lexington, on the 19th of April, 1775. A
revolutionary war of seven years' duration followed,
on the American soil,—a war of the weak against the
strong—of the few in numbers against the many—but a war successful,
in its results, to the cause of freedom. Fortunately for the colonies
the war was not confined to them alone; and as the history of the
American portion of it is doubtless already familiar to most of our
readers, we proceed to consider the new relations, between England
and the other powers of Europe, arising out of the war of the American Revolution

VII. OPENING
OF THE WAR
WITH THE
COLONIES.

9 The continental powers, jealous of the maritime and commercial
prosperity of England, and ardently desiring her humiliation in the contest which she had unwisely provoked
with her colonies, rejoiced at every misfortune that befel
her. The French and Spanish courts, from the first,
gave the Americans the aid of their sympathy, and opened their
ports freely to American cruisers, who found there ready purchasers
for their prizes; and although, when England complained of the aid
thus given to her enemies, it was publicly disavowed, yet it was evident that both France and Spain secretly favored the cause of the
Americans.

VIII. EURO-
PEAN RELA
TIONS OF
ENGLAND.

10. The capture of the entire British army of general Burgoyne
at Saratoga, in October 1777, induced France to throw
aside the mask with which she had hitherto endeavored
to conceal her intentions; and in the month of March
1778, she gave a formal notification to the British government that she had concluded a treaty of alliance,
friendship, and commerce, with the American States. France and
England now made the most vigorous preparations for the anticipated
contest between them; the English marine force was increased, but
the French navy now equalled, if it did not exceed, that of England,
nor was France disposed to keep it idle in her ports.

IX. ALLIANCE
BETWEEN
FRANCE AND
THE AMERI-
CAN STATES.

11. Although war had not yet been declared between the two nations, in the month of April, 1778, a French fleet, commanded by Count D'Estaing, sailed from Toulon for
America; and soon after a much larger naval force was
assembled at Brest, with the avowed object of invading
England   In June, the English admiral Keppel fell in with and at

X. WAR
BETWEEN
FRANCE AND
ENGLAND.

tacked three French frigates on the western coast of France, two of which he captured. The French government then ordered reprisals against the ships of Great Britain, and the English went through the same formalities, so that both nations were now in a state of actual war.

12. During the autumn and winter of 1778 the West Indies were the principal theatre of the naval operations of France and England In September, the governor of the French island of Martinique attacked, and easily reduced, the English island of Dominica,[1] where he obtained a large quantity of military stores; but in the December following the French island of St. Lucia[2] was compelled to submit to the English admiral Barrington, after an ineffectual attempt to relieve it by the fleet of D'Estaing.

13. While these naval events were occurring on the American coasts, the French and English settlements in the East Indies had also become involved in hostilities. Soon after the acknowledgment of American independence by the court of France, the British East India company, convinced that a quarrel would now ensue between the two kingdoms, despatched orders to its officers at Madras to attack the neighboring post of Pondicherry, the capital of the French East India possessions. That place was accordingly besieged in August, by a force of ten thousand men, natives and Englishmen, and after a vigorous resistance was compelled to surrender in October following. Other losses in that quarter of the globe followed, and during one campaign the French power in India was nearly annihilated.

14. In the year 1779 another power was added to the enemies of England. Spain, under the pretext that her mediation,—(which she

XI. WAR BETWEEN SPAIN AND ENGLAND.

had proposed merely as the forerunner of a rupture)— had been slighted by England, declared war, and with the coöperation of a French fleet laid siege to Gibraltar, both by sea and land, in the hope of recovering that important fortress. Early in this year a French fleet attacked and captured the British forts and settlements on the rivers Senegal and Gambia, on the western coast of Africa; and later in the season the French conquered the English islands of St. Vincents[3] and

1. *Dominica* is one of the Windward Islands, in the West Indies, between Martinique and the Guadaloupe. It was restored to England at the peace of 1783.

2. *St. Lucia* is also one of the Windward group. At the peace of Paris it was definitively assigned to England.

3. *St. Vincent* is the central island of the Windward group. By the peace of 1783 it reverted to Great Britain.

Grenada[1] in the West Indies; but the count D'Estaing acting in concert with an American force, was repulsed in the siege of Savannah.

15. Early in January 1780, the British admiral Rodney being despatched with a powerful fleet to the relief of Gibraltar, fell in with and captured a Spanish squadron of seven ships of war and a number of transports; and a few days later he engaged a larger squadron off Cape St. Vincent, and captured six of the heaviest vessels and dispersed the remainder. These victories enabled him to afford complete relief to the garrisons of Gibraltar and Minorca, after which he proceeded to America, and thrice encountered the French fleet, but without obtaining any decisive success. In August the English suffered a very heavy loss in the capture of the outward bound East and West India fleets of merchant vessels, by the Spaniards, off the western coast of France.

16. The position which England had taken in claiming the right of searching neutral ships for contraband goods, together with her occasional seizure of vessels not laden with exceptionable cargoes, were the cause of a formidable opposition to her at this time, by most of the European powers, who united in forming what was called the "Armed Neutrality" for the protection of the commerce of neutral nations. In these proceedings, Catherine, Empress of Russia, took the lead, asserting, in her manifesto to the courts of London, Versailles, and Madrid, that she had adopted the following principles, which she would defend and maintain with all her naval power:—1st, that neutral ships should enjoy a free navigation from one port to another, even upon the coasts of belligerent powers, except to ports actually blockaded: 2d, that all effects conveyed by such ships, excepting only warlike stores, should be free: 3d, that whenever any vessel should have shown, by its papers, that it was not the carrier of any contraband article, it should not be liable to seizure or detention; and 4th—it was declared that such ports only should be deemed blockaded, before which there should be stationed a sufficient force to render the entrance perilous. Denmark, Sweden, Holland, Prussia, Portugal, and Germany, readily acceded to the terms of the "armed neutrality;" France and Spain expressed their approval of them, while nothing but fear of the consequences which must have resulted from the re

XII. ARMED NEUTRALITY AGAINST ENGLAND.

---

1. *Grenada* is one of the most southerly of the Windward group. About the year 1650 it was first colonised by the French, from whom it was taken by the British in 1762. In 1779 it was retaken by the French, but it was restored to Great Britain at the peace of 1783.

fusal, induced England to submit to this exposition of the laws of nations, and the rights of neutral powers.

17. Since the alliance between France and the United States, mutual recriminations had been almost constantly pass-
TILL RUPTURE BETWEEN ENGLAND AND HOLLAND.
ing between the English and the Dutch government, the former accusing the latter of supplying the enemies of England with naval and military stores, contrary to treaty stipulations, and the latter complaining that great numbers of Dutch vessels, not laden with contraband goods, had been seized and carried into the ports of England. A partial collision between a Dutch and an English fleet, early in the year 1780, had increased the hostile feelings of the two nations; and in December of the same year Great Britain declared, and immediately commenced, war against Holland, induced by the discovery that a commercial treaty was already in process of negotiation between that country and the United States. The Dutch shipping was detained in the ports of Great Britain, and instructions were despatched to the commanders of the British forces in the West Indies, to proceed to immediate hostilities against the Dutch-settlements in that quarter.

18. The most important of these was the island of St. Eustatia,[1] a free port, abounding with riches, owing to the vast conflux of trade from every other island in those seas. The inhabitants of the island were wholly unaware of the danger to which they were exposed, when, on the 3d of February, 1781, Admiral Rodney suddenly appeared, and sent a peremptory order to the governor to surrender the island and its dependencies within an hour. Utterly incapable of making any defence, the island was surrendered without any stipulations. The amount of property that thereby fell into the hands of the captors was estimated at four millions sterling. The settlements of the Dutch situated on the north-eastern coast of South America soon after shared the same fate as Eustatia.

19. In the month of May the Spanish governor of Louisiana completed the conquest of West Florida from the English, by the rapture of Pensacola. In the West Indies the fleets of France and England had several partial engagements during the month of April, May, and June, but without any decisive results. In the latter part

---

1. *St. Eustatia* is one of the group of the Leeward Islands, a range extending north-west of the Windward isles. This island was taken possession of by the Dutch early in the seventeenth century. It has, since then, several times changed hands between them, the French, and the English, but was finally given up to Holland in 1814.

of May a large body of French troops landed on the island of Tobago,[1] which surrendered to them on the 3d of June.   In the month
of August a severe engagement took place on the Dogger Bank,[2]
north of Holland, between a British fleet, commanded by Admiral
Parker, and a Dutch squadron, commanded by Admiral Zoutman.
Both fleets were rendered nearly unmanageable, and with difficulty
regained their respective coasts.

20. In the meantime the war had been carried on, during a period
of more than six years, between England and her rebellious American colonies; but the latter, guided by the counsels of the immortal
Washington, had nobly withstood all the efforts of the most powerful
nation in the world to reduce them to submission, and had finally
compelled the surrender, at Yorktown, of the finest army England
had ever sent to America.   After the defeat and surrender of Corn-
wallis, at Yorktown, in October, 1781, the war with the United States
was considered, virtually, at an end; but between England and her European enemies hostilities were carried on more vigorously than ever.
The siege of Gibraltar was ardently prosecuted by the Spaniards;
and the soldiers of the garrison, commanded by governor Elliot, were
greatly incommoded by the want of fuel and provisions.   They were
also exposed to an almost incessant cannonade from the Spanish batteries, situated on the peninsula which connects the fortress with the
main land.   During three weeks, in the month of May, 1781, nearly
one hundred thousand shot or shells were thrown into the town.   But
while the eyes of Europe were turned, in suspense, upon this important fortress, and all regarded a much longer defence impossible,
suddenly, on the night of the 27th of November, a chosen body of
two thousand men from the garrison sallied forth, and, in less than
an hour, stormed and utterly demolished the enemy's works.   The
damage done on this occasion was estimated at two millions sterling.

21. In the month of February following, the island of Minorca,
after a long siege, almost as memorable as that of Gibraltar, surrendered to the Spanish forces, after having been in the possession
of England since the year 1708.   During the same month the former
Dutch settlements on the north-eastern coast of South America were

---

1. *Tobago* is a short distance north-east of Trinidad, near the northern coast of South
America.   It was ceded to Great Britain by France in 1763, but in 1781 was retaken by the
French, who retained possession of it till 1793, since which it has belonged to England.

2. The *Dogger Bank* is a long narrow sand bank in the North Sea or German Ocean, extending from Jutland, on the west coast of Denmark, nearly to the mouth of the Humber, on the
eastern coast of England.

recaptured by the French. St. Eustatia had been recaptured in the preceding November. Other islands in the West Indies surrendered to the French, and the loss of the Bahamas[1] soon followed. For these losses, however, the British were fully compensated by an important naval victory gained by Admiral Rodney over the fleet of the Count de Grasse, on the 12th of April, in the vicinity of the Carribee islands.[2] In this obstinate engagement most of the ships of the French fleet were captured, that of Count de Grasse among the number, and the loss of the French, in killed, wounded, and prisoners, was estimated at eleven thousand men. The loss of the English, including both killed and wounded, amounted to about eleven hundred.

22. During the year 1782 the fortress of Gibraltar, which had so long bid defiance to the power of Spain, withstood one of the most memorable sieges ever known. The Spaniards had constructed a number of immense floating batteries in the bay of Gibraltar; and one thousand two hundred pieces of heavy ordnance had been brought to the spot, to be employed in the various modes of assault. Besides these floating batteries, there were eighty large boats, mounted with heavy guns and mortars, together with a vast multitude of frigates, sloops, and schooners, while the combined fleets of France and Spain, numbering fifty sail of the line, were to cover and support the attack. Eighty thousand barrels of gunpowder were provided for the occasion; and more than one hundred thousand men were employed, by land and sea, against the fortress.

23. Early in the morning of the 13th of September the floating batteries came forward, and at ten o'clock took their stations about a thousand yards distant from the rock of Gibraltar, and began a heavy cannonade, which was seconded by all the cannon and mortars in the Spanish lines and approaches. At the same time the garrison opened all their batteries, both with hot and cold shot, and during several hours a tremendous cannonade and bombardment was kept up on both sides, without the least intermission. About two o'clock the largest Spanish floating battery was discovered to emit smoke, and towards midnight it was plainly seen to be on fire. Other batteries began to kindle; signals of distress were made; and boats

1. The *Bahamas* are an extensive group of islands lying east and south-east from Florida. They have been estimated at about six hundred in number, most of them were cliffs and rocks, only fourteen of them being of any considerable size.

2. What are sometimes called the *Carribee Islands* comprise the whole of the Windward and the southern portion of the Leeward islands, from Anguilla on the north to Trinidad on the south.

were sent to take the men from the burning vessels, but they were interrupted by the English gun boats, which now advanced to the attack, and, raking the whole line of batteries with their fire, completed the confusion. The batteries were soon abandoned to the flames, or to the mercy of the English.

24. At the awful spectacle of several hundred of their fellow soldiers exposed to almost inevitable destruction, the Spaniards ceased firing, when the British seamen, with characteristic humanity, rushed forward, and exerted themselves to the utmost to save those who were perishing in the flames and the waters. About four hundred Spaniards were thus saved,—but all the floating batteries were consumed, and the combined French and Spanish forces were left incapable of making any farther effectual attack. Soon after, Gibraltar was relieved with supplies of provisions, military stores, and additional troops, by a squadron sent from England, when the farther siege of the place was abandoned.

25. The siege of Gibraltar was the last act of importance during the continuance of the war in Europe. In the East Indies the British settlements had been engaged, during several years, in hostilities with the native inhabitants, XIV. WAR IN THE EAST INDIES. who were conducted by the famous Hyder Ali, and his son Tippoo Saib, often assisted by the fleets and land forces of France and Holland. Hyder Ali, from the rank of a common sepoy, had raised himself, by his abilities, to the throne of Mysore,[1] one of the most important of the kingdoms of Hindostan. His territories, of which Scringapatam[2] was the capital, bordered on those of the English, which lined the eastern coast of the peninsula; and as he saw the possessions of the Europeans gradually encroaching upon the domains of the native princes, he resolved to unite the latter in a powerful confederacy for the expulsion of the intruders. After detaching one of the powerful northern princes from an alliance with the English, and

1. *Mysore*, a town of southern Hindostan, and capital of the State of the same name, is three hundred miles north of Cape Comorin, and nine miles south west from Seringapatam. The State of Mysore, comprising a territory of about thirty thousand square miles, is almost entirely surrounded by the territory of the Madras presidency; and although the government is nominally in the hands of a native prince, it is subsidiary to the government of Madras. From 1760 to 1799 Mysore was governed by Hyder Ali and Tippoo Saib.

2. *Seringapatam* is a decayed town and fortress of Hindostan, in the State of Mysore, two hundred and fifty miles south of Madras. It was besieged by the English on three different occasions: the first two sieges took place in 1791 and 1792, and the third in 1799, on the 4th of May of which year it was stormed by the British and their allies, on which occasion Tippoo was killed, with the greater part of his garrison, amounting to eight thousand men. On an eminence in the suburbs of Seringapatam is the mausoleum of Hyder Ali and Tippoo Saib.

having introduced the European discipline among his numerous troops as early as 1767 he began the war, which was continued with scarcely any intermission, but with little permanent success on the part of the natives, down to the period of the American war, when the French united with him, and the war was carried on with increased vigor.

26. In the year 1780 Hyder Ali and his son Tippoo Saib, at the head of an army of one hundred thousand natives, and aided by a body of French troops, fell upon the English forces in the presidency of Madras, and killed or captured the whole of them,—Madras, the capital, alone being saved from falling into their hands. In the following year the English were strongly reënforced, and Hyder Ali, at the head of two hundred thousand men, was defeated in three obstinate battles; but these successes were _ interrupted by the loss of an English force of three thousand men, which was entirely cut to pieces by Tippoo Saib in the year 1782.

27. On the death of Hyder Ali, in the same year, Tippoo Saib succeeded to the throne, and in the following year, after the restoration of peace between France and England, he concluded a treaty with the English, in which the latter made concessions that greatly detracted from the respect hitherto paid to their name in Asia. But this native prince never ceased, for a moment, to cherish the hope of expelling the British from Hindostan. In 1790 he began the war again, but was eventually compelled to purchase peace at the price of one half of his dominions. His last war with the English terminated in 1799, by the storming of Seringapatam, his capital, and the death of Tippoo, who fell in the assault.

28. On the 30th of November 1782, preliminary articles of peace were signed between Great Britain and the United States, which were to be definitive as soon as a treaty between France and Great Britain should be concluded. When the session of parliament opened, on the 5th of December, considerable altercation took place in respect to the terms of the provisional treaty, but a large majority was found to be in favor of the peace thus obtained. The independence of the United States being now recognized by England, the original purpose of France was accomplished; and all the powers at war being exceedingly desirous of peace, preliminary articles were signed by Great Britain, France, and Spain, on the 20th of January, 1783. By this treaty France restored to Great Britain all French acquisitions in the West Indies during the war, excepting Tobago,

XV. TREATY OF 1782.

XVI. GENERAL TREATY OF 1783.

while England, surrendered to France the important station of St.
Lucia.   On the coast of Africa the settlements in the vicinity of the
river Senegal were ceded to France,—those on the Gambia to Eng.
land.   In the East Indies France recovered all the places she had
lost during the war, to which were added others of considerable importance.   Spain retained Minorca and West Florida, while East
Florida was ceded to her in return for the Bahamas.   It was not till
September, 1783, that Holland came to a preliminary settlement
with Great Britain, although a suspension of arms had taken place
between the two powers in the January preceding.

20. Thus closed the most important war in which England had
ever been engaged,—a war which originated in her ungenerous treatment of the American colonies.   The expense of blood and treasure
which this war cost England was enormous; nor did her European
antagonists suffer much less severely.   The United States was the
only country that could claim any beneficial results from the war,
and these were obtained by a strange union of opposing motives and
principles on the part of European powers.   France and Spain, arbitrary despots of the Old World, had stood forth as the protectors
of an infant republic, and had combined, contrary to all the principles of their political faith, to establish the rising liberties of America.
They seemed but as blind instruments in the hands of Providence,
employed to aid in the dissemination of those republican virtues that
are destined to overthrow every system of political oppression throughout the world.

VI. THE FRENCH REVOLUTION.—1. The democratic spirit which
had called forth the war between England and her American colonies,
and which the princes of continental Europe had encouraged and fostered, through jealousy of the power of DEMOCRATIC
England, to the final result of American independence, SPIRIT.
was destined to exert a much wider influence than the royal allies of
the infant Republic had ever dreamed of.   Borne back to France by
those of her chivalrous sons who, in aiding an oppressed people, had
imbibed their principles, it entered into the causes which were already at work there in breaking up the foundations of the rotten
frame-work of French society, and contributed greatly to hurry forward the tremendous crisis of the French Revolution.

2. At the time of the death of Louis XV., in 1774, the lower
orders of the French people had been brought to a state of extreme

indigence and suffering, by the luxuries of a dissolute and despotic court, during a long period of misrule, in which agriculture was sadly neglected, and trade, commerce, and manufactures, existed but in an infant and undeveloped state. The nobility had been, for a long period, losing their power and their wealth, by the gradual elevation of the middling classes; and the clergy had lost much of their influ ence by the rise of philosophical investigation, which was not only attended by an extraordinary degree of freedom of thought, but was strongly tinctured also with infidelity.

3. Louis XVI., who came to the throne at the age of twenty years, was poorly calculated to administer the government at a critical period, when resolute and energetic measures were requisite. He was a pious prince, and sincerely loved the welfare of his subjects; but the exclusively religious educa- tion which he had received had made him little acquainted with the world, and he was exceedingly ignorant of all polite learning—even of history and the science of government. Ignorance of politics, weak- ness, vacillation, and irresolution, were the fatal defects in the king's character.

II.
Louis XVI.

4. To find a remedy for the disordered state of the French finances, and the decline of public credit, was the first difficulty which Louis had to encounter; nor did he surmount it until he found himself involved in the vortex of a Revo- lution. Minister after minister attempted it, sometimes with partial success, but oftener with an increase of evil. Turgot would have introduced radical and wise reforms by an equality of taxation, and by the suppression of every species of exclusive privilege; but the nobility, the courtiers, and the clergy, who were interested in main- taining all kinds of abuses, protested against any sacrifices on their part; and the able minister fell before their combined opposition. Turgot was succeeded by Neckar, a native of Geneva, an economical financier, who had amassed immense wealth as a banker; but his projects of economy and reform alarmed the privileged orders, and their opposition soon compelled him to retire also.

III. FINAN-
CIAL DIFFI-
CULTIES.

5. The brilliant, vain, and plausible Calonne, the next minister of finance, promulgated the theory that profusion forms the wealth of a State; a paradox that was highly applauded by the courtiers. His system was to encourage industry by expenditure, and to stifle discontent by prodigality; he liquidated old debts by contracting new ones,—paid exorbitant pensions, and gave splendid entertain

men's; and while the credit of the minister lasted, his resources appeared inexhaustible. Calonne continued the system of loans after the conclusion of the American war, and until the credit of the government was utterly exhausted, when it was found that the annual deficit of the revenue, below the expenditure, was nearly thirty millions of dollars! General taxation of the nobility and clergy, as well as the commons, was now proposed, and in order to obtain a sanction to the measure, an assembly of the Notables,—the chiefs of the privileged orders,—was called; but although the assembly at first assented to a general tax, the national parliament defeated the project.

6. Brienne, who succeeded Calonne, becoming involved in a contest with the parliament, which was anxious to maintain the immunities of the privileged orders, and being unable to obtain a loan to meet the exigencies of government, was   IV. THE STATES-GENERAL. reduced to the necessity of a convocation of the States-General, a great National Legislature, composed of representatives chosen from the three orders, the nobility, the clergy, and the people, but which had not been assembled during a period of nearly two hundred years

7. When the day came for the payment of the dividends to the public creditors, the treasury was destitute of funds; much distress was occasioned, and an insurrection was feared; but the removal of Brienne, and the restoration of Neckar to office, created confidence, while the most urgent difficulties were removed by temporary expedients, in anticipation of some great change that was to follow the meeting of the States-General,—the remedy that was now universally called for. The court had at first dreaded the convocation of the States-General, but finding itself involved in a contest with the privileged classes, who assumed all legal and judicial authority, it took the bold resolution of throwing itself upon the representatives of the whole people, in the hope that the commons would defend the throne against the nobility and clergy, as they had done, in former times, against the feudal aristocracy.

8. When it was known that the great assembly of the nation was to be convened, a universal ferment seized the public mind. Social reforms, extending to a complete reorganization of society, became the order of the day; political pamphlets inundated the country; politics were discussed in every society; theories accumulated upon theories; and, in the ardor with which they were combated and defended, were already to be seen the seeds of those dissensions which

afterwards deluged the country with blood.   There was abundance
of evil to be complained of, and it was evident that exclusive privileges, and the marked division of classes, must be broken down.   The
clergy held one-third of the lands of the kingdom, the nobility another third ; yet the remaining third was burdened with all the expenses of government.   This was more than could be borne ; yet the
clergy, the nobility, and the magistracy, obstinately refused the surrender of their exclusive privileges, while, on the other hand, the
philosophic party, considering the federal republic of America as a
model of government, desired to break up the entire frame-work of
French society, and construct the edifice anew.   Such was the state
of France when the assembly of the States-General was called, a
measure that was, in itself, a revolution, as it virtually gave back the
powers of government to the people.   The Third-Estate—the Commons, comprising nearly the whole nation, demanded that its representatives should equal those of the other two classes—the clergy and the
nobility.   Public opinion called for the concession, and obtained it.   The
result of the elections conformed to the sentiments of the three classes
in the kingdom : the nobility chose those who were firmly attached to
the interests and privileges of their order ; the bishops, or clergy,
chose those who would uphold the Roman Catholic hierarchy, and
who were more inclined to political freedom than the former ; while
the commons, or Third-Estate, chose a numerous body of representatives, firm in their attachment to liberty, and ardently desirous of
extending the power and influence of the *people*.

9. At the opening of the States-General, on the 4th of May, 1789,
a difficulty arose as to the manner in which the three orders should
vote ; the clergy and nobility insisting that there should be three
assemblies, each possessing a veto on the acts of the others, while the
commons insisted that all should be united in one general assembly,
without any distinction of orders.   The commons managed with
great tact and adroitness, waiting patiently, day after day, for the
clergy and nobility to join them, but after more than a month had
thus passed away, they declared themselves the "National Assembly,"
being, as they asserted, the representatives of ninety-six hundredths,
at least, of the nation, and therefore the true interpreters of the
national will.   The nobles, alarmed by this sudden boldness of the
Assembly, implored the monarch to support their rights ; a coalition
was formed between them and the court, but the public mind was
against them, and towards the last of June, the clergy and the no-

bility, constrained by an order of the sovereign himself, took their seats in the hall of the Assembly, where they were soon lost in an overwhelming majority. "The family was united, but it gave few hopes of domestic union or tranquillity."

10. The triumph of the *third-estate* had destroyed the moral power and influence of the government: a spirit of insubordination began to appear in Paris, caused, in some degree, by the pressure of famine; journals and clubs multiplied; declaimers harangued in every street, and directed the popular indignation against the king and his family; and the very rabble imbibed the intoxicating spirit of politics. When a regiment of French troops mutinied, and their leaders were thrown into prison, a mob of six thousand men liberated them, collisions took place between the populace and the royal guards; and the former, obtaining a supply of muskets and artillery, attacked the Bastile, or state prison of Paris, tore the governor in pieces, and inhumanly massacred the guards who had attempted to defend the place (July 14th, 1789.)

V REVOLU-
TIONARY
STATE OF
PARIS.

11. Louis, greatly alarmed, now abandoned the counsels of the party of the nobles, who had advised him to suppress the threatened revolution at the head of his army, and hurrying to the National Assembly, craved its support and interference to restore order to the capital. At the same time he caused the regular troops to be withdrawn from Paris, while the defence of the place was intrusted to a body of civic militia, called the National Guards, and placed under the command of La Fayette, whose liberal sentiments, and generous devotion to the cause of American liberty, had made him the idol of the populace.

12. The union between the king and the National Assembly was hailed with transports of joy by the Parisians, and for a few days it seemed that the revolution had closed its list of horrors; but there were agents at work who excited and bribed the people to fresh sedition. The consequences of the insurrection of the 14th July extended throughout France; the peasantry of the provinces, imitating the lower orders of the capital in a crusade against the privileged classes, everywhere possessed themselves of arms; the regiments of the line declared for the popular side; many of the chateaux of the nobles were burned, and their possessors massacred or expelled, and in a fortnight there was no authority in France but what emanated from the people. These things produced their effect upon the National

Assemb y. The deputies of the privileged classes, seeing no escape

VI. GREAT POLITICAL CHANGES. from ruin but in the abandonment of those immunities which had rendered them odious, consented to sacrifice the whole ; the clergy followed the example, and in one evening's session the aristocracy and the church descended to the level of the peasantry ; the privileged classes were swept away, and the political condition of France was changed. (Aug. 4th, 1789.)

13. An interval of two months now passed over without any flagrant scene of popular violence, the Assembly being engaged at Versailles in fixing the basis of a national constitution, and the municipality of Paris in procuring bread for the lower orders of the Parisians, while the latter, imagining that the Revolution was to liberate them from almost every species of restraint, were rioting in the exercise of their newly-acquired freedom. Towards

VII. FAMINE AND MOBS. the latter part of August the famine had become so severe in Paris, (a natural consequence of the public convulsions, and the suspension of credit,) that mobs were frequent in the streets, and the baker's shops were surrounded by multitudes clamoring for food, while the most extravagant reports were circulated, charging the scarcity upon the court and the aristocrats. The leaders of the populace, artfully fomenting the discontent, instigated the mob to demand that the king and the Assembly should be removed from Versailles to the capital ; and on the 5th of October a crowd of the lowest rabble, armed with pikes, forks, and clubs, and accompanied by some of the national guards, marched to Versailles. They penetrated into the Assembly, vociferously demanding *bread*,— a slight collision occurred between them and some of the king's body guards, and during the ensuing night they broke into the palace massacred the guards who opposed them, and had it not been for the opportune arrival of La Fayette and his grenadiers, the king himself and the whole royal family would have fallen victims. After tranquillity had been partially restored, the king was compelled to set out for Paris, accompanied by the tumultuous rabble which had sought his life. The National Assembly voted to transfer its sittings to the capital. The royal family, on reaching Paris, repaired to the Tuilleries, which henceforth became their palace and their prison.

14. Several months of comparative tranquillity followed this outrage, during which time the formation of the constitution was prosecuted with activity by the Assembly. The feudal system, feudal services, and all titles of honor, had been abolished. One general

legislative Assembly had been decreed : the absolute veto of the king had been taken away; and now the immense prop- erty of the church was appropriated to the State, a meas- ure that secured the great financial resources which so long upheld the Revolution.　In the meantime the training, dividing, forming, and marshalling of parties went on.　At first, La Fayette, and those who aided him—the moderate friends of liberty—prevailed in the Assembly, satisfied with constitutional reforms, without desiring to overthrow the monarchy But there was another class—the ultra revolutionists—composed of the factious spirits of the Assembly, who afterwards obtained the control of that body.　Having organized themselves into a club, called the club of the Jacobins, from the name of the convent in which they assembled, and gathering members from all classes of society, they held nightly sittings, where, surrounded by a crowd of the popu- lace, they canvassed the acts of the Assembly and formed public opinion.

VIII. NEW CONSTITU- TION.

IX. MARSHAL- LING OF PARTIES.

15.　At one time this club contained more than two thousand five hundred members, and corresponded with more than four hundred affiliated societies throughout France.　It was the hot-bed of sedition, and the centralization of anarchy, and it eventually overturned the government, and sent forth the sanguinary despots who established the Reign of Terror.　Barnave, the Lameths, Danton, Marat, and Robespierre, were the leaders of the Jacobin faction.　Mirabeau, the first master-spirit which arose amid the troubles of the times,—a man of extraordinary eloquence and talent, but of loose principles— who had at first united with the Jacobins, foreseeing the sanguinary excess that already began to tinge the career of the Revolution, at length entered into a treaty with the court to use his great influence in aiding to establish monarchy on a constitutional basis; but his death, early in 1791, up to which period he had maintained his ascendancy in the Assembly, deprived the king of his only hope of being able to withstand the Jacobin influence in the National Legis- lature.　Mirabeau had a clear presentiment of the coming disasters " Soon,' said he, " neither the king nor the Assembly will rule the country, but a vile faction will overspread it with horrors."

16.　While the machinations of the Jacobins were convulsing France, the repose of Europe was threatened by the in- judicious movements of the emigrant nobility, large numbers of whom, estimated at seventy thousand, dis- gusted with the Revolution, had abandoned their country, resolved to

X. THE EMIGRANT NOBILITY

seek the restoration of the old government by the intervention of foreign powers. Collecting first at Turin, and afterwards at Coblentz,[1] they endeavored to stir up rebellion in the provinces, and solicited Louis to sanction their plans, and join their meditated armaments. Louis, accompanied by his queen and children, attempted to escape secretly to the frontiers, but was stopped and brought back a prisoner to his capital. (June 1791.) The Jacobins now argued that he king's flight was abdication; and the National Assembly, to appease the popular outcry, provisionally suspended him from his functions, until the constitution, now nearly completed, was presented to him for acceptance. On the 14th of September, 1791, he took the oath to maintain it against civil discord and foreign aggression, and to enforce its execution to the utmost of his power. The *Constituent Assembly*, as that which framed the constitution is often called, after having passed a self-denying ordinance that none of its members should be elected to the next Assembly, declared itself dissolved on the 30th of September, 1791.

VI. ATTEMPTED ESCAPE OF THE ROYAL FAMILY.

17. But the constitution thus established, could not be permanent, for the minds of the French people were still agitated by the passion for change, and the members of the new *Legislative Assembly* soon displayed opinions more radical, and divisions more numerous, than their predecessors. The court and the nobility had exercised no influence in the late elections; the upholders of even a mitigated aristocracy had disappeared; the assembly was thoroughly democratic; and the only question that seemed to remain for it was the maintenance or the overthrow of the constitutional throne. The chief parties in the assembly, at its opening were the constitutionalists and the republicans,—the latter were more usually called Girondists, as their most celebrated leaders, Brissot Petion, and Condorcet, were members from the department of the Gironde. The constitutionalists would have preserved the throne, while they stripped it of its power; but the Girondists, enthusiastic admirers of the Americans, despising the vain shadow of royalty, longed for republican institutions on the model of antiquity. The Jacobins, who were anarchists, men without principles, and attached to no particular form of gov-

---

1. *Coblentz*, (the *Confluentes* of the Romans,) is a Prussian town in the province of the Rhine, at the confluence of the Rhine and Moselle. Since the wars of Napoleon it has been strongly fortified, and is now deemed one of the principal bulwarks of Germany on the side of France. *Map No. XVII.*)

ernment, possessed at first little influence in the assembly, but directing the passions of the populace, and possessing the means of rousing
at pleasure the strength of the capital, they soon acquired a preponderating influence that bore down all opposition, and crushed the more
moderate revolutionary party of the Girondists.

18. The legislative assembly commenced its sittings by confiscating
the property of the emigrants, and denouncing the penalties of treason
against those refractory priests who refused to take the oath to support the constitution; but the king refused to sanction the decrees
It was the great object of the Girondists to involve the kingdom in
foreign war; and the warlike preparations of the Austrian emperor
and the German princes, evidently designed to support the emigrants,
rendered it an easy matter to carry out their designs. When an
open declaration of his objects was demanded of the Austrian emperor, he required as a condition on which he would discontinue his
preparations, that France should return to the form and principles
of government which existed at the time of the commencement of
the constituent assembly. Against his own judgment the king yielded to the force of public opinion, and on the 20th of
April, 1792, war was declared against the court of
Vienna. It must be admitted that the war which arose
from so feeble beginnings, but which at length involved
the world in its conflagration, was not provoked by France, but by
the foreign powers which unjustly interposed to regulate the laws
and government of the French people.

XII. WAR
DECLARED
AGAINST
AUSTRIA.

19. While the strife of parties continued in Paris, producing confusion in the councils of the assembly, and increasing anxiety and
alarm in the mind of the king, a formidable force was assembling on
the German frontier with the avowed object of putting down the
Revolution, and restoring to the king the rights of which he had
been deprived. The king of Prussia and the emperor of Austria
engaged to coöperate for this purpose; and their united forces were
placed under the command of the Duke of Brunswick, who, towards
the end of July, entered the French territories at the head of a hundred and forty thousand men. The threatening manifesto which he
issued roused at once the spirit of resistance throughout every part
of France; the demagogues seized the occasion to direct the popular
fury against the court, which was accused of leaguing with the enemy;
and the two prominent factions, the Girondists and Jacobins, com-

bined to overturn the monarchy, each with the view of advancing its own separate ambitious designs.

20. The dethronement of the king was now vehemently discussed in all the popular assemblies; preparations were made in Paris for a general revolt; and soon after midnight on the morning of the 10th of August, an infuriate mob attacked and pillaged the palace, massacred the Swiss guards, and forced the king and royal family to seek shelter in the hall of the National Assembly. The assembly protected the person of the king, but, yielding to the demands of the conquering populace, passed a decree suspending the royal functions, dismissed the ministers, and directed the immediate convocation of a National Convention. La Fayette, then in command of the army on the eastern frontier, having in vain endeavored to keep his troops firm in their allegiance, and being outlawed by the assembly, fled into the Netherlands, but was seized and -imprisoned by the Austrians. Dumouriez, who had adhered to the assembly, succeeded to the command, and made energetic preparations to resist the coming invasion.

XIII. MASSACRE. OF THE TENTH OF AUGUST.

21. The massacre of the 10th of August was soon followed by another of still more frightful atrocity. The prisons of Paris had become filled with suspected persons; and the leaders of the Jacobins, now occupying the chief places in the magistracy, in order to diminish the number of their internal enemies planned the massacre of the prisoners. Accordingly, at three o'clock on the morning of the 2d of September, a band of three hundred hired assassins, accompanied by a frantic mob, entered the prisons, and began the work of death. In the court yard of the first prison four and twenty priests were hewn in pieces because they refused to take the revolutionary oath. In some instances the assassins, stained with gore, established tribunals to try their victims, and a few minutes, often a few seconds, disposed of the fate of each individual. The massacres continued from the 2d to the 6th of September and during this period more than five thousand persons perished in the different prisons of Paris. A committe of the municipality of Paris, declaring that a plot had been formed by the prisoners throughout France to murder all the patriots of the empire, invited the other cities to imitate the massacres of the capital, but, fortunately, none obeyed the summons.

XIV. MASSACRE OF SEPTEMBER.

22. While these shocking excesses were perpetraxd in the capital,

the armies of Prussia and Austria, which had invaded the French territories, met with a signal repulse. Dumouriez, pursuing his suc cesses, crossed the Belgian frontier, and on the 6th of November gained the battle of Jemappes,[1] which gave him possession of all the Austrian Netherlands. With so much rapidity and decision did Dumouriez execute the skilful movements of the army, that the allies soon found there was no want of able generals among the French At the battle of Jemappes, the enthusiasm and martial spirit of the French, displaying themselves in all their brilliancy, bore down all obstacles, and redoubt after redoubt was stormed and taken, to the chant of the Marseilles Hymn.[a]

23. The National Convention, which had succeeded the Legislative Assembly, inflamed by this first great victory of the Revolution, published a decree offering the alliance of the French to every nation that desired to recover its liberties,—a decree which was equivalent to a declaration of war against all the monarchies of Europe. One step further was necessary to complete the Revolution, and that was the death of the kind-hearted and unfortunate monarch. On the ridiculous charge of having engaged in a conspiracy for the subversion of freedom, on the XV. TRIAL AND EXECU-TION OF LOUIS XVI. 26th of December Louis XVI. was brought before the Convention, and, after a trial which lasted twenty days, was declared guilty, and condemned to death by a majority of twenty-six votes out of seven hundred and twenty-one. Nearly all of those who had voted for his death subsequently perished on the scaffold, during the sanguinary " reign of Terror," which soon followed. On the 21st of January, 1793, Louis was led out to execution. He met death with magna-nimity and firmness, amid the insults of his cruel executioners. His fate will be commiserated, and his murderers execrated, so long as justice or mercy shall prevail on the earth.

1. *Jemappes* (zhem-map) is a small village of Belgium, near Mons, forty four miles south. west from Brussels. The Duke de Chartres, afterwards Louis Philippe king of the French, acted as the lieutenant of Dumouriez during the battle of Jemappes, and by his intrepidity at the head of a column aided essentially in winning the day.

a. The famous *Marseilles Hymn,* the national song of the French patriots and warriors, was composed by Joseph Rouget de l'Isle, (roozhi de leel,) a young engineer officer, early in the French Revolution. It was at first called the " Offering to Liberty," but received its present name because it was first publicly sung by the Marseilles confederates in 1792. Both the words and the music are peculiarly inspiriting. So great was the influence of this song over the ex- citable French, that it was suppressed under the empire and the Bourbons; but the Revolution of 1830 called it up anew, and it has since become again the national song of the French people.

24. The Girondists, who had been the first to fan the flame of revolution, were the first to suffer by its violence. Ardent republicans in principle, but humane and benevolent in their sentiments, they had not desired the death of the king, but they could not restrain the mad fury of the Jacobins. The latter, a base faction in the convention, taunted the former with having endeavored to save the tyrant : their partisans, throughout Paris, roused the feelings of the populace against the Girondists : a powerful insurrection[a] deprived the convention of its liberty : thirty of the leading members of the Girondist party were given up and imprisoned ; and those who had not the fortune to escape from Paris were brought to trial, condemned, without being heard in their defence, and speedily executed,[b] and all for no other crime than having tried to prevent the execution of the king, to avenge the massacres of September, and to allay the desolating storm of violence and crime that was spreading terror and dismay over their country.

[1793]
XVI. FALL
OF THE
GIRONDISTS.

25. After the fall of the Girondists, the victorious Jacobins, at the head of whom were Danton, Marat, Robespierre, and their associates, obtained control of the " Committee of Public Safety," a formidable Revolutionary tribunal, in which was vested the whole power of the convention and of the government. Some opposition was indeed made, by the magistracies of the cities and towns throughout a great part of France, to this central power, and at one time seventy departments were in a state of insurrection against the convention ; but the vigorous measures of the Parisian Revolutionists soon broke this formidable league. Revolutionary committees, radiating from the central Jacobin power in Paris, extended their network over the whole kingdom ; and these committees, having the power of arresting the obnoxious and the suspected, and numbering more than five hundred thousand individuals, often drawn from the very dregs of society, held the fortunes and lives of every man in France at their disposal.

26. The prisons throughout France were speedily filled with victims ; forced loans were exacted with rigor ; TERROR was made the order of the day ; and the guillotine* was put in requisition to do its work of death. The queen was

XVII. THE
REIGN OF
TERROR.

* *Guillotine*—so called from the name of the inventor—is an engine or machine for beheading persons at a stroke.

a. May 31st.　　　　　b. Oct. 31st.

brought to the scaffold,[a] and the dauphin, thrown into prison, ere long fell a victim to the barbarous neglect of his keepers. Irreligion and impiety raised their heads above the mass of pollution and crime: the Sabbath was abolished by law: the sepulchres of the kings of France were ordered to be destroyed, that every memorial of royalty might be blotted out; and the leaders of the municipality of Paris, in the madness of atheism, publicly expressed their determination "to dethrone the king of Heaven as well as the monarchs of the earth." As the crowning act of this drama of wickedness, the Goddess of Reason, personified by a beautiful female, was introduced into the convention, and declared to be the only divinity worthy of adoration:—the churches were closed—religion everywhere abandoned—and on all the public cemeteries was placed the inscription, "Death is an Eternal Sleep."

XVIII. TRI-
UMPH OF
INFIDELITY.

27. After the downfall of the Girondists and the party attached to a constitutional monarchy, divisions arose among the Jacobin leaders. The sanguinary Marat had already fallen by the dagger of the devoted heroine, Charlotte Corday, who voluntarily sacrificed her own life in the hope of saving her country. The more moderate portion of the Revolutionary leaders, Danton, Camille Desmoulins, and their supporters, who had so recently roused the populace against the Gironde, were ere long charged with showing too much *clemency*; and brought to the scaffold.[b] The Republican Girondists had sought to *prevent* the Reign of Terror—the Dantonists to *arrest* it; and both perished in the attempt. Thereafter there seemed not a hope left for France. The revolutionary excesses everywhere increased: those who kept aloof from them were suspected, and condemned; and the power of DEATH was relentlessly wielded by such a combination of monsters of wickedness as the world had never before seen.

XIX. FALL
OF THE
DANTONISTS.

28. Having pursued the internal history of the Revolution down to the fall of the Dantonists in March 1794, we resume the narrative of affairs at the beginning of 1793. The death of Louis XVI., which derives its chief importance from the principle which the revolutionists thereby proclaimed, excited profound terror in France, and feelings of astonishment and indignation throughout Europe. France thereby placed herself in avowed and unrelenting hostility to the established governments of the neighboring States; and it was universally felt that the period had

XX. WAR
AGAINST
EUROPE.

now arrived when she must conquer the coalition of thrones, or perish under its blows The convention did not wait to be attacked, but forthwith, on various pretexts, declared war against England, Spain, and Holland, and ordered the increase of the armies of the republic to more than five hundred thousand men.

29. Early in 1793 the English and Prussians combined to check the progress of the French in Holland, and on the 18th of March Dumouriez was defeated in the battle of Neerwinde. Soon after this repulse, the French general, disgusted with the excesses of the revolutionists in Paris, and finding himself suspected by both Girondists and Jacobins, entered into a negotiation with the allied generals for a coalition of forces to aid in the establishment of a constitutional monarchy in France; but his army did not share his feelings, and being denounced by the convention, and a price set upon his head, he was obliged to take refuge in the Austrian lines.

30. After the defection of Dumouriez, Custine was appointed to the command of the north, then severely pressed by the allies near Valenciennes; but being unable to check the progress of the enemy, he was deprived of his command, ordered to Paris, and, soon after, condemned and executed on the charge of misconduct. The revolutionary government, seeing no merit but in success, placed its generals in the alternative of victory or death, and employed the terrors of the guillotine as an incentive to patriotism. The fall of Valenciennes seemed to open to the allies a way to Paris, but, pursuing independent plans of aggrandizement, they injudiciously divided their forces, and before the close of the year, were driven back across the frontier.

31. Early in the same year Spain had despatched an army of fifty-five thousand men for the invasion of France by the way of the Pyrenees; but although the French, who advanced to meet them, were driven back, the campaign in that quarter was characterized by no event of importance. In the meantime, in the west of France, the insurrectionary war of La Vendee was occupying the troops of the convention; and on the side of Italy the allies were aided by the revolt of Marseilles, Lyons, and Toulon.

32. In La Vendee, a large district bordered on the north by the
XXI. INSUR-   Loire, and on the west by the ocean, containing eight
RECTION OF   hundred thousand souls, the Royalists, embracing nearly
LA VENDEE.   the entire population, had early taken up arms in the cause of their church and their king. This district soon became the

theatre of innumerable conflicts, in which the undisciplined peasantry of La Vendee at first had the advantage, from their peculiar mode of fighting, and the nature of their country On the 10th of June, 1793, they obtained a great victory at Saumur,[1] where their trophies amounted to eighty pieces of cannon, ten thousand muskets, and eleven thousand prisoners; but on the 29th of the same month they were defeated in their attempt on Nantes, where their brave leader Cathelineau was mortally wounded. During the summer two invasions of the country of the Vendeans was made by large bodies of the republican troops under skilful generals, who were defeated and driven back with severe loss. The convention, at length aroused to a full sense of the danger of this war, surrounded La Vendee with an army of two hundred thousand men, who, by a simultaneous advance, threatened a speedy extinction of the revolt. But the republican troops who had penetrated the country were cut off in detail—the veterans of Kleber were defeated near Torfou,[2] and before the close of September the Vendean territory was freed from its invaders.

33. Again the convention made the most vigorous efforts to suppress the insurrection. Their forces penetrated the country in every direction, and, with unrelenting and uncalled-for cruelty, burned the towns and villages that fell into their hands, and put the inhabitants, of every age and sex, to the sword. Defeated[a] in the battle of Cholet,[3] and their country in the possession of their enemies, a large portion of the surviving Vendeans, with their wives and children, crossed the Loire into Brittany, with the hope of obtaining assistance from their countrymen in that quarter. In the battle of Chateau Gonthier,[4] fighting with the courage of despair, they gained a decisive victory over the Republican forces, whose loss amounted to twelve thousand men and nineteen pieces of cannon. This victory was gained on the very day when the orator Barrère announced in the convention, "the war is ended, and La Vendee is no more." Great then was the consternation in Paris when it was known that the Republican army was dispersed, and that nothing remained to prevent the advance of the Royalists to the capital.

1. *Saumur* is on the southern bank of the Loire, in the former province of Anjou, one hundred and fifty-seven miles south-west from Paris. (*Map* No. XIII.)

2. *Torfou* was a small village in the northern part of La Vendee, a short distance south-east from Nantes. (*Map* No. XIII.)

3. *Cholet* (sh o-la) is nearly forty miles south-east from Nantes. (*Map* No. XIII.)

4. *Chateau Gonthier* is sixty miles north-east from Nantes. (*Map* No. XIII.)

a Oct. 17th, 1793.

34. But the Vendeans were divided in their councils. Induced by the hope of succors from England, they directed their march to the coast, and, after laying siege to Granville,[1] where they expected the cooperation of the English, were at length compelled to retreat, with heavy loss. Defeated[a] at Mans,[2] and having experienced a final overthrow[b] at Savenay,[3] they slowly melted away in the midst of their enemies, fighting with unyielding courage to the last. Out of nearly a hundred thousand who had crossed the Loire, scarcely three thou sand returned to La Vendee, and most of these fell by the hands of their pursuers, or, brought to a hasty trial, perished on the scaffold.[c]

35 The discontents in the south of France against the measures of the convention first broke out in open insurrection at Marseilles, which was soon reduced to submission, while a large proportion of the inhabitants fled to Toulon. In the meantime Lyons had revolted. During four months it was in a state of vigorous siege; and sixty thousand men were employed before the place at the time of its surrender in October, 1793. All the houses of the wealthy were demolished, and nearly the entire city destroyed. In the course of five months after the surrender of the place, more than six thousand of the citizens suffered death by the hands of the executioners, and more than twelve thou sand were driven into exile.

XLII. INSUR-
RECTION IN
THE SOUTH
OF FRANCE.

36. On the fall of Lyons the Republican troops immediately marched to the investment of Toulon, whose defence was assisted by an English and Spanish squadron. The artillery of the besiegers was commanded by a young Corsican, Napoleon Bonaparte, who re- mained faithful to France, in which he had been educated. By his

1. *Granville* is a fortified seaport town of France, on the western coast of Normandy, one hundred and eighty miles west from Paris. Granville was bombarded and burned by the Eng- lish in 1695, and was partly destroyed by the Vendean troops in 1793. (*Map* No. XIII.)

2. *Mans* is situated on the left bank of the river Sarthe, a northern tributary of the Loire, one hundred and twenty miles south-west from Paris. (*Map* No. VIII.)

3. *Savenay* is a town on the northern bank of the Loire, twenty-two miles north-west from Nantes. Here the Vendeans fought with the courage of despair, and their guard, protecting a crowd of hapless fugitives—the aged, the wounded, women and children—continued to resist, with their swords and bayonets, long after all their ammunition had been expended, and until they all fell under the fire of the Republicans. (*Map* No. XIII.)

a. Dec. 10th, 1793.   b. Dec. 22d, 1793.

c. The most prominent of the Vendean leaders were Larochejacquelin, Bonchamps, Cathe- lineau, Lescure, D'Elbe, Stofflet, and Charette. Nearly all of these, and most of their families, perished in this sanguinary strife, or on the scaffold. Among those who were saved by the courageous hospitality of the peasantry were the wives of Larochejacquelin and Bonchamps, who, after escaping unparalleled dangers, lived to fascinate the world by the splendid story of their husbands' virtues and their own misfortunes.

exertions a fort commanding the harbor was taken, and the place being thus rendered untenable, was speedily evacuated[a] by the allies. who carried away with them more than fourteen thousand of the wretched inhabitants—being so many saved from the vengeance of the Revolutionary tribunals.

37. Thus terminated the memorable campaign of 1793. In the midst of internal dissensions and civil war, while France was drenched with the blood of her own citizens, and the world stood aghast at the atrocities of her " Reign of Terror," the national councils had shown uncommon military talent and unbounded energy. The invasion, on the north, had been defeated; the Prussians had been driven back from the Rhine; the Spaniards had recrossed the Pyrenees; the English had retired from Toulon; and the revolt of La Vendee had been extinguished; while an enthusiastic army, of more than a million of men, stood ready to enforce and defend the principles of the Revolution against all the crowned heads of Europe.

[1794.] 38. The fall of Danton and his associates, which occurred in the early part of 1794,[b] was followed by unqualified submission to the central power of Paris, from every part of France. For a time the work of proscription had been confined to the higher orders; but when it had descended to the middling classes, and when, even after all the enemies of the Revolution had been cut off, there seemed no limit to its onward course, humanity began to revolt at the ceaseless effusion of human blood, and courage arose out of despair.

39. In the convention itself, which, long stupefied by terror, had become the passive instrument of Robespierre and his associates, a conspiracy against the tyrant was at length formed among those whose destruction he had already planned,—not of the good against the bad, but a conspiracy of one set of assassins against another: his arrest was ordered: he was declared out of the pale of the law; and, after a brief struggle, he was condemned, with twenty of his associates, by the same Revolutionary Tribunal which he himself had established, and sent to the scaffold, where he perished amid the exulting shouts of the populace. On the following day sixty of the most obnoxious members of the municipality of Paris met the same fate. Thus terminated that Reign of Terror, which, under the cloak of Republican virtue, had not only overturned the throne and the altar and driven the nobles of France into exile, and her priests into cap

XXIII. FALL OF ROBESPIERRE, AND END OF THE REIGN OF TERROR.

tivity, but which had also shed the blood of more than a million of her best citizens.*

40. The fall of Robespierre placed the direction of public affairs in the hands of more moderate men; but the genius of Carnot still controlled the military operations, which were conducted with remarkable energy and success. In consequence of the extinction of civil employments, and the forced requisition on the people, the whole talent of France was centered in the army, whose numbers, by the beginning of October, 1794, amounted to twelve hundred thousand men. After deducting the garrisons, the sick, and those destined for the service of the interior, there remained upwards of seven hundred thousand ready to act on the offensive;—a greater force than could then be raised by all the monarchies of Europe. The French territory resembled an immense military camp, and all the young men of the country seemed pressing to the frontier to join the armies.

41. England, at the head of the allies in the war against France, made preparations that were considered "unparalleled;" and it was soon easy to see that the latter was destined to become irresistible on land; and the former to acquire the dominion of the seas. In the early part of the season the French were dispossessed of all their West India possessions; the island of Corsica, in the Mediterranean, was captured; and on the 1st of June, a French fleet of twenty-six ships of the line was defeated, and six vessels taken by the English admiral Howe, off the western coast of France. But numerous victories on the land far more than compensated for these losses; and the campaign was one of the most glorious in the annals of France. At the beginning of the year the allies were pressing heavily on all the frontiers: at its close, the Spaniards, defeated in Biscay[1] and Catalonia, were suing for peace: the Italians, driven over the Alps, were trembling for the fate of their own country: the allied forces had everywhere recrossed the Rhine: Holland had been revolutionized

XXIV. THE ENGLISH VICTORIOUS AT SEA, AND THE FRENCH ON LAND.

---

1. Biscay is a district of northern Spain, on the Bay of Biscay, and adjoining France. It comprises Biscay Proper, Alava, and Guipuzcoa,—the three Basque provinces. The Basques have a peculiar language, which is undoubtedly of great antiquity. Some have attempted to trace it, as a dialect of the Phœnician, to the Hebrew. It has some similarity to the Hungarian and Turkish. (Map No. XIII.)

* The Republican writer, Prudhomme, gives a list of one million, twenty-two thousand three hundred and fifty-one persons, who suffered a violent death during this period, of whom more than eighteen thousand perished by the guillotine. In his enumeration are not included the massacres at Versailles—in the prisons, &c.—nor those shot at Toulon and Marseilles.

and subdued; and the English troops had returned home or had fled for refuge into the States of Hanover.

42. The failure of the allies in the campaigns of 1793 and 1794 was in great part owing to a want of cordial coöperation among them, occasioned by the prospect held out to Russia, Prussia, and Austria, of obtaining a further share in the partition of ill-fated Poland. While Poland was a prey to civil dissensions, it was invaded in 1792 by Russia, and early in the following year by Prussia; and the result was a second partition of the Polish territory among the invading powers, with the concurrence and sanction of Austria,—the king of Prussia assigning as reasons for his treachery and disregard of former treaties, that the "dangerous principles of French Jacobinism were fast gaining ground in that country." *[XXV. SECOND PARTITION OF POLAND.]*

43. Scarcely had this iniquitous scheme been consummated, when the patriots of Poland, with Kosciusko at their head, arose against their invaders, whom they drove from the country. But Poland was too feeble to contend successfully against the fearful odds that were brought against her. Kosciusko was defeated, wounded, and taken prisoner by the Russians; and the result of the brief struggle was the third and last partition of Poland, among Russia, Prussia, and Austria. To effect this unhallowed object, Austria and Prussia had withdrawn a portion of their troops from the French frontiers, and thus the time was allowed to pass by, when a check might have been given to French ambition. *[XXVI. THIRD PARTITION OF POLAND.]*

[1795.] 44. The first coalition against the French Republic, formed in March 1793, embraced England, Austria, Prussia, Holland, Spain, Portugal, the two Sicilies, the Roman States, Sardinia, and Piedmont; but the successes of France in the campaign of 1794 led to the dissolution of this confederacy early in 1795. The conquest of Holland decided the wavering policy of Prussia, which now, by a treaty of peace, agreed to live on friendly terms with the Republic, and not to furnish succor to its enemies; and before the first of August, Spain also, completely humbled, withdrew from the coalition; and thus the whole weight of the war fell on Austria and England. Russia had indeed already become a party to the war against France, but her alliance was as yet productive of no results, as the attention of the Empress Catherine was wholly engrossed in securing the immense territories which had fallen to her by the partition of Poland *[XXVII. DISSOLUTION OF THE FIRST COALITION AGAINST FRANCE.]*

45. During the year 1795 the reaction against the Reign of Terror was general throughout France : the Jacobin clubs were broken up the Parisian populace disarmed, and many of the prominent members of the Revolutionary tribunals justly expiated their crimes on the scaffold. As yet all the powers of government were centered in the National Convention ; but the people now began to demand of it a constitution, and the surrender of the dictatorship which it had so long exercised. A constitution was formed, by which the legislative power was divided between two Councils, appointed by delegates chosen by the people, that of the *Five Hundred*, and that of the *Ancients*, the former having the power of originating laws, and the latter that of passing or rejecting them. The executive power was lodged in the hands of a *Directory* of five members, nominated by the council of Five-Hundred, and approved by that of the Ancients.

XXVIII.
NEW CON-
STITUTION.

46. This constitution was to be submitted to the armies of the people for ratification : but the convention, composed of the very men who had at first directed the Revolution, who had voted for the death of the king, and the execution of the Girondists, and who had finally overthrown the tyrant Robespierre, still unwilling abruptly to relinquish its power, decreed that two-thirds of their number should have a seat in the new legislative councils. This measure met with great opposition, and caused intense excitement. Although the armies, and a large majority of the people, accepted the constitution, a formidable insurrection against the convention broke out in Paris, headed by the Royalists, comprising many of the best citizens, and supported by the Parisian National Guard numbering thirty thousand men, but destitute of artillery. The convention, hastily collecting to its support a body of five thousand regular troops assembled in the neighborhood of Paris, placed them under the command of General Barras, who intrusted all his military arrangements to his second in command, the young artillery officer who had distinguished himself in the reduction of Toulon— Napoleon Bonaparte. The latter was indefatigable in making preparations for the defence of the convention, and when his little band was surrounded and attacked by the Parisians, he replied at once by a discharge of cannon loaded with grape shot, firing with as much spirit as though he were directing his guns upon Austrian battalions. In a few hours tranquillity was restored; and this was the *last insurrection* of the people in the French Revolution. The new gov

XXIX. INSUR-
RECTION IN
PARIS.

ernment being established, the convention, which had passed through
so many stormy scenes, and had experienced so great changes in
sentiment, determined to finish its career by a signal act of clemency,
and after having abolished the punishment of death, and published a
general amnesty, it declared its mission of consolidating the Republic accomplished, and its session closed.   (Oct. 26th, 1795.)

47. The military events of 1795 were of much less importance
than those of the two former years. England indeed maintained her
supremacy at sea; but the Austrians barely sustained themselves in
Italy; and success was evenly balanced on the side of Germany,
while a general lassitude, and uncommon financial embarrassments,
the result of the recent extraordinary revolutionary exertions, prevailed throughout France.

[1796.]   48. In the spring of 1796 the French Directory sent
three armies into the field; that of the Sambre and XXX. INVA-
Meuse,[1] under Jourdan, numbering seventy thousand SION OF
men; that of the Rhine and Moselle, under Moreau, GERMANY
numbering seventy-five thousand; and the army of Italy under Bonaparte, numbering forty-two thousand. Jourdan and Moreau made
successful irruptions into Germany, but they were stopped in their
mid-career of victory by the Arch-duke Charles of Austria, one of
the ablest generals of his time, and eventually compelled to retreat
across the Rhine.

49. The operations of the army of Bonaparte in Italy were
more eventful. Although opposed by greatly supe- XXXI. THE
rior forces, the indefatigable energy and extraordinary ARMY OF
military talents of the youthful general crowned the ITALY.
campaign with a series of brilliant victories, almost unparalleled in
the annals of war. Napoleon, on assuming the command, found his
army in an almost destitute condition, maintaining a doubtful contest
on the mountain ridges of the Italian frontier. Rapidly forcing his
way into the fertile plains of the interior, he soon compelled the
king of Sardinia to purchase a dishonorable peace, subdued Piedmont
conquered Lombardy, humbled all the Italian States, and defeated,
and almost destroyed, four powerful armies which Austria sent against
him. The battles of Montenotte[2] and Millessimo,[3] the terrible pas-

---

1. *Sambre* and *Meuse.* The Sambre unites with the Meuse at Namur. (*Map No. XV.*)
2. April 11–12, 1796. *Montenotte* is a mountain ridge near t' e Mediterranean, a short distance west from Genoa.
3. April 13–14. *Millessimo* is a small village twenty-eight miles west from Genoa.

sage of the bridge of Lodi,[1] the victory of Arcole,[2] and fall of Mantua[3]—in fine, the brilliant results of the campaign, excited the utmost enthusiasm throughout France, and Napoleon at once became the favorite of the people. The councils of government repeatedly decreed that the army of Italy had deserved well of their country and the standard which Napoleon had borne on the bridge of Arcole was given to him to be preserved as a precious trophy in his family.

50. England had for some time been greatly agitated by a division XXXII. DIS-TURBANCES IN ENGLAND. of opinion respecting the policy of continuing the war against France; important parliamentary reforms were demanded;[a] party spirit became extremely violent; and on several occasions the country seemed on the brink of revolution.[b] Added to these internal difficulties, in the month of August, 1796, Spain concluded a treaty[c] of alliance, offensive and defensive, with France, and this was followed, in the month of October,[d] by a formal declaration of war against Great Britain. Still, England maintained her supremacy at sea, and greatly extended her conquests in the East and West Indies,[e] while a powerful expedition[f] which France had prepared for the invasion of Ireland was dispersed by tempests, and obliged to return without even effecting a landing.

1. May 10th. The bridge of *Lodi* crosses the Adda, twenty miles south-west from Milan. (*Map* No. XVII.)

2. Nov. 15–17. *Arcole* is a small village a short distance east of the Adige, thirteen miles south-west from Verona, and one hundred miles east from Milan. (*Map* No. XVII.)

3. *Mantua* is a fortified town of Austrian Italy, on both sides of the Mincio, twenty-one miles south-west from Verona. It derives its principal celebrity from its being the native country of Virgil. After the conquest of northern Italy by Charlemagne, Mantua became a republic, and continued under that form of government till the twelfth century, when the Gonzaga family acquired the chief direction of its affairs. They were subsequently raised to the title of dukes and held possession of Mantua till 1707, when it was taken by the Austrians. Mantua surrendered to Napoleon, Feb. 2d, 1797, after a siege of nearly six months. In July, 1799, surrendered to the Austrians, after a siege of nearly four months. (*Map* No. XVII.)

a. For increasing democratic power &c., for which purpose there were numerous associations throughout the kingdom, and the reformers were charged with a desire of subverting the monarchy, and establishing a republican constitution, similar to that of France.

b. Kings' carriage surrounded—pelted with stones, &c., Oct. 29th, 1795, and the monarch narrowly escaped the fury of the populace. A crisis in money matters compels the Bank of England to suspend cash payments, Feb. 1797. Discontents in the navy, and mutiny of the channel fleet, April, 1797. Second mutiny, May and June, and blockade of the Thames.

c. Of San Ildefonso.

d. Oct. 2d.

e. St. Lucia, Essequibo, and Demarara, in the West Indies, were reduced in May, 1796, and early in the same year Ceylon, the Malaccas, Cochin, Trincomalee, &c., in the East Indies. The Cape of Good Hope had been previously taken by the English.

f. The French fleet under Hoche, carrying twenty-five thousand land forces, sailed Dec. 15th, 1796. A formidable conspiracy existed in Ireland to throw off the English yoke and establish a republican government, and alliance with France

[1797.]   51. Early in the spring of 1797, Napoleon, after stimu-
lating the ardor of his soldiers by a spirited address,[a] in
which he recounted to them the splendid victories which
they had already won, set out from Northern Italy[b] at
the head of sixty thousand men, in several divisions, to
carry the war into the hereditary States of Austria.   Opposed to
him was the Arch-duke Charles at the head of superior forces, only
a part of which, however, could be brought into the field at the beginning of the campaign.   Rapidly passing over the mountains, Napoleon drove his enemies before him, and was ready to descend into
the plains which spread out before the Austrian capital, when proposals of peace were made and accepted; and in less than a month
after the first movement of the army from winter quarters, the preliminaries of a treaty between France and Austria were
signed.[c]   The final treaty was concluded at Campo-
Formio[1] on the 17th of October following.   Spain and
Holland suffered severely in this war: Austria was re-
munerated for the loss of Mantua by the cession of Venice; while
France obtained a preponderating control over Italy, and her frontiers
were extended to the Rhine.   Thus terminated the brilliant Italian
campaigns of Napoleon.   Italy was the greatest sufferer in these
contests.   " Her territory was partitioned; her independence ruined,
her galleries pillaged;—the trophies of art had followed the car of
victory; and the works of immortal genius, which no wealth could
purchase, had been torn from their native seats, and violently trans-
planted into a foreign soil."[d]

XXXIII.
NAPOLEON'S
AUSTRIAN
CAMPAIGN.

XXXIV.
TREATY OF
CAMPO
FORMIO.

52. During these events of foreign war, the strife of parties was
raging in France.   In the elections of May, 1797, the *Royalists* prevailed by large majorities, and royalist principles were boldly advocated in the legislative councils,—so great a change had been pro-

---

1. *Campo Formio* is a small town and castle of northern Italy, near the head of the Adriatic.
The negotiations for this peace were carried on by the Austrians at Udine, a short distance
north-east of Campo Formio, and by Bonaparte at the castle of Passeriano. The treaty was
dated at Campo Formio, because this place lay between Udine and Passeriano, although the
ambassadors had never held any conferences there. (*Map No. XVII.*)

a " You have been victorious," said he, " in fourteen pitched battles and seventy combats;
you have made one hundred thousand prisoners, taken five hundred pieces of field artillery,
two thousand of heavy calibre, and four sets of pontoons. The contributions you have levied
on the vanquished countries have clothed, fed, and paid the army; you have, besides, added
thirty millions of francs to the public treasury, and you have enriched the museum of Paris
with three hundred masterpieces of the works of art, the produce of thirty centuries."
b. March 10th.   c. April 9th, at Judemberg.   d. Alison.

duced in public opinion by the sanguinary excesses of the Revolution But the vigilance of the Revolutionary party was again aroused, and the Directory, who were the Republican leaders, becoming alarmed for their own existence, but being assured of the support of the army, determined upon decisive measures. On the

XXXV. ESTABLISHMENT OF MILITARY DESPOTISM IN FRANCE.

night of the 3d of September, twelve thousand troops, under the command of Augereau, and with the concurring support of Napoleon, were introduced into the capital; the Royalist leaders, and the obnoxious members of the two councils, were seized and imprisoned; and when the Parisians awoke from their sleep, they found the streets filled with troops, the walls covered with proclamations, and military despotism established.[a] The Directory now took upon themselves the supreme power, while their opponents were banished to the pestilential marshes of Guiana.[1]

53. The year 1798 opened with immense military preparations

[1798]
XXXVI. PREPARATIONS FOR THE INVASION OF ENGLAND.

for the invasion of England, the only power then at war with France. Unusual activity prevailed, not only in the harbors of France and Holland, but also of Spain and Italy: all the naval resources of France were put in requisition, and an army of nearly one hundred and fifty thousand men was collected along the English Channel, under the name of the Army of England, the command of which was given to Napoleon. But the hazards of the expedition induced Napoleon to direct his ambitious views to another quarter, and, after

XXXVII. EXPEDITION TO EGYPT.

considerable difficulty, he persuaded the Directory to give him the command of an expedition to Egypt, a province of the Turkish empire. The ultimate objects f Napoleon appear to have been, not only to conquer Egypt and Syria, but to strike at the Indian possessions of England by the overland route through Asia, and after a series of conquests that should render his name as terrible as that of Ghenghis Khan or Tamerlane, establish an Oriental empire that should vie with that of Alexander

54. Filled with these visions of military glory, Napoleon sailed from Toulon on the 19th of May with a fleet of five hundred sail, carrying about forty thousand soldiers, and ten thousand seamen He took with him artisans of all kinds; he formed a complete collection of philosophical and mathematical instruments; and about

1. *French Guiana.* See Surinam, p. 303.
Called the Revolution of the eighteenth Fructidor.

a hundred of the most illustrious scientific men of France, reposing implicit confidence in the youthful general, hastened to join the expedition, whose destination was still unknown to them.

55. The fleet first sailed to Malta,[1] which quickly surrendered[a] its almost impregnable fortresses to the sovereignty of France,—the way having been previously prepared by a conspiracy fomented by the secret agents of Napoleon. Fortunate in avoiding the fleet of the English admiral Nelson, then cruising in the Mediterranean, the armament arrived before Alexandria on the first of July, and Napoleon, hastily landing a part of his forces, marched against the city, which he took by storm before the dismayed Turks had time to make preparations for defence.

56. With consummate policy Napoleon proclaimed to the Arab population[b] that he had come to protect their religion, restore their rights, and punish their usurpers, the Mamelukes; and thus he sought, by arming one part of the people against the other, to

1. *Malta.* (See also p. 152.) On the decline of the Roman empire Malta fell under the dominion of the Goths, and afterwards of the Saracens. It was subject to the crown of Sicily from 1190 to 1525, when the emperor Charles V. conferred it on the Knights Hospitallers of St. John, who had been expelled from Rhodes by the Turks. In 1565 it was unsuccessfully besieged by the Turks; the knights, under their heroic master Valette, founder of the city called by his name, finally compelling the enemy to retreat with great loss. In 1798 it fell into the hands of Napoleon; but the French garrisons, surrendered to the English, Sept. 5th, 1800. The treaty of Paris, in 1814, annexed the island to Great Britain.

a. June 12th, 1798.

b. The population of Egypt at this time, consisting of the wrecks of several nations, was composed of three classes; Copts, Arabs, and Turks. The Copts, the ancient inhabitants of Egypt, a poor, despised, and brutalized race, amounted at most to two hundred thousand. The Arabs, subdivided into several classes, formed the great mass of the population: 1st, there were the Sheiks or chiefs, great landed proprietors, who were at the head of the priesthood, the magistracy, religion, and learning: 2d, there was a large class of smaller landholders; and, 3d, the great mass of the Arab population, who, as hired peasants, by the name of fellahs, in a condition little better than that of slaves, cultivated the soil for their masters; and 4th, the Bedouin tribes, or wandering Arabs, children of the desert, who would never attach themselves to the soil, but who wandered about, seeking pasturage for their numerous herds of cattle in the Oases, or fertile spots of the desert on both sides of the Nile. They could bring into the field twenty thousand horsemen, matchless in bravery, and in the skill with which their horses were managed, but destitute of discipline, and fit only to harass an enemy, not to fight him. The third race was that of the Turks, who were introduced at the time of the conquest of Egypt by the Sultans of Constantinople. They numbered about two hundred thousand, and were divided into Turks and Mamelukes. Most of the former were engaged in trades and handicrafts in the towns. The latter, who were Circassian slaves purchased from among the handsomest boys of the Circassians, and carried to Egypt when young, and there trained to the practice of arms, were, with their chiefs and owners, the boys, the real masters and tyrants of the country. The entire body consisted of about twelve thousand horsemen, and each Mameluke had two fellahs to wait upon him. "They are all splendidly armed: in their girdles are always to be seen a pair of pistols and a poniard; from the saddle are suspended another pair of pistols and a hatchet; on one side is a sabre, on the other a blunderbuss and the servant on foot carries a carbine."

neutralize their means of resistance Leaving three thousand soldiers in garrison at Alexandria, he set out on the 6th of July for

XXXVIII.
BATTLE OF
THE
PYRAMIDS.

Cairo[1] at the head of thirty thousand men. After some
skirmishing on the route with the Mamelukes, on the
21st of the month he arrived opposite Cairo, on the west
side of the Nile, where Mourad Bey had formed an intrenched camp, defended by twenty thousand men, while on the
plain, between the camp and the pyramids, were drawn up nearly
ten thousand Mameluke horsemen. Napoleon arranged his army
in five divisions, each in the form of a square, with the artillery
at the angles, and the baggage in the centre; but scarcely had he
made his dispositions, when eight thousand of the Mameluke horsemen, in one body, admirably mounted and magnificently dressed,
and rending the air with their cries, advanced at full gallop upon the
squares of infantry. Falling upon the foremost division, they were
met by a terrible fire of grape and musketry, which drove them from
the front round the sides of the column. Furious at the unexpected
resistance, they dashed their horses against the rampart of bayonets,
and threw their pistols at the heads of the grenadiers, but all in
vain,—the tide was rolled back in confusion, and the survivors fled
towards the camp, which was quickly stormed, its artillery, stores,
and baggage were taken, and the "Battle of the Pyramids" was soon
at an end. The victors lost scarcely a hundred[a] men in the action,
while a great portion of the defenders of the camp perished in the
Nile; and, of the splendid array of Mameluke horsemen that had so
gallantly borne down upon the French columns, not more than two
thousand five hundred escaped with Mourad Bey into Upper Egypt.

57. A few days after the battle of the Pyramids, Napoleon expe-

XXXIX.
BATTLE OF
THE NILE.

rienced a severe reverse by the destruction of his fleet
which he had left moored in the Bay of Aboukir near
Alexandria. On the morning of the 1st of August the
British fleet, under the command of Admiral Nelson, appeared off

---

1. *Cairo* (kī'-ro) the modern capital of Egypt, and the second city of the Mohammedan
world, is near the eastern bank of the Nile, about twelve miles above the apex of its delta
and one hundred and twelve miles south-east from Alexandria. Population variously estimated
at from two hundred and fifty to three hundred thousand. Cairo is supposed to have been
founded about the year 970, by an Arab general of the first Fatimate caliph. The neighborhood of Cairo abounds with places and objects possessing great interest, among which are
the pyramids, and the remains of the city of Heliopolis, the On of the scriptures. (*Map
No. XII.*)

a. "Scarcely a hundred killed and wounded."—Thiers. "The victors hardly lost two hundred men in the action."—Alison.

the harbor, and on the afternoon of the same day the attack was commenced, several of the British ships penetrating between the French fleet and the shore, so as to place their enemies between two fires. The action that followed was terrific. The darkness of night was illumined by the incessant discharge of more than two thousand cannon; and during the height of the contest the French ship L'Orient, of one hundred and twenty guns, having been for some time on fire, blew up with a tremendous explosion, by which every ship in both fleets was shaken to its centre. The result of this famous "Battle of the Nile" was the destruction of the French naval power in the Mediterranean, the shutting up of the French army in Egypt, cut off from its resources, with scarcely the hope of return, the dispelling of Napoleon's dreams of Oriental conquest, and the revival of the coalition in Europe against the French republic. Turkey declared war; Russia sent a fleet into the Mediterranean; the king of Naples took up arms; and the emperor of Austria, yielding to the solicitations of England, recommenced hostilities

58. Notwithstanding the loss of his fleet, and the storm that was arising in Europe, Napoleon showed no design of abandoning his conquests. With remarkable energy he established mills, foundries, and manufactories of gunpowder throughout Egypt, and soon put the country in an admirable state of defence. Upper Egypt was conquered by a division under Desaix, who penetrated beyond the ruins of Thebes; and finally, in the early part of February, [1799] 1799, Napoleon, leaving sixteen thousand men as a re- XL. SYRIAN serve in Egypt, set out at the head of only fourteen thou- EXPEDITION sand men for the conquest of Syria, where the principal army of the Sultan was assembling. On the 6th of March, Jaffa, the Joppa of antiquity, the first considerable town of Palestine, was carried by storm, and four thousand of the garrison who had capitulated were mercilessly put to death—an eternal and ineffaceable blot on the memory of Napoleon.

59. On the 16th of March the French army made its appearance before Acre, where the Pacha of Syria had shut himself up with all his treasures, determined to make the most des- XLI. SIEGE perate resistance. He was aided in the defence of the OF ACRE. place by an English officer, Sir Sidney Smith, who commanded a small squadron on the coast. Foiled in every attempt to take the place by storm, Napoleon was finally compelled to order a retreat, after a siege of more than two months, having in the meantime, with

only six thousand of his veterans, defeated an army of thirty thou sand Oriental militia in the battle of Mount Tabor.[1]　On the morn ing of that battle Kleber had left Nazareth[2] to make an attack on the Turkish camp near the Jordan, but he met the advancing hosts in the plain in the vicinity of Mount Tabor.　Throwing his little army into squares, with the artillery at the angles, he bravely main-

XLII. BATTLE OF MOUNT TABOR. tained the unequal combat for six hours, when Napoleon, arriving on the heights which overlooked the field of bat tle, and distinguishing his men by the steady flaming spots amid the moving throng by which they were surrounded, an nounced, by the discharge of a twelve pounder, that succor was at hand.　The arrival of fresh troops soon converted the battle into a complete rout; the Turkish camp, with all its baggage and ammuni tion, fell into the hands of the conquerors, and the army which the country people called " innumerable as the sands of the sea or the stars of heaven" was driven beyond the Jordan and dispersed, never again to return.

60. Napoleon reached Egypt on the 1st of June, having lost more than three thousand men in his Syrian expedition; but scarcely had he restored quiet to that country, when, on the 11th of July, a body of nine thousand Turks, admirably equipped, and having a numerous pack of artillery, landed at Aboukir Bay, having been transported

XLIII. BATTLE OF ABOUKIR. thither by the squadron of Sir Sidney Smith.　Napoleon immediately left Cairo with all the forces which he could command, and although he found the Turks at Aboukir strongly intrenched, he did not hesitate to attack them with inferior forces.　The result was the total annihilation of the Turkish army,— five thousand being drowned in the Bay of Aboukir, two thousand killed in battle, and two thousand taken prisoners.

61. By some papers which fell into his hands, Napoleon was now, for the first time, informed of the state of affairs in Europe.　Early in the season the allies had collected a force of two hundred and fifty housand men between the German ocean and the Adriatic, as a bar rier against French ambition; and fifty thousand Russians, under the veteran Suwarrow, were on the march to swell their numbers.　To this vast force the French could oppose, along their eastern frontiers,

1. *Mount Tabor* is twenty-five miles south-east from Acre, and fifty-three north-east from Je rusalem.　It is the mountain on which occurred the transfiguration of Christ.—Matthew, xvii 1, and Mark, ix. 2. (*Map* No. VI.)

2. *Nazareth*, a small town of Palestine, celebrated as having been the early residence of the founder of Christianity, is seventy miles north-east from Jerusalem. (*Map* No. VI.)

and scattered over Italy, an army of only one hundred and seventy thousand. In Italy the united Russians and Austrians gradually gained ground until the French lost all their posts in that country except Genoa: many desperate battles were fought in Switzerland, but victory generally followed the allied powers, while, in Germany, the French were forced back upon the Rhine: Corfu had been conquered by the Russians and English, and Malta was closely blockaded.

62. When Napoleon was informed of these reverses of the French arms, his decision was immediately made, and leaving Kleber in command of the army of Egypt, he secretly embarked for France. After a protracted voyage, in which he was in constant fear of being captured by British cruisers, he landed at Frejus[1] on the 9th of October, and on the 18th found himself once more in Paris. The most enthusiastic joy pervaded the whole country on account of his return. The eyes, the wishes, and the hopes of the people, who were dissatisfied with the existing state of things, were all turned on him : men of all professions paid their court to him, as one in whose hands were, already, the destinies of their country : the Directory alone distrusted and feared him.

63. Napoleon, perceiving that the French people had grown weary of the Directory, and relying on the support of the army, concerted, with a few leading spirits, the overthrow of the government. As preliminary measures, the Council of the Ancients was induced to appoint him commander XLIV. OVERTHROW OF THE DIRECTORY. of the National Guard and of all the military in Paris, and to decree the removal of the entire Legislative body to St. Cloud,[2] under his protection ; but the Council of Five Hundred, alarmed by rumors of the approaching dictatorship, raised so furious an opposition against him, that Napoleon was in imminent danger. As the only resource left him, he appealed to his comrades in arms, and on the 9th of November, 1799, a body of grenadiers entering the Legislative hall by his orders, cleared it of its members ; and thus military

1. *Frejus* is a town of south-eastern France, in a spacious plain, one mile from the Mediterranean, and forty-five miles north-east from Toulon. Napoleon landed at St. Raphael, a small fishing village about a mile and a-half from Frejus. Frejus was a place of importance in the time of Julius Cæsar, who gave it his own name. (*Map* No. XIII.)

2. *St. Cloud* is a delightful village six miles west from Paris, containing a royal castle and magnificent garden, which were much embellished by Napoleon. Napoleon chose St. Cloud for his residence ; hence the expression *cabinet of St. Cloud*. Under the former government the phrase was, *cabinet of Versailles*, or *cabinet of the Tuileries*.

force was left triumphant in the place of the constitution and the laws. A new constitution was soon formed, by which the executive power was intrusted to three consuls, of whom Napoleon was the chief. The "First consul," as Napoleon was styled, was in everything but in name a monarch. Not only in Paris, but throughout all France, the feeling was in favor of the new government; for the people, weary of anarchy, rejoiced at the prospect of repose under the strong arm of power, and were as unanimous to terminate the Revolution as, in 1789, they had been to commence it. The Revolution had passed through all its changes:—monarchical, republican, and democratic; it closed with the military character; while the liberty which it strove to establish was immolated by one of its own favorite heroes. on the altar of personal ambition

XLV. NAPO-
LEON FIRST
CONSUL.

CHAPTER VI.

THE NINETEENTH CENTURY.

SECTION I.

THE WARS OF NAPOLEON.

ANALYSIS. [EVENTS OF THE YEAR 1800.] 1. Napoleon's proposals for peace. Rejected by the British government.—2. Military force of Great Britain and Austria. Situation of France. Effect of Napoleon's government—3. Disposition of the French forces.—4. Successes of Moreau. [Engen. Moeskirch.] Massena is shut up in Genoa. Napoleon passes over the Great St. Bernard. [Great St. Bernard.]—5. Surprise of the Austrians. Napoleon's progress. Victory of Marengo. [Marengo.]—6. Efforts at negotiation. Malta surrenders to the British.—7. Operations of the French and Austrians in Bavaria. [Hohenlinden.] Passage of the Splugen by Macdonald. [Splugen.] Armistice. Peace of Luneville. [Luneville.]—8. Maritime confederacy against England. Its effect. Previous orders of the Danish and Russian governments.

9. [EVENTS OF 1801.] England sends a powerful fleet to the Baltic. Battle of Copenhagen. 10. The Russian emperor Paul is strangled, and succeeded by Alexander. Dissolution of the League of the North.—11. The French army in Egypt. Capitulation. General peace. [Amiens.]

12. [EVENTS OF 1802, THE YEAR OF PEACE.] Internal Affairs of France. Napoleon made consul for life.—13. Conduct of Napoleon in his relations with foreign States. Holland—the Italian republics—the Swiss cantons. Attempt to recover St. Domingo. [Historical account of St. Domingo.]—14. Circumstances leading to a RENEWAL OF THE WAR IN 1803. Hostile acts of England and France.

15. First military operations of the French, in the year 1803. [Hanover.] Preparations for the invasion of England.—16. Rebellion in Ireland. Conspiracy against Napoleon early in 1804. The affair of the Duke D'Enghien. [Baden.]—17. Hostile acts of England against Spain. The latter joins France.—18. Napoleon, emperor, May, 1804—crowned by the pope—anointed sovereign of Italy, May, 1805.

19. New coalition against France. Prussia remains neutral. Beginning of the war by Austria.—20. The French forces. Napoleon victorious at Ulm. [Ulm.] English naval victory of Trafalgar. [Trafalgar.] Additional victories of Napoleon, and treaty of Presburg, Dec. 1805 [Austerlitz.]

[1806.] 21. Conquests of the English. [Mahrattas. Buenos Ayres.] Napoleon rapidly extends his supremacy over the continent. The affairs of Naples, Holland, and Germany.—22. Circumstances which led Prussia to join the coalition against Napoleon.—23. Napoleon's victories over the Prussians. He enters Berlin. [Jena. Auerstadt.]—24. The Berlin decrees. Napoleon in Poland. Battle of Pultusk. Battle of Eylau, Feb. 1807. Fall of Dantzic. [Eylau. Dantzic.]—25. Battle of Friedland. [Friedland. Niemen.] The treaty of Tilsit. Losses suffered by Prussia. [Tilsit. Westphalia.]—26. Circumstances that led to the bombardment of Copenhagen, by the English fleet. Denmark joins France. Portuguese affairs. The French in Lisbon. [Rio Janeiro. Brazil.]—27. The designs of Napoleon against the Peninsular monarchs. Affairs of Spain, 1808. Godoy—abdication of the Spanish monarch, and his son Ferdinand. Joseph Bonaparte becomes king of Spain, and Murat king of Naples.—28. Resistance of the Spaniards and beginning of the Peninsular war.—29. Successes of the Spaniards at Cadiz, Valencia, Saragossa, and Baylen. [Baylen. Ebro.]—30. War in Portugal, and evacuation of that country by the French forces. [Oporto. Vimiera. Cintra.]—31. Napoleon takes the field in person, and the British are rapidly driven from Spain. [Reynosa. Burgos. Tudela. Corunna.]

[1809.] 32. Austria suddenly renews the war. Victories of Napoleon, who enters Vienna in May; and peace with Austria in October. [Eckmuhl. Aspern. Wagram.]—33. War with the Tyrolese. British expedition to Holland. Continuance of the war in the Spanish peninsula. Difficulties between Napoleon and the pope.—34. Napoleon's divorce from Josephine and marriage with Maria Louisa of Austria, 1810. Effects of this marriage upon Napoleon's future prospects. His conduct towards Holland. Sweden. His power in the central parts of Europe. Jealousy of the Russian emperor.—35. Continuance of the war in the Spanish peninsula. Wellington and Massena. [Ciudad Rodrigo. Busaco. Torres Vedras.]—36. The peninsula war during the year 1811. [Badajoz. Albuera.]

37. Events of the peninsular war from the beginning of 1812 to the retreat of the French across the Pyrenees. [Salamanca. Vittoria.]

38. NAPOLEON'S RUSSIAN CAMPAIGN, 1812. Events that led to the opening of a war with Russia. The opposing nations in this war.—39. The "Grand Army" of Napoleon. The opposing Russian force.—40. Napoleon crosses the Niemen, June 1812. Retreat of the Russians. Early disasters of the French army. [Wilna.]—41. Onward march of the army. Battle of Smolensko. Entrance of the deserted city.—42. Napoleon pursues the retreating Russians, who make a stand at Borodino. [Borodino.] The evening before the battle.—43. Battle of Borodino, Sept. 7th.—44. Continued retreat of the Russians, who abandon Moscow. The city on the entrance of the French. The burning of Moscow. Napoleon begins a retreat Oct. 19th. —45. The horrors of the retreat.—46. Napoleon at Smolensko. He renews the retreat Nov 4th. Battles of Krasnoi, and passage of the Beresina. [Krasnoi. Beresina.] Marshal Ney Napoleon abandons the army, and reaches Paris, Dec. 18th. His losses in the Russian campaign.

47. War between England and the United States of America. Mexico. The war in the Indian seas.

[1813.] 48. Napoleon's preparations for renewing the war. Prussia, Sweden, and Austria. Battles of Lutzen and Bautzen. Armistice, and congress of Prague. [Bautzen.]—49. War renewed Aug. 16th. Austria joins the allies. Battles. [Culm. Gross-Beren. Katsbach. Dennewitz.] Battles of Leipsic, and retreat of the French. Losses of the French. Revolts. Wellington.

[1814.] 50. General invasion of France. Bernadotte and Murat. Energy and talents of Napoleon. The allies march upon Paris, which capitulates. Deposition, and abdication, of Napoleon. Treaty between him and the allies. [Elba.] Louis XVIII. Restricted limits of France.

[1815.] 51. Congress of Vienna, and Napoleon's return from Elba. Marshal Ney. All France submits to Napoleon.—52. Napoleon in vain attempts negotiations. Forces of the allies; of Napoleon.—53. Napoleon's policy, and movements. Battles of Ligny, Quatre Bras, Wavre, and Waterloo. Second capitulation of Paris. Napoleon's abdication—attempted escape to America—exile—and death. 54. First objects of the allies. Return of Louis XVIII. Execution of Ney, and Labedoyére. Fate of Murat.—55. Second treaty of Paris. Its terms. Restoration of the pillaged treasures of art.

1. As soon as Napoleon was seated on the consular throne 01
[1800] France he addressed to the British government an able
1. EVENTS OF communication, making general proposals of peace.   To
THE YEAR this a firm and dignified reply was given, ascribing the
1800. evils which afflicted Europe to French aggression and
French ambition, and declining to enter into a general pacification until France should present, in her internal condition and foreign policy, firmer pledges than she had yet given, of stability in her own government, and security to others. The answer of the British government forms the beginning of the second period of the war—that in which it was waged with Napoleon himself, the skilful director of all the energies of the French nation.

2. War being resolved on, the most active measures were taken

on both sides to prosecute it with vigor. The land forces, equipped militia, and seamen of Great Britain, amounted to three hundred and seventy thousand men, and Austria furnished two hundred thousand. France seemed poorly prepared to meet the coming storm. Her armies had just been defeated in Germany and Italy; her treasury was empty, and her government had lost all credit; the affiliated Swiss and Dutch republics were discontented; and the French people were dissatisfied and disunited. But the establishment of firm and powerful government soon arrested these disorders; the finances were established on a solid basis; the Vendean war was amicably terminated; Russia was detached from the British alliance; many of the banished nobility were recalled; confidence, energy, and hope, revived; and the prospects of France rapidly brightened under the auspices of Napoleon.

3. At the opening of the campaign the French forces were disposed in the following manner. The army of Germany, one hundred and twenty-eight thousand strong, under the command of Moreau, was posted on the northern confines of Switzerland and north along the west bank of the Rhine: the army of Italy, thirty-six thousand strong, under the command of Massena, occupied the crest of the Alps in the neighborhood of Genoa; while an army of reserve, of fifty thousand men, of whom twenty thousand were veteran troops, awaited the orders of the first consul, ready to fly to the aid of either Moreau or Massena.

4. Moreau, victorious at Engen and Moeskirch,[1] drove the Austrians back from the Rhine, and, penetrating to Munich, laid Bavaria under contribution. Massena, after the most vigorous efforts against a greatly superior force, was shut up in Genoa with a part of his army, and finally compelled to capitulate. Napoleon, on hearing the reverses of Massena, resolved to cross the Swiss Alps and fall upon Piedmont. Taking the route by the Great St. Bernard,[2] on the 17th

---

1. *Engen* and *Moeskirch* are in the south-eastern part of Baden, near the northern boundary of Switzerland. (*Map* No. XVII.)

2. *Great St. Bernard* is the name given to a famous pass of the Alps, leading over the mountains from the Swiss town of Martigny to the Italian town of Aosta. In its highest part it rises to an elevation of more than eight thousand feet, being almost impassable in winter and very dangerous in spring, from the avalanches. Near the summit of the pass is the famous hospital founded in 962 by Bernard de Menthon, and occupied by brethren of the order of St. Augustine, whose especial duty it is to assist and relieve travellers crossing the mountains. In the midst of the tempests and snow storms, the monks, accompanied by dogs of extraordinary size and sagacity, set out for the purpose of tracking those who have lost their way. If they find the body of a traveller who has perished, they carry it into the vault of the dead, where it remains lying on a table until another victim is brought to occupy the place. It is

of May his army began the ascent of the mountain. The artillery wagons were taken to pieces, and put on the backs of mules, while a hundred large pines, each hollowed out to receive a piece of artillery, were drawn up the mountain by the soldiers. To encourage the men, the music of each regiment played at its head; and where the ascent was most difficult the charge was sounded.

5. Great was the surprise of the Austrians at beholding this large army descending into the Italian plains. Before the end of the month Napoleon was at Turin, and on the 2d of June, after little opposition, he made his triumphant entry into Milan. On the 14th he was attacked by the Austrian general Melas, at the head of greatly superior forces, on the plains of Marengo.[1] Here, after twelve hours of incessant fighting, victory was decided in favor of the French by the stubborn resistance of Desaix, and the happy charge of the gallant Kellerman. General Desaix, who had just arrived from Egypt, fell on the field of battle. The result of the victory gave Napoleon the entire command of Italy, and induced the Austrians to propose a suspension of arms, which, in anticipation of a treaty, was agreed to.

6. The efforts at negotiation were unsuccessful, as no satisfactory arrangements could be made between England and France, and in the latter part of November the armistice was terminated, and hostilities recommenced. In the meantime Malta, which, during more than two years, had been closely blockaded by the British forces, was compelled to surrender, and was permanently annexed to the British dominions.

7. On the renewal of the war, the Austrian army, eighty thousand strong, under the Archduke John, and the French army, somewhat less in number, under Moreau, were facing each other on the eastern confines of Bavaria. The Austrians advanced, and on the 3d of De-

then set up against the wall, among the other dead bodies, which, on account of the cold, decay so slowly that they are often recognized by their friends after the lapse of years. It is impossible to bury the dead, as there is nothing about the hospital but naked rocks. Not a tree or ush is to be seen, but everlasting winter reigns in this dreary abode, the highest inhabited place in Europe.

When the army of Napoleon crossed the St. Bernard, every soldier received from the monks a large ration of bread and cheese, and a draught of wine at the gate of the hospital: a seasonable supply which exhausted the stores of the establishment, but was fully repaid by the First Consul before the close of the campaign.

The *Little St. Bernard*, over which Hannibal crossed, is farther west, separating Piedmont from Savoy. The undertaking of the Carthaginian was far more difficult than that of Napoleon. (*Map* No. XIV.)

1. *Marengo* is a small village of Northern Italy, in an extensive plain forty-three miles south west from Milan. (*Map* No. XII.)

cember brought on the famous battle of Hohenlinden,[1] in which they were completely overthrown, and driven back with great slaughter. Moreau rapidly pursued the retreating enemy, and penetrated within sixty miles of Vienna, when, at the solicitation of the Austrian general, an armistice was agreed to on the 25th. In the meantime, in the very heart of winter, the French general Macdonald, at the head of fifteen thousand men, had crossed from Switzerland into the Italian Tyrol, by the famous pass of the Splugen,[2] more difficult than that of St. Bernard. The French forces in Italy now numbered more than a hundred thousand men, and the speedy expulsion of the Austrians was anticipated, when an armistice, soon followed by the peace of Luneville,[3] put an end to the contest with Austria.[a]

8. In the meantime Napoleon, with consummate policy, was successfully planning a union of the Northern powers against England; and on the 16th of December, 1800, a maritime confederacy was signed by Russia, Sweden, and Denmark, and soon after by Prussia, as an acceding party. This league, aimed principally against England, was designed to protect the commerce of the Northern powers, on principles similar to the armed neutrality of 1780; but its effect would have been, if fully carried out, to deprive England, in great part, of her naval superiority. The Danish government had previously ordered her armed vessels to resist the search of British cruisers; and the Russian emperor had issued an embargo on all the British ships in his harbors.

9. England, determined to anticipate her enemies, despatched, as soon as possible, a powerful fleet to the Baltic, under the command of Nelson and Sir Hyde Parker. Passing through the Sound under the fire of the Danish batteries, on the 30th of March the fleet came

1. *Hohenlinden* is a village of Bavaria, nineteen miles east from Munich. (*Map* No. XVII.) Campbell's noble ode, beginning,

> "On Linden, when the sun was low,
> All bloodless lay the untrodden snow,"

has rendered the name, at least, of this battle, familiar to almost every school-boy.

2. The *Pass of the Splugen* leads over the Alps from the Grisons to the Italian Tyrol, into the valley of the Lake of Como. It was only after the most incredible efforts that Macdonald succeeded in passing his army over the mountain; and more than a hundred soldiers, and as many horses and mules, were swallowed up in its abysses, and never more heard of. Since 1823 there has been a road over the Splugen passable for wheel carriages. It was built by Austria, at great expense. (*Map* No. XIV.)

3. *Luneville*, in the former province of Lorraine, is on the road from Paris to Strasbourg sixteen miles south-east from Nancy. By the treaty concluded here in 1801, and which Francis was obliged to give his assent to, "not only as emperor of Austria, but in the name of the German empire," Belgium and all the left bank of the Rhine were again formally ceded to France, and Lombardy was erected into an independent State (*Maps* No. XIII. and XVII.)

a. Feb. 9th, 1801

to anchor opposite the harbor of Copenhagen, which was protected
by an imposing array of forts, men-of-war, fire-ships, and
floating batteries.   On the 2d of April Nelson brought
his ships into the harbor, where, in a space not exceeding
a mile and a half in extent, they were received by a tremendous fire
from more than two thousand cannon.   The English replied with
equal spirit, and after four hours of incessant cannonade the whole
front line of Danish vessels and floating batteries was silenced, with
a loss to the Danes, of more than six thousand men.   The English
loss was twelve hundred.   Of this battle, Nelson said, "I have been
in one hundred and five engagements, but that of Copenhagen was
the most terrible of them all."

II. EVENTS
OF 1801.

10. While Nelson was preparing to follow up his success by attacking the Russian fleet in the Baltic, news reached him of an event
at St. Petersburgh which changed the whole current of Northern
policy.   A conspiracy of Russian noblemen was formed against the
Emperor Paul, who was strangled in his chamber on the night of the
24th of March.   His son and successor Alexander at once resolved
to abandon the confederacy, and to cultivate the friendship of Great
Britain.   Sweden, Denmark, and Prussia followed his example; and
thus was dissolved, in less than six months after it had been formed,
the League of the North,—the most formidable confederacy ever
arrayed against the maritime power of England.

11. While these events were transpiring in Europe, the army
which Napoleon had left in Egypt, under the command of Kleber,
after losing its leader by the hands of an obscure assassin, was
doomed to yield to an English force sent out under Sir Ralph Aber
crombie, who fell at the head of his victorious columns on the plain
of Alexandria.[a]   By the terms of capitulation, the French troops,
to the number of twenty-four thousand, were conveyed to France
with their arms, baggage, and artillery.   As Malta had previously
surrendered to the British, there was now little left to contend for
between France and England.   To the great joy of both nations
preliminaries of peace were signed at London on the 1st of October,
and on the 27th of March, 1802, tranquillity was restored throughout Europe by the definitive treaty of Amiens.[1]

12. Napoleon now directed all his energies to the reconstruction

1. *Amiens.* (See p. 279.)   The definitive treaty of Amiens was concluded March 27th, 1802
between Great Britain, France, Spain, and the Batavian Republic, (Republic of Holland.)
a. March 21st, 1801.

of society in France, the general improvement of the country, and the consolidation of the power he had acquired. By a general amnesty one hundred thousand emigrants were enabled to return : the Roman Catholic religion was restored, to the discontent of the Parisians, but to the great joy of the rural population : a system of public instruction was established under the auspices of the government : to bring back that gradation of ranks in society that the Revolution had overthrown, the Legion of Honor was instituted, an order of nobility founded on personal merit : great public works were set on foot throughout France : the collection of the heterogeneous laws of the Monarchy and the Republic into one consistent whole, under the title of the Code Napoleon, was commenced ; an undertaking which has deservedly covered the name of Napoleon with glory, and survived all the other achievements of his genius ; and finally, the French nation, as a permanent pledge of their confidence, by an almost unanimous vote, conferred upon their favorite and idol the title and authority of consul for life.

III. EVENTS OF 1802, THE YEAR OF PEACE.

13. In his relations with foreign States the conduct of Napoleon was less honorable. He arbitrarily established a government in Holland, entirely subservient to his will ; and he moulded the northern Italian republics at his pleasure : he interfered in the dissensions of the Swiss cantons to establish a government in harmony with the monarchical institutions which he was introducing in Paris ; and when the Swiss resisted, he sent Ney at the head of twenty thousand men to enforce obedience. England remonstrated in vain, and the Swiss, in despair, submitted to the yoke imposed upon them. Napoleon was less successful in an attempt to recover the island of St. Domingo,[1] which had revolted from French authority. Forces

---

1. *St. Domingo*, or Hayti, called by Columbus Hispaniola, (*Little Spain*,) is a large island of the West Indies, about fifty miles east of Cuba. It was first colonized by the Spaniards, by whose cruelties the aboriginal inhabitants were soon almost wholly destroyed. Their place was at first supplied by Indians forcibly carried off from the Bahamas, and, at a later period by the importation of vast numbers of negroes from Africa. About the middle of the sixteenth century the French obtained footing on its western coasts, and in 1691 Spain ceded to France half the island, and at subsequent periods the possessions of the latter were still farther augmented. From 1776 to 1789 the French colony was at the height of its prosperity, but in 1791 the negroes, excited by news of the opening revolution in France, broke out in insurrection, and in two months upwards of two thousand whites perished, and large districts of fertile plantations were devastated. While the war was raging, commissioners, sent from France, taking part with the negroes against the planters, proclaimed the freedom of all the blacks who should enrol themselves under the republican standard : a measure equivalent to the instant abolition of slavery throughout the island. The English government, apprehensive of danger to its West India possessions from the establishment of so great a revolutionary outpost as

to the number of thirty-five thousand men were sent out to reduce the island, but nearly all perished, victims of fatigue, disease, and the perfidy of their own government.

14. It soon became evident that the peace of Amiens could not be permanent. The encroachments of France upon the feebler European powers, the armed occupation of Holland, the great accumulation of troops on the shores of the British Channel, and the evident designs of Napoleon upon Egypt, excited the jealousy of England, and the latter refused to evacuate Malta, Alexandria, and the Cape of Good Hope, in accordance with the late treaty stipulations, until satisfactory explanations should be given by the French government. Bitter recriminations followed on both sides, and in the month of May, 1803, the cabinet of London issued letters of marque, and an embargo on all French vessels in British ports. Napoleon retaliated by ordering the arrest of all the English then in France between the ages of eighteen and sixty years.

IV. RENEWAL OF THE WAR, 1803.

15. The first military operations of the French were rapid and successful. The electorate of Hanover,[1] a dependency of England,

---

the entrance of the Gulf of Mexico, and hoping to take advantage of the confusion prevailing in the island, attempted its reduction, but after an enormous loss of men finally evacuated it in 1798. No sooner was the island delivered from external enemies than a frightful civil war ensued between the mulattoes and negroes, but the former were overcome, and in December 1800 Toussaint Louverture, the able leader of the blacks, was sole master of the French part of the island. Napoleon at first confirmed him in his command as general-in-chief, but finding that he aimed at independent authority, in the winter of 1801 he sent out a large force to reduce the island to submission. During a truce Toussaint was surprised and carried to France, where he died in April 1803. Hostilities were renewed: in November, 1803, the French, driven into a corner of the island, capitulated to an English squadron; and in January, 1804, the Haytien chiefs, in the name of the people, renounced all dependence on France. Numerous civil wars and revolutions long continued to distract the island. In 1821 that part of the island originally settled by the Spaniards voluntarily placed itself under the Haytien government, which still maintains its independence.

In 1791 St. Domingo was in a most flourishing condition, but its commerce and industry were seriously interrupted by the bloody wars and revolutions which succeeded. Moreover, it was not to be expected that half-civilized negroes, suddenly loosed from bondage, under a burning sun, and without the wants or desires of Europeans, should exhibit the vigor and industry of the latter. The Haytien government has found it necessary to adopt a "Rural Code," which makes labor compulsory on the poorer classes, who in return share a portion of the produce of the lands of their masters. Nominally free, the blacks remain really enslaved. But the island is beginning to assume a more thriving appearance; the manners and morals of the people, although still bad, are improving; and something has been done for public instruction. What are to be the final results of this experiment of negro emancipation, time only can determine.

1. Hanover is a large kingdom of north-western Germany, bounded north by the German Ocean and the Elbe, east by Prussia and Brunswick, south by Hesse Cassel and the Prussian department of the Lower Rhine, and west by Holland. A portion of western Hanover is almost divided from the rest by the grand-duchy of Oldenburg. (See Map No. XVII.) This kingdom is formed out of the duchies formerly possessed by several families of the junior branch of the house of Brunswick. Ernest Augustus, Duke of Brunswick, married Sophia, a

was quickly conquered, and in utter disregard of neutral rights the whole of the North of Germany was at once occupied by French troops, while, simultaneously, an army was sent into southern Italy, to take possession of the Neapolitan territories. But these movements were insignificant when compared with Napoleon's gigantic preparations ostensibly for the invasion of England. Forts and batteries were constructed on every headland and accessible point of the Channel: the number of vessels and small craft assembled along the coast was immense; and the fleets of France, Holland, and Spain, were to aid in the enterprise. England made the most vigorous preparations for repelling the anticipated invasion, which, however, was not attempted, and perhaps never seriously intended.

16. The year of the renewal of the war was farther distinguished by an unhappy attempt at rebellion in Ireland, in which the leaders, Russell and Emmett, were seized, brought to trial, and executed. Early in the following year, 1804, a conspiracy against the power of Napoleon was detected, in which the generals Moreau and Pichegru, and the royalist leader Georges, were implicated. Moreau was allowed to leave the country, Pichegru was found strangled in prison, and Georges was executed Napoleon, either believing, or affecting to believe, that the young Duke D'Enghien, a Bourbon prince then living in the neutral territory of Baden,[1] was concerned in this plot, caused him to be seized and hurried to Vincennes, where, after a mock trial, he was shot by the sentence of a court martial:—an act which has fixed an indelible stain on the memory of Napoleon, as not the slightest evidence of criminality was brought against the unhappy prince.

17. Owing to the intimate connection that had been formed between the courts of Paris and Madrid, England sent out a fleet in the autumn of 1804, before any declaration of war had been made, to interrupt the homeward bound treasure frigates of Spain; and these were captured,[a] with valuable treasure amounting to more than two

v. 1804.

---

rand-daughter of James I. of England; and George Louis, the issue of this marriage, became king of England, with the title of George I., in 1714; from which time till 1837, at the death of William IV., both England and Hanover had the same sovereign. On the accession of a female to the throne of Great Britain, the Salic law conferred the crown of Hanover on another branch of the Hanoverian family. During the supremacy of Napoleon, Hanover constituted a part of the kingdom of Westphalia, but was restored to its lawful sovereign in 1813. (*Map* No. XVII.)

1. The grand-duchy of *Baden* occupies the south-western angle of Germany, having Switzerand on the south, and France and Rhenish Bavaria (the Palatinate) on the west. (*Map* No. XVII.)

a. Oct. 4th, 1804.

million pounds sterling. The British government was severely censured for this hasty act. Spain now openly joined France, and declared war against England.[a]

18. On the 18th of May of this year Napoleon was created, by
decree of the senate, "Emperor of the French;" and on the 2d of
December, 1804, was solemnly crowned by the pope, who had been
induced to come to Paris for that purpose. The principal powers
of Europe, with the exception of Great Britain, recognized the new sovereign. On the 26th of May of the
following year he was formally anointed sovereign of Northern Italy.
The iron crown of Charlemagne, which had quietly reposed a thousand years, was brought forward to give interest to the ceremony,
and Napoleon placed it on his own head, at the same time pronouncing
the words, "God has given it me : beware of touching it."

VI. 1805.

19. The continued usurpations charged upon Napoleon at length
induced the Northern Powers to listen to the solicitations of England;
and in the summer of 1805 a new coalition, embracing Russia, Austria, and Sweden, was formed against France. Prussia, tempted by
the glittering prize of Hanover, which Napoleon held out to her, persisted in her neutrality, with an evident leaning towards the French
interest. The Austrian emperor precipitately commenced the war
by invading[b] the neutral territory of Bavaria ; an act as unjustifiable
as any of which he accused Napoleon. The latter seized the opportunity of branding his enemies as aggressors in the contest; and declared himself the protector of the liberties of Europe.

20. In the latter part of September, 1805, the French forces, in
eight divisions, and numbering one hundred and eighty thousand men,
were on the banks of the Rhine, preparing to carry the war into
Austria. The advance of Napoleon was rapid, and everywhere the
enemy were driven before him. On the 20th of October, Napoleon
having surrounded the Austrian general Mack at Ulm,[1] compelled
him to surrender his whole force of twenty thousand men. On the
very next day, however, the English fleet, commanded by Admiral
Nelson, gained a great naval victory off Cape Trafalgar,[2] over the

1 *Ulm* is an eastern frontier town of Wirtemberg, on the western bank of the Danube, seventy-six miles north-west from Munich. Formerly a free city, was attached to Bavaria in
1803, and in 1810 to Wirtemberg. (*Map* No. XVII.)

2. *Cape Trafalgar* is a promontory of the south-western coast of Spain, twenty-five miles
north-west of the fortress of Gibraltar. In the great naval battle of Oct. 21st, 1805, the English, under Nelson, having twenty-seven sail of the line and three frigates, were opposed by the

a. Dec. 12th, 1804. b. Sept. 9th, 1805.

combined fleets of France and Spain; but it was dearly purchased
by the death of the hero. On the 13th of November Napoleon entered Vienna, and on the 2d of December he gained the great battle
of Austerlitz,[1] the most glorious of all his victories,[a] which resulted
in the total overthrow of the combined Russian and Austrian armies,
and enabled the victor to dictate peace on his own terms.[b] The emperor of Russia, who was not a party to the treaty, withdrew his
troops into his own territories: the king of Prussia received Hanover
as a reward of his neutrality; and Great Britain alone remained at
open war with France.

21. While the English now prosecuted the war with vigor on the
ocean, humbled the Mahratta[2] powers in India, subdued the Dutch
colony of the Cape, and took Buenos Ayres[3] from the Spaniards, Napoleon rapidly extended his supremacy over the continent
of Europe. In February, 1806, he sent an army to take   VII. 1806
possession of Naples, because the king, instigated by his queen, an Austrian princess, had received an army of Russians and English into his
capital. The king of Naples fled to Sicily, and Napoleon conferred
the vacant crown upon his brother Joseph. Napoleon next placed
his brother Louis on the throne of Holland: he erected various districts in Germany and Italy into dukedoms, which he bestowed on
his principal marshals: while fourteen princes in the south and west
of Germany were induced to form the Confederation[c] of the Rhine
and place themselves under the protection of France. By this latter
stroke of policy on the part of Napoleon, a population of sixteen
millions was cut off from the Germanic dominion of Austria.

22. In the negotiations which Napoleon was at this time carrying
on with England, propositions were made for the restoration of Han-
ver to that power, although it had recently been given to Prussia. It

French and Spanish fleet of thirty-three sail of the line and seven frigates. Nelson, who was
mortally wounded in the action, lived only to be made aware of the defeat action of the enemy's
fleet. (*Map No. XIII.*)

1. *Austerlitz* (ows'-ter-litz) is a small town of Moravia, thirteen miles southwest of Brunn
the capital. (*Map No. XVII.*)

2. The *Mahrattas* were an extensive Hindoo nation in the western part of southern Hindostan
The various tribes of which the nation consisted were first united into a monarchy about the
middle of the seventeenth century.

3. *Buenos Ayres* (in Spanish bwä-noce-i-res,) is a large city of South America, capital of the
republic of La Plata. In 1811 began the revolutionary movements that ended in the emancipation of Buenos Ayres and the States of La Plata from Spain. The declaration of independence was made on the 9th of July, 1816.

a. Loss of the allies thirty thousand, in killed, wounded, and taken prisoners. Loss of the
French twelve thousand.

b. Treaty of Presburg, Dec. 27th 1805.   c. July 12th.

was moreover suspected that Napoleon had offered to win the favor of Russia at the expense of his Prussian ally. These, and other causes, aroused the indignation of the Prussians; and the Prussian monarch openly joined the coalition against Napoleon before his own arrangements were completed, or his allies could yield him any assistance. Both England and Russia had promised him their coöpera tion

23. With his usual promptitude Napoleon put his troops in motion, and on the 8th of October reached the advanced Prussian outposts. On the 14th he routed the Prussians with terrible slaughter in the battle of Jena,[1] and on the same day Marshal Davoust gained the battle of Auerstadt,[2] in which the Duke of Brunswick was mortally wounded. On these two fields the loss of the Prussians was nearly twenty thousand in killed and wounded, besides nearly as many prisoners. The total loss of the French was fourteen thousand. In a single day the strength of the Prussian monarchy was prostrated. Napoleon rapidly followed up his victories, and on the 25th his vanguard, under Marshal Davoust, entered Berlin, only a fortnight after the commencement of hostilities.

24. Encouraged by his successes Napoleon issued a series of edicts from Berlin, declaring the British islands in a state of blockade, and excluding British manufactures from all the continental ports. He then pursued the Russians into Poland: on the 30th of November his troops entered Warsaw without resistance; but on the 26th of December his advanced forces received a check in the severe battle of Pultusk. On the 8th of February, 1807, a sanguinary battle was fought at Eylau,[3] in which each side lost twenty thousand men, and both claimed the victory. In some minor engagements the allies had the advantage, but these were more than counterbalanced by the siege and fall of the important fortress of Dantzic,[4] which had a garrison of seventeen thousand men, and was defended by nine hundred cannon.

VIII. 1807.

1. *Jena* is a town of central Germany, in the grand-duchy of Saxe Weimar, on the west bank of the river Saale, forty-three miles south-west from Leipsic. The battle was fought between the towns of Jena and Weimar. (*Map* No. XVII.)

2. *Auerstadt* (ow'-er-stadt) is a small village of Prussian Saxony, six miles west of Naumberg, and about twenty miles north of the battle-ground of Jena. (*Map* No. XVII.)

3. *Eylau* (i-low) is a village in Prussia proper, or East Prussia, twenty-eight miles south from Konigsberg. (*Map* No. XVII.)

4. *Dantzic* is an important commercial city, seaport, and fortress, of the province of West Prussia, on the western bank of the Vistula, about three miles from its mouth. Dantzic surrendered to the French May 27th 1807. (*Map* No. XVII.)

25. At length, on the 14th of June, Napoleon fought the great and decisive battle of Friedland,[1] and the broken remains of the Russian army fell back upon the Niemen.[2] An armistice was now agreed to : on the 25th of June the emperors of France and Russia met for the first time, with great pomp and ceremony, on a raft in the middle of the Niemen, and on the 7th of July signed the treaty of Tilsit.[3] All sacrifices were made at the expense of the Pruss. monarch, who received back only about one-half of his dominion. The elector of Saxony, the ally of France, was rewarded with that portion of the Prussian territory, which, prior to the first partition in 1772, formed part of the kingdom of Poland : this portion was now erected into the grand-duchy of Warsaw. Out of another portion was formed the kingdom of Westphalia,[4] which was bestowed upon Jerome Bonaparte, brother of Napoleon ; and Russia agreed to aid the French emperor in his designs against British commerce.

26. Soon after the treaty of Tilsit it became evident to England that Napoleon would leave no means untried to humble that power on the ocean, and it was believed that, with the connivance of Russia, he was making arrangements with Denmark and Portugal for the conversion of their fleets to his purposes. England, menaced with an attack from the combined navies of Europe, but resolving to anticipate the blow, sent a powerful squadron against Denmark, with an imperious demand for the instant surrender of the Danish fleet and naval stores, to be held as pledges until the conclusion of the war. A refusal to comply with this summons was followed by a four days' bombardment of Copenhagen, and the final surrender of the fleet. Denmark, though deprived of her navy, resented the hostility of England by throwing herself, without reserve, into the arms of France. The navy of Portugal was saved from falling into the power of France, by sailing, at the instigation of the British, to Rio

---

1. *Friedland* (freed land) is a town of East Prussia, on the western bank of the river Alle (al'-leh) twenty-eight miles south-east from Konigsberg, and eighteen north-east of Eylau (*Map* No. XVII.)

2. The river *Niemen* (Polish nyem' en) rises in the Prussian province of Grodno, and, passing through the north-eastern extremity of Prussia, enters a gulf of the Baltic by two channels twenty-two miles apart, and each about thirty miles below Tilsit. (*Map* No. XVII.)

3. *Tilsit* is a town of East Prussia, on the southern bank of the Niemen, sixty miles north-east of Konigsberg. (*Map* No. XVII.)

4. *Westphalia* is a name, 1st, originally given, in the Middle Ages, to a large part of Germany · 2d. to a duchy forming a part of the great duchy of Saxony: 3d, to one of the circles of the German empire: 4th, to the kingdom of Westphalia, created by Napoleon: 5th, to the present Prussian province of Westphalia, created in 1815. Most of the present province was embraced in one or more of these divisions. See also Note, p 360. (*Map* No. XVII.)

Janeiro,[1] the capital of the Portuguese colony of Brazil.[2] Napoleon had already announced,[a] in one of his imperial edicts, that "the House of Braganza had ceased to reign." and had sent an army under Junot to occupy Portugal. On the 27th of November, the Portuguese fleet, bearing the prince regent, the queen, and court, sailed for Brazil; and on the 30th the French took possession of Lisbon.

27. The designs of Napoleon for the dethronement of the Peninsular monarchs had been approved by Alexander in the conferences of Tilsit; and when Napoleon returned to Paris he set on foot a series of intrigues at Madrid, which soon gave him an opportunity of interfering in the domestic affairs of the Spanish nation, his recent ally. Charles IV. of Spain, a weak monarch, was the dupe of his faithless wife, and of his unprincipled minister Godoy. The latter, secured in the French interest by the pretended gift of a principality formed out of dismembered Portugal, allowed the French troops under Murat to enter Spain; and by fraud and false pretences the frontier fortresses were soon in the hands of the invaders. Too late Godoy found himself the dupe of his own treachery. Charles, intimidated by the difficulties of his situation, resigned[b] the crown to his son Ferdinand, but, by French intrigues, was soon after induced to disavow his abdication, while at the same time Ferdinand was led to expect a recognition of his royal title from the emperor Napoleon. The deluded prince and his father were both enticed to Bayonne, where they met Napoleon, who soon compelled both to abdicate, and gave the crown to his brother Joseph, who had been summoned from the kingdom of Naples to become king of Spain. The Neapolitan kingdom was bestowed upon Murat as a reward for his military services.

IX. 1808.

28. Although many of the Spanish nobility tamely acquiesced in this foreign usurpation of the sovereignty of the kingdom, yet the great bulk of the nation rose in arms : Ferdinand, although a prisoner in France, was proclaimed king : a national junta, or council, was

---

1. *Rio Janeiro*, the capital of Brazil, is the most important commercial city and seaport of South America. Population about two hundred thousand, of whom about half are whites, and the rest mostly negro slaves.

2. Prior to 1808 *Brazil* was merely a Portuguese colony, but on the arrival of the prince regent and his court, accompanied by a large body of emigrants, January 25th, 1808, it was raised to a kingdom. In 1822 Brazil was declared a kingdom independent of the crown of Portugal. The empire of Brazil, second only in extent to the giant empires of China and Russia, embraces nearly the half of the South American continent; but its population—whites, negroes, and Indians—is less than six millions, of whom only about one million are whites.

a. Nov. 13th, 1807.   b. March 20th, 1808.

chosen to direct the affairs of the government; and the English at once sent large supplies of arms and ammunition to their new allies while Napoleon was preparing an overwhelming force to sustain his usurpation. A new direction was thus given to affairs, and for a time the European war centered in the Spanish Peninsula.

29. In the first contests with the invaders the Spaniards were generally successful. A French squadron in the Bay of Cadiz, prevented from escaping by the presence of an English fleet, was forced to surrender:[a] Marshal Moncey, at the head of eight thousand men, was repulsed in an attack[b] on the city of Valencia: Saragossa, defended by the heroic Palafox, sustained a siege of sixty-three days;[c] and, although reduced to a heap of ruins, drove the French troops from its walls: Cor'dova was indeed taken[d] and plundered by the French marshal Dupont, yet that officer himself was soon after compelled to surrender at Baylen,[1] with eight thousand men, to the patriot general Castanos. This latter event occurred on the 20th of July, the very day on which Joseph Bonaparte made his triumphal entry into Madrid. But the new king himself was soon obliged to flee, and the French forces were driven beyond the Ebro.[2]

30. In the meantime the spirit of resistance had extended to Portugal: a junta had been established at Oporto[3] to conduct the government: British troops were sent to aid the insurgents, and on the 21st of August Marshal Junot was defeated at Vimiera,[4] by Sir Arthur Wellesley. This battle was followed by the convention of Cintra,[5] which led to the evacuation of Portugal by the French forces.

31. Great was the mortification of Napoleon at this inauspicious beginning of the Peninsular war, and he deemed it necessary to take

1. *Baylen* is a town of Spain, in the province of Jaen, twenty-two miles north from the city of Jaen. It commands the road leading from Castile into Andalusia. (*Map* No. XIII.)

2. The *Ebro* (anciently *Iberus*) flows through the north-eastern part of Spain, and is the only great river of the peninsula that falls into the Mediterranean. Before the second Punic war it formed the boundary between the Roman and Carthaginian territories, and in the time of Charlemagne, between the Moorish and Christian dominions. (*Map* No. XIII.)

3. *Oporto*, an important commercial city and seaport of Portugal, is on the north bank of the Douro, two miles from its mouth, and one hundred and seventy-four miles north-east from Lisbon. (*Map* No. XIII.)

4. *Vimiera* is a small town of the Portuguese province of Estremadura, about thirty miles north-west from Lisbon. (*Map* No. XIII.)

5. *Cintra* is a small town of Portugal, twelve miles north-west from Lisbon. By the convention signed here Aug. 22d, 1808, the French forces were to be conveyed to France with their arms, artillery, and property. This convention was exceedingly unpopular in England. (*Map* No. XIII.)

a. June 14th.   b. June 28th.   c. June 14th, to Aug. 17th.   d. June 8th.

the field in person. Collecting his troops with the greatest rapidity in the early part of November he was in the north of Spain at the head of one hundred and eighty thousand men. He at once communicated his own energy to the operations of the army : the Spaniards were severely defeated at Reynosa,[a] Burgos,[b] and Tudela;[c] and on the 4th of December, Napoleon forced an entrance into the capital. The British troops, who were marching to the assistance of the Spaniards, were driven back upon Corunna,[2] and being there attacked

x. 1809.

while making preparations to embark, they compelled the enemy to retire, but their brave commander, Sir John Moore, was mortally wounded. On the following day the British abandoned the shores of Spain, and the possession of the country seemed assured to the French emperor.

32. A short time before the battle of Corunna Napoleon received despatches[e] which induced him to return immediately to Paris. The Austrian emperor, humbled, but not subdued, and stimulated by the warlike spirit of his subjects, once more resolved to try the hazards of war, while the best troops of Napoleon were occupied in the Spanish Peninsula. On the 8th of April large bodies of Austrian troops crossed the frontiers of Bohemia, of the Tyrol, and of Italy, and soon involved in great danger the dispersed divisions of Napoleon's army. On the 17th of the same month Napoleon arrived and took the command in person. Baffling the Austrian generals by the rapidity of his movements, he speedily concentrated his divisions, and in four days of combats and manoeuvres, from the 19th to the

---

1. *Reynosa, Burgos,* and *Tudela.* (See *Map* No. XIII.) Reynosa is forty-seven miles north-west from Burgos. Tudela is on the Ebro, one hundred and ten miles east from Burgos. Burgos is one hundred and thirty-four miles north of Madrid. At Reynosa Blake was defeated by the French under Marshal Victor: at Burgos the Spanish count de Belvidere was overthrown by Marshal Soult: and at Tudela Palafox and Castaños were beaten by Marshal Lannes.

2. *Corunna* is a city and seaport of Spain, at the north-western extremity of the kingdom. Sir John Moore was struck down by a cannon ball as he was animating a regiment to the charge. " Wrapped by his attendants in his military cloak, he was laid in a grave hastily formed on the ramparts of Corunna, where a monument was soon after constructed over h' uncoffined remains by the generosity of the French marshal Ney. Not a word was spoken at the melancholy interment by torch light took place : silently they laid him in his grave, while he distant cannon of the battle fired the funeral honors to his memory."—*Alison.*

This touching scene has been vividly described in one of the most beautiful pieces of poetry in the English language, beginning—

" Not a drum was heard, nor a funeral note,
As his corpse to the ramparts we hurried :
Not a soldier discharged his farewell shot
O'er the grave where our hero we buried "

a. Nov. 10th and 11th.   b. Nov. 10th.   c. Nov. 21st.
d. Jan. 16th, 1809.   e. Jan 1st, 1809.

22d inclusive, he completed the ruin of the Austrian army. On the last of these days he defeated the Archduke Charles at Eckmuhl,' and compelled him to recross the Danube. Rapidly following up his victories, he entered Vienna on the 13th of May, and although worsted in the battle of Aspern[2] on the 21st and 22d, on the 5th of July he gained a triumph at Wagram,[3] and soon after dictated a peace[a] by which Austria was compelled to surrender territory containing three and a half millions of inhabitants.

33. During the war with Austria, the brave Tyrolese had seized the opportunity to raise the standard of revolt; and it was not until two powerful French armies had been sent into their country that they were subdued. The British government also sent a fleet, and an army of forty thousand men, to make a diversion against Napoleon on the coast of Holland; but the expedition proved a failure The war still continued in the Spanish Peninsula, and Sir Arthur Wellesley was sent out by the British government with a large force to coöperate with the Spaniards. In the meantime difficulties had arisen between the French emperor and the Pope Pius VII.: French troops entered Rome; and by a decree[b] of Napoleon the Papal States[c] were annexed to the French empire. This was followed by a bull of excommunication[d] against Napoleon, whereupon the pope was seized and conveyed a prisoner into France, where he was de tained until the spring of 1814.

34. Near the close of 1809 the announcement was made that Napoleon was about to obtain a divorce from the Empress Josephine,

---

1. *Eckmuhl* is a small village of Bavaria, thirteen miles south of Ratisbon, and fifty-two miles north-east from Munich. Marshal Davoust, having particularly distinguished himself in the battle of the 22d, was raised by Napoleon to the dignity of prince of Eckmuhl. (*Map* No. XVII.)

2. *Aspern* is a small Austrian village on the eastern bank of the Danube, opposite the island of Loban, about two miles below Vienna. (*Map* No. XVII.) After two days' continuous fighting, with vast loss on both sides, Napoleon was obliged to withdraw his troops from the field, and take refuge in the island of Loban. Marshal Lannes, one of Napoleon's ablest generals, was mortally wounded on the field of Aspern, having both his legs carried away by a cannon ball. Napoleon was deeply affected on beholding the dying Marshal brought off the field on a litter, and extended in the agonies of death. Kneeling beside the rude couch, he wept freely.

3. *Wagram* is a small Austrian village eleven miles north-east of Vienna. (*Map* No. XVII.) In the battle of Wagram each party lost about twenty-five thousand men: few prisoners were taken on either side, and the Austrians retired from the field in good order. The French bulletin, copied by Sir Walter Scott, says the French took twenty thousand prisoners,—now admitted to be a grossly erroneous statement. The retreat of the Austrians, however, gave to Napoleon all the moral advantages of a victory.

a. Treaty of Vienna, Oct. 14th.   b. May 17th, 1809.
c. See Note, p.   d. June 11th

for the purpose of allying himself with one of the royal families of
Europe.   To Josephine Napoleon was warmly attached ; but reasons
of state policy were, in his breast, superior to the dearest affections

XI. 1810.   His first marriage having been annulled [a] by the French
senate, early in 1810 he received the hand of Maria
Louisa of Austria, daughter of the emperor Francis.   This marriage, which seemed permanently to establish Napoleon's power, by
uniting the lustre of descent with the grandeur of his throne, was
one of the principal causes of his final ruin, as it was justly feared
by the other European powers that, secured by the Austrian alliance,
he would strive to make himself master of Europe.   His conduct
towards Holland justified this suspicion.   Dissatisfied with his brother's government of that country, he, soon after, by an imperial de-
croe,[b] incorporated Holland with the French empire.   In the same
year Bernadotte, one of his generals, was advanced to the throne of
Sweden.   Napoleon continued his career of aggrandizement in the
central parts of Europe, and extended the French limits almost to
the frontiers of Russia, thereby exciting the strongest jealousy of
the Russian emperor, who renewed his intercourse with the court of
London, and began to prepare for that tremendous conflict with
France which he saw approaching.

35.   The war still continued in the Spanish peninsula.   Sir Arthur
Wellesley, who had recently been created Lord Wellington, had the
chief command of the English, Spanish, and Portuguese forces.   On
the 10th of July the Spanish fortress of Ciudad Rodrigo[1] surrendered to Marshal Massena, but on the 27th of September Massena
was defeated in an attack upon Wellington on the heights of Busaco.[2]
Wellington, still pursuing his plan of defensive operations, then retired to the strongly-fortified lines of Torres Vedras,[3] which defend-

1. *Ciudad Rodrigo* (in Spanish the-oo-dad' rod-ree-go, meaning, "the city Rodrigo,") is a
strong y-fortified city of Spain, fifty-five miles south-west from Salamanca.   In 1812 this city
was retaken by Wellington, an achievement which acquired for him the title of Duke of Ciudad
Rodrigo from the Spanish government. (*Map* No. XIII.)

2. *Busaco* is a mountain ridge starting from the northern bank of the river Mondego a few
miles north east of Coimbra, and extending north-west about eight miles.   On the summit of
the northern portion of this range, around the convent of Busaco, seventeen miles north-eas
of Coimbra, Wellington collected his whole army of fifty thousand men on the evening of September 26th, while Massena, with seventy-two thousand, lay at its foot, determined to force the
passage, which he attempted early on the following morning, but without success. (*Map* No
XIII.)

3. *Torres Vedras* is a small village on the road from Lisbon to Coimbra, twenty-four miles
north-west of the former.   The "Lines of Torres Vedras," constructed by Wellington in 1810,
consisted of three distinct ranges of defence, extending from the river Tagus to the Atlantic

a. Dec. 15th 1809.   b. July 9th, 1810.

ed the approaches to Lisbon. Massena followed, but in vain endeavored to find a weak spot where he could attack with any prospect
of success, and after continuing before the lines more than a month,
he broke up his position on the 14th of November, and, for the first
time since the accession of Napoleon, the French eagles commenced
a final retreat.

36. The early part of 1811 witnessed the siege of Badajoz[1] by
Marshal Soult, and its surrender to the French on the
10th of March; but this was soon followed by the battle XII. 1811.
of Albuera,[2] in which the united British and Spanish forces gained
an important victory. Many battles were fought during the remainder of the year, but they were attended with no important
results on either side.

37. The year 1812 opened with the surrender of the important
city of Valencia to Marshal Suchet on the 9th of Jan-
uary—the last of the long series of French triumphs in XIII. RUSSIAN CAMPAIGN, 1812.
the peninsula. On the same day Wellington, in another
quarter, laid siege to Ciudad Rodrigo; and the capture[a] of this place
by the British arms was soon followed [b] by that of Badajoz. Wellington, following up his successes, next defeated Marmont[c] in the
battle of Salamanca :[3] the intrusive king Joseph fled from Madrid, and on the next day the capital of Spain was in the possession of the British army. The concentration of the French forces
again compelled the cautious Wellington to retreat to Portugal; but
early in the following year, 1813, he resumed the offensive,—gained

Ocean,—the most advanced, embracing Torres Vedras, being twenty-nine miles in length,—the
second, about eight miles in the rear of the first, being twenty-four miles, and the third, or
" lines of embarcation," in the vicinity of Lisbon, designed to cover the embarcation of the
troops if that extremity should become necessary. More than fifty miles of fortifications, bris-
tling with six hundred pieces of artillery, and one hundred and fifty forts, flanked with abattis
and breastworks, and presenting, in some places, high hills artificially scarped, in others deep
and narrow passes carefully choked, and artificial pools and marshes made by damming up the
streams, were defended by seventy thousand disposable men. The French force under Massena
amounted to about the same number. (*Map* No. XIII.)

1. *Badajoz* is a city in the west of Spain, on the eastern bank of the Guadiana, about two
hundred m les south-west of Madrid, and one hundred and thirty-five miles east of Lisbon.
(*Map* No XIII.)

2. *Albuera* is a small town fourteen miles south-east of Badajoz. In the battle of Albuera,
fought May 16th, 1811, the allied British, Spanish, and Portuguese troops, were commanded by
Marshal Beresford, and the French by Marshal Soult. (*Map* No. XIII.)

3. *Salamanca* is a city of Leon in Spain, one hundred and nineteen miles north-west from
Madrid. It was known to the Romans by the name of *Salamantica*. During a long period it
was celebrated as being the seat of a University, which, in the fifteenth and sixteenth centuries,
was attended by from ten thousand to fifteen thousand students. (*Map* No. XIII.)

a. Jan. 12th. b. April 6th. c. July 22d. d. Aug. 11th.

the decisive battle[2] of Vittoria,[1] and before the close of the campaign drove the French across the Pyrenees into their own territories.

38. During these reverses to the French arms, events of greater magnitude than those of the peninsular war were occupying the personal attention of Napoleon. The jealousy of Russia at his repeated encroachments in Central and Northern Europe has already been mentioned : moreover, the commercial interests of Russia, in common with those of the other Northern powers, had been greatly injured by the measures of Napoleon for destroying the trade of England ; but the French emperor refused to abandon his favorite policy and the angry discussions between the cabinets of St. Petersburg and Versailles led to the assembling of vast armies on both sides, and the commencement of hostilities in the early part of the summer of 1812. Napoleon had driven Sweden to enter into an alliance with Russia and England ; but he arrayed around his standard the immense forces of France, Italy, Germany, the Confederation of the Rhine, Poland, and the two monarchies Prussia and Austria.

39. The " Grand Army" assembled in Poland for the Russian war amounted to the immense aggregate of more than five hundred thousand men, of whom eighty thousand were cavalry—the whole supported by thirteen hundred pieces of cannon. Nearly twenty thousand chariots or carts, of all descriptions, followed the army, while the whole number of horses amounted to one hundred and eighty-seven thousand. To oppose this vast army the Russians had collected, at the beginning of the contest, nearly three hundred thousand men : but as the war was carried into the interior their forces increased in numbers until the armies on both sides were nearly equal.

40. On the 24th of June, 1812, Napoleon crossed the Niemen at the head of the " Grand Army," and entered upon his ever memorable Russian campaign. As the enormous superiority of his forces rendered it hopeless for the Russians to attempt any immediate resistance, they gradually fell back before the invaders, wasting th country as they retreated. The wisdom of this course soon became apparent. A terrible tempest soon set in, and the horses in the French army perished by thousands from the combined effects of in-

---

Vittoria is a town in the Spanish province of Alava, on the road between Burgos and Bayonne, sixty miles north-east from the former. The battle of Vittoria almost annihilated the French power in Spain. (*Map* No. XIII.)

cessant rain and scanty forage : the soldiers sickened in great num
bers ; and before a single shot had been fired twenty-five thousand
sick and dying men filled the hospitals ; ten thousand dead horses
strewed the road to Wilna,[1] and one hundred and twenty pieces of
cannon were abandoned for want of the means of transport.

41. Still Napoleon pressed onward in several divisions, frequently
skirmishing with the enemy, and driving them before him, until he
arrived under the fortified walls of Smolensko, where thirty thousan
Russians made a stand to oppose him. A hundred and fifty cannon
were brought up to batter the walls, but without effect, for the thickness of the ramparts defied the efforts of the artillery.[a] But the
French howitzers set fire to some houses near the ramparts ; the
flames spread with wonderful rapidity, and during the night which
followed the battle a lurid light from the burning city was cast over
the French bivouacs, grouped in dense masses for several miles in
circumference. At three in the morning a solitary French soldier
scaled the walls, and penetrated into the interior ; but he found
neither inhabitants nor opponents. The work of destruction had
been completed by the voluntary sacrifice of the inhabitants, who had
withdrawn with the army, leaving a ruined city, naked walls, and the
cannon which mounted them, as the only trophy to the conqueror.

42. The division of the army led by Napoleon followed the
Russians on the road to Moscow, engaging in frequent but indecisive
encounters with the rear guard. When the retreating forces had
reached the small village of Borodino,[2] their commander, General
Kutusoff, resolved to risk a battle, in the hope of saving Moscow
On the evening of the 6th of September the two vast armies took their
positions facing each other,—each numbering more than a hundred
and thirty thousand men—the Russians having six hundred and forty
pieces of cannon, and the French five hundred and ninety. Napoleon
sought to stimulate the enthusiasm of his soldiers by recounting to
them the glories of Marengo, of Jena, and of Austerlitz ; while a
procession of dignified clergy passed through the Russian ranks, be
stowing their blessings upon the kneeling soldiers, and invoking the
aid of the God of battles to drive the invader from the land.

1. *Wilna*, the former capital of Lithuania, is at the confluence of the rivers Wilanka and
Wilna, eastern tributaries of the Niemen, about two hundred and fifty miles north-east from
Warsaw. Population nearly forty thousand, of whom more than twenty thousand are Jews
Map No. XVII.)

2. *Borodino* (bor-o-dee'-no) is a small village about seventy miles south-west from Moscow
on the small stream of the Kolotza, a tributary of the Moskwa.

a Aug. 11th.

43. At six o'clock on the morning of the 7th a gun fired from the French lines announced the commencement of the battle: the roar of more than a thousand cannon shook the earth: vast clouds of smoke, shutting out the light of the sun, arose in awful sublimity over the scene; and two hundred and sixty thousand combatants, led on in the gathering gloom by the light of the cannon and musketry engaged in the work of death. The battle raged with desolating fury until night put an end to its horrors. The slaughter was immense. The loss on both sides was nearly equal, amounting, in the aggregate, to ninety thousand in killed and wounded. The Russian position was eventually carried, but neither side gained a decisive victory.

44. On the day after the battle the Russians retired, in perfect order, on the great road to Moscow. Preparations were immediately made by the inhabitants for abandoning that city, long revered as the cradle of the empire; and when, on the 14th, Napoleon entered it, no deputation of citizens awaited him to deprecate his hostility but the dwellings of three hundred thousand persons were as silent as the wilderness. It seemed like a city of the dead. Napoleon took up his residence in the Kremlin, the ancient palace of the czars; but the Russian authorities had determined that their beloved city should not afford a shelter to the invaders. At midnight on the night of the 15th a vast light was seen to illuminate the most distant part of the city; fires broke out in all directions; and Moscow soon exhibited a vast ocean of flame agitated by the wind. Nine-tenths of the city were consumed, and Napoleon was driven to seek a temporary refuge for his army in the country; but afterwards returning to the Kremlin, which had escaped the ravages of the fire, he remained there until the 19th of October, when, all his proposals of peace being rejected, he was compelled to order a retreat.

45. The horrors of that retreat, which, during fifty-five days that intervened until the recrossing of the Niemen, was almost one continued battle, exceeded anything before known in the annals of war. The exasperated Russians intercepted the retreating army wherever an opportunity offered; and a cloud of Cossacks, hovering incessantly around the wearied columns, gradually wore away their numbers. But the severities of the Russian winter, which set in on the 6th of November, were far more destructive of life than the sword of the enemy. The weather, before mild, suddenly changed to intense cold: the wind howled frightfully through the forests, or swept over the

plains with resistless fury; and the snow fell in thick and continued showers, soon confounding all objects, and leaving the army to wander without landmarks through an icy desert.   Thousands of the soldiers, falling benumbed with cold, and exhausted, perished miserably in sight of their companions; and the route of the rear guard of the army was literally choked up by the icy mounds of the dead.   In their nightly bivouacs crowds of starving men prepared, around their scanty fires a miserable meal of rye mixed with snow water and horse flesh; but numbers never awoke from the slumbers that followed; and the sites of the night fires were marked by circles of dead bodies, with their feet still resting on the extinguished piles.   Clouds of ravens, issuing from the forests, hovered over the dying remains of the soldiers; while troops of famished dogs, which had followed the army from Moscow, howled in the rear, and often fell upon their victims before life was extinct.   The ambition of Napoleon had led the pride and the chivalry of Europe to perish amid the snows of a Russian winter; and he bitterly felt the taunt of the enemy, " Could the French find no graves in their own land ?"

46. Napoleon had first thought of remaining in winter quarters at Smolensko; but the exhausted state of his magazines, and the con centrating around him of vast forces of the enemy, which threatened soon to overwhelm him, convinced him that a protracted stay was impossible, and on the 14th of November the retreat was renewed— Napoleon, in the midst of his still faithful guards, leading the ad vance, and the heroic Ney bringing up the rear.   But the enemy harassed them at every step.   During the 16th, 17th, and 18th, in the battles of Krasnoi,[1] Napoleon lost ten thousand killed, twenty thousand taken prisoners, and more than a hundred pieces of cannon fell into the hands of the enemy.   The terrible passage of the Bere- sina,[2] which was purchased by the loss of sixteen thousand prisoners, and twenty-four thousand killed or drowned in the stream, completed the ruin of the Grand Army.   All subordination now ceased, and i was with difficulty that Marshal Ney could collect three thousand men on foot to form the rear guard, and protect the helpless multi tude from the indefatigable Cossacks; and when at length the few remaining fugitives reached the passage of the Niemen, the rear guard was reduced to thirty men.   The veteran marshal, bearing a musket, and still facing the enemy, was the last of the Grand Army

1. *Krasnoi* is a small town about thirty miles south-west from Smolensko. (*Map* No. XVII.)
2. The *Beresina* is a western tributary of the Dnieper. See *Map* No. XVII.

who left the Russian territory. Napoleon had already abandoned the remnant of his forces, and, setting out in a sledge for Paris, he arrived there at midnight on the 18th of December, even before the news of his terrible reverses had reached the capital. It has been estimated that, in this famous Russian campaign, one hundred and twenty-five thousand men of the army of Napoleon perished in battle; that one hundred and thirty-two thousand died of fatigue, hunger, and cold; and that nearly two hundred thousand were taken prisoners.

47. While these great events were transpiring on the continent of Europe, difficulties arose between the United States of America and Great Britain, which led to the opening of war between those two powers in the summer of 1812. Mexico was at this time passing through the struggles of her first Revolution; and a feeble war was still maintained between the French and British possessions in the Indian seas; but these events were of little interest in comparison with that mighty drama which was enacting around the centre of Napoleon's power, and which was converting nearly all Europe into a field of blood.

48. Notwithstanding his terrible reverses in the Russian campaign, Napoleon found that he still possessed the confidence of the French nation: he at once obtained from the senate a new levy of three hundred and fifty thousand men—took the most vigorous measures to repair his losses, and, having arranged his difficulties with the pope, on the 15th of April he left Paris for the theatre of war. In the meantime Prussia and Sweden had joined the alliance against him; a general insurrection spread over the German States; Austria wavered; and already the confederates had advanced as far as the Elbe. On the 2d of May Napoleon gained the battle of Lutzen, and a fortnight later that of Bautzen;[1] but as these were not decisive, on the 4th of July an armistice was agreed to, and a congress met at Prague to consider terms of peace.

xiv. 1813.

49. As Napoleon would listen to nothing calculated to limit his power, on the expiration of the armistice, on the 10th of August, war was renewed, when the Austrian emperor, abandoning the cause of his son-in-law, joined the allies. Napoleon at once commenced a series of vigorous operations against his several foes, and with vari-

1. *Bautzen* (bout-sn) is a town of Saxony on the eastern bank of the river Spree, thirty-two miles north-east from Dresden. (*Map* No. XVII.)

ous success fought the battles of Culm,[1] Gross-Beren,[2] the Katsbach,[3] and Dennewitz,[4] in which the allies, although not decidedly victorious, were constantly gaining strength. In the first battle of Leipsic, fought on the 16th of October, the result was indecisive, but in the battle of the 18th the French were signally defeated, and on the following morning began a retrograde movement towards the Rhine. Pressed on all sides by the allies, great numbers were made prisoners during the retreat; about eighty thousand, left to garrison th Prussian fortresses, surrendered; the Saxons, Hanoverians, and Hollanders, threw off the French yoke; and it was at this time that Wellington was completing the expulsion of the French from Spain.

50. The year 1814 opened with the invasion of France, on the eastern frontiers, by the Prussian, Russian, and Austrian armies; while Wellington, having crossed the Pyrenees, laid siege to Bayonne: Bernadotte, the old comrade of Napoleon, but now king of Sweden, was marching against France at the head a hundred thousand men; and Murat, king of Naples, brother-in-law of the French emperor, eager to secure his crown, entered into a secret treaty with Austria for the expulsion of the French from Italy. Never did the military talents of Napoleon shine with greater lustre than at this crisis. During two months, with a greatly inferior force, he repelled the attacks of his enemies, gained many brilliant victories, and electrified all Europe by the rapidity and skill of his movements. But the odds were too great against him; the enemy had crossed the Rhine, and while, by a bold movement, Napoleon threw himself into the rear of the allies, hoping to intimidate them into a retreat, they marched upon Paris, which was compelled to capitulate before he could come to its relief. Two days later the emperor was formally deposed by the senate, and, on the 6th of April, with a trembling hand, he signed an unconditional abdication of the thrones of France and Italy. By a treaty concluded between him and the allies on the 11th, Napoleon was promised the sovereignty of the

XV 1814.

1. *Culm* is a small town in the north of Bohemia, at the foot of the Erze-Gebirg mountains, about fifty miles north-west from Prague. On the 30th of August, 1813, the French under Vandamme were utterly overwhelmed by the allied Austrians, Russians, and Prussians, commanded by Barclay de Tolly. (*Map* No. XVII.)

2. *Gross-Beren* (groce-bären) is a small village a short distance south of Berlin, and east of Potsdam (*Map* No. XVII.)

3. The *Katsbach* (kats-back) is a western tributary of the Oder, in Silicia. The battle, or several battles of that name, were fought near the eastern bank of that stream, west of Liegnitz, and fifty-five miles north-west from Breslau. (*Map* No. XVII.)

4. *Dennewitz* is a small village of Prussian Saxony, seven miles north-east from Wittemberg (*Map* No. XVII.)

island of Elba,' and a pension of one hundred thousand pounds per annum. On the 3d of May, Louis XVIII., returning from his long exile, reëntered Paris: to conciliate the French people he gave them a constitutional charter, and soon after concluded a formal treaty with the allies, by which the continental dominions of France were restricted to what they had been in 1792.

51. The final settlement of European affairs had been left to a general congress of the ministers of the allied powers, which assembled at Vienna on the 25th of September; but while the conferences were still pending, the congress was thrown into consternation by the announcement that Napoleon had left Elba. An extensive conspiracy had been formed throughout France for restoring the fallen emperor, and on the 1st of March, 1815, he landed at Frejus, accompanied by only eleven hundred men:—everywhere the soldiery received him with enthusiasm: Ney, who had sworn fidelity to the new government, went over to him at the head of a force sent to arrest his progress; and on the evening of the 20th of March he reëntered the French capital, which Louis XVIII. had left early in the morning. With the exception of Augereau, Marmont, Macdonald, and a few others, all the officers, civil and military, embraced his cause;—at the end of a month his authority was reëstablished throughout all France; and he again found himself at the summit of power, by one of the most remarkable transitions recorded in history.

xvi. 1815.

52. In vain Napoleon now attempted to open negotiations with the allied powers, and professed an ardent desire for peace; the allies denounced him as the common enemy of Europe, and refused to recognize his authority as emperor of the French people. All Europe was now in arms against the usurper, and it was estimated that, by the middle of summer, six hundred thousand effective men could be assembled against him on the French frontiers. But nothing which genius and activity could accomplish was wanting on the part of Napoleon to meet the coming storm;—and in a country that seemed drained of men and money, he was able, by the 1st of June, to put

---

1. *Elba*, (the *Œtholia* of the Greeks, and the *Iloa* or *Ilva* of the Romans,) is a mountainous island of the Mediterranean, between the Italian coast and Corsica, six or seven miles from the nearest point of the former, and having an area of about one hundred and fifty square miles. It derives its chief historical interest from its having been the residence and empire of Napoleon from the 3d of May 1814, to the 26th of February 1815. During this short period a road was opened between the two principal towns, trade revived, and a new era seemed to have dawned upon the island. (*Map* No. VIII.)

on foot an army of two hundred and twenty thousand veterans, who had served in his former wars.

53. His policy was to attack the allies in detail, before their forces could be concentrated, and with this view he hastened across the Belgian frontier on the 15th of June, with a force numbering, at that point, one hundred and twenty thousand men. On the 16th he defeated the Prussians, under Blucher, at Ligny,[1] but at the same time Ney was defeated by Wellington at Quatre Bras.[2] The defeat of the Prussians induced Wellington to fall back upon Waterloo,[3] where, at eleven o'clock on the morning of the 18th, he was attacked by Napoleon in person, while, at the same time, large bodies of French and Prussians were engaged at Wavre.[4] On the field of Waterloo the combat raged during the day with terrific fury—Napoleon in vain hurling column after column upon the British lines, which withstood his assaults like a wall of adamant; and when, at length, at seven in the evening, he brought up the Imperial Guard for a final effort, it was driven back in disorder. At the same time Blucher, coming up with the Prussians, completed the rout of the French army. The broken host fled in all directions, and Napoleon himself, hastening to Paris, was the herald of his own defeat. Once more the capital capitulated, and was occupied by foreign troops: Napoleon a second time abdicated the throne, and, after vainly attempting to escape to America, surrendered himself to a British man-of-war. He was banished by the allies to the island of St. Helena,[5] where he died on the 5th of May,

1. *Ligny* is a small village on the small stream of the same name, two or three miles north-east of Fleurus, and about eighteen miles east of south from Waterloo. (*Maps* Nos. XII. and XV.)

2. *Quatre Bras* (kah-tr-brah "four arms,") is at the meeting of four roads about seventeen miles south from Brussels, and nearly ten miles south from Waterloo. (*Maps* Nos. XII. and XV.)

3. *Waterloo* is a small village or hamlet of Belgium, nine miles south of Brussels, and on the south-western border of the forest of Soignies. The great road from Brussels leading south to Charleroi passes through Waterloo, about three-quarters of a mile south of which was the centre of the position of the allies, who occupied the crest of a range of gentle eminences, extending about two miles in length, and crossing the high road at right angles. The French army occupied a corresponding line of ridges nearly parallel, on the opposite side of the valley and about three-quarters of a mile distant. In the valley between these ridges the "Battle of Waterloo" was fought. (*Maps* Nos. XII. and XV.)

4. *Wavre* is a small village on the western bank of a small stream called the Dyle, nine miles a little south of east from Waterloo, and fifteen miles south-east from Brussels. The river Dyle is not deep, but at the period of the battle it was swollen by the recent heavy rain, and the roads were in a miry state. (*Maps* Nos. XII. and XV.)

5. *St. Helena* is an island of the Atlantic Ocean, belonging to Great Britain, in fifteen deg fifteen min. south lat., and twelve hundred miles west from the coast of Benguela in South Africa. Length ten and a-half miles, breadth six and a-half miles. It is a rocky island, the interior of which is a plateau about fifteen hundred feet above the level of the sea. The highest

1821, during one of the most violent tempests that had ever raged on the island—fitting time for the soul of Napoleon to take its departure. In his last moments his thoughts wandered to the scenes of his military glory, and his last words were those of command, as he fancied himself at the head of his armies.

54. After the capitulation of Paris, the tranquilization of France, and the future peace and safety of Europe, received the first attention of the allies. Louis XVIII. following in the rear of their rmies, entered the capital on the 8th of July; but the French people felt too deeply the humiliation of defeat to express any joy at his restoration. The mournful tragedy which followed, in the execution of Marshal Ney and Labedoyére for high treason in favoring Napoleon's return from Elba, after the undoubted protection which had been guaranteed them by the capitulation of Paris, was a stain upon the character of the allies; and although Ney's treason was beyond that of any other man, to the end of the world his guilt will be forgotten in the broken faith of his enemies, and the tragic interest and noble heroism of his death. The fate of Murat, king of Naples, was equally mournful, but less unjust. On Napoleon's landing at Frejus he had made a diversion in his favor by breaking his alliance with Austria, and commencing the war; but the cowardly Neapolitans were easily overthrown, and Murat was obliged to seek refuge in France. At the head of a few followers he afterwards made a descent upon the coast of Naples, in the hope of regaining his power; but being seized, he was tried by a military commission, condemned, and executed.

55. On the 20th of November, 1815, the second treaty of Paris was concluded between France and the allied powers, by which the French frontier was narrowed to nearly the state in which it stood in 1790 : twenty-eight million pounds sterling were to be paid by France for the expenses of the war, and a larger sum still for the

---

curtain summit is two thousand seven hundred and three feet in height. Jamestown, the port, and residence of the authorities, is the only town. Longwood, the residence of Napoleon, stands on the plateau, in the middle of an extensive park. After Napoleon's death the house was for some time uninhabited, but was finally converted into a kind of farming establishment ; and recently, the room in which the conqueror of Austerlitz breathed his last was occupied as a cart-house and stable !

Napoleon arrived at St. Helena on the 13th of October, 1815, and there he expired on the 5th of May, 1821. His remains, after having been deposited for nineteen years in a humble grave near the house, were, in 1840, conveyed with great pomp and ceremony to France, where, agreeably to the wish expressed in his last will, they now repose, in the Hôtel des Invalides, in Paris.

spoliations which she had inflicted on other powers during her Revolution, and for five years her frontier fortresses were to be placed in the hands of her recent enemies; while the vast treasures of art which adorned the museums of the Louvre—the trophies of a hundred victories—were to be restored to the States from which they had oeen pillaged by the orders of Napoleon. Mournfully the Parisians parted with these memorials of the glories of the consulate and the empire. The tide of conquest had now set against France herself.—her pride was broken—her humiliation complete—and the iron entered into the soul of the nation.

SECTION II.

FROM THE FALL OF NAPOLEON TO THE PRESENT TIME.

I. THE PERIOD OF PEACE: 1815—1820.

ANALYSIS. [TREATIES OF 1815.] 1. Treaty between Russia, Prussia, Austria, and England. The "Holy Alliance." General accession to it.—2. Its authorship, objects, and effects.—3. Condition of Europe. Continued popular excitement, but change in its objects.

4. The social contest in ENGLAND. Prosperity of England during the war.—5. Disappointed expectations. Causes of a general revulsion. Scarcity, in 1816.—6. Other contributing causes—diminished supply of the precious metals, &c. Demands of the Radicals.—7. Policy of the English government. Reforms granted, Reported conspiracy.—8. Stringent measures of government. The meeting at Manchester. [Manchester.] Continued complaints. Government carries all its important measures.—9. The piratical States of Northern Africa. [Barbary.] The United States of America and Algiers.—10. Chastisement of Algiers by an English squadron, in 1816.—11. Importance of these events. Decline of the Ottoman empire.

12. Situation of FRANCE at the time of the second restoration. Change in public feeling against the Bonapartists and Republicans. Punishment of the Revolutionists demanded.—13. Religious and political feuds. Atrocities.—14. Demands, and acts, of the Chamber of Deputies of 1815. Singular position of parties.—15. Policy of the king and ministry, and coup d'état (Koo-dä-tah) of Sept. 1816.—16. Effects of the new measures.

II. REVOLUTIONS IN SPAIN, PORTUGAL, NAPLES, PIEDMONT, GREECE, FRANCE, BELGIUM, AND POLAND: 1820—1831.

I. SPAIN. 1. Spain from 1815 to 1820. Grant of a constitution in 1820. The party opposed to it. Action taken by the European powers.—2. Interference of the French in 1823. Remainder of the reign of Ferdinand. The course of England and the United States of America.

II. PORTUGAL. 1. Situation of Portugal. Revolution of 1820. Opposition to, and suppression of, the new constitution. Anarchy.—2. Don Pedro. Don Miguel's usurpation. Civil war. Foreign interference, and restoration of tranquillity.

III. NAPLES. 1. History of the kingdom of Naples previous to 1815.—2. The subsequent rule of Ferdinand. Popular insurrection in July, 1820. Grant of a constitution. Resolution of Russia, Austria, and Prussia, to put down the constitution. [Troppau.]—3. Conduct of Ferdinand. [Laybach.] An Austrian army suppresses the Revolution.

IV. PIEDMONT. 1. Account of the Sardinian monarchy. [Sardinia. Tessino.] Feelings and

complaints of the Piedmontese —2. Insurrection in Piedmont, March 1821. Success of the in
surgents, and abdication of the king. Austrian interference suppresses the Revolution.

V. The Greek Revolution. 1. History of Greece from 1481 to 1821. Proclamation of
Grecian independence in 1821. Suppression of the Revolution in Northern Greece. [Islam-
ism. Trieste.]—2. Beginning and spread of the Revolution in the Morea. Proclamation of
the Messenian senate. [Kalamatia.] Aid extended to the Greeks.—3. Rage, and cruelties, of the
Turks. Effects produced.—4. Events on the Asiatic coast, in Candia, Cypress, Rhodes, &c.
Successes and retaliatory measures of the Greeks. [Monembasia. Navarino. Tripolitza.]—5.
Defeat of the Turks at Thermopylæ. The peninsula of Cassandra laid waste by them. [Cas-
sandra.] The Turks driven from the country to the cities.

[1822.]—6. Acts of the Greek congress. [Epidaurus.] Dissensions and difficulties among
the Greeks.—7. Principal military events of 1822. [Scio. Napoli di Romania.]—8. Destruction
of Scio. Events in Southern Macedonia. [Salonica.]—8. Events in Western Greece. The
Greek fire-ships. [Tenedos.] Great loss of Turkish vessels. Taking of Napoli di Romania.

[1823.]—9. Events of the war during the year 1823. [Missolonghi.] The poet Lord Byron.
[1824.]—10. The Turks besiege Negropont, subdue Candia, reduce Ipsara, and attack Samos.
The Egyptian fleet. [1825-6.]—11. Successes of Ibrahim Pacha in the Morea. Siege and fall
of Missolonghi. [Salona.] Fate of the inhabitants of Missolonghi.—12. Danger apprehended
from the successes of Ibrahim Pacha, and treaty of London, July 1827.—13. Allied squadron
sent to the archipelago. Battle of Navarino. Rage of the Porte.—14. French and English army
sent to the Morea, 1828. War between Russia and Turkey. [Pruth.] Convention with Ibrahim Pacha. Successes of the Greeks. Retaliatory measures of the sultan.—15. Protocol of the
allies, Jan. 1827. [Cyclades.] Successes of the Russians, and peace of Adrianople. [Balkan
Mts.]—16. Unsettled condition of the country and its subsequent history.

VI. The French Revolution of 1830. 1. Beginning of the reign of Charles X. Principles
of his government and opposition of the people. The Polignac ministry, 1829.—2. The royal
speech at the opening of the Chambers in 1830. Effects. Reply of the Chambers. Dissolution
of the Chambers.—3. War with Algiers.—4. Continued excitement in France. Result of the
elections. Course pursued by the ministry. The three ordinances of July 26th. Accompany
ing report of the ministers.—5. The course pursued by the public journals. Excitemen.
throughout Paris. Apathy of the king and ministers.—6. Events of the 27th. Marmont.
Arming of the people.—7. On the 28th the riot assumes the aspect of a Revolution. The con
test during the day. Its results.—8. Renewal of the contest on the third day. Defection of
the troops of the line, and success of the revolution. Installation of a provisional government.
Louis Phillippe elected king.—9. Alarm of the continental sovereigns. The emperor of Russia.
Charles X. and his ministers.

VII. Belgium. 1. Effects of the French Revolution upon Europe. Revolution in Belgium.
—2. Vain attempts at reconciliation. Declaration of Belgian independence. Protocol of the
five great European powers. Selection of a king. [Saxe-Coburg, Gotha.] Siege and surrender of Antwerp. Prosperity of Belgium.

VIII. Polish Revolution. 1. Disposition made of Poland by the congress of Vienna. Alexander's arbitrary government of Poland.—2. The government of Poland under the emperor
Nicholas. Character of Constantine. Effect of his barbarities. Secret societies. [Volhynia.]
—3. Revolutionary outbreak at Warsaw, Nov. 1830. A general rising in Warsaw. The pro
visional government.—4. Fruitless attempts to negotiate. Russian and Polish forces. Opening
events of the war.—5. Night attacks and rout of the Russians. [Bug River.] Conduct of
Prussia and Austria.—6. Battle of Ostrolenka. [Minsk. Ostrolenka.] Death of Diebitsch and
Constantine. Conspiracy at Warsaw.—7. Dissensions among the Poles. Fall of Warsaw and
end of the war. Fate of the Polish generals, soldiers, and nobility. Result.

III. ENGLISH REFORMS. FRENCH REVOLUTION OF 1848. REVOLUTIONS IN THE
GERMAN STATES, PRUSSIA, AND AUSTRIA. REVOLUTIONS IN ITALY.
HUNGARIAN WAR. USURPATION OF LOUIS NAPOLEON.

I. English Reforms. 1. England from 1820 to 1830. Reforms obtained in 1828 and 1829.
Resignation of the Wellington ministry, 1830. The whig ministry of Earl Grey. Lord Russell'
Reform bill:—lost in the Commons.—2. Dissolution of Parliament. Result of the new elections.
Second defeat of the Reform bill 1831. Popular resentment, and riots. [Derby. Bristol.]—3

Character, and situation, of Ferdinand, who abdicates the thror e. The Hunga 1an Diet refuses to acknowledge his successor. Failure of the attempt at negotiations.—10. Defection of several of the Hungarian leaders,—but general adherence to Kossuth and the country. Want of arms—but partially supplied. Hungarian force.—11. Austrian plan of invasion. Austrians enter Peath, Jan. 1849, and the government retires to Debreczin. Concentration of the H ungarian forcer. General Bem. [Debreczin. Comorn. Eperies. Bukowina.]—12. Loss of Esseck. Bem is at first repulsed. His final successes. [Esseck. Wallachs. Hermanstadt. Cronstadt. Tom wwar.]—13. Dembinski. Operations in the valley of the Theiss. [Szegedin. Maros. Ka polna, &c.] Battles of Kapolna.—14. Gorgey. His victories over the Austrians. [Tapiobiszke, Godollo. Waitzen. Nagy Sarlo.] Siege of Buda. [Buda.]—15. Constitution for the Austrian empire. Declaration of Hungarian independence. Kossuth governor of Hungary.—16. Aus "ian and Russian preparations for a second campaign. The Hungarian forces.—17. Invasion of Hungary in June. [Presburg. Bartfeld.]—18. Gradual concentration of the enemies of Hungary. [Hegyes.] Barbarities of Haynau.—19. Gorgey's retreat to Arad. [Onod. Tokay. Arad.] Want of concert among the Hungarian generals.—20. Retreat of Dembinski. Defeat at Temeswar, and breaking up of the southern Hungarian army. Gorgey's failure to support Dembinski. His suspected fidelity. Supreme power conferred upon him.—21. Gorgey's treason, and surrender of his army, Aug. 13th, 1849.—22. Previous successes of the Hungarians in the vicinity of Comorn. [Raab.] Surrender of Comorn, Sept. 29th.—23. Fate of Kossuth, Bem, Dembinski, &c. [Widdin.]—24. The closing tragedy of the Hungarian war. Fate of the inferior officers, Hungarian soldiers, &c.

VI. USURPATION OF LOUIS NAPOLEON. 1. Election of a chief magistrate in France in 1848. The six candidates. Cavaignac, and Louis Napoleon. Election of the latter. Inauguration and oath of office.—2. History of Louis Napoleon down to the period of his election. [Fortress of Ham.]—3. His declaration of principles. Jealousy of him. Parties in the Assembly.—4. Want of confidence between the President and Assembly. Acts of the Assembly.—5. Proposed revision of the constitution.—6. President's message of November 1851. Increasing animosity of the Assembly against the President.—7. An approaching crisis,—how anticipated by Louis Napoleon. Circumstances of the *coup d'etat* of December 2d.—8. Meeting, and arrest, of members of the Assembly. The public press. Decree for an election. Insurrection of December 4th, suppressed by the military.—9. Result of the elections of December. The new constitution. Louis Napoleon President for ten years. Assumes the title of emperor.

I. THE PERIOD OF PEACE: 1815—1820.

1. On the day of the signing of the treaty of Paris, another was concluded between Russia, Prussia, Austria, and Eng-

1. TREATIES OF 1815.

land, designed as a measure of security for the allied powers, and declaring that Napoleon Bonaparte *and his family* should be forever excluded from the throne of France. On the same day a third treaty, of notorious celebrity, called "The Holy Alliance," was subscribed by the emperors of Russia and Austria, and the king of Prussia, whr bound themselves, " in conformity with the principles of Holy Scripture,—to lend each other every aid, assistance, and succor, on every occasion." This treaty was ere long acceded to by nearly all the continental powers as parties to the compact, although the ruling prince of England declined signing it, on the ground that the English constitution prevented him from becoming a party to any convention that was not countersigned by a responsible minister.

2. The terms of the Holy Alliance were drawn by the young Russian emperor Alexander, whose enthusiastic benevolence prompted him to devise a plan of a common international law that should substitute the peaceful reign of the Gospel in place of the rude empire of the sword. But the law of the Holy Alliance, although beneficent in its origin, was to be interpreted by absolute monarchs: as t was evident that its only active principle would be the maintenance of despotic power, under the mask of piety and religion, it was justly egarded with dread and jealousy by the liberal party throughout Europe, and was in reality made a convenient pretext for enforcing the doctrine of passive obedience, and resisting all efforts for the es tablishment of constitutional freedom.

3. The treaties of 1815 both closed the ascendency of imperial France in Europe, and terminated, for a time at least, the revolutionary movements in the civilized world. Twenty-five years of war had exhausted the treasures of Europe, and covered her soil with mourning, and never before had the sweets of repose been so eagerly coveted by rulers and people. But although the nations had tired of the mingled horrors and glories of military strife, the excitement occasioned by the revolutionary wars continued, and, for want of other channels of action, seized hold of the social passions of the masses : military gave place to democratic ambition—the old ante-revolutionary contest between despotism and democracy revived,—to be followed by other revolutions still, until one or the other principle shall triumph—until, in the language of Napoleon, Europe shall become either Cossack or Republican.

4. In England, the social contest, wearing a milder aspect than on the continent, displayed itself in the legal strife for government relief and parliamentary reforms. During a long and expensive war, England had enjoyed extraordinary domestic prosperity : since the year 1792 her population had increased more than four millions, notwithstanding the absorption of five hundred thousand men in the army and navy : the exports, imports, and tonnage, of the kingdom, had more than doubled since the war began ; and although the public debt had grown to an enormous amount, agriculture, commerce, and manufactures, had gone on increasing, during the whole struggle, in an unparallel d ratio

II.
ENGLAND.

5. It was confidently anticipated, not only by the ardent and en thusiastic, but also by the prudent and sagacious, that when the enormous expense of the war establishment should be removed, and

peace had thrown open the ports of all Europe to the enterprise of British merchants, the tide of national prosperity would rise still higher and higher; but never were hopes more cruelly disappointed. Exports, to an enormous amount, being suddenly thrown into countries impoverished by war, glutted the foreign market; and the consignments, in most instances, were sold for little more than half their original cost—spreading ruin throughout the commercial interests. Moreover, the opening of the European and American ports for the the supplies of grain, glutted the home market of England; and prices of every species of agricultural produce soon fell to two-thirds of what they had been during the closing scenes of the war: a season of unusual scarcity, in 1816, threatening a famine, increased the general distress, which, like a pall of gloom, enshrouded the whole kingdom.

6. Other causes, in addition to those originating in the mere transition from a state of war to one of peace, doubtless contributed to the general revulsion in business, among which may be mentioned, as the most prominent, the greatly diminished supply of the precious metals from South America,[a] owing to the unsettled state of that country then occupied with revolutionary wars, and the rapid contraction of the paper currency of Great Britain, in anticipation of a speedy return to specie payments. But the English Radical or Republican party attributed the difficulties to excessive taxation and the measures of a corrupt government; and a vehement outcry was raised for parliamentary reform, and retrenchment in all branches of public expenditure.

7. The English government, wiser than the continental powers, has ever had the prudence to make reasonable concessions to reasonable popular demands, before the spark of discontent has been blown into the blaze of revolution; and now, after a spirited contest, a heavy property tax, that had been patiently submitted to as a necessary war measure, was repealed, amid the universal transports of the people: the remission of other taxes followed, and, in one year, a reduction of thirty-five million pounds sterling was made from the national expenditure, although strongly opposed by the ministry. Still the distress continued; the popular feeling against the government increased; numerous secret political societies were organized among the disaffected; and early in the following year (1817) a com-

---

a. From 1815 to 1816 the amount of gold and silver coin produced from the mines of South America fell from about seven million pounds sterling to five and a half million pounds.

mittee of parliament reported that an extensive conspiracy existed, chiefly in the great towns and manufacturing districts, for the over-throw of the monarchy, and the establishment of a republic in its stead.

8. In consequence of the information, greatly exaggerated, which had been communicated to the committee, ministers were enabled to carry through parliament bills for suspending the privileges of the writ of habeas corpus, and for suppressing tumultuous meetings, de-bating societies, and all unlawful organizations. Armed with ex-ensive powers, government took the most active measures for putting a stop to the threatened insurrection : a few mobs were suppressed ; many persons were arrested on a charge of high treason ; and several were convicted, and suffered death. In 1819 a large and peaceable meeting at Manchester,[1] assembled to discuss the question of parlia-mentary reforms, was charged by the military, and many lives in-humanly sacrificed ; but all attempts in parliament for an inquiry into the conduct of the Manchester magistrates, under whose orders the military had acted, were defeated. Although the people still justly complained of grievous burdens of taxation, and unequal rep resentation in parliament, those evils were not so oppressive as to in-duce them to incur the hazards of revolution ; and government, having yielded to the point where danger was past, was sufficiently strong to carry all its important measures.

9. An event of general interest that occurred soon after the close of the European war was the merited chastisement of the piratical State of Algiers. During a long period the Barbary[2] powers had carried on a piratical warfare against those nations that were not suf ficiently powerful to prevent or punish their depredations. From the year 1795 to 1812 the United States of America had preserved peace with Algiers by the payment of an annual tribute ; but in the latter year the Dey, believing that the war with England would render the Americans unable to protect their commerce in the Mediterranean, commenced a piratical warfare against all American vessels that fell in the way of his cruisers. In the month of June 1815, an Ameri-can squadron, under the command of Commodore Decatur, being sent

1. *Manchester*, the great centre of the cotton manufacture of Great Britain, and the greatest manufacturing town in the world, is situated on the Irwell, an affluent of the Mersey, thirty-one miles east from Liverpool. (*Map* No. XVI.)

2. *Barbary* is the name that has been usually given, in modern times, to that portion of northern Africa bordering on the Mediterranean, and lying between the western frontier of Egypt and the Atlantic. The name *Barbary* is derived from that of its ancient inhabita ts, the *Berbers*.

to the Mediterranean, after capturing several Algerine vessels, compelled Algiers, Tripoli, and Tunis, to release all American prisoners in their possession, pay large sums of money, and relinquish all future claims to tribute from the United States.

10. In the following year, the continued piracies of the Algerines upon some of the smaller European States that claimed the protection of England, induced the British government to send out a powerful squadron, with directions to obtain from the Dey unqualified abolition of Christian slavery, or, in case of refusal, to destroy, if possible, the nest of pirates whose tolerance had so long been a disgrace to Christendom. On the 27th of August the British fleet, commanded by Lord Exmouth, appeared before Algiers, whose fortifications, admirably constructed, and of the hardest stone, were defended by nearly five hundred cannon and forty thousand men. No answer being returned to the demands of the British government, the attack was commenced in the afternoon of the same day; and although the defence was most spirited, by ten in the evening all the fortifications that defended the approaches by sea were totally ruined, while the shot and shells had carried destruction and death throughout the city. On the following morning the Dey submitted, agreeing to abolish Christian slavery forever, and immediately restoring twelve hundred captives to their country and friends. The total number liberated at Algiers, Tripoli, and Tunis, was more than three thousand.

11. The humiliation of the piratical Barbary powers by the Americans in 1815, and the battle of Algiers in the following year, were events highly important to the general interests of humanity, not only from their immediate results, but as the beginning of the decisive ascendency of the Christian over the Mohammedan world. Former triumphs of the cross over the crescent had averted subjugation from Christendom, or had been obliterated by subsequent disasters; but since the battle of Algiers, the followers of the prophet nave seen, and mournfully submitted to, their destiny; Algiers has since become a province of a Christian State; and the Ottoman empire is only saved from dissolution by the jealousies of its Christian neighbors.

12. The situation of France at the time of the second restoration of Louis XVIII., with a vast foreign army quartered upon her people, an empty treasury, and an unsettled government, was gloomy in the extreme. With a vacillation peculiar

III. FRANCE.

to the French people, public opinion had already turned against the
Bonapartists and the Republicans, who were regarded as the authors
of all the evils under which the nation suffered; and the king soon
found himself seriously embarrassed by the ardor of his own friends.
Punishment of the Revolutionists, and a restoration of the powers
and privileges of the nobility and the clergy, were violently demanded by the Royalists; but, fortunately, the extreme danger of any
violent reactionary movement was too manifest to permit the king
te intrust the government to the ultraists of his own party.

13. Had it not been for the presence of a large foreign army
France might again have been doomed to the horrors of civil war:
as it was, the party feuds of centuries between the Roman Catholics
and Protestants, revived by the imbittered feelings of the moment,
broke forth anew in the south of France : the Royalists demanded
vengeance against the Republicans; and political zeal combined with
religious enthusiasm to arouse the worst passions of the people, and
incited to numerous massacres, which recalled the memory of the
bloodiest period of the Revolution. Although the king denounced
these atrocities, and called upon the magistrates to bring the guilty
parties to justice, the latter were screened from arrest, or, if taken,
were acquitted in face of the clearest evidence of their guilt.

14. The Chamber of Deputies, at its first meeting, in the autumn
of 1815, urgently demanded of the king that those "who had im
perilled alike the throne and the nation should be delivered over to
the just severity of the tribunals :" stringent laws were passed punishing seditious words ; courts martial were established for trying political offences; and when the king, after the execution of Ney, Labedoyére, and a few others, proposed a general amnesty, the chamber
had prepared, and demanded the proscription of, a list of twelve hundred additional victims ; and in order to secure the amnesty the king
was compelled, against his inclination for moderate measures, to assent
to an amendment providing for the perpetual banishment of all those
who had voted for the death of his brother, the unfortunate Louis
XVI. France presented the singular spectacle of an ascendant Royalist party arrayed in opposition to the king, who, in order to check
their undue zeal, was compelled to ally himself with the Republi
cans, the natural enemies of his cause.

15. Although the ultra Royalists controlled the action of the legislature, there was still a powerful party of ultra Revolutionists
among the people ; and it was the policy of the king and his ministry

to guard against the danger of the ascendency of either, by conforming to the general principles which the Revolution had impressed upon the nation. As the legislative body continually thwarted the government, it was determined to alter the composition of the representatives by a *coup d'etat*, or arbitrary ordinance of the king; and accordingly, on the 5th of September, 1816, a royal ordinance was published, which dissolved the Chamber of Deputies, arbitrarily diminished the number of representatives, and secured the election of a majority of those who were attached to the measures of the ministerial party.

16. The royal ordinance of September, although conferring the right of suffrage upon only one hundred thousand out of thirty millions of the population of France, was far more democratic than accorded with the wishes of the Royalists, who feared that the new representatives, chosen mostly from the middle classes of landed proprietors, would incline towards a republican form of government, under which they might most effectually secure their own rights, and divide among themselves the honors and emoluments of office.[a] And such, indeed, was the result. The electoral law proclaimed by the king, and the subsequent creation[b] of a large body of peers taken from the Liberals and Bonapartists, soon placed the control of government in the hands of the democratic party, which was naturally antagonistic to the power which had given it influence; but the Royalists, who at the restoration had seemed the ruling party, were unwilling to resign the control of the government; and the struggle continued to increase in violence between them and the Liberals, until it finally resulted in the Revolution of 1830, and the overthrow of the monarchy.

II. REVOLUTIONS IN SPAIN, PORTUGAL, NAPLES, PIEDMONT GREECE, FRANCE, BELGIUM, AND POLAND: 1820—1831.

I. SPAIN. 1. During the period of general peace, from 1815 to 820, Spain, under the rule of the restored Ferdinand, was in a state of constant political agitation; and in 1820 an insurrection of the soldiery compelled the king to restore to his subjects the free and almost republican constitution of 1812. The Republicans, however,

a. By the ordinance of Sept. 5th, 1816, the right of suffrage was established on the basis of the payment of three hundred francs direct taxes to the government.
b. March 5th, 1819.

who thus obtained the direction of the government, showed little wisdom or moderation; and a large party, directed by the monks and friars, and supported by the lower ranks of the populace, was formed for the restoration of the monarchy.   Several of the European powers, in a congress held at Verona, adopted a resolution to support the authority of the king in opposition to the constitution which he had granted; but England stood aloof, and to France was intrusted the execution of the odious measure of suppressing democratic principles in Spain.

2. Accordingly, early in the year 1823, a French army of a hundred thousand men, under the command of the Duke d'Angoulême, entered Spain: the patriots made but a feeble resistance, and the king was soon restored to absolute authority, on the ruins of the constitution.   The remainder of the reign of Ferdinand, who died in 1833, was characterized by the complete suppression of all liberal principles in politics and religion, and the revival of the ancient abuses which had so long disgraced the Spanish monarchy.   England and the United States severely censured the interference of France in the domestic affairs of the Spanish nation, and showed their sympathy with the cause of the oppressed by recognizing, at as early a period as possible, the independence of the Spanish South American republics, which had recently renounced their allegiance to Spain.

II. PORTUGAL.   1. The adjoining kingdom of Portugal was a prey to similar commotions.   The emigration of the king and court to Brazil during the peninsular war, has already been mentioned, (p. 488.)   The nation being dissatisfied with the continued residence of the court in Brazil, which in fact made Portugal a dependency of the latter, and desiring some fundamental changes in the frame of government, at length in August 1820 a revolution broke out, and a free constitution was soon after established, having for its basis the abolition of privileges, the legal equality of all classes, the freedom of the press, and the formation of a representative body in the national legislature.   This constitution, being violently opposed by the clergy and privileged classes, who formed what was called the apostolical party, at the head of whom was Don Miguel, the king's younger son, was suppressed in 1823, and a state of anarchy continued until the death of the king in 1826, when the crown fell to Don Pedro, emperor of Brazil.

2. Don Pedro, however, resigned his right in favor of his infant daughter Donna Maria, at the same time granting to Portugal a

constitutional charter, and appointing his brother Don Miguel regent. Although the latter took an oath of fidelity to the charter, he soon began openly to aspire to the throne, and by means of an artful priesthood caused himself, in 1829, to be proclaimed sovereign of Portugal, while the charter was denounced as inconsistent with the purity of the Roman faith. The friends of the charter, aided by Don Pedro, who repaired to Europe to assert the rights of his daughter, organized a resistance, and after a sanguinary struggle during which they were once driven into exile, they obtained the promise of support from France, Spain, and England, who in 1834 entered into a convention to expel the younger brother from the Portuguese territories. Soon after, Don Miguel gave up his pretensions, and the young queen was placed upon the throne, since which time the country has remained comparatively tranquil.

III. NAPLES. 1. The kingdom of Naples, embracing Sicily and southern Italy, nearly identical with the Magna Græcia of antiquity had been erected into an independent monarchy in 1734, under the Infante Don Carlos of Spain, who took the name of Charles III. It continued under a succession of tyrannical or imbecile rulers of the Bourbon dynasty till 1798 : the Italian portion of the kingdom was then overrun by the French, who held it from 1803 till 1815, when it reverted to its former sovereign Ferdinand, who, during the French rule, had maintained his court in the Sicilian part of his kingdom.

2. Under the rule of Ferdinand, popular education was wholly neglected ; the roads, bridges, and other public works which the French had either planned or executed, were left unfinished, or fell into decay ; and yet the people were oppressively taxed, and a representative government was denied them. At length, on the 2d of July, 1820, the growing discontents of the people broke out in open insurrection, and a remonstrance was sent to the government demanding a representative constitution. One based on the Spanish constitution of 1812 was immediately granted, and the Neapolitan parliament was opened on the 1st of October following ; but on the same month a convention of the three crowned heads who formed the Holy Alliance, attended by ministers from most of the other European powers, met at Troppau ;[1] and it was there resolved by the

1. *Troppau,* the capital of Austrian Silesia, is situated on the Oppa, a tributary of the Oder, thirty-seven miles north-east from Olmutz. From 20th October to 20th November, 1820, it was the place of meeting of the diplomatic congress, which afterwards removed to Laybach. (*Mas No. XVII*)

sovereigns of Russia, Austria, and Prussia, to put down the Neapolitan constitution by force of arms.

3. France approved the measure, but the British cabinet remained
neutral. The old king Ferdinand, who had been invited to visit the
sovereigns at Laybach,[1] was easily convinced that his promises had
been extorted, and therefore were not binding; and Austrian troops
immediately prepared to execute the resolutions of the congress
while the aid of a Russian army was promised, if necessary. An
Austrian force of forty-three thousand men entered the Neapolitan
territory, heralded by a proclamation from Ferdinand, calling his
subjects to receive the invaders as friends. A few slight skirmishes
took place, but the country was quickly overrun; foreign troops garrisoned the fortresses; the king's promise of complete amnesty was
forgotten; and courts martial and executions closed the brief drama
of the Neapolitan Revolution.

IV. PIEDMONT. 1. Piedmont is the principal province of the Sardinian monarchy;[2] and the latter, first recognized as a separate kingdom by the treaty of Utrecht in 1713, comprises the whole of northern Italy west of the Tessino,[3] together with the island of Sardinia
in the Mediterranean. The Piedmontese, never considering themselves properly as Italians, had been proud of their annexation to
France under the rule of Napoleon; and on the restoration of the
monarchy they were the first of the Sardinian people to exhibit the
liberal principles of the French Revolutionists, and to complain of
the oppressive exactions imposed upon them by the government.

2. Scarcely had the Neapolitan Revolution been suppressed, when
an insurrection, beginning with the military, broke out in Piedmont.
On the 10th of March, 1821, several regiments of troops simultaneously mutinied; and it is believed that the malcontents were secretly favored by Charles Albert, a kinsman of the royal family, who

---

1. *Laybach*, the capital of Austrian Illyria, (which latter embraces the duchies of Carinthia
and Carniola,) is situated on a navigable stream, a tributary of the Save, fifty-four miles north-
east from Trieste. It is celebrated in diplomatic history for the congress held here in 1821.
(*Map* No. XVII.)

2. *Sardinia* (Kingdom of) embraces the territory of Piedmont, Genoa, and Nice, and the
adjacent duchy of Savoy on the west side of the Alps, together with the island of Sardinia.
Savoy, which was governed by its own counts as early as the tenth century, was the nucleus
of this monarchy. Genoa was annexed to the Sardinian crown at the peace of 1815. (*Map*
No. XVII.)

3. The *Tessino* or *Ticino* (anciently Ticinus, see p. 158,) having its sources in Mount St.
Gothard, flows southward, and after traversing the Lago Maggiore in its entire length, and
forming the boundary between Lombardy and Piedmont, falls into the Po at Pavia. (*Map* No.
XVII.)

afterwards became king of Sardinia. The seizure of the citadel of Turin, on the 12th, was followed, on the 13th, by the abdication of the king Victor Emanuel, in favor of his absent brother Charles Felix, and the appointment of Prince Albert as regent. While ef forts were made to organize a government, an Austrian army was assembled in Lombardy to put down the Revolution: the new king repudiated the acts of the regent, who threw himself on the Austrians for protection: on the 8th of April the insurgents were overthrown in battle; and on the 10th the combined royal and Austrian troops were in possession of the whole country. In Piedmont, as in Naples, Austrian interference, ever exerted on the side of tyranny, suppressed every germ of constitutional freedom.

V. THE GREEK REVOLUTION. 1. In the year 1481, Greece, the early and favored seat of art, science, and literature, was conquered by the Turks, after a sanguinary contest of more than forty years. The Venetians, however, were not disposed to allow its new masters quiet possession of the country; and during the sixteenth and seventeenth centuries it was the theatre of obstinate wars between them and the Turks, which continued till 1718, when the Turks were confirmed in their conquest by treaty. Although the Turks and Greeks never became one nation, and the relation of conquerors and conquered never ceased, yet the Turkish rule was quietly submitted to until 1821, when, according to previous arrangements, on the 7th of March Alexander Ypsilanti, a Greek, and then a major-general in the Russian army, proclaimed, from Moldavia, the independence of Greece, at the same time assuring his countrymen of the aid of Russia in the approaching contest. But the Russian emperor declined intervention; the Porte took the most rigorous measures against the Greeks, and called upon all Mussulmen to arm against the rebels for the protection of Islamism:[1] the wildest fanaticism raged in Constantinople, where hundreds of the resident Greeks were remorselessly murdered; and in Moldavia the bloody struggle was terminated with the annihilation of the patriot army and the flight of Ypsilanti to Trieste,[2] where the Austrian government seized and imprisoned him.

L 1821.

1. *Islamism*, from the Arabic word *salama*, "to be free, safe, or devoted to God," is the term which the followers of Mahomet apply to their religion. The term "Mohammedism" is as objectionable as the term "popery."

2. *Trieste*, a seaport town of Austrian Illyria, is near the north-eastern extremity of the Adriatic, seventy-three miles north-east from Venice. During the middle ages Trieste was the capital of a small republic. (*Map* No. XVII.)

2. In southern Greece no cruelties could quench the fire of liberty and sixteen days after the proclamation of Ypsilanti the Revolution of the Morea began at Suda, a large village in the northern part of Achaia, where eighty Turks were made prisoners. The revolution rapidly spread over the Morea and the islands of the Ægean : the ancient names were revived ; and on the 6th of April the Messenian senate, assembled at Kalamatia,[1] proclaimed that Greece had shaken off the Turkish yoke to save the Christian faith, and restore the ancient character of the country. From that time the Greeks found friends wherever free principles were cherished ; and from England and the United States large contributions of clothing and provisions were forwarded to relieve the sufferings inflicted by the wanton atrocities of the Turks.

3. The rage of the Turks was particularly directed against the Greek clergy, many of whom were murdered, among them the aged patriarchs of Constantinople and Adrianople ; and several hundred of the Greek churches were torn down, while the Christian ambassadors of neutral powers in vain remonstrated with the Turkish divan. These excesses, and the massacre of those whom the Turks took in arms, showed to the Greeks that the struggle in which they had engaged was one of life and death ; and it is not surprising, therefore, that the Greeks often retaliated when the power was in their hands.

4. During the summer months the Turks committed great depredations among the Greek towns on the coast of Asia Minor : the inhabitants of the island of Candia, who had taken no part in the insurrection, were disarmed, and the archbishops, and many of the priests, executed : in Cyprus, where also there had been no appearances of insurrection, the Greeks were disarmed, and their archbishop and other prelates murdered. The most barbarous atrocities were also committed at Rhodes, and other islands of the Grecian Archipelago, where the villages were burned, and the country desolated. But when in August the Greeks captured the strong Turkish fortresses of Monembasia[2] and Navarino,[3] and in October that of Tripolitza,[4]

---

1. *Kalamatia* is near the head of the Messenian Gulf, now called the Gulf of Kalmatia. Its ancient name was *Calama*. It is east of the Pamisus river—now the Pamitza. (*Map* No. I.)

2. The fortress of *Monembasia* is in the vicinity of the ancient Epidaurus, on the eastern coast of Laconia, forty-three miles south-east from Sparta. (*Map* No. I.)

3. *Navarino* is on the western coast of Messenia, near the ancient Pylus. It stands on the south side of a fine semi-circular bay of the same name, cut off from the sea by the long narrow island of Sphagia—anciently *Sphacteria*. (*Map* No. I.)

4. *Tripolitza*, a town of modern origin, and, under the Turks, the capital of the Morea, is about five miles north of *Tegea*, in the ancient Arcadia. Its name *Tripolitza*, "the three

they took a terrible revenge upon their enemies; and in Tripolitsa alone eight thousand Turks were put to death.

5. On the 5th and 6th of September the Greek general Ulysses defeated, near the pass of Thermopylæ, a large Turkish army which had advanced from Macedonia; but on the other hand the peninsula of Cassandra[1] was taken by the Turks, when three thousand Greeks were put to the sword; women and children were carried into slavery, and the flourishing peninsula converted into a desert waste. The Athenian Acropolis was garrisoned by the Turks, and the inhabitants of Athens fled to Salamis for safety; but in general, throughout all southern Greece, the Turks were driven from the country districts, and compelled to shut themselves up in the cities.

6. The year 1822 opened with the assembling of the first Greek

II. 1822.
congress at Epidaurus,[2] the proclaiming of a provisional constitution on the 13th of January, and the issuing, on the 27th, of a manifesto which announced the union of the Greeks under an independent federative government, under the presidency of Alexander Mavrocordato. But the Greeks, long kept in bondage, and unaccustomed to exercise the rights of freemen, were unable at once to establish a wise and firm government: they often quarreled among themselves; and their captain, or captains, who had exercised an independent authority under the government of the Turks, could seldom be brought to submit to the control of the central government. The few men of intelligence and liberal views among them, and the few foreign officers who entered their service, had a difficult task to perform; and all that enabled them to continue the struggle was the wretchedly undisciplined state of the Turkish armies.

7. The principal military events of 1822 were the destruction of Scio[3] by the Turks, the defeat of the Turks in the Morea, the successes of the Greek fire-ships, and the surrender of Napoli di Romania[4]

---

alias," is supposed to be derived from the circumstance of its having been constructed of the ruins of the three cities Tegea, Mantinea, and Pallantium. (*Map No. I.*)

1. The peninsula of *Cassandra* is the same as the ancient *Pellene*, at the eastern entrance of the Thermaic Gulf, now Gulf of Salonica. (*Maps Nos. I. and X.*)

2. *Epidaurus.* See Monembasia.

3. *Scio* (anciently *Chios*) is a celebrated and beautiful island, about thirty-two miles in length, near the Lydian coast of Asia Minor. In antiquity, and in modern times down to the dreadful catastrophe of 1822, the island, although for the most part mountainous and rugged, was cultivated with the greatest care and assiduity. It was called the "paradise of modern Greece." Scio aspired to the honor of being the native country of the first and greatest of poets,—

"The blind old man of Chio's rocky isle."

4. *Napoli di Romania* (the ancient *Nauplia*, the port of Argos) is situated on a point of land at the head of the Argolic Gulf, or Gulf of Nauplia. (*Map No. I.*)

to the Greeks. The Greek population of the flourishing and defenceless island of Scio had declined every invitation to engage in the Revolution, until a Greek fleet appeared on the coast in March 1822, when the peasants arose in arms against their Turkish masters attacked the citadel, and put the Turkish garrison to the sword. To punish the Sciots, on the 11th of April five thousand of the most bar barous of the Turkish Asiatic troops were landed on the island, which was given up to indiscriminate pillage and massacre; and in a few days the paradise of Scio was changed into a scene of desolation. According to the Turkish accounts, twenty thousand individuals were put to the sword, and a still greater number, mostly women and children, sold into slavery Soon after, one hundred and fifty villages in southern Macedonia experienced the fate of Scio; and the pacha of Salonica[1] boasted that he had destroyed, in one day, fifteen hun dred women and children

8. In the meantime the Turks had made extensive preparations to conquer western Greece—the ancient Epírus, Acarnánia, and Ætólia and relieve the Turkish garrisons in the Morea; but after some successes they experienced a series of defeats so disastrous, that, during the month of August alone, more than twenty thousand Turks perished by the sword. In June, soon after the destruction of Scio, forty-seven Greeks rowed a number of fire-ships into the midst of the fleet of the enemy, and blew up the vessel of the Turkish admiral, with more than two thousand men on board. The admiral himself, mortally wounded, was carried on shore, where he died. On the 10th of November, seventeen daring sailors conducted two fire-ships into the midst of the Turkish fleet off the island of Tenedos,[2] and fastened one of them to the admiral's ship, and the other to that of the second in command. The former narrowly escaped; the latter blew up with eighteen hundred men on board. Several of the Turkish vessels were wrecked on the Asiatic coast; others were captured; and out of a fleet of thirty-five vessels that had sailed for the relief of the

1. *Salonica*, (anciently Thessalonica, at the head of the Thermaic Gulf in Macedonia,) is now celebrated city and seaport of European Turkey, at the north-eastern extremity of the Gulf of Salonica. The town was known to Herodotus, Thucydides, and Æschines, by the name of *Therma*, but Cassandra changed its name to that of his wife Thessalonica, the daughter of Philip, and sister of Alexander the Great. In Thessalonica the Apostle Paul made many converts, to whom he adressed the Epistle to the Thessalonians. (*Maps* Nos. I. and X.)

2. *Tenedos* is a small but celebrated island of Turkey, in the Ægean Sea, (Archipelago,) fifteen miles south-west from the mouth of the Dardanelles, and about five miles west from the Asiatic coast According to Virgil, (Æneid ii.) it was the place to which the Grecian fleet made the feigned retreat before the sack of Troy. (*Map* No. III.)

Morea, only eighteen returned, much injured, to the Dardanelles. Finally, to crown the successes of the year, on the 12th of December the strong Turkish fortress of Napoli di Romania was carried by assault.

9. During the year 1823 the war was carried on with results generally favorable to the Greeks. In Thessaly and Epirus
III. 1823.
there was a suspension of arms: on the 22d of March the Greek fleet gained a victory over an Egyptian flotilla: daring expeditions were made to the coast of Asia Minor: a Turkish army of twenty-five thousand men, that attempted to invade the Morea by way of the Corinthian Isthmus, was repulsed by the brave Suliot leader Marco Botzaris, who fell in the moment of victory: and the Turks failed in repeated attacks on Missolonghi.[1] In the summer of this year the illustrious poet, Lord Byron, arrived in Greece, and took an active part in aid of Greek independence; but he died at Missolonghi on the 19th of April following.

10. The Turks commenced the campaign of 1824, while dissensions
prevailed among the Greek captains, by seizing Negro-
IV. 1824.
pont, subduing Candia, and reducing the small but strongly-fortified rocky island of Ipsara, in which latter place the heroic Greeks blew up their last fort, after two thousand of the enemy had entered it, and thus perished with their conquerors. The Turk-ish fleet next made an attempt on Samos, but was driven away in terror by the skill and boldness of the Greek fire-ships. A large Egyptian fleet, sent to attack the Morea, was frustrated in all its de-signs, and the campaign terminated gloriously to the Greeks.

11. The campaign of 1825 was opened by the landing, in the Morea,
of an Egyptian army under Ibrahim Pacha, son of the
V 1825.
viceroy of Egypt, whom the sultan had induced to engage in the war. Navarino soon fell into his power; nor was his course arrested till he had carried desolation as far as Argos. In the meantime Missolonghi was closely besieged by a combined land and naval Turkish force, which, on the 2d of August, after a contest of several days, suffered a disastrous defeat, with the loss of nine thou-sand men. But Missolonghi was again besieged, for the fourth time, the siege being conducted by Ibrahim Pacha alone, who had an army of twenty-five thousand men, trained mostly by French officers. Af-ter repelling numerous assaults, and enduring the extremities of

1. *Missolonghi* is on the coast of Ætolia, about ten miles west of the ancient Chalcis (Map No. 1.)

famine, Missolonghi at length fell, on the 22d of April, 1826, when eighteen hundred of the garrison cut their way through the enemy, and reached Salona[1] and Athens in safety. vi. 1826. Many of the inhabitants escaped to the mountains; large numbers were captured in their flight; and those who remained in the city, about one thousand in number, mostly old men, women and children, blew themselves up in the mines that had been prepared for the purpose Five thousand women and children were made slaves, and more than three thousand ears were sent as a precious trophy to Constantinople.

12. Ibrahim Pacha was now in possession of a large part of southern Greece, and most of the islands of the Archipelago or Ægean Sea; and the foundation of an Egyptian military and slave-holding State seemed to be laid in Europe. This danger, connected with the noble defence and sufferings of Missolonghi, roused the attention of the European governments and people: numerous philanthropic societies were formed to aid the suffering Greeks; and, finally, on the 6th of July, 1827, a treaty was concluded vii. 1827. at London between England, Russia, and France, for the pacification of Greece—stipulating that the Greeks should govern themselves, but that they should pay tribute to the Porte.

13. To enforce this treaty, in the summer of 1827 a combined English, French, and Russian squadron, sailed to the Grecian Archipelago; but the Turkish sultan haughtily rejected the intervention of the three powers, and the troops of Ibrahim Pacha continued their devastations in the Morea.   On the 20th of October the allied squadron entered the harbor of Navarino, where the Turkish-Egyptian fleet lay at anchor; and a sanguinary battle followed, in which the allies nearly destroyed the fleet of the enemy.   The Porte, enraged by the result, detained the French ships at Constantinople, stopped all communication with the allied powers, and prepared for war.

14. In the following year the French cabinet, in connection with England, sent an army to the Morea: Russia declared war for violations of treaties, and depredations upon her commerce; viii. 1828. and on the 7th of May a Russian army of one hundred and fifteen thousand men, under command of Count Wittgenstein, crossed the Pruth,[2] and by the second of July had taken seven for

---

1. *Salona* is the same as the ancient Amphissa, in Locris. See *Amphissa*, p. 96. (*Map* No 1.)

2. The river *Pruth*, forming the boundary between the Russian province of Bessarabia and the Turkish province of Moldavia, enters the Danube about sixty miles from its mouth. (*Maps Nos.* X. and XVII.)

tresses from the Turks. In August a convention was concluded with Ibrahim Pacha, who agreed to evacuate the Morea with his troops, and set his Greek prisoners at liberty. In the meantime the Greeks continued the war, drove the Turks from the country north of the Corinthian Gulf, and, towards the close of the year, fitted out a great number of privateers to prey upon the commerce of the Turks in the Mediterranean. In consequence of these measures the sultan banished from Constantinople all the Greeks and Armenians not born in the city, amounting to more than twenty-five thousand persons.

15. In the month of January, 1829, the sultan received a protocol from the three allied powers, declaring that they took the Morea and the Cyc'lades' under their protection, and IX. 1829. that the entry of any military force into Greece would be regarded as an attack upon themselves. The danger of open war with France and England, together with the successes and alarming advance of the Russians, now commanded by Marshal Diebitsch, who, by the close of July, had crossed the Balkan' mountains and reached the Black Sea, and on the 20th of August, took Adrianople, within one hundred and thirty miles of the Turkish capital, induced the sultan to listen to overtures of peace. On the 14th of September the peace of Adrianople was signed by Turkey and Russia, by which the sultan recognized the independence of Greece, granted to Russia considerable commercial advantages, and guaranteed to pay the expenses of the Russian war.

16. The provisional government of Greece, which had been organized during the Revolution, was agitated by discontents and jealousies ; for some time the country remained in an unsettled condition, and the president, Count Capo d'Istria, was assassinated in October 1831. The allied powers, having previously determined to erect Greece into a monarchy, first offered the crown to Prince Leopold of Saxe-Coburg, (since king of Belgium,) who declined it on account of the unwillingness of the Greeks to receive him, and their dissatisfaction with the boundaries prescribed by the allied powers. Finally,

---

1. The *Cyc'lades* is a name given by the ancient Greeks to that large cluster of islands in the Ægean Sea lying east of southern Greece. (*Map* No. III.)

2. The *Balkan* mountains are the same as the ancient *Hæmus*, which formed the northern boundary of Thrace, separating it from Mæsia. (See *Map* No. IX.) The Balkan range extends from the Black Sea westward a distance of about two hundred and fifty miles, dividing the Turkish provinces of Bulgaria and Roumelia, and the waters that flow into the Danube on the north from those that flow into the Ma itza on the south. (*Map No. X.*)

the crown was conferred on Otho, a Bavarian prince, who arrived at Nauplia in 1833.

VI. THE FRENCH REVOLUTION OF 1830. 1. On the death of Louis XVIII., in 1824, the crown of France fell to his brother Charles X,, who commenced his reign by a declaration of his intentions of con firming the constitutional charter that had been granted the French people at the time of the first restoration. But the new king, bit terly opposed to the principles of the Revolution, and governed b the counsels of bigoted priests, labored to build up an absolute mon archy, with a privileged nobility and clergy for its support; while, on the other hand, the people, persuaded that a plot was formed to deprive them of their constitutional priviléges, talked of open resist ance to the arbitrary demands of the court. A ministry, which the popular party had forced upon the king, was suddenly dismissed, and in August, 1829, an ultra-royalist ministry was appointed, at the head of which was Prince Polignac, one of the old royalists, and an early adherent of the Bourbons.

2. At the opening of the Chambers in March 1830, the speech from the throne plainly announced the determination of the king to overcome, by force, any obstacles that might be interposed in the way of his government, concluding with a threat of resuming the concessions made by the charter. As soon as this speech was made public the funds fell; the ministers had a decided majority opposed to them in the Chamber of Deputies, and a spirited reply was returned, declaring that " a concurrence did not exist between the views of the government and the wishes of the people; that the administration was actuated by a distrust of the nation; and that the nation, on the other hand, was agitated with apprehensions which threatened its prosperity and repose." The king then prorogued the chambers, and on the 17th of May a royal ordinance declared them dissolved, and ordered new elections,—measures that produced the greatest ex sitement throughout France.

3. In the meantime the king and his ministers, hoping to facilitate their projects, and overcome their unpopularity by gratifying the taste of the French people for military glory, declared war against Algiers, the Dey having refused to pay long-standing claims of French citizens, and having insulted the honor of France by striking the French consul when the latter was paying him a visit of ceremony. A fleet of ninety-seven vessels, carrying more than forty thousand soldiers, embarked at Toulon on the 10th of May,—on the 14th of

June effected a landing on the African coast,—and on the 5th of July compelled Algiers to capitulate, after a feeble resistance. The Dey was allowed to retire unmolested to Italy; and his vast treasures fell into the hands of the conquerors.

4. The success of the French arms in Africa occasioned great exultation in France, but did nothing towards allaying the excited state of public feeling against a detested ministry. The elections, ordered to be held in June and the early part of July, resulted in a large increase of opposition members; and the ministerial party was left in a miserable minority. The infatuated ministry, however, instead of withdrawing, madly resolved to set the voice of the nation at defiance, and even to subvert the constitutional privileges granted by the charter. They therefore induced the king to publish, on the morning of the 26th of July, three royal ordinances,—the first dissolving the newly-elected Chamber of Deputies—the second changing the law of elections, sweeping off three-fourths of the former constituency, and nearly extinguishing the representative system—and the third, suspending the liberty of the press. In the ministerial report, published at the same time with these ordinances, the ministers argue, in favor of the latter measure, that "At all epochs, the periodical press has only been, and from its nature must ever be, an instrument of disorder and sedition"!

5. In defiance of these ordinances the conductors of the liberal journals determined to publish their papers; and on the evening of the same day, the 26th, they published an address to their countrymen, declaring that "the government had stripped itself of the character of law, and was no longer entitled to their obedience,"—language that would probably have exposed them to the penalties of treason if the contest had terminated differently. It was late in the day before intelligence of the arbitrary measures of government was generally circulated through Paris: then crowds began to assemble in the streets: cries of "down with the ministry," and "the charter forever," were heard: the fearless harangued the people; and during the night the lamps in several of the streets were demolished, and the windows of the hotel of Polignac broken. So little had the king anticipated any popular outbreak, that he passed the day of the 26th in the amusements of the chase; and it appears that the infatuated ministry had not even dreamed of a Revolution as the consequence of their obnoxious measures.

6. On the morning of the 27th several of the journalists printed

and distributed their papers; but their doors were soon closed, and
their presses broken by the police.   This morning the king appointed
Marsha. Marmont commander-in-chief of the forces in Paris; but it
was not till four in the afternoon that orders were given to put the
troops under arms, when they were marched to different stations
to aid the police, and overawe the people.   The latter then began to arm: some skirmishing occurred with the troops: during the
night the lamps throughout the city were demolished; and, under
he cover of darkness, many of the streets were barricaded with
paving-stones torn up for the purpose.   At the close of the day Mar-
mcnt had informed the king that tranquillity was restored; and
therefore no additional troops were sent for; nor were the great
depots of arms and ammunition guarded.

7. At an early hour on the morning of the 28th, armed multitudes
appeared in the steets; and numbers of the National Guard, which
the king had previously disbanded, appeared in their uniform among
the throng, and with them the famous tri-colored flag, so dear to the
hearts of all Frenchmen.   To the surprise of Marmont, the king,
and the ministry, the riot, which, on the previous evening, they had
thought suppressed, had assumed the formidable aspect of a Revolution.   By nine o'clock the flag of the people waved on the pinnacles
of Notre Dame, and at eleven it surmounted the central tower
of the Hotel de Ville, which was afterwards, however, retaken by
the royal troops.   Marmont showed great indecision in his movements: his columns were everywhere assailed with musketry from
the barricades, from the windows of houses, from the corners of the
streets, and from the narrow alleys and passages which abound in
Paris; and paving-stones and other missiles were showered upon
them from the house-tops.   The royal guards were disheartened:
the troops of the line showed great reluctance to fire upon the citizens; and the 28th closed with the withdrawal of the royal forces
from every position in which they had attempted to establish themselves during the day.

8. The contest was renewed early on the morning of the third day,
when several distinguished military characters appeared as leaders of
the people, and among them General Lafayette, who took command
of the National Guard; but while the issue was yet doubtful, several
regiments of the line went over to the insurgents, who, thus strength
ened and encouraged, rushed upon the Louvre and the Tuilleries,
and speedily overcame the troops stationed there.   So suddden was

the assault that Marmont himself with difficulty escaped, leaving be
hind him more than twenty thousand dollars of the public funds.
About half past three P. M. the last of the military posts in Paris
surrendered ; the royal troops who escaped having in the meantime
retreated to St. Cloud, where were the king and ministry, now in consternation for their own safety.   The Revolution was speedily completed by the installation of a provisional government : on the 31st
Louis Phillippe, Duke of Orleans,[a] the most popular of the royal
family, accepted the office of lieutenant-general of the kingdom :
when the Chambers met he was elected to the throne ; and on the
9th of August took the oath to support the constitutional charter.

9. The results of the revolutionary movement in France, and the
overthrow of the elder branch of the Bourbons, in defiance of the
guarantees of the congress of Vienna, spread alarm among the sovereigns of continental Europe ; and the emperor of Russia went so
far as not only to hesitate about acknowledging the title of the citizen king of France, but, as is believed, was preparing to support the
claims of the exiled Charles X., when the popular triumph in Eng
land, in the passage of the Reform Bill of 1832, by converting a
former ally into an enemy, raised up obstacles that arrested his
measures.   Charles X., after having abdicated the throne, was permitted to retire unmolested from France ; but his ministers, attempting to escape, were arrested, and afterwards brought to trial, when
three of them, including Polignac, were declared guilty of treason,
and sentenced to imprisonment for life.   At the end of six years they
were released from confinement,—indignation towards them having
given place to pity.

VII. Belgium.   1. The French Revolution of 1830 produced a
powerful sensation throughout Europe, and aroused an insurrection
ary spirit wherever the people complained of real or fancied wrongs,
while the continental sovereigns, on the other hand, alarmed for the
safety of their thrones, looked with jealousy on every political movement that originated with the people, and prepared to suppress, by
military force, the incipient efforts of rebellion.   The Belgians, who
had been compelled by the congress of Vienna to unite with the Hollanders in forming the kingdom of the Netherlands, having long been
goaded by unjust laws, and treated rather as vassals, than as subjects,

a. Louis Phillippe, Duke of Valois at his birth, Duke of Chartres on the death of his grand-
father in 1785, and Duke of Orleans on the death of his father in 1794, was the son of Louis
Phillippe Joseph, Duke of Orleans,—better known under his Revolutionary title of Philip
Egalité.

of the Dutch king, judging the period favorable for dissolving their union with a people foreign to them in language, manners, and interests, arose in insurrection at Brussels, in the latter part of August, and, after a contest of four days' duration, drove the Dutch authorities and garrison from the city.

2. In vain were efforts made by the Prince of Orange to reconcile the conflicting demands of the Dutch and the Belgians, and again unite the two people under one government. The proposals of the prince were disavowed by his father the king of Holland, and equally rejected by the Belgians; and on the 4th of October the latter made a formal declaration of their independence. Soon after, the representatives of the five great powers,—France, Great Britain, Prussia, Russia, and Austria, assembled at London, agreed to a protocol in favor of an armistice, and directed that hostilities should cease between the Dutch and Belgians. The Belgians, having decided upon a constitutional monarchy, first offered the crown to the Duke of Nemours, the second son of Louis Phillippe; but the latter declined the proffered honor on behalf of his son; after which the Belgian congress elected Leopold, prince of Saxe-Coburg-Gotha,[1] for their king. As the Dutch continued to hold the city of Antwerp, contrary to the determination of the five great powers, a French army of sixty-five thousand men, under Marshal Gerard, entered Belgium in November 1832, and, after encountering an obstinate defence, compelled the surrender of the place on the 24th of December. Since her separation from Holland, Belgium has increased rapidly in every industrial pursuit and social improvement.

VIII. POLISH REVOLUTION. 1. By the decrees of the congress of Vienna, most of that part of Poland which Napoleon had erected into the Grand Duchy of Warsaw, and conferred upon his ally the king of Saxony, (see p. 487,) was reëstablished as an independent kingdom, to be united to the crown of Russia, but with a separate constitution and administration; and on the 20th of June, 1815, the Russian emperor Alexander was proclaimed king of Poland. The mild character of Alexander had inspired the Poles with hopes that he would protect them in the enjoyment of their liberties; but his

1. *Saxe-Coburg-Gotha* is a duchy of central Germany, consisting of the two principalities, Saxe-Coburg, and Gotha;—the former on the south side of the Thuringian forest, and the latter on the north side. Area of the whole, seven hundred and ninety-seven square miles: population one hundred and forty thousand: chief towns, Coburg, and Gotha. The government is a constitutional monarchy. The house of Saxe-Coburg has intermarried with the principal reigning families of Europe. (*Map* No. XVII.)

fine professions soon began to prove delusive: ere long none but
Russians held the chief places of government: the article of the
constitution establishing liberty of the press was nullified: publicity
of debate in the Polish diet was abolished; and numerous state
prosecutions imbittered the feelings of the Poles against their
tyrants.

2. On the accession of Nicholas to the throne of Russia, in De
cembe 1825, although the lieutenancy of Poland was intrusted to a
Pole, yet the real power was invested in the king's brother, the
Archduke Constantine, who held the appointment of commander-in-
chief of the army. Constantine proved to be the worst of tyrants—
a second Sejanus—delighting in every species of judicial iniquity
and ministerial cruelty. The barbarities of Constantine, sanctioned
by Nicholas, revived the old spirit of Polish freedom and nationality;
and the successful examples of France and Belgium roused the Poles
again to action. Secret societies, organized for the express purpose
of securing the liberty of Poland, and uniting again under one government those portions that had been torn asunder and despoiled by
the rapacity of Russia, Prussia, and Austria, existed not only in Poland proper and Lithuania, but also in Volhynia[1] and Podolia, and
even in the old provinces of the Ukraine, which, it might be supposed, had long since lost all recollections of Polish glory.

3. The fear of detection and arrest on the part of some members
of one of these societies, led to the first outbreak at Warsaw, on the
evening of the 29th of November, 1830. The students of a military
school at Warsaw, one hundred and eighty in number, first attempted
to seize Constantine at his quarters, two miles from the city; but
during the struggle with his attendants, of whom the Russian general
Gendre, a man infamous for his crimes, was killed, the duke escaped
to his guards, who, being attacked in a position from which retreat
was difficult, lost three hundred of their number, when the students
returned to the city, liberated every State prisoner, and were joined
by the school of the engineers, and the students of the university. A
party entered the only two theatres open, calling out, "Women
home—men, to arms!" The arsenal was next forced, and in one
hour and a half from the first movement, forty thousand men were
in arms. Constantine fell back to the frontier. Chlopicki was first
appointed by the provisional government commander-in-chief of the

1. *Volhynia* is a province of European Prussia, formerly comprised in the kingdom of Poland, lying south of Grodno and Minsk. (*Map* No. XVII.)

army of I oland, and afterwards was made dictator; but he soon re signed, and Adam Czartoriski was appointed president.

4. After two months' delay in fruitless attempts to negotiate with the emperor Nicholas, who refused all terms but absolute submission, the inevitable conflict began—Russia having already assembled an army of two hundred thousand men under the command of Field Marshal Diebitsch, the hero of the Turkish war, while the Poles had only fifty thousand men equipped for the fight. On the 5th of February, 1831, the Russians crossed the Polish frontier: on the 18th their advanced posts were within ten miles of Warsaw; and on the 20th a general action was brought on, which resulted in the Poles retiring in good order from the field of battle. On the 25th forty thousand Poles, under Prince Radzvil, withstood the shock of more than one hundred thousand of the enemy; and at the close of the day ten thousand of the Russians lay dead on the field, and several thousand prisoners were taken.

5. Skryznecki, being now appointed commander-in-chief of the Polish forces, concerted several night attacks for the evening of the 31st, which resulted in the total rout of twenty thousand Russians, and the capture of a vast quantity of muskets, cannon and ammunition. These successes were so rapidly followed up, that before the end of April the Russians were driven either across the Bug into their own territories, or northward into the Prussian dominions. The conduct of Prussia, in affording the Russians a secure retreat on neutral territory, and furnishing them with abundant supplies, while in all similar cases the Poles were detained as prisoners, destroyed all advantages of Polish valor. Austria, likewise, permitted the Russians to pass over neutral ground to outflank the Poles, but detained the latter as prisoners if they once set foot on Austrian territory. Thus Russia and Austria interpreted and enforced the principles of the "Holy Alliance."

6. While the Poles were stationed at Minsk,[2] Skryznecki, uniting all his forces in that vicinity, to the number of twenty thousand, suddenly crossed the Bug and forced his way to Ostrolenka,[3] a distance

---

1. The *Bug*, a large tributary of the Vistula, forms a great part of the eastern boundary of the present Poland. Another river of the same name, running south-east through Podolia and Kherson, falls into the estuary of the Dnieper, east of Odessa. (*Map* No. XVII.)

2. *Minsk* is a small town of Poland, about twenty-five miles south-east of Warsaw. A large city of the same name is the capital of the Russian province of Minsk, formerly embraced in Poland. (*Map* No. XVII.)

3. *Ostrolenka* is a small town sixty-eight miles north-east from Warsaw. (*Map* No. XVII.)

of eighty miles, where, on the 26th of May, he engaged in battle with sixty thousand Russians. The combat was terrific—no quarter was asked, and none was given. The Poles, led by the heroic General Bem, lost one-fourth of their number. The loss of the Russians was less in proportion, but they had three generals killed on the field. In the following month, both the Russian commander-in-chief, Marshal Diebitsch, and the Archduke Constantine, died suddenly. About the same time a conspiracy for setting at liberty all the Russian prisoners, thirteen thousand in number, was detected at Warsaw.

7. Dissensions among the Polish chiefs, and the want of an energetic government, soon produced their natural consequences of divided counsels, and disunited efforts in the field; and by the 6th of September, during the strife of factions at Warsaw, a Russian army of one hundred thousand men, supported by three hundred pieces of cannon, had assembled for the storming of the city. Although defended with heroism, after two days' fighting, in which the Russians had twenty thousand slain, and the Poles about half that number, Warsaw surrendered to the Russian general Paskewitch—the main body of the Polish army, and the most distinguished citizens, retiring from the city, and afterwards dispersing, when no farther hopes remained of serving their ill-fated country. Large numbers crossed the frontiers and went into voluntary exile in other lands: most of the Polish generals, who surrendered under an amnesty, were sent to distant parts of the Russian empire; and the soldiers, and Polish nobility, were consigned by thousands to the dungeons and mines of Siberia. The subjugation of Poland is complete: her nationality seems extinguished forever

III. ENGLISH REFORMS. FRENCH REVOLUTION OF 1848. REVOLUTIONS IN THE GERMAN STATES, PRUSSIA, AND AUSTRIA. REVOLUTIONS IN ITALY. HUNGARIAN WAR. USURPATION OF LOUIS NAPOLEON.

I. ENGLISH REFORMS. 1. From the death of George the Third, in 1820, to the death of George the Fourth, in June 1830, England was agitated by a continued struggle between the two great parties which divided the nation—the whigs and the tories. Civil disabilities of all kinds were loudly objected to, and political abuses denounced with a plainness and force never before known in England. In 1828 the reform party obtained the abolition of the test act, which, though nearly obsolete in point of fact, still imposed nominal disabilities on Protestant dissenters; and in 1829 the barriers which had

so long excluded Roman Catholics from the legislature were removed
At the time of the accession of William IV., in 1830, a tory ministry
headed by the Duke of Wellington, was in power; but the decided
sentiment of the nation in favor of reform in all the branches of government, occasioned its resignation in November of the same year. A
whig ministry, pledged for reform, with Earl Grey at its head, then
came into power; and on the first of March of the following year
Lord John Russell brought forward in parliament the ministerial
plan for reforming the representation of England, Scotland, and
Ireland, which, if adopted, would extend the right of suffrage to half
a million additional voters, disfranchise fifty-six of the so-called rotten or decayed boroughs, and more nearly equalize representation
throughout the kingdom. After a long but animated debate the bill
passed a second reading in the House of Commons by a majority of
only one, but was lost on the third reading, the vote being two hundred and ninety-one for the bill, and two hundred and ninety-nine
against it.

2. By advice of the ministers, the king hastily dissolved parlia
ment, and ordered new elections for the purpose of better ascertain-
ing the sense of the people. The elections took place amid great
excitement, and the advocates of reform were returned by nearly all
the large constituencies. The new parliament was opened on the
14th of June, 1831. The reform bill, being again introduced, passed
the commons by a majority of one hundred and thirteen, but was rejected by the lords, whose numbers remained unchanged, by a majority of forty-one. The rejection of the bill by the lords led to
strong manifestations of popular resentment against the nobility:
serious riots occurred at Nottingham and Derby;[1] and at Bristol
many public buildings, and an immense amount of private property,
were destroyed; ninety persons were killed or wounded; five of the
rioters were afterwards executed, and many were sentenced to trans
portation.

3. On the 12th of December Lord John Russell a third time in
troduced a reform bill, similar to the former two; and on the 23d
of March, 1832, it passed the Commons by a majority of one hundred
and sixteen, but was defeated in the House of Lords by a majority

1. *Derby* is a large town on the Derwent, one hundred and ten miles north-west from London
2. *Bristol* is a large and important city and seaport of England, at the confluence of the
Avon and the Frome, eight miles from the entrance of the former into Bristol Channel, and
ndred and eight miles west from London. The city extends over six or seven distinct
d their intermediate valleys, amidst a picturesque and fertile district. (*Map* No. XVI.)

of forty. The ministry now advised the king to create a sufficient number of peers to insure the passage of the bill; and on his refusal to proceed to such extremities, all the members of the cabinet resigned. Political unions were now formed throughout the country; the people determined to refuse payment of taxes, and demanded that the ministers should be reinstated. There were no riots, but the people had risen in their collective strength, determined to assert their just rights. The king yielded to the force of public opinion and Earl Grey and his colleagues were reinstated in office, with th assurance that, if necessary, a sufficient number of new peers should be created to secure the passing of the bill. When the lords were apprized of this fact they withdrew their opposition; but it is worthy of remark that many of them, and all the bishops, left their seats on the final passage of the bill, which, having been rapidly hurried through both houses, received the royal assent on the 7th of June.

4. The passage of the Reform bill was, to England, a political revolution—none the less important because it was bloodless, and carried on under the protection of law. Thereby the electoral franchise, instead of being confined to a varied and limited class in the interest of the aristocracy, was extended, not to the whole citizens, as in America, but to a large body comprising the middle classes of society, who were thus, in effect, vested with supreme power in the British empire. An entire change in the foreign policy of the country was the consequence. The French Revolution of 1830 had elevated to power the middle classes of the French people also; and the ceaseless rivalry of four centuries between France and England was, for the time, forgotten: the political interests of the two great powers of Western Europe were united; and the Russian autocrat, in full march to overturn the throne of the citizen-king, and put down republicanism in France, was arrested on the Vistula, where his arms found ample employment in crushing the last remnants of Polish nationality. As to England herself, none of the many evils arising from democratic ascendency in the government, so often predicted by the aristocratic party, have yet followed in the train of reform; but, on the contrary, the peace, power, and prosperity of the country, have increased thereby.

5. The reign of William IV. was terminated on the 19th of June, 1837, when the Princess Victoria, daughter of the Duke of Kent, and grand-daughter of George III., succeeded to the throne, at the age of eighteen years One effect of the descent of the crown to

female was the separation from it of Hanover, after a union of more than a century. On the 10th of February, 1840, her majesty was married to Albert, prince of Saxe-Coburg and Gotha, a duchy of central Germany.

II. FRENCH REVOLUTION OF 1848. 1. The most important events that distinguished the reign of Louis Phillippe were the abolition of the hereditary rights of the French peerage in October 1831; he siege of Antwerp, and its surrender by the Dutch, after a long nd vigorous resistance, in 1832; an attempt of Louis Napoleon Bonaparte, nephew of the emperor Napoleon, to excite an insurrection at Strasbourg, in October 1836, for the purpose of overthrowing the government; the second attempt of Louis Napoleon to excite a revolution in France, by landing at Boulogne in August 1840, and his subsequent condemnation to perpetual imprisonment; and, in December of the same year, the splendid pageant of the restoration of the remains of the emperor Napoleon to France.

2. Louis Phillippe had been selected to fill the throne of France chiefly through the instrumentality of the venerable Lafayette, who, thinking France still unfitted for a republic, preferred for her " a throne surrounded by republican institutions." Placed in this anomalous position, Louis Phillippe, in the vain attempt to conciliate both monarchists and republicans, had a difficult game to play; and while he was laboring to consolidate his power, a large and influential party, that he dare not openly denounce, was zealously striving to undermine it. Yet for a time, with an immense revenue, and unbounded patronage, and the numerous means of political corruption which they placed at his disposal, the government of Louis Phillippe seemed to be steadily acquiring solidity, and by its success in keeping down domestic factions, and maintaining friendly relations with foreign powers, acquired a high reputation for wisdom and firmness.

3. Yet amid all this seeming security, the middle and lower classes, disappointed in their expectations as to the results of the Revolution of 1830, were daily growing more and more discontented with the measures and policy of the government; and it was this all-pervading feeling of discontent, which, without any serious aggressions on the part of government, and without any previous conspiracy on the part of the people, led to the unpremeditated Revolution of February 1848,—a revolution which, in its completeness and importance, and the bloodless means by which it was accomplished, is without a parallel in history.

4. During the winter of 1847–8 numerous political reform banquets were held throughout France; and the omission of the king's health from the list of toasts on these occasions was a circumstance that added much to the jealousy with which these displays were regarded by the government. The leaders of the opposition having announced that reform banquets would be held throughout France on the 22d of February, Washington's birthday; on the evening preceding the 22d, the administration forbade the intended meeting in Paris, and made extensive military preparations to suppress it if it were attempted, and to crush at once any attempt at insurrection. In the Chamber of Deputies, then in session, this arbitrary measure of government was warmly discussed, when the opposition members, consenting to give up the meeting for the morrow, concurred in the plan of moving an impeachment of ministers, with the expectation of obtaining either a change of cabinet, or a dissolution of the Chamber and a new election, which would test the sense of the nation.

5. On the morning of the 22d the opposition papers announced that the banquet would be deferred, when the orders for the troops of the line to occupy the place of the intended meeting were countermanded, and picquets only were stationed in a few places; but no serious disturbance was anticipated, either by the ministry or its opponents. The announcement of the opposition journals, however, came too late; and at noon a large concourse, chiefly of the working classes, had assembled around the church of the Madeline, where the procession was to have been organized. But the multitude exhibited no symptoms of disorder, and were dispersed by the municipal cavalry without any loss of life. In the evening, however, disturbances began: gunsmiths' shops were broken open; barricades were formed; lamps extinguished; the guards were attacked; the streets were filled with troops; and appearances indicated a sanguinary strife on the morrow.

6. At an early hour on Wednesday, February 23d, crowds again appeared in the streets, barricades were erected, and some skirmishing ensued, in which a few persons were killed. Numbers of the National Guards also made their appearance, and a portion of them, having declared for reform, sent their colonel to the king, to acquaint his majesty with their wishes. He immediately acceded to their requests, dismissed the Guizot cabinet, and requested Count Molé to form a new ministry. This measure produced a momentary calm; but the rioters continued to traverse the streets, often attacking, and

sometimes disarming, the municipal guards. Between ten and eleven in the evening a crowd, passing the Hotel of Foreign Affairs, was suddenly fired upon by the troops with fatal effect. The people fled in consternation, but their thirst for vengeance was aroused, and the cry, " To arms! Down with the assassins! Down with Louis Phillippe! Down with the Bourbons!" resounded throughout Paris.

7. The attempt to establish a Molé administration having failed, the king sent, late at night, for M. Thiers, and intrusted to him the formation of a ministry that should be acceptable to the people ; and on the following morning, the 24th, a proclamation to the citizens of Paris announced that M. Thiers and Odillon Barrot had been appointed ministers—that orders had been given the troops to cease firing, and retire to their quarters—that the Chamber would be dissolved, and an appeal made to the people—and that General Lamoriciere had been appointed commandant of the National Guards. The order to the troops to retire, which occasioned the resignation of their commander, Marshal Bugeaud, after a protest against the measure, was a virtual surrender, on the part of government, of the means of defence ; and the king and royal family soon found themselves at the mercy of an excited populace. The troops quietly allowed themselves to be disarmed by the mob, who then, to the number of twenty thousand, and accompanied by the National Guard, directed their course to the Palace Royal and the Tuilleries, and demanded the abdication of the king. In the course of the day the king signed an abdication in favor of his grandson, the young Count of Paris ; but before this fact was generally known the armed populace broke into the palace, made a bonfire of the royal carriages and furniture, and after having carried the throne of the state reception room in triumph through the streets, burned that also. Meanwhile the ex king and queen escaped to St. Cloud, whence they pursued their way to Versailles, and thence to Dreux, from which latter place they escaped in disguise to England, whither they were followed by M. Guizot, and other members of the late ministry.

8. On the day of the king's abdication the Chamber of Deputies assembled ; but, being overwhelmed by the crowd, the greatest confusion prevailed, and amid shouts of " No king! Long live the Republic," the members of a provisional government were named, and adopted by popular acclamation. Although a majority of the deputies seemed opposed to the establishment of a republic, and it was by no means certain that there was any great party out of Paris in

its favor, every attempt to adjourn the question was the signal of renewed shouts and disorder; and amid the turbulent demonstrations of the Parisian populace the French Republic was adopted, and proclaimed to the nation. Royalty had vanished, almost without a struggle,—blown away by the breath of an urban tumult,—and the strangest revolution of modern times was consummated.

9. The leading member of the provisional government was M Lamartine, to whom belongs the renown of saving the country from immediate anarchy. By his noble and fervid eloquence the passions of the mob were calmed; and by his prompt and judicious measures, among the first of which was the declaration of the abolition of capital punishment for political offences, tranquillity and confidence were at once restored. On the 26th the bank of France was reopened; the public departments resumed their duties; and with unparalleled unanimity the army, the clergy, the press, and the people, in the provinces as well as in Paris, immediately gave in their adhesion to the new Republic.

10. The Revolution of February, 1848, was accomplished by the union of the two great sections of the democratic party—the Moderate and the Red Republicans. The principles advocated by the former were the right of self-government, civil and religious liberty, and universal suffrage. The latter went much farther, and, adopting the leading principles of the Socialists, demanded the establishment of new social relations between capital and labor; a new distribution of wealth, the elevation of the laboring classes at the expense of the wealthy, labor and food to all, by government regulations, and the working out, on a national scale, of the grand problem of Communism. Believing that it is the duty and in the power of government to remedy most of the many evils of society, the people soon began to manifest the hopes which they expected the Revolution to transform into realities. Deputations from all trades and callings—even to shoe-cleaners, waiters, and nursery-maids—waited on the provisional overnment, making known their grievances, and demanding relief, which generally consisted of freedom from taxation, the establishment of national workshops, fewer hours of labor, higher wages, and more holidays.

11. Although the Moderate and Red Republicans had united in overthrowing the monarchy, no sooner was tranquillity restored than the animosities of the two sections revived; and when it was found that the Moderates had control of the provisional government, their

opponents determined upon its overthrow. On several occasions during the month of April, the working classes of Paris assembled in mass to make a demonstration of their numbers; but the fidelity of the National Guard showed that the real physical power of Paris was still in the hands of the provisional government. The elections, held in April, also showed a large majority in favor of the Moderate party; and on the ballot, in May, for an executive committee of the government, consisting of five members, not one of the avowed Red Republicans was elected; and Ledru Rollin, the most violent and ultra of the committee, was the lowest on the list.

12. On the 15th of May the National Assembly was surrounded by the populace, led by Barbés, Blanqui, Hubert, and other Communist leaders, who, after having driven the deputies from their seats, and assumed the functions of government, proclaimed themselves the national executive committee, and through Barbés, one of their number, declared that a contribution of a thousand millions of francs should be levied on the rich for the benefit of the poor—that a tax of another thousand millions should be raised for the benefit of Poland—that the National Assembly should be dissolved—and, finally that the guillotine should be put in operation against the enemies of the country. But in the meantime the National Guard was called out, the rioters were soon dispersed, their leaders arrested, and the provisional government reinstated.

13. Owing to the fear of another demonstration against the government, the full command of all the troops in Paris was given to General Cavaignac, the minister of war; and all the approaches to the National Assembly, and the different ministries, were strongly guarded. In June, the government, finding the burdens imposed on the public treasury too heavy to be borne, determined to send out of Paris, to the provinces, about twelve thousand of the workmen then unprofitably employed in the national workshops. This was the signal of alarm: disturbances began on the evening of the 22d: on the 23d the most active preparations were made by both parties for the coming contest, and some blood was shed at the barricades erected by the insurgents. At one o'clock on Saturday morning, the 24th, General Cavaignac declared Paris in a state of siege, and the struggle began in earnest. From that hour until four o'clock in the afternoon when the insurgents were driven from the left bank of the Seine, the musketry and cannonade were incessant, and Paris was a vast battlefield. The fight was renewed at an early hour on Sunday morning

and continued during most of the day, and it was not till noon on Monday that the struggle was terminated, by the unconditional surrender of the last body of the insurgents. The number killed and wounded in this insurrection—by far the most terrible that has ever desolated Paris—will never be known; but five thousand is probably not a high estimate.

14. The exertions and success of General Cavaignac in defending the government procured for him a vote of thanks from the Assembly and the unanimous appointment of temporary chief-executive of the nation, with the power of appointing his ministers. Many of the leaders of the insurrection, among them Louis Blanc and Caussidiére, fled from the country: a small number of those taken with arms in their hands were condemned to transportation; but the great majority, after a short confinement, were set at liberty. The Assembly, in the meantime, proceeded with its task of constructing the new Constitution which was adopted on the 4th of November, 1848, by a vote of seven hundred and thirty-nine in its favor, and thirty in opposition. It declared that the French nation had adopted the republican form of government, with one legislative assembly, and that the executive power should be vested in a President, to be elected by universal suffrage, for a term of four years. Its principles were declared to be liberty, equality, and fraternity; and the basis on which it rested, family, labor, property, and public order.

III. REVOLUTIONS IN THE GERMAN STATES, PRUSSIA, AND AUSTRIA. 1. As soon as the first accounts of the French Revolution of the 24th of February, 1848, reached Germany, the whole of that vast country was in a ferment: popular commotions took place in all the large cities; and the people demanded a political constitution that should give them a share in legislation, establish the liberty of the press, and otherwise secure them their just rights. On the 29th of February deputations from every town in the Grand Duchy of Baden demanded of the Grand Duke liberty of the press, trial by jury, th right of the people to bear arms, and meet in public, and a more popular representation in the national diet at Frankfort.[a] On the

a. The present confederation of Germany, organized in 1815, embraces nearly forty States, some of very small dimensions, but each possessing an independent government, and only liable to be called on to furnish its proportionate contingent to the army of the Confederation in case of danger. The emperor of Austria, being the sovereign of many territories that were considered fiefs of the German empire, is a member of the Germanic Confederation; and his minister has the right of presiding in the Confederate Germanic Diet, held at Frankfort. The Austrian German provinces belonging to the Germanic Confederation are the arch-duchy of

the 2d of March the Duke yielded to their demands, and appointed a ministry from the popular party.

2. Similar demonstrations were made in nearly all the German States. At Cologne, a riot ensued, the town-house was stormed, and the authorities made prisoners. At Munich the people stormed the arsenal, and, having possessed themselves of the arms it contained, forced from the Bavarian king the concessions which he had refused to make. At Hanau,[1] in Hesse Cassel,[2] the Elector yielded only after a severe conflict. Within a week from the revolution in Paris the demands of the people had been acceded to throughout nearly all the south and west of Germany.

3. In a popular convention held at Heidelberg[3] on the 5th of March, the necessity of the reforms demanded by the people was insisted upon; and at the same time the Federal Diet, sitting at Frankfort, invoked the different German States to take the measures necessary for a new constitution of the Diet, providing that the people as well as the rulers should be represented in it. King Frederick William of Prussia, after having in vain resisted a popular revolution in Berlin, unexpectedly to all placed himself, foremost in the ranks of the reform party, with the hope, it is believed, of reuniting the German States in one great empire, and placing himself at its head. The king of Saxony was compelled to grant the requests of his subjects, who had pronounced in favor of reform : the king of Hanover also yielded, but with much reluctance, and only when farther delay would have cost him his throne. On the 26th of March, Sleswick and Holstein,[4] the two southern duchies of Denmark, which had always considered

1. *Hanau* is a town of fifteen thousand inhabitants in the electorate of Hesse, eleven miles north-east from Frankfort. (*Map* No. XVII.)

2. *Hesse Cassel* is an irregularly-shaped State of Germany, consisting of a central territory and several detached portions, the whole lying mostly north of north-western Bavaria. The government is a limited monarchy. Hesse Darmstadt, or the Grand Duchy of Hesse also a limited monarchy, is divided by Hesse Cassel—part of it lying north and part south of the river Mayn. (*Map* No. XVII.)

3. *Heidelberg* is a city of northern Baden, on the south side of the Neckar, forty-eight miles south of Frankfort. (*Map* No. XVII.)

4. *Sleswick* and *Holstein*. See p. 403, and *Maps* Nos. XIV. and XVII.

Austria, the kingdom of Bohemia, with Moravia and Silesia, part of Galicia, the county of Tyrol, and the duchies of Styria, Carinthia, and Carniola, with the town of Trieste. The other States of the Austrian empire have no connection with the German Confederation. The king of Prussia, in the same manner as the Austrian emperor, is a member of the Confederation. The empires of Austria and Prussia, and the kingdoms of Bavaria, Saxony, Hanover, and Wirtemburg, have, each, four votes in the German Diet; and the smallest State, the free city of Hamburg, containing an area of only forty-three square miles, has one vote: the principality of Lichtenstein, with a population of only seven thousand, has also one vote.

themselves as governed by the king of Denmark in his capacity of a prince of Germany, long dissatisfied with the Danish rule, and irritated by the refusal of the king to accede to any of their demands, declared themselves independent of Denmark, and solicited admission into the Germanic Confederation. Being assisted by twenty thousand Prussian and Hanoverian volunteers, they waged a sanguinary war against the Danish king until foreign intervention terminated the contest.

4. For some time there had been much political excitement in those portions of the Austrian empire embracing Galicia,[1] Hungary, and northern Italy; but down to the period of the French Revolution, in February 1848, the German provinces of the empire had remained tranquil. When, however, news of the downfall of Louis Phillippe reached Vienna, a shock was felt which vibrated throughout the whole Austrian empire: the public funds immediately fell thirty per cent.: the people, sympathizing with the Parisians, expressed themselves upon the great subject of reform with a freedom and earnestness altogether foreign to their habits; and the royal family, panic-stricken by the gathering tempest, were closeted in deep consultation. All the royal family and the imperial cabinet, with the exception of the Archduke Louis, uncle of the emperor, and the minister Metternich, were in favor of making immediate concessions to the people, as the only means of retaining the provinces, if not of preserving the throne. Metternich tendered his resignation, but was persuaded to retain his post only on condition of being, as hitherto, unobstructed in his administration of the government.

5. At the opening of the Diet of Lower Austria, at Vienna, on the 13th of March, an immense concourse of citizens, headed by the students of the University, marched to the hall of the Assembly, and there presented their petition in favor of a constitutional government, a responsible ministry, freedom of the press, a citizens' guard, trial by jury, and religious freedom. The crowd increasing, the Arch duke Albert ordered the people to disperse, but, not being obeyed, commanded the soldiers to fire upon them. Many victims fell, and the greatest excitement was occasioned, which was only partially calmed by an order from the emperor for the military to withdraw.

6. The city guard had in the meantime sided with the people, and

---

1. *Galicia* and *Lodomeria*, now constituting a province of the Austrian empire, and lying north of Hungary, include those territories of Poland which have fallen to Austria in the several partitions of that country. (*Map* No. XVII.)

opened to them the arsenal. Metternich and the Archduke Albert resigned. On the next day, the 14th, the emperor abolished the censorship of the press, and assented to the formation of a National Guard; and forty thousand citizens enrolled their names, and were furnished with arms. On the following day, the 15th, all the other demands of the people were complied with, and a promise given that a convention of deputies from each of the provinces should be assembled as speedily as possible for the purpose of framing a constitution for the empire. This announcement was received with ex·pressions of the greatest joy; and the supposed dawn of Austrian liberty was celebrated by triumphal processions and illuminations.

7. The first period of the Revolution terminated with the triumph of the people, and was followed by apparently sincere efforts on the part of the government to fulfil its promises and carry out the reforms projected. But·serious difficulties intervened. The various races in the empire—Germans, Magyars, Slavonians, and Italians—were jealous of each other, while their wants and requirements were dissimilar: the people, generally, were unprepared for free institutions; and the government was undecided to what extent concessions were expedient. During the whole of April and May, the mob, guided by the students, who often conducted themselves disgracefully, ruled in Vienna: the liberty of the press degenerated into licentiousness: a shameful literature flooded the city: violations of law and order were frequent: the Reign of Terror commenced; and finally, on the 18th of May, the emperor, anxious for his personal safety, secretly left Vienna and repaired to Innspruck[1] in the Tyrol. But the withdrawal of the emperor was not what the people wished, and they desired him, now that Metternich was removed, to lead them onward in the way of reform. Returning in August he strove in vain to resume the reins of government: the students of the university and the democratic clubs usurped the entire control of the city, and, in the name of democracy, exercised a most cruel and unmitigated despotism.

8. In the meantime the Bohemians, of Slavic origin, opposed to every measure tending to identify them with the German Confederation, had demanded of the emperor a constitution that should give them a national existence, equivalent, in its relations with the empire, to that enjoyed by the Hungarians. Being refused their demands, a

1. *Innspruck*, the chief city of the Tyrol, is on the river Inn, two hundred and orty miles south-west from Vienna

congress of the Slavic nations of the Austrian empire had assembled at Prague early in June, and was discussing the various plans of Slavic regeneration, when a vast assemblage of citizens and students addressed a "Storm Petition" to Prince Windischgratz, the military commander of the city, demanding the withdrawal of the regular troops, and a distribution of arms and ammunition for the use of the people. The petition not being granted, the people rose in open revolt ; a most fearful and bloody conflict ensued within the city, which was also bombarded from the surrounding heights, and after almost an entire week of fighting, on the 17th the city capitulated. The Slavic congress was broken up; the bright visions of Bohemian nationality vanished; and subsequently the strong national feelings of the Slavonic population, and their hatred alike of Magyars and Germans, rendered them the chief supporters of the Austrian throne and government.

9. At this time Hungary[1] was striving for a peaceable maintenance of her rights against Austrian encroachments; and Croatia,[2] which was considered as an integral part of the Hungarian monarchy, encouraged by Austria, had revolted, and her troops were already on their march towards the Hungarian capital. Austria now openly supported the Croats; and an order of the emperor, on the 5th of October, for some troops stationed in Vienna to march against Hungary, produced another Revolution in the Austrian capital. The people, sympathizing with the Hungarians, opposed the march of the troops : a sanguinary contest followed; the insurgents triumphed; the ministry was overthrown; the minister of war murdered; and the emperor fled to Olmutz,[3] attended by the troops that remained

1. *Hungary*, taken in its widest acceptation, includes, besides Hungary proper, Croatia, Slavonia, the military frontier provinces, the Banat, and Transylvania. The Carpathian mountains form the boundary of Hungary on the north-east, separating it from Galicia and Lodomeria. The greater part of the kingdom consists of two extensive plains ;—the plain of Upper Hungary, north of Buda, traversed by the Danube from west to east ; and the great plain of Southern Hungary, south of Buda, watered by the Danube and its tributaries, the Drave the Save, and the Theiss, with the numerous affluents of the latter. The whole of thi lower plain, an exceedingly fertile territory, embracing thirty-six thousand English square miles, is in scarcely a single point more than one hundred feet above the level of the Danube. (*Map* No. XVII.)

2. *Croatia*, (Austrian) regarded as forming the maritime portion of Hungary, has Slavonia, Turkish Croatia, and Dalmatia, on the east and south-east, and the Adriatic on the south-west. The Drave separates it from Hungary proper. The Croats are of Slavonic stock, and speak a dialect which has a greater affinity with the Polish than any other language. About the year 1180 Croatia was incorporated with Hungary. (*Map* No. XVII.)

3. *Olmutz*, a town of Moravia, and one of the strongest fortresses of the Austrian empire, is on the river March, forty miles north east of Brünn. Olmutz was taken by the Swedes in the

faithful to his cause. Fortunately for the emperor, a large and faith
ful army in other parts of the empire enabled him soon to concentrate
an overwhelming force around the chief seat of rebellion: Prince
Windischgratz from the north, and Jellachich the ban or governor
of Croatia from the south, united their forces before Vienna: on
the morning of the 28th of October they opened their batteries on
the city; and on the 31st, after a great destruction of life and property, compelled an unconditional surrender. Of sixteen hundred
persons arrested under martial law, nine only were punished with
death.

10. While these events were occurring at Vienna, a Hungarian
army of twenty or thirty thousand men, which had pursued Jellachich
to the Austrian frontier, had remained there many days awaiting an
invitation from the Viennese to come to their aid. At last, on the
28th of October, the Hungarians took the responsibility of advancing
into the Austrian territory: on the 30th and 31st they met the imperialists, when some skirmishing ensued; but the fatal blow had
already been struck at Vienna, and the Hungarian army recrossed
the frontiers.

11. The second Revolution of Vienna was a riot, neither national
nor liberal in its character, and not participated in by the other
parts of the empire; but its suppression, in connection with the
scenes of anarchy which preceded it, produced an unfavorable effect
on the cause of freedom throughout the whole of Germany. A reaction had already taken place in the popular mind: peace, under
imperial rule, began to be preferred to the unchecked excesses of the
mob: the emperor Ferdinand, yearning for repose, resigned his
crown in favor of his nephew the Archduke Joseph: the government
resumed its despotic powers; and Austria fell back to her old position. In Prussia, Frederick William, imitating the Austrian emperor, and calling the army to his aid, dissolved the assembly which he
had called for the purpose of constructing a constitution, and forgot
all his promises in favor of reform and constitutional liberty. With
Prussia and Austria against them, the smaller German States, divided in their counsels, could accomplish nothing; and the project
of German unity was virtually abandoned.

IV. Revolutions in Italy. 1. Since the fall of Napoleon, Austrian influence has been predominant in Italy. The Congress of

---

Thirty Years' War: ; was besieged unsuccessfully by Frederick the Great in 1758; and Lafay
ette was confined there in 1794. (*Map No. XVII.*)

Vienna assigned to Austria the whole Milanese and Venetian provinces, now included in Austrian Lombardy : at the same time the dependent thrones of Tuscany, Modena,[1] and Parma,[2] were filled by members of the house of Hapsburg; and it was not long before Austria, in her steady adherence to the principles of despotism, had exacted treaties from all the princes of Italy, stipulating that no constitution should be granted to their subjects. When, in 1820, the Neapolitans established a constitution, Austria suppressed it by the force of arms, (see p. 516) : in 1821 she interfered in Piedmont and in 1831 and 1832, in the Papal States' also, for the purpose of suppressing all liberal tendencies, whether in the government or the people.

2. The election in June 1846, of Cardinal Mastai, to fill the pontifical chair, with the appellation of Pius the Ninth, threatened the subversion of Austrian influence throughout a great part of Italy. The pope, a plain upright man, earnestly desiring to ameliorate the condition of his people, immediately commenced the work of reform; and the liberal course pursued by him at once revived the spirit of nationality throughout the entire peninsula. Austria, alarmed by these movements, used every means to change the course of the pope; and on the 19th of July, 1847, the Austrian army entered Ferrara,[4] a northern frontier town of the Papal States. The occupation of Ferrara was the signal for a general rising against the emperor of Austria, not only in Rome, but also in Florence, Bologna,[5] Lucca,[6] and Genoa, without regard to their distinct governments. In De-

1. The *Duchy of Modena* is a State of northern Italy, having Austrian Lombardy on the north, the northern division of the Papal States on the east, Parma on the west, and Tuscany, Lucca, and the Mediterranean, on the south. *Modena*, the ancient *Mutina*, is the capital. The government, an absolute monarchy, is possessed by a collateral branch of the House of Austria.

2. The *Duchy of Parma* adjoins Modena on the west, and has Austrian Lombardy on the north, from which it is separated by the Po. Government, an absolute monarchy. Capital, Parma, thirty-three miles south-west from Mantua.

3. The *Papal States*, or the "States of the Church," occupying a great part of central, with a portion of northern Italy, have Austrian Italy on the north, from which they are separated by the Po ; Modena, Tuscany, and the Mediterranean, on the west ; the Neapolitan dominions on the south ; and the Adriatic on the north-east.

4. *Ferrara*, formerly an independent duchy belonging to the family of Esté, and now the most northern city belonging to the pope, is on the west bank of the Volano, five miles south of the Po, and fifty-three miles south-west from Venice.

5. *Bologna*, the second city in rank in the Papal States, is at the southern verge of the valley of the Po, twenty-five miles south-west from Ferrara. Bologna, which has always assumed the title of "Learned," has given birth to eight popes, nearly two hundred cardinals, and more than one thousand literary and scientific men and artists.

6. *Lucca*, a duchy of central Italy, and, next to San Marino, the smallest of the Italian States, has the duchy of Modena on the north, and the Mediterranean on the south-west. Lucca, its capital, is eleven miles north-east of Pisa, and thirty-eight west of Florence.

cember the Austrian army was withdrawn; and the right of the States of Italy, not under Austrian rule, to choose their own forms of government, seemed to be conceded.

3. The Austrian emperor, fearing for the safety of Lombardy which was already in commotion, increased his forces in that province, until, in the beginning of March 1848, the different garrisons numbered a hundred thousand men. The proclamation of a republic in France hastened the crisis in the Austrian portion of Italy, and, by the unexpected tidings of the Revolution in Vienna, the climax was precipitated. On the 18th of March the citizens of Milan arose in insurrection, and after a contest of five days drove the Austrian troops, commanded by Marshal Radetsky, from the city. At the same time the Austrians were driven out of Parma and Pavia; and nearly all the Venetian territory was in open insurrection. On the 23d of March the king of Sardinia, Charles Albert, issued a proclamation in favor of Italian nationality, and marched into Lombardy to aid in driving the Austrians beyond the Alps. The Austrian general, Radetsky, a skilful and veteran commander, retreated until he could concentrate all his forces, when he returned to meet the Italians, who, gradually overpowered by superior numbers, were soon compelled to retire; and one by one the Austrians regained possession of all the cities from which they had been driven. After defeating the Sardinian king in several engagements during the latter part of July, on the 5th of August Radetsky was again before Milan: all Lombardy submitted; an armistice was agreed upon; and Charles Albert retired to his own dominions.

4. After some attempts of England and France to mediate between the contending parties, the armistice was terminated by Charles Albert on the 20th of March, 1849, on the avowed ground that its terms had been repeatedly violated by the Austrians; but, in reality in obedience to the clamors of his people, and as the only chance of saving his crown, and preventing Sardinia from becoming a republic. Sardinia was poorly prepared for the conflict: her forces were badly organized, and her officers incompetent; while opposed to them was one of the most efficient and best-disciplined armies in Europe, under the command of an able and experienced general. At twelve o'clock on the 20th, the moment that the armistice expired, Radetsky entered Piedmont, while the Sardinians were utterly ignorant of his movements; and by the 24th the war was at an end. Charles Albert, defeated in three battles and rightly judging that more favor would

35

be shown his countrymen if the supreme power were in other hands, abdicated in favor of his son Victor Emanuel on the evening of the 23d, and in a few hours left the country—bidding adieu not only to his crown, but his kingdom also. Victor Emanuel purchased peace by the payment of fifteen millions of dollars as indemnity for the ex penses of the war.

5. While these successes were attending the Austrian arms in Piedmont, an Austrian army was blockading Venice, which on the 22d of March, 1848, had proclaimed the " Republic of Saint Mark." Venice held out until her provisions were exhausted, and an immense amount of property had been destroyed—not less than sixty thousand shot and shells having been thrown into the city during the last few days of the siege. In the last days of August 1849, Venice surrendered to Marshal Radetsky;—and with the fall of the Republic of Saint Mark, Austria recovered her authority throughout all northern Italy.

6. During this period the southern portions of the peninsula were far from enjoying tranquillity. The subjects of Ferdinand, king of Naples[1] and Sicily, had risen early in 1848, and their demands for a constitution were acceded to ; but the promises of the king to the Sicilians were broken, and Sicily revolted from his authority, and elected for her sovereign the Duke of Genoa, the second son of Charles Albert king of Sardinia. A sanguinary war between the Neapolitans and Sicilians followed : Messina, after two days' bom bardment, fell into the hands of the Neapolitans : the Sicilians were defeated in a desperate battle at Catania ; Syracuse, terror stricken, surrendered without a blow : Palermo,[2] the last stronghold of the islanders, fell after a short struggle ; and Ferdinand of Naples re-sumed his former sway as unlimited monarch of the two Sicilies.

7. From the well-known liberal character of Pius the Ninth, and the manner in which his reign began, it was to be expected that, in the Papal States at least, liberty would find a quiet asylum. For a time prince and people were united in the noble cause of the political regeneration of Italy ; but the people soon outran the pope in the march of reform, and began to murmur because he lingered so far behind them. He granted liberty of the press, and its license alarmed him : he placed arms in the hands of the people, but could

---

1. The *Kingdom of Naples*, otherwise called the " Kingdom of the two Sicilies," nearly identical with the Magna Græcia of antiquity, comprises the southern portion of Italy, together with Sicily and the adjacent islands.

2. *Palermo : see Pan ormus*, p. 117.

not control the use of them : he named a council to assist him in the administration of civil affairs, but was dismayed at the cries for a representative assembly that should share in the government of the country.

8. In the summer of 1848 symptoms of reaction began to appear. Pius signified to the Roman Chamber of Deputies that it was asking too much; and his appointment of Rossi to the post of prime minister exasperated the people, and diminished his own popularity Rossi's avowed hostility to the democratic movement led to his assassination on the 15th of November, as he was proceeding to open the Chambers; and eight days later the pope fled from Rome, and took up his residence in Gaeta,[1] in the territory of the king of Naples. On the 9th of February following, a National Assembly, elected by the people, proclaimed that the pope's temporal power was at an end, and that the form of government of the Roman States should be a pure democracy, with the name of " The Roman Republic."

9. Month after month Pius remained at Gaeta, unwilling to demand foreign aid to reinstate him in his temporal sovereignty, and hoping that his people, acknowledging their past misconduct, would recall him of their own accord; but no signs of any change in his favor being exhibited, he at length availed himself of the only resource left him. The Roman Catholic powers of Austria, Naples, Spain, and France, responded to his appeal for aid : the Austrians entered the Papal States on the north—the Neapolitans on the south—a body of Spanish troops landed on the coast—and, to the shame of republican France, towards the close of April a French army, under the command of General Oudinot, was sent to southern Italy, under the avowed pretence of checking Austrian influence in that quarter, but, in reality, as the sequel proved, to restore papal authority on the ruins of the Roman Republic.

10. The pretended " friendly and disinterested mission" of the French army was resisted with a heroism worthy of the days of the early Roman Republic, and the first attack of the French upon the city of Rome resulted in their defeat; but the assailants were reënforced, and after a regular siege and bombardment, on the 30th of June, 1849 Rome surrendered. When the French troops entered the city they were received with silence and coldness on the part of the people;

---

1. Gaeta is a strongly-fortified seaport town, forty-one miles north-west from Naples, and seventy-two miles south-east from Rome. Cicero was put to death, by order of Antony, in the immediate vicinity of this town.

the Roman guards could not be induced to pay them the customary salute; the common laborers refused to engage in removing the barricades from the streets, and the French soldiers were compelled to perform this task themselves. Pius the Ninth returned to Rome, stealthily, and in the night, a changed man. Three years of political experience had changed his zeal for reform into the most imbittered feelings towards all democratic institutions: political tolerance gave place to the most determined support of absolutism; and the blessings with which his people once greeted him were changed to curses.

V. HUNGARIAN WAR. 1. It has been mentioned that the immediate cause of the second Revolution in Vienna, in October 1848, was the order to some Austrian troops stationed in Vienna to march to the aid of the Croats, who had revolted from Hungary. The Hungarian and Croatian war soon became a war between Hungary and Austria. In order to understand the true character of this important war it will be necessary to explain the previous political connection between the two countries.

2. The Magyars, from whom the present Hungarians are descended, were a numerous and powerful Asiatic tribe, which, after overrunning a great part of central Europe, settled in the fertile plains of the Danube and the Theiss,[1] about the close of the ninth century. For a long period the government of the Magyars was an elective monarchy, and in the year 1526 Ferdinand of Austria, of the house of Hapsburg, was elected to the throne of Hungary; and this was the first connection between the two countries. Seven succeeding Austrian princes of the same house were elected in succession by the Hungarian Diet, until, in the year 1687, the Diet declared the succession to the Hungarian throne hereditary in the house of Hapsburg; yet the independence of the kingdom was not affected thereby, although Hungary, with all its dependent provinces, among which was Croatia, became permanently attached to the Austrian dominions. The same as Bohemia, it acknowledged the Austrian emperor for its monarch; but Austria, Hungary, and Bohemia, were still separate *nations*, each governed by its own laws.

3. In the year 1790 Leopold the Second, emperor of Austria, yielded to the demands of the Hungarian Diet, and signed a solemn

---

1. The *Theiss*, (ancient *Tibiscus*,) a northern tributary of the Danube, is a large and navigable river of Hungary, flowing south through the great Hungarian plain. The area of its basin is estimated at six thousand square miles. (*Map* No XVII.)

declaration that "Hungary is a free and independent nation in her entire system of legislation and government," and that "all royal patents not issued in conjunction with the Hungarian Diet, are illegal, null, and void." After the peace of 1815, Francis the Second re- solved to govern Hungary without the aid of a Diet, in violation of the laws which he had sworn to support; but after a long period of confusion he found it necessary, in 1825, to yield, and again summon the Diet. His attempt to subvert the constitution of Hungary, ter- minated in renewed acknowledgment of the constitutional rights of the Hungarians, and a reiteration of the declaratory act of 1790.

4. Ferdinand the Fifth, who succeeded his father Francis in 1835, took the usual coronation oath, acknowledging the rights, liberties, and independence of Hungary; and the project of incorporating Hungary with Austria seemed to be abandoned; but still the empe- ror, by the exercise of the royal prerogative in making appointments to office, could command a majority in the House of the Magnates, and, by the influence which he could exert in the elections, hoped to secure an ascendency in the House of Deputies. Moreover, the af- fairs of Hungary, instead of being regulated in Hungary by native Hungarians, were managed by a bureau or chancery in Vienna, under the direct supervision and control of the Austrian cabinet. Austrian influence very naturally produced an Austrian party in the country, opposed to which was the great mass of the Hungarians, who took the designation of the Liberal or Patriotic party.

5. At a most opportune moment, just after the first Revolution in Vienna, in March 1848, when the emperor had conceded to the people of his hereditary States the rights and privileges which they demand- ed, a deputation from Hungary appeared, asking, for their kingdom, the royal assent to a series of acts passed by the Hungarian Diet, providing for its annual meeting, the union of Transylvania and Hungary, the organization of a National Guard, equality of taxation for all classes, religious toleration, freedom of the press, and a re- sponsible ministry. After some delay these acts received the roya. assent, and on the 11th of April were confirmed by the emperor per sonally, in the midst of the Diet assembled at Pesth,[1] the capital of Hungary. These concessions were received with the utmost joy throughout the Hungarian nation.

---

1. *Pesth*, which, in conjunction with Buda, is the seat of government of Hungary, is on the east side of the Danube, immediately opposite Buda, with which it is connected by a bridge of boats. Population about sixty-five thousand. It is one hundred and thirty-five miles south east from Vienna. (*Map No. X. LL.*)

6. The sudden change from the restraints of a rigid government to the enjoyment of constitutional liberty, exerted, among the masses who had hitherto enjoyed no political privileges, and especially in the provinces dependent upon Hungary, an influence the most adverse to rational freedom. Liberty was construed to mean license: in some places the Jews were plundered and maltreated: officers and jurors who did their duty were sacrificed to the vengeance of the mob: the imbittered feelings and prejudices of race were kindled into all their fury; and the most horrid atrocities were committed, while the new government, scarcely organized, was too feeble to afford protection to the persons and property of the more peaceful inhabitants. Calls upon the Austrian government for assistance from the Austrian troops in the provinces to suppress this anarchy were unheeded; and the indifference thus shown to the welfare of Hungary gave rise to the first threats of separation.

7. A more alarming danger to Hungary was the opposition against her in her own provinces, first secretly encouraged, and afterwards openly aided, by the Austrian government. The Hungarian dominions embrace a population of about fifteen millions, of whom only six millions are Magyars; and unfortunately the other eight millions were so jealous of the Magyar ascendency as to be found either cold to the cause of Hungary, or openly joining the Austrian party. First the Croats, a portion of the southern Slavi, or Slavonians,[1] after demanding entire independence of Hungarian rule, and showing a disposition to place themselves in more immediate connection with Austria, also a Slavonic nation, took up arms against Hungary, and rejected all advances towards reconciliation. Notwithstanding the unconstitutionality of their position, the emperor sided in their favor, and sent Austrian armies to their aid. Portions of Slavonia proper joined the Croats; and the Serbs,[2] or Servians, in eastern Slavonia, distinguishing their revolt by the greatest atrocities, with unrelenting fury laid waste the Magyar villages, and massacred the unresisting inhabitants. The actual beginning of the war on the part of Hungary was the bombardment, on the 12th of June, 1848, of Car-

---

1. The *Slavonians* comprise a numerous family of nations, descendants of the ancient Sarmatians. The Slavonian language extends throughout the whole of European Russia; and dialects of it are spoken by the Croats, Servians, and Slavonians proper, and also by the Poles and Bohemians.

2. The *Serbs* or Servians, who belong to the wide-spread Slavonian stock, are inhabitants of the Turkish province of Servia; but many of the Serbs are scattered throughout the southern Hungarian provinces.

lowitz,[1] the metropolis or holy city of the Serbs. The city made a brave defence : the Ottoman Serbs hastened across the frontiers to the assistance of their brethren, and the Magyars were driven back into the fortress of Peterwardein.[2] The whole Servian race in the Banat[3] then rose in rebellion, and the peninsula[a] at the confluence of the Theiss and the Danube became the theatre of a furious conflict between the hostile races. Finally, on the 29th of June, the Austrian cabinet, throwing off all disguise, announced the intention of Austria to support Croatia openly. It soon appeared, also, that the altered condition of Austria, consequent upon the late triumphs of the imperial arms in Italy, had determined the emperor to revoke the concessions recently made to Hungary.

8. The Hungarian Diet, now convinced that the constitution and independence of Hungary must be defended by force of arms, decreed a levy that should raise the Hungarian army to two hundred thousand men. In the meantime Jellachich, the ban, or governor, of Croatia, had advanced unopposed into Hungary, at the head of an Austrian and Croatian army, and had arrived within twenty miles of Pesth, when the eloquence and energy of Kossuth, one of the leaders of the patriot party, collected a considerable body of troops, and on the 29th of September Jellachich was repulsed and the capital saved. The ban fled, and on the 5th of October the rear guard of the Croatian army, ten thousand strong, fell into the hands of the Hungarians.

9. Hitherto both parties, the invaders and invaded, appeared to be acting under the orders of the emperor-king, a kind-hearted man, but of moderate abilities, and unfitted for the trying situation in which he found himself placed. Wearied by the contentions in different parts of his empire, desiring the good of all his subjects, but distracted by diverse counsels, and involved, by a series of intrigues, in conflicting engagements, Ferdinand abdicated the throne on the

1. *Carlowitz* is a town of Slavonia, on the right bank of the Danube, four miles south-east of Peterwardein. (*Map* No. XVII.)

2. *Peterwardein*, the capital of the Slavonian military frontier district, and one of the strongest fortresses in the Austrian empire, is on the south bank of the Danube, in eastern Slavonia. It derives its present name from Peter the Hermit, who marshalled here the soldiers of the first crusade. (*Map* No. XVII.)

3. The *Banat*, or Hungary-beyond-the-Theiss, is a large division of south-eastern Hungary having Transylvania on the east, and Slavonia on the west. (*Map* No. XVII.)

a. " The very spot that was, in 1697, the theatre that witnessed the splendid victories of Eugene of Savoy over the Turks, and which were followed by the peace of Carlowitz, that memorable era in the history of the house of Austria and of Europe."—*Stiles' Austria*, ii. p. 68. See p. 398.

2d of December, but a short time after the second Revolution in
Vienna, (see p. 542;) and, by a family arrangement, the crown was
transferred, not to the next heir, Ferdinand's brother, but to his
nephew Francis Joseph. The Hungarian Diet, declaring that Ferdinand had no right to lay down the crown of Hungary and transfer
it to another—that the same was settled by statute on the *direct* heirs
of the house of Hapsburg—and, moreover, that Francis Joseph had
not taken the requisite oath, in the Hungarian capital, to preserve in
violate the constitution, laws, and liberties, of the Hungarians,—denied the right of the new emperor to reign over their nation. The
Hungarians, however, averse to a war with Austria, attempted negotiations for a settlement of all difficulties; but the Austrian cabinet,
desirous of setting aside the constitutional privileges recently granted to Hungary, had resolved upon the unconditional submission of
the Hungarians; and the new emperor yielded himself to the course
of policy dictated by his ministers.

10. With the alarming prospect of a desperate conflict with the
whole power of the Austrian empire, several of the Hungarian leaders,
who had thus far supported all the measures of the movement party,
withdrew altogether from the struggle; but the great mass of the
Hungarian people, more than one-half of the high aristocracy, and
nearly all the untitled nobility, and both Romanist and Protestant
clergy, rallied around Kossuth, and sided with the country. Although
the peasantry, whom the constitution had elevated from the condition
of serfs to that of freemen, rose *en masse*, arms and ammunition
were wanting, and the regular troops of Hungary were still in Italy,
fighting the battles of Austria. Manufactories of powder and arms
had to be established; but they arose as if by magic; and in every
town the anvils rang with the clang of the arms which the artizans
forged by night and by day. But, after all possible efforts, the Hun
garian army, at the actual opening of the campaign in December
1848, amounted to only about sixty-five thousand men, which was as
nothing compared with the forces which Austria was concentrating
for the subjugation of the country.

11. The plan of Prince Windischgratz, commander-in-chief of the
Austrian forces, consisted in invading Hungary from nine points at
the same time—all the lines of attack tending to a common centre,
the capital of the kingdom   The main divisions of the Austrian
army, entering Hungary from the north and west, met with but little
opposition from the Hungarian general Gorgey, who had the com

mand in that quarter, and on the 5th of January, 1849, both Win-dischgratz and Jellachich entered Pesth without striking a blow. Kossuth and the government retired to Debreczin [1] in the south-eastern part of the kingdom, leaving a strong garrison, however, in the almost impregnable fortress c Comorn,[2] while the Hungarian forces gradually concentrated in the valley of the Theiss, from Eperies[3] to the Danube. To protect the rear, General Bem, a Pole was sent to Bukowina,[4] at the eastern extremity of Transylvania, a 'no head of ten thousand men.

12. On the 30th of January the Hungarians lost the strong for-tress of Esseck[5] in Slavonia, which surrendered with about five thou-sand men. About the same time Bem was driven from Bukowina, and, after repeated disasters, from Transylvania also,—the Saxons and Wallachs,[6] who form the bulk of the population, having joined the Austrians. The Szeklers, however, a wild, restless, and warlike race of southern Hungary, espousing the side of the Hungarians, placed themselves under the command of Bem, who, thus reënforced, was soon in a condition to resume the offensive. Again he entered Transylvania, at the head of a well-disciplined corps of twenty thou sand men; and although ten thousand Russian troops had crossed the frontiers to aid the Austrians, he repeatedly defeated their united forces, took Hermanstadt[7] after a severe battle, and entered Cron-stadt[8] without opposition. In a few weeks Bem was complete master

1. *Debreczin*, the great mart for the produce of northern and eastern Hungary, is situated in a flat, sandy, and arid plain, one hundred and fourteen miles east of Pesth. Population forty-five thousand. (*Map* No. XVII.)

2. *Comorn*, situated on a point of land formed by the confluence of the Waag and the Dan-ube, is forty-six miles north-east of Buda. The citadel is one of the strongest fortresses in Europe, and has never been taken. (*Map* No. XVII.)

3. *Eperies* is a fortified town of Upper Hungary, on an affluent of the Theiss, one hundred and forty miles north-east of Pesth.

4. *Bukowina*, ceded by the Turks to Austria in 1774, is now included in Galicia and Lodo-meria. (*Map* No. XVII.)

5. *Esseck*, (ancient *Mursia*,) the capital of Slavonia, is a strongly-fortified town situated on the Drave, thirteen miles from its confluence with the Danube. It is one hundred and thirty-four miles south of Buda. *Mursia*, founded by the emperor Adrian, in the year 125, became the capital of Lower Pannonia. (*Map* No. XVII.)

6. The *Wallachs*—properly the inhabitants of the Turco-Russian province of Wallachia, are the descendants of the ancient Dacians. (Pronounced Wol'-laks: Wol-la'-ke-a.)

7. *Hermanstadt*, the capital of the "Saxon land," a Saxon portion of Transylvania, is situated in an extensive and fertile plain, on a branch of the Aluta, in the southern part of Transyl-vania. (*Map* No. XVII.)

8. *Cronstadt*, the largest and most populous, as well as the principal manufacturing and commercial town of Transylvania—also in the "Saxon land"—is seventy miles east of Her-manstadt. (*Map* No. XVII.)

z

of Transylvania, from which he passed into the Banat, and captured Temeswar,[1] its capital.

13. In the meantime important events had occurred in the valley of the Theiss. About the first of February General Dembinski, also a Pole, was invested, by Kossuth, with the command-in-chief of the Hungarian armies. Although the appointment of Dembinski aroused the jealousy of the native Hungarian officers, who seconded him with little cordiality, yet his plan of operations was judicious. Leaving strong garrisons at Szegedin[2] and on the Maros,[3] about the middle of February he concentrated his forces in the upper valley of the Theiss, to meet the Austrians, then advancing in full force under Windischgratz. In the vicinity of Kapolna,[3] on the 26th and 27th, a severe battle was fought between forty thousand Hungarians and sixty thousand Austrians, without any decisive result; but had it not been for the inactivity of Gorgey, who restricted himself to a defensive position, the Austrians would have suffered a total defeat.

14. Early in March Dembinski resigned, and General Vetter was appointed commander-in-chief of the Hungarian forces; but owing to the illness of Vetter the command soon devolved on Gorgey, under whom was gained a series of victories by which the Austrians were for a time driven out of Hungary. On the 4th of April Jella-chich was defeated at Tapiobieske,[3] and on the 6th the corps of Windischgratz at Gödöllö:[3] on the 9th Gorgey took Waitzen[3] by storm: on the 19th the Ausrians were defeated in a desperate battle at Nagy-Sarlo;[3] and on the 20th Gorgey relieved the fortress of Comorn, which the Austrians had closely besieged during several months. In a few days the main body of the Austrians was driven from the right bank of the Danube, when nothing but a routed army remained between the Hungarians and the city of Vienna. Had Gorgey then followed up his successes, as he was strongly urged to do by Kossuth, in two days his forces might have bivouacked in the Austrian capital; but he remained inactive eight days at Comorn, and then proceeded to the siege of the fortress of Buda,[4]

1. *Temeswar*, the capital of the Banat, is a strongly-fortified town, seventy-five miles north-east of Peterwardein. It was taken from the Turks in 1716 by Prince Eugene. The Bega canal, seventy-three miles in length, passes through the town. Temeswar is supposed to represent the ancient Tabiscus, to which Ovid was banished. (*Map* No. XVII.)

2. *Szegedin* is a large town of Hungary, situated at the confluence of the Maros and the Theiss, one hundred miles south-east of Pesth. (*Map* No. XVII.)

3. For the river Maros, and the towns Kapolna, Tapiobieske, Gödöllö, Waitzen, and Nagy-Sarlo, see *Map* No. XVII.

4. *Buda*, situated on the right bank of the Danube, one hundred and thirty-five miles south

which was carried by storm on the 21st of May. Buda was the bait which the retreating army left behind them to lure the Hungarians, and its siege was the salvation of Vienna, and, perhaps, of the Austrian empire.

15. On the 4th of March the Austrian emperor had made known the project of a constitution for his empire, the effect of which would have been to rob Hungary of her independence and constitutional rignts. This measure, in connection with the well-known fact that Russia had been invoked to lend her aid in suppressing the Hungarian rebellion, induced the Hungarian Diet to make, on the 14th of July, 1849, the declaration of Hungarian independence. The Diet also decreed that, until the form of government to be adopted for the future should be fixed by the nation, the government should be conducted by Louis Kossuth and the ministers to be appointed by him. Kossuth was thereupon unanimously declared governor of Hungary, with little less than regal powers.

16. The demand which the Austrian emperor had made upon the Czar for assistance was neither rejected nor delayed; and preparations for a second campaign against Hungary were speedily completed. Four hundred thousand men, of whom one hundred and sixty thousand were Russians, were assembled on the Hungarian frontiers early in June,—the whole being placed under the command-in-chief of the Austrian general Haynau, of whom little was then known, except that he had served under Radetsky in Italy, where he had distinguished himself by his atrocities. To meet this force the Hungarians had raised an army of one hundred and forty thousand men, with four hundred pieces of artillery. Of these, forty-five thousand, under the immediate command of Gorgey, were on the upper Danube, between Presburg[1] and the capital. The other principal divisions of the Hungarian forces consisted of thirty-five thousand men under General Perczel in the Banat, thirty-two thousand under General Bem in Transylvania, and twelve thousand under Dembinski t Eperies, near the Galician frontier.

17. Almost simultaneously, in the early part of June, Haynau, at the head of fifty thousand men, entered Hungary at Presburg;

east of Vienna, is, in conjunction with Pesth, the capital of Hungary. Attila occasionally made Buda his residence. Arpad, the Magyar chief, made it his head-quarters in the year 900; and it then became the cradle of the Hungarian monarchy. (*Map No. XVII.*)

1. *Presburg*, once the capital of Hungary, is on the north bank of the Danube, thirty-four miles east of Vienna. The castle, now in ruins, is memorable as the scene of the appeal made in 1741 by Maria Theresa to the Hungarian States, which was so generously responded to by the latter. See p. 420. (*Map No. XVII.*)

Paskiewitch at the head of eighty-seven thousand Russians, passed the frontiers of Galicia, and descended into the valley of the Theiss by way of Bartfeld[1] and Eperies; and forty thousand Russians and fourteen thousand Austrians entered Transylvania from the south and east. Smaller divisions entered at other points—the whole designed to enclose the Hungarians within a circle of armies, in the plains of the Theiss and the Danube.

18. The plan of the Austrians and Russians was too successfully carried out. The Russians, after encountering a heroic resistance, drove Bem from Transylvania: Jellachich, after experiencing the most disastrous defeat in the defile of Hegyes,[2] marched up the Theiss: the Russians, under Paskiewitch, in two divisions entered Debreczin on the 7th of July, and Pesth on the 11th. Haynau fought his way from Presburg to the vicinity of Comorn, near which place he fought, on the 11th of July, a severe battle with Gorgey, in which the latter had the advantage. On the 19th he reached Pesth, where he renewed those brutal scenes which had marked his whole career in Hungary. To his own everlasting infamy, and the deep disgrace of the Austrian government, he repeatedly ordered ladies of great respectability and high rank to be publicly flogged for having held communication with the insurgents,—and one, the daughter of a professor in Raab, for having turned her back upon the emperor as he entered the city. Brave officers were hanged by him for no other crime than that of defending their country. Haynau, by his barbarities, fully earned the title which has been given him,—that of "Hungary's Hangman."

19. From Comorn, Gorgey, constantly harassed by the enemy, retreated to Waitzen, and thence to Onod,[3] and on the 29th crossed the Theiss at Tokay,[4] from which place he turned south, and, pursued by the enemy, continued his retreat, until, on the 8th of August,

---

1. *Bartfeld* is at the foot of the Carpathian mountains, in northern Hungary, on the Tope, an affluent of the Theiss. It formerly enjoyed considerable distinction as a seat of learning. It is one hundred and fifty-five miles north-east from Pesth. (*Map* No. XVII.)

2. *Hegyes* is a small town of Southern Hungary, thirty-five miles north-west of Peterwardein. (*Map* No. XVII.)

3. *Onod* is on the western bank of the Theiss, ninety-five miles north-east of Pesth. (*Map* No. XVII.)

4. *Tokay* is a small town, situated at the confluence of the Bodrog with the Theiss, one hundred and thirteen miles north-east from Pesth. Tokay derives its whole celebrity from its being the *entrepôt* for the sale of the famous sweet wine of the same name, made in a hilly tract of country extending twenty-five or thirty miles north-west from the town. The finest quality of the wine is that which flows from the ripe grapes by their own pressure, while in heaps (*Map* No. XVII.)

he reached the fortress of Arad,[1] on the Maros. Petty jealousies
between the Hungarian generals frequently prevented concert of
action and a union of forces when the safety of whole armies depended upon it; and the ambition of Gorgey, in particular, who was
possessed of both skill and courage, seemed to be to show himself a
great general. His country's safety was a secondary consideration.

20. Dembinski, in the meantime, had retreated south, and crossed
the Danube also in the Banat. After almost constant fighting on
the 5th, 6th, 7th, and 8th of August, on the latter of which days he
was severely wounded, on the 9th his army, commanded by Bem,
fought with Jellachich and Haynau the decisive battle of Temeswar,
in which the Austrians were at first repulsed with great loss; but
the failure of ammunition in the Hungarian lines finally gave the
victory to the Austrians. The southern Hungarian army was com
pletely broken up by this disaster: many laid down their arms and
returned home: some escaped into Turkey; and some thousands fell
into the hands of the pursuing enemy. On the 8th Gorgey had
reached Arad with forty thousand troops, within half a day's march
of the spot where Dembinski was fighting; but instead of joining his
countrymen at that opportune moment, when he might have turned
the scale of victory, he was then engaged in efforts for obtaining the
dissolution of the government, and procuring for himself the appointment of dictator. Gorgey's fidelity to the Hungarian cause had
long been suspected, even by Kossuth himself, yet he had been retained in command of the largest division of the Hungarian army;
and now, when he declared that he alone could and would save the
country if dictatorial powers were conferred upon him, Kossuth,
considering the cause of Hungary desperate, took the important step
of dissolving the government and conferring upon Gorgey the supreme civil and military power. (Aug. 10th.)

21. It soon appeared that Gorgey had long maintained a treason-
able correspondence with the enemy. He had long disobeyed, at his
pleasure, the orders sent him by the government; and he now made
such a disposition of his forces that the Russians might enclose his army,
of which, in spite of its corrupt condition, he still stood in fear. On
the 13th he surrendered to the Russian general Rudiger, without
any conditions, his entire force, with one hundred and forty-four cannons. When the troops were drawn up for surrender, grief and in-

---

1. *Arad* is a strongly-fortified town, situated on both sides of the Maros, twenty-seven miles
north of Temeswar. (*Map* No. XVII.)

dignation were visible throughout the ranks : one officer broke his sword, and threw it with curses at Gorgey's feet : many a hussar shot his noble charger, that it might not survive the disgrace of its master ; and some regiments burned their standards, determined never to surrender them to the enemy.

22. A few days before Gorgey's treacherous surrender, one parting gleam of success shed its lustre on the Hungarian arms. At mid-night on the 3d of August the garrison of Comorn, commanded by General Klapka, sallied from the fortress, and drove back the Austrians with dreadful slaughter ; and so great was the panic that on the 5th of August Raab[1] was taken, and with it supplies and ammunition to the value of several millions of dollars. The peasantry in the valley of the Danube rose *en masse*, and Klapka thought seriously of marching upon Vienna itself, when the news of Gorgey's surrender paralyzed all farther effort. Comorn surrendered on the 29th of September, on favorable terms ; and with the fall of that important fortress, terminated the military operations in Hungary.

23. After the surrender of Gorgey, Kossuth left Arad and directed his course to the Turkish frontier, and, finding that no hope remained of serving his country, delivered himself up to the Ottoman garrison at Widdin.[2] Austria in vaid demanded him of the Turkish government. When he was finally permitted to leave the country he came to the United States. The attentions there bestowed upon him for his noble efforts in the cause of Hungarian freedom, called forth, from the Austrian government, a remonstrance, which was nobly answered by Mr. Webster, the American Secretary of State. Bem also fled into Turkey, where, after receiving a command in the Turkish army, he died in 1850, of wounds received in the Hungarian war. Dembinski and a few others followed the fortunes of Kossuth.

24. On the 6th of October, 1849,—a day rendered forever memorable for infamy in the annals of Austria—thirteen Hungarian generals and staff officers, who had surrendered, were shot or hanged at Arad : many of the Hungarian ministers and other civil officials were also executed : an immense number of inferior officers were sent to fortresses to be imprisoned for life, or a term of years; and about seventy thousand Hungarians, who had taken part in the contest,

1. *Raab* is situated south of the Danube, twenty-two miles south-west of Comorn. It was a strong post under the Romans. In 1809 an Austrian force was routed by the French under its walls. (*Map* No. XVII.)

2. *Widdin* is a fortified town of Bulgaria in Turkey, on the southern bank of the Danube, one hundred and sixty-five miles so ith-east of Peterwardein. (*Map* No. VII.)

were forcibly enlisted in Austrian regiments. Thus terminated the struggle of Hungary for freedom. Her national existence, preserved through a thousand years, was annihilated, not so much by the overwhelming power of two great empires, as by the faults and treason of her own sons.[a]

VI. Usurpation of Louis Napoleon. 1. After France had adopted a republican constitution in 1848, the election of a chief magistrate, to hold the executive power of the nation for four years became the absorbing subject of thought and discussion with the French people. Six candidates were in the field,—Lamartine, Ledru Rollin, Raspail, Generals Changarnier and Cavaignac, and Louis Napoleon. Lamartine, who had saved the country from anarchy in the Revolution of February, but had made a feeble president of the provisional government, soon virtually withdrew from the contest, by requesting his friends to make no efforts in his behalf: the adherents of Ledru Rollin, although earnest and active, were, comparatively, few in number: Raspail and Changarnier possessed no peculiar recommendations for the office; and it was soon evident that the choice would lie between General Cavaignac and Louis Napoleon—the former, popular with the Assembly and the leading republicans, a man of tried integrity, and possessing every requisite qualification for the office—the latter an adventurer, who had made two foolhardy attempts to usurp the throne of France, viewed with jealousy and distrust by the republicans, and treated with coldness by the politicians of all parties, but strong in the prestige of a name, and hailed by the people as the living representative of that worldrenowned emperor whom France can never forget. The result of the election surprised every one. Seven and a-half millions of votes were polled in the nation, and, of these, five and a-half millions were cast for Louis Napoleon, who was inaugurated President on the 20th of December. He then solemnly swore " to remain faithful to the Democratic Republic, and to fulfil all the duties which the constitution imposed upon him."

2. Louis Napoleon, the son of Louis Bonaparte and Hortense Beauharnais, the king and queen of Holland, was born in the palace

a. When Kossuth, with the members of the provisional government, was retreating from point to point as the Austrian and Russian armies advanced, he carried with him the Hungarian regalia—the royal jewels, and the crown of St. Stephen—objects of almost religious veneration to the Hungarian people. It long remained a mystery what had become of them, but after years of search by individuals sent out by the Austrian government, they were discovered n Sept. 1853, buried in an iron chest near the confines of Wallachia.

of the Tuilleries on the 20th of April, 1808, and, being the first
prince of the Napoleon dynasty born under the imperial régime, and
the only one living at the time of his election as President of the
French Republic, considered himself, and was acknowledged by the
Bonapartists, as the legitimate representative of the emperor Napoleon, and the heir to his empire. After his second attempt, in
August 1840, to excite a Revolution against Louis Phillippe, he was
confined in the castle of Ham,[1] from which he made his escape in
May 1846, after an imprisonment of more than five years. Being
in London at the time of the Revolution of February, 1848, he immediately repaired to Paris, but was so coldly received by the members
of the provisional government that he again left the country. Soon
after he was informed that he had been elected a member of the Assembly from three different departments; but the hostility against
him in the Assembly was so great that, deeming it unsafe to take
his seat as a delegate, he resigned the office. · In the election to fill
vacancies, in August, he was reëlected, when he returned to France,
and at the 26th of September took his seat as the representative of
Paris, his native city. But even then, nearly all the members, regarding him as a secret enemy of the government, treated him with
marked coldness and neglect; nor did the icy reserve wear away
when the suffrages of nearly six millions of his countrymen had
elevated him to the first place in the Republic.

3. The first act of Louis Napoleon was to make a public declaration of the principles of his government, which he avowed to be
strictly republican; yet from the outset it was assumed by a large
portion of the Assembly that he would prove unfaithful to his oath,
and endeavor to establish an imperial dynasty. The Assembly was
composed of several parties,—first, the Legitimists, who were adherents of the elder branch of the Bourbons:—second, the Orlean-
ists, who desired to see the heir of Louis Phillippe raised to the
throne:—third, the Republicans, both moderate and ultra;—and,
finally, the Bonapartists, who openly expressed their desire for the
restoration of the empire, and were encouraged by Louis Napoleon,
although he remained professedly attached to the Republic.

4. From the beginning there was no mutual confidence between
the President and the Assembly; and while the conduct of the

1. *Ham*, celebrated for its strong fortress used as a State Prison, is a town in a marshy plain
in the former province of Picardy, seventy miles north-east from Paris, and thirty-five south-east
from Amiens. Here Prince Polignac and other ministers of Charles X. were confined for six
years.

former exhibited marked dishonesty of purpose in furthering his ambitious views, the whole career of the latter was a series of intrigues against the President, of party contests, and encroachments upon popular rights. The Assembly introduced severe restrictions upon the liberty of the press : it placed the entire control of education in the hands of the Roman Catholic clergy : it made restrictions upon the right of suffrage, which disfranchised three millions of electors; and it united with the President in sending an army to crush the rising Republic of Rome.

5. The constitution of 1848 provided that it might be revised by a vote of three-fourths of the Assembly during the last year of the Presidential term, and that the President should be ineligible to reëlection until after an interval of four years. This latter provision would therefore render the continuance of Louis Napoleon in power impossible, without a revision of the constitution. Early in 1851 the question of revision was brought before the Assembly, and after being the subject of some very exciting and stormy debates, in which any change was vehemently opposed by the republicans, the motion to revise failed by nearly a hundred votes.

6. In his annual message in November the President strongly urged upon the Assembly the extension of the right of suffrage, a measure which greatly increased his popularity with the French people; but the bill introduced for that purpose was rejected by the Assembly. Soon after, the increasing animosity of the Assembly towards the President was exhibited by the proposal of a law authorizing his impeachment in case he should seek a reëlection in violation of the constitution. His accusation and arrest on a charge of treason were also hinted at.

7. The strife of parties in the Assembly was fast bringing matters to a crisis that would probably have ended in anarchy and civil war, when suddenly—unexpectedly—and quietly, Louis Napoleon put forth his hand, and with a degree of skill that would have done honor to his great name-sake, grasped the reins of power, and, crushing the constitution, overwhelmed all opposition to his will. On the night of Monday, December 1st, the palace of the President was the scene of a gay assemblage of the fashion and beauty of Paris; and it was remarked that the President was in the highest spirits, and unusually attentive to his guests. On the following morning the inhabitants of Paris awoke to find the city filled with troops, and every commanding position in the vicinity occupied by them, while the Presi-

dent's decree, posted on every wall, announced the dissolution of the National Assembly, the restoration of universal suffrage, and the establishment of martial law throughout Paris. The chief members of the Assembly, together with Generals Cavaignac, Changarnier, Lamoriciere, and others, had been seized in their beds, and were already in prison : not a man was left of sufficient ability and popularity to rally the people; the *coup d'etat* was entirely successful, and Louis Napoleon was absolute dictator of France.

8. On Tuesday the 2d of December about three hundred members of the Assembly, finding the doors of the hall of legislation guarded, met in another part of the city, declared the President guilty of treason and proclaimed his deposition ; but scarcely had they signed the decree when they were surrounded by a band of soldiers, and all marched to prison. The Assembly being destroyed, measures were next taken to disarm the power of the press; and none of the journals, except the government organs, were allowed to appear. On Wednesday, the 3d, a decree was promulgated, convening the whole people for an election to be held between the 14th and 22d of December—the questions submitted to them being whether Louis Napoleon should remain at the head of the state ten years, or not, with the power of forming a new constitution on the basis of universal suffrage. On Thursday, the 4th, troops were called out to suppress an insurrection in Paris : no quarter was given, and about a thousand of the insurgents were killed, when tranquillity was restored. In some of the departments the people rose in great strength against the usurpation ; but the army remained faithful, and in the course of two or three days all resistance was quelled.

9. It had been arranged that the army should vote first on the great question submitted to the nation ; and, as had been anticipated, its vote was nearly unanimous in favor of Louis Napoleon. The official returns showed nearly seven and a half millions of votes in his favor, and but little more than half a million against him. Thus the nation sanctioned his usurpation of the 2d of December, and virtually proclaimed its wish for the restoration of the empire. On the 1st of January, 1852, the result of the election was celebrated at Paris with more than royal magnificence, and on the 14th the new constitution was decreed. It was avowedly based on the constitution which the emperor Napoleon had given to the French nation. I intrusted the government to Louis Napoleon for ten years, made him commander-in-chief of the army and navy, gave him control over legislation, and the power to declare war and make treaties. He was all but in name an emperor ; and before a year had passed he assumed that title, apparently with the consent, and by the desire, of the nation. France had accepted the Napoleon Dynasty as a refuge from anarchy—as the only compromise between Bourbonism, or the past, and Republicanism, or the future.

GENERAL GEOGRAPHICAL AND HISTORICAL VIEWS,

(IN ADDITION TO THE NOTES THROUGHOUT THE WORK.)

ILLUSTRATED BY THE FOLLOWING MAPS.

ANCIENT AND MODERN GREECE. Map No. 1.

A general description of both Ancient and Modern Greece may be found on pp. 21 and 22—Grecian Mythology, 22 to 27—Ancient History of Greece, 27 to 123—Modern History 31 to 523. For descriptive accounts of the Grecian States, and important towns, cities, rivers, battle grounds, &c., see the "Index to the Descriptive Notes" at the end of the volume.

The following is a brief synopsis of the leading events in Grecian History, beginning with the Persian wars, which ended B. C. 469. The Peloponnesian wars lasted nearly thirty years, B. C. 431-404. Subjugation of Greece by Philip of Macedon, B. C. 338, after which came the conquests of Alexander, the Achæan League, and then the Roman conquest, B. C. 146, from which time, during thirteen hundred and fifty years, Greece continued to be either really or nominally a portion of the Roman empire. The country was invaded by Alaric the Goth, A. D. 400, and afterwards by Genseric and Zaber Khan, in the sixth and seventh, and by the Normans in the eleventh century. After the capture of Constantinople by the crusaders in 1204, Greece was divided into feudal principalities, and governed by a variety of Norman, Venetian, and Frankish nobles. It was invaded by the Turks in 1438, and conquered by them in 1481. It was the theatre of wars between the Turks and Venetians during the sixteenth and seventeenth centuries; but by the treaty of Passarovitch, in 1718, it was given up to the Turks, who retained possession of the country till the breaking out of the Greek Revolution in 1821.

The present kingdom of Greece embraces all the Grecian peninsula south of the ancient Epirus and Thessaly, as seen on the accompanying map, together with Eubœa, the Cyclades, and the northern Sporades. Thessaly, now a Turkish province, retains its ancient name and limits; Epirus is embraced in the Turkish province of Albania, for which, see Map No. VII.

The Modern Greeks are described as being, generally, "rather above the middle height, and well-shaped; they have the face oval, features regular and expressive, eyes large, dark, and animated, eyebrows arched, hair long and dark, and complexions olive colored." They retain many of the customs and ceremonies of the ancients; the common people are extremely credulous and superstitious, and pay much attention to auguries, omens, and dreams. They belong mostly to the Greek Church; they deny the supremacy of the pope, abhor the worship of images, and reject the doctrine of purgatory, but believe in transubstantiation. The priests are generally poor and illiterate, although improving in their attainments; and their habits are generally simple and exemplary.

The inhabitants of Northern Greece, or Hellas, are said to have retained "a chivalrous and warlike spirit, with a simplicity of manners and mode of life which strongly remind us of the pictures of the heroic age." The inhabitants of the Peloponnesus are more ignorant and less honest than those of Hellas. Previous to the Greek Revolution, remains of the Hellenic race were found, in their greatest purity, in the mountainous parts of the country—in the vicinity of Mount Parnassus in Northern Greece, and the inhospitable tracts of Taygetos in Southern Greece, whither they had been driven from the plains by their ruthless oppressors. The *language* of the modern Greeks bears, in many of its words, and in its general forms and grammatical structure, a strong resemblance to the ancient Greek—similar to the relation sustained by the Italian to the Latin; but as the pronunciation of the ancient Greek is lost, how far the modern tongue corresponds to it in that particular cannot be ascertained.

Travellers still speak in the highest terms of the fine views everywhere found in Grecian scenery;—and besides their natural beauties, they are doubly dear to us by the thousand hallowed associations connected with them by scenes of historic interest, and by the numerous ruins of ancient art and splendor which cover the country—recalling a glorious Past, upon which we love to dwell as upon the memory of departed friends, or the scenes of happy childhood—"sweet, but mournful, to the soul."

> "Yet are thy skies as blue, thy crags as wild;
> Sweet are thy groves, and verdant are thy fields,
> Thine olive ripe as when Minerva smiled,
> And still his honied wealth Hymettus yields.
> There the blithe bee his fragrant fortress builds,
> The freeborn wanderer of thy mountain air;
> Apollo still thy long, long summer gilds,
> Still in his beam Mendeli's marbles glare;
> Art, Glory, Freedom fall, but Nature still is fair.

> "Where'er we tread, 'tis haunted, holy ground;
> No earth of thine is lost in vulgar mould,
> But one vast realm of wonder spreads around,
> And all the muses' tales seem truly told,
> Till the sense aches with gazing to behold
> The scenes our earliest dreams have dwelt upon;
> Each hill and dale, each deepening glen and wold,
> Defies the power which crush'd thy temples gone:
> Age shakes Athena's tower, but spares gray Marathon."
> *Childe Harolde*, canto ii.

ANCIENT GREECE.

Among the monuments of antiquity which still exist at Athens, the most striking are those which surmount the Acrop'olis, or Cecropian citadel, which is a rocky height rising abruptly out of the Attic plain, and accessible only on the western side, where stood the *Propylæ'a*, a magnificent structure of the Doric order, which served as the gate as well as the defence of the Acrop'olis. But the chief glory of Athens was the *Par'thenon*, or temp.e of Minerva, which stood on the highest point, and near the centre, of the Acrop'olis. It was constructed entirely of the most beautiful white marble from Mount Pentel'licus, and its dimensions were two hundred and twenty-eight feet by one hundred and two—having eight Doric columns in each of the two fronts, and seventeen in each of the sides, and also an interior range of six columns in each end. The ceiling of the western part of the main building was supported by four interior columns, and of the eastern end by sixteen. The entire height of the building above its platform was sixty-five feet. The whole was enriched, within and without, with matchless works of art by the first sculptors of Greece. This magnificent structure remained entire until the year 1687, when, during a siege of Athens by the Venetians, a bomb fell on the devoted Par'thenon, and setting fire to the powder which the Turks had stored there, entirely destroyed the roof, and reduced the whole building almost to ruins. The eight columns of the eastern front, however, and several of the lateral colonnades, are still standing, and the whole, dilapidated as it is, still retains an air of inexpressible grandeur and sublimity.

North of the Par'thenon stood the *Erechthéivm*, an irregular but beautiful structure of the Ionic order, dedicated to the worship of Neptune and Minerva. Considerable remains of it are still existing. In addition to the three great edifices of the Acrop'olis, which were adorned with the most finished paintings and sculptures, the entire platform of the hill appears to have been covered with a vast composition of architecture and sculpture, consisting of temples, monuments, and statues of Grecian gods and heroes. Among these may be mentioned statues of Jupiter, Apollo, Neptune, Mercury, Venus, and Minerva; and a vast number of statues of eminent Grecians—the whole Acrop'olis having been at once the fortress, the sacred enclosure, and the treasury of the Athenian nation, and forming the noblest museum of sculpture, the richest gallery of painting, and the best school of architecture in the world.

Beneath the southern wall of the Acrop'olis, near its eastern extremity, was the *Theatre of Bacchus*, which was capable of containing thirty thousand persons, and whose seats, rising one above another, were cut out of the sloping rock. Adjoining this on the east was the Odéum built by Pericles, and beneath the western extremity of the Acrop'olis was the Odéum or *Musical Theatre*, constructed in the form of a tent. On the north-east side of the Acrop'olis stood the *Prytanéum*, where were many statues, and where citizens who had rendered service to the State were maintained at the public expense. A short distance to the north-west of the Acrop'olis was the small eminence called Areop'agus, or hill of Mars, at the eastern extremity of which was situated the celebrated court of the Areop'agus. About a quarter of a mil south-west stood the *Pnyx*, the place where the public assemblies of Athens were held in its palmy days, a spot that will ever be associated with the renown of Demosthenes, and other famed Athenian orators. The steps by which the speaker mounted the rostrum, and a tier of three seats for the audience, hewn in the solid rock, are still visible. A short distance south of the Pnyx was the eminence called the *Muséum*, that part of Athens where the poet Musæus is said to have been buried.

In the *Ceramicus*, north and west of the Acrop'olis, one of the most considerable parts of the ancient city, were many public buildings, some dedicated to the worship of the gods, others used for stores, and for the various markets, and some for schools, while the old *Forum*, often used for large assemblies of the people, occupied the interior. North of the Areop'agus is the *Temple of Theseus*, built of marble by Cimon. The roof, friezes, and cornices, of this temple, have been but little impaired by time, and the whole is one of the most noble remains of the ancient magnificence of Athens, and the most perfect, if not the most beautiful, existing specimen of Grecian architecture.

South-east of the Acrop'olis, and near the Ilissus, is now to be seen a cluster of sixteen mag nificent Corinthian columns of Pentelic marble, the only remaining ones of a hundred and twenty, which mark the site of the *Temple of Jupiter Olympius*. On the left bank of the Ilissus was the *Stadium*, used for gymnastic contests, and capable of accommodating twenty five

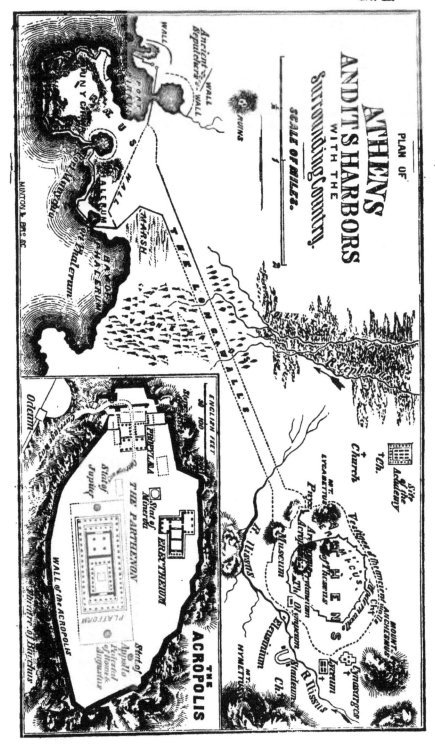

thousand persons. The marble seats have disappeared, but the masses of masonry which formed the semi-circular end still remain.

Just without the ancient city walls on the east was the *Lyceum*, embellished with buildings, groves, and fountains,—a place of assembling for military and gymnastic exercises, and a favorite resort for philosophical study and contemplation. Near the foot of Mount Anchesmus was the *Cynosar' ges*, a place adorned with several temples, a gymnasium, and groves sacred to Hercules. Beyond the walls of the city on the north was the *Academy*, or Public Garden,—surrounded with a wall, and adorned with statues, temples, and sepulchres of illustrious men, and planted with olive and plane trees. Within this enclosure Plato possessed a small garden, in which he opened his school. Thence arose the *Academic* sect.

Athens had three great harbors, the Pirœ' us, Munych' ia, and Phal' erum. Anciently these ports formed a separate city larger than Athens itself, with which they were connected by means of two long walls. During the prolonged conflict of the revolutionary war in Greece, from 1820 to 1827, Athens was in ruins, but it is the now capital of the kingdom of Greece.

The philosophical era in the history of Athens has been beautifully alluded to by Milton.

> " See there the olive grove of Academe,
> Plato's retirement, where the Attic bird
> Trills her thick-warbled notes the summer-long ;
> There flowery hill Hymettus with the sound
> Of bees' industrious murmur oft invites
> To studious musing ; There Ilissus rolls
> His whispering stream : within the walls then view
> The schools of ancient sages ; his who bred
> Great Alexander to subdue the world,
> Lyceum there, and painted Stoa next ;
> * * * * * * *
>
> To sage philosophy next lend thine ear,
> From Heaven descended to the low-roofed house
> Of Socrates ; see there his tenement,
> Whom, well inspired, the oracle pronounced
> Wisest of men ; from whose mouth issued forth
> Mellifluous streams that water'd all the schools
> Of Academics old and new, with those
> Surnamed Peripatetics, and the sect
> Epicurean, and the Stoic severe."

ISLANDS OF THE ÆGEAN. Map No. III.

The *Ægean Sea*, now called the Archipelago, is that part of the Mediterranean lying between Greece, the islands Crete and Rhodes, and Asia Minor. It embraces those groups o .ands, the Cyc' lades and the Spor' ades ;* also Eubœ'a, Lesbos, Chios, Tenedos, Lemnos, &c , nearly all of which cluster with interesting classical associations. Mentioning only the most important in history, and beginning in the northern Archipelago, we have *Thasos*, now Theso or Tasso, early colonized by the Phœnicians on account of its valuable silver mines :—*Samothraca*, where the mysteries of Cybe.e, the "Mother of the Gods," are said to have originated :—*Lemnos*, known in ancient mythology as the spot on which Vulcan fell, after being hurled down from heaven, and where he established his forge :—*Tenedos*, whither the Greeks retired, as Virgil relates, in order to surprise the Trojans :—*Lesbos*, celebrated for its olive oil and figs, and as being the abode of pleasure and licentiousness, while the inhabitants boasted a high degree of intellectual cultivation, and, especially, great musical attainments :—*Chios*, now Scio, called the garden of the Archipelago, and claimed to have been the birthplace of Homer :—*Samos*, early distinguished in the maritime annals of Greece for its naval ascendency, and for its splendid temple of Juno :—*Icaria*, whose name mythology derives from Ic' arus, who fell into the sea near the island after the unfortunate termination of his flight from Crete :—*Patmos*, to which St. John was banished, and where he wrote his Apocalypse :—*Cos*, celebrated for its temple of Æsculapius, and as being the birthplace of Hippocrates, the greatest physician of antiquity :— *Nisyrus*, said to have been separated from Cos by Neptune, that he might hurl it against the

---

* The division between the Cyc' lades and Spor' ades, on the accompanying Map, should include the islands *Ascania*, *Thera*, and *Anaphe*, among the latter.

ISLANDS of the ÆGEAN SEA, With the COASTS OF GREECE AND ASIA MINOR.
Scale of Miles

giant Po ybæ' tes:—*An' aphe*, said to have been made to rise by thunder from the bottom of the sea, in order to receive the Argonauts during a storm, on their return from Colchis:—*Thera*, now called Santorin, said to have been formed in the sea by a clod of earth thrown from the ship Argo:—*Astypalæ'a*, called also Trapedza, or the "Table of the Gods," because its soil was fertile, and almost enamelled with flowers:—*Amorgus*, the birthplace of the Iambic poet Simon' ides:—*Ios*, claimed to have been the burial place of Homer:—*Melos*, now Milo, celebrated for its obstinate resistance to the Athenians, and its cruel treatment by them, (see p. 63):—*Antiparos*, celebrated for its grotto, of great depth and singular beauty:—*Paros*, famed for its beautiful and enduring marble:—*Naxos*, the largest of the Cyc' lades, celebrated for the worship of Bacchus, who is said to have been born there:—*Seriphus*, celebrated in mythology as the scene of the most remarkable adventures of Perseus, who changed Polydec' tes, king of this island, and his subjects, into stones, to avenge the wrongs offered to his mother Danæ:—*De' s* (a small island between Rhenea and Mycanos,) celebrated as the natal island of Apollo and Diana:—*Ceos*, the birthplace of the Elegiac poet Simonides, grandson of the poet of Amorgus. The Simonides of Ceos was the author of the celebrated inscription on the tomb of the Spartans who fell at Thermopylæ:—"*Stranger, tell the Lacedæmonians that we are lying here in obedience to their laws.*" Ægina, Salamis, Crete, Rhodes, &c., have been described in other parts of this work. See Index, p. 846.

ASIA MINOR. Map No. IV.

ASIA MINOR, or Lesser Asia, a celebrated region of antiquity, embraced the great peninsula of Western Asia, about equal in area to that of Spain, and bounded north by the Black Sea, east by Armenia and the Euphrates, south by Syria and the Mediterranean, and west by the Euxine Sea or Archipelago. The divisions by which it is best known in history are the nine coast provinces, Cilicia, Pamphylia, and Lycia, on the Mediterranean; Caria, Lydia, and Mysia, on the Ægean; Bithynia, Paphlagonia, and Pontus, on the Euxine; and the four interior provinces, Galatia, Cappadocia, Phrygia, and Pisidia. All of these were, at times, independent kingdoms, and at others, dependent provinces.

The most renowned of the early kingdoms of Asia Minor was that of Lydia, situate between the waters of the Hermus and the Mæander, and bounded on the east by Phrygia. Under the last of its kings, the famous Crœsus, renowned for his wealth and munificence, the Lydian kingdom was extended so as to embrace the Grecian colonies on the Euxine coast, and nearly all Asia Minor as far as the Halys. On the overthrow of Crœsus by Cyrus the Persian, B. C. 566, the Lydian kingdom was formed into three satrapies belonging to the Medo-Persian empire, under which it remained upward of two centuries. The Macedonian succeeded the Persian dominion, B. C. 331, from which time, during nearly two centuries, Asia Minor was subject to many vicissitudes consequent on the changing fortunes of Alexander's successors. During the century immediately preceding the Christian era, the western provinces of the peninsula fell successively into the hands of the Romans, under whom they formed what was called the proconsulship of Asia, (see Map No. IX.,) the same which the Greek writers of the Roman era call Asia Proper, and in which sense we find the word Asia used in the New Testament, (Acts, 2: 9,) although in some passages Phrygia is spoken of as distinct from Asia. (Acts, 16: 6, and Revelations.) The decline of the Roman power exposed the peninsula to fresh invasions from the East; and at the period of the first crusade the Mohammedans had spread over almost the whole peninsula. Asia Minor now constitutes a pachalick of Asiatic Turkey, under the name of *Natolia*, or *Anatolia*—a corruption of a Greek word, (ανατόλη,) meaning *the East*, corresponding to the French word *Levant*.

The Greek colonists of Asia Minor, who spread themselves along the coast from the Euxine to Syria, were at least equal, in commercial activity, refinement, and the cultivation of the arts, to their European brethren. Among the Grecian poets, philosophers, and historians of Asia Minor, we may mention, in poetry, Homer, Hesiod, Sappho, and Alcæus; in philosophy, Thales, Pythag' oras, and Anaxag' oras; and in history, Herod' otus, Ctesias, and Dionysius of Halicarnassus. *Anatolia* is now occupied by a mixed population of Turks and Greeks, Armenians and Jews; besides wandering tribes of Kurds and Turcomans in the interior, engaged partly in pastoral, and partly in marauding occupations.

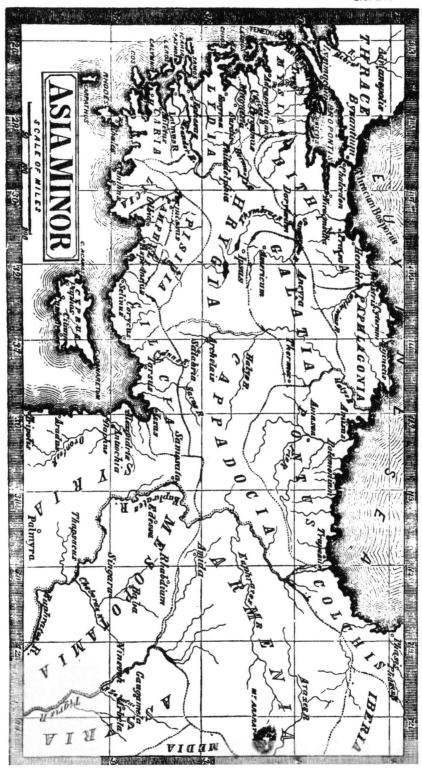

PERSIAN EMPIRE. Map No. V.

ANCIENT PERSIA comprehended, in its utmost extent, all the countries between the rivers Indus and the Mediterranean, and from the Euxine and Caspian Seas to the Persian Gulf and Indian Ocean; but in its more limited acceptation it denoted a particular province, bounded on the north by Media and Parthia, on the east by Carmania, on the south by the Persian Gulf, and on the west by Susiana. (See Map.) This was the original seat of the conquerors of Asia.

Great obscurity rests on the early history of the nations embraced within the limits of the Persian empire; but about the middle of the sixth century B. C., Cyrus, supposed by some to have been grandson of Astyages, the last Median monarch, being elected leader of the Persian hordes, became, by their assistance, a powerful conqueror, at a time when the Median and Babylonian kingdoms were on the decline, and on their ruins founded the Persian empire, which properly dates from the capture of Babylon, B. C. 536. Cambyses, generally supposed to be the Ahasuerus of Scripture, succeeded Cyrus; then followed the brief reign of the usurper Smerdis, after whom Darius Hystaspes was elevated to the throne, 521 B. C. Darius was both a legislator and conqueror, and his long and successful reign exerted a powerful influence over the destinies of Western Asia. Under his rule the Persian empire attained its greatest extent. (See Map.) His vast realm he divided into twenty satrapies or provinces, and appointed the tribute which each was to pay; but his government was little more than an organized system of taxation. The attempts of Darius to reduce Greece to his sway were defeated at Marathon; (B. C. 490;) and the mighty armament of Xerxes, his son and successor, was destroyed in the battles of Sal' amis, Platæ'a, and Myc' ale. The Medo-Persian empire itself was finally overthrown by Alexander the Great, in the battle of Arbela, B. C. 331.

The Macedo-Grecian kingdom of Alexander succeeded to the vast Persian domains, with the additional provinces of Greece, Thrace, and Macedon—thus exceeding the Persian kingdom in extent. About the middle of the third century B. C., the Parthians, under Arsaces, one of their nobles, arose against the successors of Alexander, and established the Parthian empire, which, under its sixth monarch, Mithridates I., attained its highest grandeur – extending from the Euphrates to the Indus. (See Parthia, p. 179.) The Parthian empire lasted nearly four hundred and eighty years—from B. C. 250 to A. D. 226, at which latter period the Persians proper, taking advantage of the weakened state of the empire under the Seleucidæ, rebelled, and founded a new dynasty, that of the Sassanidæ. (See Note, Persian History, p. 249.) The Persian empire under the Sassanidæ continued until the year 636, when it was overthrown by the Moslems in the great battle of the Cadesiah. (See p. 249.) Persia then continued a province of the caliphs for more than two centuries, when the sceptre was wrested from them by the chief of a bandit tribe. After this period Persia was wasted, for many centuries, by foreign oppression and internal disorder, (see pp. 287—311—351,) when, toward the end of the sixteenth century, order was restored, and Persia again rose to distinction under the government of Shah Abbas, surnamed the Great, (p. 351.)

The present kingdom of Persia is reduced to the limits of the ancient provinces of Persia, Media, Carmania, Parthia, the country of the Matieni, and the southern coasts of the Caspian Sea. The Turkish territories extend some distance east of the Tigris; Russia is in possession of the country between the Euxine or Black and Caspian Seas, embracing a part of Armenia; and on the east the now independent but constantly changing kingdoms of Cabool and Belohistan embrace the ancient Bactria, India, and Gedrosia, together with parts of Margiana and Aria, (now eastern Khorassan,) and the country of the ancient Sarangæi. The present Persia has an area of four hundred and fifty thousand square miles, with a population of eight or ten millions. The most striking physical features of Persia are its chains of rocky mountains; its long arid valleys without rivers; and its vast salt or sandy deserts. The population is a mixture of the ancient Persian stock with Arabs and Turks. The language spoken is the Parsee,—simple in structure, and, like the French and English, having few inflections. The religion of the country is Mohammedanism (of the Sheah sect, or adherents of Ali,) which seems, however, to be rapidly on the decline.

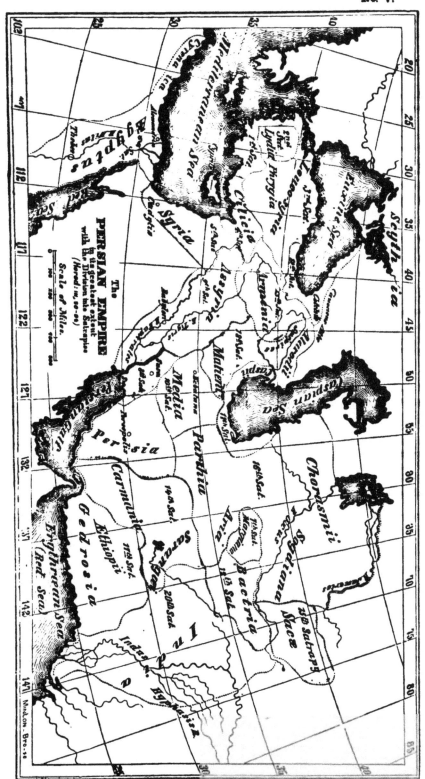

The
PERSIAN EMPIRE
with its greatest extent
with the Division into Satrapies
(Herodotus, III. 90–94.)

Scale of Miles.

PALESTINE. Map No. VI.

A brief geographical account of PALESTINE has been already given on page 40:—accounts of the Moabites, Canaanites, Midianites, Philistines, Ammonites,—and of the Jordan, Jabesh-Gilead, Gilgal, Gath, Gilboa, Hebron, Tyre, Sidon, Joppa, Syria, Damascus, Rabbah, Edom, Samaria, Gaza, Bethoron, Mount Tabor, &c., may be found by referring to the Index at the end of the volume.

Joshua divided Palestine, or the Holy Land, among the twelve Israelitish tribes, whose localities may be learned from the accompanying map. The Children of Israel remained united under one government until the death of Solomon, when ten of the twelve tribes, under Jeroboam, rebelled against Rehoboam, the son and successor of Solomon. The tribe of Judah, with a part, and part only, of the little clan of Benjamin, remained faithful to Rehoboam. From this time forward Judah and Israel were separate kingdoms. The dividing line was about ten miles north of Jerusalem, between Jericho and Gibeah,—the former belonging to Israel, the latter to Judah. Edom, or Idumea, and the possession of the capital, Jerusalem, therefore fell to Judah; but four-fifths of the territory, and the sovereignty over the Moabites, belonged to Israel. The Syrians (Aramites) and Ammonites, after this, were no longer under subjection.

The history of ISRAEL from the time of Jeroboam to the carrying away of the ten tribes captive to Assyria, (B. C. 721,) was a series of calamities and revolutions. The reigns of its seventeen princes average only fifteen years each; and these seventeen kings belonged to seven different families, which were placed on the throne by seven sanguinary conspiracies. With the captivity, the history of the ten tribes ends. Josephus assures us that they never returned to their own land.

The history of JUDAH, after the revolt of the ten tribes, is little more than the history of a single town, Jerusalem. After the lapse of three hundred and eighty nine years Jerusalem was taken by Nebuchadnezzar, (B. C. 606, and afterwards, B. C. 587,) and Judea became tributary to the king of Babylon. The termination of the captivity of Judah, after a period of seventy years, was the act of Cyrus, soon after the conquest of Babylon, B. C. 530; but it was a common saying among the Jews, that "only the bran, that is, the dregs of the people, returned to Jerusalem, but that all the fine flour stayed behind at Babylon." At the time of the Persian conquest by Alexander, Judea, along with the rest of the Persian provinces, passed under the Macedonian dominion. After the death of Alexander we find Palestine alternately subject to the kings of Syria and Egypt; about the middle of the second century B. C., Judea was rendered independent by the Maccabees, (pp. 112—114,) and in the year 63 B. C. it was conquered by Pompey, when it became a part of the Roman empire. (See p. 177.)

Under the Roman dominion, Palestine was divided into five provinces, viz.: Upper and Lower Galilee, Samaria, Judea, and Peræa,—situated as follows: The divisions of Asher and Naphtali, (see Map,) embracing the country of the Sidonians, formed Upper Galilee;—the tribes of Zebulun and Issachar, embracing the country of the Perizites, formed Lower Galilee;.—the half tribe of Manasseh west of the Jordan, and the tribe of Ephraim, embracing the country of the Hivites, formed Samaria;—the tribes of Benjamin, Judah, and Simeon, embracing the countries of the Jebusites, Amorites, Hittites, and Philistines, formed Judea;—the tribes of Reuben, Gad, and the half tribe of Manasseh east of the Jordan, embracing the countries of the Moabites and Ammonites, and the kingdom of Bashan, formed Peræa.

Palestine remained under the Roman dominion (part of the time under the Eastern or reek empire) until the year 636, when Omar conquered Jerusalem, (see p. 249:) after being more than four hundred years subject to the Arabian caliphs, the country fell into the hands of the Turks, (see p. 268,) who proved more oppressive masters than any of their predecessors. Then followed the Crusades; and about four hundred and sixty years after the conquest of Omar, the Holy city was rescued from the Mohammedan yoke, (see p. 283;) but after a series of changes, in the year 1519 Jerusalem came finally into the hands of the Turks, whose flag has ever since floated over its sacred places.

The inhabitants of Palestine are a mixture of various races—consisting of the descendants of the ancient inhabitants of the country, their Arab conquerors, Turks, Crusaders, wandering Bedouins, Kurds, &c., but all now equally naturalized, and distributed into various classes or tribes according to their several religions systems.

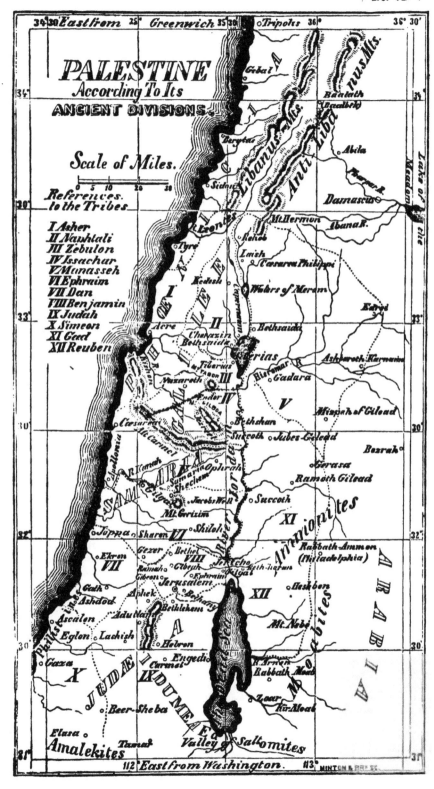

No. VI.

PALESTINE
According To Its
ANCIENT DIVISIONS.

Scale of Miles.

References.
to the Tribes

I Asher
II Naphtali
III Zebulon
IV Issachar
V Manasseh
VI Ephraim
VII Dan
VIII Benjamin
IX Judah
X Simeon
XI Gad
XII Reuben

East from Greenwich

Tripolis
Gibal
Berytus
Sidon
Tyre
Kedesh
Acre
Chorazin
Bethsaida
Tiberias
Nazareth
Casarea
Mt. Carmel
Samaria
Shechem
Jacobs Well
Mt. Gerizim
Joppa
Sharen
Ekron
Gezer
Bethel
Ramah
Gibeon
Jerusalem
Aphek
Ashdod
Gath
Ascalon
Adullam
Bethlehem
Eglon
Lachish
Hebron
Gaza
Engedi
Carmel
Beer-sheba
Elasa
Tamar
Amalekites
Valley of Salt

Baalath
Baalbek
Abila
Damascus
Mt. Hermon
Abana R.
Imish
Cæsarea Philippi
Waters of Merom
Edrei
Bethsaida
Ashtaroth Karnaim
Gadara
Mizpah of Gilead
Bethshan
Succoth
Jabes-Gilead
Bezrah
Gerasa
Ramoth Gilead
Succoth
Rabbath Ammon
(Philadelphia)
Heshbon
Mt. Nebo
R. Arnon
Rabbath Moab
Zoar
Kir-Moab

Libanus Mts.
Anti Libanus Mts.
PHŒNICIA
GALILEE
SAMARIA
JUDÆA
IDUMEA
Philistia
River Jordan
Dead Sea
AMMONITES
ARABIA
Moabites
omites

East from Washington

MINTON & BRO. SC.

EUROPEAN TURKEY, including Moldavia, Wallachia, and Servia, which are con'ected w.th we Porte only by the slenderest ties, is bounded on the north by Slavonia, ll ingary, and Transylvania—divisions of the Austrian empire—from which it is separated by the Save, the Danube, and the eastern Carpathian mountains; on the north-east it is separated from the Russian province of Bessarabia by the Pruth; on the east it has the Black Sea, the Bosporus, the Sea of Marmora, and the Hellespont; on the south the Archipelago and Greece; and on the west the Mediterranean, the Adriatic, and the Austrian province of Dalmatia. Area of European Turkey about two hundred and ten thousand square miles; population about fifteen millions.

The leading events in the history of European Turkey may be stated as follows: The ancient Byzanteum founded by Byzas the Megarean, B. C. 656:—destroyed by Septimius Severus in his contest with Niger, A. D. 196:—rebuilt by Constantine, who gave it his own name, and made it the capital of the Roman empire, A. D. 323:—captured in 1204 by the Crusaders, who retained it till 1261:—taken in 1453 by the Turks, who thus put an end to the Eastern or Greek empire, and firmly established their power in Europe. The Turkish arms continue to maintain their ascendency over those of Christendom until their check in 1683 by the famous John Sobieski, in the siege of Vienna. (See p. 389.) Then began the decline of the Ottoman power: it received a severe blow by the victories of Prince Eugene in 1697, (see p. 390;) since which period province after province has been dismembered from the empire, which, during the last century, has been saved from dissolution only by the mutual jealousies and animosities of its Christian neighbors.

The divisions by which European Turkey is best known in history are Rumilia, Bulgaria, Moldavia, Wallachia, Servia, Bosnia, Turkish Croatia, Her-egovina, Albania, Thessaly, and Macedonia,—for which, see the accompanying Map. *Rumilia*, bordering on the Black Sea, the Sea of Marmora, and the Archipelago, containing the cities of Adrianople and Constantinople, and watered by the Maritza, the ancient Hebrus, is coterminous with the ancient Thrace, (p. 71.) *Bulgaria*, separated from Rumilia by the Balkan range of mountains, having Sophia for its capital, and the Danube for its northern boundary, corresponds to the ancient Moesia Inferior, (p. 200.) *Moldavia* and *Wallackia*, separated from Transylvania by the Carpathian mountains, correspond to the ancient Dacia conquered by Trajan, (p. 200–3.) The inhabitants, descendants of the ancient Dacians, call themselves *Roumuni*, or Romans. *Servia*, peopled by Slavonians—corresponding to the ancient Moesia Superior, formed an independent kingdom in the Middle Ages. It was conquered by the Turks in 1365; but since that period it has frequently rebelled against its Turkish masters. The internal government is now wholly in the hands of the Servians, who pay a small annual tribute to the sultan. *Bosnia*, now a pachalic of Turkey, comprising also under its government Turkish Croatia and Hersegovina, and occupying the north-western extremity of the empire, was anciently included in Lower Pannonia. In the Middle Ages it first belonged to the Eastern empire, and afterwards became a separate kingdom dependent upon Hungary. It was conquered by the Turks in 1490, after a war of seventeen years; but it was not till 1522 that Solyman the Magnificent finally annexed it to the Turkish dominions. *Albania*, a large province bordering on the Adriatic, is nearly the same as the ancient Epirus, (p. 44.) *Thessaly* and *Macedonia* preserve their ancient names and limits.

CONSTANTINOPLE, the capital of the Turkish dominions, occupies a triangular promontory near the eastern extremity of the province of Rumilia, at the junction of the Sea of Marmora with the Thracian Bosporus. It is separated from its extensive suburbs Galata, Pera, &c., on the north, by the noble harbor called the Golden Horn. Like Rome, Constantinople was originally built on seven hills. The city is about thirteen miles in circuit—comprises an area of about two thousand acres—and has a population, exclusive of its suburbs, of about five hundred thousand. The *seraglio*, containing the palace, mint, arsenal, public offices, &c., occupies the site of the ancient Byzantium, (see p. 218,) at the apex of the triangle. It is about three miles in circuit, and is entirely surrounded by walls. The *Bosporus*, or Channel of Constantinople, is about seventeen miles in length, with a width varying from half a mile to two miles. The channel is deep; the banks abrupt, with stately cliffs; and the adjacent country is unrivalled for beauty.

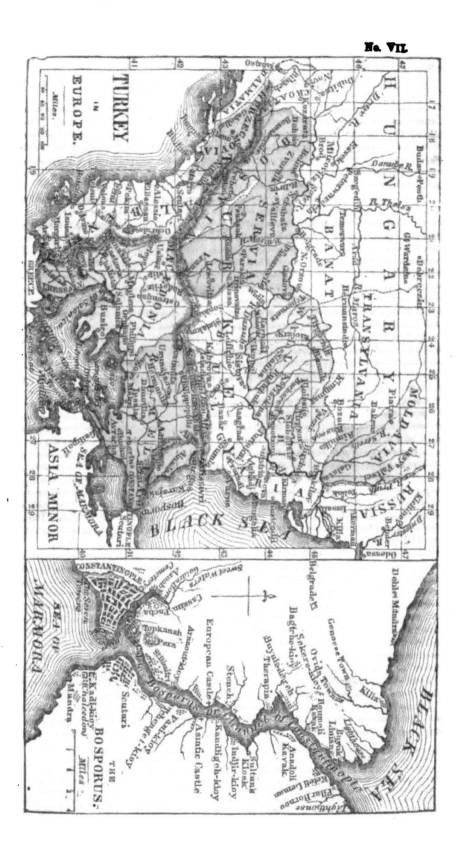

ANCIENT ITALY was called by the Greeks Hesperia, from its western situation in relation to Greece; and from the Latin poets it received the names Ausonia, Saturnia, and Œnotria. (See also p. 123.) About the time of Aristotle, (B. C. 380,) the Greeks divided Italy into six countries or regions,—Ausonia or Opica, Tyrrhenia, Iapygia, Ombria, Liguria, and Henetia; but the divisions by which it is best known in Roman history are those given on the accompanying Map,—Cisalpine Gaul, Etruria, Umbria, Picenum, the country of the Sabines, Latium, Campania, Samnium. Apulia, Calabria, Lucania, and Brutiorum Ager.

Cisalpine Gaul, or *Gaul this side of the Alps*, embracing all northern Italy beyond the Rubicon, was inhabited by Gallic tribes, which, as early as six hundred years B. C., began to pour over the Alps into this extensive and fertile territory. *Etruria*, embracing the country west and north of the Tiber, was inhabited by a nation which had attained to an advanced degree of civilization before the founding of Rome. *Umbria* embraced the country east of Etruria, from the Rubicon on the north to the river Nar, which separated it from the Sabine territory on the south. *Picenum*, inhabited by the Picentes, was a country on the Adriatic, having the river Æsis on the north, the Matrinus on the south, and on the west the Apennines, which separated it from Umbria. The *Country of the Sabines*, at the period when it was marked out with the greatest clearness and precision, was separated from Latium by the river Anio, from Etruria by the Tiber, from Umbria by the Nar, and from Picenum by the central ridge of the Apennines. (See also Map No. X.) *Latium* was south of Etruria and the country of the Sabines, from which it was separated by the Tiber and the Anio. *Campania*, separated from Latium by the river Liris, was called the garden of Italy. The Campanian nation conquered by the Romans was composed of Oscans, Tuscans, Samnites, and Greeks; the latter having formed numerous colonies in southern Italy. *Samnium*, the country of the Samnites, bordered on the Adriatic, having Picenum on the north, Apulia on the south, and Latium and Campania on the west. The ambitious and warlike Samnites not unfrequently brought into the field a force of eighty thousand foot and eight thousand horse. *Apulia*, inhabited by the early Daunii, Peucetii, and Messapii, bordered on the Adriatic on the east; and, on the west, on the territories of the Samnites, the Campanians, and Lucanians. *Calabria*, called also by the Greeks Iapygia, embraced the south-eastern extremity of the Italian peninsula, answering nearly to what is now called Terra di Otranto. *Lucania*, inhabited by the warlike Lucani, who carried on a successful war with the Greek colonies of southern Italy, was separated from Apulia and Calabria on the north-east by the Bradanus. *Brutiorum Ager*, the Country of the Brutii, comprised the southern extremity of the peninsula, now called Calabria Ultra. The Brutii, the most barbarous of the Italian tribes, were reduced by the Romans soon after the withdrawal of Pyrrhus from Italy.

Since the downfall of the Roman empire Italy has never been united in one State. After having been successively possessed by the Heruli, Ostrogoths, Greeks, and Lombards, Charlemagne annexed it to the empire of the Franks in 774: from 888 till the establishment of the republic of Milan in 1150, it generally belonged, with the exception of the territory of the Venetians, to the German emperors. In 1535, Milan, then a duchy, came into the possession of the emperor Charles V. Since the war of the Spanish succession, the duchies of Milan and Mantua have generally belonged to Austria, with the exception of the short time they formed a part of the Cisalpine republic and the French empire. Venice was a republic from the seventh century till 1797. It was confirmed to Austria by the treaty of 1815. The present Italian States are the kingdom of Lombardy and Venice, forming a part of the Austrian empire—kingdom of Sardinia—kingdom of Naples and Sicily—Grand-duchy of Tuscany—States of the Church—Duchies of Parma, Modena, and Lucca—and the little republic of San-Marino.

The French rule in Italy was a great blessing to that unhappy country; "but the coalition," says Sismondi, "destroyed all the good conferred by France." The state of the people contrasts very disadvantageously with the fertility of the soil and the beauty of the climate.

"How has kind Heav'n adorn'd the happy land, And scattered blessings with a wasteful hand! But what avail her unexhausted stores, Her blooming mountains and her sunny shores, With all the gifts that Heav'n and earth impart, The smiles of nature and the charms of art, While proud Oppression in her valleys reigns, And Tyranny usurps her happy plains? The poor inhabitant beholds in vain The redd'ning orange and the swelling grain. Joyless he sees the growing oils and wines, And in the myrtle's fragrant shade repines: Starves, in the midst of nature's bounty curst, And in the laden vineyard dies for thirst."

THE ROMAN EMPIRE. Map No. IX.

REGAL ROME, or Rome under the Kings, occupying a period of about two hundred and forty years, from the founding of the city, 753 B. C., to the overthrow of royalty, 510 B. C., ruled over only a narrow strip of seacoast, from the Tiber southward to Terracina, an extent of about seventy miles, (see Map No. X ;) but it already carried on an extensive commerce with Sardinia, Sicily and Carthage.

REPUBLICAN ROME, occupying a period of about four hundred and eighty years, from the overthrow of royalty 510 B. C. to the accession of Augustus, 28 B. C., extended the Roman dominion, not only over all Italy, but also over all the islands of the Mediterranean—over Egypt, and all Northern Africa from Egypt westward to the Atlantic Ocean—over Syria and all Asia Minor—over Thrace, Achaia or Greece, Macedonia, and Illyricum—and over all Gaul, and most of Spain.

IMPERIAL ROME occupies a period of about five hundred years, extending from the accession of Augustus, 28 B. C., to the overthrow of the Western empire of the Romans, A. D. 476. Under Augustus, the Roman dominion was extended by the conquest of *Mœsia*, corresponding to the present Turkish provinces of Bulgaria and Servia—of *Pannonia*, corresponding to the eastern part of southern Austria, and Hungary south of the Danube, Styria, Austrian Croatia, and Slavonia, and the northern part of Bosnia—of *Noricum*, corresponding to the Austrian Salzburg, western Styria, Carinthia, Austria north to the Danube, and a small part of south eastern Bavaria—*Rhætia*, extending over the country of the Tyrol and eastern Switzerland—and *Vindelicia*, corresponding to southern Wirtemberg and Bavaria south of the Danube. (See also Maps Nos. VII. and XVII.) On the death of Augustus, therefore, the Roman empire was bounded by the Rhine and the Danube on the north ; by the Euphrates on the east ; by the sandy deserts of Arabia and Africa on the south ; and by the Atlantic Ocean on the west.

The southern part of Britain, or Brittania, was reduced by Ostorius, in the reign of Claudius ; and Agricola, in the reign of Domitian, extended the Roman dominion to the Frith of Forth, and the Clyde. With this exception, the empire continued within the limits given it by Augustus, until the accession of Trajan, who, in the year 105, added to it *Dacia*, a region north of the Danube, and corresponding to Wallachia, Transylvania, Moldavia, and all Hungary east of the Theiss and north of the Danube. Trajan also, in his eastern expedition, descended the Tigris from the mountains of Armenia to the Persian Gulf, and for a brief period extended the sway of Rome over Colchis, Armenia, Mesopotamia, and Assyria ; and even the Parthian monarch accepted his crown from the hands of the emperor. In the time of Trajan, therefore, who died A. D. 117, the Roman empire attained its greatest extent,—being, at that period, the greatest monarchy the world has ever known,—extending in length more than three thousand miles, from the Western Ocean to the Euphrates, and more than two thousand in breadth, from the northern limits of Dacia to the deserts of Africa,—and embracing an area of sixteen hundred thousand square miles of the most fertile land on the face of the globe. Well might it be called the Roman WORLD.

Adrian, or Hadrian, the successor of Trajan, voluntarily began the system of retrenchment which was forced upon his successors. In order to preserve peace on the frontiers he abandoned all the conquests of his predecessor except Dacia, and bounded the eastern provinces by the Euphrates. The unity of this mighty empire was first broken by the division into Eastern and Western in the year 395. In the year 476 the Western Empire fell under the repeated attacks of the barbarians of Germany and Scythia, the rude ancestors of the most polished nations of Europe. The Eastern Empire survived nearly a thousand years longer, but finally fell under the power of the Turks, who took Constantinople, its capital, in the year 1453, and made it the capital of the Ottoman empire.

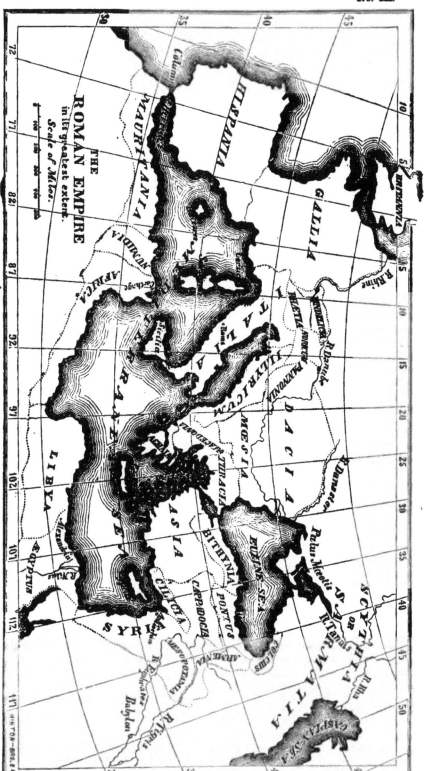

THE
ROMAN EMPIRE
in its greatest extent.

Scale of Miles.

In describing ANCIENT ROME our attention is first directed to the relative localities of the Seven Hills on which Rome was originally built—the Aventine, Cœlian, Palatine, Esquiline, Capitoline, Viminal, and Quirinal—all included within the walls of Servius Tullius, built about the year 550 B. C. About two hundred and eighty years later the emperor Aurelian commenced the erection of a new wall, which was completed by Probus five years afterward. The circumference of the Servian town was about six miles; that given it by the wall of Aurelian, which extended to the right bank of the Tiber and inclosed a part of the Janiculan mount, was about twelve; although the city extended far beyond the limits of the latter. The modern rampart surrounds, substantially, the same area as that of Aurelian.

The greater part of Modern Rome covers the flat surface of the Campus Martius, the Capitoline and Quirinal mounts, and the right bank of the Tiber from Hadrian's Mausoleum, (now the Castle of St. Angelo,) south to and including the Janiculan mount. The ancient city of the Seven Hills is nearly all contained within the old walls of Servius. Almost the whole of this area, with the exception of the Capitoline and Quirinal hills, is now a wide waste of piles of shattered architecture rising amid vineyards and rural lanes, exhibiting no tokens of habitation except a few mouldering convents, villas, and cottages.

Beginning our survey at the Capitoline hill, on which once stood the famous temple of Jupiter Capitolinus, we find there no vestiges of ancient grandeur, save about eighty feet of what are believed to have been the foundations of the temple. At the northern extremity of the hill we still discern the fatal Tarpeian Rock, surrounded by a cluster of old and wretched hovels, while ruins encumber its base to the depth of twenty feet.

The open space between the Capitoline, Esquiline, and Palatine hills, is covered by relics of ancient buildings interspersed among modern churches and a few paltry streets. Here was the *Great Roman Forum*—a large space surrounded by and filled with public buildings, temples, statues, arches, &c., nearly all of which have disappeared ; and the surface pavement on which they stood is now covered with their ruins to a depth of from fifteen to thirty feet. The space which the Forum occupied has been called, until recently, Campo Vaccino, or the Field of Cows ; and it is in reality a market place for sheep, pigs, and cattle.

In early times there was a little lake between the Capitoline and Palatine hills. In time this was converted into a marsh ; and the most ancient ruin which remains to us, the *Cloaca Maxima*, or great drain, built by the Tarquins, was designed for carrying off its waters. This drain, still performing its destined service, opens into the Tiber with a vault fourteen feet in height and as many in width. The beautiful circle of nineteen Corinthian columns near the Tiber, around the church of Santa Maria, has been usually styled the *Temple of Vesta*—supposed to belong to the age of the Antonines.

On the Palatine hill Augustus erected the earliest of the *Palaces of the Cæsars* ; Claudius extended them, and joined the Palatine to the Capitoline by a bridge ; and towards the northern point of the Palatine, Nero built his "Golden House," fronted by a vestibule in which stood the emperor's colossal statue. The Aventine rises from the river steep and bare, surmounted by a solitary convent. On the Cœlian are remains of the very curious circular *Temple of Faunus*, built by Claudius. Southward are the ruins of the *Baths of Caracalla*, occupying a surface equal to one-sixteenth of a square mile. The building, or range of buildings, was immense,—containing four magnificent temples dedicated to Apollo, Æsculapius, Hercules, and Bacchus,—a grand circular vestibule, with baths on each side for cold, tepid, warm, and sea-bathing—in the centre an immense square for exercise—and beyond it a noble hall with sixteen hundred marble seats for the bathers, and, at each end of the hall, libraries. On each side of the building was a court surrounded by porticoes, with an odeum for music, and, in the middle, a spacious basin for swimming. There was also a gymnasium for running, wrestling, &c., and around the whole a vast colonnade opening into spacious halls where the poets declaimed, and philosophers gave lectures to their auditors. But the immense halls are now roofless, and the wind sighs through the aged trees that have taken root in the pavements.

South of the Palatine was the *Circus Maximus*, which is said to have covered the spot where the games were celebrated when the Romans seized the Sabine women. It was more than two thousand feet in length, and, in its greatest extent, contained seats for two hundred

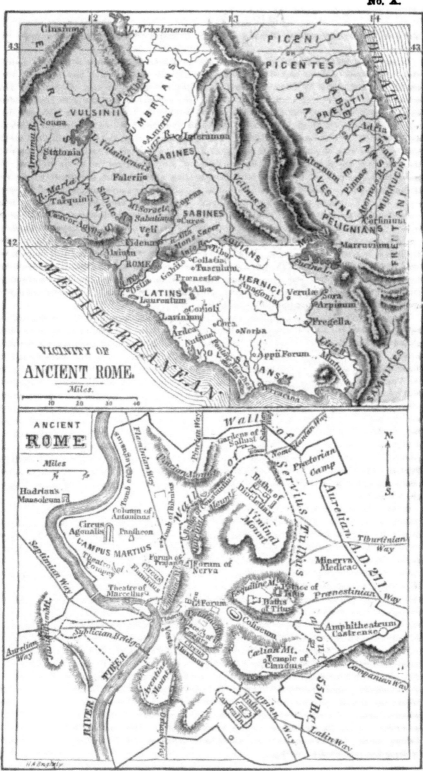

VICINITY OF
ANCIENT ROME.

Miles.

ANCIENT
ROME

Miles.

and sixty thousand spectators. We can still trace its shape, out the structure has entirely disappeared.

In the open space eastward of the Great Forum stands the *Coliseum or Flavian Amphitheatre*, the boast of Rome and of the world. This gigantic edifice, which was begun by Vespasian and completed by Titus, is in form an ellipse, and covers an area of about five and a-half acres. The external elevation consisted of four stories,—each of the three lower stories having eighty arches supported by half columns, Doric in the first range, Ionic in the second, and Corinthian in the third. The wall of the fourth story was faced with Corinthian pilasters, and lighted by forty rectangular windows. The space surrounding the central elliptical arena was occupied with sloping galleries resting on a huge mass of arches, and ascending towards the summit of the external wall. One hundred and sixty staircases led to the galleries. A movable awning covered the whole, with the exception of the Podium, or covered gallery for the emperor and persons of high rank. Within the area of the Coliseum, gladiators, martyrs, slaves, and wild beasts, combated on the Roman festivals; and here the blood of both men and animals flowed in torrents to furnish amusement to the degenerate Romans. The Coliseum is now partially in ruins; scarcely a half presents its original height; the uppermost gallery has disappeared; the second range is much broken; the lowest is nearly perfect; but the Podium is in a very ruinous state. From its enormous mass " walls, palaces, half cities have been reared;" but Benedict XIV. put a stop to its destruction by consecrating the whole to the martyrs whose blood had been spilled there. In the middle of the once bloody arena stands a crucifix; and around this, at equal distances, fourteen altars, consecrated to different saints, are erected on the dens once occupied by wild beasts.

The principal ruins on the Esquiline, a part of them extending their intricate corridors on the heights overlooking the Coliseum, have been called the Baths and the Palace of Titus; but although it is evident that baths constituted a part of their plan, the design of the whole is not known. What is called the Temple of Minerva Medica, in a garden near the eastern walls, is a decagonal ruin, supposed to belong to the age of the Antonines. The *Baths of Diocletian*, on the Viminal mount, appear to have resembled, in their general arrangement, those of Caracalla. Still farther to the north-east are the remains of the camp erected by Sejanus, the minister of Tiberius, for the Prætorian guards. In the beautiful gardens of the historian Sallust, on the eastern declivity of the Pincian mount, are the remains of a temple and circus, supposed to belong either to the Augustan age, or to the last days of the Republic. On the western ascent of the thickly-peopled Quirinal, whose heights are crowned by the palace and gardens of the pope, are extensive ruins of walls, vaults, and porticoes, belonging to the baths of Constantine. They are now surrounded by the beautiful gardens of the Colonna palace. Farther south, between the Quirinal and Capitoline, some striking remains of the Forums of Nerva and Trajan are still visible.

Of the numerous ruins in the Campus Martius, we have room for only a brief notice. Of the *Theatre of Marcellus*, eleven arches of the exterior walls still remain. Of the *Theatre of Pompey*, the foundation arches may be seen in the cellars and stables of the Palazzio Pio. The *Flaminian Circus* and the *Circus Agonalis* are entirely in ruins. The *Column of Antoninus* and the *Tomb of Augustus* are still standing, with their summits much lowered.

The *Pantheon*, the most perfect of all the remains of ancient Rome, is a temple of a circular form, built by Agrippa. It was dedicated to Jupiter the Avenger, but besides the statue of this god, it contained those of the other heathen deities, formed of various materials—gold, silver, bronze, and marble. The portico of this temple is one hundred and ten feet long by forty-four in depth, and is supported by sixteen Corinthian columns, each of the shafts consisting of a single piece of Oriental granite, forty-two feet in height. The bases and capital are of white marble. The main building consists of a vast circular drum, with niches flanked by columns, above which a beautiful and perfectly preserved cornice runs round the whole building. Over a second story, formed by an attic sustaining an upper cornice, rises, to the height of one hundred and forty-three feet, the beautiful dome, which is divided internally into square panels supposed to have been originally inlaid with bronze. A circular aperture in the dome admits the only light which the place receives. The consecration of this temple (A. D. 608) as a Christian church, has preserved, for the admiration of the moderns, this most beautiful of heathen fanes. Christian altars now fill the recess where once stood the most famous statues of the gods of the heathen world.

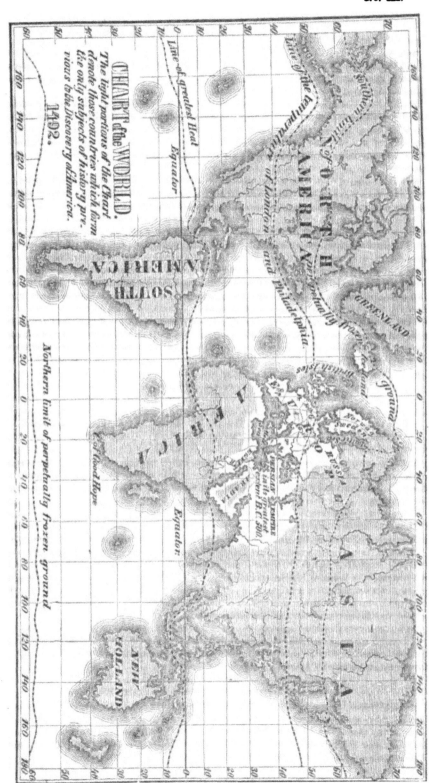

CHART of the WORLD.
The light portions of the Chart denote those countries which form the only subjects of history previous to the Discovery of America.

1492.

Map No. XI. is a CHART OF THE WORLD on Mercator's projection—a *Chart of History*, ex hibiting the world as known to Europeans at the period of the discovery of America—and a *Chart of Isothermal lines*, or lines of equal heat, showing the comparative mean annual tem perature of different parts of the Earth's surface.

It will be observed that Gene al History, previous to the discovery of America, is confined 'o a small portion of the Earth's surface ; as represented by the light portions of the Chart; while the whole Western Continent and Greenland, most of Africa and Asia, and their islands, and parts of Northern Europe and Iceland, were unknown to Europeans, and in the darkness of barbarism. It would seem, therefore, that the history of THE WORLD has but just com menced.

The Isothermal lines show that the temperature of a place does not depend wholly upon its latitude. Thus the southern limit of perpetually frozen ground in the northern hemisphere (at a mean annual temperature of thirty-two degrees Fahrenheit) follows a line ranging from below fifty-five degrees of latitude to above seventy. The mean annual temperature of London, at fifty-one and a-half degrees north latitude, is fifty degrees of Fahrenheit, the same as that of Ph iladelphia, which is eleven and a-half degrees of latitude farther south. The line of greatest heat, (at a mean annual temperature of eighty-two and four-tenths degrees of Fahrenheit,) is more than ten degrees of latitude north of the Equator in South America, in Africa, and southern Hindostan ; and about eight degrees south of the Equator in a part of the Indian Ocean be tween Borneo and New Holland. The sea is, generally, considerably warmer in winter than the land, and cooler in summer. Continents and large islands are found to be warmer on their western sides than on the eastern. The extremes of temperature are experienced chiefly in large inland tracts, and little felt in small islands remote from continents. Had the Arctic regions been entirely of land, the intense heat of summer and the cold of winter would have been equally fatal to animal life.

BATTLE GROUNDS OF THE WARS OF THE FRENCH REVOLUTION AND THE WARS OF NAPOLEON. Map No. XII.

The wars growing out of the French Revolution, of which those of Napoleon were a con tinuation, embrace a period of nearly twenty-three years, from the defeat of the Austrians at Jemappes on the 17th of November, 1792, to the defeat of Napoleon at Waterloo on the 18th of June, 1815.

The accompanying Map presents at a glance the vast theatre on which were exhibited the thousand Scenes in this mighty Drama of human suffering. The thickly-dotted Spanish penin sula may be regarded as one great battle-field, where Frenchman, Spaniard, Portuguese, and Briton, sank in the death struggle together. Those dark spots where the " pealing drum," the " waving standards," and the " trumpets clangor," invited to slaughter, cluster thickly around the eastern boundaries of France, including Belgium and northern Italy ;— they are seen in far-off Egypt and Palestine, recalling Napoleon's dreams of Eastern conquest ; and they strew the route to Moscow, where, from the fires of the Kremlin, and amid the snows of a Russian winter, the French eagles commenced a lasting retreat.

As we look over this vast gladiatorial arena of frantic, struggling Life, and agonizing Death, our thoughts naturally turn from its mingled horrors and glories to rest upon the commanding genius,—the wizard spirit,—of him " who rode upon the whirlwind and dire ted the storm"— of him whom Byron well describes as a mighty Gambler.

> " Whose game was empires, and whose stakes were thrones,
> Whose table earth, whose dice were human bones."

But the French Revolution and the wars of Napoleon, with all the suffering which they oc casioned, have not been unattended with useful results in urging forward the march of European civilization. The moral character of Napoleon, the most prominent actor in the drama, has been variously drawn by friends and foes ; but the towering height, the lightning-like rapidity and the brilliancy, of his genius, have never been questioned by his most bitter revilers.

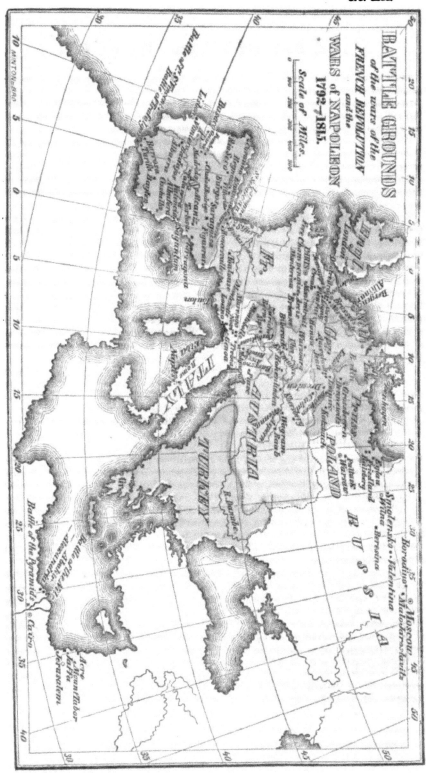

BATTLE GROUNDS
of the wars of the
FRENCH REPUBLIC
and the
WARS of NAPOLEON
1792–1815.

Scale of Miles.

FRANCE, (ancient *Gaul*,) bordering on three seas, and being enclosed by natural boundaries on all sides except the north-east, where her natural limits are the Rhine, is admirably situated for a commanding influence in European affairs; and, besides, her large population, the active spirit of her people, the fertility of her soil, and the amenity of her climate, place her among the foremost of the great nations of the earth in power and resources.

When first known to the Romans, Gaul was divided between the Belgæ, the Celtæ, and the Aquitani; the Belgæ or Belgians between the Seine and Lower Rhine;—the Celts between the Seine and Garonne; and the Aquitani between the Garonne and Pyrenees; but the Romans under Augustus, made four divisions of Gaul;—Belgica, in the north-east;—Lugdunensis, between the Seine and Loire;—Aquitania, between the Loire and Pyrenees;—and Narbonensis, in the south-east.

None of the barbarian tribes of Europe passed through a more agitated or brilliant career than the ancient Gauls, the ancestors of the French people. They burned Rome, conquered Macedonia, forced Thermopylæ, pillaged Delphi, besieged Carthage, and established the empire of Galatia in Asia Minor; but, after a century of partial conflicts, and nine years of general war with Cæsar, they yielded to the overshadowing power of Rome. When Rome fell, Gaul was overrun by the Germanic nations: then came the beginning of the empire of the Franks—the encroachments and defeat of the Saracens—the vast empire of Charlemagne—and then the increasing power of the feudal nobility, until, in the year 987, the last of the Carlovingian princes possessed only the town of Laon! Under Hugh Capet even, dukes, counts, and minor seigneurs, shared among themselves nearly all of the modern kingdom. But by degrees the great fiefs, one after another, fell to the crown: and before the close of the seventeenth century all France was united under one monarchy in the person of Louis XIV.

Thus, with her history, the geography of France has been continually changing; but those divisions of her territory best known in general history are the old Provinces, as given on the accompanying Map. These provinces, during the Middle Ages, were all either duchies or minor seignories ruled by the feudal nobility; and their history is, therefore, virtually, for a long period, that of separate kingdoms. (See description of Provence, Brittany, Normandy, Aquitaine, Burgundy, Roussillon, &c., pp. 300, 371-2, 379.)

At the period of the French Revolution the thirty-three provincial divisions were abolished, and France was then divided into eighty-six Departments or Prefectures; these into three hundred and sixty-three Arrondissements; these into two thousand eight hundred and forty-five Cantons; and these latter into thirty-eight thousand six hundred and twenty-three Communes.

SPAIN, anciently *Hispania*, a name given to the entire peninsula beyond the Pyrenees, was not fully conquered by the Romans till the time of Augustus, who made three divisions of the country;—1st, *Bætica*, in the south of Spain, embracing the more modern province of Andalusia;—2d, *Lusitania*, embracing all Portugal south of the Douro, and, in addition, most of Estremadura and Salamanca;—and, 3d, *Tarraconensis*, embracing the remainder, and greater portion, of the peninsula.

About the time of the subversion of the Western empire of the Romans, Spain was overrun by the Vandals, and other Gothic tribes; and, a century later, the Christianized Visigoths established their supremacy in every part of the peninsula. At the beginning of the eighth century the Moors from Africa overran the whole country, but after their defeat by Charles Martel in France, (see p. 253,) the Christians began to make head against them, founded the kingdom of Leon about the middle of the eighth century, and, from that period, gradually extended their power until, in 1492, Granada, the last Moorish kingdom, yielded to the arms of Ferdinand of Aragon, and, soon after, the whole Spanish peninsula was united under one government. In 1139 PORTUGAL became an independent kingdom: from 1580 to 1640 it was a Spanish province; but at the latter period it regained its independence. For historical accounts of Navarre, Aragon, Castile, Leon, and Granada, see p. 317,—Portugal, 318.

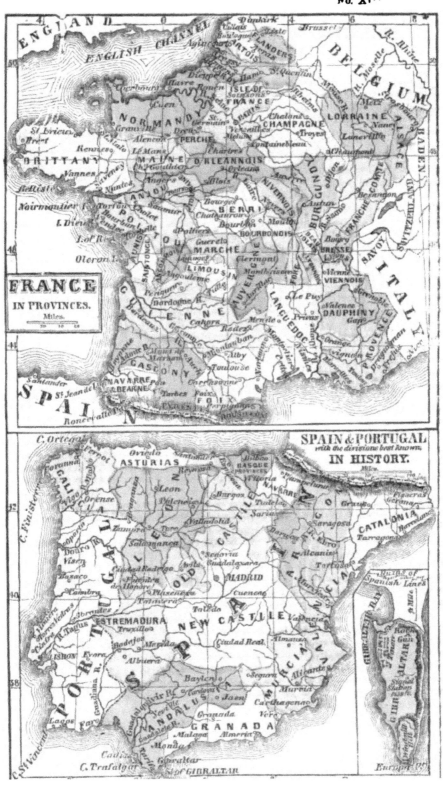

SWITZERLAND, DENMARK, AND PARTS OF NORWAY AND SWEDEN. Map No. XIV.

As a brief outline of the history of SWITZERLAND has already been given on page 290, and of DENMARK, SWEDEN, and NORWAY, on page 308, we shall here confine our attention principally to the physical geography, government, population, &c., of those countries.

SWITZERLAND is a republic formed by the union of twenty-two confederated States or cantons, whose total area is about fifteen thousand square miles, or about one-third of that of the State of New York. Population, about two millions two hundred thousand, of whom nearly two-thirds are Protestants. More than half of the Swiss people speak a German dialect about four hundred and fifty thousand speak French; and about one hundred and twenty-five thousand a corrupt Italian.

The greater portion of Switzerland consists of mountains; and the geographical appearance of the country has, not improperly, been compared to a large town, of which the valleys are the streets, and the mountains groups of contiguous houses. Both the Rhine and the Rhone, and several other important rivers, have their sources in Switzerland; but the Aar drains the greater part of the country, passes through the lakes of Brienz and Thun, and, after a course of about one hundred and seventy miles, unites with the Rhine. The lakes of Switzerland are numerous—all navigable—and remarkable for the depth and purity of their waters, and their great variety of fish. Lakes Thun and Brienz are nineteen hundred feet above the level of the sea—the lakes of Geneva and Constance about twelve hundred. Not only is Switzerland much colder than the adjacent countries, owing to its elevation, and the influence of its glaciers in cooling the atmosphere, but the cold has increased in modern times, and many tracts are now bare that were formerly covered with forests and pasture grounds.

The kingdom of DENMARK, properly so called, comprises only Jutland, or the northern half of the ancient Cimbric Chersonese, together with the islands between Jutland and Sweden, and the island of Bornholm in the Baltic. To these possessions have been added the duchies of Sleswick and Holstein, which originally formed part of the German empire; and as sovereign of which the Danish king now ranks as a member of the Germanic confederation. Iceland, part of Greenland, the Faroe isles, and some possessions in the East and West Indies, also belong to Denmark.

The surface of the Danish peninsula is remarkably low and level; and along the whole western coast of Sleswick and Holstein the country is defended, as in Holland, against irruptions from the sea, by immense mounds or dikes. The soil is various, but, generally, very fertile. There are no mountains, and no rivers of any magnitude; but the inlets of the sea are numerous, and penetrate far inland. Since the year 1660 the government has been perhaps as absolute a monarchy as any other in the world; but the sovereigns have generally exercised their extensive powers with great moderation. The Lutheran is the established religion. Population but little more than two millions.

The kingdom of SWEDEN comprises, with Norway and Lapland, the whole of the Scandinavian peninsula, west of the Baltic. Sweden is, in general, a level, well-watered country, but the soil is poor. Sweden extends so far north that, near Tornea, the sun is visible, at midsummer, during the whole night. The government of Sweden is a hereditary monarchy, with a representative diet consisting of four chambers, formed, respectively, of deputies from the nobility, clergy, burghers, and peasants, or cultivators.

NORWAY, forming the western part of the great Scandinavian peninsula, is a mountainous country, and is characterized by its lofty mountain plateau in the interior, and the deep indentations or arms of the sea all round the coast. Although Norway is under the same crown with Sweden, it is, in reality, little connected with the latter country. Its democratic assembly, called the Storthing, meets for three months once in three years, by its own right, and not by any writ from the king. If a bill pass both divisions of this assembly in three successive Storthings, it becomes a law of the land without the royal assent—a right which no other monarchico-legislative assembly in Europe possesses.

THE NETHERLANDS, NOW EMBRACED IN THE KINGDOMS OF HOLLAND AND BELGIUM. Map No. XV.

Nearly the whole kingdom of Holland, (often mentioned in history as the "Low Countries,") with the exception of a few insignificant hill ranges, is a continuous flat—a highly fertile country—in great part conquered by human labor from the sea, which, at high tide, is above the level of a considerable portion of the surrounding country. The latter is at all times liable to dangerous inundations. Where there are no natural ramparts against the sea, enormous artificial mounds or dikes have been constructed; but these are sometimes broken down by the force of the waves. That extensive arm of the sea called the Zuyder Zee, occupying an area of about twelve hundred square miles, was formed by successive inundations in the course of the thirteenth century. The surface of the country presents an immense network of canals, the greater number being appropriated to the purposes of drainage. When the sea is once shut out by the dikes the marsh is intersected by water courses; and wind-mills, erected on the ramparts, are employed to force up the water. Sometimes the marsh is so far below the level of the sea—even twenty-five or thirty feet below the highest tides—that two or more ramparts and mills, at different elevations, are requisite. There is no other country where nature has done so little, and man so much, as this. The north and west provinces of Belgium are very similar in their flatness, fertility, dikes, and canals, to Holland.

Goldsmith's description of Holland is peculiarly appropriate.

" To men of other minds my fancy flies,
Embosom'd in the deep where Holland lies:
Methinks her patient sons before me stand,
Where the broad ocean leans against the land;
And, sedulous to stop the coming tide,
Lift the tall ramparts artificial pride.
Onward, methinks, and diligently slow,
The firm compacted bulwark seems to grow;
Spreads its long arms around the watery roar,
Scoops out an empire and usurps the shore:
While the pent ocean, rising o'er the pile,
Sees an amphibious world beneath him smile,
The slow canal, the yellow-blossom'd vale,
The willow-tufted bank, the gliding sail,
The crowded mart, the cultivated plain,
A new creation rescued from his reign."

Holland and Belgium were partially subjected by the Romans: in the second century Holland was overrun by the Saxons: in the eighth both were conquered by Charles Martel; and they subsequently formed a part of the dominions of Charlemagne. From the tenth to the fifteenth century they were divided into many petty sovereignties, most of which successively passed into the possession of the house of Burgundy, thence to that of Austria, and, about the middle of the sixteenth century, the whole fell under the rule of Charles V., king of Spain and emperor of Germany. The arbitrary measures of Philip Ii. of Spain, the son and successor of Charles V., led to a general rebellion in the Netherlands: the independence of the "Republic of the United Provinces," embracing the States of Holland, was acknowledged by Spain in 1609, while the ten southern provinces, which had either remained loyal to Spain or been kept in subjection, had in the meantime passed under the sovereignty of the house of Austria. From this period the southern provinces have been generally distinguished by the name of Belgium. After having been several times conquered by the French, and recovered from them, they were incorporated, in 1795, with the French republic, and divided into departments. In 1806 the republic of Holland was erected into a kingdom for Louis, a brother of Napoleon; and on the downfall of the latter, the Congress of Vienna, in 1815, united Holland and Belgium to form the kingdom of the Netherlands, which latter, by the Revolution of 1830, was dissolved into the present kingdoms of Holland and Belgium. A portion of Luxembourg, entirely detached from the rest of the Dutch dominions, belongs to Holland.

Of the inhabitants of Holland, numbering about two millions six hundred thousand, about two millions are Dutch, who speak what is called the Low Dutch, as distinguished from the High Dutch or German—the two great divisions of the Dutch or Teutonic language. The population of Belgium numbers about four millions three hundred thousand, divided among three principal races,—the Germanic, which comprehends the Flemings and Germans; the Gallic, to which belong the Walloons, who speak a dialect of the ancient French; and the Semitic, which comprehends only the Jews. The French language is used in public affairs, and by all the educated and wealthy classes.

NETHERLANDS;
now divided into
HOLLAND & BELGIUM.

Scale of Miles.

10 20 30 40 50 60 70 80

Provinces of
BELGIUM.

1 West Flanders
2 East Flanders
3 Hainault
4 Antwerp
5 South Brabant
6 Namur
7 Limbourg
8 Liege
9 Luxembourg

Mouths of the
Meuse & Rhine

Eastern Scheld

W. Scheld

Schiermonn

Amland

Ter Schelling

Vlieland

Vlieland

Wieringen

Texel

Leeuwarden

GRONINGEN

Groningen

FRIESLAND

Assen

Helder

Steenwyk

Bergen
Alkmaar

DRENTHE

OVERYSSEL

ZUIDER ZEE

Zwolle

Deventer

Haarlem

Old Rhine

GUELDERLAND

Harderwick

Leyden

Utrecht

Hague

UTRECHT

Arnheim

Greenlo

Ryswick

R. Rhine

R. West

Rotterdam

Nymegen

Bois le Duc

Cleves

NORTH   BRABANT

R. Rhine

Breda

Bergen op Zoom

Helmont

Turnhout

Dusseldorp

Antwerp

Hereutbals

4

Hamont

Lier

Malines

7

Bruges

Ghent

Furnes

1   2

Hasselt

Ypres

Louvain

Colegne

Courtrai

BRUSSELS

Tirlemont

Maestricht

Oudeuarde

5

Waterloo

Aix la Chapelle

Grammont

Wavre

Lilleo

Ramillies

Liege

Tournay

3

QuatreBras

8

Fontenoy

Jemappes

Ligny

Meuse R.

Mons

Fleuruso

Namur

Malmedy

Valenciennes

Charleroi

Malpluueto

R. Sambre

Dinant

Marche

Cambray

Charlemont

Givet

6

Baslogne

St Quentin

Bocruy

9

Vervius

Neufchateau

Moselle R.

Mesieres

Arlon

Treves

Leon

R. Aisne

Montmedy

Luxembourg

Soissons

Compiegne

Rheims

Verdun

Metz

R. Morne

Epernay

Chalons

Menehould

R. Meuse

R. Moselle

J. MINTON, SC.

The UNITED KINGDOM OF GREAT BRITAIN AND IRELAND consists of the islands Great Britain and Ireland, the former including the once independent kingdoms of England and Scotland, and the whole constituting not only the nucleus and the centre, but also the main body and seat, of the wealth and power of the BRITISH EMPIRE. The colonies and foreign dependencies belonging to the United Kingdom are of great extent and importance, consisting principally of the British possessions in North America, the West Indies, the Cape of Good Hope, Australia, and the East Indies. The British East India possessions alone embrace an area of one million two hundred thousand square miles. It is doubtless the common opinion that the United Kingdom is indebted to its territorial possessions for a large portion of its wealth and power; but many able writers have come to the conclusion that these colonies and dependencies occasion an enormous outlay of expense without any equivalent advantage, and that they are a source of weakness rather than of strength.

No country ever existed more favorably situated for the centre of a mighty empire than the United Kingdom. Its insular situation gives it a well defended frontier, rendering the country comparatively secure from hostile attacks, and affording unequalled facilities for commerce; while its soil enjoys the fortunate medium between fertility and barrenness that excludes indolence on the one hand, and poverty on the other. Its harbors are numerous and excellent: its principal rivers, the Thames, Trent, and Severn in England, and the Shannon in Ireland, are all navigable to a very great distance: iron is found in the greatest abundance: its tin mines of Devon and Cornwall are the most productive of any in Europe: its salt springs and salt beds are alone sufficient for the supply of the whole world; and its *inexhaustible* coal mines, the principal source and foundation of its manufacturing and commercial prosperity, are more valuable than would have been the possession of all the gold and silver mines in the world. But England has an enormous public debt: her government is very expensive; and consequently, with all her wealth and prosperity, the burdens of taxation are unusually heavy. In 1838 her public debt, contracted in great part during the American Revolution, and the French revolutionary wars, amounted to nearly *eight hundred million pounds sterling*. Her expenditures during the same year were upwards of fifty millions, of which more than twenty-nine millions were appropriated to defray the interest and expense of managing the public debt!

The inhabitants who occupied the British isles at the period when the Romans first landed in England, fifty-five years before Christ, belonged partly to the Celtic, and partly to the Gothic family—the Celts having very early passed over into England from the contiguous coasts of France; and the Belgic Goths having at a later period driven the Celts northward and westward into Scotland, Wales, and Ireland, and occupied the eastern, lower, and more fertile portions of England. The Romans conquered England and the more southern portions of Scotland, but appear not to have visited Ireland. After the departure of the Romans, about A. D. 409, the Caledonian Celts overran the country, when the Saxon chiefs, Hengist and Horsa, were invited over to aid their English brethren. The conquest of England by the united Saxons, Jutes, and Angles, occupied a period of about one hundred and thirty years, from the landing of Hengist. In the ninth and tenth centuries occurred the repeated inroads of the Danes, who, at length in 1017, under their leaders Sweyn and Canute, became masters of the kingdom, which, however, they only held till 1041. In the year 1066 occurred the conquest of England by William of Normandy. Through William and the princes of the house of Plantagenet, more than a third part of France was placed, by inheritance, marriage, conquest, &c., under the immediate jurisdiction and sovereignty of the kings of England; but during the reign of John, surnamed Lackland, the French recovered most of their provinces. In 1169 Henry II. began the conquest of Ireland.

The leading epochs in later English history are, the Civil Wars of the Two Roses, terminated by the battle of Bosworth Field in 1484: the union of the *crowns* of England and Scotland in 1604: the great Civil War in the reign of Charles I., followed by the execution of that monarch in 1649: the Restoration in 1660: the Revolution of 1688: the *legislative* union of England and Scotland in 1707: the accession of the House of Hanover in 1714, (see Hanover p. 482:) the American War, 1776-1784: the war with revolutionary France, 1793-1815: the legislative union of Ireland with England and Scotland, 1799: the repeal of the Test Act, 1828: Catholic Emancipation, 1829; and passage of the Reform Act, 1832.

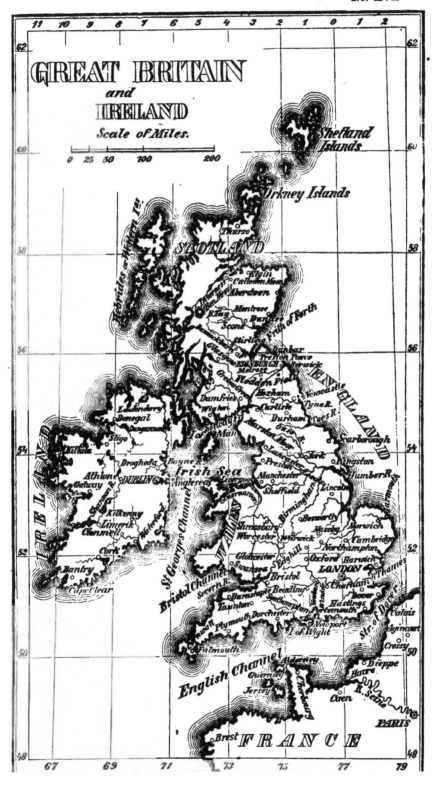

GREAT BRITAIN
and
IRELAND
Scale of Miles.

0   25   50   100   200

CENTRAL EUROPE, TOGETHER WITH POLAND, HUNGARY, AND WESTERN RUSSIA. Map No. XVII.

CENTRAL EUROPE may be considered as embracing the present numerous German States and Switzerland; including in the former those portions of the Austrian and Prussian empires which, previous to the French Revolution, belonged to the German empire.

The "German Empire" occupies a prominent position in the history of Continental Europe, but it has passed through so many changes in limits, divisions, and government, that the reader of history, unless he is familiar with them, will often be perplexed by apparent contradictions. Thus the emperor of Austria is often mentioned as the emperor of Germany; and portions of Germany are spoken of as belonging to Austria. The following sketch of the *German Empire*, and the *Germanic Confederation*, it is believed will explain these seeming inconsistencies, and render German history more intelligible to the general reader.

The first Carlovingian sovereigns of Germany were hereditary monarchs; but as early as 887 the great vassals of the crown deposed their emperor, and elected another sovereign in his stead; and from that period down to the dissolution of the German empire in 1806, the emperors of Germany were elected by the most powerful vassals of the empire, some of whom were monarchs within their own domains. From 1745 to 1806 the Austrian emperors exercised a double sovereignty,—as emperors of Austria, and emperors of Germany also; but a portion of the Austrian dominions were not included in the German empire.

At the period of the outbreak of the French Revolution, the German empire was divided into what were termed Ten Great Circles, each of which had its diet for the transaction of local business; but affairs of general importance to the empire at large were treated by the imperial diet summoned by the emperor. The Ten Great Circles were, 1st, the Circle of *Austria;* 2d, The Circle of *Burgundy,* (including most of the present Belgium, and belonging to Austria;) 3d, the Circle of *Westphalia;* 4th, the Circle of the *Palatinate;* 5th, the Circle of the *Upper Rhine;* 6th, the *Suabian* Circle, (including Wirtemberg and Baden; see Suabia, p. 270;) 7th, the Circle of *Bavaria;* 8th, the Circle of *Franconia,* (see Franconia, p. 270;) 9th, the Circle of *Lower Saxony,* (including the duchies of Magdeburg, Holstein, &c.: the latter a part of Denmark;) 10th, the Circle of *Upper Saxony,* (including Pomerania, Brandenburg, the electorate of Saxony, &c.) In addition to these Circles the empire embraced the kingdom of Bohemia; the margraviate of Moravia; the duchy of Silesia, (Austrian and Prussian;) and various small territories held directly of the emperor. The Swiss cantons had revolted from the empire, and maintained their independence. Thus the German empire, consisting of a vast aggregation of States, from large principalities or kingdoms down to free cities and the estates of earls or counts, comprised all the countries of Central Europe, and was bounded north by northern Denmark and the Baltic; east by Prussian Poland, Galicia, and Hungary; south by the Italian Tyrol and Switzerland; and west by France and Holland. The Austrian monarch was at the head of this vast empire; but he had also other States, such as Hungary, Galicia, Slavonia, &c., which had no connection with the German empire. Most of Prussia, and the southern half of Denmark, were also included in the German dominions.

Napoleon made important changes in the political geography of the German empire. By the treaty of Campo Formio in 1797, (see p. 467,) the frontiers of France were for the first time extended to the Rhine; and the Circle of Burgundy was thus cut off from the German dominions. The treaty of Presburg in 1805 was followed by other changes, Austrian Tyrol being given to Bavaria, and Hanover to Prussia; and, in 1806, by the Confederation of the Rhine, (see p. 485,) population of sixteen millions was taken from the Germanic dominion of Austria. Under these circumstances, on the 6th of Aug. 1806, the Austrian emperor solemnly renounced the style and title of emperor of Germany. The war with Prussia in 1807 deprived the Prussian monarch of nearly one half of his dominions; and Westphalia was soon after erected into a kingdom for Napoleon's brother Jerome.

The downfall of Napoleon restored Germany to its geographical and political position in Europe, but not as an empire acknowledging one supreme head. A confederation of thirty-five (afterwards changed to thirty-four) independent sovereignties, and four free cities, replaced the old elective German monarchy. In this Confederation are embraced all the Austrian and Prussian territories formerly belonging to the German empire; also Holstein, (a part of Denmark,) and Luxembourg, (a part of Holland;)—the emperor of Austria, and the kings of Prussia, Denmark, and Holland, becoming, for their respective German territories, parties to

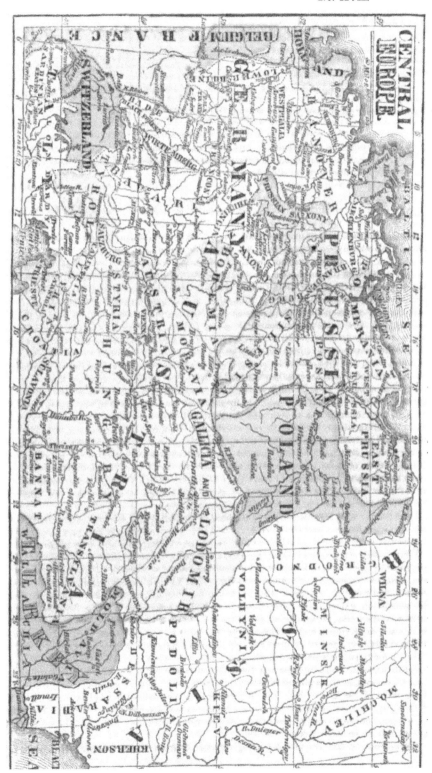

the league. The affairs of the Confederation are managed by a diet, in which the representative of Austria presides. Until a very recent period each of the German States had its own custom houses, tariff, and revenue laws, by which the internal trade of the country was subjected to many vexations and ruinous restrictions; but chiefly through the influence of Prussia this selfish system has been abandoned; free trade exists between the States; and a commodity that has once passed the frontier of the league may now be conveyed without hinderance throughout its whole extent.

For notices of Russia, Poland, and Hungary, see pp. 287, 311, and 542.

THE UNITED STATES OF AMERICA. Map No. XVIII.

The UNITED STATES occupy the middle division of North America, extending from the Atlantic to the Pacific Ocean, and embracing an area of about three millions two hundred thousand square miles. Physical geography would divide this broad belt into three great sections; 1st, the Atlantic coast, whose rivers flow into the Atlantic; 2d, the Valley of the Mississippi, whose waters find an outlet in the Gulf of Mexico; and 3d, the Pacific coast, embracing an extensive territory west of the Rocky Mountains. The section between the Alleghanies and the Atlantic, embracing the thirteen original States, has a soil generally rocky and rough in the north-eastern or New England States; of moderate fertility in the Middle States; and generally light and sandy in the Southern Atlantic States. The immense Valley of the Mississippi, included between the Alleghanies and the Rocky Mountains, and drained by the Mississippi, Missouri, Ohio, Arkansas, and Red rivers, is one of the largest and finest basins in the world, embracing an area of more than one million square miles—nearly equal to all Europe, with the exception of the Russian empire. In the eastern and middle sections of this valley the soil is generally of very superior quality; but extensive sandy wastes skirt the eastern base of the Rocky Mountains. The country west of the Rocky Mountains exhibits a great variety of soil. Washington and Oregon territories are divided into three belts or sections, by mountain ranges running nearly parallel with the coast. The eastern section is rocky, broken, and barren; the western fertile. Most parts of Utah and western New Mexico are an extensive elevated region of sandy barrens and prairie lands: the northern and eastern sections of California are hilly and mountainous: the only portion adapted to agriculture being the southern section, and a narrow strip along the coast, forty or fifty miles in width. The vast mineral wealth of California gives that country its chief importance.

The United States seem destined to become, at no distant day, in population, wealth, and power, the greatest nation of the earth. In the year 1850 their population numbered more than twenty-three millions; and if it should continue to increase, for a century to come, as it has during the past twenty years, at the end of the century it will number *one hundred and sixty millions*, and then be only half as populous as Britain or France. Hardly any limits can be assigned to the probable wealth of so extensive and fertile a country, intersected by numerous canals and navigable lakes and rivers, bound together by its roads of iron, bordering on two oceans, and commanding the trade of the world. In commerce it is even now the second country on the globe, being inferior only to Great Britain: in its agricultural products it has no equal; and in manufactures it has already risen to great respectability. Its revenue, which has arisen chiefly from customs on imports, and the sale of public lands, was sufficient in January 1837, not only to complete the payment of the public debt contracted during the two wars with Great Britain, but also, after retaining five million dollars in the treasury, to distribute more than thirty-seven millions among the States. In 1838 the United States was entirely free from debt, while at the same time Great Britain owed a debt of nearly eight hundred million pounds sterling, equal to more than *thirty-five hundred millions of dollars !* the annual interest on which, at the low English rates, was more than three times the amount of the total annual expenditure of the American government.

The national existence of the United States commenced on the 4th of July, 1776, when they

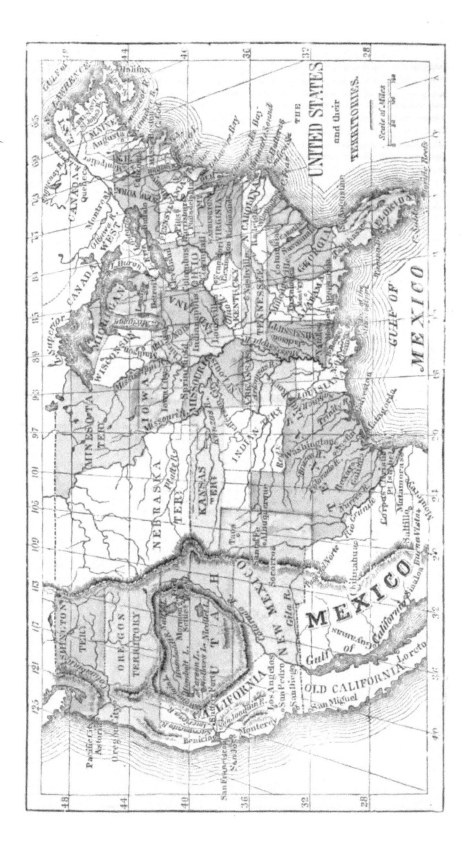

declared their independence of Great Britain. The seven years' war of the Revolution followed: the definitive treaty of peace was signed September 30th, 1783 · the present Constitution was ratified by Congress July 14th, 1788; and on the 30th of April, 1789, Washington was inaugurated first President of the United States. In 1803, Louisiana, embracing a vast and undefined territory west of the Mississippi, was purchased from France for fifteen millions of dollars; and in 1821 Florida was ceded to the United States by Spain. On the 4th of June, 1812, the American Congress declared war against Great Britain: peace was concluded at Ghent, Dec. 14th, 1814. In the year 1845 the Republic of Texas was annexed to the United States. In April 1846 a war with Mexico began: California was conquered by the Americans during he summer of the same year; on the 27th of March, 1847, Vera Cruz capitulated; and on he 14th of September the American army entered the city of Mexico. In February, 1848, treaty was concluded with Mexico, by which the United States obtained a large increase of territory embracing the present New Mexico Utah and California.

INDEX.

TO.

THE GEOGRAPHICAL AND HISTORICAL NOTES.

THE

AMERICAN EDUCATIONAL READERS.

A NEW GRADED SERIES, fully and handsomely illustrated, excelling all others in Manufacture, Gradation, and in Cheapness. The most beautiful Series of School Books ever issued.

This is an entirely new series of Readers. They have been published to meet a want not heretofore supplied, in respect to size, gradation, and price. The books contain less pages than those of the old popular series, and are much cheaper in price. They have been compiled by several eminent educators who have acquired, by a life-long experience in the work of elementary education, a familiarity with the wants of pupils and teachers in this department of instruction.

The *plan* of the American Educational Readers will be found to embrace several new features. That of the first reader combines the *word method*, the *alphabetic method*, and the *phonic method*. The word and phonic methods are used to teach the elementary sounds and their simplest combinations. Words are taught by associating them with the pictorial representations of familiar objects, and their analysis leads to a systematic and logical presentation of *letters* and their *sounds*, as the components of the words. The whole system is logical and systematic from the beginning to the end. The *regular* combinations are carefully presented at the commencement, and the pupil is made to pass by slow degrees to what is *anomalous* and *complex*. *Articulation* and *pronunciation* are secured before the pupil's mind is very much occupied with other considerations. Here the *phonic method* has been kept steadily in view in the arrangement of the exercises.

In the more advanced books of the series, while elocutionary principles have been carefully elaborated, and illustrated by appropriate exercises, the important object of instructing the pupil himself by means of his own reading, has not been lost sight of. Hence, the lessons will be found to embody much valuable information, upon scientific and other subjects, entirely divested, however, of an abstruse or technically scientific character. In these books, while it has not been deemed requisite to encumber the pages with a mass of minute questions—such as any teacher of even ordinary tact and intelligence could readily construct without aid—brief *analysis* have been appended to many of the lessons, containing a summary of the matters contained therein. These will be found very useful in conducting exercises to develop the intelligence of the pupils or training them in habits of attention and correct expression.

The *Illustrations* of these books will be found very far in advance of those of any other series, in beauty and accuracy of drawing and engraving. They have been drawn by the most eminent and talented artists, and engraved expressly for these books. No books in the market are more copiously and beautifully illustrated than the *New Graded Series*.

The *printing* and *paper* are of a high order of excellence, the former being the best style of the work of the well-known University Press at Cambridge.

☞ *Full descriptive* CIRCULARS *of the series, with titles and prices, will be sent by mail on application.*

₊ THE EDUCATIONAL REPORTER—Full of interesting and valuable Educational information, is published three times a year, bearing date respectively January, May and September, and will be sent to teachers and educationists, without charge, on application.

Ivison, Blakeman, Taylor & Co.

EDUCATIONAL PUBLISHERS,

138 & 140 GRAND ST., NEW YORK.   133 & 135 STATE ST., CHICAGO.

The American Educational Series.

SCHOOL RECORDS.

We publish the following School Records, to which we invite the attention of Teachers. We shall be pleased to send sample pages of any or all of them, without charge, on application.

No. 1. ALPHABETICAL REGISTER. 204 pages. Cap folio. Indexed. Price $3.75.

No. 2. ROUGH REGISTER; or, Admission Book. 48 pages. Cap 4to. Price 60 cents.

No. 3. DISCHARGE BOOK. 40 pages. Cap 4to. Price 60 cents.

No. 4. DAILY ATTENDANCE AND WEEKLY REPORT BOOK. 100 pages. Cap folio. Price $2.50.

No. 5. RECITATION RECORD; or, Class Book. 80 pages. Medium 4to. Price $1.25.

No. 6. ROLL BOOK; or, Class Attendance Book. 80 pages. Medium 4to. Price $1.25.

No. 7. SCHOOL DIARY. No. 1 (for Pupils), to last six months. Price per dozen, $1.00.

No. 7. SCHOOL DIARY. No. 2 (for Pupils). Same as No. 1, with the addition of blanks for communication from Teacher to Parent, or from Parent to Teacher, Summary, &c. Price, per dozen, $1.00.

No. 8. ALPHABETICAL LIST, to show the number of days and months each pupil was present during the year. 80 pages. Cap folio. Indexed. Price $1.75.

No. 9. AMERICAN SCHOOL, DAILY, WEEKLY, AND QUARTERLY REGISTER. Price 90 cents.

No. 10. GENERAL RECORD OF RECITATION AND ATTENDANCE. Medium size. Bound. Price $4.00.

No. 11. WEEKLY AND TERM REPORT CARDS. Price, per dozen, 60 cents.

No. 12. AMERICAN SCHOOL CLASS RECORD. Price $1.25.

No. 13. TEACHERS' COMPLETE POCKET RECORD. Price 63 cents.

The SCHOLAR'S POCKET RECORD. A Weekly, Monthly, or Quarterly Register of Attendance, Deportment, &c. $1.00 per dozen.

*** THE EDUCATIONAL REPORTER—Full of interesting and valuable Educational information, is published three times a year, bearing date respectively January, May and September, and will be sent to teachers and educationists, without charge, on application.

Ivison, Blakeman, Taylor & Co.,

EDUCATIONAL PUBLISHERS,

138 & 140 GRAND ST., NEW YORK. 133 & 135 STATE ST., CHICAGO.

Milton Keynes UK
Ingram Content Group UK Ltd.
UKHW042313190124
436367UK00003B/141